John & Mila

USA TODAY BESTSELLING AUTHOR

KENNEDY FOX

John & Mila

BISHOP FAMILY ORIGIN, #3

USA TODAY BESTSELLING AUTHOR

KENNEDY FOX

Copyright © 2023 Kennedy Fox
www.kennedyfoxbooks.com

JOHN & MILA
Bishop Family Origin, #3

Includes: *Chasing Him,*
Wrangling the Cowboy, & Winning the Cowboy

This special edition Bishop family origin collection consists of three books from the *Bishop Brothers World.*

Chasing Him
John & Mila

Wrangling the Cowboy
Gavin & Maize

Winning the Cowboy
Grayson & Mackenzie

Bishop Brothers World

The parents get their stories in the first generation, the *Bishop Brothers* series.

Their children get their stories in the second generation, the *Circle B Ranch* series.

GRANDPARENTS
Scott & Rose Bishop

PARENTS
Evan Bishop
John Bishop
Jackson Bishop
Alex Bishop

KIDS
Riley
Maize
Elizabeth
Rowan
Ethan
Mackenzie
Kane
Knox
Kaitlyn

Reading Order

Each book in the Bishop Brothers World can read as standalones but if you wish to read the others, here's our suggested reading order.

BISHOP BROTHERS SERIES
Original Bishop Family
Taming Him

Needing Him

Chasing Him

Keeping Him

SPIN-OFF'S
Friends of the Bishops
Make Me Stay

Roping the Cowboy

CIRCLE B RANCH SERIES
Bishop Family Second Generation
Hitching the Cowboy

Catching the Cowboy

Wrangling the Cowboy

Bossing the Cowboy

Kissing the Cowboy

Winning the Cowboy

Claiming the Cowboy

Tempting the Cowboy

Seducing the Cowboy

Chasing Him
JOHN & MILA

John Bishop isn't your typical single dad.
Reserved, impatient, and utterly clueless.

Running the family's bed and breakfast has many perks. Working long hours, picking up after the guests, and hearing couples going at it all night long aren't any of them. Hooking up with girls who come to the ranch for horseback riding lessons? Best perk of them all.

That is until a baby shows up at his doorstep with a note claiming it's his. Growing up on a ranch was anything but easy, but raising a newborn is proving to be the hardest task he'll ever tackle. Leaving the bachelor life behind, his only priority is to hire a nanny who can teach him a thing or two about parenting—except he doesn't anticipate her being gorgeous and quirky with an unhealthy football obsession.

Mila Carmichael has many talents—making balloon animals, creating origami art, and remaining in the friend zone. Often seen as one of the guys, she's struck out more times than a rookie baseball player. Seeking a new adventure, she flies to Texas to visit family and is offered a position she can't refuse. Helping out a new dad should come easy to her, considering her past experience, but what she doesn't anticipate is him being an attractive Southern temptation. But that's only the beginning.

While growing close to his family and falling madly in love with the baby girl who's stealing their hearts, things are bound to get complicated. Everyone knows not to mix business with pleasure. That means no late movie nights, no stolen glances, and definitely no kissing behind closed doors. Too bad the universe has other plans—one that'll threaten taking away the main thing that binds them together.

You could break my heart in two
But when it heals, it beats for you

"Back to You"
-Selena Gomez

John

TEN MONTHS AGO

"You smell like shit," Jackson, my idiot twin brother, says the second I walk through the side door of the bed and breakfast I manage.

"Thanks for noticing," I grunt. Reaching behind my neck, I pull off my T-shirt that's filled with sweat and dirt and use it to wipe off my forehead and neck. "Maybe if you were on time for once, I wouldn't have had to do *your* job."

"I would've done it," he insists, but I know better. The horses need to be fed on a schedule, especially when they're giving trail rides in the afternoons. Jackson decided to sleep in after partying all night, which happens to be a regular occurrence. Running my family's B&B doesn't give me that luxury, because guests know when they're being fed late. If I stay out all night, I still have to get my ass up the next morning for work.

"Well, there wasn't any time to wait since we have to go to San Angelo for our tux fitting in an hour and a half," I remind him, and by the way his face drops, I know he forgot. "Stay here and man the desk while I shower."

I don't give him a chance to respond before heading toward the back door. Breakfast is being held in the main room downstairs, so I sneak out before anyone can stop and talk to me.

Luckily, the house Jackson and I share is within walking distance from the B&B, so once I make it outside, I jog home, kick off my shoes, and shed the rest of my clothes as soon as I step into the mudroom.

Once I've showered and dressed, I grab Jackson, put my assistant manager in charge for the rest of the day, and then we head out.

Alex, our youngest brother, is getting married soon, and Mama has been all over our asses about making sure everything is ready. She knows Jackson's a loose cannon, so she puts me in charge of making sure he gets his shit done. We might be identical in looks—dark brown that turns dirty blond during the summer as well as our trimmed facial hair—even down to the same tattoos we got when we turned eighteen. But our personalities have never matched. In fact, if we didn't have the same face and body build, I'd swear he was adopted.

"This has to be a joke." Jackson groans as soon as he walks out of the dressing room wearing a fitted black tux with a cowboy hat. "I look like a tool."

"You are." I snort, shaking my head. Evan, our oldest brother, and Alex are still in their dressing rooms, but as soon as they come out, I look at the four of us and chuckle. Evan has long, dark blond hair that he normally pulls back when he's working in the ER, and Alex is the only one who's a true blond and has it cut shorter than any of us. We've called him the "pretty boy" ever since he got drunk and pierced his damn ears. You'd think by now Alex would've taken them out, but he enjoys toying with our mother who absolutely hates them. His fiancée, however, must not mind them too much.

"We look like—" I continue.

"A bunch of classy hillbillies," Evan finishes for me, laughing at all of our expense. "I, on the other hand, just look classy." He smirks like an arrogant bastard. Out of all of us, Evan is the only one who's had to dress like this in any real capacity. Hell, he probably has a few tuxedos and suits in his closet.

"How are we doing over here?" a sweet voice asks from behind, and when I look over my shoulder, I see a gorgeous woman with dark brown hair—so dark it's almost black—pulled to the side in a long braid. She's wearing a tight pencil skirt with a ruffled shirt, and her piercing green eyes watch me as I study every inch of her. Her tan legs stop my gaze as an obnoxious cough pulls my attention away. Looking up, I see Alex glaring at me.

I shrug unapologetically for noticeably checking out his wedding consultant. He told me about her before but forgot to mention how hot she is.

"You have anything less...dorky?" Jackson asks, breaking the tension. Evan shakes his head, unamused, but Alex ignores him completely.

"I think y'all look great," she states, folding her arms in front of her. "Could lose the attitude, though." She flashes a smug grin, and I'm about ready to bow at her feet for putting Jackson in his place. Not many women do that—well, except for his childhood crush, Kiera.

"Ooh, you're feisty. What's your name, darlin'?" Jackson activates his smooth-talking voice, but it's not working on her, and that absolutely thrills me.

"Stop harassing her," I interject, stepping in to push Jackson back before he starts humping her leg.

"Don't worry 'bout me," she reassures. "He's not the first cowboy to waltz in here thinking he's a real-life John Wayne." She smirks, keeping her gaze on me. "I'm Bailey."

When she holds out her hand, I take it and introduce myself along with Jackson, so she doesn't fall for his switch-trick. He likes faking people out, which was funny when we were kids, but now that we're in our early thirties, it's just annoying.

"I'm the hot twin, clearly." Jackson winks, holding out his hand and purposely interrupting our conversation.

"Is that so?" she asks, reluctantly taking his hand in hers. "How do ya figure?"

Evan and Alex snicker as they stand by watching Jackson being shot down, something he's apparently not used to.

"Well, we may look identical in obvious ways, but, darlin', I'd be willing to show you in not-so-obvious ways later tonight." He winks at her again.

Bailey raises her eyebrows, obviously not taking the bait, but it's still hilarious to watch the train wreck.

"As tempting as that offer sounds, I'm gonna have to pass. I have a strict no-dating-clients rule." She shrugs and purses her lips as if she's really disappointed.

"No worries, sweetheart. I'm not your client. I'm your client's groomsman so—"

"So take the hint," I blurt, setting my jaw tight as I slap a hand on his shoulder and push him toward Evan and Alex. "Go change so we can go."

"Leave me your number!" Jackson shouts as Evan drags him back to the changing room.

Fortunately, Bailey is laughing and shaking her head instead of scowling like she ought to be. At least she has a good sense of humor.

"We usually leave him at home, but we have to take him out once a month for fresh air and socialization," I quip, smiling when I get a loud belly laugh out of her.

"You're funny." She steps closer, and our gazes lock on each other. "The tux looks great on you." She blinks when she realizes we're not alone. "All of you," she adds quickly.

The rest of the groomsmen show up shortly after and Bailey gets them all fitted. We chat throughout the appointment, and when I tell her I manage the Circle B Bed & Breakfast, she squeals in excitement.

"Oh my gosh, I've wanted to check that place out for forever!"

"Yeah?" I smile. "You should come out, and I'll personally give you a tour of the ranch."

Jackson snorts, and I curse when I realize he's behind me. "I bet you will."

"Shut up," I snap at him. "I'd love to take you out on the horse trail and show you around." I direct my attention back to Bailey who lights up like a Christmas tree.

"Actually..." Jackson interjects, *again*. "I'm the B&B's horse trainer. I'd be happy to give you a ride." He throws his signature wink her way while biting down on his lower lip. I swear if he weren't my brother, I'd pound into him without thinking twice. My hands ball into fists, but I force myself to calm down. Giving Jackson a black eye before Alex's wedding would make my life a living hell, regardless if it's deserved or not.

"Okay, Jackson," Evan intervenes just in time, smacking a hand on his shoulder and squeezing. "Let's go change before John punches in your face."

Bailey chuckles again, and the sweet sound brings my attention back to her. Once the room clears, and it's just the two of us, I offer her my number.

"Sure, I'd love that! I've never been horseback riding if you can believe it."

I smile, nodding. "Actually, I can. You grew up in the city?" I arch my brow.

"Sure did," she confirms my suspicions. "Is it that obvious?" She bites on her lower lip.

"Well…" I lower my gaze down her body and purposely check her out without apology. "I can usually tell. But don't worry, I'll choose a good horse for ya." I wink, and she blushes, which is adorable against her tanned skin.

A week later, Bailey calls me, and when I invite her over, horseback riding isn't the only thing I plan to teach her. The moment I return the horses to their stalls, her hands and lips are all over me. I pin her up against the wall and claim her mouth, feeling how turned on she is when she rubs her hard nipples against my chest. Moaning, I slip my hand into her panties, and my suspicions are confirmed—she's so goddamn wet and aroused.

I take Bailey to my house where she strips off her clothes and allows me to memorize every inch of her sweet body. She scrapes her nails along my hard stomach and screams my name as I push her ankles up to her shoulders and bring her to an ecstasy she'll never forget.

The following morning, Jackson is all over my ass after I walk Bailey to her car and we exchange goodbyes. He's pissed I kept him up all night, but I'm not one bit sorry because he puts me through the same shit on a weekly basis. But I know he's mostly pissed that Bailey was interested in me and not him. His poor little ego is bruised.

"I'm gonna be useless today, thanks to you," he huffs, slamming cupboard doors as he searches for something in the kitchen.

I snort, smirking. "Sounds like every day, so I don't know what you're talkin' about."

"Fuck off, asshole. You don't even give lessons, but all of a sudden, you're a Cowboy Smooth-Talker."

I roll my eyes at his stupid nickname. "Perks of working on the ranch, brother." I pat his shoulder. "Chicks dig guys who don't try so hard."

He jerks his shoulder, pushing my hand off him. "Says the guy who met his hookup at a bridal shop." Jackson chuckles.

I shrug, not letting his sour attitude bring down my mood. "Still ended up in my bed, so that's all that matters," I taunt. "Better invest in some earplugs. I might invite her over for round two later," I call out as I walk down the hallway. "Unless listening is your thing!"

"Fuck off!" is the last thing I hear him shout before I hop in the shower and start my day on a damn good note.

CHAPTER ONE

Mila

I love the feeling of a new year. The old saying "New Year, New Me" is officially my motto. I've started exercising again, filled out a ton of job applications, and even gave up chocolate—which might actually kill me— but after eating sugar like my life depended on it all through college, I know I need to lay off it for a while. My best friend and I have a running bet how long these resolutions will last—he says two months; I say at least six—but only time will tell.

The late evening rain pounds against my window, and though it's only six, it's practically dark outside. It's one indication that winter is still here, but I'm treating it as an extended vacation. After doubling up on my classes the last few semesters and working my ass off so I could graduate a semester early, I decided I'd relax for a few months. I've chosen to enjoy myself and not stress while I wait for several different elementary schools to review my résumé. Though I'm registered to substitute teach, I haven't been called in a few weeks, which is somewhat disappointing.

"Mila," my mother calls from downstairs. After I find a permanent teaching job, the first thing I'm saving up for is an apartment. My parents supported me taking a short break after taking a full load of classes along with my student teaching position last semester, but I don't like asking them for money. I'd rather earn it.

"Yes, Mom?" I ask from the top of the stairs.

"Your grandma called. Don't forget to call her back sometime this century."

I roll my eyes, and before going to change clothes, I peek inside the twin's room, but they don't even notice me. Katie and Avery are typical twelve-year-old girls and in the stage of makeup, celebrity crushes, and obsessed with their iPhones. Pretty soon, they'll be teenagers, which completely blows my mind since I've basically helped raise them.

I check in Becca's room, but she's not home from soccer practice yet. She's sixteen and recently got her license, so it's almost impossible to catch her. I try to be a great big sister, and since I'm the third oldest out of seven, I try to show them that I really care and love them because eventually I'll move out and things will change. I cried when Sarah and Andrew moved out, especially since we're so close in age. Piper is three years younger than I am and a freshman in college, so she only makes it home on occasion or when she wants money.

Tonight, I'm meeting up with my best friend, Cade, at a sports bar across town to watch football recaps from last season. It's typically how we spend our Thursday nights. He loves football, I love football, and together, we're a match made in heaven—if only he thought so. I've been securely placed into the friend zone since we met our freshman year in college, and I doubt that'll ever change, though a part of me holds out hope that one day he'll wake up and see who's been in front of him all along.

Letting out a sigh, I slip on a pair of jeans and boots and wrap a scarf around my neck before walking downstairs. Through the patio doors, I can see Mom on the phone. She waves me outside where she has the small gas firepit lit, and I head over so I can tell her I'm going out for the rest of the night.

As soon as I step outside, the Georgia cold smacks me in the face. Mom's cup of coffee is steaming. Though I've lived here all my life, I'm not sure I'll ever get used to the briskness in the air. Thank goodness for central heat. I swipe the hair from my forehead and adjust my ponytail.

Mom points to the phone and mouths, "It's your grandma."

I shake my head and show her the time on my phone, gesturing I have to go.

"Sure, she's right here," Mom says with a devilish grin. I somehow knew I wasn't getting out of this one.

I shake my head at her and take the phone. "Hey, Gigi."

"Mila. You promised me you'd come to visit, and I want to know when you're coming. The church is hosting a big cakewalk and pie sale for Valentine's Day, and I know how much you used to love that when you were little."

I smile. It's hard to be annoyed when I'm chatting with her, though she doesn't know when to end a conversation. Not that I take her for granted; I love my Gigi more than anything in the world, but I really do have a football date.

"I'll have to check and see how much tickets are," I tell her, knowing I promised I'd spend time with her once I'd graduated and had more free time. I hear papers shuffling, and I'm sure she's looking through the notepad she writes everything in.

"Before you say anything else, I know it's short notice, but Papaw said he'd pay for your plane ticket if you came. We miss you, sweetie. And your cousins miss you, too. Plus, since you graduated and are takin' some time off, maybe you could spend a few weeks or even a month visitin', comin' to church, helpin' around the ranch, collecting eggs from the coop—just like old times."

I smile. I used to spend a month or two of my summers there each year, but when I started taking summer classes, the tradition broke. Mom looks at me with a grin as she rocks in a chair my older brother made in woodshop in high school. The heat from the firepit licks my face, and I'm tempted to tell Cade to meet me here instead.

"Yeah, Gigi. I'll come. It'll be fun." I reminisce as she explains the cool weather, how Papaw's doing, and how I used to love visiting when I was younger. We'd go horseback riding and collect farm eggs and feed the pigs. It's the only time I felt like a true Southerner.

"I know you usually come with your brother and sisters, but you don't need them to visit your Gigi. It'll just be me, Papaw, and you for a few weeks," she explains, though my mind is made up already. "And of course, Katarina," she adds, mentioning my cousin who I'm pretty close to. I could use some adventure and take some time to relax after a hectic four years of school and really think about my future.

"You've convinced me. I'll be there. But I really gotta go. I love you." I hurry and hand the phone to Mom before I get stuck chatting all night and reminiscing about old times. I whisper and tell Mom where I'm going and give her a side hug before I leave. We've always had a close relationship mainly because I'm more like my mother than any of my sisters. Though she sometimes pries a little too much, she respects my privacy when I need it.

I walk to my car and send a quick text to Cade, letting him know I'm on my way. I get a thumbs up emoji in response. I laugh, crank the car, and head across town with the heat and music blaring. After finding a parking spot, I walk inside and see he's at the bar—with a girl I don't recognize—which takes me by surprise. Sucking it up and forcing a smile on my face, I head toward them and interrupt their intimate moment.

"Mila!" He stands and gives me a big side hug. "You have to meet my friend, Kristi."

He glances at her, and just by that one look, I know they're more than just *friends*. Jealousy creeps up and reveals its ugly face, but I try to force it away. Why wouldn't he tell me he was bringing someone? At least then I wouldn't have been blindsided by her. The thoughts and questions continue to swirl, but I try to forget it as we greet one another.

"Hey! It's nice to meet you."

"You too," she states as she eyes me—sizing me up. "I've heard a lot about you."

"I hope it's all good." Somehow, I manage to be sincere as I sit at the bar on the other side of Cade and order a chicken salad. At times like this, I don't want to follow my resolution and eat healthily. I want to drink beer and eat a double cheeseburger, but honestly, listening to them flirt kind of ruins my appetite.

Throughout the night, we chat about the replays and quarterbacks, but I can't help feeling like a third wheel. Their conversation drifts to a more private one, and I take their closeness as my cue to leave before the situation becomes more awkward than it already is.

"I'm going to head out," I tell him, just as they order another round of drinks.

"No, don't go. The night is still young."

Kristi laughs, and I force out a chuckle. "For you two lovebirds maybe, but I have an early day tomorrow." It's a lie, I know, but watching them flirt drives a spear into my heart. Just a reminder that I'm *only* a friend, and that's all I'll ever be to him.

"I'll walk you out," Cade offers, and I can't deny him. It'll be the first time tonight we've had any private time, but all I want to do is go home, put on my comfy pants, and eat my weight in ice cream.

Once we're outside and crossing the parking lot, he asks me what I think about her.

"She's nice," I add, unlocking my car and watching the lights flash, hoping they'll distract me.

"I really like her. She kind of reminds me of you," Cade tells me, breaking my heart even more. Why would he say something like that? Can't he see I've been here for him this whole time?

I keep a smile—the only security blanket I have at this point. "Then you should go for it."

"You think so?" He searches my face, and I give him the approval he's looking for.

I let out a laugh. "It's not up to me. I don't have to date her."

He stops and grabs my hand. "No, but you're my best friend. I want to know what you really think."

For a moment, I consider everything I want to say to him and almost lay it all out on the table. I want to ask why I'm not good enough, why he's never thought of me that way, and what Kristi has that I don't since she apparently reminds him of me anyway. It'd be easy for me to throw my feelings and heart on the pavement, but instead, I let out a shaky breath.

"I think if you like her, you should see where it leads. That's the honest truth."

That million-dollar smile of his returns, and I hate that my heart lurches forward at the sight of it. "Thanks, Mila. Text me when you get home, okay?"

"I will," I promise as we exchange a quick hug. When we pull apart, I feel the electricity soaring between us, but by the platonic way he looks back at me, I know it's one-sided. As he walks away, I slip inside the car and crank it, leaning against the headrest. How horrible of a friend would I be to sabotage his new relationship? It's too risky to say anything now, not when it's new and fresh and after he admitted how he feels about her. The realization that I'll be sitting on the sidelines *again*, waiting for him to wake up, hits me hard.

By the time I make it home, my parents are already in bed, which I'm thankful for. My mom knows I've had feelings for Cade for years, and she'll know something's up if she seems my face right now. I climb up the stairs, change into a baggy T-shirt, and crawl under the blankets for warmth.

As I toss and turn, I can't stop thinking about Cade, and the weight on my chest becomes heavy. Being supportive of his bad decisions is what I do. It's what I've always done and what I'll continue to do because I know him well enough to know he'll do what he wants anyway. Just before I click on the television, my older sister Sarah, calls me.

"What are you doing tomorrow?" she asks as sweet as pie. I already know what she wants just by her tone, and I smile—happy for the distraction. Sarah's four years older than I am, so we've always been really close. Mom's told me stories about how excited she was to have a little sister and always enjoyed helping take care of me. We quickly bonded even when we were in different stages of our lives. She's always been someone I can count on and vice versa.

"Um, well, I'm actually swamped. I plan to sleep until noon, stuff my face with junk food, and watch Netflix all while staying in my sweats all day."

I'm pathetic.

"Do you think you could break plans with yourself and watch Graham? I have a doctor's appointment that I totally forgot about, and an old friend wants to meet for brunch afterward. Please, please, please! I'll pay you whatever you want, and I'll even grab a bottle of your favorite red wine."

I let out a laugh. "You don't have to pay me. What time?"

"Eightish? Um, maybe make it seven?" Her voice fluctuates as if she's not entirely sure.

"I'll be there, but I'm feeding him chocolate milk all day, so he'll be good and wired when you get back," I tease.

"Bad idea considering he's lactose intolerant. The joke would be on you, *literally*," she retorts.

I chuckle, and a big yawn escapes me, causing her to do the same. I didn't realize how tired I actually was until now. "Yeah, never mind on that one. Anyway. I'll see you tomorrow, bright and early."

"Thank you. I love you!"

"Uh-huh, love you too."

I end the call and set my alarm. I'm feeling restless, so I turn on the TV. Too many thoughts swarm through my head, and they keep going back to Cade and Kristi. Jealousy rears its ugly head again, and I hate that I feel this way. I should be happy for him, yet I replay every stolen glance, every smile —all of the little moments we've shared—and the thought of them together almost hurts.

I close my eyes, listening to the soft sounds of the television, not caring what channel it's on. I don't watch it but allow the sounds and flashing lights of it to distract me. Though my eyes are closed, and my body's relaxed, I can't fall asleep, which frustrates the hell out of me. I need as much rest as I can get because Graham is a handful—especially now that he can walk. Giving up, I sit up in bed, remembering I was supposed to let Cade know when I made it home. Grabbing my phone, I send him a text.

MILA

I made it home.

MILA

We should probably talk later.

I don't know what made me send that last message, but there's just too much weighing on me. Sometimes when a person's in a weird place, it's better to talk it out, and he's my best friend, so I should be able to do that, right? After I think about it, I immediately feel stupid and wish I could delete the message, but it's too late.

CADE

Yeah. I need to chat with you about some things too.

My heart races as heat rushes to my face.

19

MILA

Perfect. Tomorrow then?

CADE

It's a date.

What the hell does that mean...*a date*? I'm overanalyzing everything. I lock my phone and eventually fall asleep, though I toss and turn all night, my mind wandering.

My body is awake before my alarm, and I'm exhausted. I slip on some clothes and make my way downstairs. As soon as my foot hits the top step, I can smell the coffee brewing in the kitchen and hear the soft mumbles of my parents chatting in the kitchen. That's one thing I'll miss about moving out —my parents. Though a pain in my ass at times when it comes to being nosy in my personal life, I love them so much. Once I come into view, Mom and Dad both turn and stare at me like they've seen a ghost. The twins are arguing about something as they eat cereal at the table. Becca comes from downstairs with earbuds in, humming to her music and ignoring everyone as she pops some bread in the toaster. Mom is digging in the fridge for the twins' lunches, and Dad is searching for something in the cupboards. Since Becca can drive, Mom has one less errand in the morning before work because Becca takes the twins to school. The chaos doesn't even faze me anymore. This is a typical morning at the Carmichael house.

"What are you doing up so early?" Dad looks down at his watch then back at me. He knows I usually roll out of bed a few hours after the kids leave for school now that I don't have my student teaching or classes to worry about.

"I told Sarah I'd watch Graham today." I stumble to the coffeepot, pull a to-go mug from the cupboard, and fill it to the brim.

"You're so nice. I'm sure she appreciates it." I look over my shoulder and see Mom smiling.

"Yeah, yeah." I laugh, blowing on my coffee after adding some creamer. I give them both hugs before I leave and tell my sisters bye.

The morning coolness hits my skin, and I wish I could sit in front of the fireplace all day and watch ESPN. However, considering my sister doesn't really have anyone else she can depend on, other than family, I don't want to leave her hanging. Her divorce was a messy one, and now that she has full custody of Graham, I try to help her as much as I can.

I drive a few blocks down the road and park at her house. As soon as I get out of the car, she's meeting me at the door with Graham in her hands.

"He's in a special mood this morning," she warns as he leans his head against her shoulder, looking as cute as ever.

"Hey, Graham Cracker. Wanna see your favorite aunt?" I sweet-talk him, holding out my arms, and he instantly reaches for me. Mom always says I have a magic touch when it comes to kids, and I should open a daycare instead of teaching first graders. Since I've grown up helping my parents with my younger siblings and spent several summers watching newborns at the church nursery, I'd almost agree with her. Babies love me, and I love them, and one day, I want to have at least four of my own. Growing up in a household with six siblings shaped the person I am today, and I've always dreamed of having a big family once I marry and move out. I smile at the thought when Graham tugs at my hair talking in gibberish.

"Okay, well I'll see you in a few hours." I smile at Sarah. She gives Graham a big kiss on his chubby little cheek and tells me thank you several times before I shoo her away. As soon as I try to set Graham down, he screams at the top of his lungs, and I fully understand what Sarah was referring to.

"Graham the Man," I tease. "No screaming like that or Aunt Mila isn't going to play with you," I warn him, and he looks at me with a death glare and returns his head to my shoulder.

"No!" he tells me, and I know exactly where he got his little attitude from—Sarah.

Once he's done clinging to me, Graham and I play on the floor with his trucks, Legos, and dinosaurs. He shows me every truck and lines them up. I watch in amazement at how big and smart he's getting. My heart tugs knowing his father is missing out on experiencing this, but I know it's his choice not to be involved anymore. It also tugs for Sarah's sake. She didn't choose to get pregnant and be a single mom all on her own. Her happily ever after bubble was popped, and now I feel sad that she's without companionship.

After a couple of hours of playing, I turn on the TV and sit on the couch holding Graham because I know he needs his late-morning nap. We both end up dozing off to the background noise of the TV.

When I wake up, my arm is numb, and a toddler is talking in my face about his toys again, and I let out a small laugh. That hour nap has him so wired; it's as if Sarah gave him sugar before she left. He scoots himself off the couch and begins picking up dinosaurs and special delivers them all to me. The couch is stacked high. I wish I had half the energy he has before ten o'clock in the morning.

Our day continues forward with snack time, more playing, reading a few books, and just before I'm preparing lunch, Sarah comes home. She's smiling and hands me a brown bag with what I assume is a bottle of wine.

"You might need it more than I do," I tell her with a laugh, looking back at Graham.

"It's your favorite, a gift from me." She gives me a hug and thanks me for everything. I finish making Graham's lunch, and just as I set his plate in front of him, he dives in and starts stuffing his face. "Slow down, buddy," I tell him when the spaghetti sauce starts to cover his face and hands.

"Someone's in a better mood." She looks at him, then back at me. "Thank you again."

Just as I'm about to tell her to stop thanking me, my phone buzzes and interrupts my thoughts. I pull it from my pocket and see it's a text from Cade asking when I can meet up today and have our talk. My heart flutters, and Sarah looks at me with her brows raised.

"Why don't you just tell him how you feel? Get it over with?" she asks. "What's the worst that could happen?"

I give her a disapproving look. "It could ruin our friendship since I'm ninety-nine percent sure he doesn't feel the same. Also, we both know neither of us are pros when it comes to relationships." Considering most of mine have ended with one-sided feelings or in heartbreak, that statement couldn't be truer.

"So there's a chance?" she quips, giving me a sad smile. "You're right, though." She scrunches her nose. "But to be fair, Tim was a dick."

"Not arguing there." I shrug before hugging her and saying goodbye.

I agree to meet him at a sandwich shop across town, and I replay everything I want to say in my head. Should I say something about how I've always felt or push those feelings back? How will it affect our friendship if I do and he's already falling for Kristi? I go over different options and scenarios in my mind and decide that I'm going to let him tell me his news first. Maybe he'll tell me how he feels, and then it won't be so awkward.

Ha! A girl can dream.

After parking, I walk inside and find him sitting at a booth by the windows that overlook the streets. It looks like a typical winter day, colorless, but I love living here. We order our food, and while we wait, I study him. He's biting his lower lip, which makes me even more nervous.

"So," he starts.

"Yeah?" I lift my eyebrows and take a drink of water, my mouth feeling dry.

"Well last night…" He pauses, causing my palms to sweat. I sit silent and wait. Seconds pass, but it feels like hours.

"Cade. Just spit it out," I encourage.

"Yeah okay. Last night, Kristi told me she's pregnant. And the baby's mine."

Holy shit! I hadn't expected that *at all*. I swallow hard, making sure not to let my emotions show. My heart races and everything spins. There are too many questions that I want to ask, but instead, I choke them back and smile. "Wow. Really?"

He nods with a small grin. "Yeah, we've been seeing each other off and on the past few months," he explains, and I feel slightly betrayed at the fact I didn't know he was seeing someone. I tell him almost everything, and I thought he did the same, but I guess not.

"I see." I glance over, grateful our food is being delivered. I thank our waiter before giving Cade all my attention. "So how do you feel about it?"

"I was shocked, and I think it's still sinking in, but I think I'm going to ask her to marry me. It's the right thing to do, and I really do like her a lot. I told my mother this morning, and she freaked out."

I search his face, wishing I could read his mind. "Do you *love* her?"

"I think I could," he admits. "I hadn't planned on settling down so soon, but she's carrying my child now, and I think I need to give it a chance for the baby's sake, ya know?"

"You're a good guy, Cade." I slide my hand on top of his. "Go with your gut instincts because they'll never let you down," I tell him with a sincere smile though it pains me to know this is going to change everything between us.

He nods, his gaze following to where our hands are. "Thanks, Mila. I don't know what I'd do without you."

Slowly, he's breaking down, the stress of him becoming a dad and possibly a husband is written on his face. As I glance up at him, I almost don't recognize my best friend or the man I've had a crush on for the past few years. But if there's one thing that's certain, Cade is a genuine and sweet soul, so this Kristi girl better realize what she has.

We finish eating, and sadness washes over me as he talks about his new future, and I know there's not going to be much room for me in it anymore. This isn't exactly the life he planned for himself, but I know he's too much of a gentleman to do anything other than what he believes is right. I'll support his decision, whatever it is, because that's what friends do.

After lunch, Cade walks me to my car and pulls me into a big hug. We stand there for a while, his scent overpowering my senses. He's always smelled good, and his cologne easily became my favorite the first time he wore it. When I push away, I see the worry in his eye.

"Wait, weren't you going to tell me something?" he asks.

"Oh, right." I think of something quickly. "Just that I'm going to visit my grandma in Texas for a month, so I won't be around to watch old football reels with you on Thursdays for a little while." I wink, fidgeting with my shirt and hoping he can't see right through my lies.

He takes in a deep breath. "I guess that's okay. You have my permission," he jokes.

I grin.

"Thank you, Mila." His expression turns serious, and I'm worried about all the pressure he's going to be putting on himself now.

I laugh, unlocking my car. "For what?"

"For being a good friend. You're the only person in the world I trust, and I can breathe a little easier knowing I have your support."

"You're welcome." I smile, though it's forced. I love that he trusts me so much, but it makes me wonder why he kept Kristi a secret until yesterday, and if she hadn't told him this news, would he have ever told me? "And you'll always have my support no matter what," I remind him before climbing into my car.

I wave as I drive away, and he walks to his car in higher spirits than before. I feel just like the rookie player who never gets to be a starter, watching everyone's life progress forward as I sit on the sidelines. I drive home in a daze, replaying everything that's happened in the past twenty-four hours. As I pull into the driveway and look up at the gray sky that perfectly describes my mood, my phone rings, and I see it's my grandma. A smile fills my face, and I happily answer the call because the new plan is to leave as soon as I can.

CHAPTER TWO

John

Jackson needs a boot in his ass. It's the only thought that fills my head when I saw the horses out of their stables and scattered all around the front pasture of the B&B.

He must've left the gate open again, which infuriates me, especially since I haven't even had my morning coffee first. Fog lines the ground, and my surroundings are coated in an orange hue due to a sliver of sun peeking over the horizon. Letting out a sigh, I walk to the barn, tuck some feed in my jacket pocket, and grab a few lead ropes. It's cold, considering it's January, and this is the last thing I want to be doing right now. Actually, the more I ponder on it, Jackson needs two boots in his ass. Just thinking about rounding these horses up alone as he sleeps infuriates me. Fuck this!

I storm back toward the house where he's happily sleeping. Walking in, the door slamming behind me, I go straight to the kitchen to fill a pitcher to the top with cold water. I even put a few ice cubes in it for good measure.

Without wasting any more time, I open Jackson's door, see him hanging halfway off his bed in his boxers and throw the water on him.

"What the mother fuck!" he yells, rolling out of his bed and hitting the floor with a loud thud. I hold back a laugh as he stands with water dripping from his body, looking as pissed as ever. He looks down at his wet boxers, then at me, and charges for me. I shake my head, move my body out of the way and watch as he slams into the wall behind me.

"Now, you and I both know you shouldn't get yourself all worked up before coffee," I taunt him. His chest rises and falls with anger. "So before you start throwing a little dick fit, you should know that all the horses are out roaming around the B&B," I explain, walking back to the kitchen and grabbing the lead ropes I left hanging on the back of a barstool. I don't even wait for him before I step outside to round up the horses. Moments later, I hear the door slam behind me.

"You're an asshole for waking me up that way," Jackson yells. I shake my head and keep walking. I pass the steps of the porch of the B&B and see all the plants that once lined the bed have been eaten to nothing. Mama's gonna be pissed, but I'll let Jackson answer for his mistakes.

A white mare is chewing grass, and I tuck my hand in my pocket, pull out some feed, and walk up to her. At first, she's hesitant but then comes to me, taking the bait. I click the lead rope to the metal ring on her halter and lead her back to the barn. I pass Jackson and roll my eyes at him, scoffing. He doesn't say a word because he knows I have a right to be pissed at him. My guess is he was out trying to impress a girl and forgot to lock the gate because that seems to be the reason more times than not.

After I walk two more horses back to the stables, I let Jackson handle the rest. I'm done. He made this mess, and it's time for him to clean it up alone. Considering most of the horses were out wandering around, I'm not surprised when I see my brother Alex and Dylan drive up. They both get out of the truck and help. I mutter a few curse words under my breath when a guest stops me.

"'Scuse me," the woman says, her hair wrapped tightly in curlers. She's wearing a furry housecoat with matching slippers, both bright yellow. "You gonna brew some coffee?"

I smile at her before walking over to the coffeepot. "You like it strong?"

She pretends to fluff her hair and looks me up and down before throwing a wink my way. "The same way I like my men."

Chuckling, I shake my head and start the coffee. The woman is about the same age as Mama, but it doesn't surprise me. I've been running the bed and breakfast for years, and I've learned that many people go on vacation for a quick hookup. Although Miss Daisy is definitely reaching out of her league.

I give her a smile, hand her a coffee cup, and walk away. Getting the hell out of awkward situations seems to be my specialty.

I open the curtains in the common room so when the sun rises, it'll peek through the windows and cast a warm glow throughout. Old lady McFlirty asks if I can light the fireplace for her, and I do. I bend over to stack freshly chopped wood inside the hearth. Instantly, the fire starts crackling, and when I turn around, she's staring at my ass. I hold back an eye roll and force a smile as she settles on the couch with her coffee.

As I'm walking toward the phone, Jackson comes barreling in. He looks at the older woman sitting on the couch and tilts his hat at her. "Howdy, Ma'am."

"Oh, so there's two of you?" Her voice rises in excitement, and I groan. She continues mumbling something about her fantasies, and I'm happy Jackson keeps walking. Getting him riled up is the last thing I want to deal with today. It's already been a clusterfuck.

"We're still missing three horses," he tells me, leaning against the counter. "Alex and Dylan are searching, but I don't know where they could've gone."

I glare at him. "Well, considering they've probably had all night to wander around, there's no telling where the hell they are."

"I'm sorry! Okay? I was showing Amanda around the stables last night, and one thing led to another, and I must've forgotten to lock the main gate. Throw a dog a bone every once in a while."

A dog is right.

Shaking my head, I flip through my to-do list for the day. "You're tellin' Dad."

"Can't we just keep it to ourselves this time?"

I look up at him, brows raised. "You really believe Dad doesn't already know? The last time, Old Betsy was over at the Lakefields' property eatin'

Mrs. Lakefield's flower garden. Thank God they were equestrian safe, or that would've been your ass. All I'm saying is the longer they're out, the more trouble you're gonna be in."

Jackson rolls his eyes. "You need to get laid."

The older woman chuckles but doesn't look over at us or—thankfully—volunteer herself.

"And you need to quit being an irresponsible horndog," I retort.

"No can do, bro. Living my best life, which you'd know something about if you actually had one." Jackson laughs, gives me a sarcastic smile, then walks out the back door. I hear him going on about something and look through the window where the other three horses are grazing in the distance. *Of course.* Makes me wonder when his luck is going to finally run out.

For most of the morning, I spend my time making sure the house is warm enough for everyone. Considering it's mid-January, and most of our guests like to spend their time inside by the fire, I find myself chopping more wood than usual, and before lunch, my arms and legs are sore from carrying loads into the B&B. Just as I'm taking a break to catch my breath, I see my brothers Alex and Evan bustling through the side door. Evan's girlfriend, Emily, is following behind them.

"What the hell is this?" I ask as soon as they're within earshot. "This can't be good." I cross my arms over my chest. Emily is smiling so big that it's hard not to smile with her.

"It's not bad news," she finally says, holding out her hand to show me the rock on her hand.

"Well, damn!" I relax and smile. I figured Evan would be popping the question any day now, considering they're expecting their first baby soon and have just finished building their dream house on the ranch. "Looks like we have another weddin' to plan soon. Congrats, you two!" I pat Evan on the shoulder and nod. He deserves every bit of happiness coming his way. They both do.

"Baby first, then wedding," Emily confirms. "I'm not walking down the aisle ten months pregnant."

Jackson snorts. "Another party! Yeehaw!" He hip thrusts the air, and Evan punches him in the shoulder.

"I'm shooting you with a tranquilizer," Evan deadpans.

"I'll help you," Alex adds.

"Can't stop, won't stop," Jackson taunts, spinning around and shaking his butt. He looks over his shoulder, then slaps his ass just to get a rise out of us.

"Oh my God." I groan. "Stop it. You're giving my face a bad name."

"I'm the only reason you're getting laid, and you know it," Jackson retorts, and it takes all my willpower to keep from smacking the shit out of him.

"Speaking of laid, Emily and I have plans that don't include any of you." Evan drags Emily by the hand toward the front door.

"Don't be rude." Emily smacks his shoulder.

"Trust me, John wants us out as much as we do." Evan jerks his head toward me, and I confirm with a nod. I have to get back to work.

"Yes, and take the evil twin with you," I reply, glaring at Jackson who then wraps his arms around my shoulder and makes a big show out of kissing me on the cheek.

Alex shakes his head, grabbing Jackson by the arm and thankfully pulling him away. "C'mon. The horses won't feed themselves."

Everyone's in good spirits as I follow them toward the front door. I love seeing Evan so happy after everything he's been through and the sacrifices he's made to do what he loves, which has always been helping others.

"Congrats again. I'm so happy for you guys," I tell them one last time before remembering it's also Emily's birthday, so I wish her a happy birthday too. I try to give her a hug, but she's so pregnant that it's almost impossible. She lets out a groan, and I remind her that my niece will be here soon enough. I love being an uncle and spoiling all my nieces and nephews.

Evan opens the door, but all three of them come to a stop, and I hear commotion in front of me about a baby.

"Is that a baby?" Jackson asks.

"A what?" Gasping, I step between them and see a sleeping infant in a car seat on the porch. It's the middle of January, so it's chilly—even for Texas—and I look at everyone else and then the baby again; we're all confused as hell.

"A baby," Emily confirms, her mouth slightly open in shock.

"Whose baby?" Evan asks what we're all wondering.

We all turn and look at Jackson.

"You think this is *my* baby?" He sounds offended, which is comical. "I double wrap my shit, thank you very much."

Emily snorts, knowing very well that Jackson has a reputation. "There's a note!" she says before reaching down and grabbing it. Her expression drops. "Oh, no." Evan leans over and reads the name written on the front, his brows raised in shock.

"It's for you." Emily hands me the envelope, and all the blood drains from my face when I realize what she just said. My heart is racing so hard in my chest, that it almost hurts.

"Shit, I didn't see that coming!" Jackson howls, and I'm tempted to throat punch him, so he learns to shut up.

I take it from her hand, and though I'm surrounded by my brothers, I feel as if I'm standing alone, the cold air brushing over me, as I open the envelope and pull out the letter.

John,

If you're reading this, then my lawyer has been informed of my death and brought you our daughter. First, I want to tell you how sorry I am. I'm sorry this is how you're finding out about her. It pains me to write this letter to you, and I wish I didn't have to. I find myself wishing for a lot of things these days. I wish for more time to be a mother to our daughter and time to watch her grow up and all the milestones I'll miss. After our time together, I knew you were someone special, but I wasn't in a place in my life to have a relationship, and I didn't think you were either. I did often wonder if what we shared was real or if we'd ever cross paths again. When I found out I was pregnant, then I knew it had to be real. She's a miracle, John. A true miracle. When I was twenty-two, I was diagnosed with PCOS and was told my chances of having a baby were less than ten percent, yet here she is. Completely perfect in every way.

I was weary through my first trimester, always expecting to miscarry. Then I made it through my second and finally my third. I knew I was lucky and even more grateful to even be experiencing the feeling of her kicking inside me. Once the shock wore off, I knew I needed to tell you, but I was scared. It crippled me, and every day, I told myself that was the day I'd call you. The guilt of not telling you nearly destroyed me, and the longer I waited, the harder it became. I should've tried harder to tell you, but knowing you moved on, I couldn't bear your rejection of a baby I was so thankful for.

So this brings me to now. As I'm writing this, I'm weaker than I've ever been and can't stop crying that my time with our baby is ending. I'd been having some health problems and blamed the symptoms on the pregnancy, but when I blacked out at work, I was taken to the ER where they found I had a brain tumor. I even saw a neurologist, hoping the diagnosis was wrong or not as bad as originally thought. I was told it was too advanced, and that surgery could be an option, but it wasn't a guarantee. The risks were high. I could die on the table, or they could get inside and realize the tumor was too invasive to remove. My other option was to do chemo to shrink it and give myself more time, but it would've aborted the baby. My last option was not to have the surgery or chemo and give our sweet child a chance at life. By the time she was born, those options were completely out. But I wanted to meet her, hold her, kiss her sweet face. I knew I'd never get to do that if I picked the first two options, and I wasn't about to put my life above hers, not when she had already proven to be such a miracle. The cancer had already spread so quickly, and the chances of survival were slim to none. Now, I have no chance at all.

But I don't regret it. Getting to spend these last nine weeks with her has been a blessing and the best weeks of my life. I chose our baby, John. Please take care of her. She's the best thing that's ever happened to me, and I know you'll fall in love with her too. She looks a lot like you actually, which makes me happy. My time to go is almost here. My body is shutting down, and no amount of treatment can help me now. Knowing I was leaving her behind has made me an emotional wreck, but I couldn't stand the thought of our precious girl being sent to foster care or worse—being raised by my parents. As far as I know, they don't know about her, and I'd like to keep it that way.

Her name is Maize Grace Kensington-Bishop. I listed you as her father on the birth certificate, so you have full guardianship rights.

She needs you now more than ever. I can't give her the life I wanted, but you can. When she's older, please tell her I loved her more than anything—more than my own life—more than words can describe. Tell her I'll see her again someday and will always be watching over her.

Tell her stories of how we met and us horseback riding together. Those nights we spent together were the most magical nights of my life, and I hope you can forgive me for not telling you sooner, but I tried. It was selfish of me, but after she was born, I wanted to spend what little time I had left with her and soak up every minute. I love you for *making me a mom, John Bishop. She's special in so many ways, and I hope you can understand why I had to do this.*

Love,
Bailey Kensington

P.S. All her paperwork is tucked into the side of her car seat. I'm so sorry.

The word *daughter* repeats in my mind as I blink and see everyone staring at me with anticipation. I become a tight ball of emotions as I hold the letter tight, but my arms fall lifelessly to my side.

"She's mine," I say barely over a whisper, glancing down at the baby girl with a pink blanket wrapped tightly around her, sleeping so peacefully. There's a pink bow in her dark hair. Swallowing, I continue. "Her name is Maize."

Jackson's mouth falls open, and even I don't know what else to say. I'm just as blindsided about this as they are. On cue, Maize opens her eyes, takes one look at all of us hovering over her, and releases a scream from her lungs. I look around, not really sure what to do. Emily kneels, picks her up, and then holds her gently against her chest. Standing up, she rocks her body back and forth to soothe her.

"Shh, it's going to be alright, little Maize. We're all going to take good care of you," Emily whispers, calming her and me at the same time.

"What did the letter say exactly? Who's the mother?" Evan asks, watching Emily calm the baby. She's already a natural, which doesn't surprise me.

"Do you remember Alex's bridal consultant who we met during our tux fittings?"

"The one you stole from me?" Jackson taunts.

I roll my eyes and ignore him. "Her name was Bailey, and she came for horseback riding lessons, and well, we hooked up." I lower my eyes, trying to really grasp the fact that she's gone. Honestly, I don't think this will ever sink in, or maybe I'm just in a state of permanent shock.

"You hooked up with my wife's bridal consultant?" Alex shifts on his feet and folds his arms.

"Yeah, why? Was she off-limits or something?" I scoff.

"Wait…" Evan interrupts. "Her name was Bailey?" he asks as if he's trying to remember that day.

"Yeah, apparently she was diagnosed with a brain tumor and—"

Evan and Emily look at each other, and an uneasy feeling surrounds me. "What?" I ask.

"Do you think…could it be?" Emily asks Evan, and he gives her a look.

"What's going on?" I wave my hand between their faces.

"Can I read the letter?" Evan asks me sincerely, and I reluctantly hand it over to him. I trust him.

I wait impatiently as Evan and Emily read over the letter, trying to hold back their emotions. Staring at Maize sleeping peacefully in Emily's arms, I still can't believe she's really mine. She definitely looks like a Bishop with the trademark nose and pouty lips.

"I can't believe this," Emily finally says.

"What?" Alex and Jackson ask at the same time.

"We had a patient come into the ER about four months ago who was in her third trimester and diagnosed her with a brain tumor just like this," Emily explains, the blood draining from her face. "Her name was Bailey, and she had chosen not to be treated."

"That must've been her," I mutter, my eyes glossing over as I think about Bailey going through that alone. If she's not close with her parents, I can only imagine how scared she was to make such a life-changing decision.

"It was her," Evan confirms. "Same last name and everything."

I release a deep breath, stunned by this realization. "You told her not to take the treatment?"

"No!" Emily quickly responds. "Our jobs are to explain all the options with risks and possible outcomes. She could've waited to get the treatment until after the baby was born, but even then, surgery was risky. She wanted to spend as much time with the baby as she could, and doing chemo could've prolonged her life, but she would've been sick for months. We told her everything and encouraged her to do what she felt was right." Emily's words should comfort me, but I feel nothing. Numb.

I can't believe this. How am I going to raise a baby on my own?

"So wait…what happened to her?" Alex interrupts.

"She only had a few months to live," Emily explains.

"Which is why she had the baby sent here," I continue, my vision going fuzzy.

Evan places his strong hand on my shoulder. "We're going to help you. We won't let you do this alone," he reassures me. Jackson, with zero jokes and all seriousness, tells me he'll help however he can. Alex pipes in too, telling me how great of a dad I'm going to be, and that he and River will do anything they can to pitch in, too. At this moment, I'm so proud to have these men as my brothers.

"I'm going to need all the help I can get." I brush a hand through my hair, not knowing where to even begin. Sure, I've helped with Riley, but this is different. This baby girl will depend on me for everything, and the weight of that is almost too much to comprehend. I almost feel as if I'm in a dream state, but there's no chance of me waking up. This is now my reality.

Emily looks over at me with a smile. "You should hold her," she says softly.

I take Maize and hold her gently in my arms. My body tenses at first, but then she opens her eyes and looks up at me, and I relax.

"I promise to give you the best life I can," I tell her. All eyes are on me, but there's no judgment. Instead, the bunch of them are smiling at me. It takes everything I have not to break down as the realization sets in that this is really happening.

Holy shit!

I'm a dad.

CHAPTER THREE

Mila

A smile hits my face as soon as the plane touches down in San Angelo. The elephant that's been sitting on my chest for the last week might actually move on, though each time I think about Cade, my heart hurts. After we deplane, I walk to the luggage carousel and grab the suitcase I plan to live out of for the next month. By the time I make it out of the sliding doors, Gigi and Papaw are waiting by the curb in their big Dodge Ram truck. Gigi gets out and walks over to me, looking as pretty as ever with her silver hair pulled back into a tight ponytail. As soon as we're within arm's reach, we exchange a big hug.

"There you are, sweetie!" *Gah, it's good to finally be back in Texas.*

Oddly enough, it feels like home. Though I've never lived here, I have handfuls of wonderful memories attached to this place.

"How was the flight?" she asks as we walk toward the truck where Papaw is sitting with a big grin on his face.

"It was fine. No turbulence at all. Even got a window seat and basically took pictures the whole time." I throw my suitcase over the tailgate of the truck and hop in the back seat.

"Good to see you, Mila."

"You too, Papaw! You didn't have to come to pick me up. I know how busy you are." I lean forward, patting his shoulder.

Shaking his head, he continues. "Wouldn't pass up the opportunity to see my favorite granddaughter." He flashes a wink over his shoulder.

Gigi slaps him on the arm because she has over twenty grandchildren and hates it when he calls favorites, but the truth is, he says that to all of us, and I kinda like it. Makes me feel special because when I'm with them, I get their full attention for the time being.

We drive toward Eldorado where they've lived their whole lives, down the twisting and turning country roads with speed limits closer to a hundred than not. I stare out the window, trying to take in the rolling hills and grayish sky. It's much colder here than I expected it to be, and my warm breath causes the window to fog.

As we pass through the old wrought-iron gate and travel over the cattle guards, I smile. After traveling a while down the old rocky road, the ranch home with the big wraparound porch comes into view. I can't wait for Papaw to stop the truck, so I can take in the cool, fresh air, then run inside and get warm by the fireplace. Something is sacred about Gigi's house. It always smells like sugar cookies, and it's the coziest place on the planet.

Once the truck is parked, I step out and take in my surroundings. The smile on my face doesn't falter, and as I look around, I realize this is exactly what I needed—nothing but peace and solitude. My grandparents' ranch is a small piece of heaven on earth that somehow washes away all the sadness.

Papaw grabs my suitcase from the back of the truck, and I'm half-tempted to run over to the tire swing I used to play on as a kid, but I don't. I'm almost shocked to see it's still hanging.

"Mila!" Gigi calls as I make my way toward the porch. "Kat wanted you to call her as soon as you arrived."

"Will do!" I say with a smile. My cousin Katarina and I have always been close, and we tend to get into trouble when we're together, but I'm looking forward to hanging out with her for the next month.

Papaw unlocks the door, and I step inside, taking in the time capsule from my childhood. Not much has changed, and it makes me happy. The same pictures are on the walls, and the old quilts are lapped over the back of the couch. Walking up the stairs, dragging my suitcase behind, I go into the bedroom where I always stay. I throw my suitcase on top of the bed and run my hand across the top of the quilt my great-great-grandmother made just as my phone buzzes. Pulling it out of my pocket, I see it's Kat and hurry and unlock the screen.

> **KAT**
> Hooker. You here yet?

> **MILA**
> Just arrived!

> **KAT**
> I'm coming to pick your ass up. We need to catch up.

> **MILA**
> Let's do it!

I go downstairs and catch Gigi up with my life as she mixes the dough for my favorite cookies. I tell her about my last semester of school and how hectic it was trying to finish early while doing student teaching, and she tells me what they've been up to around here, which actually is quite more than I expected. We laugh, and I help her scoop the dough into balls and place them on the cookie sheet. Shortly, Kat is walking through the door and basically tackles me when I come into her view.

"You two girls favor each other so much." Gigi admires us with a proud smile. Kat and I look at each other and laugh. When I'd visit in the summer, we used to tell people we were twins separated at birth because we look so much alike. We're the same height, have dark brown hair, blue eyes, and high cheekbones with dimples.

Gigi puts the cookies in the oven, and less than twenty minutes later, she's pulling them out and stacking them on a cooling rack. I take one as soon as Gigi turns around. It's hot as hell, but that doesn't stop me.

"I'm supposed to be watching my sugar," I admit after taking a large bite of the warm, gooey cookie.

"Why?" Gigi looks me up and down. "You could use some meat on those scrawny bones of yours."

I playfully roll my eyes and take another bite as Katarina basically pulls me out the door by the arm.

"Don't y'all be going and getting into any trouble," Gigi warns us.

"I'll try," I say right before I close the door.

We walk out to Kat's car, and I smile. "I wish it wasn't so damn cold, so we could take the top off this baby."

She runs her hand across the hood of her Camaro convertible. "We can take the top down."

Just the thought of it makes me shiver. It's cold enough outside without her driving seventy.

"I'm good," I tell her, but she doesn't listen and takes the top down anyway.

"It'll be good for you." She laughs. "And I'll turn the heat on."

"You're nuts, but that's why you're my ride or die."

Thankfully, she has heated seats and blasts the heat on my feet, but it's almost not enough. We drive down the old twisting country roads all the way into town where she takes us to the local diner. Once she parks, she looks over at me with a funny expression, and I know my hair is just as windblown as hers. My cheeks are as cold as ice, and I can't feel my toes.

"Let's get some coffee and pie," she finally says as she presses the button that puts the top up. *Thank God.* We both place our hands over the vents to warm them.

"That was such a bad idea," I tell her, shivering.

"You're right," she finally admits but shrugs. Kat isn't always about logic and reason, which is why she's known for being a troublemaker. Hearing about the messes she's gotten into is the only adventure I get in Georgia, but I do wish she'd take life more seriously now that we're getting older. She's almost twenty-three now.

We walk inside and find a booth as far away from the door as possible, so we don't feel the cold breeze blowing in. After we order our coffees, she tries to fill me in on the family drama I've missed over the past month. Kat's mom and dad own half of Eldorado, and she's always lived in style. Though we're basically the same age, Kat has spent more time talking about the future than actually making plans for it. I love her to death, but she's never had to work a day in her life for anything, which is probably how she got her nickname, Rebel Princess, during high school. She's never had to deal with real consequences because of who her daddy is, but since everyone knows everyone, nothing slips past her parents.

"...and apparently Kelly thinks it's okay to let her husband cheat as long as he comes home to her every night."

I shake my head in disbelief. Her sister married her high school sweetheart right after graduation, and it's been drama ever since.

"She won't listen to any of us, so we're just waiting for her to snap. Thankfully, they don't have kids, so hopefully, when she finally leaves his cheatin' ass, it'll be a clean break."

A waitress sets a carafe of coffee on the table and asks for our order. We order a piece of apple pie and a piece of cherry pie with extra whipped cream.

Kat looks at me. "So tell me what's going on with you. It's been about a month since we last talked."

"I know. Student teaching and grading took over my life. They practically killed me on top of studying." I sigh, taking a small sip of coffee.

"I bet!" She cringes on my behalf. "So how's Cade?" She gives me a smirk.

I roll my eyes, and her demeanor changes. "Oh, that can't be good."

A sarcastic laugh escapes me, and that's when I realize how bitter I really am about the whole situation. "Apparently, he'd been secretly seeing someone."

"And didn't tell you? I thought you told each other everything?" she asks, just as confused as I was when I found out.

"Exactly! That's what I thought anyway. But get this...apparently, she's pregnant."

Kat gasps and nearly chokes. "Couldn't wait to tell me that when I wasn't takin' a drink?" she teases.

I chuckle. "Sorry. Put the cup down because there's more." She does and gives me her full attention. "He's told me he's going to propose because it's the right thing to do." The annoyance in my tone is evident, though I try to remind myself I should be happy for him even if I disagree with it.

Kat practically picks her jaw up off the floor before she can form a sentence. "Wow. Did not see that comin'."

"I don't think anyone did, or at least, I'm pretty certain no one would because one minute he was single, and the next, he's having a baby and getting engaged. So yeah, I need to get over him because nothing is ever going to change between us now, and even if I did tell him my true feelings, it'd be too late. I'm not going to be *that* girl who tries to ruin a happy family."

"Geez, Mila. I'm so sorry." She reaches across the table and squeezes my hand.

I shrug, knowing I can't do anything about it now. I missed my chance, and it's something I'll regret forever.

"We haven't chatted in a few days since he told me, and I'm still trying to process it all. I'm basically building that wall so I can let go and move on, but I'll be there if he needs me. We're officially at two different places in our lives at this point, so it's only a matter of time before he pushes me out completely." I take another sip of my coffee, needing to warm up my nerves.

"Well, that happens in every friendship. One day, you're both partying it up, and the next, your best friend has a husband and kids, and you have no idea where the time went. Before you know it, you're nearly twenty-three, wondering how to even sort your laundry."

I chuckle, biting my lip because I know she's referring to herself, but she's good at making light of it.

"Well, if I had someone to do my laundry, I wouldn't bother to sort mine either." We're both laughing now. "Oh, I didn't tell you the best part!" I slap my free hand on the table much louder than I meant to. "He told me she reminded him of me. Can you believe that shit?"

"That rat bastard!" Kat says in a hushed voice between her gritted teeth. "There's no way she's as pretty, smart, sweet, and loyal as you are. There's only one Mila Carmichael," she states matter-of-factly, making me chuckle at how serious she sounds. Kat might have her flaws, but she really knows how to cheer me up.

"I know I'm better off, honestly. I've had some time to think about it and soul search, and I want him to be happy. If he ever had feelings for me, he would've said something or made a move. It was probably nothing but a stupid crush that I held on to for too long. We never even kissed. How pathetic is that?"

Our warm slices of pie are placed in front of us, and just the smell of the sugar makes my mouth water.

"You know what you need?" Kat says while we both take a bite of our dessert. "To find you a nice Texas cowboy, get married, have a bunch of babies, and live happily ever after right here in Eldorado!" Kat laughs, but her tone is serious. "Or…" She pauses before continuing, "you just need to get laid right now."

I pinch my lips together, moving them side to side and not exactly hating her ideas. "All of the above?" I chuckle.

"Deal. I'm going to help make this happen," Kat says once she swallows a large bite.

"No matchmaking, please. That never works out for me. Actually, relationships don't work out for me, period. They either put me safely in the friend zone and treat me like 'one of the guys' or they introduce me as their friend, who's 'like a sister.'" I cringe at the dozens of times I've heard that. It's like any chick who wears a football jersey can't possibly have a vagina. I shrug, exhaling a deep breath of frustration. "Maybe I'm doomed. I'll be a celibate cat lady who makes balloon animals for the neighborhood children, and then when I die, my cats can eat my corpse."

"Ew, gross. Why are you so morbid?" Kat laughs. "And depressing. Jesus. It's worse than I thought. Mission: *Get Mila Laid* is in full effect immediately." As soon as the words leave her mouth, my phone buzzes in my pocket.

CADE

She said yes!

A picture of Kristi smiling so happy with the ring on her finger comes right after the text. Another is sent where he's sitting beside her with his arm around her. They both look ecstatic, which is good I guess. I don't know anything about this chick, but if he likes her—loves her—then I want them to work out.

I turn my phone around and show the photo to Kat. By the look on her face, I can tell she's not impressed either.

"I really want to be happy for him, but man, I can't help feeling a tad jealous and maybe even a little bitter. Where did this chick come from, and why is she better than me, especially since she apparently reminds him of me? How does that even make sense?" I'm rambling now, so I shove the rest of the pie in my mouth to shut me up.

"Because you've been friend zoned since the day you met him and feeling rejected is hard considering you've had feelings for him for years. It'd be easy to understand your feelings of jealousy, Mila. They're completely valid, but you have to decide if you're going to let yourself wallow and be depressed or get yourself back out there and find your own happy."

"You know, for a relationship-phobe, you hit the nail right on the head." I smile, thankful that I have someone like Kat to talk to about this. I suck in a deep breath, pick up my phone, and type 'congrats' with a smiley face and tons of exclamation marks before hitting send and locking my phone. There's a reply, but I don't rush to read it. Kat's right. Rejection, jealousy, being put into the friend zone...it's like I set myself up to feel this way without even realizing it.

"Tonight, I'm staying at Gigi's too. After they go to bed, we'll sit by the fireplace, drink the bottle of whiskey I've been saving for a rainy day, and talk all this shit out like we used to do each summer when we were teenagers."

I snort and refill my coffee cup. "When we use to underage drink."

She chuckles and nods. "Yeah, but we both turned out just fine. You think Gigi ever knew?"

Nodding, I laugh. "Without a doubt. Our breath, bodies, everything smelled like whiskey. I didn't drink for years after that summer. Just the thought makes me deathly ill."

"Being teenagers in love is hard. We had to drink and talk out all our woes," she admits as she places her credit card at the edge of the table. The waitress picks it up and gives me a smile before walking away.

"Being an adult in love is hard," I mumble.

After our check is paid for, Kat stands and stretches.

"You know what? Fuck love," she says matter-of-factly.

We make eye contact as we exit, and I grin. I think that might be my new motto for the rest of the year. Hell, the rest of my life at this rate.

CHAPTER FOUR

John

Oh my God, what the hell is this? I hold up the contraption and rotate it back and forth, trying to make sense of what it does. It has a bunch of pointy sticks and holes. This can't be safe for anyone.

"It's a bottle drying rack, John," Emily tells me after she watched me for a good minute trying to figure it out. "Goes by the sink so when you wash the bottles in hot water, you can put them on the rack and air dry them."

"Why not just throw them in the dishwasher?" The words roll out of my mouth before I can stop myself. "Never mind. Dumb question." I shake my head, feeling frustrated with all these new gadgets that have quickly taken over my house. The kitchen, living room, and my bedroom. I have no idea how I'm going to do this.

As soon as I called Mama, she rushed over to the B&B and nearly had a stroke when I told her the news. I expected her to chew my ass out or hit me upside the head, but she took Maize into her arms and cried. Knowing Mama, she'd gladly accept anyone into our family, and my baby is no different. I let her read Bailey's letter, and then she started crying all over again, which then made Maize cry.

After realizing she needed to be changed and was probably hungry, I found a few supplies in her diaper bag that was left to the side of her car seat. Bailey left me a note in there as well, explaining her current schedule and how often she needs to be changed, bathed, and fed. And then *I* nearly had a stroke when she wrote that Maize wakes up every two to three hours during the night to eat.

Shortly after, Emily volunteered to go into town with Evan to buy everything I need. Since they've been preparing for their own baby to arrive, I trusted they knew exactly what to buy, so I handed them my credit card and thanked them for helping me out. I wouldn't have the first clue of what to get or where to even start.

Luckily, Mama let Maize and me stay at the main house for the first few nights since she had everything set up for Riley already. She helped me with swaddling, changing, and making and checking the temperature of the formula, and although the first night was rough, we made it through.

Now it's been a week, and I'm wondering if I'll ever get the hang of this. Emily's been in the nesting mood lately, and since their new house and nursery are all set up, she's claimed my house to clean and organize.

Not that I even mind.

Evan and Alex come walking into the kitchen from my room wearing scowls on their faces. Alex's shirt is off, and Evan is unbuttoning his.

"Why the fuck is it so hot in here?" Evan removes his shirt.

"I don't want her to get cold," I tell them. Maize's so tiny that I can't imagine her body being able to stay warm.

"She has like thirteen layers of blankets on her," Evan remarks.

"I'll go turn it down," Emily offers. "And check on her quick."

My brothers came over to help set up the crib and rocking chair. I don't want Maize far from me at night, so I had them set everything up in my room since Jackson occupies the other bedroom. Emily told me about co-sleeping when she brought over a co-sleeper that stands next to the bed, so I've been using that for now. I like being able to roll over and make sure she's still breathing. I had no idea I'd be so paranoid. Every sound sends me into a panic, and I find myself just staring at her to make sure she's all right.

Hell, I had no idea what it took to be a dad. A single dad, at that.

"She's fine. That swing is a miracle, I'll tell you that." Emily smiles proudly. I didn't even know what a swing was—shocker—but I have to agree with her. It's been a godsend for when I need to take a quick shower or put her down so I can eat something. She loves to be held, so anytime I lay her down, she'd start crying, but she definitely loves her swing and new vibrating chair. Alex found Riley's old one and brought it over for me to use.

It's truly amazing how wonderful my family's been, and it makes me think about Bailey, wishing I could've been there for her during those early days.

"Well, everything's set up," Alex announces. "We left the mattress raised so you can move it down once she gets older," he explains, knowing I wouldn't know.

"But you can still use the co-sleeper," Emily interrupts. "Lots of parents do for the first six months or so."

"Then why did I just spend my day off sweating my ass off to put it together?" Evan retorts, giving Emily a look.

"Because I said so." Emily flashes him an over-the-top grin. She has about two months to go before my niece is here, which means her hormones aren't one to mess with at the moment, and by the look on Evan's face, he knows it, too.

Alex snickers, covering his mouth with his hand as he tries to hide his smile. Even though he's the youngest brother, he has more fatherly experience than Evan and me combined.

"The mattress sheets and blankets have all been washed and are ready and so are all her new clothes, bibs, and receiving blankets," Emily informs me, and I'm already lost. She sees the concern on my face and before I can respond, speaks up again. "I'll go put everything away and make sure the crib is ready." She pats my cheek like a mother would to their clueless child.

Yep, that's me.

As if on cue, Maize starts crying, and I bolt between my brothers to get to her. The swing is no longer moving, and I figure the timer must've stopped. It's been a couple of hours, so I take her out and immediately smell her.

"Dang, girl. You put your uncles to shame." I scrunch my nose and walk us toward my room where all the diapers and wipes are stocked. Emily's eyes light up as soon as she sees Maize's awake.

47

"Hey, pretty girl," she coos, and Maize immediately stops crying.

"You're never leavin'," I tell Emily, only half-joking. "I think she thinks you're Bailey," I say sadly at the realization that she misses her mama and is too young to understand why she's not here. I've been so busy and tired that I hadn't even thought of how confusing this must be for Maize even if she's only ten weeks old. She spent nine weeks with her, feeling her touch, smelling her, being held by her weak arms. I imagine the day when she's old enough to ask questions, and I'll have to explain this all to her.

"Let me help, John," Emily says, breaking me out of my thoughts. "I can tell your mind is spinning."

I brush a hand through my hair and sigh. "When hasn't it been this week? I think I'm still in shock, honestly. I haven't had time to even really think about the next day, let alone years from now. What am I going to tell her? How? What do I even say?"

Emily grabs Maize and gently sets her down on the bed. I hand her a diaper and the box of wipes and watch as she effortlessly unsnaps her onesie and gets her diaper off in less than twenty seconds. That would've taken me two minutes, minimum.

"You're going to tell her what a warrior her mama was," Emily begins, making smiley faces at Maize as she continues to change her. "You'll explain how brave and selfless she was and how her mama loved her so much that she gave up her own life so Maize could live hers. And then you'll tell her it's okay to be sad, but it's also okay to be happy."

My eyes water without permission, and I look up at the ceiling to contain them. The less sleep I get, the more broken down I feel. Everything Emily just said has me wrapping my arms around her and thanking her.

She turns toward me and rests her palm on my cheek with a small smile. "And then you're going to tell her all about the day you became a dad. You'll continue about how hard and draining it was and how you never thought you'd sleep again, and before the conversation is over, you'll explain how she was worth it all. How happy you were to find out you had a daughter and how she changed your life for the better because John, there's no better feeling than being a parent. And even though our little one isn't here yet, I know I'd do anything for her. I see the same look in your eyes, and I know you'll be a great dad. It's hard right now, but you'll

48

eventually form a schedule and a rhythm, and you won't even remember what life was like before Maize."

Hearing those words are like music to my ears, and I can't believe Emily just poured her soul out to me like that. I know she's extra emotional lately, but as I watch the tears fall down her cheeks, I'm not embarrassed that I'm crying right along with her. This has been the hardest and most emotionally draining week of my life, but Emily's right. I'd do anything for Maize because my life is no longer just about me.

"Do I need to get my gun?"

We both snap our heads toward the door when we hear Evan's annoyed voice. I quickly look down to wipe my face on my sleeve and wait for Emily to explain before Evan threatens my nuts with his shotgun.

"Calm down, caveman," Emily teases. "I was just giving John a good parent pep talk."

"Well, can you do that without touching him?"

Alex snorts, and I hadn't even realized he was behind Evan.

"You're just jealous I'm getting more action than you," I taunt, knowing he's been extra careful with Emily lately since he's worried she'll go into premature labor if they have sex. He's a doctor, for God's sake, yet he treats Emily like she's made of glass and will break at any moment.

"Don't push me, John. You don't get a pass just because you're a new dad now."

"Yeah, we'll see when things are vice versa in a month or so," I mock.

"Who's gettin' action?" Jackson barges in as per his usual. Only interested when the conversation is about getting laid.

"No one," I say, dismissing him. "And keep it down."

"Why? She's not sleeping. She's wide-awake," Jackson states, stepping in and walking right toward Maize. "And she's a happy girl, I see." He smiles, which makes all of us laugh because Jackson doesn't know shit about babies any more than I do, yet somehow, he turns to mush anytime he sees her. "Not that I'm surprised. Her favorite uncle is home now," he gloats before reaching down to pick her up.

"Be careful!" I remind him. "Hold her head."

Jackson brings Maize to his chest and rests his palm over her tiny head. "You don't have to coach me every single time," Jackson barks. "I may be a lot of things, but I know how to hold a damn baby. Isn't that right, Maze?"

I roll my eyes, not wanting to argue with him while Maize's awake and currently not screaming her head off. This past week, I haven't slept more than three hours at a time. I'm behind on my chores, my laundry, bookings and schedules at the B&B, and just about everything else. But I look at Maize who's currently content in Jackson's arms and wonder if I'll ever get the hang of being a single dad.

Bailey's been on my mind nonstop, and I often wonder about her parents and family. We talked briefly about her childhood and how she grew up but never got into too many details about it. She didn't like talking about it, and we only dated for about a month before things fizzled out. Regardless, it makes me sad because I can't imagine trying to do all this without my family. Knowing she did it alone gives me the motivation to keep going even when I feel like giving up.

"Knock, knock." We all turn toward the door when Kiera's voice echoes down the hallway. Jackson immediately perks up but tries to cover his smile.

"We're in John's room," Emily announces. "Hope you don't mind. I invited her over. She wanted to meet Maize." She looks at me with pitiful eyes.

"It's fine," I say. I've known Kiera since we were kids, and she's basically a Bishop with how often she's here.

"Oh my gosh," Kiera squeals as soon as she spots Jackson. "She's adorable!" Kiera reaches out and grabs Maize out of his hands and starts making googly eyes. "There is no denyin' she's yours, John," she teases, walking closer as she studies her features.

"Or mine," Jackson taunts. I give him a look, daring him to test my limits right now. "But considering she has John's temperament and scowl, I can't even pretend it could be an option."

Kiera snorts and rubs her finger along Maize's cheek. Just like she does with Emily, Maize looks up and flashes a little smile. My chest tightens, knowing that she's not only going to miss Bailey but an actual mother figure in her life. I only hope I can be enough for her, so she doesn't feel the void.

"You look pretty natural holding that baby," Emily comments, giving Kiera a knowing look. If I had to guess, it has something to do with Kiera wanting to get married and start her own family soon. She and Emily went to college together and are the same age, so with Emily settling down, Kiera's been more vocal about wanting that too.

Jackson growls in protest, but everyone ignores it. He only pretends that he doesn't care who she dates, but we all know better. He's been in love with her since before either of us knew what it meant.

Kiera Young is a strawberry blonde bombshell and always has been one of the prettiest girls around, yet she's always struggled in the relationship department. The rest of us have our suspicions as to why they never worked out. Kiera's been in love with Jackson, too, but since he insists on sleeping with half the female population in town, she's never told him—though, to be honest, she hasn't exactly been discreet about her feelings.

She's been dating our local vet, Trent Laken, since early last year, and it's made Jackson turn into a complete dumbass—well more than usual anyway. Instead of telling Kiera how he feels, he whores around and denies wanting her. No one really understands why.

Her parents and our parents have been family friends since we were kids, and ever since Jackson could chase her around the ranch in diapers, they've been inseparable. They'd be perfect for each other if he could get his head out of his ass and man up; otherwise, we all know what's going to happen—she's going to find someone who realizes how amazing she is and scoop her up for good.

He continues to pretend they're just friends no matter how many times we tell him he's gonna be too late if he doesn't say something soon. The denial was believable in our teen years, but as we got older, it became more evident. They talked and hung out all the time, and anytime one of her boyfriend hurt her, Jackson would knock his teeth out and console her. If he had any brains at all, he would've used those opportunities to finally make his move.

"Please don't tell me you want to have babies with the vet?" Jackson scoffs, crossing his arms.

I smack him and narrow my eyes at him.

"So what if I do?" Kiera retorts. "I'm not gettin' any younger."

Noticing things are about to get heated, I step in and take Maize from her arms. "I'm just going to go feed her, so she lays down for a nap," I explain. Emily gives me a funny look, knowing damn well Maize just woke from a nap.

"So that means having babies with just anyone?" Jackson snickers.

"Trent is not *just* anyone," Kiera argues. "Plus, it's not like there's a line of guys offerin' to start a family with me."

"Oh, so you're just goin' to settle?" Jackson grunts, and I should really walk away, but this whole scene is like a car wreck.

I can't look away as he continues to dig his grave deeper.

"I'm not settlin'," she confirms. "Now you listen here, Jackson Bishop." She pokes a finger in his chest and steps right into his space. "You don't get to tell me who I can and can't have babies with, ya hear? You're supposed to be my friend, and last I checked, friends are supportive and caring, not super jackasses like you're being."

"Why don't we go check on the horses," Alex interrupts, likely trying to defuse the situation. This isn't the first time Kiera's had to put Jackson in his place, and the fact that she's the only person who can says something right there. If it were anyone else telling him off, Jackson would be pushing right back.

"Yeah, fine," Jackson says as Alex pulls on his arm toward the hallway. He walks around Kiera without saying another word.

"Well, that was entertaining. Can we leave now?" Evan says, breaking the awkward tension once Jackson and Alex are gone.

Kiera visibly relaxes and releases a deep breath. "I swear to God, that man makes me want to stab him sometimes."

"Oh, is that all? He makes me want to choke him with a rattlesnake in his sleep," I tell her.

Emily and Kiera chuckle.

"I'm going to get her bottle now," I say before thanking Evan again for putting together the crib before he and Emily head out.

"Do you mind if I hold her once more before I go?" Kiera asks, reaching for her. "I have to load up the trailer and get back to the ranch soon."

"Of course," I say, handing her over. She follows me out to the kitchen with Maize in her arms.

Kiera's a horse trainer, and we outsource our horses to her often when we have more than we can handle. She trains them for trail riding and helps run her family's ranch, so we see each other a lot, which means anytime Kiera comes around, Jackson acts stupider than usual. I think he does it to get a rise out of her.

"She's seriously beautiful, John." Her voice is soft and sincere, not anything like it was a few minutes ago. Kiera doesn't have a mean bone in her body except when it comes to her tolerance for Jackson's behavior.

"I know." I grab the formula from the cupboard and scoop it into a bottle before I mix it with water. "Her mother was gorgeous too."

"I believe it." I turn around and see Kiera smiling wide. "I know I shouldn't be in a rush to have babies, but I can't help it. I'm not in my twenties anymore, which means I only have five or so years left before complications could arise."

"Well, I hear the Bishop sperm is pretty powerful." I chuckle, shaking the bottle to mix it up. "I'm actually surprised Jackson is the only one who doesn't have a baby, considering his reputation."

Kiera rolls her eyes as if she's thought the same thing. "That's because he's too selfish to ever consider having a family and kids. He wants to be on his own time clock and do whatever the hell he wants. It was cute at twenty-one maybe, but ten years later, it's pathetic."

"Geez, Kiera. Don't hold back," I tease, reaching for Maize again.

Her shoulders drop, and she releases a frustrated breath. "Sorry, I shouldn't unload on you like this. He's just so…frustrating."

"Welcome to my life twenty-four seven." I groan.

"Why does he refuse to grow up? I don't understand," she asks as I take Maize from her hands.

I sit at the table where I can hold and feed her. She happily takes the bottle and starts sucking away, staring up at me as if I'm her whole world.

"Jackson has always been the wild child," I say. "He's rowdy, likes to play pranks, be obnoxious, and hasn't yet figured out that he's not a teenager anymore. He needs a good dose of tough love to crack through his stupidity sometimes."

"What he needs is a swift kick in the ass," she remarks, twisting her finger around a lock of her hair.

I chuckle and nod. "That too."

CHAPTER FIVE

Mila

"**I**s that what you're wearing?"

Looking at my reflection in the mirror, I gaze down my body at the outfit I picked out. "Yeah, what's wrong with it?" I ask Kat, who's staring at me as if I have a third eye.

"Are you going to a Valentine's fundraiser or a funeral?" She narrows her eyes at me, disapproval of my black shorts written all over her face.

"That depends. Considering I'm going to a church event on Valentine's Day, it very well could be the death of my social life."

Kat snorts. "Well, as much as I'm diggin' this Gothic chic look, it's gonna scare away any potential men suitors, so let me pick something out for you. Something a little less…*sad*."

Rolling my eyes, I cave and take off my black dress and sneakers. I've been here for three weeks now, and Kat has used every opportunity to try to find me a man or, rather, a *cowboy*—her words, not mine. Though I'm perfectly content to just spend time with my grandma and be back on the ranch again, she seems to think I need a guy to get over my feelings for Cade.

Kat tosses me a bright red top with black cut-off shorts and then tells me I can borrow a pair of cowboy boots.

"Much better!" Kat praises. "Definitely bangable now."

I burst out laughing and double-check myself in the full-length mirror. "These boots really bring out the hillbilly in me," I tease, clapping them together.

"Girls!" Gigi knocks on the door. "Time to go."

I'm not sure how I got talked into going, but I find it hard to say no to Kat and especially Gigi. She's an active churchgoer, but Kat and I both know it's because it's more of a gossip gathering than anything.

Once we're packed into the truck with Gigi's famous lemon pound cake, we head into town, and Kat fills me in on all the details. There's a cakewalk, private auction, games for kids, and other activities to help raise money. All the profits of the annual event goes to the local food bank, which cements my decision to participate.

"I've died and gone to cake heaven," I say as soon as we walk into the banquet hall and inhale the sweet scents. The crowd is already overwhelming, but if I'm being honest, I didn't have anything else to do.

Gigi sets her cake on the table and walks us around, introducing me to all her friends. I'm not sure why Kat thought this would be a good place to meet guys because, at this rate, the only guys here are under ten or over seventy.

"I'm not sure if you're aware, but I'm not looking for a sugar daddy," I tease Kat when we're alone.

"It's all about networking," Kat reassures me. "They all have grandchildren, ya know."

"And that helps me how?"

Kat faces me and flashes a devilish smile. It's all I need to suspect she's up to something.

The event begins when an older woman grabs everyone's attention and starts explaining the details of the cakewalk. Squares with numbers are placed on the floor, and when the music ends, a number will be called out and whoever is standing on that number gets to choose a cake to buy. This continues until no cakes are left, and since I'm determined to get a cake, I'm playing to win.

Only three cakes are left when my number gets called.

"Yes! Finally!" Kat and I high-five, then she helps me pick one. "Triple layer chocolate it is! I plan to eat this in one sitting."

"Then plan to puke it all up later." Kat snickers.

"It'd be totally worth it."

"Yeah, you can taste it going down *and* back up!"

Laughing, I pick it up and bring it to my nose. Yep, would totally be worth it.

Before walking away, I feel a tap on my boot, and when I look down, I see a small hand from underneath the tablecloth. Setting my cake back down, I pull back the tablecloth and see a little boy. He can't be older than two years old.

"Hey." I smile, kneeling to his level. "What's your name?"

"Riwey."

I laugh when he tries to say his name. "Nice to meet you, Riwey. I'm Mila. So what are you doing down here?"

At first, he's shy but then grins wide. "Hiding." He puts a finger up to his lips to signal me to keep quiet.

"Oh, who are you hiding from?" I whisper with a smile.

"My grammy," he responds, peeking his head out to look around.

I look over my shoulder and spot an older woman walking toward us, calling out his name. "Riley Bishop! Come here before I paddle your behind."

Riley giggles, sinking farther under the table. Now I definitely know this is a one-sided game of hide and seek.

"I think your grammy is looking for you."

He shakes his head and covers his mouth with both hands.

Dropping the tablecloth, I look over the table and see his grandmother searching around, growing frustrated as she asks another woman if she's seen her grandson. After a minute, I make eye contact with her and jerk my head at the table, so she gets my signal. With a grateful smile, she walks over and plays along.

"Hmm, I wonder where he could be," she says loudly. Both of us hear Riley giggling, and we both smile and laugh. "Riley, come out."

I peek under the tablecloth again and see him shaking his head.

"Don't you wanna come out and play?" I ask and realize I'm trying to negotiate with a toddler.

"No!" He stands his ground.

The woman releases a frustrated breath, and I can tell she's not in the mood to crawl under there and grab him.

"Your daddy is waitin' for us, so you best get your behind out here before I come after you," she threatens, but Riley doesn't budge.

"Let me see if I can help," I say to her softly.

I crawl completely under the table until the tablecloth drops back down, and Riley and I are alone.

"So how old are you?"

He holds up a finger. My guess is he's closer to two than one, but I smile and nod.

"What's your favorite color?"

He shrugs.

"Favorite food?"

"Candy!"

I chuckle. "Me too. Well, cake. And ice cream. Really anything that's sweet and delicious."

"I love iscream!"

"Yeah?" I perk up, acting overly excited. "Should we go get some? I heard they have a sundae bar with sprinkles, cookies, and chocolate sauce!" I hold out my hand, hoping he takes the bait.

I'm relieved when he finally takes my hand and agrees to come out from under the table. He lets me pick him up and giggles when his grandma gives him a stern look.

"Were you hiding from me?" she teases.

"You found me!" he says, and we both laugh.

"I kind of promised him a sundae," I tell her, worried about her reaction about my bribing.

"Well, what a coincidence. I was on my way over there too." She winks at me, and the three of us make our way the kitchen area.

"Vanilla or chocolate?" I ask Riley, and he points at the chocolate. "A man after my own heart. That's my favorite!" I grab a bowl of the chocolate and set him down so he can point out which toppings he wants.

"Oreos, gummy bears, and sprinkles. Your daddy is never gonna trust me with you again," his grandma teases.

"Well, you blame me if you need to," I say, laughing at the mountain of candy Riley picked out. You can't even see the ice cream anymore. Carrying his bowl, we walk over to an open table and sit.

"What's your name, dear?" she asks.

"Oh, sorry. My name's Mila Carmichael." I hold out my hand, and she takes it with a big smile.

"Lovely to meet you, Mila. I'm Rose Bishop."

"Nice to meet you too. You have a very energetic grandchild."

"Very much so. Good thing I'm the grandma and can sugar him up before sending him home."

Laughing, I look at Riley who already has a mouthful of ice cream and candy.

"You're good with him," she says after a moment. "He doesn't normally take to people so quickly."

"I have six brothers and sisters and a couple of nieces and nephews. I've had my fair share of talking kids out from under a table."

"Wow, big family! You're a natural." She smiles widely. "I haven't seen you here before."

"Oh, I'm actually visiting from Georgia. My grandma and cousin are here somewhere." Just as I start looking around, I spot Gigi and Kat walking toward me.

"Rose!" Gigi exclaims. "You met my granddaughter, Mila."

"She's yours? Well, I shouldn't be that surprised." Rose smiles, wrapping her arm around Gigi and motioning for her to take a seat. "Katarina, hello dear! You look lovely tonight."

"Good to see you, Mrs. Bishop," Kat says, giving her a side hug. "Thank you!"

"I'm so excited y'all came!"

"Of course," Gigi says. "Mila's only here for a month, so Katarina and I are showing her all around."

"Only a month, huh?" Mrs. Bishop frowns, which confuses me. "That can't be long enough."

"Well, I don't want to overstay my welcome," I interrupt.

"Oh, you'd never," Kat blurts. "Plus, you aren't leaving till you meet a real Southern gentleman."

I roll my eyes and sigh. "I actually did!" I wrap my arm around Riley's little shoulders and smile. "We both like ice cream, which is more in common than I've ever had with any other guy, so I'm thinking he's the one," I tease, crossing my fingers and getting a rise out of Kat.

Mrs. Bishop and Gigi both laugh as Kat frowns.

"You should come tour our ranch," Mrs. Bishop says, grabbing my attention. "Plenty of Southern gentleman stock." She smirks, giving me one of those looks, and I know she's up to something. What is with these Southern women always trying to play matchmaker?

"Ooh yes, we definitely need to go! Ranch hands galore! Not to mention, Mrs. Bishop has four sons of her own!"

"Yes, but two are taken," she states.

"That leaves the twins," Gigi interrupts with a laugh, though I'm not sure what's so funny. This is starting to feel like a meat market, and I'm on display.

"No setups," I blurt. "I'm fully capable of finding my own dates," I tell Gigi and Kat, though I don't even believe my own words.

"Clearly." Kat snorts, jerking her head toward Riley.

"I never said they were age appropriate," I mock.

"Well still, you should come out before you leave, okay?" Mrs. Bishop insists.

"Sure, that'd be great," I say to appease her.

Once Riley has tapped out and is on a full-out sugar high, Mrs. Bishop concludes that's her cue to leave and get him home before he starts jumping off the walls. Gigi, Kat, and I leave shortly after, and as we're driving home, I think about Cade and how fast his life is moving now and wonder if I've been holding back all this time waiting on something that was never mine.

CHAPTER SIX

John

"What's this?" I ask when River holds out a book as thick as the Bible. I fell asleep in the rocking chair again with Maize on my chest. I felt a tap, and when I peeled my eyes open, River was standing in front of me.

"What to Expect the First Year," she answers, setting it on my lap and taking Maize from me. "It was my saving grace with Riley. There's a ton of information, and it'll help ease your mind by answering some basic questions you might have. Talks about milestones and all that too."

I blink a few times, trying to wake myself up, though it's late and Maize's bedtime, which means I should go to bed while she sleeps because it'll only be a matter of hours before she's up again.

"Oh, well, thank you." I scan my eyes over the cover and flip through the pages. "I need all the help I can get." I release a deep breath. I'm currently living on the three hours of sleep I got last night and can barely

"Speaking of help, why don't you get some?" she asks pointedly, rocking her body back and forth as she snuggles Maize to her chest.

Furrowing my brows, I give her a look and huff. "Are you offerin'?"

"Sure, let's trade. Riley's already into the terrible twos."

"The terrible twos?" That doesn't sound good at all.

"That'll be in the next book." She chuckles. "But seriously, you can't keep going on like this. It's been almost a month, and you're doing this alone—all night long. You have bags under your eyes, you're running on zero energy, and you can't possibly think that's best for Maize."

I sigh, already over this conversation. I've heard it plenty. Mama watches her while I sneak into work for a couple of hours each day, but other than that, it's just been Maize and me from the beginning.

"It's only been a month," I remind her. "I'm still adjusting to her schedule."

"Exactly my point, John," she says. "But you have to eventually go back to work full-time. We all know Jackson can't run the B&B for shit, and Alex and Dylan can only take over Jackson's work for so long. You're going to burn everyone out, including yourself."

"Well, aren't you Miss Pessimistic." I grunt.

"More like Mrs. Reality," she retorts. "Plus, you're really becoming a cockblock since my husband comes home dead tired every night and passes out the second his head hits the pillow. Or maybe it's a vagina block?" She thinks to herself, and I'm completely lost. "Whatever. Either way, I'm not getting laid, and it's your fault."

"I'm...sorry?" I offer, not really sure how this conversation turned into her and my brother's sex life, which is weirding me out.

"You should be. I'm trying to give you another niece or nephew, and that's pretty impossible when I'm not getting any." The tone in her voice is bitter, and I hold back a chuckle when I think about my brother being too tired for sex, considering she got pregnant within the first two weeks they met. Her blonde hair is pulled up into one of those messy knots, and by the death glare she's shooting at me, I know she's serious.

"You're trying to get pregnant?" Definitely news to me.

"Yeah, well, not preventing, but kind of trying. Between our crazy work schedules, it doesn't give us a lot of time, so when I greet my husband in lingerie, and he's too tired to even rip it off, I take it a little personally."

I scoff, really wishing she would change the subject. "You know it's not because of you. This is a busy time on the ranch, trying to get everything ready for early spring." I brush my hand through my hair, pushing the longer strands on one side to the back and out of my eyes.

"Every time is a busy time of year," she says robotically as if she's heard it time and time again. "But this isn't helping, and you know you can't keep going on like this. Get some help so you can actually be a dad to Maize instead of a zombie."

"She just needs to get on a sleeping schedule, and then I'll be fine."

"And then what? You're just going to wear her on your chest all day long as you do schedules and make coffee at the B&B?" She quirks a brow, and I know she's right, but I don't tell her that.

"Well, I was hoping Mama would watch her when I'm back to work full-time, but I'd like to be able to pop in at home and see her during my breaks, but I guess that's not really an option since she has Riley during the day right now."

"And once Emily goes back to work, Mama already volunteered to watch their baby too."

"So what are my options? Hire a babysitter?" I ask, hoping she has all the answers because she's acting like she does. I know she means well; I'm just too tired for a dose of honesty right now.

"Babysitter or nanny. Someone who can stay at the house while you work so you can just walk over and visit during your shifts. Someone who knows about babies and can help get Maize on a good schedule for you, so you don't look like the walking dead. Then that way you aren't far away, and you can keep an eye on them," she replies. "Plus, I'm pretty sure your mama is already on a mission to find you someone, whether you agree to it or not."

Groaning out in frustration, I scrub a hand over my jaw. "Shit. Knowing Mama, she'll send a nanny, housekeeper, and the National Guard to come in and help me."

"I honestly wouldn't put anything past that woman." She quietly laughs, and I do, too, because Mama is predictable in that she's unpredictable.

"So let's say I agree to get someone to come help. How am I going to even find someone qualified and trustworthy?"

"Well…" She snickers. "It's the twenty-first century. Welcome to Google and nanny services. They do full background checks and interviews. Or if you don't want to hire a stranger, I'm sure someone around here knows someone who's good with babies."

"Okay, well, I'll start looking online tomorrow and see what I can find," I tell her to put her at ease.

She hands Maize back to me and kisses her little chubby cheek. "You better because if I don't see my husband and get a baby out of this, I'm comin' back for you." She points her finger at me, and I roll my eyes at her threat.

Once Maize's asleep in the co-sleeper, I make myself something to eat and think about what River said. Grabbing the heavy-as-hell book she left me, I open it to the first chapter and begin reading.

An hour later, I'm in bed with the book and thinking about how I'm going to continue living like this. I know Mama only wants what's best for me, and River is only saying what's true, but that doesn't help me in knowing what to do. Maize's still so new in my life, and I'm so terrified I'm going to screw this up for her. Alex tells me every dad feels that way, but I feel it on a deeper level because she's already lost so much.

It's 3:00 a.m. and Maize's screaming her lungs out. Every time she wakes up in the middle of the night, it scares the shit out of me. You'd think after three weeks, I'd be used to being woken up by her, but I'm always in such a dead sleep that it nearly has me jumping out of bed in a panic.

"We need to get you on a better sleep schedule, Little Miss," I tell her as I walk us toward the kitchen. "Daddy needs more than a few hours." In my half-asleep daze, I stub my toe on the leg of the dining table, and a variety of curse words fly out of my mouth. "Son of a bitch, that hurt."

Maize doesn't give me an ounce of pity as she continues crying, and I hop on one foot. I do my best to one-hand prep her bottle and warm up the water before mixing the formula in. As soon as I start shaking it up, liquid goes everywhere. On the walls, ceiling, cupboards, floor, and me. It's then I realize I forgot to put the lid on.

"Shit!" I slam the bottle down on the counter and look at the mess. I'm so goddamn tired, and with Maize bellowing in my ear, I can't think straight.

"What in the hell happened here?" Jackson comes stumbling in wearing only his boxers and a blonde attached to his arm in nothing but one of his T-shirts. Just fucking great.

"Oh my goodness, what an adorable baby!" the blonde says in an English accent, taking me by complete surprise. "Is she yours?"

"That's what everyone says, but she's too cute to be his," Jackson blurts out, and I'm ready to smack him for his smartass comment when I realize Maize has stopped crying.

"Can you take her for a second, so I can clean this up quick and get her a bottle?" I hate asking Jackson for help or, rather, anyone in general, but I can't do this one-handed again.

"I'd be happy to hold her," the blonde says.

"Sorry, no disrespect, but I don't know you, so I'd rather not," I tell her, handing Maize over to Jackson instead.

"Sure, I totally understand. I'm Hanna, by the way." By the look on Jackson's face, he hadn't even known that was her name. Or perhaps he just stopped listening once she gave him a second of attention.

"I'm John. And I assume you know my twin brother, Jackson?" I tease.

"Twins? And you live together? How sweet!" She beams.

"Well I tried gettin' rid of him, but he just keeps comin' back...kind of like a stray dog," I quip, walking back to the mess and cleaning it up.

"Don't listen to him, Maze." Jackson rocks back and forth. "It's all lies."

Hanna watches him with doe-eyes. Jackson may be a lot of things, but he's actually really good with kids and even Maize.

Once I have everything wiped clean, I prepare another bottle and this time screw on the top before shaking it and testing the temperature.

"Thanks," I say, reaching for Maize and taking her from Jackson so I can finally feed her. "Sorry to wake you."

"No worries," Jackson says then wraps his arm around Hanna and pulls her in for a kiss, which I could've lived without witnessing. "We weren't sleeping anyway." He winks, and I fight the urge to roll my eyes.

Hanna giggles when Jackson picks her up and carries her to the kitchen table then sets her down.

"Oh, for fuck's sake." I groan. "I eat breakfast there."

"Well, then you might not wanna watch what I'm about to eat—"

"Jackson!" Hanna squeals, swatting his bare chest. I take that as my cue to get the hell out of here.

"And now breakfast is ruined for me," I mumble to myself, taking Maize back to my room. As she's sucking down her bottle, I get a whiff of something that I know is coming from her.

Laying her down on the bed, I prop her bottle up against my pillow so I can change her while she continues to eat. If I take it away from her now, she'll scream the entire time, and I need to get us both back to sleep before I completely lose my mind.

"Why are there so many damn buttons on this sleeper thing?" I ask aloud while trying to maneuver her chubby legs out of her pajamas. The smell gets worse, making my eyes water like a damn pussy. "In one end and out the other," I joke, but Maize doesn't even look at me. "What? You can't appreciate a good dad joke yet?"

Chuckling to myself and realizing just how exhausted I must be to tell jokes to my three-month-old baby is an indication as to just how sleep deprived I am. Between stopping in at the B&B, keeping up with laundry, dishes, and other household chores, as well as getting up with her every few hours, I'm second-guessing my sanity.

Just as I undo her diaper, I realize the sight is much worse than the smell.

Complete. Massive. Blowout.

That's what I get for trying to get her bottle before changing her.

Fuck my life.

I manage to get her footie pjs off while carefully trying not to knock the bottle over. It's then I notice the blowout has completely gone up her back, and it's the exact moment Maize decides to kick her legs.

"Maize, no." I groan, torn between crying and laughing at the entire situation. "Okay then. Bath time."

I pick her up without a diaper or jammies and head to the bathroom. Normally, I'd wash her off in the kitchen sink, but I'm not going to subject Maize to what Jackson and Hanna are probably doing on my kitchen table.

Just the thought of them in there right now boils my blood all over again.

Reaching for the shower hose, I turn the water on and wait for the water to warm up before stepping into the shower and rinsing her off. I hold her to my chest and try to hum to her, so she doesn't scream again. Luckily, I was only in boxers, so I don't have to worry about being drenched.

When we're both rinsed and dried, I put Maize in a new diaper and a clean pair of footie pajamas, then tuck her back into the co-sleeper. She sucks on her pacifier and is back to sleep in five minutes.

Falling back onto my pillow, I exhale in relief. Turning to look at the time on my phone, I see it's right after four in the morning. Shit.

Maybe River and everyone else are right.

I need help.

CHAPTER SEVEN

Mila

The moment I wake up, I dress in a pair of shorts and a T-shirt for a morning run. Considering Gigi's delicious homemade cooking and all the baking she does, I'll easily gain twenty pounds eating her food. As soon as I heard the roosters crow this morning, I got up for another gorgeous day. It's nice not to have any responsibility other than helping around the ranch. Though it's work, it doesn't really feel like it because I enjoy it so much.

The brisk morning air brushes across my skin, but once I'm warmed up, I want to start removing layers of clothes. After an intense three-mile run from the house to the end of the rock road and back, I feel exhilarated.

As soon as I walk inside the house, I've got my arms on top of my head, trying to catch my breath. I hear Gigi in the kitchen on the phone, and as soon as she sees me, she flashes a smile and waves me over.

"Yeah, Rose. She actually just walked in. You wanna talk to her?"

I'm confused, but take the phone when she hands it over.

"Hello?" I politely say, just as Gigi places bacon in a hot iron skillet. The hearty smell fills the kitchen, and my stomach begins to growl as the meat sizzles and pops.

"Good mornin', sweetie. This is Rose Bishop. We met at the church fundraiser last week."

I nod as if she can see me. The one with the feisty grandchild. "Yes, ma'am. I remember."

"Well, I noticed how great you were with Riley and how well he took to you. I'm looking for a nanny, and your grandma told me you might be looking for a job, too, so I thought I'd call and see whatcha think."

I look at Gigi, but she just keeps humming along as she flips the bacon. She's so guilty. She knows I'm supposed to leave in a week, so I'm sure this has something to do with trying to keep me in Texas longer.

"Okay," I say. "Well, can you tell me more about the position?"

"Oh, absolutely. My son needs some help with his three-month-old baby girl. She's the most precious little angel you've ever laid eyes on, but she's not on any kind of sleeping schedule and is just as stubborn as he is. He needs to get back to work and needs someone to watch her during the day and possibly some nights too." She starts off sounding like a proud grandma, but her tone quickly changes halfway through the sentence. At that moment, I know I never want to cross Mrs. Bishop. She's as bad as Gigi. Sweet as pie but has a scary side too.

"I love babies," I admit. I love everything about them—the way they smell, how they're so vulnerable, their little coos, and how precious they look when they sleep. Heck, I even think their cries are cute.

"Your grandma told me all the experience you have with kids and how you just graduated with a degree in elementary education. Then seeing the way you handled Riley at the cakewalk, you'd honestly be a godsend for my son."

Considering I haven't heard anything back from any of the schools I've applied to, it seems like it would be a good opportunity for me to earn some extra cash. And since there's nothing or no one waiting for me back home, I *could* stay here longer.

"Can I think about it?" I finally ask.

"Oh sure, honey. Take as much time as you need," Mrs. Bishop says before we end our conversation. I set the phone down on the counter and look at Gigi with raised brows.

"What?" she asks, pulling the bacon from the skillet and placing it on a plate. She grabs a few eggs, cracks them, and then begins frying them in the bacon grease.

"You know *what*!" I say.

She shrugs and gives me a wink. "I'm supposed to fly home next week," I explain.

"To do what, exactly?" She narrows her eyes at me, but her smile doesn't fade.

"I guess nothing." I shrug. "Might be nice to get some extra job experience."

"So you're staying?" she asks, flipping the eggs, cooking them exactly the way I like. Once the eggs are finished, she slides them on a plate with the bacon and hands it to me.

I playfully roll my eyes. "Yes, I'll stay."

In two small steps, she has her arms around me. "Good. That means I get to see more of ya. We can call Rose tomorrow and let her know. Sometimes I like to make her sweat." She chuckles.

Like clockwork, Papaw comes down the stairs, and Gigi makes him a plate. We all sit at the dining room table, and Gigi tells him the news. Though he listens, I can tell he doesn't care about any of the details.

"Guess that means you'll be in Texas longer." He gives me a wink.

"Yes, sir. Happy to be, actually. I love it here," I tell him. It's definitely a nice distraction too.

"We love having you here," Gigi tells me.

"You two keep saying that, and you might have to force me to leave," I joke between bites, and they both laugh.

"You can stay as long as you'd like. Heck, you can stay forever," Gigi says, which makes me smile.

Papaw tells Gigi what he plans to do today, and their conversation moves to a list of things they need to grab from town. When I look at my grandparents together, my heart is so full. They are the epitome of everything I've ever wanted in life—a happy marriage, a big family, and true love.

The next morning after my run, I walk inside, and I almost feel like I'm living the same day again. Gigi is on the phone and waves me over, and I already know it's Mrs. Bishop on the other line.

"Hello?"

"Hey, Mila! It's Mrs. Bishop. Your grandma told me that you'd like to take the job. How about today?"

"Today?" I ask, glancing over at Gigi who's eagerly nodding. These Texans sure like to rush things.

"Yeah, today's as good a day as ever," Mrs. Bishop says.

"Um. Okay, yeah sure. I need to shower and take care of some small things, but I can be over afterward."

"Perfect. Gigi knows the address. Thank you so much, Mila. I just know little Maize's going to adore you. We'll see you after lunch." I'm almost in shock as I end the call. Gigi makes me a scrambled egg sandwich, and I eat it really quick before running up the stairs and jumping in the shower. I try on several different outfits, but all of them scream college student. I send my mother a text and tell her to ship me a box of clothes since I'm staying in Texas longer than I expected.

In the bottom of my suitcase, I find a dressier shirt and choose the nicest pair of jeans I have. Considering I only brought boots and sneakers, I go for the boots. When I look in the mirror, I wonder if I'm trying too hard, but I roll my eyes and decide to go with it anyway. By the time I make it downstairs, Gigi has cleaned up the kitchen and is sitting at the table reading the newspaper.

"So tell me how to get there again," I say, opening the notes on my phone and writing it out because I know GPS is wonky out here. One time it told me to turn down an old dirt road that I knew wasn't right.

"You'll go up the road and turn when you see a rusty truck on the corner. You'll head down about eight miles with lots of twists and turns in the road, and you'll see a red barn on the right. About a quarter of a mile from that, you'll see the sign for the B&B."

I glare at her. "Did you seriously just give me landmark directions?"

"You'll find it, dear. Can't miss it," she tells me matter-of-factly.

I stand and give her a hug, grab the keys to her Cadillac, and head out the door. Sitting behind the steering wheel, I try to get ahold of my nerves as I crank the car. I unlock my phone, read over the crazy ass directions, and then head out.

When I finally see the sign for the Circle B Bed & Breakfast, I somewhat relax, but I'm still tense and nervous as hell.

Taking my time, I drive down the old rock road, kicking dust up in my wake. I pass a large white house that looks like it should be on a postcard and keep driving. At the end of the road, a huge house with a wraparound porch and gorgeous bay windows come into view. I park beside the other cars, but I don't go inside. I walk around the side of the house and down a sidewalk that Mrs. Bishop told me about. It leads me straight to a country ranch-style home. Before knocking, I brush my hands through my hair, smooth the wrinkles from my shirt, and take a deep breath.

I knock a few times, but no one answers. Not really sure what I should do, I call Mrs. Bishop.

"Hello?" she answers sweetly. I hear crying in the background, and it sounds like Riley's having a fit.

"Hey, Mrs. Bishop. It's Mila. Um. I'm at the house, but no one is answering the door."

"Oh honey, just walk on in. They're home. It's no big deal."

I swallow, feeling weird about barging in. "Okay, I will. Thank you. Sorry for bothering you."

"You're fine, sweetie. Talk to you soon."

I end the call and open the door.

"Hello?" I say, shutting the door behind me and looking around. I catch a glimpse of photographs on the wall, all of horses and cowboys. There isn't much else to look at, and I can definitely tell this is a bachelor pad. Walking in farther, I call out again as I look down one of the hallways.

"Can I help you?" a deep voice booms and echoes off the wall, causing me to twist around and gasp.

"Shit!" I say loudly, nearly jumping out of my skin. "You scared me half to death."

It takes everything I have to keep my mouth from falling open. I swallow hard and can't stop staring at rock hard abs. There's a man standing in front of me wearing nothing more than a towel wrapped low on his waist. Water drips from his hair, down his chest, and my eyes nearly bulge out of my head.

"Jackson's not home. So you can find your way out," he says, rudely.

I tilt my head at him like he's lost his damn mind.

"No sorority parties happening here either." He walks toward the door, and I see the muscles cascading down his back as he reaches for the knob and turns it, showing me my way out.

"Wait, who's Jackson?" I finally ask, furrowing my brows when he turns and looks at me.

He narrows his eyes at me, both of us obviously puzzled. "Who are you?" The cool air from outside fills the room, and I shiver.

"Mila Carmichael." I hold out my hand to shake his, but he doesn't take it. I awkwardly shove my hands back into my pockets. "Who are you?"

"This is my house. I'm John. You sure you're not looking for my brother, Jackson?" He looks me up and down, his expression hardening, and I'm not sure what to make of it. "He's the same height and build, looks a lot like me." *Oh God. There's two of them?*

"Actually, I don't know who I'm looking for. Mrs. Bishop sent me. She said a nanny was needed for her new grandbaby, Maize. Maybe I have the wrong house. I'm sorry for intruding." I take a step toward the door, but he closes it before I can walk out.

"My mama sent you over here?" He shakes his head, annoyed.

"Yeah, I guess. You're the one with the baby?" I ask, almost surprised. He's nothing like I imagined, and now I'm second-guessing this whole thing.

"Yes, but I told her I didn't need any help finding a nanny, and you don't exactly look like one," he hisses, walking past me down the hall. "I'll be right back."

Wait. What the hell does that even mean? Nannies have a certain look?

Once he's gone, the baby starts crying in the other room.

I walk toward the crying and find the beautiful baby girl lying in a co-sleeper next to the bed. Gently, I pick her up and place her against my chest. I rock my body slowly to comfort her and spot her pacifier on the bed.

"Hi, baby Maize. It's nice to meet you," I say in a soft voice as she fusses.

Reaching down, I grab her pacifier and place it in her mouth. I'm sure having a stranger picking her up isn't helping either, but after a few moments, she stops crying and looks up at me.

"She likes you." I turn around and see John standing in the doorway wearing a tight-fitting button-up shirt and blue jeans. His muscular arms cross over his broad chest, and I see a sparkle in his eyes and am relieved he's not pissed I just waltzed in here and picked up his baby. Most new parents are very protective over their children, but I've been told I have a very trusting demeanor, so I use it to my advantage.

"How old is she?" I ask softly. Mrs. Bishop told me, but my brain suddenly went blank the moment I walked in here.

"Three and a half months," he responds.

"She's beautiful," I tell him, glancing between him and Maize. "She has your nose." I smile.

The corner of his mouth lifts up just the tiniest bit before he speaks. "Thanks. She looks a lot like her mother too."

"Well, I'm available and would be happy to help you get her on a better schedule. Now that she's almost four months old, she can start taking more milk at a time, and that'll hopefully hold her off longer between feedings," I explain. "Mrs. Bishop didn't tell me what days you needed, but if you and your wife or girlfriend have specific hours in mind—"

"There's no wife," he corrects me, cutting me off. "No girlfriend either. Just me and Maize."

Heat rushes to my cheeks, and I try to hold my nerves at bay, but I'm at a loss for words. A single dad. I hadn't expected that. Honestly, I'm not sure what I expected, but it most definitely wasn't him. I want to ask a million questions, but I'll save those for another day. At this point, I'm not really sure I have a job, considering he'd been so dead set on kicking me out of his house since the moment I walked in.

"Oh, okay." I look down at Maize—who's happily sucking on her pacifier—and avoid his stare. "I have a pretty open schedule and am available if you do want the help," I tell him, glancing at him again.

"Alright, Mila." He pushes himself off the doorframe and walks toward me. "To appease my mother, who's determined to drive me crazy before I'm forty, I'll give you a trial run. One week to see how things go. Then we'll reassess from there."

I can't hold back the grin that fills my face. "I won't let you down," I reassure him. "I'm from a large family and am known as the baby whisperer at home." I flash a sheepish smile, trying to hold in my excitement that he's giving me a chance.

"I believe it," he says and grins for the first time since I arrived, which does things to me. He should smile more often, showing those perfectly straight teeth. The man is gorgeous, but when I look at him, I finally see a glimpse of exhaustion on his face.

"I need to shave really quick if that's okay," he says.

I give him a nod.

The connection we briefly shared is broken when he walks away. When I hear the bathroom door click closed, I hold Maize just a little tighter and try to calm my racing heart.

CHAPTER EIGHT

John

"Fuck," I whisper to myself as I walk to the bathroom and finish drying off. I should apologize for being such an asshole, but I was caught off guard. Who just walks into a stranger's house like that? It's something Jackson's lady friends would do, so I wasn't out of line assuming as much.

However, considering how pretty Mila is, I'd say Mama is trying to play matchmaker again while finding me a nanny. Kill two birds with one stone type of deal. The woman can't be trusted until all her boys are married, so I wouldn't put it past her to use the opportunity. As soon as I get a free moment, Mama's getting a call. Nannies aren't supposed to be attractive or young or full of temptation. Nannies are supposed to be older ladies around Mama's age who just adore being around babies and knit in their rocking chairs.

I slip on my jeans and a button-up shirt before heading out of the bathroom. Going back to my bedroom, I see Mila's still holding Maize like she's her lifeline. My heart leaps forward seeing how gentle she is with her, but I force it back.

"When can you start? Now?" I ask.

She nods, smiling at me. Her blue eyes stare into mine, and it's so intense, I look away. "Your mama told me to start today. Something about you needing to get back to work."

Shaking my head, I walk past her and grab my cell phone off the nightstand. "Sneaky. What else did she say?"

Mila softly chuckles as she places Maize back in the co-sleeper. "That you're stubborn," she states, turning around to face me.

My lips move into a firm line. "Of course she'd say that." I grab my watch off my dresser and snap it on. My hair is still wet, so I run my fingers through it quickly. "But anyway. I work at the B&B during the day. I've actually not been working very much for the past few weeks, but since you're here, I'd like to try to catch up. I have a few questions first," I tell her.

"Sure…go ahead," she says, following me into the living room.

I sit on the couch, and she sits at the other end. Turning my head, I look over at her and notice how nervous she is under my gaze.

"What experience do you have with babies?"

She laughs. "Lots. I have four younger siblings who I basically helped raise. One of my sisters is five years younger than me, the other is three years younger, and I have twin sisters who are ten years younger. I helped my mom do everything while my dad was at work. Every day after school, I'd come home and help with feedings and changing diapers, and as they got older, I was in charge of keeping them out of trouble. I guess you could say I've been around babies and kids for the past decade. I also have a degree in elementary education, and when I wasn't enrolled in summer school, I worked in the nursery at my church. I've always been passionate about kids, which is the main reason I've always wanted to be a teacher."

I swallow hard, watching her talk about kids, and by the way she lights up, I know she's not bullshitting me.

"You've never been a nanny before?" I ask.

She shakes her head. "Not an *actual* nanny, like with the title and all that, but trust me when I say I'm more than qualified. I watch my two-year-old nephew often and have since he was born. And he's a handful."

Confidence. I like that.

"Well, it certainly sounds like you know what you're doing. I guess I should show you around," I say. I lead her into my bedroom that's been a makeshift nursery since the moment Maize came into my life. I show Mila where all the extra diapers, creams, and clothes are kept. We walk through the kitchen where I point out the extra bottles and formula.

"Do you have any questions for me?" I ask her, leaning against the counter.

"Not that I can think of at the moment, but I'll be sure to tell you if I do." She smiles.

"Okay." I look her up and down and feel confident that Maize will be in good hands with Mila. A part of me feels nervous as hell leaving my baby with a woman I just met, but another part of me knows Mama probably found out every little detail about her before sending her over here, which gives me a bit of relief.

She grins at me. "Shouldn't you be going to work now?"

I let out a breath, finding it hard to walk out the door, but I know I have to. I give her a firm head nod. "If you have any issues, call me ASAP."

She swallows hard, then follows behind me. "Um. I don't have your number."

As she pulls her phone from her back pocket and unlocks it, I slip it from her hand. I open the text messages, type my number in, and text myself. "Now you do."

She looks up at me and gives me a reassuring smile. I flash a small grin before finally leaving. There haven't been many moments since Maize came into my life that I've left her alone with anyone other than family, so I'm a bit nervous. Knowing Mila has tons of experience is the only thing that's keeping me sane as I walk into the B&B. I go to the office and look around and see nothing is where I keep it, which frustrates the fuck out of me.

"Nicole," I call, opening the door. Nicole is my assistant and has been filling in for me and helping Jackson run the B&B for the past month.

"Yes, sir?" she asks, peeking her head inside the office.

"Where's my duty book?" I look at her.

"Not sure."

Considering I'm exhausted, and things aren't where they're supposed to be, I try my best not to be rude or moody toward her because I know it's not her fault. "Okay, thanks."

She takes it as her cue to leave and walks away. I overhear her talking to a guest about changing the sheets in one of the rooms, and when she goes upstairs, I find my book stuffed under a stack of rodeo magazines at the check-in counter. This has Jackson written all over it. Out of the two of us, I'm the organized one, and since he's been filling in for me, none of my daily tasks have been checked off. I wish Mama would've let Alex fill in for me instead because he, at least, takes his job seriously. For the most part, Jackson just glides by unless it has to do with horses—or chicks. After I take a mental note of what needs to be done, I sit on the stool behind the counter and look out the window. My eyes are heavy, and I slightly close them. My breathing slows, and my body relaxes for the first time in weeks. The next thing I know, I'm being woken up by Jackson slamming his hand on the counter. I have no idea how long I'd been there, but my arms hurt from laying on them for so long. Glancing down at my phone, I realize an entire hour has passed.

"Shit," I say, rubbing my hands over my face.

"Sleepin' on the job now?" He flashes a shit-eating grin.

"Shut the hell up. I'm tired as fuck," I admit and look at him, and he looks just as tired as me.

"Tell me about it. Speaking of..." He leans against the counter and nods at the ladies who walk by. A couple of them blow kisses at him over their shoulders, and I shake my head as he winks in their direction.

"Yeah?" I interrupt his flirt session.

"I think I'm gonna move out. I talked to Dad about the house I was supposed to be working on when I moved in..."

"Yeah, wondered if you were ever gonna finish that, honestly," I add.

"It was easier just to live with you. But things change. I'm gettin' real sick of my brothers knocking up chicks and basically being kicked out each time," he admits with a chuckle, and I roll my eyes. I didn't mind Jackson living with me—for the most part—but the Friday night whiskey parties and the different girl each week got annoying quick.

"I'm not kicking you out," I remind him.

"I know, just givin' you a hard time."

A few years ago, he and Alex lived together, but then River moved in when she found out she was pregnant, so Jackson moved in with me. I almost feel guilty that he has to move again, but I think he wants to because a baby means no more parties or late nights being loud. I actually might miss him being around. Though he's a pain in my ass most of the time, he's still my twin brother, and my life wouldn't be the same without him in it.

"Yeah, yeah. Anyway, how long until it's ready?" I'm successfully able to bring the conversation back. If I've learned anything over the years, it's to avoid traveling down conversation rabbit trails with Jackson.

"I've hired the contractors that built Evan and Emily's house, and they said a few months to finish it, so I'm gonna stay at the ranch hand living quarters until then. If I don't get any sleep, I might actually start looking as shitty as you do." He lets out a chuckle.

"Are you sure?" I ask, not wanting to force him to leave. It's understandable, and I'm sure if the roles were reversed, I'd do the same. Maize wakes up a minimum of three times during the night, and if hearing Jackson and his ladies through the walls are any indication, he can hear Maize's screams.

"Yeah. It's time. Plus, it's hard to bring girls back to the house knowing there's a baby trying to sleep. I'm an asshole, but I'm not *that* much of an asshole."

"If you need anything, let me know," I tell him.

He gives me a smile before walking out. "Same, brother."

After double-checking reservations for the upcoming week, I tell Nicole I'm heading home as the kitchen staff prepares dinner. Dishes clink and clank, and I step in and tell everyone hello. It's two of Mama's church friends and an older gentleman, but they're here each day cooking breakfast, lunch, and dinner for our guests.

"How's the baby doin', John?" Mrs. Tellie asks.

"She's doin' real good. Goin' to check on her now," I tell her with a smile. The cool air brushes across my face as I step outside, and I place my hands in my pocket. The winter is much colder than usual, which I can't complain about too much, considering I work inside a majority of the time, but it makes me think about my dad and brothers who are out in this weather. Being as quiet as I can, I walk into the house and find Maize sleeping on Mila's chest, who is also asleep.

When the door clicks shut, her eyes flutter open. She looks at me with a sleepy gaze. "Sorry," she whispers.

"Already sleeping on the job?" I smirk, but she takes me seriously.

"I-uh."

"No, it's fine. Everything go okay?" I ask. She has no idea how tempted I've been all day to come home and check.

"Perfect, actually. She's such an easy baby. We've had a really good day. We played peek-a-boo, did a few minutes of tummy time—which she hates, by the way—then she napped for a few hours. After she woke up, she ate and had a poop explosion, so I gave her a quick bath in the sink. Then she ate again an hour ago, and then we both fell asleep," Mila whispers with a smile, before repositioning her body. Sounds like everything did go well, which makes me happy.

I take Maize from her arms. "Hey, baby girl," I whisper, kissing her forehead. She looks up at me with admiration, and it's times like this that affect me emotionally. Maize attached to me from the moment we met. Even when I was filled with uncertainty, one thing I did know was I wanted to give her everything that life had to offer.

Mila sits up straighter on the couch and watches me before she stands and stretches. "What time should I be here tomorrow?"

"Seven?" I ask.

"Sure. See ya then." She grabs her phone from the table and tucks it into her pocket, then slips her boots on her feet.

"Thanks, Mila," I finally say. "Thanks for your help. It's really appreciated."

All she does is smile as she heads to the door.

It's been three days since Mila started working for me, and so far, she's been a complete blessing. I know Maize's in safe keeping, and that's all I've ever wanted, though I can't say I'm getting any more sleep than before.

After lunch, I fall asleep again, and this time, I'm woken up by a guest bitching about a toilet issue. Usually, I'm friendly and have a smile plastered on my face, but honestly, I'm pissed. Mama caught wind of me snapping at someone and practically threatened to fire me, which I know would never happen, but it was a wake-up call that I need more sleep at night, and that's not going to happen until Maize's sleeping in longer stretches. Any noise I hear, I'm wide-awake, and then I can barely fall back to sleep. By the time I do, it's time to get up for work. I feel as if I could sleep for a week straight.

After falling asleep for the third time today, I force myself to stand the rest of my shift. I've had so many ridiculous things happen that I swear it's Friday the thirteenth. By the time I make it home, I'm so fucking exhausted that I can barely keep my eyes open. When I walk in, I see Jackson flirting with Mila, and it annoys the fuck out of me.

"Jackson, kitchen," I bark when Mila walks into the room to check on Maize.

"What?" He looks at me slyly.

Leaning against the counter, I cross my arms over my chest and give it to him straight. "Listen. There's a few rules you need to adhere to."

He sarcastically nods his head, which pisses me off further.

"Don't look at my nanny like that ever again."

"Like what?" he asks.

I narrow my eyes because he knows damn well what I'm talking about. "I don't need you scaring her away and leaving me without help. So don't hit on my nanny. Don't flirt with her, ask her out, and don't you dare fuck my nanny."

He arches a brow and crosses his arms as if to ask if I'm done—as if to challenge me on everything I just listed.

"Basically, stay away from my nanny. Got it?"

Jackson bursts out into laughter. He's doubled over, trying to catch his breath, but I'm as serious as a heart attack, ready to punch him in the chest and threaten his life if he breaks my rules.

"Why? Are *you* fucking her?" he asks, laughing with amusement. "God knows you're worse than I am."

"No. *Hell no.* Those rules are for everyone, and if you break them, I'll break your fucking neck."

He leans over and whispers loud enough for just me to hear. "But you want to."

"Shut the hell up." I shove him, and he takes a few steps back, still laughing, then returns to packing up his room. After a few seconds, Mila enters the kitchen and grabs a bottle of water from the fridge. She's already made herself at home, which is perfectly fine. I want her to feel comfortable here.

"John." She looks me up and down, swallowing tightly. "I can tell you're exhausted. You have bags under your eyes," she says. I finally make eye contact with her, not wanting to admit how damn tired I am even though it's obvious at this point. "And if you don't mind me sayin', a tad grouchy."

"I'm just not sleeping well," I admit.

"I can stay around the clock if you need me to. I have nothing going on, and your mama was right; you need help," she tells me.

I ignore the last part, but it's true. I need all the help I can get.

"I'll be fine." I grunt, not wanting to admit that I can't handle this on my own. Bailey did it on her own all through her pregnancy and the first nine weeks of Maize's life, so I should be able to suck it up.

"Are you going to be stubborn about this?" She crosses her arms over her chest. I've only known her for a few days, but she's already figured me out in that short amount of time. And shit, she's bossy too.

"Probably," I confess, grabbing a beer from the fridge. "How are you going to watch Maize during the day *and* get up with her at night? You'll be a zombie like me."

"Well, it'll basically be like the last four years of my life when I went to school all day, worked in the evenings, and then studied half the night away. It's something I'm used to if that helps to know. Plus, Maize's much cuter to be woken up by than my textbooks." She grins as if she's solidifying her response. "It can be a trial run if that makes you feel better, but if you don't get some rest, you'll get sick, and that's the last thing Maize needs." She takes my beer and replaces it with her bottle of water instead. I give her a look, but she ignores it completely. "You're going to burn out."

Jackson walks back in the room and sees us in close proximity. He lifts his eyebrows at me, then winks at Mila before walking out the door.

"I can't believe he's your brother." She chuckles. "Your personalities are so different."

"He's off-limits," I warn her, my tone coming out much harsher than I mean to.

She snorts. "Don't have to worry about that. I'm not attracted to him at *all*," she says, but the ghost of a smile plays on her lips.

"Pretty sure I should be offended by that," I mumble, opening the fridge and grabbing myself another beer.

She shakes her head at my stubbornness. "I'm going to pack an overnight bag. Give me an hour, and I'll be back. Gotta tell Gigi what's going on, too, so she doesn't worry."

"I didn't agree to anything yet," I say as she follows me down the hall and to the living room where I take a seat on the couch with my beer in hand.

"You don't have to. Your mama already did."

CHAPTER NINE

Mila

Jackson Bishop is like that fun older brother I never had. Sure, I have an older brother, but he's all business and no play. It feels good to be around someone who's so carefree, and it doesn't hurt that he's the spitting image of John, who I haven't stopped fantasizing about since I saw him in that towel with water dripping down his chest. Without any kind of warning, I can tell what kind of guy Jackson is—heartbreaker number one, which means nothing but trouble. And I've had enough trouble with guys to last me a lifetime.

As soon as John walked in and saw us laughing and Jackson flirting, something in the room shifted. Just to get away from John's mood, I go and check on the baby. As I'm standing in his bedroom, where Maize's peacefully sleeping, I overhear their conversation. My heart races as John gives him the "official nanny rules," but I have a feeling no one tells Jackson what to do, not even the man who wears the same face.

"Why? Are *you* fucking her?" Jackson asks with a laugh. "God knows you're worse than I am."

My heart stammers against my chest, and I feel the heat hit my cheeks. Does that mean what I think it means? I've only been here a few days, and I'm already a forbidden cliché.

"What? No? Those rules are for everyone, and if you break them, I'll break your fucking neck," John tells him matter-of-factly, and by the tone in his voice, I wouldn't want to cross him. I'm off-limits, that much is known, and somehow it feels just as bad as being friend zoned for all those years. Not that I want anything to happen, but it sucks to always be outside of everyone's range. Half of me wants to barge out there and explain that it's not like that at all, but they become quiet, and I hear shuffling around and wonder what else was said. I take a deep breath, trying to get ahold of myself and walk out there.

Jackson is in his room packing his belongings, and John is leaned back against the counter in the kitchen. He looks exhausted from head to toe, just as his mama told me he would be. This morning, while he was at work, she called me and asked me if I'd consider pulling a few twenty-four-hour shifts. She explained how John was losing his patience at work and falling asleep on the job. As I study his face, I realize how right she is, and my heart kind of hurts for him. He's doing the best he can as a single dad, but it's still not enough.

After I tell him how it's going to be and walk outside, I suck in a deep breath. On the way to the car, I pull out my phone and text Kat.

MILA

Girl. These Bishop boys...

KAT

Told you. They're all trouble. Even the taken ones.

MILA

Thankfully, I've only met Jackson.

KAT

And he's the worst of them all.

I let out a laugh. Poor Jackson has gotten a bad rap. Even Gigi warned me about him.

MILA

He and John were arguing about me today, and he told Jackson to basically back off. Then Jackson asked him why, and if he was fucking me.

The bug-eyed emoji she sends says it all.

MILA

I know. And I'm already a nervous wreck around John as it is.

KAT

Because you like him.

MILA

No. I just think he's hot as fuck. There's a difference.

KAT

And what's the difference?

I let out a laugh and start the car.

MILA

The difference is he's my boss, and my job is to take care of his baby. Not him!

She sends me an eye-roll emoji before changing the subject.

KAT

What you doin' tonight? Want me to come over?

MILA

I'm staying the night at John's house to try to help get Maize on a schedule so he can get some sleep. He's so tired he can barely function.

KAT

And this is how it all starts.

She sends a GIF of two dogs humping. I burst out laughing, shaking my head as I turn on the heat. My heart hammers in my chest as I think about John in a towel, water dripping down his perfect torso all the way to his…

Fuck. I shake the dirty thoughts from my mind and remind myself that I'm not here to date or sleep with anyone. I got out of Georgia to recover my shattered heart, not find another reason to have it split in two.

MILA

OMG Stop it! Maybe YOU need to get laid. Plus, I'd never sleep with my boss. I have morals, ya know?

KAT

Good thing you're being paid by his mother then.

Well, she's not wrong, but I don't admit that to her.

MILA

I'm off-limits, remember?

KAT

Forbidden love is the best kind there is! ;)

MILA

You're ridiculous.

KAT

Nah! Just truthful. Mama Bishop is the boss in that family. Everyone knows it. You'll be fine, don't worry about it.

I laugh and totally believe her.

MILA

I'm just nervous, you know. If this becomes long-term, it'll be the first time I haven't lived at home. I really want to help him get the baby on a schedule because once she sleeps soundly through the night, he won't need me around the clock. I've made it my mission, plus it's a challenge, and I want to keep my baby whisperer title.

My honesty makes me laugh.

KAT

> You'll do fine. You're a professional and still have the reigning title of the baby whisperer. Just take it one day at a time.

I smile at her reassurance, something I need desperately right now as I second-guess everything. Am I really moving in to be a live-in nanny? Two months ago, I would've never believed this was my life, but even after a handful of days, I've already fallen in love with little Maize Bishop. I'm doing this for her too.

Kat sends an eggplant emoji for good measure, and I let out a big laugh.

MILA

> LOL! I'm heading to Gigi's. I'll text you when I get there.

I lock my phone and back out of the driveway and head back to my grandparents' house. Gigi already knows about the arrangement I'm sure because she and Mrs. Bishop are great friends. If they didn't talk about it, I'd be more surprised at this point. By the time I arrive, Gigi has a bag of cookies waiting for me.

"Do you know everything?" I ask with a grin.

"Grandmas and mamas know it all," she reminds me—something she used to say to Kat and me when we were younger.

"Thanks, Gigi," I tell her, giving her a hug and a kiss on the cheek.

"Anytime, honey. If you need anything or if that Bishop boy is being a pain in the ass, you let me know, and I'll have his mama take care of it."

The fact Gigi expects me to tattle on John like we're back on a playground or something makes me chuckle to myself, but I know she's just protective of me. "He's been a perfect gentleman," I reassure her before walking upstairs and packing my suitcase for a few days. I don't know how long these clothes will last me, but I'm sure I'll be visiting my grandparents soon.

Once I'm packed, I text Kat and tell her I'm heading back to John's house.

KAT

Don't do anything I wouldn't do. Actually, do everything I would do. John Bishop is S-E-X on legs!

MILA

I'm deleting this whole thread. It could be used as evidence in your murder later.

As a matter of fact, I need to delete it from my brain.

By the time I make it to John's, he's passed out on the couch sitting straight up. I quietly walk toward him and gently pat his arm.

"John," I say softly, trying not to startle him but fail miserably. He nearly leaps off the couch in a panic. "Crap, sorry." I cringe, feeling awful that I startled him.

"Scared the shit out of me," he admits, brushing his hands over his face. "You're back."

"Yes, and you're not going to be able to survive off naps forever. Go take a shower," I tell him, smelling his manly scent mixed with sweat.

He nods and pushes himself off the couch, his large frame hovering as he kicks off his boots and walks toward the bathroom. I check on Maize who's sleeping soundly in the swing, then grab my suitcase.

I want to ask him about Maize's mother, but I know that if he wanted me to know, he would tell me. Still, I'm curious and wonder what situation led him to be a single dad to a three-month-old baby. I can't imagine how hard this has been on him on top of all his other responsibilities.

Soon after, John is standing in front of me dressed in a T-shirt and a pair of low-rise sweatpants. They hang on his hips as if the smallest tug would make them fall, but I quickly snap my gaze up to his face and try to focus on what he's saying.

"You can stay in Jackson's room, but I'd change the sheets before you do. Actually, you might want to bleach them. Better yet, burn the bastards." He chuckles, glancing at my suitcase next to my feet. He picks it up for me and leads me to Jackson's old room. He walks out and comes back, placing an extra set of sheets on the foot of the bed. "There's extra blankets and towels in the hallway closet if you need them. There's only one bathroom, so I made some room on the counter for your things."

"Okay, thanks." I look around the bare room and let out a deep breath. "Home sweet home, for now," I say with a smile.

"So about Maize. I'd like for her to stay in the co-sleeper next to my bed, if possible. I'm not ready to detach yet," he admits, and I think it's cute how in love with her he is. "I won't be able to sleep with the anxiety of her not being close to me, so I hope you understand that you'll have to come in and grab her when she cries." I nod, listening to his instructions.

"Sure, that's no problem. We can put a baby monitor in my room, and when she cries, I'll grab her so, you can go back to sleep right away. I'll put some diapers and wipes in my room, and on nights I'm here, put the rocking chair in there too, so you don't hear her fuss. Then once she's changed and fed, I'll rock her back to sleep and tuck her back in the co-sleeper. At first, I'm sure you'll wake up, but hopefully, after you realize she's being taken care of, you'll be able to fall back to sleep pretty quickly," I tell him.

"You really are the baby whisperer, aren't you?" John tilts his head at me, smiling.

"I am," I say proudly.

"Now let's put Maize to bed and get the baby monitor so you can get some sleep."

I follow John to the living room where Maize's swinging quietly, and once he grabs her, we walk back to his room. I follow behind, inhaling his fresh soapy scent. I love how clean his skin smells right out of the shower. Once Maize's settled, he takes the rocking chair from his room and walks it over to mine. After he returns, he grabs the baby monitor and hands it over.

"Hopefully you don't snore," I tease, grabbing a stack of diapers and wipes to stock in my room.

"I don't. Well, at least I don't think so. I've had zero complaints." He shrugs, sitting on the edge of his bed, yawning.

"Well, goodnight. Get some sleep." I turn on my heels for the door before this gets any weirder. Being this close to him, in his room, is overwhelming my senses, and I need to set boundaries before my body turns on me.

"Goodnight, Mila. Thank you again. You have no idea how much I need this." He looks over at Maize, then back at me.

He needs me. It's the only thought that plays over in my head as I walk back to Jackson's room, which I guess is now mine. After I change the sheets, I fluff the pillows and turn on the small flat screen television that hangs on the wall.

Before crawling under the blankets, I slip into a tank top and some pajama shorts. I'm thankful Jackson didn't take his TV yet because my mind's too busy for sleep. For at least an hour, I flip through channels but don't find anything interesting; not that I could pay attention to it anyway. Just as I close my eyes, I hear my phone buzz on the nightstand. I roll over and grab it, unlocking the screen.

CADE

Can't wait to hang out again! You've been gone too long.

My heart hammers in my chest at his message. Cade and I were basically inseparable, and now I'm the awkward third wheel.

MILA

Me too! Though I might not be able to for a while.

CADE

Aren't you coming home next week?

I release a shaky breath.

MILA

No, sir. Decided to stay longer.

I keep my messages short, not wanting to get into the details of this new arrangement.

CADE

Oh, really? How much longer?

MILA

Not sure. Could be a few more weeks or months. Just playing it by ear right now.

Since the engagement, we haven't talked much. He's been so busy to notice, and truthfully so have I.

CADE

Oh bummer. Why? Everything okay?

MILA

Perfect. Couldn't be better. Just want to spend more time with my family.

It's not a complete lie, but I don't want to give him all the details right now.

Just as I'm waiting for his reply, I hear Maize's little cries on the baby monitor. I don't hesitate as I throw my phone on the bed and rush to the other side of the house. Not used to all the lights being off, I bump into a coffee table, almost knocking a lamp on the floor, then stub my toe, holding back all obscenities. I quietly open John's bedroom door and see him reaching for her.

"I've got her," I tell him, leaning into the co-sleeper and grabbing Maize. He looks at me in a sleepy daze and nods before re-adjusting his comforter over his shirtless body. Blinking, I snap my eyes away from him and walk Maize out of the room, careful to shut the door behind me without making too much noise.

"Hey, sweet girl," I say softly, hoping to calm her. "Are you hungry? I bet you are." I walk us to my room, so I can check her diaper, and once she's changed, I prepare her bottle in the kitchen and settle us in the rocking chair to feed her.

I hum a song to her as I hold her bottle and rock her. It's the same song my mother used to sing to me when I was a baby. Maize looks up at me, her fingers playing with the fabric of my shirt and making me smile at how precious she is. I don't know much about John's backstory, but I know Maize's one lucky little girl to have him as a dad.

Within thirty minutes, she's fed and back asleep. After wrapping her back up in her blanket, I walk back to John's room and place her in the co-sleeper. The moonlight splashes through the room, and I almost feel like a creeper staring at John sleeping so peacefully, but he's just so damn beautiful. Forcing myself away, I walk back to my room, ready to get some sleep before Maize wakes up again.

I settle in bed and lay on my cold phone. I pick it up and see Cade texted me back almost forty minutes ago.

CADE

Well that's good. Haven't heard from you much while you've been gone. If I didn't know better, I'd say you had a boyfriend there or something.

The message has me laughing out loud, and I roll over and send a text back.

MILA

Not a boyfriend. Just been busy helping someone out with his baby girl. She's so precious. I'm already in love with her.

The thought makes me smile. Each day, Maize and I have girl talk. Though she sleeps through most of it, I tell her all my secrets. Mrs. Bishop was right; little Maize has already stolen my heart, and I'd do anything for her. It might actually be a record. Even for me—the baby whisperer.

CHAPTER TEN

John

At 5:00 a.m., I wake up to the sound of my alarm, and just like the past two weeks, I feel rested and ready to go. Ever since Mila's been staying here, I've finally been able to sleep through the night.

I turn off the low sound of the beeping and roll over to check on my baby girl, and she's not there. Sitting up in bed, I look around and don't see her or Mila anywhere. In a panic, I jump out of bed and rush down the hall in search of Maize.

When I hear bacon sizzling and eggs frying, I stop at the end of the hallway that leads to the kitchen and spot Mila chatting up Maize like they're best friends. A smile instantly fills my face as I lean against the doorframe and watch her move around the kitchen in skimpy pajama shorts and a tank top that shows her stomach and lower back. There's way too much skin, and I'm finding it hard to look away. This is not how a nanny should to look. I scrub my hand over my face, trying to wake myself up.

Mila starts the coffee and dances and sings to Maize who's in her vibrating chair, watching her every move.

"You're such a pretty girl," Mila praises her, making sweet kissing noises. Maize's eating it all up as she smiles and kicks her little legs. My face stretches into a wide smile, relieved at how well Maize has adjusted to having Mila in our lives in such a short amount of time. I hate that Bailey isn't here to witness our baby grow up, but I have to keep reminding myself that I'll do whatever it takes to make sure she never goes without. Mila's a true miracle for coming to our rescue.

Turning toward the cabinets, Mila looks through them and pulls out some plates, then stands on her tiptoes to reach a coffee cup. The coffeemaker beeps, and she fills the cup to the top. Turning around, she finally spots me and nearly drops the mug.

"Jesus, you scared me!" She rests a hand on her chest as she catches her breath. She places the small of her back against the counter and relaxes her shoulders.

"Sorry," I say with a grin. "Was just enjoyin' watchin' you and Maize have a party in here."

"Well ya know, gotta start the morning off right," she says with a hint of embarrassment that I'd been watching her dance around. Her eyes travel down my body, then up again, and I notice her eyebrows are raised. "Um, you might want to get dressed before we sit down to eat."

I look down my body and curse. "Shit," I mutter, realizing I'm still in my boxers and hard as a goddamn rock. Fuck, how embarrassing. I turn and walk as fast as I can to the bedroom, trying to think of horrible thoughts so my dick will settle down. At this point, I need a cold ass shower, but somehow, I calm myself before getting dressed.

By the time I return to the kitchen, Mila has two plates of food waiting along with coffee. She hands me a fork before she sits with a proud smile. I can't remember the last time anyone other than Mama cooked for me. The microwavable pizzas Jackson makes don't count.

"You didn't have to do this," I tell her, taking a bite of fresh farm eggs covered with cheese.

"I know." She shrugs. "But breakfast is the most important meal of the day. Didn't your mama teach you that?"

I laugh. "Actually, yes. But I haven't had the time or energy to make anything, so I usually just grab a breakfast bar or something."

"Well, lucky you that I'm a great cook," Mila tells me matter-of-factly. "I learned at a young age and cooked for my siblings all the time, so I know from experience that you need sleep and food. The essentials. Speaking of, how'd you sleep last night? When I came in for Maize, you were snoring like you were out cold."

"Are you sure it was me?" I tease, and she gives me a look that tells me what a ridiculous question that is. "I slept great. Actually, since you've been here, I've been sleeping better than...well, since becoming a dad," I admit, taking a bite of bacon.

"Must've been a rough four months." She chuckles, and I almost feel guilty for not telling her the full story. I decide to save it for another day since she's staying on full-time. It's not an easy story to tell, especially since it's still so fresh and the wound is still open.

"Yeah," I say instead, though, in reality, it's been almost two months. "Oh. I almost forgot. Mama called me last night and asked if we'd like to do lunch today. Though I think she just wants to see Maize and wouldn't care if either of us showed, I told her it shouldn't be a problem. I hope that's okay."

Mila smiles and nods with a mouthful of food. After she swallows, she speaks. "I've heard your mama is one of the best cooks in all of Eldorado."

"She's known for it. But I've got her beat with my brisket."

"Oh, that sounds like a challenge," Mila gets out right before Maize starts crying. Just as if she knew this would happen, Mila lifts her into her arms and pulls a bottle full of formula from the counter.

"I'm impressed," I tell her. "It's like you knew."

Mila gives me a wink as she feeds Maize. I offer to take her so Mila can finish eating breakfast, but she shoos me away. Instead of insisting, I sit and clean my plate. After Maize's fed, Mila puts her back in her chair and cleans out her bottle in the sink. I watch as she places it on the weird bottle drying rack and brings the carafe with coffee to the table. An awkward silence fills the room, and we both open our mouths to speak at the same time and then close them.

"Go ahead," she says.

"No, you go first."

Mila shakes her head as she refills her coffee cup and then reaches across the table to refill mine.

"I was just going to say that I appreciate everything you've done for me —us—so far. I know it's only been a couple of weeks, but after finally getting some decent sleep, I feel like a brand-new person."

Her eyes meet mine. "Good. Even if this is *only* a trial run." That's a hint of amusement in her tone, which I'm sure is on purpose.

"I think we're past that point, Mila," I drawl out slowly. "Maize and I need you." As soon as the words come out, I worry how they'll be interpreted, but regardless, we do need her. She's been a godsend, and I wouldn't be functioning without her help. At first, I was dead set on not allowing anyone but family watch Maize, but after seeing how well Mila takes care of her, I knew that'd be a mistake.

"Well, I'm not going anywhere for now." She smirks, grabbing her empty plate off the table and walking to the sink.

After Mila cleans up, she tells me she's going to rock Maize and get her down for a nap. I head to my room to grab my phone and finish getting ready for work. Less than ten minutes later, Mila carries Maize into my room and sets her in the crib. While I'm at work, Maize sleeps in her crib, which, according to the baby book River gave me, is healthy for the weaning process when she's too big to sleep next to my bed.

I look at my precious little angel sleeping peacefully. I've always heard people say they didn't really know what love truly meant until they had kids, and I fully understand that now. In a blink, my life changed, and though it was scary at first, I wouldn't want it to be any other way. Maize's the best thing to happen to me, and even if I wasn't prepared, I can't help thinking that I now need her just as much as she needs me.

Glancing over at Mila, I catch her looking at Maize with the same love and adoration in her eyes. I give her a quick smile, tell her I'm heading to work, and grab my jacket before walking out the door.

As I make my way to the B&B, I'm elated with being back on schedule and feeling like a normal human being. Two weeks ago, I was nothing more than a bag of bones. Today, I feel like I could conquer the world—or my daily duties—but one thing at a time.

After helping set breakfast out, I find Mrs. Jefferson, the woman I snapped at, and apologize for being such a dick a few weeks ago. Once I explain I'm a new dad and everything, her face softens, and she gives me a hug.

"Being a parent is the hardest job you'll ever have, but it eventually gets easier," she informs me before biting into a homemade blueberry muffin. Mama's famous recipe.

I hold on to her words like they're my saving grace. It gets easier, which means there'll eventually be a light at the end of the tunnel.

After I put in a few hours of work, I look down at my phone and realize I need to head home and pick up Mila and Maize before we all head to my parents' for lunch.

As soon as I walk into the living room, I see Mila in tight blue jeans and a low-cut shirt that shows way too much cleavage.

"Nope." Resting my hands on my hips, I look at her, trying not to stare at her chest. It doesn't help that her nipples are hard as a damn rock either. Fuck. Eyes up.

"Nope, what?" she asks, furrowing her brows in confusion as she grabs Maize out of the swing.

"You can't wear that shirt. Actually, we should probably set some ground rules since you'll be staying here around the clock."

Mila rolls her eyes and kneels in front of the car seat. She's dressed Maize in an outfit that says something about Grandma being her favorite, and I know Mama's going to love it. "Is that what you do 'round here? Make rules for everyone?" She arches an eyebrow with a cocky smirk on her face.

Tilting my head, I narrow my eyes and study her. "What's that supposed to mean?"

"Ask Jackson." She carefully places Maize in the car seat and straps her in. I suck in a deep breath remembering the nanny rules I'd given Jackson—the ones she wasn't supposed to hear.

"Jackson needs rules. He has zero boundaries. And it's not like he listens to anyone anyway. Trust me. It's an open invitation to flirting and ridiculous comments from him. So you can't be wearing shirts like that around him."

"…or I can't be wearing shirts like this around you?" she quips, not paying any attention to how frustrated I'm becoming. "I think I can handle Jackson, so stop worrying yourself."

"Whatever, Mila."

She straightens up and looks me dead in the eyes. "You're my boss, and you can make any crazy rules you want when it comes to your baby, but you don't get to tell me what I can and can't wear, unless you're instituting a dress code for me, and if that's the case, I want a raise and a clothes allowance then."

I scoff, crossing my arms over my chest that's rising and falling rapidly. "How much for you to wear baggy overalls and turtlenecks every day?"

"You've got jokes, do you?" she mutters, not amused. "Why not just put a chastity belt on me, too, while you're at it?"

I grunt, thinking that's not a bad idea actually.

After Maize's strapped in, she picks up the car seat, and we walk toward the door. I grab the handle from her and carry her instead. Even though Maize's almost four months old, she gets heavy in this thing. Mila grabs her coat and the diaper bag off the chair and looks over her shoulder at me. "I'm not changing."

"Fine, suit yourself. I'm willing to bet after five minutes around my brother, you'll wish you would've."

"We'll see," she tells me as she walks toward the truck. I open the back door and try to snap Maize's seat in, but the damn thing won't click in.

"Dammit," I curse, fiddling with the base that never seems to work for me. Alex had to come to help me the first time because I didn't realize the car seat faces backward or even how to buckle it in.

"Let me do it." Mila pushes her tiny self between the door, and our bodies are so close, I can feel her heart beating against her chest. Noticing our proximity, I step back and let her in. "You have to put the back end in first and then push it forward until you hear the click." She does it in a matter of seconds and then tickles Maize's belly and smiles. She adjusts her straps once more and tucks in her pacifier.

The drive over to my parents' is awkwardly silent. Mila stares out the window, not saying much to me, and I wonder if I really pissed her off. Everything seemed fine this morning when I left for work, so I'm sure she's annoyed with how I reacted to her outfit, but I couldn't help it. There needs to be boundaries, especially if she's living in my house and will be around my brothers. I know how Jackson acted around River and Emily when Alex and Evan first brought them around, and it was primarily to piss them off.

However, Mila isn't mine, which, to Jackson, means she's available for the taking—but she definitely isn't.

I'm tempted to ask her what her problem is just to get her to speak to me again, but as soon as I open my mouth, her phone buzzes, and she's lost in it as soon as she gets a text. We arrive at the house, and once I park, Mila gets out, unlatches the base, and I carry Maize inside.

As soon as we enter the house, Mama is greeting me at the door with open arms. She hugs and kisses me as if she hasn't seen me in years and does the same for Mila. "Good to see you, honey. John treating you well?" she asks.

"Yes ma'am," she says, but keeps it short.

The smell of roasted chili fills the room, and my mouth waters thinking about Mama's homemade cornbread.

"Can I take her out?" Mama asks and reaches for Maize before I even respond. Mila kneels, unstraps Maize, then shows off her shirt.

"Oh, my goodness gracious, look how cute she looks in that," she says, grabbing Maize out and holding her close. Maize smiles up at Mama as she makes goofy faces.

"Mila picked it out," I tell her with a smile.

"Mila, honey. I already love you." Mama holds Maize close to her chest and talks about how much she loves the way babies smell. She's at her happiest with her grandkids, and though none of us were remotely prepared for another baby to be added, Mama's been my biggest supporter.

"Bowls are on the counter. Cheese is in the fridge. Help yourselves," she says just as Jackson and Alex come barreling in.

Mama gives them the evil eye, and when they see Maize, they bring their volume from a ten to a one in an instant.

"Mila, this is Alex, my youngest brother," I introduce. Alex gives her a smile, and she holds her hand out to shake his, but he pulls her into a side hug. "We're huggers 'round here. You'll learn that soon enough. Nice to meet you. Thanks for saving my brother's ass." He lets out a small chuckle.

Dad enters through the back door, goes straight to the sink to wash his hands, and then darts over to where Mama and Maize are. He holds out his arms.

"No, sir. I planned this lunch so I could get a little love from my grandbaby." I shake my head at their antics as I grab two bowls. After filling them both, I set them down on the table and then grab the shredded cheese.

"You want some homemade cornbread?" I ask Mila over my shoulder, and all she does is give me a nod. I groan out in frustration but decide now's not the time for a heated discussion.

Mama sweet-talks Maize but reluctantly hands her over to Dad a minute later. Out of everyone in the family, he's surprised me the most. From the moment he saw Maize, it was love at first sight, which made me so happy and relieved. When I told Dad the news of being a father, I was so damn nervous about his reaction. Since I had called Mama first, she told me it was my responsibility to tell him too. Maize and I were sitting in the living room that first night, and when Dad came in from the pastures, he looked like he'd seen a ghost. I stood, carrying Maize over, and told him she was mine. He was silent at first but then patted my shoulder and said he wanted to go clean up, then we'd talk. I told him about Bailey and the note, and that I was all she had now. He turns to mush now anytime she's around. Dad helped raised four boys and a girl, so I know firsthand how soft he gets around girls. Courtney got away with murder growing up, and I suspect that won't be any different with Maize either.

It's actually brought us closer, which is nice too. Dad's quiet and a hard shell to crack on his best days, but Maize has brought all of us together. He lights up when he sees her, and a smile that I've never seen before fills his face. Maize and Dad have a special bond that I don't think can ever be broken.

I break my attention away from my parents quietly arguing over who gets to hold and feed her and look over at Jackson. Just as I suspect, once he lays his beady eyes on Mila, he starts in with his flirting, but this time, he doesn't go light. He's full on trying to piss me off. We sit around the table, holding quiet conversations as Mama and Dad get their alone time with Maize.

"So Mila, you got a boyfriend back home?" Jackson asks, and Alex rolls his eyes. We can all see through his bullshit. But Mila, being as polite as she is, appeases him. If I didn't know better, I'd say she was flirting back, which irritates the fuck out of me.

"No boyfriend," she answers with a seductive smile.

"That's the best news I've heard all day considerin' I'm single and ready to mingle." He shoots her a wink, and I think I see her blush before lowering her eyes back to her food.

"Enough," I pipe in. The room grows silent, but it's short-lived.

"Sorry, my brother's a bit of an asshole. Quiet a majority of the time, but still an asshole. Though he's got the same good looks as I do, he's a total party killer." Jackson leans over and tells her loud enough for everyone in the room to hear except Mama who's paying zero attention to any of us.

"Jackson," I warn, pushing him back in his seat. "Shut the hell up and eat."

"Have you always been a nanny?" Alex asks her with a smile, changing the subject, which I'm thankful for.

"Actually, no. This is my first time. I have six brothers and sisters and helped my mom with my younger siblings growing up. I also help my older sister with my nephew when she needs me. Recently, I graduated from college with a teaching degree and hope to teach elementary kids in the fall in Georgia," she tells Alex, and that's when I realize there's still so much I don't know about her. I knew she had a large family and a degree, but I didn't know she was from Georgia. I figured she wasn't from around here since her accent is a bit different, but I had no idea she was from out of state. Thankfully, Mama hired her and probably knows everything from her blood type to her social security number, but it makes me feel like a dick for not asking basic questions and learning more about her. Though it's only been a few weeks, the realization sets in that I practically have a stranger living in my house.

"Wow, seven of you? I bet your mama is crazier than ours," Jackson says with a laugh.

"I heard that," Mama says over her shoulder.

Mila chuckles in agreement. "My mama is fierce. With one look, she makes us all shudder in fear. Taught us manners at a young age and how to follow the rules." On the last word she turns her head and looks at me. "But as the third Carmichael kid, I wasn't one to always follow the rules."

I narrow my eyes at her but don't say a word. She's testing me, and Jackson is eating it up like a fat kid at a buffet.

"A rule breaker. You sound like my kind of woman," Jackson adds, and they have a laugh together, which makes me roll my eyes. If they keep it up, they might roll straight out of my head and hit the floor.

"Your kind of woman is loose and will fuck anything with a dick, even a dirty one," I lean over and mumble to Jackson, purposely trying to get under his skin.

"Mama!" he says, and she turns and looks at him with a death stare.

"You're over thirty, and you're gonna play the tattletale game? I oughta..." she warns him.

Mila laughs. "Yes, that exact look. My mama has the same one."

Mama winks at her and walks into the living room with Maize, leaving us to our antics. Dad follows behind her, and I know being left without any adults to intervene is bad news.

I try to stay quiet and hope everyone else will too, but when Jackson asks Mila on a date in front of me just to get me stirred up, I lose my shit.

"So whaddya say? You, me, drinks." He works his charm like he always does, reaching over to brush a piece of hair out of Mila's face. Fuck this.

"Jackson, shut the hell up. She doesn't want to go on a date with you."

He smiles at me as if I didn't say a word, and Mila turns her body toward me, shooting daggers at me. "You don't get to decide what I do and don't want to do, either," she hisses between gritted teeth.

"Finally, a woman who has balls." Jackson laughs, then glances over at me before bringing all his attention back to Mila. "So is that a yes?" he asks eagerly—desperation in his tone which makes me want to knock him on his ass right here in the kitchen.

"Sure, just let me know when," Mila tells him in her sugary sweet tone, driving a knife into my last nerve.

Alex stands, excusing himself from the shitstorm, and I stand as well. I'm annoyed and frustrated with this whole situation, but she's right. I can't tell her what to do outside of taking care of Maize, but if she wants to go on a date with my horny brother, there will be rules put in place that she *will* follow before that happens. I can't risk Jackson fucking her only to break her heart, then her leaving me and Maize high and dry after it all comes crashing down. And knowing Jackson's reputation, that's exactly what will happen.

Jackson can make a sweet, innocent girl become a crazy lunatic. I've seen it a dozen times over the years and even more since he's lived with me. Considering we're identical twins, I've even experienced the craziness firsthand, and I've honestly wondered how many times he's pretended to be me to get out of a confrontation. Probably more than I want to know.

As they continue talking and flirting, I place my bowl in the sink and go into the living room where Mama is rocking Maize in the wooden rocking chair she's had since my older brother Evan was a baby. Seeing her love Maize with so much of her heart, even after everything, makes me so damn happy. My little girl is so loved. I'm so lucky to be a Bishop and to have such a supportive family, even when mistakes happen and babies are born in secret.

"She's perfect," Mama says.

"Isn't she? I love my little Maize Grace." I bend down to kiss her head that smells like fresh baby soap.

"I wasn't talking about Maize." Mama gives me a pointed look.

I narrow my eyes at her, then shake my head. I really hope she's not trying to play matchmaker like I've suspected all along, and she's just talking about how great of a nanny Mila is. Not wanting to open that can of worms, I keep quiet because if I give any hint that I think she's even remotely attractive, the grandma brigade will start planning a wedding before the first date. I've seen how this works too many times.

Mama shrugs when she doesn't get a response from me and continues as if she knows something I don't. "You better not let Jackson ruin this for you," she says, nonchalantly. "You've got a good thing going."

CHAPTER ELEVEN

Mila

I didn't really plan on going on a date with Jackson, and once John's out of earshot, I tell him as much. We share a good laugh about making John squirm, and he seems to have the same idea as me. Though, if I wasn't working for John and looking for a good time with no strings attached, Jackson would be a good distraction. The man oozes confidence like no other, and he's not afraid to say exactly what's on his mind—a big change from his brother. Not many men I've met are like that. But Jackson is one of those lady-killers—number one heartbreaker—and I've had enough of that for a lifetime. The fact that I'm still off-limits to everyone hits me full force. Always the bridesmaid, never the bride—it's been my life motto since I can remember.

After I thank Mrs. Bishop with a hug for a delicious lunch, we walk out to the truck. John has to get back to work, and Maize needs her afternoon nap. We ride in silence, which is obviously driving John insane. He's squeezing the steering wheel, and his lips are in a firm line. God, those lips. Always pouty and looking delicious.

Shit.

Not delicious.

John catches me staring at him and looks as if he's trying to read me, but before either of us can get a word out, Maize starts fussing in her seat.

Looking over my shoulder, I do my best to reach her behind John's seat. "Oh shoot, she lost her pacifier." Unbuckling my seat belt, I turn my body and can almost grab it, but it's wedged between her leg and the bottom of the car seat.

"It's okay, sweetie." I try to soothe her, but it only makes her scream louder. I know we're almost back to the house, but I hate hearing her cry like that. She's hungry and tired, and I know she'll fall asleep within minutes of rocking her. "I can't quite reach it," I say, turning around, so I'm completely facing the other direction. I lean over the center console, angling my body as far as I can, but it doesn't work. Since she's behind the driver's seat, I can barely reach her, so I put one knee on the center console and brace my other leg on the seat. As soon as I reach for the pacifier, I let out a relieved breath, until my bracelet snags on the car seat, keeping my hand firmly in place.

Maize's screaming bloody murder in my ear, so I place both knees on the console to try to grab her pacifier with the other hand. The bumps in the road make it more of a struggle, but eventually I grab it. "There we go." Sticking my finger inside of it, I place the pacifier back in Maize's mouth and wait for her to take it.

"That girl has some strong lungs." John finally speaks.

"Yeah, probably takes after her uncles." I snicker.

Once I'm sure Maize's settled, I slip my finger out of the pacifier and try to unhook my bracelet as John hits another pothole. "Shit." I'm stuck on my knees, bent over the center console with my ass right in his face. I could tug hard, but it would probably break the tennis bracelet Gigi gave me for Christmas last year. This is exactly why I don't ever wear jewelry. John starts laughing hysterically, and I can only turn just enough to see his profile. "Are you seriously laughing at me right now?"

He brings a hand up and smacks my ass. "Best view I've had in a long time."

I groan, trying to swat him away from me with my free hand. "You're an asshole."

"I warned ya," he gloats.

"Warned me about what?"

"Wearing that would get you in trouble, and now your ass and thong are hanging out of your pants as we drive by all the ranch hands on their lunch breaks." He's still laughing, and as soon as I'm able, I'm smacking that grin right off his too-perfect face.

To emphasize his point, he begins honking, and when I look out the side window, I see half a dozen guys hootin' and hollerin' at us.

"Oh my God." My cheeks heat. "I'm so gettin' you back for that."

"Yeah, we'll see about that, sweetheart. Jackson's my twin brother, remember? I have *years* of getting even."

A low groan releases from my throat as he continues to fuel my anger. "Can you pull over and help me?"

"Nah, I'm enjoying this a little too much, and we're almost home."

I try with everything I have to get unhooked, but considering I can't see what my bracelet is stuck on, it's no use. Maize looks at me with big blue eyes, and it makes me smile.

Minutes later, we arrive at the house, and as soon as he puts the truck in park and turns it off, he turns toward me so I can see his face over my shoulder.

"I'll help you on one condition," he states, looking tempting and serious all at once.

"What?"

"You don't go on a date with my brother."

I narrow my eyes, waiting for the punch line, but it never comes. Didn't I just tell him not thirty minutes ago that he wasn't the boss of my personal life? Why does he even care?

"Hmm…which brother?" I taunt, trying like hell to keep a straight face.

He grunts in response. "Okay fine. Enjoy watching Maize on your knees."

John turns and reaches for the door. He opens it and takes a step out before I finally cave.

"Okay fine!" I shout.

He turns and faces me but doesn't move. "Fine, what?"

"Oh my God." I groan, releasing a frustrated breath as I try to wiggle myself out again. "I won't go out on a date with your brother. There. Happy now?"

"Very." He grins, stepping out of the truck and just as I'm about to shout at him for leaving me here, I watch the back door open. Carefully, he finds what my bracelet is stuck on and loosens the hold on me. As I'm trying to catch my breath and rest my wrists on the middle console, he opens the driver's door with a smirk and checks out my ass one last time before his eyes meet mine.

"Didn't realize you were so good on your knees," he tells me.

"Yeah, well, I guess that's what happens when you're naturally flexible." I lick my lips to taunt him. I watch his throat tighten as if those words affected him.

Good.

That's what he gets for messing with me.

"I'll grab Maize." He finally breaks the tension and moves to the back seat to grab her.

Once we're back in the house, I take the bracelet off, then make Maize a bottle. Just as I'm turning around to go back to her, I walk straight into John's torso.

"Sorry," we both say as he places his hands on my shoulders. His body invades my space, taking the breath right out of my lungs as we stand awkwardly. "I was just coming to tell you I'm heading back to work. Probably be home around six or so."

Home.

It feels so intimate, yet it's not. This is his home, not mine, though I know it's supposed to be temporarily. I like the idea of John coming home to Maize and me.

As soon as the thought fills my head, I quickly push it out.

"Okay, sounds good. I can have dinner done by then," I say, looking up into his eyes.

He steps back, releasing my shoulders before brushing a hand through his messy hair. I love the way the longer strands fall to one side but are clean cut on the other. If I didn't know John and only saw his appearance, I'd never guess he'd be a dad or even a business owner. I know he manages the B&B for his parents, and I know a lot comes with that, including finances, schedules, expenses, bookings, and more. He's smart, and even though he's all business the majority of the time, he's starting to let his playful side show, which only makes me want to see that part of him more.

"You know you aren't required to cook for me, Mila," he reminds me, rubbing a hand casually over his groomed jaw.

"Yes, I know." I'm just about to tell him the truth about Jackson and that a date wasn't going to happen, but he speaks up before I do.

"And once I'm home, you don't have to stay stuck in the house. I don't want you to feel like you're trapped or something."

"Well, the only place I'd go is my grandma's, and she plays Bingo on Thursday nights or hangs with my cousin, Kat, but I'm content with staying in too. I see them on the weekends." John only works morning shifts on Saturdays and Sundays, so his mama watches Maize, and I actually get to sleep in. It's nice having time off, but I'm still bored—mostly. On a rainy Sunday last week, I was snuggled up on the couch watching a movie, and John walked in, looking all rugged and western with his cowboy hat and boots, and took a seat on the other end of the couch. He'd been working on the ranch before the rain came down and still smelled like country air. He lifted my feet and rested them on his lap, and we just stayed like that until the movie was over.

I ended up drifting asleep shortly after the credits rolled, and I felt his thumb rub circles on my ankle. It was sweet but confusing as John is with everything he says and does. Spending every day around him, in his space, with his daughter feels like we're playing house, and even though it's only been a couple of weeks since I've been here, it feels so much longer.

But that doesn't make him any less confusing.

I watch as John's tongue runs over his bottom lip as he takes in my words. I'm not sure what kind of answer he was expecting, but it seems to affect him in a weird way.

"Okay well, I just wanted you to know. And I'm sorry for teasing you in e truck. If you want to go on a date with Jackson, then I definitely can't o you. Might be good for you to get out anyway."

His words give me whiplash, and I furrow my brows, utterly confused. minute, he's demanding I don't date Jackson, and the next, he's telling a good idea? *What the hell?* I don't even want to go on a date n!

"Oh, okay," I slowly drawl out. "So you're okay with me going out with Jackson?" I ask to confirm.

"Sure. Doesn't bother me any. But if he pisses you off, you can't up and quit on me."

Is that the only reason he didn't want me to in the first place? Or is there something more to it? My head is spinning with questions that I know I can't ask without making things even more awkward.

"I'd never do that, John. I love watching Maize."

"Good. Then I have nothing to worry about then."

"Okay. Right." My words stumble out because I feel like I just had a conversation with two different people.

"Alright, well, I'll see you around six. Text me if you need anything," he tells me before rushing out the door.

I feed Maize her bottle while rocking her, and she falls asleep in no time. Once she's in her crib, I grab my phone and send a text to Kat.

MILA

OMG!! Why are men so confusing?!?!

KAT

You're just now asking yourself that question?

MILA

I'm serious, Kat! John got all caveman-like and crazy when Jackson asked me out on a date after blatantly flirting with me. I said yes just to appease him, but as soon as John walked away, I told Jackson no. John tells me I can't and makes me promise him I won't. Then ten minutes later, he's telling me I should! So WTF!

KAT

OH MY GOD! Bishop brother sandwich! So what's the problem?

I groan, ready to throw my phone.

MILA

I hate you.

KAT

Oh, come on, Mila! Isn't it obvious?

I scrunch my nose, narrowing my eyes as I re-read her message.

MILA

Isn't what obvious?

KAT

Two words, my friend. REVERSE. PSYCHOLOGY.

MILA

What do you mean?

I'm so damn frustrated over this that I walk into the kitchen and kneel under the sink and grab all the cleaning supplies I can find in the cupboard. Once my arms are full of sprays and paper towels, I set everything out on the table and reach for my phone again.

KAT

John knows that Jackson doesn't ever listen to him, so if he tells you not to date him, that's just going to be another reason Jackson goes after you. But if he tells you to go for it and acts like he doesn't care, then maybe you'll reconsider since he won't be "off-limits." He's mind-fucking you.

MILA

He's fucking with me! Damn him!

KAT

LOL! You gonna tell him you know?

I flash a devilish smile and type out a response.

MILA

Nope!

Three hours later, the entire house is spotless. The more I thought about what Kat said, the more annoyed I became. If I wanted to play these kinds of games, I would've stayed in high school. Whether or not he's purposely messing with my head, it doesn't make me any less infuriated. While Maize slept, I took all that frustration out on the house. I cleaned up the kitchen, swept, and mopped after doing all the dishes, cleaned the counter and table, and organized his fridge.

Next, I moved to the living room and vacuumed, dusted the TV and furniture, washed the blankets and folded them neatly by the fireplace, and even lit some candles to get the permanent ranch smell out of the carpets.

And that was only during the first hour.

I went to the bathroom next, scrubbed the shower, sink, and counter, then swept and mopped. I made his toilet shine like a damn Golden Globe Award. After putting a load of towels in the washer, I moved to his bedroom next. Since Maize was asleep in the crib, I tiptoed around to dust, changed the trash, organized his dresser and nightstand, and grabbed his hamper of dirty laundry. Then I went back in and grabbed Maize's hamper too.

Three loads of laundry later, I'm sweating my ass off at everything I accomplished. My adrenaline spiked, and once I got started, I couldn't stop. My mom always called it my angry cleaning marathon. When I get really upset over something, I busy my mind by cleaning nonstop until everything is done.

Once the towels and John and Maize's clothes are all folded and put away, I look around the house and dread crawls into my mind.

"Oh my God," I mutter to myself. "He's going to think I'm batshit crazy."

"Who's going to think you're batshit crazy?"

I spin around so fast, I nearly twist my ankle in the process. A girl I've never met before is standing in the living room with her foot cocked out and a hand on her hip.

"You scared the shit out of me." I press a hand to my chest over my racing heart.

"Sorry, babe. I knocked, but no one answered, so I just walked in," she explains, which I can't really blame her considering I'd done the same thing. "I'm Kiera." She holds her hand out for me, and I find myself wondering if she's John's girlfriend by the way she just let herself in. She has her reddish blonde hair pulled up into a ponytail and is absolutely gorgeous with her tanned skin and bright green eyes. It wouldn't surprise me because she looks like she actually belongs here with her cowboy boots and worn jeans, but John's never mentioned having a girlfriend. The thought of him having one all this time cripples my anxiety.

"Hi, I'm Mila," I finally respond, taking her hand in mine.

"I know. The nanny."

"Right." I pinch my lips together, wondering why she's here. "If you're looking for John, he's not home. He's at the B&B until six."

"Oh, I'm not here for John. I just wanted to come to meet you and maybe snuggle Maize for a few minutes," she responds with a polite smile.

"Meet me? I'm sorry, but who are you exactly? John hasn't told me anything about you so—"

"I'm a family friend. I'm one of the horse trainers. I work with John and Jackson sometimes, but my family has a ranch not far from here," she explains, relief settling in and hoping she's not a psycho stalker who's in love with John or something.

"Oh, okay. Well, just give me a minute."

As I walk to John's room, I quickly send him a text asking if it's okay that she's here. Once he gives me the approval that she's not going to murder me with the heel of her boot, I carefully lift Maize out of her crib and talk to her while she slowly wakes up. I lay her on John's freshly made bed and change her diaper.

"Is it okay to come in?" I hear Kiera and turn my head toward the door. "John give you the reassurance and approval?" She grins as if she knew I was going to double-check.

I exhale and smile. "Yeah, you're all good." I chuckle as she opens the door wider and steps in. "Sorry, I just didn't want to be one of those stories posted on the internet of a naïve woman who let a stranger in and ended up chopped into pieces."

Kiera laughs as she bends down to give Maize a kiss on the head. "No worries. Probably a good thing you validate any woman who comes here, considering the number of girls who would die to be in your shoes right now."

"What do you mean?" I ask, putting Maize's bottoms back on then tossing the diaper into the trash. "To watch the baby?" I pick her up and hand her over to Kiera's waiting arms.

"Yes, because she's just the sweetest, prettiest baby girl there ever was," she says in a high-pitched baby voice to Maize. Then she looks at me and grins. "Because John is one of the most eligible bachelors around here, and he doesn't let just anyone into his life."

"Well, I wouldn't consider being the nanny as being in his life. He needs help, and that's all I'm doing here." We walk out of the room and toward the kitchen, so I can get Maize a bottle. "Plus, he's barely here."

"Oh, trust me, babe. You're in his daughter's life, which means you're in *his* life."

"Well, even so, we're just…" I bite my lower lip as I think of the right words. Mixing the formula and water together, I shake the bottle up before handing it to Kiera. "He's my boss, and that's it. Plus, I only met him the day I started."

"Yeah, but these Bishop boys have a way of making you feel like you've known them forever." There's definitely some truth to her words, but even so, crossing that line would only end in heartbreak, considering I'm planning to go back to Georgia at the end of the summer.

"Well, I can't deny that his family's very welcoming." I chuckle as I follow Kiera to the living room where she holds Maize and feeds her. We sit on the couch facing each other, and already it feels like I've known Kiera all my life. She has a warm presence about herself that's hard to resist.

"The Bishops are amazing. I've known their whole family since I was born. My parents knew them growing up, and I basically grew up with them too."

"Oh, so you're close with them?"

"Yeah, I am, but I was always closer to Jackson. We both had a passion for horses early on, and his obnoxious behavior made hanging out together a blast."

"Oh yeah, I can totally see that. I've only met him a couple of times, and he already used me as a pawn to tick John off."

She rolls her eyes as if she's not at all surprised to hear that. "Jackson refuses to grow up basically, even though his brothers and sister have. He thinks life is a nonstop party, which is why he butts heads with John so much."

"It's hard to believe they're twins," I say. "John is so quiet and serious most of the time."

"He's always been that way. All about business and work, but he has a side to him he doesn't let a lot of people see."

"Oh yeah?" I ask, my curiosity piqued.

"Yeah. I'm pretty sure you'll be seeing that side of him really soon," she says with so much certainty I'm tempted to ask her what she means by that, but I stop. *Boundaries*, I remind myself. John was clear on setting them, and though I'm not sure why, I can't help smiling at the thought of John showing me that side of him.

"Why do I feel like you're not telling me something?" I cock my head and study her features.

"Like what?" she asks, innocently, making more goofy faces at Maize as she finishes her bottle.

I give her a pointed look to tell her I'm not buying it.

"Okay look, I'll tell you, but you cannot tell John I said a word, okay? He'd be the one to murder me into a million pieces."

I chuckle and agree.

"John and Jackson are always competing against each other. They always have, and well, when it comes to chicks, it can sometimes get intense."

"What? Like they fight over the same girl?"

"No, not exactly. Neither of them has lacked in that department, trust me. But Jackson enjoys toying with John and getting him pissed off, especially when it comes to something he wants."

"Something he wants?"

She's not talking about me, right?

"You're really attractive, Mila. Like really gorgeous, so it's not surprising that John would feel uneasy about you being around Jackson given his track record."

"Wait. Hold up. What?" I circle my hands around and motion for her to rewind before going any further.

"Why the hell would John care? He's the one who told me we needed to have rules and boundaries and using stupid reverse psychology to tell me to go out on a date with Jackson."

Kiera's smirking as she sets Maize up to her shoulder and starts patting her on the back. Things aren't adding up, and I feel like I'm in the twilight zone.

I continue. "John doesn't like me. He just doesn't want me to date Jackson and mess things up. He's afraid I'll end up quitting if Jackson pisses me off or something."

"Mm-hmm," she hums, pursing her lips together as if she's not buying it.

"No, really. He told me the only reason he was pissed about Jackson is because of how he tends to break girls' hearts, and if he breaks my heart, he's afraid he'd lose me, and he'd be without a nanny again."

"The only thing John Bishop is afraid of is his own feelings. So while he's feeding you that pathetic little story, consider this. Jackson has denied his feelings for me our entire lives, and now I'm dating the local vet. His name is Trent, by the way, and I'll tell you more about him later." She grins wide and looks like the heart-eyed emoji. "Even after I finally moved on because I was sick of waiting for him, he still couldn't admit he had feelings for me. Instead, he sleeps around with random chicks to prove that he doesn't."

"What? Really?" My eyes widen, completely shocked by this news.

She nods, then smiles when Maize finally burps. "Jackson acts like a wild horse. Untamed and can buck you off at any given moment without even a second glance to make sure you landed on your feet."

Damn. That sounds harsh.

"So what does that have to do with John and me?" I ask.

"Jackson knows John well enough to know he's attracted to you, but he also knows John wouldn't pursue anything since you're here to watch Maize, which could make things complicated if it doesn't work out. So Jackson being the man-child he is taunts John by flirting with you in front of him and waiting to see how far he can push his buttons before John cracks and finally admits what he's feeling."

Her words shock me, and I'm not sure how to feel. Relieved? Confused maybe?

"And is this something that happens…often?" I dread her response, but I need to know I'm not just another pawn in their games.

"In some ways, yes, but never to this extent. Jackson has tried to steal a girl from John a time or two, but it's never fazed him before. With you, it definitely fazes him."

116

CHAPTER TWELVE

John

The fact that Kiera is over at the house with Mila right now makes me feel uneasy and edgy. I like Kiera, and we have a decent friendship, but I don't trust either of them not to gossip. I sent Mila a text over an hour ago and still haven't gotten a response.

Yeah, that can't be good.

I'm sitting in my office when Nicole comes barging in. She takes a seat across my desk and crosses her legs.

"Sure, come in," I deadpan.

She starts going on and on about something, and once I finally get her to leave, I pack up to head out myself. I can't wait to see Maize even though I did this afternoon.

It's crazy how much I miss her when I'm gone even if I'm only a few feet away.

I let my staff know I'm on my way out and wave before rushing out the side door. I love that I have a short walk to get home to Maize. Although I'm not sure what I'll be coming home to tonight, considering how lunch went.

The moment I walk in, a mixed aroma of bleach and meat hit my senses. The first thing I notice when I step into the living room is how tidy everything looks. Did Mila clean?

"Hello?" I call out, setting my jacket on the arm of the couch.

"We're in here!" I hear her call from the kitchen with a cheery voice, and I hope that means there's no more awkwardness between us.

The moment I spot her, I see how wrong I am.

Not only is the house spotless, but she made dinner—more like a damn feast. There's a spread on the table, Maize's in her little vibrating chair, and Mila's dolled up in a tight dress, heels, and her dark hair is curled into waves. She has an apron tied around her waist, and she looks like she walked out of a Southern cookbook. My eyes gaze down her body from the curves of her breasts to her long, lean legs that are seriously testing my willpower.

What the hell is she thinking wearing that? It barely qualifies as a dress. That apron, though, has me thinking all kinds of inappropriate thoughts about how she'd look wearing only that.

Bent over my seat like she was earlier, running her mouth and testing my limits.

Fuck me.

"Hey!" She turns around with a wide smile. Her makeup's heavier than usual and her bright red lipstick is distracting me in every way possible. "Dinner is almost ready if you wanna wash up. I made your favorite!"

Flicking my eyes to the table, I see she's made chicken fried steak with mashed potatoes, white gravy, and corn on the cob. It's a feast, and I'm thoroughly confused why she'd go out of her way to make my favorite dishes, considering the way things ended this afternoon with her all pissed and ready for a fight. Though now that I'm seeing this side of her, I can't complain either.

"Wow...it smells amazing," is all I can say. "How'd you know?" I blink my eyes away from her and concentrate on Maize as I walk toward her.

"I called your mama, and she told me," she states proudly.

After unstrapping Maize, I hold her to my chest and feather kisses on her chunky little cheeks. "Did you have a good afternoon?" I ask her as if she understands.

"She did," Mila responds. "Well, she napped mostly. And I cleaned. Then Kiera came over and visited, and then I started dinner. But I did get her on the floor for some tummy time, which she hates with a passion still, and then we read a couple of stories, danced to some music, and I was just telling her all the secrets I'm learning about you." She grins, and there's a sparkle in her eye that makes me suspicious. So not only did she talk with Kiera this afternoon but Mama as well. Just *great*.

"That sounds highly productive," I say, impressed. "You really didn't have to, Mila. I mean, I appreciate it, but I'm not paying you to clean up after me."

She sighs, her shoulders relaxing as she steps into my space and leans in to give Maize a kiss. "I know. You tell me that at least every other day. But I need to keep myself busy. I just graduated from college, so I'm used to doing something. When she naps, I'm bored."

I put Maize back in her chair and buckle her before facing Mila. "Well, thank you. It's nice having someone to come home to." I flash her a genuine smile and look at her dress more closely. "Why are you so dressed up?"

The timer on the stove beeps, and she turns to shut it off before pulling a pan of rolls out of the oven. "I'm going out tonight. Made some plans after you told me I should get out more, so I figured, why not?" She sounds super giddy about it, which ticks me off. Not about her going out but if that person is my devious twin brother, I might blow a gasket.

"Oh. I see." I want to ask her where and with whom, but it's not my business. I'm the one who told her to get out of the house and that we need boundaries, but I'm dying to know anyway. I stick Maize back in her seat and notice there's a bottle ready to go on the table as well.

"Okay, everything's ready!" she announces, placing the bread on the table, and that's when I realize there's only one place setting.

"Aren't you eating?" I ask, taking a seat. "I can't possibly eat all of this, and Maize isn't a big eater," I tease.

She chuckles, waving me off. "Actually, no. I have to head out in a few minutes. But you enjoy, okay? Put the leftovers in the fridge, and then I'll warm it up for lunch tomorrow if you want."

"You have to eat, Mila," I say, grabbing her wrist to pull her back as she steps away.

Her eyes gaze down to where my hand is, but I don't remove it. Adding pressure, her arm relaxes in my grip, and I love feeling her warmth even if it's wrong. Aside from bumping into one another at random times, I've done my best to physically distance myself to avoid touching her, but now that I am—even just a small part—I don't want to let go.

She clears her throat when neither of us speaks. "I will, promise. I'll eat when I'm out."

At that revelation, I release her and swallow, directing my eyes back to the food in front of me.

"Okay, Maize Grace. You be good for your daddy, okay?" Mila leans over and presses kisses to her small hands. Maize responds with cooing and kicking her feet.

"I think she'll be ready for a jumper soon," she informs me. "Usually between the four to six-month range."

"What's that?" I ask, furrowing my brows as I grab the tongs and grab a piece of chicken.

"Well for my sister's kid, I got him a Jumperoo where it holds them in place, and they can bounce and spin around to play with toys. It's good in helping strengthen their muscles for crawling and walking. My nephew loved his, and it gives you some time to set them down when all they want to do is be held."

I try to imagine what this contraption looks like but honestly have no clue. I'm so out of my element when it comes to this stuff, and it feels like I'll never fully grasp it. She must see the confused look on my face because she bursts out laughing.

"I'll find a link and text it to you, so you know what I'm talking about." She glances over at the clock and then grabs her phone from the counter. "I gotta run, but I'll be back by ten at the latest to grab Maize for her first night feeding."

"Uh, okay. Have fun." I pinch my lips together to keep myself from asking the handful of questions I have. I know I don't have a right to, but that doesn't stop me from wanting to find out. "Oh and Mila…" She stops just as she steps into the hallway and leans back to peek her head into the kitchen. She has her brows raised as she waits for me to speak. "Be safe."

"Don't worry, boss." She winks at me with a devilish smile that makes me want to tear that dress right off her. "If I can handle you, I think I can handle anything."

"What the hell does that even mean?" I ask Emily and groan, tilting my head back to finish off my third beer of the night. Maize's asleep already, but I'm too anxious, waiting for Mila to return, to go to bed.

I called to talk to Evan, but as soon as he realized it was to talk about chicks, he passed the phone to Em instead.

Bastard.

She's laughing, clearly amused by my situation. "John, how can a guy like you be so dense?"

"Oh look, the Evan charm has rubbed off on you. Never mind."

I'm about to hang up when she shouts at me to wait. "You Bishops are a lot to handle. Why don't any of y'all realize this?"

Emily's about to pop any day now with my niece, and while I'm excited as hell for them, it's voided any kind of filter on her. She's edgy, grumpy that she's still pregnant and not getting a lot of sleep, and according to Evan, horny as hell.

I could've gone without knowing that last bit.

"What does that have to do with anything?" I ask. "If she can handle me, she can handle anything? Like I'm so difficult?" I grunt, wondering if I should be insulted by that or not. "I just know she's out with Jackson. She said she visits her grandma and cousin on the weekends, so who else would she know 'round here?"

"So what if she is? You did tell her she could, right?"

I hear Evan laughing his ass off, which means I've been on speaker this whole time. They both suck.

"You dumbass," Evan taunts. "You baited her right into Jackson's slutty arms."

I lean back on the couch, rolling my eyes until they close. I only said that so she wouldn't think I was acting like a jealous ex-boyfriend but a boss concerned about her feelings. Obviously, that all backfired on me now.

"That's it. I'm going over there."

"Maize," is all Emily says, reminding me that I can't just leave my house. Not without my baby at least.

"Fine. I'm calling him then."

Emily chuckles, and I can just imagine her shaking her head at me, judging me with her pregnant gaze.

"Okay, well good luck with that," Evan says. "If he's bangin' her, the last thing he's gonna do is answer your damn call."

And with that remark, I hang up and immediately dial Jackson.

Motherfucker better answer his goddamn phone.

It rings and rings, and I start getting ready to unleash the wrath on his voicemail when he finally picks up.

"What's up?" he asks, breathlessly. "I'm kinda busy. Whatcha need?"

"Uh, just wonderin' what you're doing. Wanna come over for a beer?" I ask and immediately wish I could put the words back in my mouth. I rarely ask him to hang out so now he's definitely going to suspect something's up.

"Well, actually..." he begins but is soon interrupted by laughter. A girl's laughter. It's too far in the distance to know if it's Mila's or not, and considering Jackson's track record with women, it's not unusual for him to be with someone right now. However, my gut tells me he's with her.

"Is that Mila?" I grind out, needing to know so I can pummel his ass later.

"That's not really any of your business, now is it?" he taunts with amusement, and if Maize wasn't sleeping right now, I'd pack her up and haul ass over to his place.

"Jackson," I warn, sitting up. "Don't push me."

"Bro, relax. She's not yours to claim. Unless..." he lingers, and I know exactly what he's going to say. *Unless I want to fuck her.* Damn asshole enjoys pissing me off.

"Fuck you." I hang up on him, realizing I'm not going to get any answers anyway, and while I shouldn't be reacting this way to the thought of Mila out with him, or any other guy, I can't stop the thoughts from haunting me.

Not only is she stunning in a way that makes me wonder how this girl is even single in the first place, but she's kind, caring, passionate, and funny. She gets along with everyone, and if she wasn't someone I hired to watch my baby, I would've made a move on her the first time we met. Except that isn't the case, and if I don't remind my dick of that, I'm going to be the first man known to die from blue balls.

I flip through channels while I impatiently wait and let out a sigh of relief when I finally hear her coming in at ten to ten. She walks into the living room as I'm lying on the couch with my arm resting over my head. The only light comes from the TV, but I can make out her silhouette as she crosses the room. I don't make a sound or move as I wait to see what her next move is. Just as I exhale, thinking she's turning off the TV, she surprises me when she returns with a blanket. She covers me up, and I almost feel guilty for not letting her know I'm awake.

"I'm home," she whispers above my head in that sweet, sultry tone of hers. I feel her hand linger on my other arm that's resting across my stomach as she places the blanket over me. "Goodnight, John," she says softly and begins to step away, and before I can stop myself, I reach out and grab her leg.

"Oomph," she mutters, nearly falling but luckily catches herself on the arm of the couch. "You scared me. You always do that."

"Sorry, I didn't mean to." I shift my body, so I can look up at her and study her face. "You have a good time tonight?" I ask, gauging her reaction before I assume anything.

She smiles wide, almost as if she's reliving it. "Yeah." She nods. "Yeah, I did. It was fun."

I swallow hard, pulling myself up, so I'm sitting upright. She looks content, and I should be happy about that, but I can't stop the wave of jealousy that surfaces. I hate feeling this way; in fact, I *never* feel this way, which irritates the fuck out of me even more.

"Well, I better get to bed. Five a.m. comes way too early." Standing up, I get a better view of Mila and notice how messy her hair is and smudged her makeup looks. Pursing my lips into a firm line, I don't say another word before I walk away.

CHAPTER THIRTEEN

Mila

"Oh, Maize!" I laugh even though I really want to cry. She spits up on me for the third time today, and I'm starting to question why I even wear shirts around her now. "I hope you aren't allergic to your formula or something." I make a mental note to talk to John about it later so he can talk to her doctor—just in case.

It's been just over a month since I've been taking care of Maize, and I still don't know anything about her mother. I want to ask and find out where she is or why she isn't in the picture, but John's been distant and weird, and I feel like I'm in the way half the time when he's home. I continue cooking him dinner every night after work, and when I stick around on those nights to eat with him, we sit in awkward silence or use Maize as a buffer. I'll catch him looking at me, and he'll look away as if keeping eye contact with me is physically painful for him or something. I don't get it. I don't get him.

"You think your daddy's gonna be in a good or a crabby mood today?" I ask Maize when I place her in the swing so I can find a clean shirt. She giggles at my baby talk, and I laugh right along with her. "Yeah, I agree. He's been a tad crabby lately, hasn't he?"

I toss my shirt over my head, and even though I'm in a sports bra, it feels nice having the cool air against my skin. It's been getting warmer out, which means it's humid and muggy too. Just as I turn to walk to my room for a clean shirt, my phone rings and distracts me.

I notice it's my mother and immediately pick up. "Hey, Mom!"

"Sweet girl, hey! How's it goin'? I miss you!"

"I miss you too, Mom!" I kneel beside Maize's swing and make funny faces at her. "Sorry I haven't called in a few days. Things are going well. Maize's growing like a weed right before my eyes." I scrunch my nose and lean into Maize to kiss her precious cheeks.

"Just wanted to call and see how everything was going so far. Was thinking about sending you a care package. Anything you need?"

"Um, not that I can think of. Maybe some more clothes? Other than that, I think I'm doing pretty good. I'll have to send you some more pics of Maize. I know it's only been a little over a month, but she's growing up so fast."

"That's how babies do. I still remember holding you in my arms and how precious you were. You're still making me proud, Mila. Always were so independent and still are."

Mom and I chat for the next twenty minutes, and I'm so lost in the conversation and tickling Maize, I don't even hear the door click closed.

"Hot damn!" I hear Jackson howling behind me. I look at him over my shoulder, and he flashes me a seductive wink. "No wonder John's been in a shit mood."

"I gotta run, Mom. I'll call you later to check in. Okay. Love you too. Bye."

I lock my phone and scowl at Jackson. "What does that mean?" I ask, offended. He makes an extra effort to stop in when John isn't home, and I've suspected it was either to check up on me or to get under John's skin.

I've assumed the latter, but I've also learned these Bishop boys are anything but predictable.

"Well babe, it means you walkin' around half naked is making every guy's fantasy come to life, except John won't make a move, so he's sportin' the biggest case of blue balls thinking about it."

I nearly choke on his words. "What are you talking—" I stop myself as I quickly remember I forgot to put on a clean shirt. I'm still in my sports bra and work out shorts. "Shit," I mutter, feeling my cheeks heat.

"It's hot as fuck, so it's not like I blame you, but you gotta know it's killin' him," Jackson adds, and I feel so lost that I stand, picking Maize up with me and walk toward my room.

"First off," I begin with Jackson on my heels as I open my door. "Maize spit up on me, and I had every intention of changing, but then my mother called, and I got sidetracked. Second, I literally have no idea what you're talking about."

I set Maize down on my bed and walk to the dresser for a T-shirt. Tossing it over my head, I pull my arms through and smooth the material down my stomach.

"You seriously don't know?" He cocks a brow, leaning against my doorframe with his arms crossed. He looks pretty hot in his dark jeans, blue shirt, and black cowboy hat. He wears the look so effortlessly, and I can see why Kiera's been smitten with him since she was a teen.

I lift my arms up and let them drop to my sides. "I seriously don't know."

"What did you do last night?" he asks, and his sudden change of subject gives me whiplash.

"Um…I watched a movie, stuffed my face with popcorn, and then passed out after Maize's first feeding."

"And the night before that?"

"I went into town to meet up with my cousin, Kat, and we went to the mall and dinner before I came back here and got up with Maize. Three times." I groan. She's starting to teeth, and I only suspect it's going to get worse.

"And tonight?" he asks.

"Well, tomorrow is Saturday, so I'll get to sleep in, but I'll probably just take a bath, read, or watch another movie." I pause, thinking about how sad my life sounds right now. "Okay and now you just made me realize how pathetic I am. Thanks."

He chuckles, shaking his head. "And what did John do those nights?"

I have no idea where he's going with this, but I play along anyway. "Well, we normally eat dinner together, and then he plays with Maize for a while or gives her a bath, then he'll either read to her or rock her to sleep. Then about an hour later, he goes to bed."

"And that's been his routine since the day Maize arrived," Jackson adds. "No going out, dating, drinking, having a social life. He's made Maize his number one priority."

Picking Maize up, I walk us out of my room and to the living room so I can set her in the new Jumperoo I told John to order. "What does that have to do with what I've been doing?" I pause, then continue. "Wait. What do you mean since she arrived? You mean since she was born?" I turn and ask Jackson once I make sure Maize's settled.

"Uh, yeah. Well, kinda." He sucks in his lower lip as if he's unsure he should discuss it.

"Where is her mother?" I ask, taking a seat on the couch next to Jackson. "He never talks about her, and I've been too nervous to ask."

Jackson rubs the back of his neck, obviously torn between telling me or not but then opens his mouth to speak. "It's not really my story to tell. John doesn't talk about it much anymore, so I'm leaving that up to him to tell you."

My shoulders fall, feeling so out of the loop about the whole thing. I know it's not my business, but I can't help being curious considering I'm watching over Maize every day.

"Okay, I can understand that. I just wish he'd let me in a little, ya know? One minute, he seems fine, and the next, he's pushing me away. I always feel like I did something wrong."

"John can be a difficult egg to crack," he admits. "But my whole point before was he's changed a lot recently and having you around scares him. You're in his house, around his baby, wedging your way into our lives, and it's not something he's familiar with. He likes to deny it, but he's attracted to you, and my theory is, he feels guilty about it. John likes to play by the rules, mostly, so you're off-limits in his mind. He pushes you away when he feels like he's getting too close and thinks he should only be focused on Maize. He's not one to put himself first—ever."

This all shocks me, considering it's coming from Jackson of all people. I don't know how much truth his words hold, but I can't discredit them just yet. Part of me wants to believe he's right, but the other part refuses to accept it.

"You know, this is pretty ironic coming from you, Jackson," I tease, pushing his buttons. "Don't think I haven't heard the rumors about you."

He starts laughing, obviously not caring if I know or not. Shrugging, he gives me a look like he's guilty and knows it.

"You should be taking your own advice and stop running away from what's right in front of you."

"Nah." He smirks. "What fun is that anyway?"

I roll my eyes at his attempt to act like he doesn't care. I have a feeling not many girls get to see this side of Jackson, and I understand why he'd be easy to fall for too. If only he'd admit his feelings for Kiera to himself. Typical.

Jackson rises from the couch and leans down to give Maize a kiss on the head. "Oh," he says, turning around to face me. "John thinks you and I hooked up the night you went out not too long ago. I didn't exactly deny it, so he might be less grumpy if he knew the truth."

"Oh my God! Jackson Bishop!" I shout, laughing at his pathetic expression. "You're awful! No wonder he's been avoiding me like the black plague."

"Well, keep walking around without a top on, and he'll be *on* you like chicken pox."

I let Jackson's words swirl in my mind all afternoon. I've suspected John was attracted to me that first morning he walked into the kitchen with a hard-on, but then I figured morning wood was the cause of that. It's hard not to notice the way he looks at me and how he tries to keep his distance but then finds any reason to be near me. I've lived in the friend zone so long that I always doubt I could ever be more than that to a guy I'm equally attracted to.

However, now I'm certain I know the truth, and I want to give John every opportunity to tell me himself. Does he really think I'd go out with

Jackson after it was evident he didn't want me to? Is that why he's been extra moody lately and why he sees me as off-limits?

Questions dance in my head along with my old friend doubt. Am I off-limits because I'm his nanny, or does he think I'm too young? It hasn't been brought up, but it's something I thought when he randomly made a comment about not having life experiences.

I graduated college early, have lived at home my entire life, and now I live here. I've never truly been "on my own," but at twenty-two, the opportunity to be on my own just hasn't arose yet.

Still, I don't think that'd be the reason. If John had a relationship with Maize's mother and things ended badly, he could be avoiding women in general.

Tonight, I decide, I'm going to get to the bottom of this.

John got home about an hour ago, and though I'm technically off duty, I love watching him play with Maize. I made a simple pasta dish for dinner, and right after, he hopped in the shower. I stayed in the living room and put Maize on the floor to do some tummy time.

"You're getting so strong, baby girl," I praise as she holds her neck up and bounces up and down. She fusses at first, wanting to roll over or be picked up, but I don't give in just yet.

Grabbing the small book that's next to a pile of toys, I start reading to her in hopes it distracts her, and she doesn't give up on her tummy just yet. I'm finishing up the last page just as John walks in wearing a pair of low hanging gray sweatpants, the very ones that always make me do a double take, except this time he's not wearing a shirt. I notice it's still in his hand but silently pray it combusts into a million tiny pieces, so he doesn't put it on.

"She's getting good at that," he says as he watches us play on the floor.

Looking up from my heavy eyelashes, I focus on the deep chiseled muscles across his stomach and the little droplets of water that are dripping down. Not to mention the tattoo on his side.

There's no way he's not messing with my head right now. Which if he is, isn't fair because I'm fully clothed, and my hair is up in a messy knot, and I barely have any makeup on. In fact, I look quite rough, but considering I'm getting up with Maize at night and then taking care of her all day until he gets home from work, I have every right to look like I've been run over by a truck.

"Uh, yeah. I think she'll be rolling over within a couple of months, and then you'll have to watch out because next comes the crawling, then the walking."

"I'm not sure I'm ready for that," he admits. "I'll have to baby proof the entire house it seems."

"Yeah but you can use baby gates to keep her out of certain rooms and locks on cabinets. Though that never stopped my twin baby sisters from getting into everything in sight."

He sits on the floor and crosses his legs before picking Maize up and kissing her cheek. "You have twin sisters?"

I sit up, knowing I told him this during my interview, but I also know he was pretty sleep deprived then. "Yep. My mom got pregnant with them when I was ten, and they were like my real-life dolls. As I got older, I started helping out a lot more and basically helped raise them. I have two other younger sisters, and we're a few years apart, so our house was pretty crazy most of the time."

"Wow, yeah sounds like it. Did you like having that many siblings?" he asks, placing Maize in his lap and successfully blocking my view of his tattoo and abs.

"Yeah, I always loved having a big family. It felt special, ya know? I loved taking care of them, and I guess I was just born with a maternal instinct. As soon as my parents needed something, I was there ready to pitch in. I learned to change diapers at a young age and helped potty train my sisters along with lots of other stuff."

"You want to have a big family of your own too?"

I smile wide. "I do. I think it'd be awesome."

He nods.

"However, I'm not sure it'll ever be in the cards for me. Guys don't tend to see me that way."

John arches a brow as if I've said the craziest thing ever. "I doubt that."

I snort. "I don't. The guy I've crushed on for four years took me by surprise before I came to Texas by not only forgetting to tell me he was seeing someone, but that she's pregnant and they're getting married!"

John's eyes widen, and I'm sure I sound like a jealous lunatic, but I've had time to think it over since leaving Georgia.

"I'm happy for him, though. It's made me realize I shouldn't wait to tell someone how I feel about them." The air between us grows thick, and when he sucks in his lower lip, I wonder what he's thinking. "Which leads me to this."

He blinks, his body straightening as I continue. "I didn't go out with Jackson when I was all dressed up. Kiera invited me to go out with her, and we spent the night sharing a margarita and talking about her boyfriend, Trent."

"What?" His expression softens, but I can't tell if it's due to relief or confusion of bringing it up.

"Jackson was over this afternoon and told me you thought we went out, but I just wanted you to know that I have no interest in going on a date with him. Never did."

"I'm gonna kill him," he mutters, which makes me chuckle. He inhales a deep breath before bringing his gaze back to mine. "What else did he say?"

"Basically, that you're stubborn and how Maize's been your only priority since she's arrived."

He holds his stare on me, and I know he's wondering if there's more.

"He didn't tell me much else, but I did ask him about Maize's mother. He said it wasn't his story to share, which is why I'm bringing it up now."

John looks down at Maize with pain in his eyes, and I feel sad that her mother isn't in her life for whatever reason.

"He also told me you haven't dated anyone since then."

John rolls his eyes and grunts. "So, what? You guys hung out while I was at work and discussed my life without me?" He sounds pissed, which I guess I should've considered, but it was the only way to get him to open up to me.

"No, actually, he normally stops in to say hi and play with Maize for a few minutes."

"He does?" His brows raise in shock.

"Yeah. It's cute actually. He loves her a lot."

"Yeah, well he's a real pain in the ass a lot, so..." he mumbles.

"While I don't deny that's true, I know he only wants what's best for you, and he can see that you're going through some shit that you refuse to talk about."

"Mila," he says in a low, warning tone that sends shivers down my spine. "I don't know what he's all told you, but you should consider ninety-nine percent of it is bullshit."

"Really?" I raise my brows right back at him. "So you don't consider me off-limits and you're not denying you're attracted to me?"

His jaw clenches with anger as he purses his lips into a firm line. Kneeling, he sets Maize in the Jumperoo with her pacifier and stands.

"Stay with her. I'll be right back," he orders as he starts walking away.

Quickly, I get to my feet and chase after him. "John, wait." I grab his arm and pull myself in front of his body. "Why are you running away? I've been living in your house for over a month, and I still feel like you're a mystery to me. Why can't you talk to me and open up about what you're really feeling?"

"Mila, move."

"No. Not until you talk to me."

"I don't have anything to say, so please get out of my way so I can go murder my brother."

He tries walking around me, but I press my palms against his chest and stop him. "Tell me," I say softly. "Tell me what happened to her mother."

The pain flashes across his face, and I feel awful bringing it up because I can see how much he's holding back his emotions.

His eyes meet mine as we stand chest to chest.

"Did something happen to her?"

"Yes." He brushes a hand through his hair, the longer strands sticking to his fingers as he stares up at the ceiling. "I didn't know Maize existed until she was nine weeks old, and she was dropped off on the porch of the B&B."

"Oh my God," I whisper in shock, taking a step back. "Someone just dropped her off and left?"

"Yeah, I guess. It was her lawyer fulfilling Bailey's last wishes."

Bailey.

The moment her name crosses his lips, he cringes as if it was painful to say aloud.

"She passed away," I say, already knowing the answer.

"Yeah. She did. I hadn't even known she was sick. Or pregnant."

"Wow. I'm so sorry. I don't know what to say, John. But you can talk to me about her anytime you want."

His eyes lower to the floor, and he doesn't speak for several seconds before wrapping a hand around the nape of his neck and releases a slow breath.

"You're off-limits because you work for me, Mila." He finally speaks, but his words are like a punch to the gut, and I immediately wish I hadn't asked him in the first place. "It'd be inappropriate to cross those boundaries, which is why I push you away most of the time. You're gorgeous, and I'd have to be blind not to notice. But it's more than that, too," he states but doesn't explain.

I don't know how to respond, so all I do is nod as if I understand his reasoning, which doesn't feel any different than the constant friend zone I've lived in for the past four years.

"You're an easy person to get along with, and that's not something I've ever had before. I've never really wanted to get to know a girl on a deeper level, but watching you with Maize every day, the way you've opened your life to be with her, and the way you've helped me learn about her needs, has affected me in ways I didn't even realize until it was impossible not to have you on my mind. You walkin' around in those tiny shorts with your hair up in those messy buns, exposing that soft part of your neck, and the way you dance around my kitchen as you make breakfast has made it impossible not to have you on my mind, Mila."

I swallow hard at his unexpected confession, and it stuns me silent. I want to reach out and touch him, but I'm frozen in place.

"But that doesn't change the fact that you're Maize's nanny and you're living in my house. I don't know what your future plans are, but I doubt it's to live in small-town Texas on a ranch."

I tilt my head and give him a look as I cross my arms over my chest. "And how would you know what I want?"

"You're too young to know," he states, and it feels like a direct punch to the throat. "You just graduated college and have so much ahead of you still."

"So what...you just decided for both of us what I want? That hardly seems fair."

"Well, life isn't fair. Just ask Maize who doesn't get to grow up with her mother because she died of a brain tumor."

His words are harsh and hit me so hard, I drop my arms and gasp. "A brain tumor? I'm...sorry."

I can't even imagine, and sadness washes over me as I think about little Maize not ever getting the chance to have her mother in her life. I couldn't live without my mother, and I find myself tearing up at the thought of losing her.

Things start to make sense now, and I can't stop the words from spewing out of my mouth. "You feel you don't deserve to be with anyone," I finally say after a minute of awkward silence. John's hard expression softens just enough to know I'm onto something. "She's not here, and Maize doesn't have a mother, so you feel you don't get to be happy, right? Whether or not it's because I work for you or because I've invaded your life, you don't want to cross a line that could lead to something you think you aren't allowed to have now. Well, I can't speak for anyone else, but you deserve everything, John Bishop." I take a step closer, placing my hand on his cheek and feeling the warmth on my palm. He doesn't flinch like I anticipate so I bring his face to mine and press my lips ever so lightly against his. "You deserve to be happy, and one day you'll realize that, but when you do, you just might be too late to get the happiness you were after."

"Mila," he whispers, placing his forehead against mine as he sucks in a breath. Even though the kiss was brief, his lips were so warm and inviting, and it takes willpower I didn't know existed not to maul his mouth completely.

"I'll stay and watch Maize," I say when he doesn't finish his thoughts.

Stepping around him, I somehow manage to walk away with my tears in tact and go toward Maize who's happily jumping away and playing. A few moments later, I hear the front door open and shut with a slam.

I get Maize ready for bed and rock her to sleep. Thinking back to only a couple of hours ago, I'm quite certain things will forever be changed between John and me. The uncertainty of whether I should've pushed him or not fills my head, but I can't keep doing this dance with him every day. Although parts of him are still a mystery to me, I can't help the way I feel when he's around, invading my thoughts and my life.

Once Maize's asleep in her crib, I go to my room and turn on the baby monitor. I'm not sure how late John plans to stay out, so I want to be able to hear her just in case.

I must've fallen asleep because the last thing I remember is my head hitting the pillow. Maize's crying, and when I look at the clock, I see it's close to midnight already.

"Oh, shit," I mutter, jumping out of bed. Once I get to John's room, I see he's passed out in bed and hasn't even flinched to Maize's cries.

"It's okay, sweetie. Daddy's tired, so why don't we get a bottle and rock back to sleep in my room." I speak as quietly as I can while picking her up.

Once her bottle is made, I place her on my bed and change her. I make silly noises to distract her, and once she's clean again, I place her on my chest to rock her. My phone lights up on the nightstand, and when I reach for it, I see it's Kiera who texted me.

KIERA
> Hope I'm not waking y'all but just got the call that Emily's in labor! Not sure on the details but Evan said he'll text when there's an update.

MILA
> Oh yay, that's exciting! John's sleeping, but I'll let him know when he wakes up.

KIERA
> Aren't you off duty tonight?

MILA
> Technically, yes. Realistically? No.

KIERA
> LOL! Fill me in tomorrow. I'm going to bed so I can get to the hospital tomorrow after my morning chores.

I send her one last text before setting my phone down and rocking Maize back to sleep. It doesn't take long, and once she's out cold, I walk back to John's room and place her in the co-sleeper next to him. Right after I tuck her in and make sure she's secure, I turn to walk out, but John reaches his hand out at me and scares the shit out of me.

"Jesus," I breathe out, placing a hand to my chest. "Why do you always do that?"

He flashes a lazy smile. "Sorry," he whispers. "Just wanted to say thank you. And I'm sorry for the way I left."

The corners of my lips tilt up just the slightest, so he knows I heard him. "We can talk about it later." I step to walk out but then remember the news. "Oh! Emily's in labor, so you'll probably hear from Evan in the morning."

His eyes widen a bit. "Oh, that's awesome. I bet Evan's losing his mind right now," he says with a low chuckle.

"Good thing he has a couple of brothers he can go to for fatherly advice then." I wink, hoping he finds it comforting.

CHAPTER FOURTEEN

John

Considering I'm back on a sleeping schedule these days, I get up early to help at the B&B while I wait to hear from Evan, so I can head to the hospital. I don't typically work full days on the weekends, but I like to help out when I can, especially if we're short staffed or are fully booked. It's a good way to keep my mind busy.

Before walking out the door, I find Mila, trying to forget that she kissed me just hours ago, but it's still fresh in my mind, driving me insane. They're both in the kitchen already, and I give Maize a kiss on my way out. Mila's grabbing breakfast as she makes a bottle. I love getting to see Maize before I leave for work instead of having to rush her off to a sitter. Mama normally watches her on Saturdays, but since she's already on her way to the hospital to be with Evan and Emily, Mila stepped in to save my ass once again.

As I head toward the B&B, I see Jackson parking his truck on the side of the building. I owe him a boot in the ass for running his mouth to Mila. He hops out in an extra good mood this morning, and walks toward me.

"You're up bright and early," he says in an annoyingly cheerful way. I'm actually surprised he's not hungover from his infamous Whiskey Friday parties.

I point a finger at him, scowling. "I owe you a punch in the face, but considering Mama's gonna want some pictures with the family and new baby, I'll spare you a black eye. This time."

"Oh, c'mon. I did you a favor. You should be thanking me." He presses a hand to his chest as his words come out serious but the expression on his face is taunting.

"You're more delusional than I thought if you think I'd thank you after talking to Mila about me."

"I only said the truth, so be pissed all you want, but I opened her eyes and gave her insight to the things you'd never say."

"Well, that wasn't for you to tell her, now was it?"

"Are you saying things didn't go well?" He arches a brow, crossing his arms. He's challenging me, which works my nerves.

"I'm saying fuck off and stop talking to Mila."

"No can do, bro. She secretly wants me."

Without thinking, I grab his collar and push him to the ground. Jackson laughs as he lands on his ass.

"Dude, you're so easy. You need to get the wrench out of your ass."

I grunt, holding my hand out, so I can help lift him back to his feet. "Go do your job so we can go visit Evan and Em when it's time."

"I'm going to feed the horses really quick, then head up there and wait around." Jackson tucks his hands in his pocket and gives me a shit-eating grin.

"Evan said to wait until the baby was born. Didn't you get his message?"

All he does is laugh. "And do I follow the rules or what Evan directs ever?"

"Right, forgot about that one." I walk up the back steps of the porch. "I'm gonna go inside, make coffee, check on breakfast, then I'll come help you with the horses."

"Perfect," he tells me, before turning and walking to the stables.

Considering it's dark out, I know most of our guests are still sleeping soundly. Being here each day at a decent time allows me the ability to get to know them and their habits, which changes on a daily basis.

I walk in, and the warm glow of the lamps light the way. Walking through the common area, I begin opening the curtains and turning on some lights. I walk over to the coffeemaker, add in water and the grounds, and start a pot. As I walk through the B&B double-checking everything, the smell of fresh coffee fills the room. I go into the kitchen and see the cooks have already started making gravy and rolling out homemade biscuits.

"Good morning," I tell them with a smile, and they all begin chatting me up.

I lean against the counter with a smile as the older women ask me about Maize. I love talking about her as much as they do. After I realize I've been there for way too long, I take another walk around the B&B and make sure things are exactly how they should be before helping Jackson. Once I feel confident they are, I head outside toward the stalls. My phone vibrates in my pocket, and I pull it out to see it's a message from Evan.

EVAN

Hourly update. Still no baby. Emily is ready to tear off my nuts, though.

JOHN

Ha. Thanks for the update. Be careful. Saying a prayer your balls survive this.

EVAN

Thanks. I guess. I'll update you soon.

I lock my phone and tuck it in my pocket. When I walk into the barn, Jackson is busy on his phone, and I know he's texting Evan.

"Glad I'm not having a baby," he says. "No offense, of course, but I'm good. I like my nuts too much."

"So does everyone else," I quip. "But don't jinx yourself, that's all I'm saying." I walk into the feed room and look around. Jackson throws me an extra pair of leather gloves that are on the shelf and begins to put his on so carrying all the buckets doesn't hurt as bad. He's already got the buckets lined up and begins scooping grain into them. He's lucky he gets to be out here with the horses. While I love the business aspect of the B&B and meeting all the people who stay, I also enjoy being out here too. Just the smell of the fresh hay, grain, leather, and the horses brings back so many good memories of my childhood. It's a distinct smell that's unforgettable.

For a slight moment, I think about Bailey and being in here with her. Randomly, she sneaks into my mind, and sometimes it still hurts, considering how things ended between us. Our relationship progressed too quickly in the few weeks we were together, and then she stopped talking to me as if I didn't exist. The only person who really understands this pain of losing someone is Evan, considering the girl he had crushed on before he met Emily tragically passed away.

It's not like I can just go to Bailey and have a chat about our differences or issues. It's a pain that runs deep, and some of the questions I have will never be answered. Sometimes it's a hard reality to deal with. There will be a day when our daughter understands and begins to ask questions about her mother. Unfortunately, there's so much I don't know, and I'll never be able to explain it all. Bailey died with her secrets.

Jackson clears his throat, interrupting my thoughts, as he picks up as many buckets as he can carry, four in each hand. "Did you hear me?"

"Sorry, no." I follow his lead and grab the rest. Jackson walks to the opening of the barn and whistles loudly. Some of the horses sleep in the stables while others choose to roam around the open pasture. We don't typically keep them in the stables overnight and like to give them as much freedom as possible. He's trained them so well that when he lets out a whistle, they mosey up to their designated stall. It's actually impressive. Jackson should train professionally like Kiera but would never do it since he wouldn't want to compete with her business. Actually, he's better than Kiera but chooses to send new horses we purchase to her because his undeniable love runs so damn deep.

Jackson turns and looks at me and breaks me from my thoughts. "Time to wake up, little brother. We got shit to do."

"Little brother? You're two minutes older than me."

"In a woman's world, those two minutes matter." He chuckles.

All I can do is shake my head as he stops at each of the stalls in the main barn and pours grain into the feeders. He stacks the buckets, and I keep walking to the barn on the other side of the corral since we have a few barns where the extra horse stalls are.

"After we're done here, I'm gonna call everyone who has lessons today and cancel," he says from behind me.

"Good idea," I tell him, walking across the way. The horses are waiting for feed, so I go one by one and pour the grain in and begin stacking all the buckets and carry them back.

"Don't you have a horse being delivered today?" I ask, remembering a young quarter horse Jackson bought a few weeks ago.

"Shit, what's today?"

"March 28th," I remind him.

"Shit, shit. Yes. That was today. Totally slipped my mind." He pulls the gloves from his hands, and I do the same. I throw them at him, and he takes them into the tack room and returns them back to the shelf.

"I might call Kiera and ask her if she can pick him up instead since she'll be doing the training," he mutters, mostly to himself. "She owes me one anyway."

"You two frustrate the shit out of me," I say, standing in the doorway as he secures the top on the feed barrel.

Jackson keeps his head down. "Mind your own damn business."

"Look who's talking," I shoot back. "Hi Pot, meet Kettle."

He grunts, not wanting to admit I'm right about this.

"It's so painfully obvious why you continue sending horses her way when you could do it yourself."

"I can't do it all myself," he retorts.

"Maybe, maybe not, but you know if you didn't you'd need another excuse to see her," I say.

"She has a boyfriend, jackass," he tells me, his mood instantly souring.

"And when has that ever stopped you?" I snort. "Plus, I see the way she looks at you, though—well I'm pretty sure we all do—and have since we were teens. So boyfriend or not, that's gotta mean something, right?"

He finishes what he's doing and removes the cowboy hat from his head, runs his fingers through his hair, then glares at me. "It wouldn't matter anyway. It's too late."

"It's not too late until she's no longer here, okay? Then it's too late. I'm just saying, don't wait until you regret it. It fucking sucks." I don't wait for his reply and walk back toward the B&B.

"Didn't realize you were so prophetic these days," Jackson yells across the way, and I keep walking toward the B&B, shaking my head.

"You're welcome!" I mock over my shoulder as I flip him off for his last comment. I hear his devilish laugh echo across the way.

I take the steps up the back porch and call Nicole, letting her know she'll most likely be in charge at some point today, which I know she doesn't mind. The entire ranch has had a game plan set for the moment when Emily went into labor. We agreed to go to the hospital *after* the baby was born, instead of crowding the halls and waiting room. Evan actually demanded it, and considering he's a doctor and it's his baby, we agreed to do what he wanted.

Keeping my mind busy, I start with my everyday tasks and pull out the scheduling book to see who's reserved the rooms for next week and compare it to the current checkout dates. I like to have everyone lined up and scheduled, so there's no guessing where they'll stay when they arrive. I log in to the laptop that's in the small office in the corner and begin checking emails and write down more confirmations for the summer. The sun begins to rise, filling the B&B with a yellow hue. I actually love this part of the morning.

Soon, guests begin waking up and grabbing a coffee while breakfast is being served. I walk around, greeting everyone, making sure they're happy and chat about everything and nothing. It's a part of the job, which I used to hate, but the older I've gotten, the more I've enjoyed it. So many people who visit us are from all different walks of life and different areas of the world. It amazes me each time we have someone from out of the country visit. We're a small family-owned operation, and we're making a difference in people's lives by showing them what true Southern living is like without all the cheesy clichés. Many become regulars, which makes me happy, plus it helps the ranch thrive.

After I help clean the dirty plates from breakfast, my phone buzzes. I hurry and wipe my hands, grab it, and unlock it.

EVAN

Still no baby. My nuts have survived, but barely. Keep you updated.

JOHN

Ha-ha, okay! We're heading that way as soon as you say the magic word.

EVAN

Hopefully sooner than later. Crossing my fingers!

I smile and tuck my phone back in my pocket. I'm kind of sad I didn't get to experience this part of Maize's life. I wonder if Bailey had anyone there happy for her, celebrating what she did, and it hurts my heart to think otherwise.

"Hey John," Nicole says, grabbing my attention. "I'm here. Still no baby?"

I shake my head. "Not yet. I'm sure Emily is about ready to kill Evan, though. Actually, I know she is."

Nicole laughs. "Well, she has told me how big the Bishop babies are, so yeah, he deserves it all."

My phone buzzes in my pocket and I hurry and pull it out.

EVAN

THE BABY IS HERE! BUT DON'T SPEED COMING HERE! Em and baby are doing perfect!

I look up at Nicole, my mouth falls open, and she laughs. "Go!"

"I'm gonna have another niece!" I yell out, running toward the back door. I don't stop running until I'm in the house, and when I walk in, Mila is smiling big as she packs up Maize.

"We gotta get going!" she says, all excited.

"Let's do it!" I yell out, so excited for Evan. Maize's kicking her legs in her car seat. "You're going to have a cousin that you'll be able to get in lots of trouble with," I say, sweetly.

"Cousins are trouble," Mila tells me. "Kat was a horrible influence, but I love her."

"No one knows about bad influences until they have Jackson as a brother. I've got tattoos to prove it."

She smiles. "Oh, I was wondering about that."

I narrow my eyes at her as I grab the car seat and we head toward the truck. "That one was an impulse decision when we were eighteen. We really are identical, down to the tats."

Opening the door to the back seat, Mila takes the car seat from me and locks it into the base. Once it's secure, we get in to drive the hour to the hospital, though I'm going to take it slower to give Evan and Emily more time to be alone.

"This is one of my favorite parts," Mila says, smiling. I think she may be more excited about the baby than I am.

"The birth?" I ask.

"Yes. They're so small and vulnerable, and their little cries warm my heart. It's just a beautiful thing, giving life to a tiny human." She smiles, and I can't help but notice how beautiful she looks when she's genuinely happy. My heart jumps forward, and I force my eyes to stay on the road and keep my attention there.

"You're something else," I say.

"In a good way, I hope." She bites her bottom lip.

I glance over at her. "Of course. In the best way."

Mila turns her head and looks out the window at the vast land that goes on for miles. I glance over at her and see her reflection in the window and true happiness shines through. I want to bring up last night and apologize again for my temper and how I reacted, but instead, I bring the conversation back to Evan and Emily, and she asks more questions about them.

"So how'd they meet again? Like the real story," she says.

I let out a chuckle. "The short story? They met at Alex and River's wedding. Hooked up. She gave him a fake name. And then, she stole his clothes and left him butt ass naked at the B&B."

Mila bursts out into a hearty laugh. "No way."

"Yep. Then he went to work on Monday, and she was there."

"Emily is a savage," she says.

"It would take a savage to tame Evan. Feisty as hell, kinda like you." The last part slips out, but they're both sassy. Must be a Southern thing.

She playfully rolls her eyes. "I am *not* feisty."

I pop an eyebrow and look over at her.

"Okay, maybe a little bit."

Soon we're pulling into the hospital parking lot, and it's almost like a family reunion as we get out of the car. I took my time driving over, and it's been over an hour and a half since Evan texted me. Jackson and Alex rode together, and I see them get out of Jackson's truck. When we make eye contact, they grin real big. Mila waves at them, and they wave back.

"Mama and Dad are already in there," Alex says. "You know Mama wouldn't wait. River joined her with Riley since she's off today and I had shit to finish at the ranch."

"Didn't expect her to," I say. I turn and look at Jackson. "I thought you were coming early."

"Mama said if I did, she'd throat punch me."

Laughter breaks out.

"She did not say that," Mila says as I take the car seat from her once she's unlocked it from the contraption that still confuses the hell out of me.

"I swear it and the tone of her voice when she said it was deadly. Basically went back to the stalls and oiled saddles until Alex said he was ready. I was legitimately scared," he tells her. We walk into the hospital and go to the elevator and take it to the labor and delivery floor. River meets Alex as soon as the elevator doors open, and they basically maul each other. She's wearing a huge smile and can't stop kissing him.

"Get a room," Jackson says, loudly.

"Shut up," River tells him. "This way," she says, walking past us. "Emily did really well. No complications other than delivering a ten-pound Bishop baby. You guys are deadly with your big ass babies." River snorts.

"That's not the only thing that's big," Jackson adds, and Alex elbows him in the stomach.

We make it to the room, and we all stop and look at each other, the moment becoming more serious, though we're smiling. River turns the handle and opens the door, looking at each of us as we walk in. The first thing I see is Evan holding his baby girl in his arms, and I fully understand the happiness that's written all over his face. Mama is standing by Emily, holding her hand, smiling so damn big. I see Emily's family as well, and Jackson, Alex, and I walk toward Evan to get a look at the sleeping baby and congratulate him. She looks so peaceful, and even though she's only a few hours old, I can already see so much of Emily and Evan in her features. Dad has Riley on his lap who's talking about babies. Mama spots Maize and comes over and takes her from the car seat. Mila and I go to Emily and chat with her, though I know she's dead tired.

"How're things goin', Mama?" Mila asks.

She gives us a sweet smile. "Really good. But I feel like a punching bag. No amount of reading books or being a doctor prepares a person for this.

Elizabeth's healthy as can be, all the testing went great, and she already ate like a champ." Emily yawns.

"Oh, I love her name! What made you pick that?" Mila asks.

"Elizabeth is after the first female doctor, Elizabeth Blackwell, and her middle name is after Mama Rose," she explains, smiling contently.

"Oh, of course, you two would. Doctor stuff." Mila chuckles.

Emily smiles sweetly but yawns again.

Evan walks over and offers us the baby to hold. Mila's eyes light up immediately as she opens her arms. "She's so precious," she murmurs. "Looks so much like you Bishops already."

"That's right," Emily chimes in. "Spend nine months carrying the baby, making sure to eat right and exercise, go through hours of labor, and for what, you ask?" she mocks, looking up at Evan with a devilish smile. "Baby comes out looking just like her dad."

All of us laugh at her teasing when Mama comes over. "Try having five babies coming out looking like their dad."

We laugh again, Mama sounding so serious too.

"What can I say? Bishops have strong genes," Dad says, pulling Riley up as he stands and walks toward the group.

"You wanna hold her?" Mila nudges my arm, and when I look down at her holding Elizabeth, I can't help the thoughts spinning in my mind. She's such a natural with babies and seeing her with Maize or any other baby continues to mess with my head.

"Sure, I'd love to."

Mila hands her over, and I carefully hold Elizabeth in my arms. I can't believe how tiny she feels compared to Maize and those feelings of missing her early days come back full force.

Mama comes over and places Maize close by. "Here's your new cousin," she tells them. "You two are going to give us all a run for our money, aren't you?" she asks, and we all chuckle at how close in age they're going to be growing up.

"Looks like you're gonna be in charge of them, Riley," Emily teases him when Dad sets him down, and he hides behind Mama's legs.

Elizabeth starts to fuss, and Emily takes her back to feed her again.

"We should give you some alone time. You're exhausted," I say, grabbing Maize from Mama.

"Good luck," Emily says. "You might need a forklift to make them all leave."

"Oh crap," I mutter, remembering I was supposed to FaceTime Courtney so she could meet the baby too. I hurry and dial her number, and as soon as she sees my face, she squeals.

"It's about time! I was beginning to think you forgot about me!" she scolds. I turn the volume down on my phone because Courtney can be...energetic.

"I'd never forget about you, sis," I reassure her with a laugh.

"Where's Emily?" she asks. I hand the phone to her once Elizabeth is settled on a pillow in her lap.

Courtney immediately starts talking and goes on and on about how she needs to use this time to rest and not be afraid to kick people out of the room. Emily chuckles and shakes her head, knowing she'd never win that battle with a family like ours.

"Can I see her?" I hear the excitement in Courtney's tone. Emily turns the phone around, and Courtney lets out a big aww when she sees Elizabeth.

I stand to the side with my arms crossed and can't stop smiling. Scanning the room, taking in everyone's happiness, I see Mila, and she's looking at me. I smile a little bigger, and she blinks slowly. At the moment, it feels as if we're having a silent conversation. She tucks her lips into her mouth, and before I completely lose myself in her gaze, Emily is handing the phone back to me. About fifteen minutes pass, and when the nurses walk in to do a regular checkup, Evan nonchalantly kicks us all out. The hoard of us go to the waiting room, and he comes out to chat with us with joy written all over his face.

"Sorry, y'all, Mom needs some rest; she's had a long day already," he explains. He comes over and chats with us. Courtney's still on the phone, being passed around to everyone. By the time I finish chatting with Evan, I search for Mila, who is chatting with Courtney. Though Court isn't here, somehow, she made her way around the room as if she were. I walk up to Mila. Our arms brush together, and I feel her tense.

"What are you talking about?" I put myself into view, and Courtney tilts her head at me.

"Just meeting your work wife." As soon as the words leave Courtney's mouth, Mila blushes. I open my mouth to say something, but Courtney interrupts me. "I was just kidding. Geez, you two. So uptight. How's my little Maize doing these days?"

I tell Courtney how happy and good Maize is and how she's finally on a real schedule thanks to Mila's help. Chatting with Courtney about baby things reminds me of the moment I told her about Maize. Instead of calling her, or texting her, I FaceTimed her. Considering I don't do it often, she answered my call immediately and assumed something was wrong. I knew, without a doubt, Courtney would be the most supportive out of everyone. Of course, she was shocked like everyone else and even asked if I was sure it wasn't Jackson's—just like the rest of them did—but once I explained the letter and Bailey to her, there wasn't another snide comment about it. She's been helpful and even sent packages of baby girl clothes that hers had outgrown. That's one thing I can say about my sister—she's generous and caring, regardless of the distance between us.

"Oh, please let me chat with Evan one last time before I hang up. It was nice meeting you, Mila. I have a good feeling about you." Courtney winks. "Get my number from John, and if you ever get bored, feel free to call or text me. We can have FaceTime playdates, and I can give you all the dirt on John. The *real* dirt."

Mila laughs and agrees before I cut in and walk across the room with the phone.

Courtney leans in and whispers. "So are you two dating or something?"

"Seriously?" I give her a look that tells her how annoyed I am with that assumption. "You offer her gossip and then ask if we're together?" I narrow my eyes at her, though I can't stay mad at my sister for long. "She's just Maize's nanny."

"Really?" She looks at me with disbelief.

"*Really.* There's nothing going on." I keep a straight face because it's the truth, as long as one kiss doesn't count.

"Not yet at least," Courtney adds with a laugh.

I shake my head. "Sometimes, you're just as bad as Mama."

She lets out a hearty laugh, and I happily hand the phone to Evan.

As tempting as it is, I cannot go there with my nanny, regardless of what my heart is saying.

CHAPTER FIFTEEN

Mila

The Bishop family has been in a constant state of happiness since baby Elizabeth was born. Though it's been a few weeks, the excitement is still there. We celebrated Easter together, and the Bishop family got together to dye eggs to bring to the church hunt. Evan and Emily dressed Elizabeth in a poofy little dress and giant flower headband that matched Maize's, and the two of them were the life of the party. At the Easter egg hunt last weekend, I promised Gigi I'd visit after church this week, which passed in a blink. Each day, time feels like it's going by so slow, but when I think about the big picture and how I've been here for almost two months, I realize it's actually not. Another reminder that interviews will start for the next school year soon.

Before I leave, I let John know what my plans are. On the weekends, I'm free to do whatever I'd like, but as a courtesy, I let him know I'm leaving for a few hours—just in case.

I grab my phone, tell Maiz, and John bye, and hop in the car. Gigi's let me keep her car, so I have transportation while I'm here since she has a second car to use. On the way over, I roll down the windows and take in the warmth. There's still a briskness to it, but otherwise, spring is in full force. Along the highway, random flowers have begun to bloom, and the grass has woken up.

It doesn't take long for me to make it to her house, and just seeing it come into view puts a smile on my face. I park the car, make my way up the steps, and walk in. Gigi is sitting in her chair with her feet kicked up, napping. I almost feel bad for waking her because she looks so peaceful.

"Gigi," I whisper.

Her eyes flutter open, and she smiles. "Mila, what time is it?"

I glance down at my phone. "Almost two."

"Oh Lord. I invited some ladies over to play cards at five." Gigi pops up out of her chair and goes straight to the kitchen to pull down ingredients for her famous oatmeal cookies.

"I can help," I tell her, measuring out the oatmeal like I used to do when I was a kid. She looks over at me, gives me a wink, then grabs the farm eggs off the counter.

"How're things going so far? Summer's 'bout to be here, and I know that means you'll be going back to Georgia for interviews."

I swallow hard, knowing this question would eventually come up. When I talked to my mom earlier this week while Maize was taking a nap, I somehow avoided it completely. But I know I can't easily change the subject with Gigi. "It's going great. Haven't gotten any news yet. I just plan to take it one day at a time and cross that bridge when I get a call."

Gigi gives me a sweet smile. "Maybe you should apply for some positions here?"

I laugh. "Gigi! You're determined to keep me in Texas, aren't you? You're not even trying to be sly about it anymore!"

"If it were up to me, I'd have the whole family move here," she admits, cracking the eggs into a bowl, then adding butter, brown sugar, white sugar, and a tablespoon of vanilla.

"I know you would. I do love it here, though. We'll see how things work out," I say, placing the butter in the fridge.

"Oh, honey. Forgot to tell you. Your mother sent a huge box, and it came in the mail yesterday. It's in the living room." She continues mixing the dough.

I can't help but smile as I go in search of the box. When I see how large it is, I let out a happy squeal. Running to the kitchen, I grab a pair of scissors and go back to the box and cut the tape because it looks like Mom used a whole roll sealing it. I drop to my knees on the floor and open it as quickly as I can. Inside is my favorite Green Bay Packer poster of Rodgers and Matthews, my Aaron Rodgers jersey, some of my favorite Packer T-shirts with sayings like *Go Pack Go* and *Cheesehead Pride*, a green and gold Packer blanket, my fluffy robe and slippers, and tons of candy I love. She even sent some of my favorite clothes like I asked, which will save me from doing laundry every few days. There are photos of the family in nice frames, and a picture of Graham holding a sign that says he misses me. Somehow, Mom always knows how to play with my heartstrings.

"What'd she send?" Gigi walks into the living room, and I hand her the silver framed photo of the group of us.

"Aww, that was sweet."

"I know, right? I think they might actually miss me." I let out a laugh, but it's the first time I've let my homesickness sneak in since leaving. Staying in Texas this long was never a part of the plan, and I never could've predicted I'd be the nanny to a sweet, precious little girl. It's almost hard for me to imagine leaving, though I know I will have to eventually. Soon, many school districts will begin their interview process for the fall, which adds additional stress wondering if I'll even get a call. Right now, life is easy, and I'm going to enjoy that as long as I can.

"I told Rose you wouldn't be staying past the middle of July," she adds, before returning to the kitchen. I stand and follow her.

"Why's that?" I ask. There's no malice in my tone; I'm just curious.

"Honey, I know you're gonna get a call for one of those schools you applied to. It's best the Bishops know ahead of time, so they can replace you once you leave. As much as I want you to stay, we all knew it wasn't a permanent situation." Gigi pulls another empty pan from the cabinet and rolls parchment paper on top. Her words hit me like a ton of bricks. That's only three months from now. This whole time, have I been living in a fantasy world and just playing house with John and Maize? The thought of it weighs heavy on my heart, but I force a smile.

"You never know, Gigi. Haven't gotten a call yet. Might not get one at all this school year. Competition is fierce in small towns," I tell her, almost hopeful about it.

She lets out a laugh. "With your grades and experience student teaching, they'd be stupid to let a good thing like you slip through their fingers."

I let out a sigh, and she wipes her hands on a dish towel. "I know that look."

She places the second tray of cookies in the oven and sits across from me at the bar. Gigi searches my face, and I'm sure she already knows what my issue is.

"You love that little girl too much, and now you're attached." She hit the nail on the head.

"Yes, ma'am. It's gonna be so hard leaving her. She needs me, Gigi. We have a special bond—the two of us—and she's grown up so much in the short time I've been here."

Placing her hand on top of mine, she gives me a little squeeze. "Honey, now listen to me. Sometimes in life, we're faced with forks in the road, decisions that will change the outcome of our entire future. It seems to me that you're comin' up on one of those. But no matter what, you gotta listen to what your heart says. Just promise me that. If going back to Georgia to follow your dreams is what you want, then do it. Papaw and I will be here till our end days, and you can come to visit at any time. Besides, I'm sure Rose will happily send you photos of that pretty little grandbaby. No matter what you do, it won't be the end of the world. You're young. You still have time to figure out the big stuff." She holds my gaze for a moment before checking her watch.

"Thank you," I tell her. "You always know what to say to make me feel better."

"It's 'cause grandmas always know best. You know, at one point or another in everyone's life, there can be real tough decisions to make. Just think, if I would've moved to California and pursued my dreams of being an actress, I woulda never met your Papaw, your mother wouldn't have been born, and you wouldn't be sitting right here right now talking to me about it."

I smile. "Dang, Gigi. That's deep. That one moment changed the outcome of everything."

My mind wanders, and I feel my phone vibrate in my pocket, but I ignore it and try to spend as much time as I can with Gigi before her friends arrive to play cards. After she's baked several trays of cookies, and the house smells like sugar and oatmeal, I realize how long we've sat around and talked about ranching, Texas history, and the bachelor auction this fall that I should come back for.

"A what?" I ask again to make sure I understood her correctly. We never have the fun stuff where I live.

Gigi is tickled to death. "You mean to tell me Rose hasn't invited you yet? Each year, she always holds a big fundraiser for the county food bank, rounds up all the boys, ranch hands, and any other bachelors she can rope in, and forces them to go on dates with all the grandmas. If we're willing to pay."

"No way. Y'all are crazy down here." I snatch a cookie off the tray, and it's so delicious, it basically melts in my mouth.

"Apparently, the building where it's held is going through renovations at the moment, so she's moved it to the middle of October. If you're free, you should come, but you should start saving now. Some of those young ladies are savages when it comes to those Bishop boys," Gigi explains.

"But aren't half of them taken?" I think about Alex and Evan, their relationships, and how they both have babies.

"Rose is relentless. She makes them participate regardless and tells their women they better bid big. Gigi snickers. I laugh, too, because I can imagine River and Emily fighting women off their men. Mama Rose is something else, and I understand why she and Gigi are such good friends.

Once I hear the car doors slam outside, I know her friends have arrived, so I give Gigi a big hug goodbye.

"Don't be a stranger, you hear?" she tells me and pats me on the shoulder.

"I won't. Promise."

Being the way she is, she hands me a ziplock bag full of cookies. I've learned to never say no to Gigi and willingly take them. On the way to the door, I grab the giant box Mom sent over as Gigi turns the doorknob. If I wouldn't have been carrying the huge box, I'm sure I would've gotten squeezed by every woman I passed with a smile.

I place the heavy box in the back seat of the car then wave to Gigi as she chats with her friends. Smiling, I get into the car, crank it, and head down the rock road. By the time I make it to John's, his truck is missing, and I'm sure Maize's with him wherever he ran off to. I park off to the side, lift the box, and carry it into the house, barely making it to my bed. I search around the house for the two of them, but my suspicions were correct—they're not here. Probably visiting with Emily and Evan or at Mama's.

Taking my time, I unpack everything Mom sent. She even went the extra mile and sent sticky-tack, so I could easily hang my posters of the hottest quarterback in the entire league—Aaron Rodgers. I put the one of him with a full beard next to my bed just to ensure sweet dreams.

In the bottom of the box, I see Mom included a onesie for Maize that reads *Go Pack Go,* and I can't wait to see John's face when she's proudly sporting it. He actually might shit himself. He's probably a Cowboys fan like everyone else around here, but that doesn't mean I can't influence Maize to the better team. Though the thought of him seeing her wear it has me laughing to myself.

Once the posters are hung, the clothes are put away, and my Packers throw blanket is spread across my bed, I let out a happy sigh. It almost feels like home now. Wanting to call my mom to give her a big thank you and tell her how much I love her, I pull my phone from my pocket and try to find the place in my room where I have service. Seeing that she was the one who called while I was at Gigi's, I decided to check my voicemail first. The prompt tells me I have three messages, so I press one to check them.

The first one is from Sarah and Graham, and he's telling me about the new dinosaurs he got. I quickly save it, because I do that with every message my family leaves, and then move to the next one.

The next message is a man's voice, and it slightly catches me off guard.

"Ms. Mila Carmichael, this is Shawn Demry, the Morgan County School District Superintendent. I've reviewed your application for the first-grade position available at Morgan County Primary School and saw you were highly recommended based on the student teaching you completed last semester. It's noted in your file that a position was discussed, and I wanted to know if you're still interested. If so, please call to schedule an interview as soon as possible. I can be reached at 706-720-9891 during normal business hours. Thanks."

My body freezes. I replay the message, and it seems like it was left sometime last week. I don't always get the greatest cell reception in the house, and I'm not the best at remembering to check my voicemail. It seems as if my time here could come to an end much sooner, and the thought crushes me. I go to the next message, and it's Mom asking if I received the box and to tell me that a Mr. Shawn Demry called the house to set up an interview, and she gave him my cell phone number. She sounded so excited, too, which leaves me with mixed feelings.

I sit on the edge of my bed and stare at my phone. I really thought I'd have more time to decide what I wanted to do. Even though it's only been a couple of months since I've been here, it doesn't feel long enough. I know I wouldn't have to go back to Georgia for a few more months, but that leaves me open to growing more attached to Maize and the entire family. It's been my dream to become a teacher, so why am I not more excited to finally hear from a school?

Moments pass as I stay lost in my thoughts, and I'm startled by a deep voice that makes me jump.

"Hey," John says, standing in the doorway holding Maize. "Everything okay?"

Instantly, I smile. "Yes, it's great. I was looking for you two when I got back." I stand and go to Maize. "There's my sweet girl." I kiss her pinchable cheeks before taking her from John's arms.

He places his hands on his hips, and his mouth falls open as he scans my newly decorated room.

"What?" I ask, pretending not to have a clue.

"Aaron Rodgers? The Green Bay Packers? Are you kiddin' me? Don't you know we fly the blue and white in this household?"

"Not in this area of the house, we don't," I tell him, holding Maize, as he walks around the room and looks at all my Packer gear.

"You're as bad as River. Packer nation is her territory. Disgusting." He pretends to shiver. "I think I need a shower after being around this trash. I might sleep in my Cowboy's jersey tonight just to wash away the green and gold stank."

I scoff. "So you're a *shi*-crap talker? Oh man. You better be glad football season isn't for a few more months. I'm a die-hard football fan and will out-game anyone."

"There's always preseason, baby. America's team all the way!" John shouts, leaving the room. I hurry and grab the onesie that Mom sent and change Maize into it. She's such a good sport about it, which makes this even better. We walk into the living room, and I don't say a peep about it, waiting to see how long it'll take him to realize.

I place Maize in her Jumperoo, pull it around, and sit next to him on the couch as he flips through the channels.

He glances over at me, and when our eyes meet, it's as if all the air leaves the room, and I'm no longer able to breathe. I watch as he swallows hard, and I open my mouth to say something, but I'm not sure what I was going to say. There's too much flowing between us, too many unspoken words, and I feel my cheeks heat. His eyes dart over to Maize and widen.

"What in the world do you have on my daughter?" He stands up to go to her, and I quickly jump up and block him.

"Mila Carmichael! You should move outta my way!" He tries to give me his best stern voice.

"Nope," I tell him with a cocky smirk.

"This is your last chance," he warns with a grin.

I shake my head, and that's when his hands slither their way onto my sides, and he begins tickling me. I scream out in laughter and try to push him away, but he's too strong. Losing my balance, I grab on to his shirt, and soon we're both falling onto the couch laughing. Our faces are mere inches apart, and I feel the warmth of his breath brush against my cheek. We both still, staring into one another's eyes, before he pushes himself up. Thankfully, he changes the subject back to the Packers onesie Maize's wearing. She's jumping and kicking her feet, smiling.

"See, she loves it." I stand, brushing the loose hairs from my face.

"She doesn't know she bleeds blue and white yet. Not fair trying to push your cheese head tactics on an infant. You should be ashamed of yourself." He laughs, lightening the mood. "You're from Georgia. Why Green Bay?"

Crossing my arms over my chest, I shoot him a sexy smirk. "Because Aaron Rodgers is hot and obviously good with his hands."

"You're kiddin', right?" He gives me a disapproving look, and his pouty lips have me remembering the way I kissed him the other night. Actually, I haven't stopped thinking about it, but neither of us has brought it up either.

I shake my head and plop back on the couch as he continues to stand.

"You're telling me you're a super fan because of scrawny Rodgers?" John looks at me like I've lost my mind.

"Yep, I'd have his babies. *All* his babies," I say nonchalantly.

This causes him to laugh *at* me. "You want Green Bay babies from a goofy looking dude?"

"A girl can dream." When I close my eyes, I'm not thinking about football or Aaron Rodgers. No, I'm thinking about John and Maize, which causes my heart to lurch forward.

"Hate to interrupt you while you're in fantasyland, but Mama packed up some leftovers for our dinner tonight. I'll warm them up after I take a shower if that's okay?"

I nod, and he walks to the bathroom. With a smile, I glance over at Maize who's as happy as can be wearing her Packers onesie. She's blinking up at me with the pacifier in her mouth that she must've grabbed from the tray, and I pick her up and hold her against my chest. Each time she rests her head against my shoulder, I have the urge to hold her just a little tighter. I try to take in each precious moment we share together.

Time passes, and soon John is walking into the living room wearing a T-shirt and some low-hanging sweats. I feel him watching me, and a burning sensation travels through my body. He moves across the room and sits next to me on the couch. "She really likes you."

When our eyes meet, it's as if nothing else matters but the three of us. He opens his arms, and I gently pass Maize to him. John holds her on his lap and begins speaking. "Bell, fell, sail, mail, trail."

I start giggling. "What in the world are you doing?"

"Rail. Tail. Yell. Shell." He glances over at me. "River gave me a baby book. It said to do rhyme time to help with reception skills. There was something about saying them in different tones to watch the baby's reaction too."

"Where's this book? I'd like to read it," I offer. I actually think I came across it one day when I was cleaning but never thought anything of it.

He chuckles. "It's beside my bed. That thing was my baby bible before you showed up. Now I've got the baby whisperer."

I nod with a smug grin. "Told you so."

"She's growing up so fast," he says, bringing his attention back to Maize as he lightly bounces her on his lap. She's smiling, loving every minute with her dad.

"Pretty soon, she'll be dating and driving," I add.

"Nope. Not happening. She's not allowed to date until she's fifty," he tells me matter-of-factly.

"You're gonna be one of those scary dads, aren't you?"

With a popped eyebrow, his eyes meet mine. "What do you think?"

Smiling, I stand and walk to the kitchen and pull the leftovers that Mama packed for us.

"Are you hungry now?" I ask John.

"Yeah, but I'll take care of dinner tonight." He stands, places Maize back in the Jumperoo, and nearly glides into the kitchen. I can't seem to take my eyes off him as he walks around me and pulls plates from the cabinet. His muscles are practically bulging through his shirt that fits him in all the right places.

Moving flawlessly around me, he takes the containers from the fridge and places them in the microwave. He grabs two wine glasses from the cabinet, pours them to the top with red wine, and hands me one.

"What's the occasion?" I ask, taking a sip. My taste buds do a little dance. It's been too long since I've had wine.

"You."

I nearly choke as I'm swallowing. Just as I open my mouth to say something, the microwave beeps and John begins pulling the containers out and setting them on the counter.

"Maize's doing so great and basically on a schedule. You've really done a great job, Mila, and I can't imagine doing this without you."

"Well, she's a great baby. I've enjoyed spending time with her and watching her grow." I glance at the floor, feeling my cheeks heat at his compliment. Before he can respond, I go back to the living room to grab Maize and put her in the bouncy chair that's in the kitchen. She's not quite big enough for a big girl high chair, but she'll be starting on cereal soon.

Once Maize's buckled in, John hands me a plate, and I place some fried chicken and scoop out some rice and gravy. It smells delicious. Mama's cooking reminds me so much of home.

We share small talk while we eat and discuss Maize. Once we're both finished, I clean up and put our plates in the dishwasher. The wine rushes through my bloodstream because, of course, we didn't just have one glass each. I check the clock and realize it's creeping up on Maize's bedtime. I make a bottle before handing it over to John, so he can feed her and get her to bed.

Once Maize's passed out, John tells me he's calling it an early night, and though the sun's barely set, I feel tired too. After I take a quick shower, I head to my room, climb under the blankets, and quickly fall asleep.

Hours pass, and I wake up to the sound of Maize crying. I'm always on alert and have gotten so good at hearing the slightest sound from her that I'm in John's room before he even wakes. My eyes feel heavy, but I make a bottle and change her before heading to my room to rock and feed her. I swear she has an internal clock, and she's either a few minutes ahead or behind, but she's typically on time with when she wants to eat.

Once she finishes the bottle, I softly pat her back until she burps, then take her back to John's room and lay her back down in the co-sleeper. As soon as I stand to walk out, she begins to fuss, so I sit on the edge of the bed and rub her little tummy.

"You gotta go to sleep, baby girl," I whisper after a yawn. Each time I try to stand, she becomes more vocal, so I lie on my side and watch her. As long as I'm here, she's quiet. Though my eyes are heavy, I wait for her to fall asleep, but somehow, I beat her to it.

CHAPTER SIXTEEN

John

Smooth, warm skin presses against my bare chest as I snake my arms around a small waist. I hear a low moan as a perky ass pushes against my hard dick, which causes my eyes to bolt open. I'm holding Mila as she sleeps soundly in my arms. I'm wrapped around her—our bodies are the closest they've ever been—and it scares the shit out of me how good it feels. As fast as I can, I roll out of bed and stand, trying to put as much distance between us as possible. Mila rolls over, her eyes flutter open, and the realization of where she is flashes on her face.

She gets out of my bed just as quick as I did and stands on the other side of the room, but her eyes glance down to my dick that's at full salute. Not allowing another awkward second to pass, I walk out of the bedroom, go into the bathroom, and shut the door. All that can be heard is the beating sound of my heart that's about to explode out of my chest.

Just as I lean against the cool wood, two soft knocks ring out.

"I'm sorry," Mila says quietly on the other side, and it feels like the door may just cave in. "I didn't mean to fall asleep," she explains, and the tenderness of her voice nearly breaks me in two. I don't think I can look at her right now because there's too much going on inside my head. That was never supposed to happen nor was it supposed to feel so natural.

I scrub my hands over my face, trying to get ahold of myself, before I face my fears, grab the knob, and crack it open.

"It's okay. Don't worry about it, but don't let it happen again." I snap it shut, turn on the faucet, and splash cold water on my face before I let out a deep breath. Ten minutes pass and I feel more at ease than I did before and decide to pretend like it didn't happen. It's better that way for both of us; otherwise, it may be too awkward being around her.

Once I'm back in my bedroom, I change into a pair of jeans and a T-shirt. I notice Maize isn't in the co-sleeper and know that Mila grabbed her. As soon as I open the door, the smell of bacon hits my senses, and the moment I walk into the kitchen, I see Mila placing eggs and bacon onto two plates. The air in the room goes still, and I feel as if I can't breathe. It's uncomfortable, exactly how I didn't want it to be, and I'm confused by how I feel. We sit, both keeping our eyes down.

"Are we going to talk about the elephant in the room?" Mila finally asks, looking at me.

"Nope," I say in a beat. "There's nothing to talk about."

She moves her eggs around on her plate, playing with her food instead of eating. When I look up again, she's glaring at me. Once she realizes I'm not saying a word about her being in my arms this morning, Mila quickly finishes her breakfast, places her plate in the sink, then picks Maize up from her chair with a bottle in her hand.

After I've cleared the food on my plate and rinsed it, I grab my phone and let Mila know I'll see her at lunch. Before I leave, I give Maize a kiss on her cheek, and though Mila's eyes are boring into me, I try my best to avoid her gaze. As I walk to the B&B, I hope today is one those times when being away means "out of sight, out of mind," but if it's anything like every other day since she arrived, the thought of her will be the highlight of my day. I'm so fucked.

Luckily, as soon as I walk into the B&B, I'm distracted by Jackson who's busy making coffee in the serving area.

"What the hell you doin' here so early?" I ask.

"Jesus, do you just sneak up on people like that all the time?" He glares at me.

"Maybe." I chuckle.

"The damn coffeepot in the ranch hand quarters broke, so I'm desperate. I can't wait until my house is finished. It's like living in a frat house."

"Then you should fit right in, considering my house felt the same way when you lived there," I add.

Jackson gives me a huff and an eye roll then goes back to watching the coffee drip like it's his life blood. Once the coffee finishes, I grab a cup and fill it to the top, considering I left the house without drinking any this morning.

"What's your deal?" Jackson takes a sip of hot ass coffee, not caring that it's steaming. He acts like he didn't just burn the shit out of his mouth, but I know the truth.

"I don't have a deal," I say, but he knows better.

"Okay. Whatever you say. Anyway, gotta feed the horses. Do you ever just wanna call in sick? No? Just me? Today was one of those days, but the ranch hands woulda snitched me out. Bastards."

He continues complaining, and I try to ignore him, but he's impossible. I asked for a distraction and got a grumpy Jackson—perfect. A few guests come downstairs, and thankfully, Jackson moseys his way to the barn.

Hours pass, and I get lost in confirming reservations and writing a marketing plan to help book more riding lessons for the summer. It's an easy way to exercise the horses and build the B&B's brand. We're coming up on the busiest time of the year, and it's important to accommodate our guests. When I look up from my notes, I see it's almost time for lunch, so I suck it up and walk to the house. When I enter, I can see it's spotless again, basically gleaming, and instantly know Mila is pissed.

"Mama sent over some lunch," Mila says from the couch, barely showing any attention to me when I walk in.

"Okay, great." I see the containers on the table and walk over and make a plate of fried fish, French fries, and homemade hush puppies. I sit at the table alone and hate how much this is bothering me. Once I'm finished eating, I wash my hands and have my short playtime with Maize.

"I think you're overreacting. I've already said I'm sorry. What else do you want me to do?" Mila stands and walks to the kitchen to grab a bottle of water.

"Can we just pretend it didn't happen and move on?" As much as I've tried to pretend, the thought of holding her close against me again hits me in full force.

"That's what you want?" She unscrews the top and takes a big drink.

I nod, but just thinking about her soft skin makes my mouth dry too.

"Okay, then." The attitude in her voice isn't lost on me.

I place Maize in her jumper, give Mila a smile, then go back to the office. On the way over, I curse myself for being so fucking stubborn. Mila doesn't deserve that, but some things are better left buried, hidden away. If discussed, light will be brought to feelings we shouldn't have, and it's easier to just not.

Walking up the back porch, I run my fingers through my hair and push it all away. As soon as I walk into the B&B, I place a smile on my face. A woman stops me in the front common area and asks me questions about horseback riding.

"I've never been on a horse before, and I'm an old lady. Can't risk falling and breaking a hip or anything. You think I'll be okay?" she asks slightly concerned.

"We have horses specifically for beginners. Basically, a toddler could ride and be fine. Plus, my brother is the best teacher in Texas. Swear by it." I smile.

"It has always been a bucket list item for me." She grins, thinking it over.

"Great, when would you like to start? Tomorrow? I think Jackson has an opening right after lunch if you're interested." I just looked at the schedule and know that for a fact.

Beaming, she nods her head. "Yes, sign me up. I'd like that a lot."

"It's a date then." I give her a wink.

She gives me a side hug, and I can tell she's excited about riding. I love introducing people to horseback riding and being able to provide that service. We continue with small talk about the weather, and I follow her to the front door and open it for her. Just as she's telling me goodbye, I notice a brand-new solid black Mercedes creeping down the driveway. I place my hands on my hips and watch as the car slows in front of the house. Probably one of those fancy real estate agents trying to buy the property again.

Instead of entertaining the thought, I walk inside. I really don't have time for this today. I send Jackson a quick text to give him a warning about my suspicions just in case he needs to step in. Though I'm pretty direct that we're not selling this property ever, Jackson has a way with words. The thought makes me laugh, especially considering he's in a mood today.

While waiting for the driver to get out of the car, I step back into my office and pull up the wholesale supplies website and make an order for extra cleaning products, new towels, and other things we're running low on. Almost fifteen minutes pass before a well-dressed couple walks into the B&B. The woman is slim and pretty in her own way. Her hair is cut into a short blonde bob, and her lips are pursed. The man is older, wearing a tailored suit, just as nice as the tuxedos we rented for Alex's wedding. He looks tired—frail almost—with sunken-in eyes and a hard expression. They glance around, studying the B&B, and I wonder what kind of offer they'll make. People trying to buy us out isn't anything new, but it's still early in the season for that.

As soon as they make eye contact with me, I smile, but their expressions don't change. I notice the giant ring on the woman's finger when she brushes the hair from her eyes, though her hair hasn't moved an inch since she entered. They walk to the counter, and I treat them just as I would any other person who enters the B&B.

"Hi y'all, how can I help you?" I wait for it, the million-dollar offer, with a smile on my face.

"We're actually looking for John Bishop," the man says. His voice is deep and gruff, not what I expected from him.

"I'm John, and you are?" My smile doesn't falter.

The woman opens her mouth and closes it quickly before looking over at the man. Guests begin to filter in from downstairs, and the room fills with chatter.

"I'm Mr. Bradley Kensington, and this is my wife, Barbara."

I glance over at the woman, and she grabs his hand. My body stiffens as I look at Bailey's parents. The grandparents of my daughter. This will be the first time we've formally met. It's hard to concentrate with so many people around, so I politely ask if we can bring the conversation to the back porch.

Once we're outside, I look at them and try to keep my manners, but it's hard. Too many side glances and I can tell they're judging everything about me all the way down to my boots, which doesn't sit well with me. Considering the few stories Bailey told me about her parents, I know they're here for a reason.

"How can I help you?" I ask, crossing my arms across my chest.

"Well sir, we'd like to talk to you about our daughter's baby," her dad says.

"You mean, our baby. My baby."

He ignores my words and acts as if I didn't speak.

"Right, we understand how much this all has probably burdened you. Having a baby, having to take care of her in your current situation." He looks around at the B&B, allowing his elitism to ooze from his ass.

"Anyway, what we're trying to say is, what's your number?"

I'm confused by what he's asking me, and the look on my face says as much. "My number?"

Her mother pipes in. "Yes, how much would you like for us to take the baby off your hands. I think her name is…Macy?"

"It's Maize. And actually, I'm appalled that you'd have the audacity to march your uppity asses up here and offer a dollar amount for my goddamn child. If you know what's best for you, you'll hop in that fancy car of yours and drive straight to hell."

Her father chuckles, which only causes me to burn with anger.

"Fifty thousand," he says with eyebrows raised.

"Excuse me?"

"Seventy-five thousand," Mr. Kensington throws out before I even have a chance to fully process what the hell is happening.

"Get the fuck out," I hiss, trying to keep my voice down since there are guests inside.

"A hundred thousand," Mrs. Kensington offers frantically.

"Y'all have lost your damn minds," I mutter, shaking my head in disbelief.

Mrs. Kensington straightens her shoulders as she continues speaking. "This is no place for a child to grow up. What do you really have to offer her anyway? I'm sure you weren't prepared to take care of her. You're a smart and good-looking young man; I'm sure you'll see we're giving you an out, so you can get back to the life you had before this slight inconvenience."

If she wasn't a woman, I'd deck her between the eyes. Luckily, Mama taught me manners, and being Jackson's brother taught me tolerance, but right now both are being tested. I stare at them, so disgusted with the fact that they're offering to buy my child from me—my own flesh and blood.

"It's the only piece of our daughter we have left. We want to raise her the *right* way. Send her to all the best private schools. We can afford to give her the life you can't," Mr. Kensington says.

"And treat her like you treated your own daughter?" I throw in their faces. "Keep her under your thumb and control her life like you did Bailey?" The expressions on their faces tell me they hadn't realized I'd known about that part of her life, and even though our time together was short, she did share some personal things.

"With all due respect—" Mrs. Kensington begins, but I'm quick to cut her off.

"No, you listen. I might not have a fancy car, a vacation house on the beach, or money to throw around like it's nothing, but that child has experienced more love than you ever gave Bailey. Now I've declined your offers, so pardon my French, but you need to get the fuck outta here before there's an actual issue." I take a step forward, closing the gap between Mr. Kensington and me.

I'm past the point of angry, and the only thing that pulls me back to reality is seeing Mila in the distance as Jackson steps up on the porch, ready to break apart a fight

"This is no place for a child," Mrs. Kensington adds, acting as if she's disgusted she even had to set foot on this land. Guaranteed, she's not feeling nearly as disgusted as I am at the moment.

"What's the problem here?" Jackson asks, looking back and forth between us, only catching the tail end of the heated discussion.

"Nothing. They were just leaving," I tell him, keeping my stance as I narrow my gaze at them.

The Kensingtons look back and forth between us, realizing there's two of us, but don't say anything about it. As Mr. Kensington goes to leave, wrapping his arm around his wife, he looks over his shoulder with a smug ass look on his face. "Give me a number. We'll pay whatever you want for the baby."

"Over my dead body," I throw back at them, taking a step toward them, but Jackson steps in front to block me.

He quickly realizes what's going on, and his expression goes rigid once he puts the pieces together. "Get the fuck out of here and don't you ever set your bald, ugly ass on this property again or you'll be dealing with me. And I'm a lot worse than my brother," he spits out before the Kensingtons leave.

"You're a disgrace. You'll be hearing from our lawyer," Mr. Kensington says, opening the door. I walk around Jackson to go after him and give him exactly what he deserves, but Jackson's quick to jerk me back.

My chest rises and falls, and I'm so mad that I reach back and punch the wooden post on the back porch. It fucking hurts, but the adrenaline rushing through me has me not giving a shit. Blood covers my knuckles, and I know I'm going to have a cut, but I'm so riled up, I can't even think straight. There are too many things running through my mind, and I'll be damned if I allow them to treat me or Maize that way. She's not an animal that can be sold. She's my daughter.

"Go take a breath. Get your mind right. I'll watch over everything, okay?" Jackson squeezes my shoulder, and I walk off the back porch, knowing I need to get my emotions together. For once, I'm thankful for Jackson being there for me. If he hadn't shown up, I may have assaulted Bailey's father, which is probably what they wanted just to prove I was unfit to raise a child.

I see Mila out of the corner of my eye but keep my head down. I hate that she witnessed me losing my shit, but my reaction was valid. Feeling the blood drip down my hand, I wipe it on my shirt and realize there are three nasty gashes. It burns the moment I rub it against the fabric, and I know I'll need to clean it out.

I know this is far from over, but I'll fight with everything I have for my little girl. I won't be intimidated by an asshole in a suit driving a Mercedes, regardless if they're Maize's biological grandparents. I understand now why Bailey warned me about them in her note and why she left their house as soon as she was able to afford to. No telling what she'd say about their offer, but it seems as if they're used to buying everything, so it might not be shocking at all.

Unfortunately for them, money can't and won't ever buy what they want from me. The thought alone has me rolling in anger all over again.

CHAPTER SEVENTEEN

Mila

Well, that wasn't awkward or anything.

As soon as John leaves after lunch, I know things between us are never going to be the same. He can act like it never happened all he wants, but I know deep down he feels the connection just as much as I do.

I still can't believe I fell asleep in his bed, then woke up in his arms. It was also the best sleep I've had in a long time. His large body engulfed mine, and I'd felt so safe and secure in his warm embrace. His breath tickled my neck, and when his arm wrapped around my waist and pulled me closer, I moaned aloud at how amazing it felt.

As soon as the bed dipped and he was gone, I realized something was wrong.

Then reality set in. I was in John's bed, wrapped up in him as his erection pressed against my butt.

The strangled groan that released from his throat the moment his eyes met mine told me everything I needed to know. He's fighting his emotions and the longer he pretends the connection between us doesn't exist, the faster his walls are crumbling down.

Breakfast was another awkward moment, and even though I apologized for being in his bed, he's blowing it off. I'm basically the major of pretending-shit-didn't-happen-ville and queen of we're-only-friends-land, but John Bishop deserves his own island for being the most confusing man on the planet.

"Alright, Maize." I finish getting her dressed for the third time today. "No more blowouts, okay? Can we make a deal? You save them for when your daddy's on duty, and I'll put a good word in for you to get your own pony."

She smiles up at me, warming my heart the way she does every time I talk to her. Her dark hair is getting longer, so I grab one of the bow headbands on her dresser to keep her hair back. She's already changed so much in the couple of months I've been here, and it's hard to believe she's just over five months old. Watching her grow and change in just two months has been one of the most rewarding parts of this job. I saw how fast my twin sisters grew, but I didn't appreciate it back then. Now they're twelve years old, crushing over boys, and glued to their iPhones. They'll officially be teenagers this summer.

I texted John shortly after lunch and asked about a stroller, so I could take Maize for a walk after her nap, and once I sent him a picture of what one might look like, he told me there was one in the storage shed behind the house.

"I need to get your daddy a picture book," I tell Maize with a chuckle as I snap her car seat into the stroller. "Let's go for a walk and get some sun. Whatcha say, baby girl?"

I place a little sun hat on her head, and she smiles for me, so I snap a picture and send it to John. Maybe it'll break some of the weird tension between us.

MILA

Hi Daddy! Look at how cute Mila dressed me :)
Can't wait to see you tonight!

I've only texted him a few times with pictures of her because I always worry I'll be bothering him at work, but I just couldn't resist today. The bright colored hat on her head is too cute.

JOHN

She looks adorable. Thanks for sending that.

MILA

No problem. We're heading out for our walk.

JOHN

Have fun. It's beautiful out today. Wish I could take her myself.

MILA

I'll leave the stroller out from now on in case you want to take her after work one of these nights.

JOHN

Great, thanks.

If I thought John was hard to read in person, he's impossible to read in text messages. But at least we're chatting, even if it is about Maize. Guess he really meant what he said this morning—wants to act like us waking up together in his bed never happened.

No amount of drinking into a self-loathing coma could make me forget.

Once Maize and I are out of the house, we walk down the path toward the stables. Kiera's truck and trailer are pulled up to the barn, so we head over to see her and Jackson.

"Hey!" I say as we approach them. Kiera's dressed up more than usual in a sundress that shows her long tan legs, and by the look on Jackson's face, he's noticed too.

"Hi, y'all!" She smiles, walking toward the stroller. "How's my sweet girl?" She peeks into the stroller, and Kiera's eyes light up as soon as she notices Maize's little sun hat. "Oh my goodness, how precious is that?"

"Isn't it cute?" I gush.

"What the hell did you do to my niece?" Jackson barks behind me. "She going to a tea party?"

"She looks adorable. Shut up, Jackson," Kiera retorts, and I laugh at their banter.

"She needs a cowgirl hat, not whatever the hell that is." He moves to take it off her head, then groans when he sees the bow headband. "Seriously?"

"Well, until she has one, this hat is staying on. It's keeping the sun off her face," I remind Jackson as I yank the hat from his hand and place it back on Maize's head.

He snarls, crossing his arms as if he has a say in this. "Don't worry, kid. Uncle Jackson will get you the right gear for livin' out here." He winks, and the tone of his voice has Maize kicking her feet and smiling like crazy. It's ridiculous how much she responds to him, but not at all surprising, considering he looks like John.

"I'm her favorite," Jackson taunts.

I snort, laughing. "That's because she thinks you're Daddy. You share the same face, so don't go getting a big head about yourself."

"Too late," Kiera chimes in. "It's so big, he has to get custom-made hats to fit his rather large ego."

"The only thing large around here is your mouth," Jackson shoots at Kiera. If looks could kill, Kiera's glare would've brought him to his knees begging for mercy.

"So..." I turn toward Kiera to change the subject. "What are you doing here all dressed up?"

She chews on her lower lip as her eyes light up. "I was just dropping off a horse before I head out of town. Trent took a few days off, so he's taking us to Fredericksburg for a little getaway as soon as I'm done here."

"Oh, nice! That's exciting."

"It is! We really need some time alone. Between our work schedules, we barely find time to really be together, so I'm looking forward to it."

Jackson's mood instantly changes, and it's no secret as to why. He rolls his eyes and starts to walk away before a black sedan pulls up and parks near the B&B. It catches all of our attention.

Jackson returns, crossing his arms as he studies the vehicle.

"What is it?" I ask, noticing his expression.

Before he can respond, his phone chimes.

"Great," he mutters, reading over the message on his cell. "Looks like a realtor bringing clients out again," he responds.

"Again?" I ask.

"Rich, high-profile oil tycoons from the big cities come to ranches like these to try to talk the owners into selling by throwing around big numbers," Kiera explains. "They come around my parents' ranch about once a year, and I'm constantly forcing them out, threatening to put my boot in their ass."

"But they don't normally come to the B&B like this," Jackson explains. "Usually go right to the main house, where Mama shoos them away."

"Maybe they're trying a new tactic," Kiera suggests.

"Won't matter anyway. We'll never sell to money-hungry city twats." Jackson shakes his head as if he's disgusted at the thought of it.

"Why would they want to buy ranches?" I ask, curiosity eating at me.

"Because ranch land like this is worth a fortune, especially considering the hundreds of acres we own. Most want to capitalize by building extravagant corporate hunting ranches, where they stock the land with large game, like elk, to allow rich assholes to kill for fun. They don't even keep the meat and actually eat it. Motherfuckers."

"Way out here?" I ask, stunned.

"That'd just be the start. They'd eventually try to expand and push the ranches out to start fracking without consequence," Jackson explains.

"That or..." Kiera adds. "They also buy the land, so they can split it up and sell it to numerous buyers and keep just enough property to stay profitable."

"Whatever they want to do won't matter because there's no way Mama and Dad will sell. Even when they pass away, the ranch will get split up between the five of us. It's our inheritance. The ranch is our life and has been passed down for five generations. Can't put a price on that."

We end up talking for another ten minutes as we watch a gentleman and woman finally walk into the B&B. Jackson says John will put them in their place, so he's not even worried about it until a few minutes later when we hear commotion and loud voices coming from the back of the B&B.

"Shit," he mutters, jogging down the path that leads to the back porch.

"Watch Maize, I'll be right back," I tell Kiera, and she nods in agreement.

I follow behind Jackson, not exactly sure what I'll be walking in on, but the moment I see John, I can tell something's wrong. His arms are crossed, his face is red, and by the vein popping in his forehead, he's boiling. Jackson gets to the porch just in time to block John from making a move that'd inevitably come back to bite him in the ass. I can't tell exactly what's being

172

said, but Jackson tells the couple he's worse than his brother, which can't be good.

Somehow, I don't doubt that.

Once the couple of walks back into the B&B, John throws a punch at a wooden post, making me jump and cringe as I watch him self-destruct. I can't even imagine what was said to make him that angry.

I want to go to him, but considering the way things started this morning, I don't think that'd be the best thing right now. I watch as Jackson puts his hands on John's shoulders and speaks quietly to him. A moment later, John's walking off the porch with his head down, avoiding my gaze. Turning my eyes toward Jackson for clarification, he shakes his head at me.

The black sedan backs out of the drive as John rounds the front of the B&B. I wait and watch until John makes his way into the house before following Jackson inside.

"What happened?" I ask frantically, pulling on Jackson's arm to stop him.

He turns around, and his face has anger written all over it. Not good.

"Were they trying to buy the ranch?" I ask.

Jackson shakes his head, and I notice the way his jaw tightens. "Worse."

Furrowing my brows, I'm confused by what that means as he licks his lips and releases a deep breath.

"Those were Maize's grandparents. They offered John money in exchange for the baby; said she'd be better off with them instead, and when John declined their offer, it got nasty."

"Oh my God," I mutter, gasping. "They wanted to *buy* Maize?"

"I guess." He shrugs. "I only caught the last bit of it, but it seemed they were implying John couldn't give her the life they could."

My blood boils at the thought of someone saying that to him. "What a bunch of assholes," I snarl.

Jackson agrees. "Yeah, I sent him to the house to cool down and told him I'd watch things here for a bit."

"Okay. I'll let Kiera know." I turn to walk toward the door when Jackson stops me.

"Mila…" I turn and look at him. "He could probably use a friend right now, even if he doesn't think so."

The corner of my lips tilts up just the slightest. Nodding my head in understanding, I go outside and back to Kiera and Maize.

"Mila!" Kiera says as soon as she sees me coming back. "What happened? Is everything okay?"

I shake my head and frown. "John put his fist into the wooden post, and he's pretty upset. Would you mind watching Maize for a second while I go check on him? Jackson's watching the B&B."

"Yeah, sure. Take as long as you need. Miss Maize and I were talking to the horses anyway," she reassures me sweetly.

I make my way back to the house, and as soon as I open the door, I hear John cursing in the bathroom. Grabbing the first aid kit I found in the back of the linen closet, I go to the bathroom and knock.

"John, it's me."

"What do you want, Mila?" His voice is gruff, and I know he's in agony.

"Let me clean up your hand."

"I'm fine," he clips. "Go back outside."

I hear the water running and figure it's safe to walk in, so without warning, I turn the knob and enter.

"You're not fine," I retort as he rinses his hand under the stream. "Let me take a look, at least." I hold up the kit in my hand as I step toward him. I unzip the pack and start taking things out. He doesn't say another word as I take his hand and pat it dry. He has two cuts on his knuckles and a small gash on his middle finger.

I feel his eyes bearing into my face as I inspect his wounds. My heart drums hard in my chest as I take his hand in mine, gently holding it. Swallowing hard, I dab some alcohol onto a cotton ball and prepare him. "This might sting a little."

As soon as I place it over the cuts, he stiffens. I know the alcohol burns against an open wound, so I try to be as careful as possible. When he flinches, I hold back.

"Sorry," I say softly. "Just trying to make sure it's clean."

"It's fine."

Keeping my eyes down, I rub some ointment on the cuts before placing a bandage around his hand to cover the knuckles and finger. He winces slightly. "Sorry," I say again. "I gotta make sure it's tight enough." I cringe, hating to bring him more pain.

"Stop apologizing, Mila," he demands. "It's not your fault."

"Okay, sorry," I say, then laugh. The faintest smile appears on his face but quickly vanishes the moment he sees me looking at him.

Once I finish wrapping his hand, I throw out the garbage and zip the kit together. The silence puts me on edge, and I hate the tension stewing between us.

"Jackson told me what happened," I speak up, blinking as I look in his eyes. His gaze hasn't faltered since the moment I walked in. "I don't blame you for reacting the way you did. They sound like horrible people."

His jaw twitches, and that vein in his forehead starts throbbing again. I know he's still heated about it, so I figure I'll leave him alone now that his hand is cleaned up.

"I better get back to Maize," I say softly, reaching for the kit and turning toward the door to leave.

"Mila, wait." The urgency in his tone has me stopping in place. I turn halfway around until our eyes meet, and seeing the way he's looking at me has my entire body shivering. "Thank you." When I blink at him in confusion, he holds up the hand I just bandaged. "You're good at taking care of people."

A smile touches my lips as I take him in. "Yeah, I guess I am."

CHAPTER EIGHTEEN

John

Fuck. My hand throbs like a son of a bitch, but the moment Mila barges into the bathroom, I'm no longer worried about the pain. All I can focus on is how close she is, how amazing she smells, and how soft her skin is against mine.

She's stunning, which isn't news, and every day she's here, it gets harder to deny my attraction to her. She's gorgeous on the inside and out, caring, sweet, and nurturing—all without even trying. The most attractive quality is how she treats Maize like her own and is always eager to help even though I tell her it's not her responsibility. She's so effortlessly molded her way into our lives that even thinking about losing her has me scared out of my mind.

The moment I needed her, she arrived, and though I pushed her away, she didn't let my stubbornness stop her. Mila's strong-willed, but she's so much more. She's fun to be around and is good at making people laugh, although most of the time I'm trying to avoid her, so I can get her off my

Though it never fucking works.

Waking up with her in my arms this morning was just the tip of the iceberg. It wasn't nearly enough to feed the animalistic desire that burns inside me, so when she walks out of the bathroom after bandaging my hand, the need to have her back in my arms is in full force.

Stepping forward, I walk until I can grab her by my good hand and pull her back until she crashes into my chest. She stumbles and looks up at me in a haze.

"What are—"

Covering her mouth with mine, I close the gap between us as I silence her with my lips. She startles for a beat before her body relaxes against mine, and I hold her close. Warm, delicate lips brush along mine before I slide my tongue between them and taste her. The first aid kit falls to the ground as her arms wrap around me. We both sink into the moment, and when she tilts her head back, I deepen the ever-consuming kiss that is surely going to change everything.

A vibrating moan escapes her throat, and I catch it with my mouth, the sound working up every part of my body. As I lose myself in her taste and touch, I push her up against the hallway wall. My cock throbs against my jeans, and I know she can feel it against her stomach the moment she arches her hips and presses against me.

I slide my arms around her waist and hold her hips in place as she grinds against my groin, causing my dick to harden even more. My lips move along her jaw, kissing her neck and making sure not to miss an inch of skin. A hand slides up her body and cups her breast. Her nipple hardens underneath, and I know she's not wearing a bra.

"Fuck," I mutter, moving my lips back to hers. "Pretty sure that violates the dress code," I tease, squeezing as I rub my thumb over her taut nipple.

"I already told you I wasn't going to follow one. And considering the first time we met you were in a towel, I figured clothing was optional." She smirks, making me laugh, and when she bites down on her lower lip and releases it, I cover her mouth again.

We're lost in each other, our hands and mouths exploring every inch of skin we can find. Fingers brushing through hair, tongues tangling, and chests heaving. Losing myself in Mila has never felt more right.

A door slams shut and footsteps approach, and within seconds, everything changes.

"Shit," we both mutter, stumbling apart.

"Sorry to barge in but Miss Maize—" Kiera comes to an abrupt stop when she sees us pushing away from each other in the hallway. Maize's on her hip, fussing and getting antsy in her arms. Glancing over, I notice Mila's hair is a mess, and her face is flushed. I'm sure mine is ten shades of red because it feels like we're teenagers who just got busted by an adult.

"I'll take Maize off your hands. She's probably getting hungry." Mila quickly breaks the awkward silence as she steps toward them, fixing her shirt.

Kiera gives me an odd look, and I know she suspects something. Not that I can blame her considering what she just walked in on.

"Well, she started to get cranky, and I figured she was getting hot or hungry." Kiera shrugs with an apology, and Mila tells her she'll take care of Maize, leaving Kiera and me alone in the hallway.

"What?" I finally speak, brushing my good hand through my hair, realizing there's a line of sweat along my brows.

"Why do you look like y'all just got caught rollin' around the haystacks?" She eyes me with a knowing smirk. "I thought you didn't mix business with pleasure?"

"I thought you knew how to mind your own damn business," I retort, walking around her but not before she catches my arm and stops me.

"I hope you know what you're doin'." Kiera looks at me, her green eyes meeting mine, and she's searching my face.

"What're ya talkin' about?"

"Mila Carmichael isn't a hit-it-and-quit-it kinda girl. She falls deeply, and I've gotten the impression she's pretty fond of you. So...I just hope you know what you're doin'," she cautions.

"Thanks for the warning," I grunt, walking past her toward the kitchen.

Mila is already preparing Maize's bottle, and though she's facing the other direction, her body stiffens the moment I enter.

Kiera's words are on repeat in my mind, and I wonder if I've done more damage than good. I don't know exactly how this will affect our professional relationship.

Maize's on Mila's hip, nuzzling her head in Mila's neck and hair. She adores Mila so much—not that I can blame her. It tugs at my heart every time I see them together. I often wonder if she thinks Mila is her mother, and if it'll end up confusing her if Mila ever decides to move on.

The thought of her leaving has my heart aching with sadness—for both Maize and me.

"I should get back to the B&B," I say, approaching them just as Mila turns around. Her lips are swollen, and I like knowing I'm the reason why.

"Okay. I'll probably put her down for an hour or so and start dinner."

"How about I worry about dinner tonight?"

She tilts her head, and the slightest smile forms as she bites down on her bottom lip. "Okay."

Closing the gap between us, I dip down to press a kiss on Maize's head and rub my hand along Mila's arm. I feel the goose bumps along her skin and know she's just as affected as I am.

"See you two later."

My heart is still hammering in my chest as I walk into the B&B. Between the altercation with the Kensingtons and mauling Mila's mouth in the hallway, my mind is a fucking mess.

"You doin' okay now?" Jackson asks when he sees me approaching. He narrows his eyes as if he's inspecting me.

"I'm fine." I pat him on the shoulder. "Thanks for…" I linger, trying to find the right words.

"You're welcome." He smacks me on the back. "Didn't feel like bailing you out of jail tonight anyway. Got me a hot date so that really would've fucked with my plans."

I roll my eyes and smile. "Glad you were thinking about me."

"I've got you." He grins. "Alright, well I better get back to the stables, so Kiera can go on her trip." He groans, and I know it affects him more than he'll ever admit.

"She's at my house, or at least she was when I left."

"Oh, okay. Talk to you later."

Once Jackson leaves, I head into my office and start researching family lawyers. I might need to get a restraining order on them, so they don't step foot on my property again, but I don't know the first thing about this shit. I'm not letting the Kensingtons anywhere near my daughter, and the only way to fight this is to do it legally, even if I'm tempted to do it with my fists.

"Knock, knock." I look up and see Emily in the doorway. Elizabeth is sleeping in her car seat, and when she sets her down, she shakes out her hand. "How are babies so dang heavy?"

I chuckle, agreeing. "If I didn't see it with my own eyes every day, I'd never guess what they're capable of producing."

"Yeah, well, that goes for all people." Emily has worked in the ER and as a doctor for quite some time, so I don't doubt she's seen her fair share of nightmares.

"What are you guys doing here?"

She comes and takes a seat. "I needed adult interaction before I completely lost my mind. Evan's back at work, which means Elizabeth is the only person I talk to for twenty hours a day."

"Well, you know you can always stop in at the house. I'm sure Mila and Maize would enjoy the company," I remind her.

"I just might because I'm starting to respond in baby talk when Evan calls me."

I laugh at the pathetic face she makes. "Well, maybe you can help me out with something. I told Mila I'd take care of dinner tonight without really having a plan."

"Oh dinner, huh?"

"Yes, dinner. She has dinner ready almost every night, and I just wanted to give her a night off from worrying about it. That's it."

"Mm-hmm."

"What is with everyone? Why does dinner always have to equal more?"

"Why don't you tell me?" she mocks. "Okay, so give me some ideas. You want something that says 'We're just hanging out,' or 'I want to take your clothes off.'"

Groaning, I roll my head back and squeeze my eyes shut. "Never mind. I'll figure something out."

"Or..." she continues, ignoring me. "'I like you and want to eventually get in your pants.'" She smirks. "In that case, I'd suggest some kind of pasta dish. Pasta is always a winner."

"How does pasta translate into that?" I give her a funny look but then shake my head. "Actually, don't answer that. Sorry I asked."

"Oh, John." She tilts one side of her lips up in a mock smile. "You're just too easy."

"You need a new hobby," I retort.

"I just found one."

"Picking on me isn't a hobby. Now hand me your baby, so I can hold her before I have to get back to work."

Once Emily and Elizabeth leave, I finish a few more tasks before calling it a night. I've been thinking about the words Emily said and wondering if that's what Mila thinks I'm trying to do. Mila is so much more than just a random hookup, but there still needs to be boundaries between us. I don't know what that kiss meant or what she'll read into it, but I also don't want to give her the wrong idea. I can no longer be that guy who acts recklessly without consequences. Maize's my life now, and that old lifestyle is long gone.

CHAPTER NINETEEN

Mila

"**F**ootball highlights are on tonight," Kat reminds me as we talk on the phone. "Featuring Rodgers and all the records he's broken."

"Oh crap, that's right. I wonder if John gets the channel here." I grab the remote and search for the NFL network. "Sweet, it starts at seven. I have to get my jersey on." Setting the controller down, I head toward my room, though it's only eleven and I have plenty of time before it starts.

Kat laughs, making me smile and melting away some of the tension in my body. Ever since that kiss in the hallway, I've been edgy. Every stolen glance between us feels forbidden, and though we've barely talked about it, I can't get it off my mind.

John came home that night and busied himself in the kitchen right away. He made spaghetti, which was really cute considering he didn't have the right noodles. It was more like fettuccini but with marinara sauce. He added mushrooms and tomatoes, and it actually wasn't too bad.

We kept the dinner conversation to a minimum, focusing on Maize and watching the cute little faces she'd make. Neither wanting to talk about the elephant in the room while avoiding eye contact throughout the meal. It felt like junior high all over again.

"Okay, I'm putting you on speaker, so I can change," I tell Kat and grab my Aaron Rodgers jersey from my closet. "Oh shoot. Maize, you need your onesie," I tell her as she jumps in her Jumperoo.

"You didn't. Kat snickers.

"Mom sent it in a package, so of course, she has to represent the green and gold!" I head back to John's room and search for it.

"I bet John loved that."

"Nope, but Maize and I have a deal. She wears Packers attire and doesn't listen to her daddy when it comes to football."

"Speaking of John…" Her voice lingers, and I know what's coming next. "Last I heard, there was a very steamy hallway kiss."

"That was last week's news." I snort, trying to avoid the subject, but I know Kat's not going to let it go.

"And?"

Once I'm back in the living room, I set down my phone, so I can change Maize.

"And…nothing. I don't know. It's been…weird. He made dinner that night, which was awkward, and then after I put Maize to bed, I joined him in the kitchen to help clean up, and then he apologized." I frown, thinking back to that evening.

"He apologized? For what? Not putting his dick in—"

"Kat! You're on speakerphone! Little baby ears," I remind her, laying Maize down on the couch and taking off the cute dress she had on.

"She doesn't know what I'm saying," she tells me with certainty.

"Okay but I don't want her first word to be the 'd' word either."

She laughs and then clears her throat. "Fine, we'll use code words. Did he apologize for not putting his *sword* in your *goody basket*?"

"Oh my God. You just referred to it as a goody basket."

"What? Would you prefer something else? Perhaps *pink panther, love canal,* or *whisker biscuit* suit you better?"

I mimic a gagging noise and beg her to stop. "Okay, goody basket it is."

"Alright, so what happened?"

I finish getting the Packers onesie on Maize and lay her down on the floor with a few toys. After she's situated, I take my phone with me as I head to the laundry room to grab her clothes from the dryer.

"Well, he apologized for kissing me and letting things go too far."

"Jerk. Okay, then what?"

"Then I asked him why he was apologizing for that, and if it was because he doesn't have feelings for me or because he does but thinks it's inappropriate because I'm Maize's nanny."

"And what did he say to that?"

"He said it was inappropriate, and we shouldn't cross those boundaries and blah, blah, blah." I set the phone down on the washer as I pull the clothes out of the dryer and place them into the basket. "And then I told him where he could shove those boundaries."

"Up his tight ass, I hope," she concludes.

I snort, closing the dryer and grabbing the basket in one hand and the phone in the other. "Basically. And it's been awkward-central ever since."

"That was almost a week ago, though."

"Yep." I walk to the living room where Maize's trying to roll from her back to her front. She's been trying super hard to roll over the past couple of days, and I think she'll be able to roll all the way over within the week.

"Okay, so aside from goody baskets and swords, what else is new? Any luck on the job searches?"

I sigh, not wanting to think about it yet, but knowing I have to or I'm going to be without a job come this fall.

"Yeah, well kinda," I admit, sitting on the couch so I can start folding clothes. "Mr. Demry from Morgan County called for an interview, but I haven't called him back yet."

"Are you serious? That's great! That's your dream school. Why wouldn't you call him back?" I anticipated her questions, but I don't know how to answer them without sounding like a fool. "You did your student teaching semester there. You'd be a shoo-in!"

"Ugh, I know. That's why I haven't returned the call yet." I groan. "Because I'm torn, Kat. I've wanted to teach for as long as I can remember, but then this job came along, and now everything's different. I love it here, but I also miss home. Leaving means leaving all of this behind, and I don't know if I'm ready for that."

"Well, you still have time to enjoy being here before you'd have to leave, but if you don't take the interview, the opportunity could pass you by."

"I know. I know. The thought of leaving Maize with someone else makes me sad." I frown just thinking about it.

"You mean, the thought of leaving John makes your goody basket tingle." There's a smile in her voice, but I can't deny she might be right.

I furrow my brows and hold back a laugh. "I don't even know what that means, but yes, he's partly the reason. I've been here for almost three months, and if I take the teaching job, I only have two months left. Eight weeks isn't enough time."

"I've never heard you sound so uncertain before, Mila. You worked your ass off to get through college, and now you're basically being handed the job to teach at the very school you want, so why are you letting doubt get in the way? I know you love Maize and being around the Bishops. They're an easy family to love, but you might never get this opportunity again. Someone else will gladly take that position, and then you'll always wonder about it."

Kat's words ring true, but that doesn't make the decision any easier. The thought of leaving brings tears to my eyes, but I knew coming here was only temporary. I hadn't expected to get so attached to Maize, and I never imagined I'd have feelings for John. But the fact is, we aren't in a relationship, and I have no idea where his head is about the two of us. Considering the kiss, the apology, and how we've barely talked leaves me with so much uncertainty about us.

"I'll call Mr. Demry back and see if the position is even still available."

"Good," Kat praises. "I'd just hate for you to lose out on this. You've worked so hard for it. At least get the interview and then make a decision when one needs to be made."

A noise from the kitchen startles me, but then I remember I left the window open and wind probably knocked something over. "Okay, you're right. As soon as I finish folding Maize's laundry, I'll put her down for a nap, and then I'll call."

"Perfect. Text me after, okay?"

"I will."

We exchange goodbyes, and I watch Maize play while folding the rest of the clothes. Once I'm done, I make Maize a bottle and take her and the basket of clothes into the room for her nap.

"Alright, Maze. Your laundry is put away, which means it's naptime for you," I tell her sweetly as I take her into my arms. We rock in the rocking chair while she eats, and once she's finished and fallen asleep, I lay her in the crib. "Such a sweet little angel you are." I rub the pad of my finger along her soft cheek. Sometimes, I just look at her and think what a precious gift to this family she's been and how much she's already gone through in her short life. If those thoughts make me emotional, I can only imagine how it affects John.

It's then I realize why John is so hesitant to cross the line with me. He can't just think about himself anymore, and I can't be selfish to push those limits when he has a daughter to consider.

Once I'm back in the living room, I listen to the voicemail once again and decide it's time to do it. I have to think about my future, too, and even if it's all unknown at the moment, I need to at least consider going for it.

Taking a deep breath, I dial the number and wait while the line rings. Seconds go by, and I contemplate leaving a voicemail, but a man answers, greeting me with a polite hello.

"Hi, this is Mila Carmichael calling for Mr. Demry. I'm sorry—"

"Ms. Carmichael? Yes. I was worried we weren't going to hear from you," he says sincerely.

"Yes, I'm so sorry for the delay. I'm in Texas at the moment and hadn't realized I had a voicemail. The reception out here isn't the greatest."

"Well, I hope we can schedule something. I've heard nothing but praise for your accomplishments and skills, and I think you'd be a great asset to our district. Your references couldn't speak highly enough about you. I'd love to have you come in for an interview, and we can discuss everything. When will you be back in Georgia?"

His words make me blush, and though I should be happy to hear it, I still feel insecure about all of this.

"Well, I'm not sure. I'm actually working as a nanny right now, and I didn't anticipate coming back until the middle of July. Is there any way we could schedule a phone interview, or do you need me to come there?"

I chew on my bottom lip, waiting for his response. If I had to leave for a day or two, I'm sure it wouldn't be an issue, and Mrs. Bishop could watch Maize, but I'd hate to put John out just in case she's unable to.

"Normally, I'd want to do a face-to-face interview but seeing that you did your student teaching here and you're our number one pick for the position, I think a phone interview will suffice. We'll have to schedule something maybe a week out, though, because it might take a couple of hours to get through everything. What do you think about that?"

I smile, grateful I wouldn't be missing the opportunity or have to fly home. "That'd be perfect. Thank you, Mr. Demry. I sincerely appreciate this."

"Excellent." I hear the smile in his voice, and my nerves settle. "I'll have my secretary contact you in the next day or two once I look at my schedule, and she'll give you a couple of options for us to talk. Sound good?"

"Perfect."

I thank him again before hanging up, and relief washes over me.

This is exactly what I've been wanting, and it feels like it's within arm's reach now.

Only, I can't shake the feeling of disappointment as I think about what leaving means.

I text Kat and my mother to tell them the news, and of course, they're both ecstatic for me. I really want to be, too, and decide I'm not going to worry about it right now. I wouldn't have to leave for another couple of months, so I have to enjoy my time here while I can.

The afternoon flies by quickly as I do more cleaning and wash my own laundry before folding and putting it all away. Maize takes a nice nap and is ready to eat and play as soon as she wakes up.

"Are you ready to try some cereal?" I ask in a high-pitched voice that always makes her smile and kick her chubby legs.

Since Maize's already five months old, I figured I'd try adding cereal into her routine, so she can get used to eating off a spoon and swallowing thicker textures. It might help her stay full longer between her night feedings, but that's *if* she lets me feed it to her.

"Vrooooooooooom…" I mimic an airplane motion with the spoon in my hand and try to sneak it into her mouth before she clamps her lips together. "Did any even get in your mouth?"

I scrape the side of her mouth with the edge of the spoon and try tricking her into opening her mouth for me again. "C'mon, Maize. Open wide for me." She takes her fist and rubs it into her eye before covering her face. "Oh, so it's gonna be like that," I tease. "Stubborn just like your daddy."

Laughter echoes behind me, making me jump, and when I turn around, I see John standing in the doorway of the kitchen with a sexy-as-sin smirk on his face.

"Jesus!" I hiss, resting a hand on my chest. "You nearly made me pee myself." Maize's giggling like this is the funniest thing in the world, and I realize she's smiling at her daddy. She's not the only one excited to see him, though.

"Well…" He shrugs his shoulder, unapologetically. "That's what you get for making my kid wear that god-awful onesie. You parading around in that jersey doesn't help your situation either."

I roll my eyes and turn back to Maize. "He's just a sore loser. Don't listen to him. Rodgers all the way!" Grabbing her arm, I hold up her hand to give me a little high-five. "See…" I say over my shoulder, watching him as he walks closer to us. "She agrees."

"She doesn't even know she has toes, so I don't think she's a reliable source," he mocks, coming up to Maize and kissing her head.

"Of course, she knows," I say, disagreeing in a singsong voice, tickling Maize's foot and squeezing her little toe. "She knows that this little piggy went to market…this little piggy stayed home…this little piggy had roast beef…this little piggy had none…and this little piggy went weeeeeee all the way home!" I grab each one of her toes and squeeze them as I sing.

Maize giggles and smiles and lights up the entire room as I sing and laugh with her. John's standing next to us with a big fat grin on his face, and for a moment everything feels right.

"You know…" John begins, smiling as if he's trying to hold back. "That's a real morbid nursery rhyme."

I narrow my eyes at him in confusion. "What? How do you mean?"

He grabs Maize's big toe and wiggles it. "This little piggy went to market…" John looks at me with a raised brow. "And this little piggy stayed home."

"Okay?"

"The first piggy goes to *market*. Like...the slaughterhouse. And the second piggy stayed home, who's probably now a widow."

"That's not right!" I argue.

"Sorry to ruin your day, sweetheart. But it's right." He winks at me, making my insides melt. "And the one getting roast beef? They're fattening him up to be next."

"There is *no* way that's true. Who would make up a nursery rhyme like that?"

"Lots of old nursery rhymes have hidden meanings. They were created during dark times."

"Don't listen to him, Maize," I turn and tell Maize who has no idea what's going on. But I like to pretend she does and that we're on each other's side anyway. "Your daddy's just bitter that this is a green and gold household now." I tickle under her chin to get another little smile and giggle out of her.

"Keep pushin' me, Mila," he taunts, poking me in the side. "And you'll be out on your ass like the trash you're wearing."

I gasp, my eyes widening at his little threat. "Better watch that filthy mouth, Daddy," I tease, glancing over at Maize who's watching us. "You're so lucky I won't be here for football season. I would *crush* you!" The words slip out of my mouth, and I playfully punch him in the shoulder, but his mood goes somber.

"Why won't you be here?" he asks. My heart drops to my toes, and I'm grateful Maize uses that exact moment to scream her head off.

Picking her up, I wipe her face with a burp rag and start moving around the kitchen to make her a bottle. John is still standing, watching.

"So what's the occasion for the jerseys anyway?" he finally asks, digging around the fridge.

"There's a special on tonight featuring Rodgers and all the kick as—er—butt records he's dominated."

John grabs a beer and takes a swig as his eyes continue staring into my soul. He chugs half of it before he sets it down.

"Well, I better take Maize off your hands then. You'll want to be able to focus for those twenty seconds," he taunts, reaching out to grab Maize from my arms.

"Pretty big sh—er—crap talker for someone who roots for a team whose best record is for having the most player arrests without getting suspended." I place my hands on my hips, daring him to talk his way out of that one.

"Damn," John howls. "You go right for the jugular."

"Hey…you mess with the bull, you get the horns." I mimic a set of horns with my fingers and point them at him. "But not you, Maize," I tell her sweetly, wrinkling my nose at her while John holds her. "You're way too sweet to be a Cowboy's fan."

"Didn't realize I had a football guru in my house." He snorts, taking the bottle from the counter.

I walk around him and look over my shoulder. John's studying me, and I catch his eyes on my ass. "I'm not all long legs and boobs, ya know?"

He clears his throat and starts feeding Maize her bottle to distract me from the fact he just got busted. "Don't worry. Your smartass mouth hasn't gone unnoticed," he retorts, his lips slightly tilting up in a mock smile.

"And neither has your bad taste in football teams."

CHAPTER TWENTY

John

As I was walking back from the barn, I decided to sneak into the house and see Maize. One of the benefits of working at the B&B is seeing my baby girl anytime I want. I walk through the front door and see Maize on the floor. I crawl down to her level and give her some kisses. As soon as I get back to my feet, I hear Mila chatting on speakerphone with someone in the laundry room. I stand there for a moment, contemplating if I should interrupt or not, but she's so caught up in her conversation I decide not to. Instead, I go into my bedroom to grab a clean shirt. Jackson needed help unloading a horse, and somehow, I ended up with shit all over me.

After I change shirts, I head into the kitchen for something to drink and can overhear Mila's conversation as she sits on the couch. Just as I'm about to let her know I'm in here, the person on the other line asks Mila about teaching jobs and if she's had any calls for interviews. When Mila responds that she has a voicemail for a job opportunity in her hometown, my heart shrivels like a raisin. I realize how much of a dick I've been this last week as I avoided her.

Why hadn't I asked Mila what her future plans were? I knew she wasn't from around here, but I hadn't anticipated the probability of losing her as a nanny this soon. By the tone of her voice, I know it's not something she wants to discuss right now. Before she turns around and catches me eavesdropping, I make my way out the back door with a racing heart.

I walk down the back porch and find Jackson sleeping on a bench. I nudge him until he rolls off and hits the ground with a thud.

"You're the biggest dick I know," he tells me, rubbing his face.

"And I have the biggest one too." I laugh. "Hate to interrupt your naptime, but can you watch the B&B? I need to go talk to Mama really quick."

Jackson huffs. "You ruin all the fun."

"Learned it from you, bro!"

As Jackson walks toward the B&B, I hop in my truck and drive over to my parents' house. Anytime I need someone to keep me grounded, Mama's the best person to talk to. She has a way of helping me understand things no one else can, and right now, I need some of that logical advice.

As soon as I walk inside the house, she's up on a step stool dusting a ceiling fan.

"Hey honey, what's the occasion?" She brushes the hair from her face with the back of her hand and steps down from the stool.

"I just need to chat with someone who's not going to judge...too much," I say with a small smile.

Mama sits on the couch and pats the spot next to her. "What's on your mind?"

"I think Mila is going to leave soon," I admit. The thought makes me sick.

With a small smile, Mama nods. "I knew this day was gonna eventually come. Her grandma said something about Mila applying for teaching positions back in Georgia before I even asked if she'd come work for us. I can help you look for a replacement. There's a woman in my book club at church who has nanny experience. She watched her grandchildren, and the last one just started school this past fall, so I could always ask her if she

192

could. Now that Maize's on a schedule, you probably don't need someone to stay twenty-four hours a day anyway."

"No, Mama. It's okay. I'll figure it out on my own this time."

Shaking her head, she grabs my hand. "You knew Mila wasn't gonna be a long-term solution." Mama searches my face, and that's when I watch her features soften. "Oh honey, you're in love with her."

I swallow hard. "You know how I feel?"

"I see the way you two look at each other. A person would have to be as blind as a bat not to notice. And I know it complicates things even further with her leaving so soon, which means your time is running out."

My eyes widen, and it's the first time I've heard it said aloud. I enjoy Mila's company, love being around her, and can't imagine her not being in Maize's or my life. I've never felt this way about anyone before—not even Bailey. The realization almost takes my breath away, but without a doubt, it steals my words. The thought of her leaving nearly cripples me, and as much as I want to be selfish and ask her to stay, I'd never stop her from following her dreams and keep her in Nowhere, Texas, with me and all of my emotional baggage.

"I can't ask her to stay, Mama. I'd feel terrible for holding her back."

She smiles again. "Mila's a smart girl, and she'll do what she wants, but you have to break out of your shell and tell her how you really feel before someone else snatches her up. If she leaves, there's no guarantee she'll ever come back. I know that bull saying that if you let something go and all that, but why would you even risk it? Don't be stubborn, son."

Running my fingers through my hair, I suck in a deep breath and exhale through my nose. I can't stop thinking about Bailey and how I should've told her how I really felt, how I shouldn't have given up so quickly. Though the cancer was inevitable, at least then I could've been there with her to the end, giving her the love and support she needed. I've lived with so much regret ever since I read her note. Regret that's buried so deep in my soul that I'm not sure I'll ever be able to get over.

Relationships haven't really been my thing, and now with Maize in the picture, they're the last thing I need. But it's not like that with Mila. She's already a part of the family, and when I watch Maize look at her and smile, it slowly builds a bridge from the dark place in my soul that's full of regret to where Mila's standing in the light. The woman has changed me for the better. She loves to give me hell and doesn't take my shit, and each time I get a sprinkle of her sass, it makes me smile.

"I'm scared. I'm scared what this will mean for us. I'm afraid of holding Mila back and asking her to stay here with me. What if it doesn't work out? Mama, this could be a Bailey situation all over again, and I don't know if I can handle losing someone else that means so much to me." I feel my walls crumbling, and it takes everything I have to keep my composure. The exhaustion from the past few months may have finally caught up to me, but I'm thinking more clearly than before.

"Honey, this isn't another Bailey situation. I don't know much about you and that girl, and I don't want to know the details, but you created a beautiful little baby who's loved by so many. I know it's a different situation, though, just by everything I've witnessed. What happened to Bailey was very tragic, and it breaks my heart, and there's nothing I can say to ever make it better. I pray for her family, as much as I don't really like 'em, and I hope that one day they can find peace. I hope one day you can find peace too, John." Mama's sincere when she speaks, keeping her voice soft.

"I will eventually, Mama. It's just going to take time, I think."

Mama stands up. "You need a drink."

I follow her to the kitchen, and she takes a glass from the cabinet, then pulls the whiskey from under the counter. My eyes widen when she pours two shots' worth in the glass and hands it to me.

"Time is something you don't have right now. It's running out. You know what you have to do. And if I know my son, you'll do the right thing for the both of you."

I hold the glass in my hand, look down at it, then drink it dry. It burns going down, a pain I welcome but haven't felt since Jackson's Friday night whiskey parties at the house. I let out a chuckle, looking at the empty glass, then set it in the sink.

"Thanks, Mama." I walk to her, giving her a big hug and a kiss on the cheek. She squeezes me hard.

"Love you so much," she tells me as we loosen our embrace. "I'm always here whenever you need me."

"Love you too, Mama." I know what I have to do. I give her a smile, then head toward the door. My heart breaks a little when I think about Maize not having a mother to speak to like this; someone who always makes her feel at home and loves her unconditionally no matter what. I'll have to be both parents for her as best as I can, and I've got one of the best examples to follow on the planet. Each day, I'm thankful for Mama and Dad. They showed us what it meant to love and be loved, and that's something I promised myself I'd teach my daughter.

I walk out onto the front porch and look up at the sky. Instead of going to my truck, I go back inside and find Mama tidying up.

"Mama," I say, and she jumps.

"I thought you left! Scared the crap out of me." She points the duster right in my face.

Taking a step back, I let out a laugh. "Can you watch Maize tonight?"

Her eyes meet mine. "Sure, honey. Bring her over whenever you're ready." My smile stretches from ear to ear, and I give her another hug before rushing out. The grin on my face doesn't falter as I drive across the property toward the B&B. I relieve Jackson of his duties, and of course, there's attitude and words exchanged as usual. The day seems to move as slow as molasses, and by the time my shift is over, I'm practically running home. In my heart, I know what I have to do, and that's going to happen tonight.

Once I'm parked, I try to get my nerves together. Letting out a laugh, I suck in a deep breath and walk up the steps to the porch. I pause for just a moment before turning the doorknob and walking inside. Mila is on the couch intently watching Aaron Rodgers' touchdown passes, and I groan. I find myself taking a mental snapshot of how beautiful she looks without even trying. She turns and looks at me, waves, and I give her a head nod before walking to Maize and giving her a big kiss on the cheek. She's wearing a sleepy face, and I leave her there because I know any moment she'll doze off, as Mila obnoxiously, but quietly, swoons over the Packers.

I look through my closet and find something nice to wear and throw it on the bed. A few minutes pass and Mila knocks on my bedroom door. I tell her to come in, and wearing a smirk, I turn to face her with my arms crossed over my broad chest. She walks past me with Maize in her arms, who's practically already asleep. Mila looks at the clothes laid on the bed, a button-up shirt, slacks, and of course, my special occasion boots.

"Are you going somewhere?" she asks with a smile as she lays Maize down in her crib.

"As a matter of fact, I am."

"Oh, who's the lucky lady?" I see something flash in her eyes—jealousy maybe? Instead of breaking the news to her that she's to be my date, I decide to play it out just a tad longer so I can watch her squirm. Payback for the whole going on a date with Jackson the first week she was here.

"Someone special." I grin, watching her fidget with the bottom of her shirt.

"Yeah? Well, good for you. What time are you leaving? Just so I know about Maize," she quickly adds. I can almost see her begin to boil over.

"I'm taking her with me," I say nonchalantly. "So I'll need an overnight bag packed for her if you wouldn't mind getting one together for me while I finish getting ready."

This takes her by surprise, and her mouth almost falls open, but she catches it. "Oh. Um. Okay. Sure, I'll get right on that."

Mila walks past me, and when she does, I grab her hand and lightly pull her to me. Her chest presses against mine, and when she looks up at me, her warm breath brushes across my cheeks. "Will you do me the honor of being my lucky lady tonight?"

Her breath catches, and she smiles. "You're a terror."

"Why?" I softly chuckle.

She narrows her eyes. "You know why."

"Mama's gonna watch Maize tonight because I've got a hot date. So pick you up at eight?"

An eyebrow pops up, and she chews on her bottom lip. "Are you taking me out on a date? Isn't that nepotism or something. Getting advantages from the boss?"

"Technically, that only refers to relatives, and since you are definitely not my sister, it doesn't count," I tell her matter-of-factly. "Are you saying no?" I ask, but I already know the answer, just by how she's looking at me with hooded eyes. It takes everything I have not to kiss her and remind her how perfect our lips match together, but I'm not trying to scare her away. It's just I can't ignore this feeling, or her, any longer.

"No. I mean, yes. I mean, oh my gosh, yes, I'll go."

"Good, I've got somewhere special I want to take you. I know you just put Maize down, but I'm going to get dressed, then take her to Mama. That'll give you about an hour to get ready." I smile because she's grinning so big it's contagious. I've not seen her this excited before, and it causes my heart to do somersaults.

"Oh, what should I wear?" she asks, before leaving the room.

"Anything as long as it's not Packer related," I joke.

She narrows her eyes at me. "Guess I'm going naked." She turns and walks away, but I know she's smiling.

"I won't complain," I say loud enough for her to hear.

When she laughs, I feel the walls that've held us back for so long are slowly crumbling away. Soon, they'll be dust. At least that's what I hope.

CHAPTER TWENTY-ONE

Mila

M y heart is having palpitations. I'm confused, but I don't know why. This is something I've wanted for so damn long, but I'm actually shocked it's happening. I keep second-guessing everything, and maybe he just used the term date, but we're really just going out, like as friends. I get so many mixed signals, and considering my history, I don't know what to believe, though my heart is telling me this is not just a hanging-out situation. I'm going on a *date* with John.

I hear the door shut, and I know John has Maize with him because he was opening and closing cabinets to pack her bag just moments earlier. I'm smiling a real smile, and my insides are squirming at what all this means. Excitement mixed with confusion means I need a drink. I have to pinch myself to make sure I'm not living in fantasyland. Nope, it's real. When it comes to dates, I'm a little rusty, so I text Kiera and ask for some advice since she knows the Bishop boys so well that she could probably write a

> **MILA**
> I NEED HELP!

KIERA
Holy Caps Queen. Is everything okay?

> **MILA**
> Yes…I think. John asked me on a date tonight, and I don't know what to wear. I don't know what to think. I don't know what to say. I think I might be losing it.

KIERA
Calm down, sister. Dates are fun.

> **MILA**
> A dress? Nice jeans? Naked?

KIERA
Naked. Just kidding. Where are you going?

I let out a groan.

> **MILA**
> I have no clue.

KIERA
Well. Hmm. If I were John Bishop, where would I take my smoking hot nanny that I've wanted to sleep with since the day she arrived?

> **MILA**
> Now you're making me want to vomit.

KIERA
My advice. Wear whatever makes you feel most comfortable. If I know them as well as I think I do, it'll be an outside thing. So dress accordingly, show some cleavage, wear a dress if you want that ass seen.

I burst into laughter, but the reality is, I need to just choose something. Considering it's warm outside, even with the sun going down, I decide on a sundress that goes mid-length and put on my cowboy boots for good measure. It's sexy and sassy all in one. I hurry and brush my teeth, fix my hair, and add some makeup, but my heart is racing one hundred beats per minute. Trying to calm down, I take in a deep breath and try to relax as I hear the front door close.

Closing my eyes tight, I give myself a small pep talk.

"Ready?"

Just the sound of his voice has me jumping off the ground.

"Stop doing that!" I tell him, noticing the smile on his face. My gaze wanders down to his outfit that fits him like a glove. Damn, he's gorgeous, and when he looks at me like that, like I'm the most beautiful thing he's ever laid his eyes on, it makes me nervous and happy all at the same time.

"You looked like you were making a wish or something. I was trying to check to see if you were clicking your boots together like Dorothy."

I shake my head and place my hands on my hips. "So this is how the night's gonna be?"

He laughs and gives me a wink before I grab my phone and walk past him. Glancing over my shoulder, I catch him staring at my ass but don't say anything. I try to hold back a laugh because Kiera was right about the dress.

John follows me, and we walk toward the front door. Once we're on the porch, I take the steps down that lead to the truck, and he laughs.

"No, ma'am."

That's when I really become confused. John nods his head toward the barn, and I narrow my eyes at him, wondering what he's really up to. We walk in sync together; our arms lightly brush against one another. It has me on edge, and I try to get ahold of the way I already feel. Butterflies flutter inside, and I feel like if I open my mouth, a swarm of them will come flying out. The sound of my heartbeat blends with the crickets, and I can't help but smile as I look at the pinks and purples splashed across the sky. We may have close to an hour before sunset, so it makes me even more curious.

We continue to walk in silence, the sound of our boots crunching across the ground until we walk into the large opening of the barn. Once inside, I see a black stallion saddled and ready to go.

I turn and look at John. "Now I'm even more confused."

"We're going riding," he says, proudly moving his hand to display the horse like a game show host as if I hadn't figured out that much.

"Um…there's only one horse tied up." I move my hand in the same motion.

John leans in, his hand brushing against mine, and gives me the sexiest smirk. "It's because we're riding double." His voice is gruff but smooth all at the same time, and it causes me to swallow hard.

He walks closer and runs his hand against the smooth black coat of the horse. "This is Shadow. Courtney broke him one summer before she left for college. He's got spunk; that's why I like him so much. But we understand each other."

I can't help but notice there's no saddle on the horse, only a saddle blanket covers his back.

My eyes go wide.

"Do you know how to ride?" he asks, paying no attention to me.

I turn and look at him. "I've been riding since I was a kid. That's all I did during the summers when I'd visit Gigi. But there's one issue. Where's the saddle?"

A hearty laugh escapes him. "Well, I didn't realize I was dealing with the rodeo queen. 'Scuse me, milady. We don't need a saddle. We're going bareback."

My mouth falls open, then closes. "Bareback?"

He leans in and whispers, and his mouth grazes the shell of my ear. "Can you handle it?"

Fuck. Me. He's trying to drive me absolutely wild.

I nod, wondering how I'm actually going to get on, considering I'm wearing a dress. Realizing my confusion, John grabs a stepladder that I'm sure they use for the kids they give lessons to.

"Hold the blanket, then hop on." He unhooks the lead rope from Shadow's bridle, then grabs the reins and hands them to me. Carefully, I stand on my tiptoes and loop my leg over the top of Shadow, scooting the saddle pad back to the middle with my butt, trying not to reveal too much, considering my choice of clothes. I'm going to be so sore tomorrow from riding.

"Good job," he says, looking up at me with a proud smile before he takes the step up and swings his leg over too. He's sitting right behind me. Our bodies are closer at this moment than they've ever been; well, if you don't count the accidental spooning.

John snakes his arms around me, and goose bumps cover my body as he takes the reins from my hand and steers from behind. He clicks his mouth and gives Shadow a little nudge with his heels, and soon, we're riding out of the barn toward a trail.

Though I've lived on the ranch for a few months, I've not been given a grand tour. But with John sitting behind me, his body so damn close to mine, I can barely concentrate on anything at all. I try to focus on not sliding off Shadow because it's much harder to stay on without stirrups. I'm holding on as tight as I can with my legs, and John notices.

"Relax, sweetheart. We're gonna stay at this pace," he tells me, his breath and mouth so close to my skin I feel as if I'm on fire.

The sun continues to set, casting a burst of dark purple across the horizon. I can't help but look around at the rolling hills, and I try to take it all in. The sound of the crickets, the way the sun casts a warm glow in the afternoons, and the smell of fresh air. This place is so beautiful, it takes my breath away, and I already know I'm going to miss it so much. The thought of not being in Texas for much longer makes me queasy.

"What are you thinking about?" he asks as if he felt my mood change.

"Nothing really." I try to lie, and though he's not buying it, he doesn't push it any further.

The trail changes, and we begin to climb in elevation. At the top of the hill, I can see for miles. We continue down the other side, and when we make it to the bottom, I see a large pond and smoke. There's a fire built and a few wooden benches surrounding it. I can tell this is a regular hangout or a stopping point for the riders when they take the trails with Jackson.

I try to look at him over my shoulder, impressed with the freshly burning fire. "How'd you manage this?"

"Bishop Brother magic." He laughs, but I have a feeling he put Jackson up to it.

Once we're close to the small fire, John moves off the side of Shadow, like it's no big deal, then takes the reins and ties him up to a bar by a nearby tree.

He opens his arms to catch me since there's no ladder over here. At first, I'm slightly scared because Shadow is so tall, and it's a long way to the ground.

"Trust me." John scoots closer and opens his arms. He has no idea how much I do trust him. Somehow, I get my leg over Shadow without revealing too much in this dress and slip right into John's arms. He holds me tight, and we stay like that for a moment before he sets me down, and I feel the shift between us.

He takes my hand and leads me over to the small campfire, and on the bench is a package of marshmallows, chocolate, and graham crackers. Instantly, I think of Graham the man and my sister, and my family back in Georgia. For once, I wish the thoughts would just go away so I can actually enjoy being alone with John.

"Do you like s'mores?" he asks.

"Oh yeah. I love them, probably a little too much," I admit, knowing I could eat a handful of them. "We'd do lots of campfires at my grandparents' when all the kids would visit, and it became a tradition."

John places some firewood on the flames and sits on the bench. He pats the space next to him, inviting me to sit. The sun has long dipped under the horizon, and the only light we have is the warm glow of the wood burning. It's nice to sit in silence and not say anything at all because we don't have to.

"Mila…" He finally speaks, breaking me from the flames, though when I look at him, he's the one who sets my body on fire. "I know you're leaving soon."

My mouth falls open, and I close it. There's nothing I can say because my time here was always temporary.

"I overheard you talking on the phone today."

I'm shocked. He sees through me like glass.

"I was talking to Kat. How much did you hear?" I ask, turning my body to face him.

"Something about a goody basket." He chuckles, though I hear the slight sadness in his tone.

"No, you didn't," I mumble, my face going hot.

"I also know about the interview too, Mila." He glances at me, our eyes meet, then he looks back at the fire, but I can't take my eyes off him. Not right now, not as I study how sexy the stubble on his chin is or how his tongue darts out and licks his full lips.

"Oh, that." I never imagined we'd be sitting here having this conversation right now. I wanted to wait until I knew for a fact I had the job, though I'm certain what the outcome will be. Even Kat knows I'm a shoo-in. That's just how small-town politics and jobs work.

"I hope you give it a chance especially after hearing Kat's words about how much this means to you."

He glances over at me.

"I wasn't eavesdropping. Or at least I hadn't meant to. I got horseshit on me when I was helping Jackson, so I came home to get a clean shirt and to see Maize before heading back to the B&B. When I walked in, you were on the phone in the laundry room, and I didn't want to interrupt you. So after changing my shirt, I went to the kitchen, and you were still on the phone while folding clothes. The conversation sounded important, so I waited for a moment to tell you I was home, but then realized there were things I shouldn't be hearing," he adds.

"Are you Houdini or something?" I let out a stifled laugh, surprised I didn't hear him, though I do recall a noise in the kitchen. I should've known, but I was sucked into Kat's and my conversation. "I'm sorry, John. That's not the way I wanted you to find out. I just didn't want to make a fuss over something that wasn't a for sure thing yet. I hope you understand that. I did plan on telling you once I knew, though."

He nods, but the conversation goes silent. "I'm the one who should be apologizing right now."

"There's no need for all that." I suck in a deep breath, trying to find my words. I think back to all the times I should've told Cade the truth and how different my life would've gone had I just confessed my feelings to him. Now, I'm thankful I didn't, but I can't leave Texas without telling John the truth. Out of anyone, he deserves to know, considering if I do fly back to Georgia, he and Maize—who I've grown so damn attached to—will be missing me. My heart lurches forward. They need me, and I need them just as much. There's so much conflict inside me that I don't know what to do anymore.

"Since I was a little girl, my dream was to teach at the same elementary school I went to. It's in my hometown, which is pretty small, but I always knew a position there wasn't guaranteed, considering it's a small school. However, that didn't stop me from getting my degree. I've always wanted to make a positive impact on kids, inspire them, spoil them, teach them. Most people can remember their first-grade teacher's name for that reason alone. It sets them up for their whole educational career, which is why it's always appealed to me. So when I got a call to interview there, I knew I should've felt ecstatic. But the truth is, I don't know what I want anymore. I know that I miss my family and home, though."

John's expression drops, and I can see a hint of sadness in his eyes too.

"But," I add, "I feel like I have a family here too. One that needs me. I love Maize so much, and the thought of leaving her, not hearing her little laughs or cries, and having tummy time with her, dancing with her, or sharing all my secrets absolutely crushes me. She's become an integral part of my life, and I've become more attached than I ever thought possible. Then there's your family who's welcomed me from the very first day. And my new friends—Emily, River, and Kiera—they're like another set of sisters. Then, of course, Gigi and Papaw and my cousin Kat are all here too. There's so much here, but there's so much at home too." I take a deep breath, realizing I'm pouring my heart out to him, and it feels right to do so. "I wasn't prepared for any of this," I tell him honestly. "I thought I'd help with a baby, make some money while I wait for job offers, and then go back home before the school year started. But it's become much more than that. Texas is home too. It always has been, and I've always loved being here." I pause for a moment as John watches me. "And then there's you."

A moment passes, his eyes staying glued on me, and then his strong hand wraps around my neck as his lips crash into mine. I don't pull away. I taste him, all of him, as our tongues mingle together. My body and soul are on fire, and by the time we break our embrace, my mind is reeling, and it all feels like a dream. My lips are numb, and when my eyes flutter open, he smiles. "You have no idea how badly I've wanted to kiss you again."

"I know," I whisper. "I was starting to wonder if I'd ever get to again."

Grabbing my hand, he looks directly at me. The mood shifts to a more serious one, and I'm almost worried what he'll say. "I'd never hold you back, Mila, and I won't beg you to stay. Even though the selfish part of me really wants to, you have to do what's right for you. Sometimes, it's easier when someone else makes the decision for us, but this is one I can't make. You have to listen to what your heart says. Teaching is such a wonderful gift that not everyone is blessed to have, and I know you'll positively impact hundreds of children throughout your career. I could never take that away from you and ask you to stay here on the ranch with Maize and me. It wouldn't be fair to you. I have a lot on my plate between being a dad and running the B&B, so it's definitely a different lifestyle out here, and I know it's not for everyone. A part of me wants to be greedy and keep you all to myself, but that's just not who I am." He lets out a stifled laugh. "For once, I wish I was more like Jackson."

My emotions bubble. Watching John, listening to his words and how sincere they are doesn't make leaving any easier.

"I know there's a lot to think about and consider," I finally say. "And I love your lifestyle. You've got Maize and your career, and all of this."

He gives me a small smile and thankfully changes the subject as the wood cracks and pops. "I'm happy that I get to raise Maize on the ranch. Growing up here has shaped who I am today. Being a part of a large, loud family, I've had a good life. I learned that I won't always get my way, but it's important to mean what you say and say what you mean. But ranch life isn't easy. I worked my fair share of younger years doing grunt work, getting kicked by animals, and falling head first into a pile of mud. It's been a lot of hard work, blood, sweat, and even tears."

"You're lucky, though. I'm envious of your view, and how there's always something to do. Growing up in suburban Georgia, well let's just say there weren't too many adventures. Unless you consider the time my one neighbor had an affair with the pool boy and was a real-life cliché of being a money-hungry housewife."

He smirks. "Jackson created enough adventures for us both."

I grab a metal poker from beside me and open the marshmallows. After I place one on the end of the stick, I hand the other one to John. I'm serious about my s'mores and melt my marshmallow from above while John places his right in the flame until it's on fire.

"Do you like being a twin?" I ask.

He pulls his marshmallow from the fire, and it's burnt to a crisp. "There are times when I do. Times when I don't. Sometimes, it's hard to be an individual when I'm always standing in Jackson's shadow. Though I don't mind it. I love him, though sometimes I want to strangle him. He has a good heart, just stubborn."

I set my stick on the bench and open the graham crackers, placing a piece of chocolate on them as John eats his marshmallow plain. "You two aren't that different after all."

Once my s'more is put together, I take a bite, and it's the most perfect thing I've ever tasted. I think this is the first time I've ever had a s'more on a date, and the thought makes me grin.

"Was that a direct jab at my stubbornness?" He licks his fingers.

I nod because my mouth is full of sugary goodness.

"I've always wondered what it'd be like to have a twin and have someone who's on your side at all times, who understands you on a deeper level. Sure, I've got tons of siblings, but it's different when you have someone who looks exactly like you. I bet y'all got into a lot of trouble."

He rubs his hands on his pants, then glances over at me. "When we were younger, we used to pretend to be each other. Though Mama will say she knows her boys, there were times when she couldn't even tell us apart."

I burst into laughter. "No way."

"Yep. We even switched classes at school. All I had to do was be loud and act out, and everyone thought I was Jackson."

"So did y'all ever girlfriend trade?"

He rolls his eyes. "He for sure wanted to, but do you think I want anyone Jackson's been with? Also, I'm not the type of man to share, not even with my brother, but I think he'd be all about it."

I laugh, but I can't stop thinking about feeling his lips against mine again. As if he reads my mind, he places one hand on my bare leg and the other wraps around my neck, and he pulls me close. Instead of kissing me immediately, John pulls my bottom lip between his teeth and tugs. I let out a sigh right before his lips brush lightly against mine. Not rushing, he continues to tease me until I'm two seconds from mauling him. Our kisses deepen, becoming more passionate, and I end up straddling him, his hands holding my ass, and I can feel how hard he is, which only turns me on further.

"I want you so fucking bad," he says between kisses.

"I wanted you first," I admit, resting my forehead against his.

John smiles against my lips. "That's probably true."

It shouldn't feel like home being with him like this, but it does.

CHAPTER TWENTY-TWO

John

I stand and grab Mila's hand and walk her over to Shadow.

"There's no way I can get on," she tells me looking up at me then glancing at the dress she's wearing. I lead Shadow to the bench close to the fire, place my leg over until I'm sitting tall. She stands on the wood, and I hold my hand out for her, pulling her up, allowing her leg to swing over until she's sitting behind me. Her hands snake around my waist tightly, and I place one of my hands on hers as I hold the reins with the other.

"We're gonna go slow," I tell her and hear her gulp behind me, which makes me chuckle. I don't correct her assumptions and explain I was talking about riding because the truth is, I don't want to rush with Mila. I want to spend every second I can with her and cherish it all while I can because soon, she'll be in Georgia, taking my heart with her.

She holds me tighter, leaning her head against my back.

"The stars are beautiful," she whispers. "I've never seen so many in my

"What stars?" I tease. "You're the only beautiful thing I see around here." The silence between us lingers on, and I wish I could see her face and try to figure out what she's thinking. Sometimes she's an enigma, a hard egg to crack, while other times I can read her like a book. Maybe this time, I stepped over the line, and perhaps she's regretting it all. Now I'm stuck in my head, second-guessing everything. Regardless, I won't be the man who holds her back from her dreams, regardless if she looks at me like she wishes I'd beg her to stay.

"It's going to be different when you're gone," I finally say as the barn lights come into view. I asked Jackson to leave them on after he put hay out for the horses tonight.

"Shh. Let's not talk about it anymore." Her voice is light, but I understand. I've been trying to forget about it since I heard her on the phone with her cousin.

"Okay. Not another mention of it tonight." I promise myself I won't, though it's the only thing running through my mind right now.

"Thank you." She squeezes me a little tighter, and it hurts my heart.

We continue forward, entering the barn, and I pull back the reins. Shadow stops beside the stepladder, and I look over my shoulder at Mila with a grin. The wind blows her dark brown hair in her face, and she tucks it behind her ears before repositioning her body to slide off. I jump off the other side, grab the saddle pad and place it upside down in the tack room to let it dry. Mila watches me as I brush him down, remove his bridle, and let him loose. Barely allowing me to move out of his way, Shadow takes off in a full sprint to the pasture, bucking as soon as his hoofs hit the grass, which makes me chuckle.

The barn light casts down on Mila, and as cheesy as it sounds, she looks like a cowgirl angel in her white sundress and cowboy boots. Absolutely stunning. She sucks on her bottom lip before I go to her. It takes all of five steps to close the space between us. Grabbing her face in my hands, I kiss her like I'll never get to kiss her again, and where it stands, I might not. I pour every bit of emotion I have left and feel her tension unravel by my touch. Taking a few steps back, the only thing that stops us from completely toppling over is a stall door. We almost lost control, again, but this time without interruption. Or that's what I think until I hear muffled laughter behind me.

Mila freezes, and I turn and look at Jackson who's standing with a shit-eating grin spread wide across his face. His arms are crossed over his chest, and all I want to do is throat punch him. It's almost as if the universe is against us, or Jackson is.

"Peculiar," he says, rubbing his hand across the stubble he's grown, to copy me.

I huff. "Don't you have someone else's life to ruin right now?"

I glance at Mila who straightens her stance, and by the look on her face, it seems as if she wants to punch Jackson too. Her lips are swollen, her hair is tousled, and there's no denying where that would've led without a rude interruption.

"I thought there wasn't anythin' going on between you two." He narrows his eyes, looking at the both of us. "I knew it. And now Alex owes me a hundred bucks. Thanks, bro." Jackson walks closer until he's standing a few feet from us.

"What are you doin' here anyway?" I ask, placing my arms over my chest. I almost feel as if I'm looking in the mirror, by his stance.

"I came to double-check the riding schedule tomorrow and noticed the lights were still on so wanted to make sure you got back safely, and I didn't need to send out a rescue team or anything."

"Please. You know I know those trails like the back of my hand."

He laughs. "Yeah, just fuckin' with you. Wanted to catch you with the nanny. Put the hay out for the horses and waited around." Jackson smiles real big as if he's proud of himself.

"You're an asshole." I grab Mila's hand and pull her past him.

"Did you find what you were looking for?" she asks.

"Sure did," he tells her, laughing.

As we walk toward the house, the lights in the barn flicker off. Mila looks up at the stars, and it makes me smile. "We'll have to come out really late one night, so you can see the Milky Way. It'll blow your mind. Sometimes, it's so bright, it actually lights up the ground."

"Really? That almost seems unbelievable." She stops and continues to look up. I wrap my arm around her shoulder, and we stand there for a moment, enjoying the view.

"I can see about three stars in Atlanta. Have to drive farther out of the city to see more than a handful," she explains.

Jackson walks past us, his boots kicking up dust. "Y'all have a *good* night."

"Shut up," I mumble, but all he does is laugh as he walks toward his truck.

After a few more moments, we watch his taillights fade in the distance, and Mila and I walk inside the house. The silent conversation streaming between us is so intense that it draws us closer together. Mila's chest rises and falls as I grab her cheeks in my hands. I search her face, asking for approval, before her eyes fluttered closed and her lips trace mine. We take it slow, not rushing, as our tongues tangle together. Though we're both gasping for air, neither of us stop. We can worry about breathing later. Mila's fingers find the button to my pants, then my zipper, and I stop her before she pushes my jeans to my ankles.

"Mila, are you sure about this?" I ask lowly, considering she's bringing this to the next level.

She places her finger over my mouth and smiles. "I've never been surer about anything in my life."

My lips gravitate to hers, and I run my fingers through her long hair until we're entirely desperate for one another. I grab her hand and lead her into my bedroom. Once inside, I click on the small lamp next to the bed, allowing it to cast a warm glow throughout the room. Our eyes meet, and it's all the permission I need.

Mila takes a few steps toward me, wraps her arms around my neck, and pulls my face to hers. As she kisses me, her hands find her way to the buttons on my shirt, and she carefully undoes each one. She moans against my mouth as she unzips my pants and pushes my jeans down along with my boxers. Glancing down, she palms my dick and strokes her hand up and down until it's hard and firm in her grip. She sucks on her bottom lip before running her tongue across it, which causes me to release a throaty moan. I've fantasized about this very moment for months.

Not wanting to wait any longer, I kick off my boots and step out of my jeans. I run my fingers up Mila's thighs and pull her dress over her head. Goose bumps cover her skin as she stands confidently in her bra and panties. I pepper kisses along her shoulder and up her neck until I reach the shell of her ear.

"You're so goddamn beautiful, Mila." I reach behind her, unclasping the white silk bra from her body. It falls to the ground, and I can't help admiring her perky breasts. I dip down, placing one nipple in my mouth and flick my tongue against the peak. Her head falls back as her breathing increases. I softly run my fingers down her body, between her legs, and place my hand on the outside of her panties.

"You're so wet," I say, hooking my fingers at the top of her panties and pushing them down so I can explore more of her.

"You do that to me," she admits with a devilish grin on her face as she steps out of her panties. She's standing completely naked in my room with nothing on but cowboy boots, and it's the hottest fucking thing I've ever seen.

I pop up an eyebrow, studying every inch of her beautiful body. "Really?"

"Every damn day." She comes closer to me and just when I'm about to throw her on my bed, she surprises me and falls to her knees. Mila tilts her head back and makes eye contact with me as she takes me into her mouth, and fuck, it's the sexiest fantasy to ever come true.

Slowly, she teases me with her tongue. I feel weightless as she starts stroking and sucking at the same time. I close my eyes, enjoying her as she runs her fingers up my thighs. For the past few months, I thought Mila was nothing more than an innocent woman, but as she takes all of me between her lips, that image of her melts. I like this side of her, the one where she has full control and takes what she wants.

Carefully, she cups my balls and the sensation of her warm mouth on my cock has my entire world spinning around me. It's so intense that it feels as if my knees may buckle out from under me. When I open my eyes and see Mila watching me, the intensity between us heightens to a level I've never felt before. She licks her tongue up my length before wrapping her lips around the tip and sucking until her cheeks go hollow.

Being with Mila like this is nothing I could've ever imagined. It's more than just a hookup and each kiss and touch we exchange brings truth to that. The attraction has been undeniable from the beginning, but what we share is much more than that. With each stroke, I'm unraveling from the core, and I need to stop her before I explode in her pretty, wet mouth. I don't want to come this soon already even though she begs with her eyes to bring me there.

Grabbing Mila's hand, I place her on the bed, just enough where her perky ass hangs off the edge.

"My turn," I tell her as I remove her cowboy boots and throw them behind me. She props herself up on her elbows, watching me as I part her legs and loop one over my shoulder. I press the softest of kisses on her ankle, then up her calf, and toward her inner thigh until I reach paradise. She puts her bottom lip in her mouth as I tease her perfectly shaved pussy with kisses. The stubble on my face presses against her sensitive parts, and she pushes harder against me as I tease her to the max. She lets out a sigh of frustration, and I chuckle against her skin.

Before she can say a word, I lick up her slippery slit, and when my tongue presses against her hard nub, she releases a loud, throaty moan. I continue, giving her everything she's begging for. I take my time with her, enjoying her sweet taste, and when she grabs the blanket with tight fists and arches her back, I know she's close. I place one finger inside and groan at how tight she is, and when she writhes around me, I add a second finger.

"Yes, yes," she whispers, grinding her hips harder against my face, telling me exactly what she wants. My tongue circles her clit in slow, calculated movements, and I know she'll explode any minute. Instead of giving her the release her body begs for, I feather kisses on her thighs.

"Please," she begs as her chest rapidly rises and falls. "Don't stop."

"Patience, sweetheart." I smile against her skin, moving back to her sweet spot. As her orgasm continues to build, Mila's moans become more intense, but I continue taking my time until she spills over with relief. She buckles beneath me, gasping and moaning, unraveling from the core. I grab her ass, pulling her closer to me, opening her thighs farther apart, wanting to taste every drop of her sweetness.

I stand and look at her, watching her as she's completely lost in her own world. She scoots farther up the bed, and I crawl over her body, hovering above her mouth. Our lips slam together with desperation, and I don't know how much longer I can wait to be inside her. Mila scratches her fingernails down my back, mixing pleasure with pain, and looks up at me with her big blue eyes.

"I need you," she begs as my dick plays against her slick opening.

Keeping my eyes tranced on her, I enter and claim her with everything I am. She gasps, and her mouth falls open as I fill her with my length. I wait for a moment as her body adjusts, and feeling how tight she is, I don't want to hurt her. Once she gives me the slightest nod of approval, I dip my head down closer.

Placing my face in her hands, she leans up and kisses me as I slowly move in and out of her. Our moans mix with pleasure, and I feel as if I'm losing myself, completely unraveling with her with each movement. We're ravenous animals, fulfilling the other's need, but allowing ourselves to be vulnerable to the way we feel, the way I think we've both always felt.

"John," she whispers, her eyes fluttering open. "I'm so close."

I don't speed up but continue at the same pace, giving it to her deeper. I know I'm close as well, and I need to feel her, all of her, as she comes.

"Oh my—" It's the only words she gets out before she buckles beneath me. Pulling me closer as she arches her hips, begging for more. There's an overwhelming sense of need with each thrust, and then she loses herself. As Mila trembles underneath me, her head tilts back as she wraps her legs around my waist and moan-screams my name. So goddamn sexy.

Her pussy tightens around me, and I can't hold back any longer. We're tumbling together, lost in the sensation, only to find full satisfaction. The smiles on our faces don't falter, and I plant soft kisses on her lips, not ever wanting to stop.

"That was..." she lingers, still panting.

"Fucking incredible," I finish for her with a smile.

"Yes," she agrees with a laugh.

I kiss the top of her nose. "Let's get you cleaned up."

Once we're back in my bed, I lie on my side and look over at Mila who's staring at me with a sheepish grin. When our eyes meet, I feel as if I'm falling, and I hope I never find the ground. She scoots closer, and I wrap my arms around her small frame and hold her tightly in my arms.

My fingertips brush across the softness of her skin, and she hums against my chest as I kiss her forehead. Our bodies tangle together, holding the other like we never want to let go, and for the first time in my life—I don't. I feel our hearts beating in rhythm, together in motion, and I can't help but smile for the thousandth time since Mila barged into my life and turned it upside down.

And I hope it never goes back.

CHAPTER TWENTY-THREE

Mila

John's fingers trace along my arm without realizing the way it affects me. It sends shivers down my spine and fills my stomach with butterflies. Everything about him has an effect on me, and the fact that we've finally succumbed to the inevitable doesn't stop my body and heart reacting to every look, touch, and kiss.

"So…you want to explain the tattoo on your inner thigh?" I break the silence while trying to hold back my laughter. "Or should I just conclude all of your tattoos are due to stupidity with Jackson?"

He holds me tighter, and when I tilt my head to look up at him, he's chuckling as a hint of blush surfaces.

"Saw that, did ya?" He looks at me with a smirk.

"Well for a split second, I thought it was real and about to attack my face." I wrap my arm around his waist tighter, wanting to feel as close to

He laughs again, and I love the way it sounds in my ear. "My dick or the tattoo?"

My head falls back with laughter again, and just when I'm about to tell him to stop stalling, his mouth latches to mine. His hand slides up my body and cups my breast, teasing my nipple as he deepens his tongue.

"Wait a minute…" I say against his mouth, pushing him back. "Don't distract me with your kisses."

"Why not?" he asks, bringing his mouth to my neck. "You don't like my kisses?"

I moan, enjoying his kisses. *A lot*. "You're avoiding my question."

"It was a dare," he finally responds, bringing his mouth back to mine.

I pull back, so I can look at him. "Another dare? Is there nothing better to do down here than dare each other with tattoos?" I quip.

"Oh, there is…much worse than tattoos." He grins.

"Somehow I don't even doubt that," I say. "Okay, so why a scorpion?"

"You mean why *not* a scorpion!"

I narrow my eyes, confused about this whole thing.

"Scorpion are known for passion, attraction, and sexual energy."

"Y'all pretty fond of yourselves." I deadpan, pretending not to be amused. "So does Jackson have one of those too?"

"Yes but…"

"Don't even tell me. I want to be able to look him in the eyes without picturing *it*."

"Hate to break it to ya, sweetheart. Jackson and I are identical down to the same birthmarks."

"That's creepy." I laugh. "You two can barely stand each other."

"Yep. Ironically enough, we get along when we're out drinking, and somehow his dumb ideas sound like good ones."

"The start to every country song ever." I laugh, loving this softer side of John. He's so easy to talk to that I could spend hours with him without even realizing the time.

"You don't have any tattoos or birthmarks?" he asks.

"Nope. I knew that I wanted to be a teacher and figured any tattoos would need to be hidden and nothing stuck out enough to get it inked on my body. Maybe someday, though."

"What would you get? And where?"

"Well, as weird as it sounds, I've thought about getting the shape of Texas because I spent many summers here when I was a kid, and it always felt like my second home. But I could never decide how I wanted it to look. Plain with just the outline or with an image inside. However, now…it might just represent something else."

"Oh yeah?"

"Yeah, Jackson's really had an effect on me—"

John covers his body over mine, pinning my wrists to the bed as he covers his mouth with mine and steals my breath. I chuckle against his lips, knowing he purposely kept me from finishing that sentence.

"Time for me to look for the perfect spot for a tattoo." He leans back, grabbing my thigh and wiggling his way between my legs. "I bet I can find just the right place." He makes his way down my body, feathering kisses between my breasts, down my stomach, and landing on my clit. My knees bend and my legs rest on his shoulders as his mouth explores, working me back to the edge.

Once his lips are coated in my juices, he grips my hips and tells me to flip over. Looking over my shoulder at him, I'm shocked to see he's hard and ready to go again. What's even more shocking is how badly I want him to fuck me over and over.

My sex life up to this very point had been nearly nonexistent, pathetic, and admittedly sad. Twice in one night was unheard of until John Bishop bends me over and slides inside me, fitting us together like we were always meant to be. His large hands hold me in place as he thrusts in and out; the sounds of our heavy breathing and skin slapping together echo throughout the room.

I fist the blankets and arch my ass up as he brings me to a level I've never been to before. My entire body stiffens and shakes as I tighten around him and cry out a moan. The intensity of it all has me rocking back and forth against him, wanting him to experience the exact same thing he just made me feel.

The sound of a hand cracking against my ass has my eyes widening in surprise. John leans forward until his palm wraps around my breast, and he's thrusting deeper than before. His lips press against my ear before he's whispering all the ways he wants to make me come.

And then like that, I die and go to heaven.

Somehow, he pulls our bodies up while we're still connected and drives fast inside me. John wraps his arms around my waist, holding us in place as his hand slides between my legs and circles my clit until I'm begging for relief.

"John, please," I whimper. "I can't take anymore." My head falls back on his chest, in disbelief that he's managed to work me up again within the short time span.

"I've got you, sweetheart," he tells me seductively. "Play with your tits, baby. Let me see how you get your nipples hard."

Oh my God.

His low, gravelly voice nearly has me unraveling on the spot. I palm my breasts for him as his lips press against my neck. Knowing he's watching makes me eager to please him, and when his body tightens, I know he's close too. The buildup is intense, and within moments, it overtakes both of us.

John holds me as we ride it out together, and I love hearing his groans in my ear as he comes undone. It's the sexiest sound I've ever heard, and if I could, I'd have it on repeat all day long.

We collapse on the bed, panting and sweaty. Neither of us talks as we catch our breaths, and when the bed dips, I know John's left to clean up again. He returns a minute later, and once I'm clean, he takes me into his arms and kisses my lips softly until we both drift off to sleep.

If there was a magazine called *Sexy Single Dads* and they needed a cover model, John Bishop would be their first pick.

Or at least he's my first pick—my thoughts are consumed with him from the very moment I wake up in his bed, surrounded by the scent of him. The other side of the bed is cold, so I put one of his shirts on and go in search of him.

And the view that has me thinking he should be a magazine cover model is the moment I find him in the kitchen at the stove, wearing only his boxers as he cooks. There's already a fresh pot of coffee made, and the smell of sausage has me smiling. Now this is what dreams are made of.

"If this is what waking up in your bed entails, sign me up for the premium package." I walk toward him, and when he looks at me over his shoulder, he flashes a crooked smile. It matches my own, and I know the memory of last night is still fresh in our minds.

Hell, it'll be the only thing I think about until I die.

"You got the exclusive package, baby." He winks.

I laugh, and when he leans down, I kiss his perfect lips. "So what are you making over here? It smells delicious."

"My famous triple berry pancakes and maple sausage. I only make it on super special occasions."

"Really? Well, considering you have Maize, I'm going to guess it wasn't giving away your virginity."

"There's that sassy mouth I adore so much."

"What? You think it was just for show?" I tease, walking to the fridge for some juice.

"Well, now that I know what it's capable of, I'll never doubt it again," he muses, flipping the pancakes over.

"Want some OJ?" I ask, pouring myself a glass.

Before he can answer, the doorbell rings, making both of us jump and look toward the front of the house.

"I'll get that."

John turns the stove off, then sets the spatula down. "Hold up," he tells me. "Not in that, you aren't."

I look down and realize I'm not wearing pants. Rolling my eyes, I cave. "Fine. It's probably Jackson anyway 'checking in' on us," I say with a laugh.

"That's just another reason why you shouldn't." He steps to walk past me but then stops and presses a quick kiss on my lips. "Wait here."

Once he's out of the kitchen, I tiptoe to the hallway, so I can peek and see who it is. John opens the door but towers over my view.

"I'm looking for John Bishop." I hear a man's voice, but it's not a friendly one, which has my heart racing.

"That's me. Who are you?"

There's a beat of silence before the guy speaks again. "You've been served. Have a good day."

John stands frozen in the doorway, and I wait until the guy steps off the porch before going to him and finding out what that was all about.

"What is it?" I ask as John shuts the door. His face is pale and looks like he just saw a ghost.

"I'm not sure. Just says the law firm it's from on the front."

I can sense John's confusion and worry, so I do my best to show him my support. He turns over the envelope, rips it open, then slides the papers out. I wait as he scans it over and within seconds, his features tighten, his eyes narrow, and his lips transform into a firm line.

"Son of a bitch," he mutters as his eyes continue to scan the documents.

"John, what is it?" I anxiously ask.

"Fucking unbelievable." He shakes his head, turning the pages and reading every word. "The Kensingtons are fighting for custody of Maize."

My eyes nearly bug out of my head from shock, and I'm taken aback. "What? How can they do that?"

"I have no goddamn clue, but whoever they hired is a fucking idiot, I can already tell that much. They're trying to claim I'm an unfit father for their deceased daughter's child and want to override my rights by objecting to the birth certificate that claims I'm Maize's father."

"Well can't you just prove you are with a blood test?" I ask stupidly because I feel so helpless right now. I can see how upset John is, and it breaks my heart this is happening right now.

"Of course, but it's not that simple." He flips to another page. "They'll dig into everything about my life and family's lives and then take whatever they can out of context to demonstrate their case. The fact they have money means they'll do whatever it takes to find what they need."

"John…" I whisper, placing my hand on his arm. "It's just a scare tactic. They have no real case, and a judge would see that right away and throw it out. You're Maize's father whether they like it or not."

"Well, consider me scared, Mila. In case you haven't realized, I'm not living on a gold mine here. I don't have the money to hire a big city lawyer like they do. I don't expect you to understand."

He walks away before I can fully process what he just said. I can't believe this turned around so quick, and suddenly, it feels like I'm the one on trial here.

CHAPTER TWENTY-FOUR

John

I can't fucking believe this.

One minute, I'm on top of the world, and the next, it's crumbling to ashes.

The Kensingtons have unlimited money to do God knows what with, and even if what they're doing is just to scare the shit out of me, it's working.

I rush to my room and get dressed. Mila stays quiet, and I feel awful for snapping at her, but my head isn't straight right now. Grabbing my keys and phone from the kitchen, I leave and walk outside. I can't be in the house right now because I'm afraid Mila will see a side of me I try so hard to keep hidden. It rarely comes to surface until something dramatic happens that really sets me off.

I hop in my truck and drive to my parents' house. I need to see Maize and bring her back home, but I also need to talk to them about what this

Gravel kicks up from my tires as I make my way down the driveway, and when I park, I jog into the house and immediately hear Mama singing in the kitchen.

"John! You scared me. I didn't expect you here so early."

I go right toward Maize who's in a high chair and attempt to take her out. "How do you unbuckle this thing?"

"What's the matter? She hasn't eaten yet."

"I just need to hold her, Mama. Can you take her out for me, please?"

She studies my face and notices my expression. Pulling the tray off and unbuckling the straps, she frees Maize and hands her to me.

"Hey, baby girl," I say, kissing her cheek, and her smile brightens the room. "Did you have fun at Grandma's?"

"She absolutely did," Mama answers for her. She gives us a minute and then adds, "So you want to tell me what the heck is goin' on?"

"Where's Dad? I need him." I hand Maize to her, so she can strap her back in the chair.

"He's in his office," she tells me, and I immediately rush down the hallway to find him.

"Hey, Dad," I say, walking in without knocking. "Have a minute?"

"Sure, son. What's goin' on?" he asks, taking off his glasses.

I hand him the envelope and give him time to look it over. He's not an easy man to read, but within seconds, his eyes narrow and features tighten at the realization of what the document is.

"Who the hell are the Kensingtons?" He looks up from the papers with a scowl.

"Bailey's parents and Maize's biological grandparents."

"Is there something you aren't telling me?"

I take a seat in the chair and rest my elbows on my knees. "They stopped at the B&B a couple of weeks ago and tried to offer me money for Maize. I told them to fuck off and to get off the property. They weren't too happy about that," I admit.

"I assume not." He sets the envelope down on the desk. "And now they're trying to get custody."

"They want to make me look like an unfit father to terminate my rights, and they have the money to do it, Dad. I don't know what I'm going to do. I emptied most of my savings out when I had to make repairs to the house last year. The rest went to bills and getting Maize everything she needed."

"You know we have a lawyer on retainer, John."

"Yeah, but not for this kind of stuff. I need a family lawyer or someone good with custody cases."

"Okay then." He slides open a drawer and takes out a checkbook.

"Dad, no. I didn't come here to ask for money," I protest. "I'll never be able to pay it back."

"Never said I wanted you to." He signs the check before handing it over to me. It's blank. "Hire the best guy you can find and do whatever it takes."

"I can't tell you how much I appreciate this, Dad. Seriously."

"Maize's family, John. I don't care how she came into this family; she's ours, and we take care of our own."

"I know, Dad." The corner of my lips tilts up just the slightest as my emotions threaten to spill over. "Thank you."

Folding the check, I tuck it into my back pocket before grabbing the envelope and heading out to the kitchen where Mama is feeding Maize.

"Everything okay?" She looks up at me and studies my face.

Taking a seat at the table, I scrub my hands over my face and exhale. "Yeah. I hope so."

Knowing Mama, she isn't going to let me leave without telling her, so I explain the situation and bring her up to speed. By the time I'm done, she's a boiling pot ready to explode.

"You get a lawyer, I don't care how much it costs, and you fight. Ya hear me?"

"Yes, ma'am. I plan to." I give her a reassuring smile.

"So?" she says after a moment.

"So what?" I ask.

"How'd your date with Mila go last night? Ya know before all this happened." She unbuckles Maize and hands her over to me, then cleans her face and hands. "Spare me any details I don't need to hear."

"Oh my God." I groan, squeezing my eyes shut.

"What? You think I'm a prude or something? You're aware you're holding your *baby* right now. Pretty sure Jackson's killed any shock factor out of my body anyway."

I chuckle, shaking my head. I figure I can give her the PG version. "It went really well. We got the chance to really talk and be open about our feelings. I took her horseback riding—"

"And then I caught them doin' the nasty in the barn."

If Maize wasn't on my lap right now, I'd get up and smack Jackson upside the head.

"Where the heck did you come from?" Mama asks, shocked.

"Dad called me in," he explains, and when he comes closer, that well-known shit-eating grin is plastered on his face. At this point, it might as well be permanent.

"He's in his office. So go away," I remark, hoping if I ignore him he'll actually do what I ask.

No such luck.

"Let me kiss my niece first," Jackson insists. "Pretty grumpy for a guy who got laid last night."

"Jackson Joel Bishop!" Mama scolds. "Where are your manners?"

"Probably the same place where John's dignity is hiding," he taunts, laughing.

"You're lucky Maize's between us right now," I warn.

"Go find your father before I beat some respect into you with a wooden spoon. I don't care how old you are, I'll whack you one." Mama's scowl is on point, and if Jackson wasn't so used to working her up, I'd actually be worried for him.

"Dang. No one knows how to take a joke this mornin'." He hands Maize back to me and turns to walk down the hall.

"You know he purposely gets you worked up, Mama."

"Of course I do." She smiles as if she hadn't just threatened Jackson. "He's been the wild child ever since he pushed you out of the way to come out first." She laughs, and the image alone has me cringing. I could've gone without hearing that information.

"Alright so…"

"I told you. We went horseback riding. Then we looked at the stars and talked. Oh, and we made s'mores."

"Is that code for somethin'? I told you to skip those parts."

"Oh my God, Mama. No." I laugh, bouncing Maize on my leg. "Then I kissed her goodnight, and we went back to our respectable rooms for the night."

"Mm-hmm." She purses her lips, knowing better. "Well, just make sure the next time you have a baby, you better be married."

"Next time?" I shake my head. "I don't even have a good hang of it as it is."

"That comes with time, darling. And age. You think I had the slightest clue what I was doing with Evan? He cried nonstop, and the second he learned to walk, he was into everything. Couple of years later, you and Jackson surprised your father and me. We had three boys under the age of four."

I never thought of it like that or how close in age we all were. "How did you do it?"

"Brandy," she blurts out.

"You drank Brandy?" I ask in disbelief. Mama hates that shit.

"No, I stuck my finger in it and then rubbed it on your gums."

"Mama!" I laugh, shaking my head at her confession.

"Helped y'all sleep like babies."

"That's mildly disturbing," I tease.

"Yeah, well, they didn't have all that fancy stuff they do now with their pills and medicine. Y'all teething was a nightmare, and I had to do something when the cold washcloth trick didn't work."

"Don't worry. I won't hold it against you," I mock.

Maize starts to get antsy, so I stand and try walking around to calm her. "I better get her home."

"Wait." Mama stops me. "I'm glad you and Mila had a chance to talk. Don't let what happened this morning ruin what you two have, alright? Let her be there for you and don't push her away just because you're scared. If she ends up going back to Georgia, you don't want to have any regrets on how you handled everything."

"I know," I agree. "I'm not used to any of this. But I'm trying."

She stands in front of me and pats my cheek like she has since I was little. "I know you are, John. You're doing a great job too. I'm very proud of you. So is your father."

I lean down and hug her. "Thanks, Mama."

The moment I walk into the house and the scent of lemon hits my nose, I can tell Mila's been cleaning and already know that's not a good sign. I've learned she cleans when she's upset, and I'm smart enough to realize it's because of me.

I set Maize down in her Jumperoo while I go search for Mila. I find her in her bedroom folding laundry, and there's music softly playing from her phone. Walking up behind her, I wrap my arms around her and feel her jump. Instead of yelling at me like she normally does for scaring her, she stays silent—also not a good sign.

Dipping my head down, I press my mouth to her shoulder and place a kiss there. She relaxes slightly, so I run my nose up the length of her neck and jaw. Her head falls back just enough to give me the access I need to kiss her soft skin. Wrapping my hand in her hair, I grip a chunk in my fist and shift her head to the side, so I can lick my tongue along her neck until I reach her ear and suck on her lobe.

Her throat vibrates with a moan, and I know she's enjoying this more than she wants to admit. I don't blame her for being mad at me, but that doesn't mean I'm going to make it easy for her to stay that way.

Towering over her, I adjust our bodies, so our lips meet, and I slide my tongue inside. She turns to face me and lets me pick her up, so I can carry her to the middle of the bed. With her legs wrapped around my waist, I hover over her and mold our bodies together as we sink into the mattress.

"Does this mean you aren't mad at me anymore?" I smirk against the dimple of her collarbone.

"No," she snarks. "Means you're a really good kisser."

I chuckle, making my way down her chest and pulling her shirt up. "Mmm…I'll be sure to use that to my advantage then." I wrap my lips around her hard nipple and suck.

"Looks like you already are," she retorts, followed by a soft moan. Arching her back, she twists her hands in my hair and tugs.

I make my way to her other nipple and give it the same attention before moving back up and stealing another kiss. She melts against me, and before I get the chance to apologize, Maize starts crying from the living room.

"Crap, Maize," Mila yells, her eyes popping open. She slams her hands against my chest and pushes me off, which takes me by surprise, and I quickly lose my balance as she jumps off the bed. I inevitably fall to the floor with a loud thud.

"Argh," I groan, landing on my ass.

"Oh my God." Mila starts laughing hysterically. "I didn't mean to push you that hard."

"Right," I tease. She walks around the bed and holds out her hand. "Don't even wanna know what happens when you're really pissed."

"That usually involves a variety of shotguns."

"Wouldn't put anything past you." I smirk, grabbing her hand. Instead of letting her pull me up, I yank her down to the ground with me.

"Maize's crying," she reminds me. "Just let me go check on her." She moves to get back to her feet.

"Probably knew we were foolin' around and wasn't havin' it." I brace myself on the nightstand and bed, pulling myself up. "If my ego wasn't bruised by you pushing me off, my ass sure is."

"That's what you get for trying to kiss your way out of trouble," she says over her shoulder, winking as she heads out to the living room.

Shaking my head, I smile. I was fully prepared to come in like a dog with my tail between my legs and beg for her forgiveness after the rude comment I made, but the moment I saw her standing in here, I couldn't resist kissing her. However, now I'll be walking around with the biggest case of blue balls at least until I get a moment with her to myself.

I find Mila in the kitchen with Maize on her hip as she makes a bottle. I can't even find the right words to express how much I love having Mila here and how at home she looks. She's taken on a much bigger role than just being Maize's nanny. She's molded herself right into our lives, fitting perfectly right where she belongs.

"What's all the screaming about?" I ask in a soft voice, taking Maize from her hold. She immediately nuzzles her head into my neck and yawns.

"I think she's ready for a nap," Mila answers, shaking the bottle.

"Mama fed her at the house when I arrived, so I'm not sure if she's still hungry," I explain. "Not sure what time she woke up either."

"I'm sure she's just tired, but we'll try a bottle too," Mila says.

"I'll rock her," I say, grabbing the bottle from her hand. I lean in and press a kiss to her lips. "Then we can talk, okay?"

"Okay, but if you're going to confess your love for Aaron Rodgers, let's just make it clear I had him first."

I grin, shaking my head at her sassy mouth. "It's a good thing you're pretty because your humor is a bit dry," I say, walking out of the kitchen.

"Aside from the fact that you just called me pretty, I take offense to that!" she shouts as if she's actually upset, but I know better. I laugh all the way down the hall until I reach Mila's room and sit in the rocking chair.

I look down at Maize as I feed and rock her. There's a blanket on the arm, and I cover her up as she slowly starts falling asleep. I love the way she clings to me, and even though she was a complete surprise in my life, I can't imagine it without her now. I'll do whatever it takes to keep her safe, and if that means fighting for my rights, I will until the day I die.

CHAPTER TWENTY-FIVE

Mila

Watching John with Maize has to be the cutest thing I've ever seen. The way he plays with her and how she lights up every time he's around has enough power to explode ovaries all across America.

It's been a week since the papers from the Kensingtons were served, and though it's a constant thing on our minds, John and I are doing our best to work through it for now. He apologized for his rude comment and the fact that he wanted to right his wrong before I even had the chance to really get mad at him shows me the kind of person he truly is.

"She's gonna be crawling soon," I tell John as he rolls around the floor with Maize. She's mastered rolling from her back to her stomach and vice versa, so it's only a matter of time before she figures out she can get from A to B being on her hands and knees. "Then the real trouble-escapades start." I slide my body down from the couch to the floor with the two of them.

"I don't know if I'm ready for that," John admits, frowning. "I can hardly

"Me either. Can you believe I've been here for over three months already?"

"It's definitely flying by," he states with a sad look on his face.

"I still remember that towel around your waist when I walked in, holding on by the grace of God because it was nearly painted on your body. I thought for sure it was going to fall at any moment. Especially when you started yelling at me and wailing your arms around like I was a trespassing sorority girl."

John's deep chuckle has me laughing right along with him. It brings me so much comfort and peace, which is what I really need right now. Today is my phone interview with Mr. Demry, and I'm a nervous wreck about it.

"Are you trying to say you weren't hoping it would fall? I saw you checking me out," he taunts.

"Oh, and you weren't checking me out? You were so obvious about it too." I playfully punch his shoulder, and he pretends it's much harder and collapses to the ground by Maize.

"Of course, I was checking you out. Long legs and perky tits. I'd be blind not to notice." He shrugs casually.

"Wow…that's some real Shakespeare poetry right there." I roll my eyes.

John sits up, grabbing my hand and pulling me between his legs. He cups my face and brings our mouths together in a sweet and soft kiss. "You're gonna do great today. Stop worrying. I can see it all over your face." He rests our foreheads together, and I exhale deeply.

"I'm not only nervous about the interview," I admit. "I'm nervous what this will mean. For us. I'm nervous about having to make a decision that'll affect all of us."

John pulls back slightly and grabs a few strands of my hair, tucking them behind my ear before looking into my eyes and smiling. "Make the decision for you," he tells me, confidently. "Maize and I will be here no matter what, rooting for you every step of the way while you make your dreams come true."

"Why are you so sweet to me? You should let people see this side of you more often." I rub my hand over his cheek.

"I have a reputation to protect," he mocks with an over-exaggerated grunt.

"Oh right. God forbid you actually have a soft side." I chuckle, pushing him.

Maize decides to roll her body toward us, attempting some kind of army crawl to get our attention. I pick her up and kiss the top of her head. "You'd miss me right, Maze?"

She squeals and smiles, then slaps her hand in my face. "Ow, right in the eye." I squint, pulling back and blinking repeatedly.

"You okay?" John grabs Maize from my hands and examines my face.

"Yeah, just made my eye blurry for a moment."

"Maize, no hitting," John tells her, but she honestly has no idea what he's saying, and even if she did, she'd do it again just to get a reaction.

"She didn't mean to," I defend. "Not my first time getting smacked in the face by a baby."

"Damn. Well, maybe you should wear goggles," John says, laughing.

"Har, har," I deadpan. "Just wait till she figures out how to kick you in the junk."

"Let's hope not." John cringes. "For both of our sakes." He shrugs, chuckling.

I roll my eyes and smile. "C'mon, Maize. Let's get you ready for Auntie River." I stand and pick her up. River's off today, so she's watching Maize while I have my interview.

"Yeah, I better get going too. Guests get cranky when they don't have their coffee first thing," he groans, shuffling to his feet.

"Yes but those cute old ladies love you," I tease when he wraps his arms around Maize and me.

"I could go without the spankings, though." He wrinkles his nose, and it's the cutest damn thing.

"Tell them hands off, or I'll have to put a sign on your butt that says *Property of Mila.*"

"Hmm...I think you should do that anyway." He leans down and presses a kiss to my lips and then one on Maize's head. "Text me as soon as your interview is done, okay?"

"I will."

Once John leaves, I get Maize dressed and her bag packed. My interview isn't for another couple of hours, but River wanted to take Riley to the zoo today, so she and Mrs. Bishop are picking Maize up before they head out.

"Okay, I think that's everything." I double-check her bag just to make sure, and once I'm positive I didn't forget anything, I text River to let her know we're all set.

They all arrive fifteen minutes later and wish me luck today before heading back out. Riley gives me a hug, and it's another tug at my heart. I love how close I've grown to everyone here.

Just as I'm about to get in the shower, my phone dings with a new text message. I grab it and see it's from my sister, Sarah.

SARAH

> Hey sis! Good luck today! I know you're going to nail it but just wanted to send you some good vibes anyway! Graham and I miss you so much! Can't wait till you're back home again!

Her message makes me smile but sad at the same time. I miss my family so much and being away would be a lot harder if I didn't have Maize and John to keep me distracted.

MILA

> Thank you!! I'm nervous but have been preparing all week for it, so I'm as ready as I'll ever be! I miss y'all so much too!! Give Graham auntie kisses from me!

SARAH

> I will! Text me when you're done, okay? Graham's wearing his Packers jersey today just for you ;) He says it's Auntie M's shirt.

MILA

> Aww! Tell him I appreciate that :) I've Packer'ed up John's house, but he doesn't seem to appreciate the green & gold like the rest of us do!

SARAH

> Better teach him, M ;)

I'm grinning from ear to ear and laugh at her last message. I love my sister so much and am sad I've not been around to chat or see her over the past few months. She doesn't have a lot of support when it comes to

Graham except our parents, and I feel bad I haven't been there to help as much as I had. Though she seems to be doing okay without me there, I can only hope she's not pretending everything is fine on my account.

I decide to send a text to Kat before taking my shower.

MILA

Tell me I'm doing the right thing.

Within seconds, she responds.

KAT

You're doing the right thing for YOU. Mila, you've got this.

I sigh, absorbing her words. Kat and I have been close since we were in diapers, and we always kept in touch while we were apart, and her encouragement means a lot to me.

MILA

Thank you. Love you.

KAT

Love you too. Text me when you're done, okay?

I chuckle to myself. I have a whole laundry list of people to text afterward.

MILA

I will.

I set my phone aside, grab my towels, and head to the bathroom. Maybe a nice hot shower will help ease my nerves, and if that doesn't work, I'll try some breathing exercises or a few yoga poses.

Mr. Demry calls at exactly eleven o'clock on the dot, and my heart goes into overdrive. Inhaling a deep breath, I release it and answer his call with a forced smile. "Fake it till you make it," or so the saying goes.

After we greet each other and he asks how I'm doing, he gets right down to business. He lets me know he has the principal of the Morgan Primary School in the room as well since I'm unable to do a sit-down interview. That news has me sweating and in need of another shower before we even get to the hard stuff.

"Mila, can you tell us the number one thing you learned from your student teaching experience?"

It takes me a moment to think before responding, and within a few seconds, I feel my heartbeat and breathing steady. I loved student teaching so much and took a lot away from it, so it takes me several minutes to fully answer the question. At first, I worry I said too much but relax when I hear them both chuckling.

This goes on for almost two hours before the principal goes into depth about the position and curriculum. I feel pretty confident by the end, which helps settle my nerves. Then Mr. Demry brings up the very topic that makes me want to vomit.

"Do you think you'd be able to return in early July?"

I clear my throat, stalling. "Well, I told my boss I was available through mid-July, and I'd hate to go back on my word since they have to find someone to replace me."

The two men start chatting, but I can't quite hear them because it's muffled as if they stepped away from the phone. I'm sure I've now said the wrong thing, and I've ruined any chance at all for this job.

"Okay sorry about that, Mila. Mid-July would be okay. We'd just need you to sign your contract before August first."

I gulp, my throat feeling like I swallowed several razor blades. "Are you offering me the position?" I ask, shocked.

I hear more chuckling on their end. "Yes. The position is yours if you want it, Mila. Your references and credentials speak for itself, and we know you'd be a positive asset to the Morgan School District."

"Wow…" I'm speechless. I hadn't expected him to offer me the job on the spot. "I'm honored, seriously."

"Well, you were a top candidate from the start."

"Can I take a few days to think it over?" I ask, hoping it doesn't make me sound ungrateful.

"Of course. We'll just need confirmation by the end of the week. That sound good?"

"Yes, thank you so much."

After our goodbyes, I collapse back on my bed and sigh. *Holy shit.*

I don't know what to think. My heart is torn in two as my dream job becomes a reality, and so does the possibility of losing the man I've fallen for.

I lie there for ten minutes, just staring at the ceiling. This is everything I've worked for over the past four years…so why doesn't it feel right?

Reluctantly, I sit up and reach for my phone, so I can text everyone.

MILA

Interview went great! Offered me the job!

I decide to copy and paste it to Kat, Sarah, and my mother. I don't feel like going into detail right now, but that should hold them over for now.

My phone beeps several times, but I don't look at it. I toss it on my bed and decide to go in search of some ice cream.

"Mila," I hear my name being called, and then my shoulder is being shaken. "Baby, wake up." I recognize John's voice and peel my eyes open to his charming face. "Hey, sleepyhead."

"Hey." I smile, blinking. "What time is it?"

"Almost five."

"Oh crap. I must've fallen asleep after my ice cream binge." I look over at the coffee table and see the empty quart of mint chocolate chip I devoured.

"Ice cream coma," John adds. "Well, I'm glad you're okay. I was getting worried when you didn't call or text me back."

"Shit, I'm so sorry." I sit up, straightening my back to the couch. "I left my phone on my bed and then was too sleepy to move."

"Well, that's much better than what was going through my head. I thought you were avoiding me."

"What? No! I was avoiding…reality." I slump my shoulders.

"Why? What happened with the interview?" John asks, sitting next to me on the couch. He shifts, so he's facing me. "Didn't go well?"

I turn so I can look at him and frown. "It went really well."

His eyes light up. "I knew it would. I'm proud of you." He leans in for a kiss, but I pull back. "What?"

"They offered me the job."

"Well, I can't say I'm surprised."

"I am," I say honestly. "That position probably had a hundred applicants."

"Just goes to prove that you're as great as I think you are."

"Stop looking so happy for me," I whine, sticking out my bottom lip. "Or I'll have to demolish the other quart of ice cream in the freezer."

John releases a throaty laugh and pulls me closer to him. "I'm happy for you because you deserve it. I'm sad as fuck it's in Georgia, but this is your dream, baby. You should be excited."

"I know." He's right.

I *should* be.

But all I can feel right now is how I'm about to break my own heart if I leave and walk away from him.

CHAPTER TWENTY-SIX

John

I force out a grin, though I'm finding it hard to do. I'm happy for Mila; however, I can't help but think about what this will mean for us. My heart hurts for her as well because I know it's not an easy decision, and the look on her face tells me as much.

"They told me I could have a few days to think it over," she adds.

"It's settled then. You have to call them back and accept the position tomorrow." I grab her hand and kiss her knuckles. "Just think about your dream job. It's what you've always wanted."

She frowns, squeezing my hand. "But think about what I'll be giving up, John." Mila is stern with her words. "How can I give up one thing to pursue another without feeling like I'm crushing my heart in the process?"

I pull her closer and kiss her forehead. "Listen to me. There's nothing to think about, so you might as well call and accept. I don't want this opportunity to pass you up. Even you said yourself that tons of people applied for the job. What we have right now is new and exciting. I don't want you to look back ten years from now and regret not taking it. You could resent me, our relationship, or no longer be happy once the newness of us wears off. You could think differently, and I don't want you to think *what if* years later," I tell her, hoping she understands where I'm coming from.

She holds my waist tightly and squeezes. "I'd never. I've wasted enough time in my life wondering *what if*. I'm not going to do it anymore."

"I just don't want you to regret anything. If it wasn't for me, you wouldn't even be struggling to make this decision. I can't let you do that. It makes me feel guilty enough that you even have to take a few days to consider it. It should've been an immediate yes."

Mila looks up at me with a somber look before letting go. She tries to walk away, but I grab her hand and pull her back to me. There's no escaping this conversation, though I don't want to be having it either.

"Talk to me, Mila." My voice is calm, and I wish I knew what she was thinking. I already feel tall walls being built around her, which is not what I want.

"I feel like you want me to go like you're already pushing me away." Her voice wavers, and it's a stab straight to my heart.

"No, it's not like that at all. I just don't want to think you're here because you're obligated to be here. I need confirmation that we're together because you actually went for your dream and it didn't work out, rather than you not going at all and never knowing. There are too many what-ifs. And I honestly wouldn't be able to live with myself knowing otherwise. The thought of how your life would've turned out if you'd taken the job would always be in the back of my mind. And I know one day it'd be in yours too. This is your dream, one you've had for years, way longer than you've known me. Go for it, baby. You're gonna do great."

She lets out a long breath. "And so what if I go and I hate it, and I'm miserable every single moment I'm away?"

I give her a side smile. "I'll make a deal with you. Accept the job, go to Georgia, and work for one school year. If it doesn't work out or you truly decide you don't like it, you'll know where I'll be. Come back here, and I'll never mention it again. I'll welcome you home with open arms, then I'll lock you up and never let you leave again." I laugh, but she doesn't think it's funny. She's too caught up in her mind.

I pull her closer. "I'm not going anywhere, Mila. I don't want anyone else. We can put us on hold to give you time to pursue your career and see if being a teacher in Georgia is what you want. You'll gain experience teaching and really know if it's for you or not. If you do that, I won't feel as if I held you back or got in the way of your passion. It won't be a black cloud hanging over our relationship, which will help remove any future regret or resentment. And once you're there, if you love it, I'll completely understand. We can always FaceTime and text. It might be hard to travel with Maize, but we'll figure it out. We can still keep in touch because no number of miles between us will ever affect the way I feel about you. I'd wait a lifetime for you to figure out what you want."

Hesitation is in her eyes as she looks at me. "I want both, and it sucks I have to pick between my heart and my career, but I understand what you're saying. It just hurts a lot. I never expected things to end up like this."

Placing my fingers under her chin, I lean in and kiss her. Sadness fills the room, and the realization that she's leaving already begins to set in. It would be easier to tell her to stay. Being together is what we both want right now, but who's to say it'll be the same six months from now or even a year? As much as I want to wrap my arms around her and keep her here with Maize and me forever, I can't do that.

"Why are you so perfect?" she asks.

"I'm far from perfect. We both know that."

"You're perfect to me." Mila interlocks her fingers with mine, squeezes, then closes her eyes. She swallows hard, and I can tell she's holding back her emotions.

"Sweetheart. Please don't cry," I beg. "This is supposed to be a really happy time for you."

Maize giggles in her Jumperoo, pulling us both away from the moment. When Mila turns and looks back at me, I tilt my head and study her face.

"I'm trying not to. I promise." Her voice cracks.

"It's not forever. It's just a trial run." I smirk, referring to that first day she showed up and said she was the nanny.

She narrows her eyes at me with a scowl, not amused by my joke. "I'm just afraid that if I leave, I won't come back to the same thing we have now. Then I think…what if I love it? What if I hate it? What if I go to Georgia and you meet someone else and what we have right now fades away?" She continues, and I eventually stop her.

"Mila. You're not going to be replaced by anyone. The only way I'll try to move on is if you do. I have the same worries as you, but I also have faith that what we have is real, and if we're meant to be together, we will be together, no matter what. But I can't have you going to Georgia worrying about me. That's why I think it's important for us to pause this. Who knows, you could meet the man of your dreams and decide to pursue that instead."

She slaps my arm and scoffs. "I already have. Truthfully, I worry about you and Maize both." She glances at me before walking to the kitchen to prepare a bottle before we go to my parents' for dinner.

I chuckle. "Mama will make sure we're both well taken care of. So no worries about that. We both know the Bishops come together when someone is in need. Maize and I will be perfectly fine. We'll miss you, but we'll manage."

"Promise me something, John. Promise me if you find someone else, you'll tell me. I don't want to hold you back either."

I look over at her and realize she's serious. "I'm not Jackson. I'm not looking for anyone else. I don't need a replacement for you, but I promise."

She smiles. "Okay." The air stills, and I check Maize's bag to make sure there are extra diapers inside. We'll most likely be at my parents' for a little while since the whole family is showing up for dinner.

"I guess we should get going if we want to make it on time," I tell Mila. She nods, tucks her cell phone in her back pocket, then places Maize in the car seat. Mila lightly taps Maize on her nose and kisses her chubby little cheek. These are the moments I'm going to miss the most when my two girls are together. I already can't help but think about Mila leaving and how different things will be without her in my everyday life.

Mila doesn't say much on the ride over, and I don't push her to speak. Sometimes, it's best to allow people to think, and right now, I know that's what she needs. Leaving means big changes for her, and I know she doesn't want to go because of what she's leaving behind, but I can't be the reason she stays without knowing she won't wake up one day wishing she'd taken the opportunity.

After I park, I walk around and grab Maize's car seat. She's growing like a weed, and I can feel her getting heavier. I glance over at Mila, grab her hand, and squeeze it. She gives me a small smile, and I pull her closer.

"It's not the end of the world. Everything will work out the way it's supposed to," I tell her to ease her mind that I know is racing a hundred miles an hour.

"It better work out the way I want it to."

I chuckle because I know we both want the same thing—each other. I love it when she's fierce.

We walk around the side of the house, and everyone is sitting around in the chairs on the back porch. Mama has the folding tables covered in plastic tablecloths with gallons of sweet tea placed in the middle. As soon as River sees us, her eyes light up. She goes straight to Maize, causing me to stop in my tracks and unbuckle her from her car seat.

"There's my pretty girl," she says, holding Maize up and kissing her cheeks. "This bow is adorable." She winks at Mila, knowing she was behind it.

"Thanks! Courtney sent a truckload of them," Mila explains.

"Sounds about right." River smiles at us both.

Before I even make it up the steps, I can already smell the meat on the pit that Dad's happily tending to. Jackson is arguing with Alex about God knows what, and Evan is busy chatting with Mama and Emily as Riley rambles on about dump trucks. The whole gang's here, and it calms me in a weird way, taking my mind off Mila leaving.

We make our rounds, telling everyone hello, and as soon as Riley sees Mila, he makes a beeline toward her. She picks him up, and she notices a bag of balloons sitting on the table.

"What are these for?" she asks.

"Oh, Riley loves balloons, so I brought a bag in case he gets bored. He likes to kick them around. It's the cutest thing," River explains.

Mila grabs the balloon pump next to the bag before digging through it and picking out two different colored balloons. Riley watches her intently as she pumps air into the first balloon. She starts with a long, green one and we all watch as she twists it around in her hands. Mila then grabs a blue one, pumps it and then wraps it around a part of the green balloon. Mila then digs in her purse until she pulls out a black Sharpie and starts drawing on the balloons. Once she's finished, she turns it around and reveals the dinosaur balloon she created. Riley squeals at the top of his lungs and claps, amused by it when she hands it to him.

"Oh my gosh, Mila! I didn't know you were a balloon pro!" River exclaims.

"It's amazing what you'll learn helping the smaller kids at the church. I can make weenie dogs too." She laughs.

I place my hand on her shoulder completely impressed with her balloon making skills.

"Well, I hope you'll mark down Riley's birthday party on your calendar, because the kids would adore this. If you wouldn't mind, that is." River smiles. "We have a bouncy house and some water games planned, too."

Mila grins real big, and I try to shake my head at River to stop the conversation, but I'm too late.

"I'd love to. When is it?" Mila is so sweet to offer, but she has no idea.

"End of July." I watch River's smile fade as she looks at Mila. She glances over at me, and I give her a somber look. I guess no one else really knew this was a temporary arrangement. It somewhat blindsided me as well.

"What?" River drops her voice and asks, but at this point, the whole family is watching us.

Mila swallows hard, aware that all eyes are on us, and she forces out a smile. "I'm taking a teaching position back in Georgia. More than likely I'll have to leave the middle of July."

Though I can see the disappointment on everyone's faces, they smile and congratulate her.

"Good for you, honey," I hear Mama say. "The kids are gonna love you." That much is true.

Thankfully, Dad announces the food is ready and serves kabobs and hamburgers. We each plop potato salad on our plates along with baked beans as Mama tends to Maize and Elizabeth so we can eat without interruption.

The subject changes to the weather and then to horses, but I can't think about anything except Mila. Once I'm finished eating, I grab her hand from under the table and interlock my fingers with hers. She glances over at me with big blue eyes, and I can't help but kiss her.

Everyone notices.

"Get a room!" Jackson says from the other end of the table, and I don't care, I kiss her again.

At this point, I don't have the time to hide how I feel anymore. Everyone already knows anyway, considering Jackson has the biggest mouth in the South.

CHAPTER TWENTY-SEVEN

Mila

A week has passed since I accepted the job position and announced to everyone I'll be leaving soon. They pretended they weren't shocked, but I knew better. It wasn't an easy thing to say, but hopefully, the more people I tell, the more I'll be excited about it, even though at this point, I doubt it.

I woke up this morning wrapped in John's arms, and it was hard for me to pull away. The only reason I did is because Maize needed to be fed. Even though it's Saturday and I'm technically off the clock, I love our morning routines. Maize looks up at me with bright blue eyes, and though she has no idea what I'm saying, I talk about everything with her—my worries and frustrations—and she hears it all.

John steps in, looking as sexy as sin in a pair of low-hanging jogging pants, and drinks his coffee with a shit-eating grin. He knows I love the way he looks in those, especially when he doesn't wear a shirt. They ride low on his hips, leaving nothing to the imagination. It takes everything I have to focus on the sausage links sizzling in the pan and not on him. This is what I'll miss the most—mornings when we're worry-free and happy.

Once we finish eating breakfast, and I hear every sexual innuendo about sausage, I throw on some comfortable clothes, my favorite Nikes, and put my hair in a high ponytail.

"Are you heading out now to go to Kiera's?" John asks, still shirtless and in his sweats, and I'm tempted as hell to cancel on her house packing party and hop back into bed. I run my fingers up his abs of steel until my hands cup his adorable face.

"Yeah, I should get going before she sends me a million messages asking where I am. I'm not really shocked she's moving in with Trent, especially after their romantic getaway," I explain with a kiss, feeling him harden against my stomach. I giggle, knowing if I give any attention to it, my plans will be canceled.

"Jackson's gonna shit bricks. It might be best not to tell him for a while. I'm sure he'll find out sooner than later though, the way the gossip train runs through town." John laughs.

I nod and try to walk away, but he grabs my arm, pulling me back to his chest. "Be quick. I don't like sharing."

"We already know that." I smile against his lips, getting lost in his touch one last time before I find the willpower to walk away. Each passing day makes the reality of leaving much harder. We're trying to make the best of my time left here and pretend nothing will change, but we both know it will.

"Already miss you," he says, holding Maize in his arms, moving her arm in a waving motion. He knows Maize's a straight shot to my heart.

"Not working," I lie, laughing at their cuteness. I force myself out the door and off the porch before I change my mind and turn around to hibernate inside all day. Kiera better be glad I like her because I'd cancel otherwise. My time left here is too precious, but I don't want to flake on her last minute. Once I'm in the car, I reverse out of the driveway and head down the old country road that leads to her house.

As soon as Kiera's cute log cabin comes into view, I see her standing on the porch with her arms on her hips and a huge smile on her face. Once I get out of the car, she runs over and gives me a big hug.

"I'm so glad you made it," she tells me. "Everyone else basically ditched me. Apparently, Elizabeth isn't feeling well today, so Emily thought it was best to keep her home, which I understand. Kat got called into work, and Trent had a house call, then there's you. Who's here. Thankfully!"

I chuckle, and she glances back at me as I follow her up the steps. "What?"

"I was five seconds from canceling," I admit with a cheesy grin, as we walk inside. "Sorry." I bat my eyes at her, hoping she forgives me.

"I'm sure Mr. Tall, Dark, and Handsome had something to do with it."

All I can do is nod. As soon as I close the door, my mouth falls opened, and I'm amazed at all the beautiful horse photographs Kiera has framed on her wall. There's a western theme going on, which doesn't surprise me, but it looks more like an art studio with hardwood floors and warm lighting. I take my time looking at all the photos until I come across one on her mantel in a small frame. Picking it up, I see it's her and Jackson in their teens. I turn and look at her.

"Look how cute y'all were," I say, glancing down at young Jackson, imagining John.

They're standing next to each other in front of a prize-winning horse. Kiera is looking at the camera smiling, but Jackson is looking at her. There are so many unspoken words in this photo, and I want to ask her every detail, but I don't. Kiera stands next to me and looks at the picture too.

"Those were the good ole days before Jackson's ego became the center of his universe, and he became an asshole." A tinge of sadness sprinkles her tone, and she immediately smiles and returns the photo back on the mantel.

"So I'm all yours. Where do you need me?" I ask, trying to change the subject. Keira leads me into her bedroom, which is a total wreck. Clothes are scattered around, and boxes are stacked against the wall. Her bed isn't made, and there are shoes, belts, and riding accessories everywhere.

"I'm a hot mess," she admits, sitting on the edge of the bed.

"Show me someone who's not." I laugh.

I feel the shift in her mood and study her face as she picks at her nails. "I know moving in with Trent is a big step for our relationship. I'm really excited about it, but I can't help but wonder if I'm doing the right thing."

"Do you love him?"

She looks up at me with twinkling eyes and smiles. I can tell she's thinking about the two of them together. "Absolutely."

"Then there's nothing to worry about. It's change. Change scares everyone. Hell, change scares the ever-living shit out of me, but it's a part of life. We accept it or stay stagnant, and we both know that's no fun." I sit next to her on the bed, thinking about my own issues.

"You're probably right. I just get nervous and second-guess myself too much. I love Trent. He makes me really happy, but…"

"But he's not Jackson," I finally add.

"Damn him," she whispers under her breath. It seems as if I hit the nail on the head.

"By what you've told me, he's had a million chances. If Jackson's too hardheaded and stubborn to admit how he feels, fuck him. I spent four long years of my life in love with a man who didn't love me in the same way. I would've waited an eternity for him to see what he had standing right in front of him. Now after everything that happened, I realize I'm better off. I found the man of my dreams. And it seems to me like you've found yours. Don't you ever let him go," I tell her.

"You sound like Emily." She pats me on my leg and stands. "The truth is, I can't keep waiting around. My ovaries are about ready to shrivel up as it is. I want the big house, white picket fence, and plenty of kids to beat up those Bishop kids. I'm ready to settle down and start a life with someone. Jackson's too busy sticking his dick in anything that has a mouth while Trent is willing to give me the world and has been for the past year. There's just no contest between them."

I think about Jackson and seriously want to slap him upside his head the next time I see him. Kiera is beautiful and in a great relationship, that she now second-guesses because of her feelings for Jackson. I make a mental note to possibly kick him in the balls because he deserves it.

Kiera begins opening her dresser drawer and throwing clothes into boxes as she continues chatting about Trent. "I would've never given him a chance if it wouldn't have been for Alex and River's wedding. I think back to that moment and how special it was to me. We did nothing but talk all night about horses, riding, and our future. Little did I know we'd be spending it together."

I love listening to Kiera swoon over Trent. It makes me think of John, and I realize I need to help speed up this packing process, so I can get back home. "All the clothes in your closet going?"

She nods and hands me a box. I open the door, and the closet is the size of a small bedroom. There are more cowboy boots than high heels and more blue jeans than dresses, but I wouldn't expect anything less. I take the hangers of jeans and fold them in the box, hoping it will save her some time when she unpacks at Trent's.

"How far away does he live?" I ask.

"Just six minutes down the road." She laughs. "I timed it."

"That's not too bad," I tell her, scooting one box of clothes into her bedroom and reaching for another. "What are you doing with your house?"

"I plan to rent it out fully furnished. It'll be a nice side income until I figure out what I want to do with it long-term. Plus, the view in the morning is to die for. Are you looking for a place?" She wiggles her eyebrows, then remembers I'm leaving in six short weeks. "Sorry. I keep forgetting."

"I wish I could. Though I doubt John would allow it anyway." I give her a small smile. "It's the hardest thing I've ever had to do in my life."

Kiera stops and looks at me with the most serious look on her face. "It's only temporary. I get what John is doing, and I can respect a man who wants his woman happy even though she's not happy about it. But I'm willing to bet money you'll be back. I'm not buying this whole you're gonna go to Georgia and fall in love with some bratty little kids at a school. There are bratty kids everywhere." She winks.

I burst into laughter. "I promised John a school year." I groan. "Nine long months."

"Whatever you say!" She lifts her hands up in the air but gives me a side eye. We continue packing until all her clothes and shoes are neatly stacked in boxes. She removes pictures from the wall and pulls her blankets and sheets from the bed. I follow her to the laundry room as she stuffs it all in the washing machine.

"I'll just need to take down all the big framed photos around the house, finish packing the kitchen, grab my books, empty the bathroom, then the rest is basically staying. This might be the easiest move I've ever had."

"Do you want me to help with the bathroom or kitchen?" I ask.

"Nah. Trent's going to come over later and help me pack some boxes, but it will probably take a week for me to finish. Since I'm already basically living with him, it's not too big of a deal. I'm just ready to get this place rented. The pictures will probably be the last thing I worry about. They're photos of all the horses I've trained."

My eyes go wide, and I'm impressed. "Really?"

"Yep. It's always hard letting go after we spend so much time together, so I like to take photos of them, have them professionally developed and framed. That way, they'll always be with me."

"That's seriously the sweetest thing I've ever heard," I say, covering my hand over my heart.

She pulls her out her cell phone and snaps a photo of me.

"You're so damn cheesy," I tell her, and she chuckles. "Well, I guess I'm gonna get going then. If you decide you need more help, let me know."

Kiera gives me a big hug and thanks me. "I'm gonna miss you, Mila."

"Stop. You even you said it yourself—I'll be back."

She walks me outside and watches me drive away. Though she's much older, Kiera is that girlfriend I always wished I had in college. On the way home, I'm lost in my thoughts. I think about Kiera and Trent, and John and Maize, and going back to Georgia. I think about my parents and brother and sisters, and Gigi. Before I realize it, I'm pulling into John's driveway. Though it's hotter than hell, I let out a sigh, feeling grateful to be here.

Once I'm out of the car and walking toward the house, I see Jackson standing by the barn complaining about someone on his cell phone. I'm tempted to give him his ball kicking right now, but considering he seems like he's in a bad mood, I save it for another time and walk up the porch.

As soon as I open the front door, I see Maize in her Jumperoo and John lying on the couch watching TV with his legs propped up. She notices me and smiles bigger. When John hears my voice, he waves me over. I go to him, and he pulls me down on top of his chest and kisses me.

"Finally," he whispers across my lips. "That took way too long."

Just as he deepens the kiss, Maize begins to cry. We laugh against each other's lips.

"I'm pretty sure she has an internal anti-kissing clock or something." John gives me another quick peck. "I got it," he tells me.

"It's okay." I sit up with a laugh, go to her, and pull her into my arms.

"You're getting heavy, little girl," I say softly. She places her head against my shoulder, and my heart flutters. A piece of me can't help but wonder what she'll think when I'm gone or how confused she'll be that I'm no longer here. It makes me feel awful knowing her mother only got nine weeks with her, and I've already had months with her.

What precious moments will I miss?

Will she forget me?

CHAPTER TWENTY-EIGHT

John

The weeks and days have passed quicker than I could've ever imagined. For once, I want time to slow down. I want Mila to stay longer and my baby girl to quit growing. I want to bottle it all up and keep us here like this forever, but considering it's close to the end of June now, the clock feels like it's ticking much faster than before.

Each morning, we have breakfast and coffee, and every day, we do a quick lunch. When I'm able to, I sneak home just to see them throughout my shifts. If I could take off the next three weeks and enjoy every moment with Mila, I would. However, summer is here, and the B&B is the busiest it's ever been, which is why taking off for mediation today frustrates the ever-living fuck outta me.

Before I'm up, breakfast is already made. Mila is acting extra sweet this morning, and I appreciate her so damn much. I quickly eat then throw on the suit and tie I have in the back of my closet for Easter Sunday and

Christmas. When I walk out, Mila gives me a popped eyebrow and sucks on her lower lip.

"If I didn't have somewhere to be…" I go to her, kissing her neck, running my lips across the softness of her skin.

"What time are you meeting the lawyer?"

"I have about two hours. He wants to go over a few things before we enter the mediation room." Though it's not necessary to have him present during mediation, I refuse to be around the Kensingtons without a witness, considering they're so vile.

Just as I'm heading out the door, Mila grabs my hand and pulls me back to kiss me. "Good luck, sexy. You're gonna do great. Don't be nervous. Remember, you've got the final say in everything, so don't let them intimidate you."

My mouth paints across hers. I'm so thankful she's my cheerleader and number one supporter. Today I really need that. "I might ask Mama to watch Maize tonight," I tell her with a grin, and she knows exactly what I'm insinuating.

"You're keeping that suit on then because I want the pleasure of taking it off." She gives me a smack on the lips, then a slap on the ass before I leave. Only Mila knows how to brighten up my sour mood.

The hour drive goes by fast, but I'm still nervous about this whole ordeal. Mama helped find the perfect lawyer to represent the case who laughed at the legal paperwork and threats. I know the Kensingtons don't have a leg to stand on, but mediation is the first step for most custody battles and will hopefully show them what rights they don't have. I was told through the grapevine they thought I'd cave and wouldn't fight back, knowing I didn't have lined pockets, but what they forgot was my parents do. Unlike them, my parents always have my back, and I wouldn't be able to do this without them. However, I'd fight to the death for my baby girl no matter what. No one can put a price tag on my child. The thought angers me all over again. I try to take in a few deep breaths and calm down as I'm pulling into the parking lot of the office space that was rented for the meeting.

My lawyer, Jason Morris, is standing on the sidewalk chatting with an older woman. If I didn't know better, I'd say he was flirting. I park and realize he's wearing snakeskin boots with his suit, and it actually looks nice with his solid black cowboy hat. He looks like a country Colonel Sanders all the way down to the white goatee and black-framed glasses. Once he lays eyes on me, he lifts his hand and waves me over.

"Ready for this, son?" he asks, patting me on the shoulder when I'm close. "Not a damn thing to worry about. But we do have some stuff to go over."

We walk inside and head toward the conference room that was booked. The mediator hasn't arrived yet, so we'll have plenty of time. I enter the large room, and we both sit at the table. Mr. Morris pulls out a stack of documents, all correspondence between the Kensingtons' lawyers and him.

"Now this is what we call legal bullshit." He slaps the papers down on the table, and I know exactly why Mama wanted me to hire him. Though we've only met a few times, he carries himself as if he takes no crap from anyone. The man should be a judge.

"So give me a rundown of what happens."

"The mediator will enter and introduce himself. You'll both get the opportunity to discuss your problem with zero interruptions. Then the mediator can either go between the two of you to try to work out the problem or speak while you're all in the room. There may be a negotiation, which is written down, and then we all go on our merry way. If there's not an agreement, basically you'll be advised on your rights. It will be a quick process, considering they have zero legal rights. It's a scare tactic meeting, which I don't take kindly to," he adds.

I continue asking questions until I feel at ease with the process. Soon, the mediator arrives and so do the Kensingtons with their lawyer. The room goes frigid, and my body tenses. I can't even look in their direction without feeling a rush of anger.

The mediator sits, introducing herself. "My name is Erin, and I'll be mediating today so that maybe we can all be on common ground and find a compromise." She continues with the rules, and when I finally glance over at the Kensingtons, I can tell they're more nervous than I am. Probably because I know my rights, and they have none.

The Kensingtons open with their introduction along with their concerns. When they state they believe I'm an unfit father for their grandchild, I'm about two seconds from interrupting them. My lawyer looks over at me, making sure I don't lose my cool, which somehow, I'm able to do. I swallow hard when they mention my finances and why they feel they'd be better guardians to raise their deceased daughter's child. By the time I'm able to speak, I'm so furious that I have to take a minute to get my words together.

"First, I'm a great father to my daughter. I've given her everything she needs—food, clothes, shelter, and most importantly, love. She has care around the clock and someone to take care of her while I'm working. I work twenty feet away if something were to happen. My issue is the Kensingtons have zero rights of my daughter. They've offered money in exchange for her. They've trespassed on my property, threatened me, and used scare tactics. My name is on the birth certificate, and a quick paternity test would prove she's mine, though she looks just like a Bishop. Since Maize's mother is no longer here, and directly warned me about them, I can only uphold her last wishes. I don't appreciate their insults when they don't get their way. I have the right to decide who my daughter sees until she's eighteen years old, and the way it stands now, she will not be around them. It's important for me to teach her how to treat other people and how to be compassionate. The Kensingtons show none of the traits I want my daughter to learn, so as it stands, I have nothing else to say regarding this matter."

The mediator looks back and forth between us, and I know she has to stay neutral, but I can tell she's not buying the Kensingtons' story.

Though my lawyer is allowed to confer, Erin was very clear about me speaking for myself. Regardless, Mr. Morris speaks up. "Let me also add, the law doesn't grant grandparents any sort of guardianship without proof of Mr. Bishop being an unfit parent, which he isn't. He doesn't have a criminal record and has never been in trouble with the law. So if there's nothin' else to discuss, my client and I will be on our way."

The Kensingtons shift in their seat as they whisper back and forth to their lawyer, who I assume is agreeing with mine. "We'd like a moment, please," they say and walk out of the room. They are gone for at least thirty minutes, seeking legal advice, I'm sure, before they return. An hour has already passed, and nothing has really been resolved.

Over the next hour, Erin asks us each open-ended questions so she fully understands what the situation is and our thoughts.

"We didn't know she had a baby until we hired a private investigator to find out more about her life. Admittedly, we weren't the best parents to Bailey. We held her back a lot of the time, and the only piece of her left is

Maize. Because of this, we feel we need to at least try to be in our only granddaughter's life. We acted out of disparity because we've not fully been able to grieve the loss of our daughter. There's a lot of guilt for us because we didn't even know she was sick. We weren't there for her when she needed us the most because she'd written us out of her life when she turned eighteen. So to find out she passed away, alone, with cancer destroyed us. To find out she had a baby before she passed gave us some sort of hope to stay connected to her. There are so many things we wished we could change but can't because she's no longer with us. It's not an excuse to treat you the way we did. We're sorry, John, and we hope one day you'll be able to forgive us because our daughter never did, and that's something we'll have to live with for the rest of our lives."

For the first time since meeting them, those words were ones I understood. They actually seem like genuine human beings, and I can't help but feel something toward them.

Erin looks at me. "Is there anything you'd like to add?"

I glance over at my lawyer, and he tilts his head, giving me the final decision. I look at the Kensingtons, making eye contact with them, and I try to believe they aren't as bad as the first impression they gave me. Though I felt as if their apology was sincere, it was still a mistake to come at me the way they did. Their threats have hung over me and my family for the past two months. I've had to speak with my lawyer on several separate occasions, wasting the precious moments I have left with Mila, and they've caused me to look over my shoulder more times than not.

With all that being said, Mama always taught us not to hold a grudge. She's all about forgiveness and giving second chances, though I find it really hard to do at times. I'm not one to punish my daughter because of the way they acted, and I feel that they deserve to be excluded from her life. I'm an understanding man, and their words about losing their only daughter and not having the time to fix their mistakes spoke to me. Knowing how much I love Maize, I couldn't imagine losing her and can't begin to put myself in their situation. Because Bailey warned me about them, I'm hesitant to allow them in her life, but I don't think it's fair to Maize until she's old enough to decide. When she gets older, the questions will come about her mother, about her mother's parents, and I don't think I'd have the heart to tell her I refused to allow them in her life. She'd hate me for it, and I couldn't live with that. They could give her way more insight on Bailey than I ever could, and I can only imagine Maize will want to know as much as possible. So many thoughts stream through my mind, and the only thing that takes me back to the moment is my lawyer clearing his throat.

"I'll consider allowing you to see her under my terms, which is supervised visitation. To be honest, I don't trust either of you as far as I can throw you, not after you put a price on my daughter's life. But she has the right to get to know you and decide if she wants you in her life, and I'll allow that—for now, at least. There will be a day when she'll want to know things about Bailey, things I don't know." I pause and look at them. "I don't owe either of you anything, and the only reason I'm doing this is because my parents taught me empathy and how to put myself in other people's shoes. But there is one condition." I swallow hard as they keep their eyes focused on me. "I want to know where Bailey is buried."

Mrs. Kensington has tears streaming down her face while Mr. Kensington consoles her. She eventually wipes them away and gives me a small smile. "We will. Thank you for this. Thank you so much."

Erin's smiling big as she writes down everything on a piece of paper. By the time I look up at the clock, we've been here close to three hours. I'm emotionally and mentally exhausted, and I can't wait to breathe in some fresh air.

Before we're dismissed, the Kensingtons tell me where Bailey is buried and draw a map on a piece of paper. We exchange phone numbers, and the mediator gives a closing statement and finishes writing up our agreement. Since our attorneys are present, we're encouraged to sign the terms, which we all do. I make it clear that they will see Maize on my terms that work with my schedule, and they wholeheartedly agree.

Once the meeting is over, I can't help but think how much easier this would've all been if they would've just asked to be in Maize's life from the beginning. All of this has been a huge waste, but I'm glad it's over for now. After the Kensingtons leave, I sit with my lawyer for a few more minutes, and he explains my rights again. I agree to meet with him next week to wrap up everything and give him a firm handshake before I leave.

I walk across the parking lot and look up at the blue skies. Relief washes over me, and I hope that this is really over without anymore meaningless threats. Maybe we'll all be able to move on and try to heal for Maize's sake. I climb into the truck and look down at the piece of paper that has the name of the cemetery written on it. Since I'm close, I decide to drive over there, though I'm not sure if I'm emotionally ready.

Our relationship started and ended so quickly. We fell too fast, and it scared the shit out of us both. She made it very clear what we had was nothing more than fun, though I was developing feelings for her that were stronger than I was used to having. We planned to meet up one day for horseback riding lessons, and she didn't show. I texted and called her, but she never responded. I left messages, and after a while, I just asked her to send me a quick text to let me know she was okay. She never did that either.

The way things ultimately ended broke my heart. But in a weird way, I understood. I thought maybe she was getting too attached as well and found it better to break it off before we became serious, which is something she was very adamant about not happening. Thinking back now, it's probably because she found out she was pregnant, but I wish she would've told me, so I could've been there for her through everything. I will never fully understand her reasons for staying away, which makes it hard not to resent her for that.

I pull into the cemetery and can't find the strength to drive to her resting place. I sit in the truck and look around at the headstones, close my eyes, and replay the few memories I have of us together. It's been over a year already, but it feels like centuries have passed since then. I'm not the same man I was. I've changed for the better, and it's all because of Maize, my little saving grace.

Regret for not fighting for Bailey, for not telling her how I really felt washes over me. It's something I'll have to live with for the rest of my life, but it's a mistake I won't make twice. Putting the truck in drive, I turn around and make my way home. There are things I need to work out with myself before I can visit her grave.

On the way back to Eldorado, my mood is somber, and I feel numb. Meeting with the Kensingtons took everything out of me, but I know when I walk inside the house, I need to leave all that at the door. When I finally arrive home, I sit in the driveway until my vision blurs, and I gain my composure. I see Jackson at the barn and wave at him before walking through the door.

Mila is asleep on the couch with Maize lying on her chest. They're both conked out, and I stand there for a moment admiring how peaceful they look. My two angels. As if she could feel me staring, Mila's eyes flutter open, and she smiles. Having her look at me like I'm her everything will never get old. I carefully lift Maize off her chest and hold her in my arms while she stays asleep.

"How'd things go?" Mila whispers, searching my face.

"It's over, I think. We found common ground. They just want to be in Maize's life, and as much as I wanted to say no, I decided to allow it. Supervised only and I set the dates and times."

"Yeah? You're a saint because I don't know if I could've done that."

I explain to her everything they said about Bailey and grieving, and she almost tears up. Mila leans over and kisses me so softly that I nearly float away.

"She can probably be put down for a nap," Mila tells me, looking down at a snoring Maize.

"I got it." I smile and stand and carry Maize to her crib. On the way to my room, I glance inside Mila's room and see most of the Packer stuff has been removed from the wall and is sitting in a box along with a few suitcases of clothes. I feel a hand on my back, and I turn around and see Mila who doesn't look very happy about it either.

"I had to keep busy, and since I only have a week left, I thought I might as well start packing."

I nod, swallowing down my emotions. Once Maize's situated, I stand in my room and run my fingers through my hair before going to Mila.

She's standing at the door of her room, looking around at everything, and I come up from behind her and pull her in my arms. I have to taste her, be with her, feel her near me. I have to enjoy the last seven days like it may be the last because it very well could be.

CHAPTER TWENTY-NINE

Mila

My room is completely empty of everything I brought here with me. The closet and dresser are empty, the bed's been stripped and replaced with clean sheets, my posters are gone, and it no longer feels like mine.

I hate it.

Yet I know I have to do this. I promised John I wouldn't pass up the opportunity even if I'm struggling with that decision. Morgan Primary School is where all the Carmichael kids went, and it's a small school, so everyone knows everyone. I've wanted to teach in my hometown's school district for as long as I can remember, and if I don't take it, I know John would constantly be worried I regretted that decision.

However, I haven't even left yet, and I'm already regretting having to leave him and Maize. I can't imagine being gone the whole school year even if that's what I told John. I already know that when I'm back in Georgia, half

I can't deny that I'm excited to see my family and give Graham six months' worth of auntie kisses. Sarah's been sending me pictures of him, and he's grown so much. She even started seeing someone a few weeks ago, so I hope to meet him soon too.

All of that aside, I'm dreading the fact that Gigi and Kat will be driving me to the airport tomorrow morning. This is my last night here for who knows how long, and I'm just not ready.

Pretty sure I'll never be ready.

"All the boxes in the truck?" Mrs. Bishop asks as I stare into my bedroom for the last night.

"Yes, Mama," John answers for me. During my time here, I accumulated so much stuff and most wouldn't fit in my suitcase, so I packed a few boxes to ship home instead. Since Mrs. Bishop is taking Maize for the night, she's offered to take them down to the post office for me.

"Everything in the diaper bag that I need?"

"Should be," I answer. "I double-checked it."

"Perfect." She rests a hand on my cheek, and I can tell she's getting emotional too. "You have a safe flight back, ya hear?"

I force out a half smile and nod, holding back the tears that are threatening to release. Mrs. Bishop pulls me in for a hug and squeezes me. I hold her just as tight because I'm going to miss her just as much.

"You call me if you need anything, dear. Anything, okay?" she whispers in my ear, and I nod in agreement.

"I will."

She steps back before leaning in to kiss my cheek. "Bye, honey. We're gonna miss you."

"I'll miss you too."

John walks over with Maize on his hip, and I know he's trying to hold it together just as much. "She's ready," he announces.

Before he hands her over to Mrs. Bishop, I hold my arms out. "Wait. Let me say goodbye to her."

John and I are spending our last night together alone, but I'm going to miss Maize so much. It's close to her bedtime anyway, but at least the three of us spent all day together. John had his assistant take over the B&B the past couple of days, so we didn't waste a minute apart.

I take Maize into my arms and hold her against my chest as I inhale her fresh baby scent. I'd been so good at controlling my emotions up to this point, but the moment Maize looks up at me, the tears pour out. I've grown so attached to her, it feels like I'm leaving my own child.

"I can't do this," I mutter, squeezing my eyes shut. "She's going to be so confused why I left." It's not fair.

"We'll FaceTime every night," John promises. "She'll still see you."

"It won't be the same," I argue. "I'm going to miss her so much."

I kiss her cheeks and hug her tightly, not wanting to let go. She's been on such a great schedule lately, only waking up once during the night. She takes regular naps and has set eating times. Now she has to get to know a brand-new sitter all over again.

"I love you, Maze. Don't forget me, okay?" I kiss her head before handing her off to Mrs. Bishop.

"She won't, honey," Mrs. Bishop promises.

John walks them both out and returns moments later.

"C'mon," he says, holding his hand out for me to take. "Let's take a shower."

I take his hand in mine, and when we step into the bathroom, he turns and wipes the tears away. Cupping my face, he presses a soft kiss to each cheek and then looks at me so damn sweetly it makes me tear up all over again.

"I should've told you this a long time ago, but I can't let you leave without saying it."

Narrowing my eyes, I ask, "What is it?"

The corner of his lips tilts up in a warm smile, and it's a particular look he's reserved only for me. "I've fallen madly and deeply in love with you, Mila Carmichael. I love you so damn much that it's hard to find words that will give justice to the way I feel. Every day we've spent together will forever be a memory I'll hold on to for the rest of my life. No amount of time or distance will take that away."

"I hate you so much right now for telling me that," I say as the tears continue falling down my cheeks. I consider myself pretty emotionally stable when it comes to handling things that are difficult, but this is completely breaking me. Taking my face in his hands, John wraps his arms around me and holds me against his chest. I can feel his heart beating and think how much I'm going to miss it.

"Let's take a hot shower, baby. I want to make love to you all night long." John pulls back and tugs at my shirt. I raise my arms and let him take it off. Next, he undoes my shorts and slips them down with my panties. Unhooking my bra last, I slide out of it and stand in front of him completely naked.

Grabbing his shirt from behind his neck, he rips it off. I watch as he continues stripping and try to memorize every inch of his gorgeous body. But it's his heart and soul I admire most.

Neither of us speaks while we wait for the water to warm. Once it's ready, he grabs my hand and leads us inside the shower. The stream cascades over us as our bodies mold together in a desperate kiss. With his hands in my hair and on my body, I wrap my arms around his waist, holding him as close to me as I possibly can.

John pushes me against the shower wall, so the water hits his back. His lips on mine are hot and greedy, and I welcome them. After a moment, I feel tears against my cheeks, and when I open my eyes, I see he's crying. I hate to see how deeply this is hurting him and nothing I say will mend either of our broken hearts.

Bringing my hands up, I cup his face and bring his mouth back to mine. "I love you, John," I say against his lips. "I love you so much it hurts."

His mouth crashes against mine, and we both know nothing else needs to be said. Our tongues dance together, and my body melts against him. John grabs my leg and wraps it around his waist, and I feel how hard he is against my stomach. In one swift motion, he slides inside me and makes love to me, expressing everything we're both feeling. His lips on my neck and jaw have me begging him for more. The way he makes me feel when he's inside me is indescribable. It overtakes all of my senses and gives me a sense of peace all at once. Our eyes lock as he continues thrusting in and out. We're both panting loudly as the love between us pours out with every movement.

My body tightens, ready to collapse as he releases himself inside me. We're both moaning against each other as he presses his lips back to mine, letting our bodies stay connected as long as possible.

"I'll never resent falling in love with you but letting you go is something

I'll always regret even if it's the right thing to do," John whispers, and I know he's falling apart right along with me.

"Leaving you and Maize is the hardest decision I'll ever have to make, and I already regret it," I admit, not even bothering to hold back the tears.

"You're making the right choice, Mila," he tries to tell me with a strong voice, but I hear it cracking underneath. "Even if it's hard to realize it right now."

John pulls me to him and kisses me slowly. He washes my body and hair for me, neither of us speaking or having to. We've said everything we need to say and know how we feel about each other.

I never expected to fall in love when I came here. Never expected John, Maize, or his entire family to mean so much to me. Life is filled with so many unexpected obstacles that I hadn't even realized coming here would change everything. Now, I have to leave it all behind.

After John thoroughly cleans every inch of my body, I return the favor and take my time memorizing him. I trace my finger along his tattoos and kiss him with a fervor I've never felt before. Once we're clean, he shuts off the water and wraps a towel around me. He dries me first and then himself. I watch him intently, smiling, and not wanting to forget a single second of our time together.

"I got you something," he tells me as we walk to his bedroom.

"What? You did?" I sit on the bed and wait for him to dig something out of his dresser.

"It's not much, but I wanted you to have it."

When he turns around, I see a picture frame with a big green G on the top, and the bottom has the words "The family that cheers together stays together" with a photo the three of us took one day. Maize's in her Packer onesies, and I'm in my Rodgers jersey, and we're both smiling wide at the camera. I made John take the selfie with us even though he was pouting about our shirts. However, in this shot, he's the only one not looking at the camera. Instead, he's looking at me.

"I can't believe you did this." I grab it from him, half-laughing, half-sobbing. My hand covers my mouth as I try to keep it together. "I love this picture so much."

"You'll always be our family, even if you brainwashed my daughter into wearing green and gold." He smirks.

"I love it." I pull him down so I can kiss his lips. "Thank you."

"It's not much, but I wanted you to have a piece of us with you."

"No." I blink, wiping my eyes for the hundredth time tonight. "It's *everything*."

John and I spend the rest of the night saying goodbye without speaking. He makes love to me over and over, and it still doesn't feel like enough. I want to crawl inside his soul and stay there forever. I'm barely able to sleep, my mind wandering way too much, and the second my alarm goes off, I know our time is almost over.

"Morning, beautiful," John whispers in my ear when I crawl on top of him and rest my body on his chest. I feel his hand on my head, brushing his fingers through my hair. "Sleep okay?"

"Shut up," I say with a teasing groan.

His body shakes underneath me as he chuckles. "Is that a no on breakfast too?"

Holding him tighter, I inhale and sigh. "You always smell so good. Have I ever told you that?"

John rolls us over so we're side by side. He brushes the hair out of my face and places his fingers under my chin, tilting my head up to look at him. "I thought I caught you smelling me a few times." He flashes a cocky grin.

"When you weren't home, I'd lie in your bed and smell your pillows."

"How weird. I did the same thing to your pillows when you weren't around."

"You're such a smartass." I laugh but then stick out my lower lip and pout. "I hate this."

"I know, baby." He brings our lips together in a soft kiss. "We're gonna figure it out, okay? I promise."

The next hour goes by too fast. We both change, and I pack up the last of my things after getting ready. Kat already texted me saying they'd be here in five minutes. I start panicking because it doesn't feel like there were enough hours in a day to tell John everything I wanted to say.

"You don't have to say anything, sweetheart," he tells me when he sees I'm struggling to speak. "I already know what's in your heart, and I hope you know what's in mine. My feelings for you will never, *ever* change, so don't you worry about that. I'll be here, waiting, for as long as you need."

Just then, I hear a car pulling up, and I know it's my ride. My eyes are burning, and I'm surprised I have any more tears left. "I love you," I tell him.

"I love you, Mila. Thank you."

I furrow my brows and release a choked laugh. "For what?"

He holds my face in his hands and kisses me again. "For *everything*."

CHAPTER THIRTY

John

"Oh my God! Maize!" I shout, racing from the hallway to the living room and tripping over a pair of shoes and stubbing my toe against the side table. "Ow, shit—er—crap!"

I hop on one foot as I maneuver to where Maize's speed crawling from one side of the room to the other.

"Look at you!" I smile, watching how fast her little legs are moving. She'd been doing some weird army crawl the past couple of weeks, but now she's on a full mission to get from point A to point B in record speed. "Daddy's gonna have to really start baby proofing now."

She looks up at me and giggles. Maize crawls over to me, and I pick her up, smooching her on the cheek. "You're getting too big, baby girl." I can't believe she's nine months old already.

And I can't believe Mila wasn't here to see this.

The thought saddens me, and I've seen the way it's affected Maize since Mila's been gone. It's been a month since she left, and it still doesn't feel real. We FaceTimed a lot at first, so Maize could hear Mila's voice and see her, but then the daily calls became every other day and then every few days as Mila's workload kept her busy. I hate the thought of how we've drifted apart already, but I'm also so proud of her.

Right after Mila flew back to Georgia, she signed all her paperwork and started getting her classroom ready. She gave me a tour once she finished and seeing the way her face lit up with excitement told me we did the right thing.

Even though it hurt like a motherfucker.

I set Maize back down on the floor and reach for my phone in my back pocket.

JOHN

You'll never guess what Maize just did!

I see it's after five, so I know I won't be bothering her in the middle of teaching.

MILA

What?!

JOHN

She just crawled across the living room floor like a speed demon! I'm gonna have to get some baby gates now.

MILA

Oh my God, no way!! Yeah, you'll definitely need to get some gates, so she stays out of the kitchen and bathroom. Next up, she'll be walking and really getting into everything.

JOHN

Can you FaceTime while Maize's awake so you can see?

MILA

I wish I could! :(I have a dinner meeting with one of the other new teachers in five minutes.

JOHN

Oh okay. Maybe tomorrow then.

MILA

I'll text you later. Love you!

JOHN

Love you too, baby.

Slipping my phone back into my pocket, I can't help feeling a wave of sadness creep up as the realization of how short our conversations have been getting hits me. I know she's busy and doing exactly what I told her to do, but I miss her like crazy every single day. Her room being bare was taunting me, so I started converting it into a room for Maize. I took the bed out and painted the walls a rosy pink color and then put her crib and dresser in it along with all her other stuff. It looks pretty good, considering I did it myself, but ironically, I miss seeing Mila's Packers posters on the wall.

Now that Mrs. Pearson, a woman from church, is watching Maize while I'm at work, I don't stop in as often. I still like popping in to give Maize kisses but the urge to every few hours vanished when Mila left. However, I'm grateful Mrs. Pearson takes Maize out for walks and will occasionally stop in at the B&B to visit.

Maize's the only reason I'm holding it together as it is. "It'll get easier," Mama told me the other day when she noticed my sour mood.

"I don't want it to get easier. That means the hope for us to work will cease to exist," I replied, wondering if that's exactly what will eventually happen. I knew her leaving wouldn't be easy, but it's been so much harder than I anticipated.

"Alright, Maze. Let's go to Grandma's," I tell her after making sure her diaper bag is packed. "Hopefully, she has some food." I chuckle, though it's a sad plea for help. Mila always made us dinner when it wasn't even required, but I'd be lying if I said I wasn't used to it. I loved our meals together even when we'd just eat in silence. It felt real to me even in those early days she was here.

Once Maize's in her car seat, I jump in the truck and drive the few minutes to my parents' house. I see Jackson's truck is here, which probably means Alex is as well.

I take her and walk us inside and immediately hear rowdy laughter. Walking through the kitchen, I find Mama with Emily, Elizabeth, River, and Riley. They immediately grab Maize out of my hands and direct me to the living room where Dad, Jackson, Alex, and Evan are talking loudly and laughing at something.

"What the hell? My invitation get lost in the mail or something?" I stand with my hands on my hips, pretending I'm butt hurt about being left out of whatever the hell this is.

"I texted you an hour ago, what are you talkin' about?" Jackson asks.

I furrow my brows, knowing I damn well didn't get one from him. "Okay, whatever. What are y'all doing anyway?"

"Celebrating Dad's birthday," Evan tells me with a popped eyebrow.

"Wait, what? It's not the—" I pause, realizing it's August 15th. "Oh shit." I brush a hand through my hair and feel terrible that I forgot. "I'm sorry, Dad. I've—"

Dad steps up in front of me and places his hands on my shoulders. "I know, son. Don't worry about it." He winks with a grin. "If it wasn't for your mother who insisted on this whole charade, I would've been happy to skip it."

"But then I wouldn't have had an excuse to get all my boys and grandbabies here," Mama interrupts, walking in with Maize on one hip and Riley on the other. "Dinner is ready."

"Wait," I say, walking over and grabbing Maize out of her grip. "We have something to show y'all." I smile as I put Maize on the floor and encourage her to come to me when I walk to the other side of the room. She giggles and gladly crawls to me, and when I look up, everyone is smiling and cheering for her. I can't help but smile, too, but not for the same reason. The fact that I have my entire family here, giving so much love and praise to my baby girl, has me feeling so damn proud. I may not be able to give Maize a glamorous lifestyle, but I can certainly make sure she's surrounded by all the love imaginable.

"Oh my goodness!" Mama beams as I pick Maize up and stand. "When did this happen?"

"Just tonight," I reply.

"Soon, she'll be walking," River says with a wide smile. "Gonna have your hands really full then."

"They're full enough." I groan. "I had to adjust her mattress already to go as low as possible so she stops trying to climb out."

"Just wait till she can," Alex adds, slapping a hand on my shoulder.

"Then she'll suddenly become a ninja, trying to escape in the middle of the night."

"Okay stop, you're scaring him." Mama comes to my defense even though she's laughing at my expense, too.

"Y'all suck," I tease.

I place Maize in one of the high chairs and sit next to her while everyone finds their seats. Just as Mama announces to hold hands for grace, the front door swings open.

"Knock, knock," Kiera's voice echoes into the living room, and as soon as she comes into view with Trent attached to her hand, Jackson releases a displeased groan. "Happy Birthday, Mr. B!" She comes behind Dad's chair and wraps her arms around him. "What are you now? Thirty?"

"You know it." He winks, patting her hand that's resting on his shoulder.

"For the twentieth year in a row!" Alex blurts out, and everyone laughs.

"Don't listen to them," Kiera comforts him. "It's not about the number; it's how young you feel anyway." She flashes him a wink and gives him a kiss on the cheek.

"Stay for dinner," Mama insists, and with Jackson sitting next to me, I see his back straighten as he tenses. He hates Trent for the sole reason he's with Kiera.

"Oh no, I couldn't intrude. I just wanted to stop in quick and drop off Mr. B's birthday card." She sets it down in front of him and encourages him to open it.

After Dad rips it open, he holds up a handful of scratch-offs. "Now, if any of those are big money winners, I expect half," Kiera teases.

"You got it, sweetie."

The fact that Dad loves Kiera like a daughter irritates Jackson even more. She's more a Bishop than any other girl in our family, and it's been that way for years.

"Okay, well I'll let y'all get back to dinner." She starts to walk away then pauses. "Oh, John." She looks at me. "Tell Mila to call me when she gets a chance!"

My face hardens at the mention of her name and my jaw clenches with frustration. "Sure."

"Okay, thanks!" She waves at everyone before leading Trent out the door.

Once Mama says grace, we all start diving in. I put small peas and carrots on Maize's plate and watching her attempt to put them on her tiny spoon makes everyone laugh. Jackson loudly scratches his chair against the floor as he stands up and walks toward the kitchen. The room goes silent as we all watch and wait until he returns with a bottle of whiskey.

"What are you doing with that?" Mama asks in a stern tone.

"I'm gonna pour me a glass or two," Jackson states without looking up. "Want one?"

"No."

The room goes eerily quiet as we continue eating, knowing damn well why Jackson's drinking. He hands the bottle over to Dad when he motions for it, and soon it's being passed around like a Christmas ham.

"If I wasn't still breastfeeding, I'd be all over that," Emily says with a groan. "Or wine. Oh man, how I miss wine."

A round of chuckles echoes, and when she passes the bottle to River, she shakes her head.

"How about you, John?" Emily asks, arching a brow as if she knows I could use a drink.

"No thanks," I say.

"Why? You breastfeeding too?" Jackson snorts, laughing.

My shoulders relax, and I give in. "Don't make me take you behind the barn and kick your butt like I used to," I threaten, pouring myself a small glass.

"Oh please," Jackson says. "I could kick your a—er—butt with one arm behind my back."

Alex and Evan start laughing, knowing when it comes to the two of us, we equally kick each other's asses and usually both end up with black eyes and bruised egos.

"So how's Mila doing anyway?" Jackson asks, and everyone's heads pop up as if it's a taboo subject no one else wanted to bring up. "She miss me yet?" he taunts.

"Shut up," I growl.

"Oh, come on. I'm just messin' with you. It's not like I'd send her away if she came crawling back like Bailey."

The room goes so silent, the only noise being heard is Jackson's loud ass chewing.

"What did you just say?" I ask. Why the hell is he bringing Bailey up now?

"Nothin'. Forget it." He shakes his head, keeping his eyes low.

"No…" I scoot my chair back and push his away from the table, forcing him to face me. "What do you mean you sent Bailey away?"

"It's nothin'. I don't know." Jackson tries to deflect by turning back toward the table, but I'm quick to grab his arm and pull him up as I stand.

"Are you saying Bailey came to the house and you sent her away? Without telling me?"

Jackson starts walking toward the kitchen, probably to find more liquor, but I follow him not allowing him to get out of this conversation.

I can hear Dad chatting in the living room quietly as the rest of them listen. It's no secret Jackson and I have our differences, but this isn't something I'm willing to let go.

"Jackson!" I shout, pulling him back when he reaches the cabinet. "Is that what happened?"

"Fine! You wanna know?" He wipes his forehead with the back of his hand. "Bailey showed up a few months after y'all stopped seeing each other. You weren't home, and I was nursing a hangover. You spent the past several weeks pining over her, wondering why she stopped taking your calls, and I thought I was doin' you a favor by telling her you moved on and she shouldn't come back again. Figured she'd then realize what a great thing she let get away and you'd get over her without getting hurt again."

I've never felt this kind of rage before in my entire life. Everything inside me tightens, and all I see is red.

The moment my fist slams into his nose, he nearly falls to the ground. He's quick to recover as he holds his face in his hands, mutter a slew of curse words.

"How could you keep that from me? You're supposed to be my brother! She was pregnant then! What the fuck is wrong with you?" As he stands up, I push him over and over until his back hits the other wall. "I should rip you to shreds, asshole."

"John." Alex and Evan are pulling me back before I even realize they're in here.

"No amount of kicking his ass will bring Bailey back," Evan tells me in a calming voice. I blink and look up at him, knowing he's been in a similar situation with a girl he lost before. "He's been drinking all afternoon. Just walk away."

I shrug their hands off me and head out toward the door, letting it slam against the wood. Instead of driving away, I take a walk.

My head is filled with so much shit, I can't sort it out. Too many what-ifs, too many missed opportunities.

I can't fucking believe this.

I walk until I end up at the horse stables and decide to take Shadow out for a ride. The only way to clear my head is to get out of it.

But the memories of Bailey and Mila both taunt me and regret surfaces as I think back to all the times I reached out to Bailey, and how she chose that specific day to come back, and I wasn't even home. Of course, Jackson was hungover—when isn't he? But I don't know how I can let this go. Knowing I could've been there for her and Maize from the start.

Fuck, what a goddamn mess.

I ride for over an hour and don't slow down until the sun sets. I don't even know what to think anymore. I feel so much anger and wish I had Mila to ground me, something she was always good at doing. And I hate that I feel like I'm losing her now too.

Finding a spot to tie Shadow's reins, I get off and sit on the grass. Lying back, I rest my arms behind my head and look up at the stars that are painted above.

"Thought I'd find you here." Evan's voice scares the shit out of me. He ties up his horse before coming next to me and lies beside me.

"Just needed to find some clarity," I admit.

"Yeah, I understand that," he says. "After Alicia's death, I thought I was losing it. I saw her face everywhere afterward, and it really fucked with my head. I kept thinking what if I hadn't been late for work that morning and stopped for coffee like I always did. What if I had finally taken five minutes to ask her out and make plans with her, would she still be alive? Would I had been able to stall her just long enough for her not to get into a car accident and die? I tortured myself for months."

I turn and look at him. Evan and I have always been close, but I never knew this about him. "That sounds horrible, man. I'm sorry you had to go through that alone. Wish I paid more attention to how it affected you."

"It's okay. I didn't let anyone know, or rather, I didn't know how to let anyone know what I was feeling or going through. It was pretty painful."

"So how'd you work through it? I mean, you didn't meet Emily till years later. What helped you move on?"

"As weird as it sounds, I started thinking that I needed to find some kind of closure to accept that she was really gone. I'd seen plenty of trauma working in the ER, yet hers was the one that crippled me. So finally, I went to her grave and decided it was time to let go. I'd never forgotten her, but I needed to let go of the guilt as hard as it was."

I swallow, hating to admit how much Jackson's betrayal hurts. He knew how much I was hurting, and he never said a damn thing. Even more so after Maize arrived. I don't know how I can just forget that.

"I've been thinking of taking Maize to Bailey's gravesite. Do you think that's weird since she's only a baby?" I ask.

"No, man. I think it's the closure you need. You never got to say goodbye, and just because she's not here with you now doesn't mean you can't tell her goodbye now."

"I want Maize to feel comfortable coming to me to talk about her mom and visiting her when she's older, but right now all I can feel is anger. You'd think punching Jackson in the face would make me feel better, but I only feel worse," I admit.

"Life is short, bro. I know you're pissed at Jackson, and you have every right to be. Jackson's an asshole most of the time, but I believe he really did have your best interest in mind. He wouldn't purposely sabotage you. He's just a fuckin' idiot and doesn't always think about the consequences of his actions."

I look at Evan, and he lets out a calm breath then looks up at the stars. "Bottom line is, if Bailey and Alicia's stories have taught us anything, it's that we can't control everything."

"I don't know how to live with this guilt when I see so much of Bailey in Maize, especially now that she's getting older. She has her dark brown hair and those tiny freckles on her nose and cheeks. I want to give Maize the world, yet I feel like I'm half-assing my way through life as it is."

"I can assure you every parent feels that way regardless of circumstances. Elizabeth is only five months old, and I already feel that way every damn day."

"She has two rockstar parents, though," I tell him with a half-smile. "I'm glad our girls are going to grow up together on the ranch."

"Yeah, but imagine the mischief they're going to get into together." Evan laughs.

"And the drama, I'm sure. We'll have to walk around with loaded guns."

"Don't even remind me." Evan sits up and leans his arms on his knees, and I do the same. "It's a good life, John. Don't forget that, okay? We grew up here, and I wouldn't change that for the world, and knowing our girls will get to experience that, too, is the only thing that reassures me I'm not a complete fuckup of a dad."

"You're right," I admit. "And as long as we don't put Riley in charge of them, we'll be golden," I say, both of us laughing. He's a good kid, but he gets into as much trouble as Alex did, which can only mean he's going to be much worse as he gets older.

We stay silent for a few moments, and I start to feel lighter now that I've been able to talk about it aloud with someone I trust. Jackson's still on my shit list, but hopefully, now I can walk back and look at him without the urge to bash his face in.

"You miss Mila," he states. "That's probably adding to your emotional state on top of everything."

"Yeah, I feel completely distraught without her. I hate it, but we made a deal. I couldn't hold her back."

"I understand why you did what you did. But remember, you only get one life—one life to make it right."

CHAPTER THIRTY-ONE

Mila

"Good morning," I greet my class of first graders as they walk in from the morning bell.

"Ms. Carmichael?" Stevie pulls on my arm.

"Yes?" I ask, kneeling to his level. "What's the matter?"

"My mommy had a baby on Monday," he tells me without smiling. "She cries a lot."

I hold back a laugh because he's frowning and it's too dang cute.

"Well, that's awesome! Now you have a baby sister." I smile wide, hoping he will too.

"Yeah, but I really wanted a baby brother." He folds his arms over his small chest.

"Ya know, I have four little sisters, and they were pretty fun to have around when I was younger. I bet you'll have fun with her too." I flash him a wink, and he shrugs as if he might consider it. "What's her name?"

"What?" I blink, thinking I heard him wrong.

"Macie," he repeats. "But I call her crybaby because that's what she is."

"Oh, well okay then. Why don't you go hang up your backpack and get seated, okay?" I stand, leading him to his locker with the other kids.

The image of Maize is front and center in my mind, and I can't help but feel sad that I'm not with her every day anymore. I miss her and John so damn much, and though I've been back in Georgia for two months now, it hasn't gotten any easier. I missed her crawling for the first time, she's babbling like crazy, and I'm worried she's starting to forget who I am. When John and I managed to FaceTime last week, Maize acted all shy like she didn't recognize me. It took at least ten minutes for her to warm up to me, which breaks my heart, considering I've known her since she was three months old.

"Who's going to be our next Student of the Week?" I ask, getting all their attention. Since it's Friday, I pick a new student for the next week, so their parents can prepare over the weekend for what they need to bring in.

A resounding wave of, "Me's," echo throughout my classroom as each student raises their arm in the air. Smiling, I stick my hand in the jar that has their names folded on a piece of paper, and once I mix it up for a few seconds, I pull out one.

"Jonathan Baxter," I call out, forcing a smile on my face as sadness washes over me. Everything reminds me of John and having two Jonathans in my class of only twelve kids doesn't help.

Students cheer for him, and I get them settled down to start our first project for the day. Lunch rolls around, and I'm finally able to refill my coffee cup.

"Looks like you're settling in well," Mr. Demry says as he stands next to me in the teacher's lounge. He only stops in every few weeks when he has meetings with the principal.

"Yeah, everyone's been very nice," I tell him. "Adjusting and all that." I give him a fake smile as I stir creamer into my coffee.

"Great to hear that, Mila!" He pats me on the shoulder. "We're really lucky to have you here."

"Thanks," I say, wincing at how guilty I feel for not appreciating this job as much as I should.

"Any exciting plans this weekend?" he asks, making himself a cup of coffee.

"Well…" I pause for a moment. "If you consider watching origami tutorials on YouTube and eating a gallon of Rocky Road exciting, then it's gonna be one hell of a party."

He laughs and then another teacher steps up, grabbing his attention. I take the opportunity to slip away and return to my classroom to look over my afternoon schedule.

Before I even make it to my desk, Mr. Rasmussen comes in. "Hey!"

"Hi," I say politely, quickly sitting in my chair. "What's going on?"

"Just wanted to see how you were doing. See if you'd be interested in maybe getting dinner tonight again?"

Sucking my lips into my mouth, I feel the awkward tension brewing. Todd's a few years older than I am and has made it very clear he's interested. He asked me out last month, and though I politely declined, he said it was just to hang out and talk since he was new to the area and didn't know many people. I felt bad since he had no friends or family and made the mistake of being too friendly. Now he's completely got the wrong idea, though I avoid him at every opportunity, he still tries to find me.

"Actually, I have plans with my sister and mom tonight," I lie but plaster a big smile on my face anyway. "Girls' night out," I add, thinking that doesn't sound like a bad idea after all. I could use a drink or five and have some girl talk.

"Oh yeah? Where are you guys going?" He stands in front of my desk with his arms crossed, holding his gaze on me.

"We actually haven't decided yet."

"Oh okay, well…have fun," he says, slowly walking backward toward the door. He's waiting for me to suggest Saturday night, which isn't going to happen anytime this century.

"Thanks. Have a nice weekend."

By the grace of God, the lunch bell rings, and I know my students will be heading back in any second.

"You, too, Mila."

I finally exhale when he leaves. Todd is nice, decent looking, and a real gentleman from what I've seen so far, but I have no interest in him. Actually, I have no interest in anyone because all I can think about is John. I've been fooling myself into believing we can make this work long-distance even if we agreed to put our relationship on pause for the time being. It feels like we're growing apart the longer I'm away, which I hate.

Grabbing my phone, I welcome my class back inside and remind them to get their reading books. Once they're settled into quiet reading time for the next fifteen minutes, I group text my mom and Sarah about meeting up tonight.

MILA

> Any chance you can get a sitter tonight, Sarah?
> Let's kidnap Mom and take her out for a girls' night!

SARAH

> Graham goes to his father's this weekend for the
> first time in months, so I could actually use a drink!

MOM

> I'd go willingly!

I laugh, hearing Mom's voice in my head.

MILA

> Dancing and margaritas, it is!

As soon as my day ends and I say goodbye to my kids, I dodge the teacher's lounge and cut through the cafeteria to the parking lot. Driving home, I decide I'm going to use tonight to really think this through. I've been holding in my feelings since arriving because this is what I've worked for my whole life and it feels like I should be more grateful. However, I'd be lying to myself if I wasn't second-guessing my decision to leave Texas.

MILA

> Hey babe! Sarah and I are taking my mom out for
> drinks tonight, so I won't be able to FaceTime, but
> I'd love it if we could tomorrow.

JOHN

> Sure, probably not until the afternoon though. We're
> swamped at the B&B, and I have a cook who's out
> sick, so I have to fill in for him tomorrow.

I can't help feeling disappointed that we won't be able to talk until later but don't tell him that. I know he's working long hours and between Maize still waking up and him getting up before the sunrise, he's dead tired by dinner.

MILA

Okay, well don't worry about it if you're tired. We can FaceTime on Sunday.

He responds that he'll let me know, and I feel him slipping through my fingers even more.

A week or two after I returned to Georgia, I finally met up with Cade for a long overdue reunion. We used to hang out so much before everything changed and now we're like strangers, but I knew it was inevitable after being gone and his life changing dramatically. After being in Texas, I can confidently say my feelings for Cade weren't anything more than a fascination and nowhere near the way I feel for John. Perhaps it took being away to see that, or it was John who helped me realize it but either way, I'm grateful.

As soon as Sarah, Mom, and I get to Kozmos' Bar, I order the biggest margarita I can.

"Rough week?" Sarah asks with a popped eyebrow.

I take the straw between my lips and suck in a large gulp. "Kinda." I shrug, being dramatic because I truly do love teaching. "Todd keeps trying to ask me out, and one of my students is pissed his mother had a baby girl instead of a boy. Oh and LeAnn, my know-it-all-student, refuses to miss a day of school so when she showed up Tuesday with the flu, she threw up her entire lunch after recess." I groan. "And then I threw up after smelling it."

Sarah starts laughing, and Mom joins in. They both ordered drinks, too, but I'm halfway done with mine before they even start theirs.

"So, wanna tell us why you're inhaling alcohol like it's Mardi Gras?" Sarah tilts her head and asks with a knowing grin.

"I bet I have an idea," Mom chimes in. "I can read it all over your face."

"No, you can't," I argue, taking another long sip.

"Sweetie," Mom says. "Are you as miserable as you look?"

"No," I lie, and they both raise their brows at me. "I love my job."

"And what about the other one hundred and twenty-eight hours of the week?" Mom asks.

I furrow my brows, then laugh. "How the hell do you just know that off the top of your head?"

"I've been pregnant six times. Four of those times, I was on bedrest because y'all decided kicking my spine was a fun way to pass the time. I had countless hours to read fun facts."

I chuckle at Mom's dramatics. She suffered with bad back pain, and from what Dad has told us, they put her on bedrest so she'd stop working and actually relax.

"Seriously, Mila," Sarah says. "You look like someone just kicked your puppy."

"Fine." I groan, grabbing my straw and sucking down the last of my drink. "I miss John and Maize and am wondering if I made the right choice to leave."

"You owe me fifty bucks, Mom," Sarah gloats, holding her hand out toward our mother.

"You were betting on the downward spiral of my life?" I pout.

"Betting you'd finally admit you hate being back home," Sarah clarifies.

"I don't hate being home," I argue. "I just wish John and Maize were with me. Or I was with them."

"No one ever said you weren't allowed to change your mind," Mom interjects. "Just because you decided you wanted to be a teacher when you were six doesn't mean you still have to want that as an adult. Circumstances change, and that's okay."

"It's not that I don't want to be a teacher. I love the job, but it feels like I gave up *someone* I love for *something* I love. I want both, and I've come to the realization that all these years I've built up the idea of working at the same school we all went to was the only place that could make me happy when, in reality, it's nothing like I imagined. Sure, it's familiar and brings me a sense of comfort, but who's to say I couldn't have that somewhere else?"

"It sounds like you've already thought a lot about it, Mila." My mother covers my hand with hers as Sarah gives me a knowing smile.

"I have over these past two months, more so in the past few weeks, and I've just felt so torn about all of it. John's worried I'll resent him down the road for not pursuing my dream and made me promise to give it a fair shot, but if I want a fair shot at us working long-term, I can't keep that promise."

"If you feel that strongly about it, then you need to go for it," Mom tells me. "You can have a career and a family without sacrificing either of them. I stayed home for a while for you girls and Andrew, but I also wanted to work and feel accomplished in other areas of my life. I was so torn because I felt like I was supposed to be the perfect stay-at-home mom, raise my babies, and have dinner on the table every night at five. It's what I always wanted—or thought I did—and though many of my friends loved that lifestyle, it wasn't for me. So I went out and got my realtor's license, worked my way up the company, and made it my full-time career the past fifteen years. And you know what?" She squeezes my hand with a big smile. "I've never looked back, and I have no regrets. Things change, and change can be good, baby. So don't be afraid to chase a new dream."

Mom's right on so many levels that I can't believe how simple it all sounds hearing it aloud. I can prove to John that it's possible to teach and be with him without sacrificing one for the other. I just need to make a plan as to how I'm to do this because chasing him is a part of my new dream.

Once the night ends, I go home and sleep off the alcohol. By the next morning, I'm feeling giddy and excited and can't wait to implement my new plan.

Grabbing my phone off my desk, I search for the right number and hit call.

"Hello?"

"Hi, Mrs. Bishop? It's Mila."

CHAPTER THIRTY-TWO

John

The morning air is cool and crisp, and I can feel that fall is officially there. I love sitting on the back porch of the B&B, drinking coffee, and watching the sunrise before the guests wake up. There are only a couple of weeks until November, and I can't wait for Maize's first Halloween. River and Emily helped me pick out her costume, so she's going trick or treating as some green fairy, which is actually super adorable on her with the wings on her back. She's close to walking on her own, and I'm pretty sure she'll be walking all by herself by her first birthday in a month.

After I drop off Maize with the sitter at my parents' house, I head home to get dressed, dreading tonight. I hate how Mama demands I participate in the bachelor auction fundraiser each year and has since the day I turned eighteen. Aside from not really having a choice in the matter, the main reason I continue to do it is because it helps raise money for the local food bank.

Considering we all have kids except for Jackson, Mama found a friend to watch them tonight, so there'd be no excuses as to why we couldn't attend. It was the last resort excuse, not having a sitter, but she beat us all to it. Marriage doesn't get us out of being auctioned off either, something River learned last time.

To make matters worse, Mama had the grand idea to make it a costume theme party and considering I had zero ideas, Jackson suggested he'd be Superman, and I could be the boring alter ego, Clark Kent. He had to mention that it'd be like 'real life'—him being super and me being boring. Since it was an easy outfit to put together, and *only* because it was easy, I agreed. But what Jackson doesn't know is, I have a little surprise up my sleeve.

It took weeks to forgive him for not telling me sooner that Bailey had come to see me. One afternoon, Jackson took me to the side and apologized. He explained how he wanted to protect me and would've never turned her away if he'd known. After looking at his face, I knew he was living the same regret I had, but nothing can change what happened. Hindsight is twenty-twenty, as they say. I've never seen him be so sincere and serious at the same time. As much as I wanted to stay mad at him forever, I couldn't, not after he fully explained his intent. The pain, the what-ifs, and the need to know exactly what happened is slowly fading away as I've tried to find closure. While it will take time, each day I get to hear my baby girl laugh and see her smile, it gets easier.

After I'm dressed in a button-up shirt, some slacks, suspenders, and slip on the authentic black-framed glasses I ordered, I grab my keys and phone, then head out the door. I send a selfie to Mila with the glasses on, and she responds with the heart eyes emoji along with the splashing drops emoji—which I've learned means she's aroused—and I laugh at her reaction.

JOHN

> Heading to the auction now. Wish me luck. I'm scared on who'll bid and win me this year. Apparently being a dad is "hot."

MILA

> Well how do you think the word DILF was penned? So I told Gigi to bid big and demanded Kat back her up if some crazy person is trying to snag you. I said sixty and above only!

JOHN

Those older ladies are the worst sometimes! They get grabby hands like you wouldn't believe.

MILA

If they know what's good for them, they'll BACK OFF. Kat's got me covered.

I smile. I don't doubt she did set up something. Even from Georgia, she's protective of me.

JOHN

Wish you were here :(

MILA

I know, baby. I can't wait to see you again!

I don't want to go on a pretend date with anyone. I'd rather sit at home with my baby girl and FaceTime Mila. Unfortunately, the past few weeks she's been overly busy, and we haven't been able to talk as much as usual, but we text as much as we can.

I've been sending her photos of Maize every chance I get because I know how much their relationship meant to her. I ask her about work, so she knows I'm still supportive of her goals, but I still wish she was here with me. We're one-third of the way through her school year commitment, and I've begun a countdown of how many days are left until she returns—if she decides to. Only two hundred and thirty-eight days.

Pretty soon, we'll be sharing Thanksgiving together since she'll get an extra few days off, which I can't wait for. It'll have been four months since we saw each other, and part of me wants to keep her hostage in my bedroom the entire time without sharing her with anyone else. She's also promised to come for Christmas and New Year's while she's on winter break, which makes me incredibly happy since she'll have almost two weeks off.

After I lock up the house, I head to town to the old bank building where the auction is being held. It took the entire summer to renovate it, and I'm actually shocked when I walk in and see how much the place has changed. It went from being an old rustic event center to a building where I expect to be served expensive wine and caviar. It's entirely too fancy for my blood.

I look around the room and see Mama went all out with the Halloween themed decorations. Giant eight-foot spiders hang from the ceiling, and black and orange balloons are scattered around the room. She even rented fog machines and has scary music playing in the background to set the mood. Smoky purple drinks with Frankenstein finger straws are served to every guest. I take one, and the first thing I taste is gin. Mama's already trying to get everyone saucy. Based on the drinks alone, this might be her most successful year yet.

"There you are!" Jackson *flies* over to me with his fist out. His red cape flutters as he runs toward me. By the look on his face and the height of the bang curl he has, I know I'm gonna need ten more of these drinks to be able to handle him tonight. "You make a perfect Clark Kent. Nerdy from head to toe. The black glasses and suspenders are a good touch."

"You can't be Clark Kent without the glasses. You're a poser." I take a sip of my drink, needing to chug it.

"No, I'm SUPERMAN!" Jackson looks at the girls walking past us and flexes as they giggle. They're both dressed like vampires and show their pointed teeth when they smile back at him. "I have something you can suck," he tells one of them, winking.

Mama comes out of nowhere and slaps him upside the head, which causes me to burst into laughter.

"Don't be disrespectful. I taught you better than that," she huffs. Mama's dressed like a Southern belle with a big poofy dress and hat that ties under her chin. It looks as if it's a period costume, and it wouldn't surprise me a bit if it's vintage all the way down to the lace. She takes this as serious as Jackson takes his whiskey parties.

"You look great, Mama," I tell her, and she gives me a curtsey.

"You do too. Emily, Evan, Alex, and River are about to arrive. I can't wait for you to see their costumes. I reserved y'all a table up in the front by the stage." She gives me a hug and eyes Jackson before patting him on his back and telling him to behave. "Watch him tonight."

I give her nod, and just as I turn, I see Evan walk through the entrance and clap my hands when I recognize all their costumes. River is Tinkerbell, Alex is Mr. Smee, Evan is Peter Pan, and Emily is Wendy.

"This is great," I tell Jackson, but I can tell he's annoyed they one-upped him.

"It's dumb. They don't even have Captain Hook," he adds, just as Dad walks through the door in full Captain Hook garb, down to the curly black hair, mustache, and burgundy hat with a feather on top.

They totally nailed it.

"Fuckin'! Epic!" I go over to them, knowing tonight they'll steal the show. They're all smiles, and it seems everyone in the room notices them too. People are pointing, and I'm trying to ignore the whole room looking at us.

"How'd you talk Dad into it?" I ask Evan.

"It was his idea, actually. We were all talking about what we were going to wear, and Dad suggested it. Apparently, he's always wanted to dress up as Hook. Anyway, Alex should've been Peter Pan, but he refused. These tights are making my nuts itch." Evan takes one of the dangerous purple drinks off the tray and downs it in three seconds. "You'd think Mama is trying to get us trashed or something."

Emily laughs at him. "The stronger the drinks, the slipperier the wallets. You know how this works. So you're Clark Kent?"

"Yeah, and apparently since I'm the boring half, it was fitting." All eyes glance over at Jackson who's standing tall in his Superman costume.

River is staring at Jackson and bursts into laughter. "Did you stuff your crotch?"

All our heads turn at the same time and look at the bulge in Jackson's tights.

"No, I'm just that big, baby," he tells her while wiggling his eyebrows.

"I call bullshit. Unless you have elephantiasis or something. Your balls aren't that big," I hear Kiera walk up and say.

"And how would you know?" Jackson's mouth practically falls to the ground when he sees Kiera dressed like Catwoman in a skintight black suit hugging all her curves. She's carrying a whip in her right hand, which is the perfect accessory, but what's scary is she knows how to use it.

Kiera bursts into laughter and Jackson's still watching her, that is until Trent walks up wearing a Batman costume. He openly rolls his eyes and walks away mumbling something about how couple costumes make him sick.

When the lights dim, we make our way past all the tables toward the front of the room. I grab another purple drink, and Evan grabs two because we know what's about to happen. Jackson flirts with random girls that walk by, and I watch as Kiera watches him. Even with Trent sitting next to her, with his arm wrapped around her, it's obvious she still has feelings for Jackson. One of the vampire girls walks by and whispers something to him, and he pulls her onto his lap where they giggle about something. I see Mama side stage glaring at Jackson who's making a fool of himself, something he does on the regular to forget about Kiera. River taps him on his shoulder and points over to Mama and Jackson shoos her away. If he doesn't stop, there's gonna be a scene like in the grocery store when we were kids, and by the look on Mama's face, it's about five seconds from happening.

"Jackson," Kiera whispers. "Jackson," she says even louder.

He turns and looks at her, a wide smile on his face. "What do you want?"

"You're acting like an ass. Stop it."

The girl on his lap looks at Kiera, whispers something in his ear, then gets up and walks away. Jackson scowls at Kiera. "Why don't you mind your own damn business?"

The look on her face is so fierce, I wouldn't be surprised if she picked up that whip and gave Jackson a run for his money. Trent rubs her back, calming her, and she turns and looks at him, not paying any mind to Jackson's antics.

Jessica, Dylan's lady, who's emceeing for the second year in a row, takes the stage with Mama just as the lights in the room dim. I look around the room, and the fake candles on the tables flicker in the low lighting. Just like every year, Mama takes the stage and introduces herself along with everyone else.

"Last year, we had a record year! So I wanted to give a big thanks to everyone who participated. We were able to earn enough money to help provide food to serve over one hundred thousand meals across the county, which is a huge deal. But I told the director of the food bank that this year will be even better. Prove me right." She smiles and nods at the audience. "So without further ado, I'll hand the mic back to our emcee, so she can get to it."

Jessica walks across the stage, dressed in a yellow ball gown. Her hair is half pulled up in a bun with a yellow ribbon. She's even carrying a couple of red roses with her. Before starting, she blows kisses at Dylan, who's also sitting at our table, and it's then I realize he's the Beast, and she's Belle.

Ugh, couples costumes. I can't escape them.

"Alright, ghouls and ghosts, is everyone ready for the fourteenth annual bachelor auction?" The women in the crowd go wild as the group of men who were threatened to participate line up next to the stage. I follow Jackson, and those who get our costumes laugh, but the Neverland group is getting all the attention, which I'm happy about.

"First up, we have Dr. Evan Bishop. He's all about saving lives, and if you're a good girl, he might give you mouth to mouth," she continues, and I watch Emily stand and bid five hundred dollars. April, Evan's stalker from last year, stands up and bids higher. Emily turns and glares at her, giving her a silent warning before bidding again. Though April is still obsessed, she sits down and pouts. I watch Evan mouth a quick, "Thank you," and walk off the stage shaking his head.

Alex is bid off to River, who has a bidding war with someone else, and I wonder why Mama just doesn't let us pay a few thousand dollars to get out of the humiliation.

Jackson nudges me. "You know I'm gonna bring in the most money like I do every year."

"Good for you. Glad you could feed the hungry wolves." I chuckle.

"Last year, I got so many phone numbers afterward that I had dates for weeks." He laughs just as Jessica calls his name.

"Next up, we've got the famous Jackson Bishop. Known for his riding skills, if you know what I mean, ladies, and his smart mouth. He likes to kiss and ain't afraid to tell, so if you're ready for a wild ride on the untamed stallion, then get your bids in." Jackson really plays it up, flexing and acting a fool. Women are literally crowding the stage, fighting over him. Pretty soon, Mama is gonna have to hire bodyguards for Jackson. I'm certain his ego loves it, though.

"Two thousand dollars," one of the vampire girls says.

"Anyone else willing to bid more than that? You're guaranteed to have a good time with this Bishop brother," Jessica adds.

"Twenty-five hundred," a woman dressed as a mummy says from the side. The bidding eventually ends at three thousand dollars. Jackson flexes, jumps off the stage, and kisses the winning girl right on the lips.

Knowing I'm next, I suck in a deep breath and walk up the stage. Jessica gives some spiel about me being a new father. "He'll be your daddy for a night, ladies. He's the hotter version of Jackson, reserved, and won't wham-bam-thank-you-ma'am."

Just as the bidding starts, I open my button-up shirt, revealing the Superman logo beneath it, and the crowd goes wild. Jackson's jaw drops open, and he stands, trying to bring the attention back to him, but it's not working.

"You can't be Clark Kent without being Superman, too, you idiot," I tell him.

The lights are shining brightly in my eyes, and I think I hear Gigi bid on me. Then a few other ladies join in.

"We're up to a thousand dollars, ladies. Dig deep and don't let this one get away," Jessica encourages with a smile.

"Was that two thousand I heard from the back of the room?" Jessica asks.

"Twenty-five hundred," another woman says. I place my hand over my eyes, trying to make out who is crazy enough to spend that kind of money on me. I find Kat in the corner, and she's shrugging her shoulders at me. Gigi is close to the front, and she's tapped out as well. *Great.*

I try to smile as another woman bids. "Five thousand dollars."

"Are you serious?" Jessica says into the microphone, then looks around. I hear shuffling in the room, and the mumbles seem to fill the large space. The lights are so damn bright that I can barely see a thing.

"Whoa, okay. Anyone else want to try to beat that?" Jessica asks, grinning, but she's just as shocked as I am. "Going once, going twice, and sold to the woman in black." The crowd applauses, and knowing Jackson, he's pissed and just as interested to know who outdid his bidding record. "Sweetie, why don't you come up here and claim your prize." Jessica tries to block the lights from her eyes as well, but it's no use. Heads turn, and I'm curious who'd spend that kind of money on me. I'm not Jackson and will not be using the date as a booty call, so it's almost a waste of money for this poor woman, though it's going to a good cause.

A small silhouette walks from the very back of the room, and I hear chatter as the woman walks toward the middle of the room. I go to the edge of the stage and wait to see who's crazy enough to spend that kind of money. The woman's wearing a black skintight suit that hugs her in all the places, and she's holding a red mask over her face as she makes her way to the front. She walks down the middle of the aisle like she's on a runway, strutting her stuff in the highest high heels I've ever seen. Glittery red devil horns sparkle in the light as she twirls the red glitter tail in her hand. Dark brown hair is in big curls, and I cross my arms over my chest and wait.

Emily and River gasp as she passes, and curiosity has the best of me. I'm actually really fucking confused. When she's close enough to the stage, she removes the mask from her face and smiles. My knees go weak, and I nearly fall.

"Mila," I whisper. My entire body trembles in happiness, and I feel as if my heart may pound out of my chest. I jump off the stage and go to her, placing her face in my hands and smile.

"You're really here?" I take a step back, looking at her from head to toe. "You *sneaky* lil' devil."

"That's me." She pops an eyebrow. She's laughing and crying all at the same time, and I'm so shocked I don't even know what else to say. I almost pinch her to make sure she's real, and when she places her arms around my body, I know she is. Not being able to wait any longer, I dip down and kiss her so intimately it causes the crowd to erupt into applause. Everything fades away, and it's just me and her standing in the spotlight. I'm the happiest I've ever been, and my world feels as if it might fall off its axis as we pull apart.

CHAPTER THIRTY-THREE

Mila

Feeling John's hands and lips on me for the first time in months has my entire body on fire. I've missed him so damn much, and keeping this a secret from him for the past several weeks has been hard but so damn worth it.

"I can't believe you tricked me," John says against my lips. "Did you really spend that much money on me?"

I nod, laughing. "Sure did, and I expect to get every penny's worth."

He releases a deep, animalistic moan, and the expression on his face tells me how much he plans to make it worth my while.

Jessica continues the auction, giving John and me the chance to escape for some privacy. He grabs my hand and leads us out until we get to an empty hallway, and then he pins me to the wall with his mouth.

"John," I say, laughing as his lips devour mine. He wraps his arms around my waist and pulls me against his body where I feel his erection.

"Ooh, Clark Kent. You're a dirty boy."

"Let's get out of here so I can show you just how dirty I can be."

"Okay, but keep those glasses on," I tease.

"As long as you keep those black heels on." He winks.

"Deal."

We laugh as he leads us out the door and to his truck. "Don't you have to tell them you're leaving?" I ask as he helps me into the passenger seat.

"My guess is they already know," he says. "You must've had the entire town in on your little secret."

"Only a few," I admit with a cocky grin.

"You're a sneaky little devil." He leans in to kiss me. "Now let me rip this off you."

We barely make it inside the house before John's mouth is back on mine, and he's tearing at my leather jumpsuit. "How the fuck do you get this thing off?"

I laugh, loving how eager he is to undress me. Turning around, I push my hair to the side and expose the zipper that goes down my back. He pulls it and helps get the fabric and my bra straps down my arms. Once I step out of the jumpsuit, I'm left in only my panties and heels. John grabs under my ass and lifts me up until my legs wrap around his waist. He starts carrying us down the hall to his room, his mouth latching to my neck and collarbone.

"I missed you so damn much," he says, setting me on the bed and lying over my body. "I still can't believe you're here."

"I hated being away from you every day. I couldn't do it anymore," I admit.

His body towers over me, and when I cup his face in my hands, I bring his lips to mine and kiss him like I've been desperately wanting to for the past four months.

"I'm glad you came," he says, leaning back to undo the rest of the buttons on his shirt. Once he takes it off, along with his tie, he pulls off the Superman T-shirt, and I chew on my bottom lip admiring the view.

"How is it you got even more ripped?"

"Maize and I have been working out." He winks, undoing his slacks next.

"You mean you've been chasing after her now that she's crawling everywhere." I chuckle.

"And pulling herself up on the furniture, giving me mini heart attacks. Girl's on a mission to kill me before I'm forty."

I snort at his dramatics and help him remove his slacks and boxers.

"I can't wait to see her. I've missed her so much too."

"She's with a sitter tonight," he tells me. "So you'll have to play with me instead."

My head falls back with laughter, and I can't believe how easy it is to fall back into our ways as if I hadn't ever left. It was part of my concern when I started planning my trip back, but all I knew was that I had to come and see for myself.

"It'll be my pleasure, Mr. Kent." I pull him down, so I can kiss him again and wrap my legs around his waist, my heels digging into his ass. "I was going to come as Lois Lane once I found out what you and Jackson were going as, but I knew Jackson would've made a comment about it since he was the 'real' Superman."

"No shit." He laughs. "Smart choice since I prefer your naughty side anyway." He kisses down my body, making his way down my stomach and my panties before helping me out of them.

"I have something to tell you first," I say, biting down on my lower lip. His mouth is between my legs, kissing my thigh as my hands thread in his hair.

"Can it wait?" He raises his head, popping a brow. "There's a reunion about to happen down here."

"Oh my God, John." I chuckle, wanting so desperately to tell him the truth, but knowing I can tell him later, I agree. "Fine."

"Actually, call me Clark. It's kinda hot."

"So are those glasses," I say, licking my bottom lip. "Mr. Clark Kent..."

"At your service, ma'am." He spreads my legs open, and the moment my back arches, his mouth is on my clit, and I see stars as he brings me to the edge over and over.

Once he's fully worked me into a frenzy, he brings his mouth back to mine and effortlessly slides inside. The moment our bodies connect, I lose it. Tears stream down my cheeks as I think how hard these past four months away from him have been. This was a true test of our love, and the way I feel with him right now only proves we belong together.

"So…when were you gonna tell me about your little addition down there?" John asks, arching his brow.

"Well, you didn't really give me much of a chance." I chuckle. "I got it a few weeks after I left."

John grabs my leg, raising it up high to get a better look. "I think it's perfect."

"Texas will always be a part of me, and you'll always have my heart. So I decided to do the outline of the state with a heart inside where Eldorado is located. The tattoo artist looked at me a little funny, but once I explained my story he said it was 'dope,'" I say, giggling.

"It's totally dope!" John mocks. He lowers his mouth to press a kiss over the ink that's on the inside of my thigh; the same spot John has his Scorpion.

"Baby, why are you crying?" He stills, worry written all over his face.

"Because I'm happy," I tell him. "You make me so happy, and I just love you so much."

"I love you, too, sweetheart. We're gonna get through the rest of this, okay? I promise."

I bring his lips back to mine and hold him so tightly, I'm sure he'll have marks from my nails digging into his skin. "I'm not leaving, John."

"Mila…" he says in a warning tone, but I'm quick to stop him before he can continue.

"I'm not letting you get away," I say matter-of-factly. "I can chase my dreams here without sacrificing my life with you, and that's what I want to do. It's already planned and done."

"Are you serious?"

"Yes," I say just above a whisper.

"You're staying? For good?" His eyes widen as if he's trying to read my face for any joking.

"For good, babe. I never want to be away from you or Maize again."

His face lights up, and it makes me laugh how excited and happy he is to hear me say that. "I don't know what I did to deserve you, Mila Carmichael, but I'm so damn grateful you're mine. Maize and I are the lucky ones."

John kisses me with a fervor I've never felt before and makes love to me until we're both screaming in ecstasy. Covered in sweat and panting, we lie in bed, and as John holds me, I know without a doubt I never want to be with anyone else.

John wakes me the next morning with his face between my legs again, and before we even get to breakfast, he's carrying me to the shower and devouring every inch of my body with his tongue.

"You need to feed me," I whine as he dries me off with a towel. "I'm completely out of fuel."

"Don't worry, baby. Mama's making a big brunch spread for everyone."

"Oh, that won't be awkward." I groan.

"Why? It's not like she thinks we were playing board games all night." He chuckles.

"Because I want to stay on her good side!" I explain.

"If she helped you plan all this, I can assure you you're on her best side. So stop worrying."

"Okay, you're probably right. But still."

"Go get dressed," he says, smacking my ass.

"Oh crap," I say, pausing at the door. "My suitcase isn't here, and I'm not wearing that jumpsuit to breakfast."

"Already here for you." He winks and kisses my cheek. "Jackson brought it over early this morning before feeding the horses."

"Oh, that was nice of him. Now I'll be able to walk in with some dignity left."

"I told him all about last night, which means everyone will know before breakfast."

"John Bishop! You did not!" I smack his arm though he barely flinches.

He starts laughing, shaking his head at me. "Yep. You're still so easy to rile up."

"You suck." I wrinkle my nose and end up cracking up right along with him.

"You always look so beautiful," John whispers, standing behind me as I look at my reflection in the mirror. He drags a hand along my shoulders, pushing my hair to one side. "And fuck, you smell so good too. To hell with breakfast…" John's mouth latches to my neck, making me laugh at how eager he is.

"Before you make us extremely late, I have to ask you something."

"Sure, what is it?" He drags his nose along my neck, then presses a kiss just under my ear.

I spin around, giving him a quick kiss on the lips. "We never got the chance to really talk about the Kensingtons' first visit with Maize or visiting Bailey's gravesite." His face falls, and I know it's a hard topic for him. I'd been so busy these past few weeks that we've only been able to chat for short moments at a time, and he hadn't had the chance to go into depth about what had happened.

"You sure you want to talk about this now?" he asks.

"Yes. I know it was a hard thing to go through, and I feel so guilty I wasn't here for it."

"Don't feel guilty, babe." He wraps my hair around my ear and kisses my forehead. Before he continues, he grabs my hand and leads me to the bed where we both sit.

"Well, first was the visitation. I told them they could come to see Maize here since it's a familiar place for her and she'd feel safe. The three of us sat in the living room while Maize played on the floor. After a while, she started bringing them toys and warming up to their company. Soon, they were both on the floor with her and seeing that made it finally feel like I had made the right choice. I'd been so torn over it knowing Bailey had warned me, but as long as the visits are on our terms, I don't worry as much."

"They sound like they want to make things right at least," I offer, remembering what they told John during their mediation.

"I really hope so because I don't want them coming in and out of Maize's life and confusing her."

"Did they ask to see her again?"

"Yeah, before they left. I told them they could come to her birthday party, and we'd go from there."

"That's good. If you're uncomfortable around them, Maize will pick up on it, and that could confuse her too. So maybe going slow will help ease your worries."

"I think so too."

"Did they go with you to Bailey's gravesite?" I ask, knowing this isn't easy for him to talk about but I want to be involved in all aspects of their lives, even the sad ones.

"No, I asked them not to, so they just gave me the location."

"So just you and Maize went?"

"Yeah, I wanted to do it with just us two first. But I hope to bring you someday too." He clasps my hand and squeezes. I smile with a nod in return. "I figure if Maize wants to keep going as she gets older, then it can be something we do together."

"Well until she understands, you can keep bringing her there, so it doesn't feel so scary for her. I'm sure she'll appreciate that with age."

"It was the first time I allowed myself to cry about her death. Standing there just made it more real and knowing she was missing out on Maize's life just really hit me. I felt like such an idiot."

"Don't say that. Crying is good for you. It's part of the closure and grieving process."

"I figured you'd say that," he says, chuckling softly. "I told Bailey how big Maize's getting and how I'm so grateful for her each day that I get to be her dad. I thanked her for giving her a chance and for bringing her into my life. I felt like an idiot talking to myself."

"I'm proud of you," I tell him, smiling up at him as his eyes gloss over. "Being vulnerable isn't easy, but I'm glad you were able to finally say goodbye. I know she'd be very grateful for how well you've been taking care of Maize. Never doubt that, babe."

"I love you." He turns, bringing our foreheads together. "Thank you."

"I love you, too, baby."

Once we finish getting ready, we drive to his parents' and are greeted by everyone. Since I didn't get to say hello to them last night, I give them all hugs. I flew in a couple of days ago but was hiding out at Gigi's house.

"Maize!" I grab her as soon as I see her and am so relieved when she doesn't shy away from me. "Look how big you are! I can't believe how much she grew."

"She's a tank," John says, leaning in to kiss her chubby cheek.

"Eats like one too," Mrs. Bishop adds.

"Well, look at who her dad and uncles are." I snort.

Riley comes up to me and gives me a big hug, too, and I couldn't be happier to be back, surrounded by all the Bishops.

"Where's Elizabeth?" I ask Emily.

"She's still napping but should be getting up in about a half hour or so."

"I bet she's gotten so big too."

"She really has. Seven months and already crawling," Emily responds.

"And ready for a little sister or brother," Mrs. Bishop blurts out.

"I think it's Jackson's turn," Evan chimes in, putting the spotlight on Jackson instead and smacking his shoulder. "You aren't getting any younger."

"Nah, you guys keep having the babies, so I can spoil them and then send them back home," he retorts. "Best part of being an uncle."

"He needs to settle down first," Mr. Bishop comes in and adds. "By the time that happens, he'll be fifty."

"Why y'all ridin' my ass? I'm the only brother who didn't knock up a girl before marriage. I deserve a medal," he states matter-of-factly, and Mrs. Bishop rolls her eyes.

"When you can start acting your age, you'll get a damn medal," Evan shoots back at him.

"Forever young, baby!" Jackson shouts.

"So, John," Mrs. Bishop knowingly changes the subject as we all find our seats at the table. "Has Mila told you what we're doing after this?"

"No, not really." John looks at me for answers, but I keep my lips sealed. "Haven't had much of a chance to talk about it," I say, hiding a smirk.

"Their mouths were otherwise occupied," Jackson blurts out.

My cheeks heat with embarrassment as everyone laughs.

"Don't make me kick your ass again before lunch," John threatens.

"Again?" My brows raise in curiosity.

"Don't worry, Mila. I let him get a couple of good hits in before I fought back." Jackson winks.

John grunts. "Yeah, you really *let* me. Okay."

"Anyway..." Mrs. Bishop clears her throat, drawing the attention back to her conversation. "We're heading to the church after this so y'all got about an hour before we have to be there."

"The church?" John asks, looking at me for confirmation.

"I'm not telling you yet," I say, keeping my head down, so his adorable pleading look doesn't wear me down.

The rest of lunch goes by quickly. I eat like I haven't eaten in days but also Mrs. Bishop's cooking is just too damn good, and I've really missed it. Once we help clean up, John and I get in his truck and tell everyone to meet us at the church.

"Give me a hint," John begs as we drive there. He squeezes my hand, and the look on his face is so damn cute, I almost give in.

"It's my plan," is all I tell him. "It's good news, I promise."

"Okay," he says, bringing my hand to his lips and kissing my knuckles.

As soon as we arrive, we park and only have to wait a couple of minutes for everyone else to arrive.

"Close your eyes," I tell him, grabbing his hand so I can lead him inside.

"Jackson, if you pants me or push me into a wall, I'm going to kick your ass six feet under," he threatens as soon as he hears Jackson behind him.

"Language," Mrs. Bishop reminds him.

"I'm offended you'd even think that," Jackson says, holding back a laugh.

"Okay, wait here," I tell John, positioning him in front of the sign. I go and flick on some more lights, so he can see it all. "Ready?" He nods, and when I take his hand, I tell him to open.

He blinks a few times, and his jaw drops slightly as he looks at everything. "W-what is this? Mila's Playground & School," he reads the sign that hangs above the arched entryway. He turns toward me, completely stunned.

"I found a way to stay," I tell him simply. His forehead wrinkles as if he's not sure about this plan, but I'm quick to explain it to him before he can say anything. "I always thought teaching at the school I went to is what I needed in order to be happy but turns out it wasn't. I love teaching, I'll always love it, but that doesn't mean I can't teach and be here with you and Maize. So I figured chasing my dream and chasing you was the same thing, and there's no reason why I can't make both happen."

"I can't believe this…" He blinks again, looking back at the sign and down the hallway that leads to classrooms. "How?"

"Your mama," I reply honestly. "And lots of helpers."

"The school shut down years ago, so I knew starting it back up would be quite the task, but we got lots of volunteers to help with getting it cleaned up again. New carpet, paint, and desks. Lots of donated toys and supplies," Mrs. Bishop answers.

"So you're going to run it?" John asks.

"Well, it's going to be a day care center for newborns up to five years old. Then I'll teach the 3k and 4k students and hire staff for the babies. Also, that way Maize can come here with me every day and start being around other children her age."

"I'm…shocked. Wow." I can tell John's mind is spinning as he tries to wrap his head around all of this. I can't blame him, though, since it's a lot to process all at once.

When I called Mrs. Bishop that day and told her I needed to find a way to come back and be able to teach, knowing that's something John wouldn't want me to sacrifice to be with him, she helped come up with a plan that would benefit everyone. Once we started the prep work, she truly was a miracle in helping get so much of the work done. I couldn't be there to make final decisions, but I trusted Mrs. Bishop one-hundred percent. She'd send me pictures for approval and ideas but just knowing I was going to be able to teach in Texas was enough. I was happy with anything and not picky at all. She's gone above and beyond to make this happen, and I couldn't be more appreciative of everything she's done.

"I wanted to come back with a plan," I start to explain. "I knew you'd be worried I was giving up teaching to be here, but I was miserable in Georgia and knew it wasn't the answer. Now I can be with Maize, still teach little kids, and most importantly be with *you*."

"I can't believe you did this," he says, brushing a hand through his hair and still looking shocked. "I'm so proud of you, though." He cups my face and kisses me. "And thank you for not giving it up. I know you love teaching, and I want you to have everything you love."

I kiss him back. "I do now."

CHAPTER THIRTY-FOUR

John

"So Mila..." River grabs her attention as we help clear the table. Mama made a huge Christmas feast, and now we're all in food comas. "I know your school isn't opening until after the new year and all, but do you think you could hold a place for me in the newborn class, say around...June or July?"

"Well, we aren't at full capacity, and I doubt we will be by then but..." Mila stops, blinks, and looks at River. "Wait. Are you pregnant?" She squeals, nearly running over to hug River.

"I knew it!" Emily shouts, joining in on their hug.

"Good job, bro," I tell Alex, slapping him on the shoulder.

"Does that mean the pressure's off me?" Jackson jokes. "Congrats, guys!"

The fact that Mama isn't plowing River and Alex down right now tells me that she already knew. I'm so excited for them, considering how long they've been trying.

"I think I deserve some credit," I say, teasing. "After River threatened my balls to get some help, I went back to work and took the extra load off you, so you could rip off your wife's clothes," I tell Alex.

"No, it's your fault it took so long," River says matter-of-factly, but she's smirking so I know she's not serious. "Actually, we're three months along already."

"Three months?" Emily and Mila gasp at the same time.

"I didn't want to say anything until we were out of the danger zone. It took so long to finally get pregnant, I kept thinking something bad was going to happen."

"It's okay, we understand," Mila tells her. "I'm so excited for you guys."

"I hope it's a girl, so the Bishop grandkids continue to outrank the boys," Emily says.

"Plus, Elizabeth and Maize need another girl cousin to get into mischief with," Mila adds.

"That or there needs to be at least one of them to talk sense into the other two," I say, cracking up laughing.

"As soon as we get through the wedding, we're trying for more," Emily announces, and by the look on Evan's face, he had no idea that was the plan. Jackson and I laugh at his expense as Emily gives him a sweet smile.

Once the table is cleared, we all gather around the tree and let the kids open their presents. Maize opened her gifts from Santa this morning, but she was only half-interested. After the third present, she was over trying to unwrap it, and Mila and I had to do the rest for her.

I haven't given Mila her gift yet, and the nerves start to hit me the closer to time it gets. For weeks, she planned her trip back to me, which has meant everything to me. Now I've been planning something amazing for her.

"Here, Mom," I whisper, handing Maize over to her. She gives me a wink, knowing exactly what I need her to go do.

"Baby," I say, grabbing Mila's attention.

"Yeah, babe?" She walks to me in the living room with a plate of pie in her hands.

"I wanna give you your gift since it's here."

Her face lights up, and she quickly swallows down the last of her dessert. "Oh, okay. I have yours here too."

"Let me grab Maize first," I tell her, leaning in to kiss her on the cheek. "Mama is changing her."

"Okay, I'll go get your present!"

As she skips over to the tree, I head to where Mama is with Maize and smile wide when I see her T-shirt. "Look at you," I say, grabbing Maize in my arms. "It's perfect." I already know Mila's going to love it.

"You ready for this?" Mama asks, patting me on the cheek.

"Been ready my entire life," I reply.

"She's a lucky girl, John."

"No, I'm the lucky one, Mama. She brings out the best in me and loves Maize as her own. I don't know what I did to deserve her," I admit, already getting emotional.

"Don't forget this." Mama hands me the box I asked her to hold on to because I didn't want Mila finding it beforehand.

"Thanks, Mama." I take it from her and put it in my front pocket.

"I love you, John. Good luck." She grins, giving me a side hug.

Holding Maize on the other side, I walk back to the living room where Mila is still digging under the tree. "I swear I put it under here," she mutters. I keep quiet, knowing exactly where it is. I had Jackson hide it when she wasn't looking so she'd stay distracted.

"Has anyone seen a gift with blue wrapping paper with silver ornaments on it?" Mila asks, moving toys and empty boxes around that have already been ripped open.

"I think I saw it in the way back by the end table," Jackson tells her, pointing to the far right.

"Do you want some help?" River asks, stalling so I can get into position.

"Sure." Mila laughs. "There's a ton of boxes down here."

While Mila and River are facing the Christmas tree, digging around the mess on the floor, I kneel behind her with Maize on my knee.

Once I'm settled, I give River a nod to signal I'm ready. She reaches between the table and couch where Jackson hid the gift and holds it up.

"Is this it?" she asks Mila.

"Ooh yes! Thank you!"

I inhale, knowing the moment she turns around she's going to see Maize and me kneeling in front of her.

Mila stands up, grabs the wrapped box from River, and as soon as she spins around, her jaw drops and her eyes widen in shock.

"Oh my God!" She clasps a hand over her mouth, dropping the present in her other hand. "What are you doing?"

"Maize wanted to ask you a question." I smirk, jerking my head down to her T-shirt.

Mila squats down to her level and straightens her shirt so she can read it. "Will you marry my daddy?" she reads aloud, tears already forming in her eyes. "Are you serious?"

I reach inside my pocket, grab the box, and flip it open, showing off the diamond ring I bought for her. "Mila, we love you more than anything, and you'd make us the happiest people in the world if you'd marry me and be ours forever."

Smiling, I watch the tears streaming down her cheeks, and she frantically nods her head. "Yes! Of course!"

Without wasting another second, I wrap a hand around her neck and pull her mouth to mine. Maize starts babbling and kicking her legs to be let down. We break apart and laugh at her.

"I can't believe you did this," Mila says, wiping her cheeks. "I love that you included her. I want her to always know that I will love her forever as my own and nothing will ever change that."

"She will, baby. We're both so lucky to have you in our lives."

"I think I'm the lucky one." She grabs my face in her hands and plants another kiss on my lips.

I punch my arm up into the air in victory. "She said yes!"

Everyone erupts into applause and cheers, Mila laughing against my lips.

Maize wiggles, and I set her down next to us. "Give me your hand." I take the ring out of the box and slide it onto her left ring finger. "It looks perfect on you."

"I'm completely shocked," she admits, looking down at the diamond. "It's so gorgeous. I still can't believe you planned this."

"I knew I wanted to marry you months ago, and I didn't see any reason to wait any longer."

"I agree." She wraps her arms around my neck and pulls me in for a deep kiss.

"No PDA on Christmas!" Jackson shouts, getting laughs from everyone. "Get a room or somethin'."

"That doesn't sound like a bad idea." I wink at Mila, grabbing her hand and helping her to her feet.

River, Emily, and Mama swarm Mila the second they're able to, wrapping their arms around her and checking out the ring. She fits right into our family, and I can't imagine our lives without her in it now. Hell, I don't ever want to.

"It's truly been the best Christmas ever," Mama says as it quiets down. "A new grandbaby is coming, and now a new daughter is joining our family." We all smile, then Mama looks over at Jackson and pops a brow.

"What?" he asks.

"Any surprises coming from you next?"

He grunts as everyone laughs.

"I'm still shocked Jackson's the only one without a kid," Dad blurts out. "Makes me wonder if all those stories he tells about women are actually true."

Evan, Alex, and I burst out laughing, knowing Jackson hates it when we bust his balls.

"Ha-ha." Jackson rolls his eyes. "It means I'm the only one who knows how to wrap his junk."

"Junk! Junk! Junk!" Riley repeats almost immediately, and we all look down at him sitting on the couch with a new toy.

"Thanks, Jackson," River groans.

"Life with boys, honey," Mama says with a knowing smirk. "If you have a girl, prepare for her to be a tomboy. I finally got mine after three boys, and she still preferred trucks and tractors over Barbie dolls and dresses."

"Sounds about right," Evan says. Courtney loved being one of the boys and always wanted to do what we were doing.

I pick Maize up off the floor and place her on my hip. "Well, I'm going to take my baby and my soon-to-be wife home for a little celebration." I wink, giving Mila a cocky smile.

"Home," she repeats in agreement. "I'll never get tired of hearing that."

I lean down and press a kiss to her lips. "You'll always be my home no matter what."

EPILOGUE

John

I roll over and pull Mila into my arms, and she hums as she snuggles closer to me. The past six months since she came back to Texas have been like a dream. We've easily settled into our old routine, though it's changed slightly since the school's opened, and I couldn't be happier to know she's my fiancée. I'm the luckiest man on the planet to have Mila in my life and my soon-to-be wife.

Maize's been giving us a run for our money now that she's walking and getting into everything. We've even gone as far as adding a baby cam in her room because she's learned to crawl out of her crib like an escape artist. No matter how low we put the mattress, she somehow finds a way to sneak out. I never imagined she'd be a mini Houdini at only a year and a half, but considering she's a Bishop and has Riley around to teach her how to act up, it doesn't surprise me. She's so damn smart and amazes me every day.

"Do you want to sleep in, baby?" I hold Mila to my chest, her body fitting with mine, and she nods. Since starting the private school, she's been exhausted. She teaches, makes sure the kids' needs are being met, all while dealing with the parents and curriculum, so she's had her hands full. Even with all of that going on, she's never been happier. The school is full of students already, and parents keep calling Mama, thinking she can easily push them to the top of the waitlist. Because so many people want to enroll their kids, Mila's considering expanding and hiring more teachers, which is amazing. Pretty soon, it might outgrow the church building, but one thing at a time, as she constantly reminds me.

I get out of bed and peek inside Maize's room and see she's sleeping soundly in her crib. I decide to close the door and make breakfast, then I'll wake up my girls. Once I'm finished cooking, I go to our bedroom, lean over the bed, and wake Mila up with a kiss. She looks at me with sleepy eyes and wraps her arms around my neck and pulls me down.

"Just a quickie," she whispers.

"Your breakfast will get cold," I warn against her mouth, though I want to have all of her right now.

"So? That's what microwaves are for." She giggles just as I hear Maize mumbling in the baby monitor.

"It's like she knows," I whisper against her mouth and kiss her again before I walk out to grab Maize.

She's standing in her crib, and as soon as I walk in, she starts jumping. "Dada." She points at me.

"Good morning, baby girl." She holds out her arms, and I pick her up and kiss her cheek. I set her on the changing table, change her diaper, and then carry her into the kitchen.

Mila brushes her hands across my back as I'm putting Maize in her high chair. I turn and look at her wearing an oversized Packer T-shirt and shake my head with a smirk. "Can't believe you're wearing that after the Cowboys destroyed your team. Poor little Rodgers...I think I can still hear him crying."

Her hair is a mess, and she rolls her eyes as she fills her cup with coffee. "Well considering Rodgers got hurt in the preseason, it wasn't a fair fight. In fact, it's the only reason your cowgirls won." Mila sits at the table and digs into her omelet. As soon as the cheesy eggs hit her lips, she moans.

I pop an eyebrow up at her, and Maize starts laughing as she picks up a berry. She loves blackberries and chopped bananas for breakfast, and it has quickly become her favorite.

After we're finished eating breakfast, we take Maize to one of Mama's friends who helps Mila at the school, because we have big plans today. Elizabeth is there too, and we give her hugs and kisses before we leave.

Once we're home, we walk over to the B&B and make sure everything is running smoothly, then make our way to the old bank building that was rented out for Evan and Emily's co-ed bridal shower.

"Are you ready for this?" I look over at Mila as we make our way into town.

"Yeah, I'm really excited for them. Can't wait to see how Mama decorated for this one. The ladies at school told me how she goes all out and is the best party planner in this part of Texas." She looks over at me and smiles.

I chuckle. "Don't tell Mama they said that, or she'll get an even bigger head about it. Just wait until the wedding. You ain't seen nothin' yet."

We pull up into the parking lot, and it's full of cars. Apparently, they had to rent this building because the whole hospital staff was invited, and Mama sent invitations to the whole town. There are easily five hundred people in that building drinking mimosas just as brunch is being set out on tables, which was the number one reason Emily wanted it at ten in the morning.

I grab Mila's hand and kiss her knuckles. "We need to start planning our parties and set an official date."

"How about a fall wedding?" She laughs, then shakes her head. "Oh wait, that won't work. I'll have the 3k and 4k students back in school and–"

I lean over and kiss her. "You're thinking too much into it. We'll find a day that works for us, or we'll pick a date and make it work. There's no rush, but I'm impatient if you know what I mean."

She smiles against my lips. "Yes, and I can't wait to officially be a Bishop, though it will be a little weird being called that because that's what everyone calls your mother, and River, and soon Emily."

"No, Emily will be *Dr.* Bishop," I remind her with a smirk. "Let's get going, babe. The quicker we can go in there, the quicker we can get hounded about our wedding and when we're going to start making Mama more babies. Guaranteed. Put on your game face and show no weakness." I wink at her, and we get out of the truck laughing.

Opening the door for Mila, I get a good look at her ass in that skirt she decided to wear. I have zero complaints, but she turns around and catches me. "Southern gentleman...my *ass*."

"And that's exactly what I was looking at."

"I know, you're not even sly about it anymore."

I grab her hand, pull her back to me, and kiss the fuck out of her in the hallway before we walk into the main room. "I don't have to be, says the ring on your finger," I say breathlessly.

She playfully slaps my arm, and I interlock my fingers with hers as we enter. A lady from church is standing at the door and hands us plastic engagement rings, then explains the ongoing game to us.

"So the one who has the most plastic rings at the end of the party will win a prize. If you hear anyone say the word wedding or the word bride, then you get to take their rings."

"Oh my gosh, this is going to be so fun. What's this game called, exactly?" Mila laughs, placing the plastic ring on her finger. It's only big enough to fit on my pinky.

"The name is Put a Ring on it," the woman tells Mila, who looks over at me and smiles.

The room is decorated in lavender and ivory, and I think this time Mama has actually outdone herself. Pictures of Evan and Emily are placed around the room along with photos of Elizabeth. Soft music plays in the background, and as soon as Emily sees Mila and me, she makes her way over to us with mimosas. She hands them to us with a smile. "You're gonna need these. Trust me."

We exchange smiles, and I see Evan on the other side of the room, cornered by co-workers. I raise my glass to him, and he gives me a nod. River and Alex walk in, and soon I see Courtney, the triplets, and her husband, Drew. Courtney smiles and makes a beeline for us. Her blonde hair is perfectly curled, and she looks great. She'll always be my baby sister to me, but she looks so grown now.

"Oh my goodness. I've missed you so damn much!" She gives us both big hugs. "Let me see the ring in person." She turns to Mila, reaching for her hand.

With a big smile on her face, Mila shows Courtney and then turns to me and smiles. "You did good, John. This ring is as beautiful as your bride-to-be." They exchange laughs, and I love how the whole family is finally together.

"Give me your plastic ring, Court," I tell her, holding out my hand.

"That's so *not* fair," she groans, handing it over.

"I've missed you," I tell her as I wrap my arms around her and laugh just as Drew walks up. Mama captured the triplets, who are now three years old already, and brings them around the room, introducing them to all of her friends.

"Hey man," Drew says, giving me a firm handshake. "How've things been?"

"Great, actually." I glance over at Mila and give them a real introduction, though she's met everyone through FaceTime.

Just as I turn my head, Jackson is walking through the door with a smirk on his face. He sees Courtney, and his eyes widen. "Dang, little sis. Didn't know you were bringing a gun show to the party," he tells her, looking at Courtney's sleeveless shirt.

"If you don't watch it, you might get shot." She balls her fist up, then pulls Jackson into her arms. The two of them have always had a special relationship, hell Courtney has a special relationship with all of us considering she's the only girl and wanted to be a part of what the boys were always doing. Evan eventually makes his way over, and for the first time in too long, all the Bishop kids are together. Mama runs over with Dad and stops someone to take a photo of the group of us, with our significant others. The triplets make funny faces, and Jackson plays along, doing the same.

"Now, can we take a serious one?" Mama asks with a smile, but she's not kidding. Just before the photo is taken, all of us make faces, which only annoys her more. "I knew I shoulda never asked." Mama thanks the woman and looks at the photo with so much admiration that it warms my heart. She turns the phone around to show us. "Look at my beautiful family."

Somehow everyone slips away and leaves Mila and me there with Mama. "So we need to start planning that wedding, so I can get some more grandkids out of this deal."

Mila's cheeks redden. "Marriage before babies. We're trying to find the perfect date. And you can go ahead and hand over your plastic ring."

"Mila, honey. You know I didn't keep that ring for more than five seconds. But a serious question, how many kids do you want?"

"Mama! Can we not talk about this now?"

Mila laughs. "Four or five," she answers. "Maybe six," she adds, and now I know she's trying to appease her.

Mama nods her head, then pats me on the shoulder. "I knew I liked her a lot."

Looking down at her watch, Mama gasps. "We need to get this party started now."

Gifts cover the table, and I already know Mama has several games planned for the party. Just as we're walking over to where Emily and Evan are opening presents, I grab Mila's hand.

"Told you so," I tell her.

"Well, then let's just elope and start poppin' babies out," she teases.

"I can have you knocked up before the Fourth of July." I wink, and she laughs.

After going through the food line, we find a place to sit and realize we're right next to Kiera and Trent. I give Trent a handshake and Kiera a side squeeze.

"Hey y'all," Mila says.

Kiera is over the moon right now wearing a shirt with the words Maid of Honor printed across the chest. "I am so happy for Emily. Finally, my best friend is getting everything she's ever wanted and deserves."

We watch as Emily opens lingerie and household items along with gift cards. Evan sits next to her, making a list of everything, and the way they look at each other has me pulling Mila even closer. After the gifts are opened, and Mama's served the cake, we're all forced to play games. By the time we've made our way around the room for the wedding scavenger hunt, I notice Kiera has about ten plastic rings on her fingers.

"Hold your rings close," I whisper to Mila. "Kiera is a savage. Look how many she has."

Mila bursts into laughter then shows me her hands, and she has just as many.

"Oh my God, you are too," I tell her.

"So the goal is to get all of Kiera's rings, so then I can win." She's always been competitive, but she has a crazy look in her eye that makes me burst out into laughter.

Jackson walks up and shows all the rings he's stolen from people too. "You're falling behind a little, brother," he tells me, wiggling his fingers.

"Looks like *you* are," Mila bumps him and shows all the ones she's gotten.

Kiera walks up and sees all their rings, and that's when I know the competition is really about to be on. Jackson teases her, trying to get her to say the magic words, but she doesn't dare. Though Trent is close by, Jackson openly flirts with her, and if I didn't know better, she's flirting back.

"You better stop it, Jackson Bishop." She laughs as he tries to tickle the words out of her.

He looks over at Mila.

"Don't you dare lay a pinky on her, or I'll break your fingers off," I warn with a smile, but I'm not joking.

"Emily's gonna sure make a beautiful..." Jackson looks at Kiera.

"You're not tricking me out of this prize, Jackson." She places her hand on his chest, just as Trent comes up from behind her. I'm standing so close I can hear him whisper the word '*wedding*' in her ear. Kiera's face lights up, and she gasps real big then turns around with her hands on her hips. My mouth and everyone else's basically falls to the floor when we see Trent on one knee holding a black box with an engagement ring inside. She covers her hands over her mouth, and when I see Emily walking over smiling, I knew this was all planned from the beginning.

"Kiera, my love. I've waited my whole life to find a woman like you. You make the bad times good and the good times better. You're beautiful, caring, and my other half—my true soul mate. You make me want to be a better man and being loved by you is my greatest accomplishment. I can't imagine my life without you in it, and I want to spend the rest of my life with you. Kiera Young, will you marry me?"

Kiera nods her head and goes to him, kissing him—long and hard. They basically topple over on the ground, and I see tears falling down her cheeks. The whole room erupts into applause. Emily hugs her and tells her congratulations, and I think everyone is just as surprised as Kiera. Totally unexpected.

"Were you in on this?" Kiera asks Emily, wiping her cheeks.

"The whole time." Emily smiles and looks over at Trent who thanks her again for her help.

"You are so sneaky." Kiera squeezes her tight again. Happiness radiates from her, and while I'm happy, I'm quite shocked.

I glance around the room, and that's when my eyes meet Jackson's. He looks as if he's seen a ghost, and for him, I'm sure it's more like a nightmare. His hands are balled into fists, and I can tell he's steaming. Jackson's been drinking, as we all have, but he looks like he's ready for a fight. Since Mila is chatting with Kiera and Emily and the whole crowd, I take the opportunity to step away. Taking a deep breath, I go to him.

"You okay?" His eyes meet mine, and I already know the answer to that.

"Is he fucking serious? It's rude and tacky to propose during someone else's party. Kiera deserves better than that shit," he tells me, his emotions bubbling over. "I should go over there and punch his pretty boy face in."

I grab his shoulder and squeeze. "Emily knew and even helped with the plan."

His eyes meet mine, and I know he's crushed. "I need to get some fresh air."

"Want me to come with you?" I ask, though I know it might be better for him to be alone, to process what this really means.

"Nah. I need some space right now." Jackson shakes his head, looks at Kiera who's happily showing off her ring, then walks out the door.

I suck in a deep breath, and Evan finds me. "Is he okay?"

"No. He's not." I put on a smile when Kiera makes her way over to us and tell her congrats.

"I'm so happy," she tells Evan. "Thank you for this. I'll never forget it."

Kiera meets Mama's open arms, and I glance over at Evan. "You knew the whole time?"

He holds up his hands in defense. "Kiera and Emily are best friends. Happy wife, happy life. There was no way I even had a fight in that. Also, Jackson's dumb ass has had plenty of opportunities to be with Kiera." Evan gives me a stern look. "He's always said it's too late, and well, now it really might be."

The party continues, and after a while, Evan and Emily thank everyone for showing up. Once it's time to go, I look around the room and notice Jackson never returned. Mila notices too.

"Is Jackson going to be okay?" she asks after we say goodbye to everyone and walk toward the truck.

I suck in a deep breath. "Honestly. I don't know. I've never seen him so distraught before."

We climb in, buckle up, and Mila looks out the window. "I *almost* feel sorry for him, but this is kinda his fault."

"I know," I tell her with a small smile. "You know, I love you, right?"

"You know I love you more."

"No, you don't. There's no way."

Before heading home, we pick up Maize from the sitter and spend the whole afternoon being together. It's moments like these that I love and look forward to every single day. I'm so grateful I found a woman who makes me feel whole again, who loves me with every inch of her being. The thought brings me back to my brother, and I feel sad for him because out of all of us, he hasn't really experienced love like this.

Or perhaps he has, which is why he's so heartbroken. He's probably loved Kiera most of his life but could never admit it.

Once we arrive at the house, I can't stop thinking about Jackson and the look on his face before he left. I send him a text, checking on him, but he doesn't respond to it. Ten minutes later, I try calling him, but it goes straight to voicemail, which means he's probably drinking his pain away or finding someone's bed to crawl into. I send him one more text, hoping he'll see it once he turns his phone back on.

JOHN

Dude, call me, okay? I'm worried about you.

The evening fades into night, and after we put Maize to bed, Mila and I hold each other like tomorrow will never come. Our lips mingle together, and soon we're making love. Being with her so intimately is indescribable. The passion soars between us, and by the time we're both satiated, we're exhausted and fall asleep naked.

Rolling over, I nuzzle my face in the crook of Mila's neck and am woken by the sound of my phone vibrating on the table next to the bed. I peel my eyes open and see an unknown number on my phone and realize it's nearly two in the morning. I hurry and answer it.

"John?" I hear Jackson ask, or at least I think it's Jackson.

315

"Yeah? What's up?"

There's a long pause, and he clears his throat. "I need you to bail me out of jail."

I sit up in bed. "What? Are you okay?"

Mila stirs beside me, her eyes fluttering open, but it's evident she's just as concerned as I am.

He sounds like he's in rough shape, his voice raspy and low, so I ask again if everything is okay.

"I'll tell you when you get here. Just promise you won't tell Mama."

You can continue reading *Wrangling the Cowboy* and *Winning the Cowboy* to get their kids' stories or you can read *Keeping Him* to get Jackson's story

Wrangling the Cowboy
GAVIN & MAIZE

Bull riding is all Gavin's known for years, but when it's time to retire, he can't let go of the reckless lifestyle. He finds a job that brings him to a small-town Texas ranch and face-to-face with the woman who snuck out after their one-night stand.

She can pretend she's over him, but he's not letting her go that easily.

Maize Bishop spends her days cooking and baking for her family's bed and breakfast. The last thing she has time for is a relationship, especially when there are no single men within a hundred-mile radius. When a mysterious newcomer flirts with her over drinks, she gives in to his mesmerizing green eyes and goes home with him.

Now that he works for her family's ranch, she'll avoid him at all costs.

There are only so many places to hide, and keeping her distance is easier said than done. After months of giving her space, Gavin's tired of waiting for Maize to admit what he knows they both want—a second round between the sheets. It may only take eight seconds to win a championship, but he'll prove to her that he can go all night long.

She's too young, he's too arrogant, and together, they're electric—the perfect recipe for disaster.

Why you gotta be so heartless?
I know you think it's harmless

Girl, why you gotta be so in between
Loving me and leaving?

"Heartless"
-Diplo, Morgan Wallen,
Julia Michaels

Gavin

"Well, it's official. I'm joining a convent."

The bartender scoffs with an eye roll as she sets a shot in front of the brunette bombshell I've been eyeing. "You're too dramatic for your own good."

The soon-to-be nun downs the clear liquid and makes a face after. "I'm serious. I decided to take a chance and sign up for a dating app, and I swear to God…" She pulls her phone from her shorts pocket and unlocks the screen. "Alright, let's start with Dennis G. *Hey, beautiful,*" she mimics in a deeper tone. "*You like those braids pulled? I'll be your cowboy and let you ride me for a night.*"

I nearly choke on my beer while I hold back my laughter.

"I mean, c'mon!" She groans. "That doesn't even make sense! You'd have to bend me over to pull my braids like reins, so he'd be riding me…"

My dick stirs at the image she created in my head, and fuck me, I like it.

"You're too literal, Maize," the bartender scolds.

Maize. Of course, she'd have a pretty name too.

I *should* stop eavesdropping and staring, but I can't. She's gorgeous, and her smart mouth has kept me hard for the past hour. After a job interview, I stopped by the Circle B Saloon to unwind before my long drive back to Houston tomorrow. I decided to sit at one of the tall tables to face the TV, and I haven't been able to take my eyes off the woman who's clearly had a rough day.

"Okay, how about this one from Gregory H." She clears her throat as she prepares to read another message.

The girl cracks up as Maize spews another horrific one-liner.

"I fuckin' quit. There are no decent, single men in Eldorado. They're either taken, swing for the other team, or talk like they dropped out of middle school. So, I'm joining a convent. At least then, my eyes would never have to be assaulted by an unsolicited dick pic ever again. And let me tell you, the last picture I got was crooked and scarred me for life anyway."

That has me doubling over with laughter, and there's no hiding it this time. Both girls snap their gaze to me as I try to control myself. I grab the neck of the beer bottle, take a swig, and act as if I wasn't listening to every word.

"Looks like one guy finds you amusing..." The bartender holds out her hand with a grin, but Maize frowns.

"I do," I say with a shrug, hoping to make her smile. "Mostly because you as a nun...I ain't seein' it."

"Really? Because I can totally picture her on her knees."

Maize's face turns beet red as she throws a straw toward the bartender. She giggles as Maize's head drops.

And now the image of *her on her knees* surfaces in my head.

"I meant, *praying!* On your knees praying," the bartender clarifies, but it's obvious she's full of shit. She's got a smart mouth too, and I quickly wonder if they're related. They do look alike.

"Excuse my sister," Maize says. "She gets a kick out of embarrassing me."

"I was right about you two," I drawl, grabbing my nearly empty beer and standing.

"Right about what?" Maize asks as I take the stool next to her at the end of the bar. She doesn't flinch when my arm brushes hers, and I take that as a good sign.

"I had a feeling you were related." I nod toward the other girl.

"My little sister," she confirms. "Kenzie."

"Her *favorite* sister." Kenzie smirks.

"My *only* sister," Maize counters, narrowing her eyes as she scowls at her again. "My pain in the ass sister."

With a palm to her chest, Kenzie gasps. "That's it. I'm cutting you off."

"Nooo!" Maize whines. "I'll read you another message," she bribes. "It'll be a really good one."

"Or I could just buy you a drink?" I interrupt.

Realization hits her as she sits taller and licks her lips. "Did you just offer to buy me a drink?"

Before I can respond, Kenzie speaks up. "Marry this man. Marry him *now*."

Maize glares at Kenzie, and I can only imagine what she wants to say to her right now, which I find comical.

"I mean, unless...do you want a dick pic first?" I flash her a smirk.

"Exactly how much did you hear?"

"I've been sitting over there for an hour, so...a lot," I admit, and her cheeks tint pink again. "It was very entertaining."

Kenzie sets a beer in front of me and a margarita in front of Maize, then looks at me. "I'll add them to your tab." She waggles her brows before leaving to help other customers at the opposite end of the bar.

"Oh my God," Maize groans. "I'm sorry about her. She assumes and—"

I reach over and put my hand over hers to stop her. "I offered, remember?"

"Yes, that's right." She nods, pulling her hand from under mine and grabbing her glass. "Thank you."

She's been burned by so many douchebags she doesn't even realize I'm hitting on her. I can't imagine any guy dumb enough to walk away from Maize, but lucky for me, she's single, and so am I.

"I'm Gavin, by the way," I say, holding out my hand and hoping to touch hers again.

"Maize." She takes the bait, and we shake. "Sorry I'm not more bubbly. You caught me on a rough night."

"No apologies needed, Maize. Maybe I can cheer you up, though."

"Oh yeah? With a non-crooked dick pic?" She arches a brow, grinning.

I chuckle, glad she's not giving me the cold shoulder. Though I've never had a problem getting a woman's attention, it's not out of the realm of reality. When I was a professional bull rider, women would flock to me, and I'd have to tear them off just to walk through a crowd. But I don't compete anymore. That life's behind me now.

"I'm too old to send explicit pictures to women."

Her eyes lower as she checks me out, then she tilts her head and studies me. "You can't be *that* old."

I suck in my lower lip as I soak in her delicate features. Light blue eyes, dark hair, and pale skin. She's undoubtedly my type, but something else about her has my blood pumping.

"I'm certain I'm quite older than you," I counter, taking a swig of my beer. "Why don't you tell me how old you are?"

"Because it's embarrassing. Most girls my age are married with a couple of kids already. And me? Well, I'm joining a convent."

"You're at least twenty-one, being that you're in a bar drinking. Definitely *not* over thirty." I tilt my head, looking at her eyes, skin, and lips. Fuck, she has the most beautiful face I've seen in a long time. "You're having a quarter-life crisis since, like you said, no husband and no babies. So, I'm gonna guess twenty-five." If I'm right, that means I'm ten years older than her.

Maize gulps down more of her drink as she watches me in amusement. "Sadly, you're correct. Well, in a few months."

I burst out laughing and shake my head. "You have plenty of time. Stop worryin'."

"That's so easy for guys to say! My grandma married my grandfather at nineteen, and they had five kids before she was thirty. Five! Granted, one pregnancy was twins, but still. I'm already behind."

"That was standard tradition thirty, forty, fifty years ago. But now, it's statistically proven that more couples wait to start their families and focus on their careers first. The average age of having their first baby is thirty. So, you still have *plenty* of time."

"Oh okay, so I only need to find a husband, convince him to marry me, get pregnant, and pop out a baby in the next five years. Noted."

"Or…" I counter, taking a long sip of my beer until it's empty. "You can just do whatever the fuck you want." Flashing a smirk, she tilts her lips up in amusement.

Before she can respond, Kenzie returns. "Another round?"

"Yes, ma'am. Keep 'em comin'. Maize and I have a game of pool to play. Loser buys shots."

"We do?" She furrows her brows as she sucks down the last of her alcohol.

"If you're gonna be a nun, you need to have as much fun as you can now. So, let's get started."

"I like him." Kenzie beams. "And if you don't marry him, I'm next in line."

"Oh, *puh-lease*. Everyone knows you and Grayson are gonna hate bang and finally admit your true feelings," Maize states.

"Don't you dare put that negative energy into the universe." Kenzie starts waving her arms around as if she's trying to push it away. "Grayson can go fuck himself for all I care."

If I knew who Grayson was, I'd be scared for him right now.

"Sounds like man-hating runs in the family." I grab the bottle Kenzie hands me.

Maize snorts and shakes her head. Once her glass is full again, I grab her hand and lead her to the pool table in the back. The pub is small and offers minimal seating, but I like it. It's a typical small-town country bar with Texas décor and pictures of cowboys on the walls. However, it's not loud and crowded, so Maize and I can actually hear each other talk and move around.

"Should I assume you know how to play, or do you need a personal hands-on tutorial?" I ask, setting my beer down. Grabbing two sticks, I hand her one, then pick up the triangle rack.

"You're quite cocky, you know that?" She bites her lip, and I notice the way her eyes rake down my body as if she wants to eat me like a snack.

"I prefer *confident*," I retort. "Though I'll say most women find that attractive in a man." I start gathering the balls from the pockets.

"Don't forget I'm becoming a nun, so my knowledge of men is lackluster at best." She sets her drink on the edge of the table and grabs the chalk. I have a feeling she knows her way around a pool table and just might give me a run for my money.

"I'd be willing to bet you know plenty. Though your execution on how to use it to your advantage might be the issue." I rack the balls and position the white ball to break. "Ladies first."

Maize narrows her gaze as she leans down and rubs the stick over her bridge hand. She pushes her ass out, which shows off her long, toned legs, and I tilt my head to get a better look.

"You keep staring like that, and you're gonna lose big time," she smarts off, then takes her shot. The balls bounce off the sides, and eventually, one goes into a pocket.

I smirk at her victorious expression.

"Looks like I'm stripes."

"Guess so. Let's see whatcha got." I fold my arms over my chest and watch in amazement as she sinks the next three balls before missing one.

We take turns calling pockets, and after fifteen minutes, we're each down to one. She talks shit the whole time, which I find cute as hell. This girl isn't trying to impress me with her body or by whispering all the dirty things she'd like to do to me. Not that I'd protest, but she's actually making conversation, and it's a breath of fresh air compared to what I'm used to.

Living on the road meant having my fair share of women available but being a bull rider—now retired—put a giant spotlight on me. Many saw the eight-pack and toned muscles and immediately stripped off their clothes. I won't deny I loved the lifestyle up until my last rodeo, but after a dozen injuries under my belt, I knew it was time to settle down.

"Corner pocket," she announces, taking her stance. I'll admit I'm a sore loser, and the thought of losing bruises my ego a bit. I find it hot as fuck that she knows how to play so well. But that doesn't mean I'm gonna give her the game.

Standing across from her, I rest my stick on the wall, then pull off my shirt. It's a bitch move since I know how she'll react, and it'll definitely distract her, but I like to play a little dirty.

"What are you doin'? We're in public," she warns.

Glancing around casually, I see three people at the bar and a couple at one of the far tables. I shrug and flex. "I don't think they mind."

326

Her throat moves when she swallows, and her hard gaze focuses on my abs as she tries to make the winning shot.

"You're tryin' to make me lose, aren't you?" She points at me and scowls. "It's not gonna work. I'm a nun-in-training and am completely *immune* to you."

"Is that so?" I puff out my chest to prove she's lying.

Maize blinks hard as if she's trying to look away but can't. "Yep. Doesn't faze me one bit. You're just wasting your time."

"Then why do you keep talkin' about it?" I challenge.

"Whatever. I'm not." She leans down again to focus on the ball. I shift my body until I'm in her line of sight, and when she goes to make her move, I grip the edge of the table as hard as I can. The veins in my hand pop out right before she strikes the cue ball, causing her to put too much force behind the shot, and the ball bounces onto the floor.

"Shit!" She slams the bottom of the stick against the floor and pouts. "You did that on purpose!"

Bending down, I grab it and walk over to her. Her breath hitches as I close the gap between us, and her eyes lower down my chest and stomach once again.

"I think you dropped this…" I hold the ball out for her, but she doesn't move.

Knowing I'm getting to her, I reach down and place the ball in her palm, then flash her a wink. "Wanna try it again?"

Finally, she blinks and steps back, putting at least a foot of space between us. "No, that'd be cheating. It's your turn."

"Alright." I grin as I take my position and call the pocket. Moments later, I sink my last ball.

She groans loudly, and I laugh.

"Problem?" I ask, looking over my shoulder.

She glares at me, shaking her head, and I bring my focus back to the eight-ball.

"Middle pocket," I say, then shoot it in perfectly.

"Looks like I'm buying shots," she says, defeated.

I put up our sticks, then tilt her chin up until our eyes meet. "Or we could skip them, and you could come home with me."

Maize looks like she's gonna pass out as she stares at me intently. I'm pretty sure I've shocked her into silence. The corner of my lips tilts up in amusement as I watch her mind spin out of control.

"It's a yes or no question, Maize. You look like you're trying to solve a trigonometric equation."

She wrinkles her nose and finally inhales a breath. "I-I'm a mess. You heard how awful I am with dating…" She holds out her hand, motioning to the bar. "And you witnessed firsthand how pathetic I am at flirting. I mean, seriously, it's sad. So, why would you—"

Before she can continue ranting, I cup her face, and our mouths collide. She's hesitant at first and barely brushes her lips against mine. When I slip my tongue inside, she finally relaxes into my touch. She tastes like lemon and salt, a combination of the alcohol she was drinking earlier.

My hand slides down her body as she wraps her arms around my neck, pulling me closer, and I know she wants this as much as I do. Maize releases a moan, and the sound goes straight to my dick. I want to hear that noise all night long—underneath me, on top of me, bent over in front of me. And there's no denying she does too.

"Maize, I need an answer before I embarrass myself here," I murmur against her mouth.

"Yes," she whispers. "Take me home with you."

"I need to pay my tab. I'll be right back," I say, somehow stepping back and releasing her. "Fuck." I adjust myself, then grab my shirt and slip it on. Maize giggles, and I notice the way she touches her swollen ruby red lips.

"Hey, Kenzie. I need to close out," I tell her, grabbing my wallet.

She gives me the total, and I hand her my card. Once I write the tip and sign the receipt, I slide it to her with a thank you.

"You're welcome. Don't forget to wear a condom!" she shouts as I make my way back to Maize, and I swear she's blushing more than before.

"You ready?" I hold out my hand.

"Dear God, yes." She grabs it, and I lead her through the back entrance to my truck. "I love my sister, but she's loud and obnoxious, which is sometimes cute, but typically embarrassing."

I chuckle as we climb inside, and I start the engine.

"She loves getting a rise outta you," I say, making my way down the street to Colt's apartment. Since I was only staying for one night, he let me use it while he visits his girlfriend in Dallas.

Five minutes later, I pull into the parking lot, and we jump out.

"You live here?" she asks as I scramble to find the key.

"No, it's a friend's place. He's not home, though."

As soon as I open the door, I flick on a couple of lights and lead her inside. "Do you want a nightcap?" I ask, gripping her hand in mine and leading her to the kitchen.

"No, thanks." She stops walking, and I quickly look at her. Maize grabs my waist and pulls herself close, then reaches for my face. I lean down and meet her lips as she pushes her tongue inside my mouth. She roams her hands over my body, lowering them to my belt buckle and zipper. Once she successfully undoes my jeans, I grab her shirt and pull it off. I wait a moment to take in how breathtaking her body is—perky tits, flat stomach, and slim waist. She's a fuckin' meal that I can't wait to devour.

"Goddamn, Maize..." I help her out of her tight jean shorts. "You're driving me insane."

"Take yours off *now*," she orders.

Once we're both down to only our underwear, I slide a hand between her thighs and feel how wet she is for me. I nearly combust when she coats my finger through the fabric of her panties.

Before I forget, I grab my wallet from my jeans. I pull out a condom, then drop the wallet on the floor. "Your sister's orders," I say, chuckling.

Maize shakes her head. "She acts like *she's* the older one."

Sliding my hands down her body, I grip her ass and lift her into my arms. Maize's legs wrap around me as my erection pushes against her. Our mouths crash together as I walk us through the living room and into the bedroom. Once she's flat on the mattress, I tower over her and sink my teeth into her neck.

"Fuck, I want you so bad," I growl into her ear. Flattening my tongue against her warm skin, I slide it over her jaw until I meet her lips again. "Say it, Maize. Tell me you want this as much as I do."

I hate that I need the reassurance, but after getting a glimpse of her doubts about men tonight, I need to be certain she does.

"I do, Gavin. I want it so bad. Fuck me...*hard*." She nearly begs as she arches her body up into mine.

"You got it, sweetheart." I move down her body and help her unsnap her bra. Covering her nipple with my mouth, I suck hard until she yelps. Then I move to the other.

"God, you're beautiful, Maize. I don't know if one night is gonna be enough to satisfy my craving for you. You're already like a sweet tooth I can't kick." I kiss down her stomach until I reach the edge of her panties. Once I remove them, I slowly slide my tongue up her slit. Her breathing grows faster, and I know the moment I dive inside her, she'll combust.

I flick her clit before sucking it and tasting her. Gliding my hand up her thigh, I spread her wider and then push a finger into her pussy. She gasps, rocking her hips as I thrust.

As her sweet juices cover my mouth and face, I devour her like my last meal. It takes only a couple of minutes before her legs clench, and she screams out her release.

I'm well practiced with control and patience, but my willpower snaps the moment she comes on my tongue. Quickly, I remove my jeans, then slip on the condom. As soon as I line up with her entrance, I push inside.

The moment our bodies connect is fucking heaven.

She wraps her legs around my waist as I pound into her, over and over, giving her exactly what she asked of me. *Hard and fast.*

As she gasps for air and lets out little breathy noises, I know she's close again, so I don't slow down until she squeezes my cock. We rock together in perfect harmony as I rub her clit and massage her breast.

"Fuuuuck, Maize. You're so tight."

"Don't stop, oh my God, it's soooo good." She bucks her hips wildly as she fists the sheets. "I'm so close. Go deeper," she begs.

I lift one of her legs until it's on my shoulder and spread her wider so I can angle myself to get deeper inside her pussy. The moment I do, her entire body shakes, and she moans out her third release.

"Holy shit," she pants.

"I'm not done with you," I tell her, shifting back. "Roll over," I demand.

As soon as she does, I get between her legs and grip her hips. Maize arches her back and sticks out her plump ass for me.

"Spank me. *Hard.*"

Raising my arm slightly, I crack my hand against her cheek and smile when I see how red it gets. "Fuckin' perfect, baby."

I position myself between her thighs and return to paradise. With one hand, I fist her hair and yank her head back until my mouth touches her ear. "I've been fantasizing about doing this to you since the moment you mentioned it at the bar tonight. Bending you over and pulling your hair... fuck, I'd been hard for hours just thinkin' about it."

"Yes," she purrs. "Pull harder."

She looks up at me with big blue eyes, and I nearly lose myself right then.

"Don't push me, Maize," I growl. "I don't wanna hurt you."

"You won't," she assures me. "I want it hard and rough with you, Gavin. Don't stop."

I do exactly as she asks. I pull her hair as I fuck her from behind, slamming my cock so goddamn deep inside her pussy she'll be feeling me there for days. Then I smack her ass again to make sure my red imprint stays too.

The moment she clenches around my cock and gasps for more air, I wrap my hand around her throat and squeeze gently. She loses control, and seconds later, I do too.

My body aches from the best sex I've ever had.

I can say that with one-hundred-percent certainty, which, considering I haven't dated a woman in over a decade, is fucking insane. One-night stands, yes, but I never get attached. And I definitely don't think about round two the next day.

But I am. I want Maize for breakfast, lunch, and dinner. Then again for dessert. The taste of her pussy and sweet skin is still on my tongue, and I need more.

I half-open my eyes and see the sun blazing through the blinds. Why in the hell Colt doesn't have curtains is beyond me, but at least this way, I'll be able to fuck Maize and admire every perfect inch of her body.

When I roll over to find her, I'm greeted with an empty bed.

What the hell?

I feel around, but the sheets are cold.

No…she couldn't leave. I drove us here.

Deciding to check around the apartment, I pull on my boxers and walk to the kitchen. When it's empty, I check the bathroom. Then the living room.

Next, I notice her clothes aren't on the floor.

She *left*.

I check the time, and it's barely eight in the morning.

No note, no phone number for me to reach her, *nothing*.

Well, shit. There really is a first time for everything, and I can't say I'm a fucking fan of getting bailed on the morning after.

CHAPTER ONE

Maize

THREE WEEKS LATER

As I get dressed for work, I can hear my parents chatting, and it makes me smile. I've been trying to soak in these little moments because eventually I'll move out and get my own place. My dad wants me to live here until I'm fifty, but that's not happening. It's one of the reasons I've been thinking about starting a catering business as a side hustle.

"Oh stop," Mom says with a giggle as I pull my hair into a tight ponytail. After all these years, they're still madly in love, and sometimes I wonder if that'll be in the cards for me. Not even my gourmet meals can snag me a man. I'm doomed to become a nun or be a single woman with twelve dogs and horses to keep me occupied. It's something I'm coming to terms with.

I'm picky, and I've got rules—well, a rule. I don't date men who work on my family's ranch. I got my heart broken and won't let it happen again. Most of the men in my small town are taken, too young, or related to me, so the pickings are really slim. Becoming a nun has been a running joke, but it *could* be my reality.

After I finish getting ready, I walk into the kitchen and pour a cup of coffee. I sit next to my dad, trying to wake up because I'll need to be on my A game once I get to the bed and breakfast. As the head chef, I have four employees to manage and plan the meals for the week. My sole responsibility is to introduce all the guests to comfort food and Grandma's favorite recipes. They deserve an authentic Southern experience for breakfast, lunch, and dinner, and I take it very seriously.

"What's on the menu today?" Dad asks as he slips on his cowboy boots. He has managed the B&B since before I was born, and he takes pride in his work. Mom smiles, and I notice she's already dressed for work in black slacks and a pink blouse. When she moved to Texas permanently, she saw a need for childcare and opened the only daycare in Eldorado. It quickly transitioned into a private school and now boasts a long waiting list due to its popularity. Once my sister, Kenzie, graduates with a degree in education, she'll work there too.

We're early risers here—well, except for Kenzie when she's bartending at the Circle B Saloon until close. Right now, she's home from college, but she'll return in a few days. I'm not looking forward to it because I always miss her when she's gone.

"Breakfast consists of the normal spread of grits, biscuits, gravy, sausage, bacon, waffles, muffins, blueberry pancakes, omelets, and scrambled eggs. For lunch, I planned fried chicken, mashed potatoes, green beans, and rolls. Dinner is beef tips with gravy and rice, corn bread and veggies on the side, and finally, triple chocolate cake for dessert."

"I'm sure the ranch hands are gonna love that," Dad says with a laugh. "I mean, the guests."

"Oh, I'm sure they will." I cut my eyes to him, but all he does is shrug. The ranch workers eating at the B&B is a tradition my uncles started in their twenties. Uncle Jackson's to blame, but everyone knows he can't be controlled. After realizing he was gonna keep eating and inviting half the ranch to join him, Grandma made it a perk for the workers. By the time I got out of culinary school, I knew exactly what I was signing up for when I took the job.

I cook quadruple servings each day because the workers eat like horses, and I still need enough for the guests. There usually aren't any leftovers, so at least nothing's wasted. Knowing people appreciate my cooking does make me feel good, but I still give them shit for liking it so much. Then again, so does Dad.

Once my mug is empty and I'm more awake, I stand and grab my keys. Mom tells me to have a good day, and Dad says he's right behind me. I give them a wave and leave. Though the sun won't be up for another hour, it doesn't bother me. I enjoy getting up before the roosters and like the stillness of my surroundings.

When I arrive, the big farmhouse lights are dimmed, and I take my time turning them on. I walk into the kitchen to grind the coffee beans and then put them in the maker to brew. After I pull out the menu I've planned, I start pulling the ingredients from the cabinets. There's no canned food or anything pre-made served here. It's all mixed and made with love.

I've wanted to be a chef since I was a little girl, thanks to Grandma. As the fifth oldest grandkid but only the second girl, I spent a lot of time with her growing up. When I was five, she had me baking homemade blueberry muffins by memory. My childhood was different from my cousins because my biological mother passed away from cancer nine weeks after I was born. Dad had no idea I existed until I was left on the porch of the B&B. Raising a newborn wasn't something he knew how to do, so he hired Mila to be my nanny and help him adjust to being a single parent. They fell madly in love, and the rest is history. She raised me as her own and is the only mother I've ever known. Soon after, they were married, and Mila got pregnant with Kenzie. Once my sister was born, our family was complete. While I wish I knew more about my biological mother at times, I'm thankful for the family I do have.

Jane and Sandra arrive right on time and immediately take over for me, then finish with the omelets, scrambled eggs, and the muffins. I restack the plates, refill the silverware bin, and then bring out the vat of coffee to the dining area. The three of us work together like a well-oiled machine. While I'm in charge, I never have to micromanage because they know what I expect them to do each day.

We have a list of a hundred different recipes we rotate in and out, and we occasionally throw in new ones to see how people like them. The ranch hands are opinionated but no one has ever hated anything we've served. If they have, they've kept their damn mouths shut and rightfully so.

We run food out to the burners, and when I look up at the clock, I'm shocked we only have five minutes until breakfast begins. It never fails to amaze me how fast time passes when I'm here.

Dad enters and gives me a grin. "Smells good."

"Thanks, Mr. Bishop," Sandra says. I look over my shoulder and give him a big smile.

After everything is set and ready for the breakfast rush, we immediately start making the second and third rounds of food because it'll go fast. Soon, the dining room is full of chatter. Sandra checks every ten minutes and makes a list of what we need to replenish.

"More sausage and pancakes," she says at the door. "And coffee, but I'll get that going."

Each morning, the three of us do this dance. I usually cook on the flat top, and Jane is at the stove while Sandra makes her rounds to top off the food and drinks.

When I turn my head, my sister and cousin Rowan barge through the kitchen door, chatting about God knows what. Kenzie carries a plate holding an omelet, and she's stuffing her face.

"What are y'all doin' here?" I ask.

"Coming to visit you, of course!" Kenzie exclaims, then shrugs. "And eat."

"Thought we'd keep you company for a little while," Rowan says with a grin, propping herself up on the counter and swinging her legs back and forth. Though I'm working and don't need the distractions, I'm glad they're here so we can catch up anyway. Considering Kenzie is going back to college in a few days, I want to spend as much time with her as I can.

Rowan looks like she's floating on cloud nine, and I'm so tempted to say something about how annoyingly in love she is with Diesel, but I refrain.

As if she can read my mind, she speaks up. "Bite me."

"So, how's the sex?" Kenzie blurts. Rowan and Diesel have been inseparable, and while it's disgustingly cute, I'm happy for her.

"Kenzie!" I scold, knowing my employees can hear every word we're saying, but they keep our secrets like vaults. Oftentimes, they're so focused I forget they're still in the room. They both have kids a little older than us, so they're hardly fazed.

"What?" She takes a bite of her omelet. "You were thinking it too. I just care enough to ask," she states with pride.

I gag, and we all start laughing. Considering the breakfast rush is nearly over, I grab the ingredients to make the homemade rolls for lunch.

"Don't be a love hater. Someday, Maze…you're gonna find *the one*."

Just the thought of it has me rolling my eyes while I mix, then beat the dough.

"Speaking of which, Diesel and Riley are coming to the bar tonight with the new guy who just got hired. You should come. Kenzie and I are working," Rowan insists.

"Hells yes, you should!" Kenzie's face lights up, and she's way too excited about it. "Stay until after my shift so I can use my newfound drinking freedom to do it *legally*." She just turned twenty-one a month ago and takes every opportunity to remind us.

I glance at her. "I'm busy tonight."

"Doing what?" Rowan asks, doubtful. "Bingeing *Love is Blind* and shoving dark chocolate into your mouth doesn't qualify as busy."

I give her my best death glare, unamused by how right she is.

"But you gotta admit, it's a train wreck you can't look away from…" Kenzie says, referring to the show. "Cameron's my favorite. I'd marry him in a heartbeat."

"See?" I hold my hand out toward Kenzie. "I need to catch up."

Rowan doesn't buy my excuse, though. "You can do it tomorrow. Tonight, you're coming to the bar! No arguing!"

I plop the dough on the counter, then break it into pieces and roll it into balls. "Damn, I thought getting laid would make you nicer," I mutter with a smirk.

"Maybe you're the one who needs to get laid, meanie," she retorts.

"I *definitely* need to get laid," Kenzie adds, and the three of us burst into laughter. I know we're being loud as hell, but I can't help it. These two bring out the best in me.

"What's all this noise I'm hearing?" Dad enters, and I hope to all things holy he didn't overhear what we were talking about. I'd be absolutely mortified.

"None of your business," I quickly say. "Girl talk. No boys allowed."

"Pretty sassy for someone who still lives under my roof," Dad teases, not that I needed the reminder.

"Kenzie and I are gonna get an apartment in the city," I say casually, wanting to change the subject quickly.

"Not a chance in hell," he snaps. "Nice try, though." He reaches over and steals one of the apple turnovers that Kat delivered this morning. Kat's a family friend who provides the B&B with gluten-free pastries. While I could prepare everything, Grandma Bishop loves to support Kat's bakery, and it's something we've done for a long time.

"Dad…" I suck in a breath. "I'm almost twenty-five and live at home. Do you know how pathetic I sound? I need my own place."

He lifts his eyebrow. "You can move out when you get married."

This response causes me to snort, considering my very single relationship status. "And did you and Mom wait till marriage to move in with each other?"

I cross my arms and wait for his answer.

"Do as I say…"

"Not as I do," Kenzie pipes in and finishes his sentence.

"That's right." Dad kisses Kenzie on the head. "Your mom isn't ready to be an empty nester yet, and frankly, I think she'll go crazy without you two there, so until you're in a serious relationship, no talk of moving out."

Rowan looks at us with a tilted head. "My parents are halfway there. I wonder if they'll get all sappy on me when I move out?" she asks.

"Knowing your mom and dad, they're ready to relive their youth days and have their privacy back," Dad says with a chuckle. "They didn't exactly take the slow and steady route."

"Thanks for the visual…" Rowan groans. "Now I need to go throw up my breakfast."

Dad chuckles, then pats her on the shoulder. "Alright, well I'm gonna leave y'all to your girl talk."

Kenzie and Rowan continue chatting, and when the clock changes to ten, crumbs are all that remain. I add fruits and pastries to different baskets we keep out for the guests, as Sandra and Jane continue prepping for lunch.

"So, you never answered the question," Kenzie reminds Rowan. "How's the sex?"

"Mind-blowing," Rowan says, then snorts.

"I gotta clean up and get ready for lunch," I tell them, wanting no part of this conversation.

"Go for it," Kenzie shoos.

After the dining room is cleaned, Jane and I peel the boiled potatoes and then mash them. While I'm adding tons of butter to the pounds of russets, Rowan turns to me.

"So about tonight. I need you to commit."

I bite the inside of my cheek, then add salt and pepper. "You're not gonna let me get out of this, are you?"

Kenzie laughs at how demanding Rowan is being.

"Nope! You're joining us. The whole gang will be there, and you deserve to have a little fun."

"Fun?" I question with a smirk. She elbows me, and I grunt.

Soon the kitchen smells of fried chicken and cornbread. I realize how hungry I am, but I don't typically have time to eat until after serving lunch. When we place the hot food in the dining room, Kenzie and Rowan are the first to grab a plate.

"Ahh, now I see why you really came."

Rowan snickers. "Nah, this is just a bonus."

Kenzie takes a seat, then stuffs her mouth full and lets out a moan. "Mmm. So good."

Soon, guests trickle in and pile their plates, and chatter fills the room. Once Kenzie and Rowan finish eating, we exchange hugs, and I start on my cleanup list as I go over the dinner menu with Donna and Becky, the ladies who work the dinner shift.

I typically do the morning and lunch rush because it's so time-consuming, but I'll help in the evening too if I'm bored. We have a short meeting, then I post the menu for the rest of the week so we're all on the same page.

Jane and Sandra finish prepping as Donna and Becky start cooking. I go through the fridge and pantry and then write down what I'll need to order next week. Just as I'm wrapping up my list, Grandma Bishop walks in wearing her million-dollar smile. Immediately, she opens her arms and pulls me into a hug. I'm pretty sure I'm her favorite grandkid.

"Maize, sweetie, I've missed you," she tells me with a tight squeeze.

"I saw you Friday!" I remind her.

"Doesn't mean I can't miss you," she retorts, then pulls away and greets my employees. They're old friends who chat about the weather and their grandbabies as they work.

Dad walks in, sees Grandma, and laughs. "Mama. Whatcha doin' here?"

"I leave the house, and y'all act like it's a Christmas miracle. I'm not *that* old yet. But since you're so concerned, I was gettin' ready for my quilt club meeting and wanted to stop by and see you two on my way out," she explains, but her smile doesn't falter.

"Checkin' up on me, Grandma?" I ask.

She grabs my cheek like I'm five. "Always, dear."

This causes Dad to let out a howl. "Maize walks a straight line, just like her father. Now, Kenzie, she's a different story."

"Okay, well, if I'm being truthful, I heard you were making double chocolate cake for dinner. I told Scott that sugar wasn't allowed in the house anymore because it's not good for our waistline. So, I thought I'd just grab a slice and be on my way."

Dad snorts. "That's cheatin, Mama."

"No, no, it's not. I said no more sugar was allowed *in* the house. The B&B isn't home, is it? Technically, I'm still following the rules I set."

I cover my mouth to hold back my laughter, then point over to the fridge where the five cakes are waiting.

"That's why you're my favorite," Grandma says, and it causes me to beam.

Dad just shakes his head. "Wait till I tell Dad about your little scheme."

"You will do no such thing, John Joseph Bishop," she warns.

"Oooh, Grandma just pulled out the middle name," I quip.

Grandma lifts an eyebrow at me as she walks over and grabs a to-go box. After cutting the biggest slice of cake I've ever seen, she places a plastic fork in the container with it and then gives me a wink.

"You never saw me. I wasn't here." She waves her hand as though she's trying to pull a Jedi mind trick on us, and somehow, it works because neither of us will tattle.

I crack up, and Dad rolls his eyes. Grandma pats me on the shoulder, then waltzes out as quickly as she walked in.

"Grandpa showed up earlier. Trust me when I say he ate a stack of pancakes with extra, extra syrup," he tells me with a shit-eating grin.

"Oh God," I let out. "They're cheaters! Both of them."

"Not technically, just found loopholes. And they wonder where Jackson gets this shit from!" he exclaims. A bell dings at the front desk, so he hurries to fill his cup full of coffee, then leaves.

As I'm washing my hands, my phone vibrates. Once I dry them off, I pull my cell from my back pocket.

> **ROWAN**
> See you tonight!

I laugh.

> **MAIZE**
> I said maybe!

> **ROWAN**
> You will be there, or I'll kick your ass.

This makes me laugh.

> **MAIZE**
> Aww. How sweet. I'd like to see you try, though ;)

> **ROWAN**
> I'm serious! Plus, who knows, you might meet a new man at the bar tonight. You just never know.

> **MAIZE**
> Oh pleaseeeee. We all know the only guys I'll see there are the regulars and ranch hands.

> **ROWAN**
> Don't be a Debbie Downer. They're coming around nine. Be there or be scared. You deserve to let loose and have a little fun!

> **MAIZE**
> You know I'm an old lady and get up early.

> **ROWAN**
> So it's time to change that. See ya there!

I send her a thumbs-up, something she hates, then I grab all the dirty rags and place them in the wash before telling everyone bye. Rowan doesn't like to take no for an answer, but I don't want to commit just yet. I'm so tired I might fall asleep before the sun sets.

Once I'm home, I kick off my shoes and relax on the couch. I close my eyes, knowing I need to shower because I smell like a mix of food and sweat.

"Are you sleepin'?" Kenzie asks.

I open my eyes and glance at her because I didn't even hear her come in. "Not yet, but if you would've left me a little longer, I might've been. Mondays are always so exhausting."

She gives me a half-smile. "Okay, just wanted to let you know I'm leaving. Get your ass rested so you can hang out with me until close."

I groan because she's just as relentless as Rowan.

She nods, then checks the time. "See you later, sis."

I give her a wave, then finally get up and head for the shower. Staying up late during the week isn't something I like to do because of how early I have to get up in the mornings, but I want to spend as much time with Kenzie before she returns to school. I really can't wait until she graduates in the spring and is home permanently. It's just not the same here without her.

After I clean up, I take an hour nap and reset my brain before I begrudgingly go to the bar. Though I may not stay until close like Kenzie wants, I hope it makes them happy to know their peer pressure still works after all these years.

CHAPTER TWO

Gavin

Over the weekend, I moved all my shit into one of the spare ranch hand cabins. Though the new place is furnished, I still had a lot to pack and bring with me. I also couldn't leave Houston without my favorite saddle and rope. I thought I could pack up and move in with little effort, but it took an entire day just to load my truck. Then it rained during the whole damn drive to Eldorado.

This morning, I woke up extra early for my first official day on the job. I've already taken a shower and drunk a cup of coffee, and I still have forty-five minutes before I have to meet with Alex Bishop, the ranch manager. Instead of waiting around and watching the clock, I decide to head out.

The directions Jackson, my new boss, gave me are comical. The map he emailed me does not have any named roads—just barns, curbs, and cactus patches—and it looks like a five-year-old drew it. It's Southern directions at their finest. After I drive over nine cattle guards, I should see a metal

Even though I live on the ranch, it's so massive it takes me nearly fifteen minutes to arrive where I need to be. The sun hasn't risen yet, but I'm grateful to see lights on in the shop and an old pickup outside. I park and enter, not sure what to expect.

Alex, who I met previously, is drinking a cup of coffee at a desk. He's Jackson's younger brother and about ten years older than me. Two guys in their mid-twenties give each other shit, and he watches them with a grin. After a moment, Alex notices me.

"Alright, if you ladies are done, Gavin's here," Alex interrupts them.

They both turn and size me up. By their expressions, I don't think they knew a new employee was starting today.

"Gavin, this is my son, Riley."

He didn't have to tell me because they look nearly identical other than their age. I take Riley's hand and shake it firmly.

"This is Diesel, he runs the cattle operation," Alex continues.

"Nice to meet you," Diesel says with a handshake and a grin.

"He's new to Eldorado and will be staying in one of the ranch hand cabins. He'll be working with Jackson on breaking in the wild horses. He has bull riding experience and trains riders too."

Diesel looks at me with a sly grin. "Bull riding?" His brows raise, a reaction I'm used to from people when they learn what I used to do. "Impressive."

"Thanks. It was dangerous work, won some competitions, got some trophies, but I'm retired now." People are always shocked by what I've accomplished. I've made enough money to do whatever I want, and I stopped riding bulls before I broke my back. However, I keep those details to myself.

"I bet you have some insane stories about traveling to rodeos and competing, huh?" Riley gives me a smirk.

"Or how much ass you got?" Diesel taunts.

The corner of my lips tilts up as I think about the past. It was a wild and crazy time. "You could say that. On both accounts."

"Maybe over a round of beers," Diesel suggests. "My girlfriend works at the Circle B Saloon in town and will hook us up. We could meet up after work."

Riley groans, and I'm not entirely sure why. Might be because Diesel mentioned his girlfriend, but I have a feeling there's more to this story than they're saying.

"Uh, sure. I've been there a couple of times." I pinch the back of my neck, thinking about the last time I was in town. Maize comes to the forefront, and I half-wonder if she'll be there. Wouldn't that be some crazy shit? I look at him. "How about nine?"

"Sounds good," he tells me.

One thing I love about this part of Texas is everyone's friendly, and I know Diesel's genuinely inviting me to make me feel welcome. It's just how people are around these parts, and the last thing I want to do is reject the offer and come off like a dick. First impressions are important.

"Alright, now that our team meeting is over..." Alex's lips tilt up. "I'm gonna give Gavin a tour of the property and get him settled in with Jackson and Kiera."

Moments later, Alex and I head out the door. Alex unlocks the truck that looks like it's seen better days, and we get inside. The bumper is bent with large scratches on the side. I buckle in, and as the sun rises, we begin the grand tour of the Circle B Ranch.

"Riley and Diesel like to rag on each other all the time. They've been best friends since they were kids," Alex explains. "And Diesel is now dating my daughter Rowan, something Riley has been against since he was five."

I laugh. "That actually explains a lot. Dating your brother's best friend... they better get married—or things might get really awkward between them."

"If he knows what's good for him, he won't break her heart," Alex clarifies. "He'll be roadkill otherwise. Rowan would murder him herself."

This makes me chuckle. I'm not a man of many words and usually listen and watch everyone else. Alex doesn't seem to mind and fills the silence with information about the ranch. I'm amazed they have thousands of acres of land. It's much different than the Houston area where I grew up.

Alex points out a large two-story home with a wraparound porch that sits off the road, telling me that's where his parents live. As we continue driving, we pass different barns, and he explains each one's purpose. Some hold extra feed for the animals while others house the equipment. An hour passes before we arrive at the training facility run by Jackson and Kiera.

When Alex parks, he turns and looks at me. "Jackson's a known prankster. Consider yourself warned."

I grin. "Thanks for the heads-up. It'll keep the days interesting at least."

"You say that now," Alex says as we head inside toward the office, where Kiera's sitting behind a big oak desk with a schedule book open. As soon as her eyes meet mine, she grins.

"God, I'm so happy you're finally here."

A minute passes, and Jackson walks in wearing a shit-eating grin followed by two young men. Twins. "Not gonna listen to any complainin' today," he warns them both. "Maybe your mom will."

Kiera groans with an eye roll. "It's too early for that. Don't start with me, or you'll be doing double," she warns."

Their jaws lock, but they don't talk back. I get the feeling they get themselves into a lot of trouble by their parents' reaction.

Kiera sweeps loose strands of blond hair out of her face. "Oh, Gavin, these are our two boys, Knox and Kane. You'll see them around doing the guided horse tours at the B&B. They also feed them in the morning and shovel shit in the afternoon, which will be the least of their worries if they keep driving me crazy."

Their faces contort, but they have manners and shake my hand.

"Nice to meet you," they say. There's no way I could tell them apart, even if I tried.

During my interview with Jackson and Kiera, they explained how busy they've been with training and how they desperately needed extra help with the wild horses. I went through all my experience, and a week later, they offered me a position. I had some other obligations at home first and couldn't start immediately, but they were willing to wait. When I got the call, there wasn't a doubt in my bones about accepting the job. The money was great, I'd have a place to stay, and the landscape was vast and beautiful. Though Houston will always be home, I was ready to escape to a small town away from the lifestyle I'd led. I fell in love with Eldorado the first time I visited. There's something magical about the ranch that I can't explain.

"I'll meet y'all outside," Alex tells the twins. One of them releases a grunt while the other rolls his eyes.

Kiera sighs once they're out of sight. "I wish they were more like their sister. Kaitlyn does things without being disrespectful."

Jackson chuckles and turns to me. "That's our youngest. She just left for her second year of college, but she'll be back during the holidays and breaks. I'm sure you'll see her around then."

The phone rings, and Keira answers and immediately begins scribbling on a notepad. "How about next week? Could probably fit you in on Monday. Yep. See ya then." She ends the call, then looks up at me. "I hope you're ready to start workin' this afternoon," she tells me.

"I sure am. Been looking forward to it," I admit, which seems to please them both. The exhaustion on their faces is evident. I'm glad I can relieve some of the pressure and stress they've had running this huge empire by themselves.

"Great," Jackson says, patting me on the back. "We've got a packed training schedule for the next five years."

My eyes widen in shock.

"That might be a slight exaggeration." Kiera snorts. "But the rest of the year and next will be really busy, though. Since our competitor closed shop, business has been booming."

"That's great." I smile.

"Have you eaten?" Jackson abruptly changes the subject, but Kiera doesn't seem to mind and goes back to her calendar.

"Actually, no," I respond.

Jackson immediately shakes his head. "Unacceptable." Swinging open the office door, he finds Alex standing by the truck talking to the twins and moves toward him. "Not feeding our new employee on his first day is ridiculous. The man has to eat!"

Alex rolls his eyes and flips him off. Jackson turns toward me. "Alex will take you to the B&B for breakfast. It's tradition. Then I'll show you 'round here."

Kiera comes outside and frowns. "Don't be a bad influence."

"Yeah, yeah. Haven't heard that all my life." He chuckles. "Really happy you took our offer. Now go eat. I'll see you back here in an hour."

"Is that a firm hour?" Alex asks. "Or do we have time?"

Jackson shrugs. "Take however long you need, considering it's his first day. Make sure he tries the blueberry pancakes," he tells Alex, then looks at me. "My niece makes the best stacks in Texas," Jackson says with a grin.

"Sounds like I need to." I smile. Alex and I climb into the truck while Knox and Kane ride in the back.

Alex drives us across the property on the road that leads to the shop. "Sorry. I should've thought about bringin' ya to the B&B for breakfast since we were so close. Slipped my mind, though."

"No need to apologize. I should've eaten before I left the house. I typically do," I explain.

"Nah. Not anymore. Breakfast at the B&B is something you should add to your daily schedule. It's served from six to ten every day with enough to feed a small army—or rather all the ranch hands on-site." He chuckles.

Alex parks in the front by a ton of other work trucks. I check my phone and see it's just past seven. Knox and Kane climb out of the bed, and I follow Alex up the steps. Once we're inside, the smell of bacon and pancakes has my stomach growling. I didn't realize how hungry I was until now.

The tall ceilings and wooden floors of the B&B give me the same feeling as when I'd visit my grandma's house. We enter the buffet area, and I am surprised by the amount of food even though Alex warned me. We grab plates, and I notice the ample seating inside the dining room for the guests.

"There's seating outside too," Alex explains, piling sausage and scrambled eggs on his plate.

"Showing him how to do it right," a man says from behind, and my brows furrow.

He holds out his hand and takes mine. "I'm John, nice to meet you."

I glance at Alex. "Jackson didn't say he was a twin, did he?" I shake my head.

"I'm the non-crazy one," John explains with a chuckle. "I run the B&B."

"Gotcha. I was slightly confused for a second," I admit.

John takes in a deep breath. "I'm sure you were. Most people are. Thankfully, Jackson's somewhat settled down in his old age, or I'm sure some sort of joke would've been played on ya. Trust me when I say it's not been easy having the same face as him."

His admission has me chuckling. "I can *only* imagine."

"Don't let me interrupt you. Enjoy your food. If you need anything, let me know," John says, then walks away to greet some of the guests who enter. It would be impossible to sleep in late with the delicious smells wafting through the house.

Alex and I sit at a table by the large windows that oversee the backyard, and Knox and Kane make their way to a bigger table. Though it's the last day of August, it's by no means cool, so hopefully, the temperatures will drop soon. The humidity here isn't like it is in Houston, but it's still hot as hell.

"So, how long has this place been here?" I ask, interested in the history of the B&B.

"Almost thirty years. It was John's idea to turn the old farmhouse into a nature getaway. Ever since we remodeled and fixed it up, we've been booked solid. Some regulars have booked the same weeks for the past few decades and have made visiting here a tradition in their family, which Mama loves."

I take a bite of the blueberry pancakes like Jackson suggested, and I swallow it down. My eyes go wide as I take bigger bites until my plate is clean.

"Good, huh?" Alex grins. "My niece, John's daughter, is the head chef. Took all Mama's recipes and added some of her culinary skills to them. She plans all the meals, and with her small team, she prepares hot food every day for every meal."

"You Bishops are the jacks-of-all-trades," I say, impressed with how much they've accomplished.

"Not to mention my older brother Evan is a doctor and so is his wife. So, if an apocalypse happens, you're in the right place." Alex says around a mouthful. It makes me smile.

Seconds later, Diesel and Riley enter, going back and forth with each other just like they were this morning, but now it all makes sense.

Alex shakes his head. "They act like that all the time."

Another guy I haven't met yet is following them. As soon as the guys see me, they walk up and give hellos and introductions.

"Grayson, this is Gavin. He's helping Uncle Jackson with the horses," Riley says, popping a piece of bacon in his mouth.

"Nice to meet ya." We say it at the same time, then laugh.

"I work with Diesel, but hope to one day be training horses too," Grayson tells me.

"I'm the best boss he's ever had!" Diesel nearly yells. Grayson rolls his eyes.

"Let's eat," Riley announces, getting antsy, and they follow him to sit with Knox and Kane.

I get up and put another stack of pancakes on my plate, then cover them with syrup. As I take a big bite of pancakes, I think about the night I had with a girl the last time I was here. I think I remember Maize mentioning someone named Grayson, and I wonder if it's the same guy. It's a small town, so it's possible.

I think about that night we spent together often and wish I would've asked her for her number. I've thought about her and the chemistry we shared. It's been impossible to get her out of my system, and it's not from a lack of trying.

We finish eating, and Knox and Kane decide to ride with Riley. Alex delivers me to Jackson, who's sweating his ass off with a shovel in his hand.

Alex rolls down the window. "Hey, old man. I brought Gavin back as demanded."

Jackson gruffs. "Thank you, captain obvious."

"Thanks for showing me around," I tell Alex as I get out of the truck.

"Anytime!" Alex says out the open window, then gives me a wave before leaving.

Jackson sets the shovel down and walks over to me, wiping the sweat from his brow. "How was breakfast?"

"Great. Reminds me of my ma's cookin'," I admit. "I think I ate ten pancakes."

"Told ya! Anyway, guess we should get you acquainted with the training area."

We walk over to the different sections and barns. Among the several corrals is enough room to train several horses at once. Before I got hired, Kiera and Jackson explained their experience and what they were looking for in an employee. For the past few years, they've been doing everything on their own with their kids' help. They want to expand, but without help, that's not possible.

"Right now, we're training eight horses. Two will be picked up by the end of the week, and one was delivered about an hour ago. The others are at different stages but only have a few more weeks to go. We're also getting some new mares on Monday."

I nod and make a mental note. We walk to the edge of the training area, and Jackson shows me an obstacle course set up for barrel racing. It's impressive, but it seems everything the Bishops do is.

"The kids usually feed the horses in the morning, and I make them clean out stalls in the afternoons. For the most part, they're doing different tasks around the ranch. They're good kids, but damn, they make me feel old."

I give him a side-grin. "My ma always said to be good growing up, or my payback would be having kids who were worse than me. Guess they're yours."

"Damn right they are," he admits, shaking his head. "Oh, that colt delivered this morning will be your first project. He's in the stable being fed but thought you could get started with him today. Spunky as hell and has a bad attitude."

"Just my type." I chuckle.

"Fireball should be a good start for you," he tells me, leading me to the barn.

The colt looks like he's around two and doesn't pay any attention to us.

"Apparently, he's a fucker, I mean bucker. Same thing, though." Jackson leans against the gate.

"Has he had any saddle practice?" I ask, wanting to know the history and what level we're starting on.

"The owners have done nothing but put a halter on him and led him on rides. He's an asshole, and they want him broken in enough for their grandkids to ride."

Fireball starts pawing his hoof on the ground, and I smile. It's been a while since I've been this excited about work. Jackson shows me the location of all the gear, then he leaves me to myself. Taking my time, I lead Fireball out to the arena, and we get started.

The afternoon passes by quickly, and I work with Fireball until we're both exhausted. I started slow with leading and saddle practice, and he hated every minute. Repetition is key when training and breaking animals. After we finish working, I rinse him down and put him in the pasture, where he immediately starts rolling.

"You are an asshole," I yell at him, then walk to the office, remembering I left my truck at the shop this morning. Jackson's got his feet up on the desk when I enter.

"Can you possibly give me a ride to the shop?" I ask, and he's more than willing.

We hop in the truck, and on the way over, he asks me how things went this afternoon.

I grin. "Great, but you're right, he does have an attitude. I think he'll realize who's in charge, though, hopefully."

Jackson chuckles. "He better."

He pulls up next to my truck, and I thank him before I get out and wave as he drives off. As I'm pulling my keys from my pocket, Riley and Diesel exit the shop. They look like they've both had a hell of a day.

"There you are," Riley says. "We both stupidly forgot to get your number earlier."

I pull my phone out, and we exchange info.

"Want me to pick you up on the way there?" Riley asks.

"Yeah, that'd be great. Just need to take a shower first."

Diesel looks down at all the dirt on his clothes. "Good idea."

"Awesome! I'll pick you up around eight-ish," Riley tells me, then turns to Diesel. "You need a ride too?"

"Nah, man, I'm gonna stay until close to hang out with your sister." He elbows him. Riley lets out a groan. A roar of laughter escapes Diesel, and I can tell he's getting a kick out of rubbing this in his best friend's face.

"I'm probably only going to stay for a drink, then go home, if that's cool with you," he tells me.

"That's fine. I gotta be up early for work in the morning anyway."

"See," Riley says with a finger to his chest. "Some of us *are* responsible adults."

Diesel laughs. "I'm responsible, ask my girlfriend."

Riley's ready to punch him in the face but doesn't. I tell them both goodbye and get in the truck and leave. I replay my day, and I realize I'm tired. By the time I walk up the steps and enter the cabin, I'm more than ready to wash off the sweat of the day.

I'm not used to being here yet, but I'm sure it will eventually feel like home. On the walls are photographs of horses and fences, rolling hills and old tractors. The décor is exactly what one would expect to see on a ranch. I go to my bedroom, grab some clothes, then take a shower.

By the time I'm finished, I still have a few hours before Riley arrives. I could have driven myself, but he's not staying that long anyway, so it's not a big deal. My eyes are tired, and I end up falling asleep on the couch until knocks tap on the door. I get up, and Riley's standing there with a smile. "Ready?"

"Yep," I tell him, grabbing my keys and walking out with him.

We drive over to the saloon, and Maize comes to mind. She was drinking her worries away, looking so goddamn gorgeous. I'm tempted to ask Riley if he knows her since this is a small town, but I don't. If we're meant to see each other again, we will.

"So how'd you end up here, considering you used to ride professionally?" he asks on the way.

"After I won a few championships, I was ready to get out of Houston. Eldorado seemed like the perfect place to settle down and not be in the hustle or bustle of a big city. It's the exact opposite of what I'm used to, and I love training horses."

"Oh, so you're from Houston. I didn't realize people were into riding and stuff there," he admits.

A lot of people think that, especially if they don't know the landscape.

"My parents live on the outskirts, not downtown or anything. But yeah, there's a lot of riding that goes on, and the Houston Rodeo is one of the biggest in Texas. It's a popular thing to do. When I watched the bull riders there as a kid, I immediately knew that's what I wanted to do when I grew up. Plus, I'm somewhat of an adrenaline junkie."

Riley laughs. "You'd have to be to get on the back of one of those animals."

We pull into the parking lot, and a small smile touches my lips when we walk inside.

"Looks like Diesel's already here," Riley mutters as we walk toward the bar. He's chatting with people, but Riley interrupts him. "Uh...anyway." He clears his throat. "This is Gavin. He'll be working with Jackson training horses."

Kenzie's eyes go wide, and recognition flashes behind them. I wonder if she remembers me from the bar that night, but she doesn't say a word. Neither do I. My heart races, and I wonder if Maize is here too.

I meet Rowan, and when I turn my head, I see Maize sitting there as pretty as ever. I have so many damn questions I can barely contain myself.

"This is my other cousin, Maize. She's the cook at the B&B."

I smirk, realizing I was eating her food this morning. "Ooh, the one who makes the amazing pancakes."

Maize slightly turns to shake my hand, and that's when she sees me. She blinks hard, as if she expects me to disappear. I wish she'd say something, and I open my mouth, but Rowan interrupts me, thankfully. There are too many people around to ask her what the hell happened that night.

"So, Gavin, where're you from?" Rowan asks, moving the conversation away from Maize, who's acting awkward as hell.

"Houston. But I've traveled a lot in the past twelve years or so. I've been all over the state."

"Gavin's a retired bull rider," Riley explains. "Trains riders now on the side."

"Oh my God," Kenzie gushes in the same tone she did the night I first met her. "That is so cool. I would love to see you ride."

I'm well aware of her personality and how she acts, and I smile at her. She has to remember me.

Taking a seat at the bar, I order a drink as Rowan walks up to Diesel. She's obviously Alex's daughter, and I don't doubt for a second he wouldn't kick Diesel's ass if he hurt her. Noticing the way they look at each other, though, I can tell it's the real deal. While I'm sipping my beer, Maize gets up and walks away, then Rowan follows her.

Diesel brings up my bull riding days, and I get lost in conversation. When I turn to order another drink, I realize Maize never returned. It makes me think that bailing on people might just be her thing.

CHAPTER THREE

Maize

"Hey, what's goin' on?" Rowan asks, coming into the bathroom where I'm hiding. "You look like you've seen a ghost."

"That guy…" I inhale sharply, hardly believing it.

"Gavin? What about him?"

"That's *Gavin*."

She blinks. "Right, I just said that."

"No, I mean, yes. That's the Gavin I slept with a few weeks ago," I reiterate.

"Wait…" She narrows her eyes. "The guy you bailed on the next morning?"

"Yes!"

Rowan quickly covers her mouth as if she's trying to hold back laughter. "Oh my God, Maze!"

"Shut up!" I smack her arm. "This is humiliating!"

"This is freaking awesome." She chuckles. "Did he recognize you?"

I sigh, rubbing my temples as a headache surfaces. "I don't know. I recognized him right away. That's why I quickly turned away."

"Well, go out there and say hi!" She pushes me toward the door, but I dig my heels into the floor.

"Hell. No!" I frantically shake my head.

"Weren't you just tellin' your daddy you were almost twenty-five years old and old enough to move out?" She cocks her hip and places a hand on it. "This isn't very mature." She snickers.

I roll my eyes and shrug because I don't care. I'm not going back out there. "I didn't realize how much older than me he was. He looks older, right?" I ask nervously.

She nods, agreeing. "He definitely does. Probably ten years older?"

"Oh my God." I drop my face into my hands. "I'm leaving through the back."

"I don't think so," she states firmly.

"Fine, then I'm staying in here."

"The bathroom?" She cocks a brow.

"Rowan, please! Help me," I plead.

"Alright, fine. I'll make sure the coast is clear." She pats my shoulder. Slowly, she opens the door and peeks around.

"Okay, you're good," Rowan says. She faces me and waves me out. I immediately rush toward the employee exit.

"Thank you!" I whisper-shout, feeling relief as soon as I step outside.

I hope Gavin doesn't notice I ditched...*again*. I'm sure I'm a sight to see, scrambling out like I just robbed a bank. By the time I climb into my truck and head home, my palms are sweaty, and my heart is racing. Gavin working for Uncle Jackson means I'll eventually have to see him again. The dread nearly consumes me, and I'm pissed I got myself into this predicament in the first place. One-night stands aren't my thing, but I was convinced I'd never see him again because I thought he was only passing through town.

Cowboys are typically a hard no, and I should've stuck by that rule.

When I was eighteen, I dated a ranch hand named Timothy. It was love at first sight, or so I thought. My family was aware of our relationship and warned against getting involved because he wouldn't be staying long term. I foolishly thought I was enough for him to stay, but I was so damn wrong.

When it ended between us, I realized how I'd been bamboozled by love. My heart was broken beyond repair, and I swore never to make that mistake again. I've avoided any men who've shown interest in me and worked on the ranch. Yet I find myself in this predicament. I just hope like hell he keeps our secret to himself and leaves me alone.

When I get home, Mom and Dad are watching TV on the couch. Before I'm bombarded with conversation, I wave, then rush to my room and dramatically fall onto my bed. The only thing that pulls me away from my humiliation is my phone vibrating. When I pick it up, I see a message from Rowan and hope she was able to come up with a good excuse.

> **ROWAN**
>
> Totally random question for no reason, but when was your last period?

> **MAIZE**
>
> Uh...I don't know? Why?

> **ROWAN**
>
> Well, any chance you could be pregnant?

What the fuck kinda question is that? Probably because all the blood drained from my face, and I rushed to the bathroom like I was gonna vomit the moment I realized Gavin was here.

> **MAIZE**
>
> WHAT? No!

Just the thought of being pregnant throws me into a panic. How the hell would I explain that to my family?

> **ROWAN**
>
> Are you sure? Like 100%?

I think back to the incredible night we had together, but the small details remain a blur. We were greedy for one another, and he worshipped my body like I was a goddess. Gavin's the type of man you run away with for a summer, not the kind you settle down with. The bull riding culture creates fuck boys, and I bet he was one.

Obviously, we were careful, but there's always a chance.

MAIZE

I'm on the pill, and we used a condom.

ROWAN

Did you remember to take your pill?

These questions aren't helping the way I feel right now.

MAIZE

I think so…I mean, sometimes I forget, but typically I do!

ROWAN

Oh my God…

MAIZE

Shut up. I swear. I'm not pregnant.

ROWAN

Then take a test.

MAIZE

We hooked up like three weeks ago. It'd be too soon to know anyway.

ROWAN

Maybe. I'm buying you a test, though, just to be sure.

I roll my eyes, though I know she will.

MAIZE

And when I prove to you I'm NOT, you owe me $100!

ROWAN

Ha! You better cross your fingers and toes you aren't. Unless you want Mr. Brooding Cowboy as your baby daddy ;)

MAIZE

I hate you so much.

I roll over and bury my face in the pillow. I'll probably never be able to live this down. Thank God no one else knows about it other than Rowan and Kenzie. As the thought crosses my mind, I get a text from her.

KENZIE

Do you feel okay?

MAIZE

Yep, I just had to get out of there.

KENZIE

Okay good. Kinda worried me. Sidenote: I can't believe Gavin's working for Uncle Jackson. What are the odds?

With a groan, I reply. I was half hoping she'd forgotten that night, but Gavin isn't the forgettable type. Not with his dark hair, blue eyes, and pouty lips. She witnessed us flirting, saw us leave together, and knows I slept with him.

MAIZE

I don't know, but I'M NOT HAPPY ABOUT THIS.

KENZIE

Why? He's hot as hell and was totally into you that night at the bar. I'm ecstatic we have some real-life cowboy man candy to drool over. Might put in a good word to Aunt Kiera and see if she can hire someone more my age, though.

MAIZE

Ugh. Can we drop this?

KENZIE

I guess, but only because I gotta get back to work!

Then again, I can't deny how damn sexy he looked in those jeans and boots. I almost ask Kenzie if he's still there but decide against it. If I close my eyes, I almost remember the smell of his skin against mine. As soon as I think about rolling around naked in the sheets with him, I push it away. Even though my mind is all over the place, I somehow force myself to sleep.

The next morning, I'm in a weird mood. It's a reminder to keep my ass home regardless of how much Kenzie and Rowan pressure me to go out. Next time, I'm sticking to my guns and watching Netflix like I wanted.

I drink a cup of coffee and leave before Dad like always. While I grab the ingredients for breakfast, I'm distracted. My employees arrive on time, and I'm thankful because when they're around, I have no time to think about my complicated but nonexistent love life.

As soon as six rolls around, the dining room quickly fills up with people. At seven, I check the buffet status, and that's when I see Gavin. Our eyes lock, and I feel as if my feet are glued to the floor. I tuck my bottom lip into my mouth, wishing I would've just stayed hidden in the kitchen, then break the hold he has on me. When I glance over again, Gavin waves me over. While I contemplate turning around and pretending I didn't notice him, it's impossible with so many roaming eyes. My heart beats rapidly, but I push it down as I walk over to the table where he's eating alone. I try my hardest not to raise suspicion especially with my cousins watching.

Gavin smiles and speaks in a hushed tone. "We've met before, haven't we?"

Panic creeps in my throat, and I hope no one can hear him. Immediately, I shake my head. "No, I don't think so."

Gavin narrows his eyes. Damn those ocean-colored eyes seem to peer straight through me as he smirks. "I'm positive we ran into each other at the bar a few weeks ago," he insists.

I shrug and force a smile. "You must be confusing me with somebody else."

"You sure 'bout that?" He waits, giving me the chance to change my tune.

"I don't remember, sorry. But it's really nice to meet you. Oh, and I apologize for running out the other night. I wasn't feeling very well. But I hope you had a good time hanging out with everyone."

He clears his throat, then sips a cup of coffee. "Hanging out with your sister and cousins."

I keep a steady smile and don't react.

"Well, welcome to the ranch. Hope you enjoy your breakfast. I gotta get back to work."

By the time I return to the kitchen, my heart's galloping at full speed.

"Are you okay?" Sandra asks, glancing at the cold sweat that's formed on my brow.

"I'm fine. We need more ham and coffee," I say, wanting to forget Gavin completely, but knowing that'd be impossible. Pretending I didn't know him was dumb as hell, and I'm positive he didn't believe me. But if I keep up the act, maybe he'll drop it, and I can go on living in an alternate universe where I didn't have the best sex of my life with him. The chemistry we shared was undeniable, but I lost control with him, and it can never happen again.

I'm pissed he wanted to bring it up here. This isn't the time or the place, and it caught me off guard, which I don't appreciate. Once breakfast is over, I text Rowan, knowing she'll get a kick out of it.

> **MAIZE**
> So...I spoke to Gavin today.

> **ROWAN**
> Did you? OMG! Details, now!

> **MAIZE**
> He asked if I remembered him, and I denied it.

I shake my head at how stupid it seems after I send the message.

> **ROWAN**
> Wait, your plan is to pretend it didn't happen?

> **MAIZE**
> Exactly! Just avoid him like he has an STD, and then hopefully it'll be like it never happened.

> **ROWAN**
> Uh. Good luck with that. Did you take that pregnancy test yet?

I growl and bite my bottom lip.

> **MAIZE**
> NO!

> **ROWAN**
> I'm buying you one today!

The lunch rush flies by quickly, and I've never been more ready to go home and lock myself in my room than I am right now. Before I leave, I walk through the kitchen and confirm the night shift has everything they need. Donna and Becky assure me they have it under control, and I know they do.

"You headed out?" Dad pops his head up from behind the check-in desk when I walk by.

"Yes, sir."

"Before you go, can you check the garden? I think your mom mentioned something about the tomatoes and squash needing picked."

My eyes light up because it's one of my favorite things to do. "Sure, I'll be happy to."

I put on the pair of boots I keep at the B&B. After grabbing a tub, I walk out to the rows of vegetables and herbs we plant each season. Dad was right. I pull as much as I can, then drop it in the kitchen before going out and picking more. Getting my hands a little dirty relaxes my busy mind.

"Told ya!" Dad says when I return with my second load.

"In a few days, there will be even more," I explain and rinse them. After I finish, I say my goodbyes and head home. I think about Gavin and his cold stare when I denied knowing him. After I shower, I eat leftovers, then go to my room. Even if I used *Love is Blind* as an excuse to ditch, I wasn't kidding about catching up.

I flick on the TV and get comfortable. As I'm dozing off, Kenzie lets herself into my room.

"I knew it! I knew I heard Cameron's voice."

Grabbing a pillow, I throw it at her, but she quickly blocks it. She's entranced by the TV, but then snaps out of it and brings the attention back to me.

"You gonna tell me what really happened between you and Gavin, without the CliffsNotes?" She tilts her head and crosses her arms. "I wasn't born yesterday, Maze. I saw the way you two were flirting at the bar a few weeks ago, and considering you needed to be picked up after my shift, I think I know what happened. I'd never forget a face like that," she says.

I sigh. "You wouldn't believe me if I tried to make something up anyway."

"Because you're a shitty liar," she reminds me.

"That's what you think," I retort.

"Your face *always* gives you away." Kenzie smirks. "So quit stalling and tell me how big his dick was." She plops down on my bed, reaches for the remote, and pauses the show.

My cheeks heat, and her mouth falls open.

"Oh my God," she whispers. "He's humongous, isn't he?"

I nod, then cover my face before I glance at her. "The sex was amazing, but I can't get involved with him."

Kenzie places a hand on her chest. "I will trade you places in a heartbeat!"

I lean my head against the wall. "You're ridiculous."

"*You* are. If he'd let me inside, I'd go to his cabin right now and save a horse. So what's the hangup? You're allowed to have fun, Maze. Amazing sex never hurt anyone."

After sucking in a deep breath, I exhale slowly. "He's so much older. I knew he was when we hooked up, but it didn't matter at the time because it was a one time thing. Not to mention we're in two different places in our lives. I want to start my catering business eventually, and he could get bored of being in the middle of nowhere and leave. Not to mention my rule—I have it for a reason."

"Yeah, yeah. I know. Timothy ruined every opportunity for anyone who works on the ranch and wants to date you, even if they're the perfect man. So how old is he?"

I look at her. "Thirty-five, I think?"

"So what if he's closer to dad's age than yours. Big deal. There are some silver foxes out there that I'd let be *my* daddy."

Nearly throwing up in my mouth, I playfully smack her. "Oh my God, stop! That's not true." I burst out laughing at the face she makes. "You say that shit to get under my skin."

She smiles wide. "Of course."

I reach for the remote, but she pulls back before I can. "We're not done talking about this. I have to know what you're going to do about this now that he's here."

A small grin forms on my lips. "Pretend I didn't have the best sex of my life with him."

"And that's it?"

I nod.

Her eyes widen in shock. "Do you have brain damage?"

"No! It's just another heartbreak waiting to happen. Pretending lets me move on with my life. The right man will come when I least expect it."

Kenzie snorts and rolls her eyes. "But what if he is *the one*, and you're just being stubborn as hell?"

"Doubtful," I huff.

"People have sex with no attachments. You don't have to get married or anything. It's called having fun."

"Not for me, Kenzie. I'm good. Also please don't tell anyone. And I mean *anyone*. Rowan knows, but no one else."

She makes a zipper motion across her lips. "Secret's safe with me, but you gotta tell me why you called me to pick your ass up if the sex was so great."

I hesitate. "I was embarrassed that we slept together so soon after meeting. I'd never done that before. I knew I couldn't face him and didn't reach out because I wasn't sure what to say."

"You were living on the edge." Kenzie snickers.

I throw another pillow, but this time, it catches her off guard and smacks her. I snag the remote and flick on the show. Being preoccupied by Cameron, she kicks off her shoes and lies on the bed. We watch and laugh at the same things. Randomly, I'll think about Gavin and the way his lips felt on my skin. His strong hands on my body is something I wish I could feel again. Just the way his tongue twisted with mine makes heat rush through me. When the episode ends, I yawn.

"I'm leaving tomorrow to go back to school," she tells me.

I stick out my lower lip. "I know. I'm gonna be sad."

"Aw, I already promised Mom I would come back as much as I could." She hugs me.

"Good," I say. "Drive safe. Text me when you get to your dorm." I sound like Mom with the reminder.

"I will! Night. Love you," Kenzie says with a grin

"Love you too."

She shuts the door, and I let out a long sigh.

What Gavin and I had was special, but it can *never* happen again. Sex without some sort of attachment doesn't exist.

CHAPTER FOUR

Gavin

ONE MONTH LATER

"C'mon, Racer. Don't gimme a hard time today," I plead with the colt who's giving me hell about wearing a bridle. He's a quarter horse, and they are usually the easiest breed to train, but it's hot as hell, so we're both agitated. He's not as wild as the others, which is why I start my days with him.

Maybe it's not just the heat that's annoying me.

It's been a month since I moved to the ranch, and though I've settled in comfortably, Maize's still trying to convince me she doesn't remember who I am. When we're in the same place, she actively dodges me as though I have a contagious disease.

And perhaps it pisses me off more than it should, but I've never had a woman who wasn't eager for my attention. She claims to have no memory of our night together, but I don't believe her, considering she screamed my name and begged me to fuck her *hard*. I haven't been able to get it out of my mind since it happened almost two months ago.

With working on the ranch and training Cooper advanced bull riding skills a few times a week, one would assume I'd be too damn exhausted to think about her, but every morning I see her at the B&B, and it's impossible not to. Maize barely glances my way as she walks in and out of the kitchen, refilling the buffet with her delicious pancakes and sausage patties. When I speak, she acts as if I'm wasting her time, and her responses are short. I'd be amused if she weren't lying to me. Regardless, I always smile at her, and though she tries to remain unfazed, the blush on her cheeks gives her away.

"That's a good boy," I tell Racer once I secure the bit in his mouth and put the bridle over his head. I slowly pet him and give positive reinforcements until he's used to the sensation. We've been working together for a couple of weeks, and he's already making good progress.

I train him for another hour—setting the saddle on his back and adding some weight so he can get used to it. Eventually, Racer will be used on guided tours.

After we're done, I put Racer in the main pasture to graze, and I get a text from Grayson.

GRAYSON

Meeting for brunch in ten.

On the early mornings when we're too busy to eat breakfast, we go after the rush. That usually means Maize isn't as busy, and I can attempt to get more than one-word responses from her.

GAVIN

I'll be there.

I park at the B&B, a place that's become my second home, and get out of the truck. After I stroll inside, I immediately scan the area for Maize. Though I don't see her, I can hear her laughter. Once I'm in the dining area, I see Grayson sitting at a table with Riley and Diesel, and he's chatting with Maize and John.

"Mornin'," I bellow, tapping my hat toward Maize as she glares at me. "You look pretty today."

She sighs, then rolls her eyes before walking away without a word.

Yeah, I'm used to that reaction. Not sure why she's hell-bent on ignoring me or denying our night together, but I'm determined to figure it out no matter how long it takes.

"Tell me again how much game you've got." Diesel barks out a laugh.

"Trust me, it's not my *game* that's the issue. It's *her*," I counter, flashing an apologetic look at her dad before he murders me for talking about his daughter.

"I've raised that girl for twenty-five years, and I'm still trying to figure her out, so good luck." John chuckles before leaving us to ourselves.

"Great," I mutter.

Once I've filled a plate with food, I take a seat next to Grayson.

"Dude, I'm telling you. These Bishop women are as complicated as hell. Don't waste your time trying to figure them out because you'll go crazy tryin'. It's a goddamn miracle Diesel ended up with one," Grayson says, stabbing a hash brown with his fork.

"Hey, that's my sister," Riley warns. Before I arrived, it came out that Diesel and Rowan had been secretly dating. While they were taking it slow, Diesel learned he was a dad. When Chelsea, the woman he had a one-night stand with, brought their son to visit, she made a move. Diesel confessed he was in love with someone else. Shortly after, the whole Bishop family knew, and Riley blew a gasket, punching Diesel in the face. I would've loved to have seen it all go down.

"I'm just callin' it how I see it." Grayson shrugs, then looks at me. "Take it from someone who's under Kenzie's wrath for no damn reason, just walk away before she fucks you up for good." I can tell he's talking from experience by the pained expression on his face. "Thank God she's back at college now. I won't have to deal with her devil glares and bad attitude until Thanksgiving."

"Maize's too nice to hate you for no reason," Diesel says, then eyes me. "So, there's gotta be more to this story."

I haven't told anyone about our night together and don't plan to. Considering she won't acknowledge what happened, she probably wouldn't appreciate them finding out from me.

"She hasn't had the best dating experience," Riley explains. "And she won't give anyone who works on the ranch a chance."

"All I've tried to do is *talk* to her," I counter. "That's it."

"It'd be in your best interest if you didn't," Riley adds. "Trust me. I nearly knocked this one's teeth out when I found out he was sleepin' with my sister behind my back. I'm not sure I could actually hurt you, but I'd try if you broke Maize's heart."

I arch a brow at his cocky bluntness, and though he's right—he wouldn't leave a single mark on me if he tried—I'd rather not piss off the men I work with.

"Still bummed I didn't get to see it go down." I laugh as I dive into my scrambled eggs.

When our plates are nearly empty, Alex enters and gives us all a look. "There y'all are. We on a break I didn't know about?"

"Just re-fueling, Dad," Riley explains. "We're almost done."

"Good. We're running behind and have a shit ton to do today." He turns around and leaves before they can reply.

Diesel groans as he cleans up his mess, then puts on his hat. "Grayson, hurry up."

"I am!" he says around a mouthful, rushing.

Since their cousin Ethan left to finish his senior year of college, they've been shorthanded. Well, not really, but they were just used to slacking while Ethan was home for the summer.

"I really can't wait to train horses," Grayson mutters, popping the rest of his biscuit into his mouth.

"Why? Horse shit ain't much different than cattle shit." Riley snorts. "You'll be cleaning barns either way."

"I know, genius. But at least with horses, I'm bonding with them as I train and ride. Cows couldn't care less if you're around, and I'd argue that their shit is *very* different. Ever step in cow shit?"

Riley chuckles.

"Sorry to say, Grayson, but you aren't leaving me for a while," Diesel tells him with a crooked grin. "I need your assistance with all my bitch work."

Grayson rolls his eyes, and I wave before the three of them head toward the door. I'm fortunate enough to make my own schedule as long as I get my work done each week. Jackson and Kiera focus on their tasks, and I focus on mine.

Since the dining room is empty, I look for any opportunity to get into the kitchen with Maize. I notice the dirty dish tub is full and decide to take it back there. She can't yell at me if I'm helping.

I peek through the little window in the door to see if she's alone. When her employees are nowhere to be found, I kick it open and waltz in. Maize immediately spins around and pins me in place with a death glare.

"What do you think you're doin'?" She scowls, putting her hands on her hips. It's the cutest fucking thing ever.

"Helpin' you with these," I explain, glancing down at all the dirty dishes. "I'm a gentleman, ya know?" I set the tub by the dishwasher and spin around to face her.

"I didn't ask for your help, so you can leave," she tells me sternly.

"What's your problem, Maize Bishop?" I cross my arms over my chest and narrow my eyes. "You throw daggers at me like you hate me or something."

"I never said I *hated* you."

I take a step toward her. "So you like me then?"

Her nostrils flare. "Definitely didn't say that either."

"Then what is it? It's either one or the other."

"I don't know you well enough to have an opinion." She takes a step back as I inch closer.

Smirking, I continue, "Now that's not true. I think you know me quite well. You're just afraid to admit it."

"I honestly have no idea what you're talkin' about. As I've said before, you must have me confused with someone else."

I shake my head in amusement. "Trust me, Maize. I'd never forget you. *Or* our night together."

"Sure you weren't dreaming or something?" She barks out a laugh, but it's fake.

"Alright then, why don't you give me a chance? Let me take you out," I offer, watching her throat tighten as she swallows hard.

"I don't date men who work on the ranch," she informs me with a mediocre grin. "It's not personal."

Furrowing my brows, I move closer, studying her. "Is that so?"

"Yep." She quickly walks around me, and I turn to watch her unload the dishes. "I have a lot of work to do, so if you don't mind…"

"I *don't* mind. I already offered to help," I gloat, then stand beside her. "So let me."

This time, I don't give her a chance to deny me and quickly take over, rinsing off the crumbs before putting them in the dishwasher.

"Fine, whatever. I need to chop veggies for lunch anyway. Since Sandra and Jane are both sick with the stomach flu, my hands are full."

Realizing she's taking care of everything alone makes me want to do even more. I go back to the dining area and pick up the rest of the dinnerware, then load the dishwasher again. Thank goodness it's a large commercial one that only takes minutes to cycle through. After that, I wipe down each table and make sure they're set for lunchtime.

Once the dishes are finished, I have a hell of a time trying to figure out where they go. After a solid minute of looking, Maize finally takes pity on me.

"Over there." She points at a shelf. "On the right."

I look, and sure enough, there are the others. "Thank you."

"You really didn't have to stay."

"Seems like you needed some company today. It's quiet in here."

"I don't mind being alone," she says. "Silence doesn't happen much 'round here. My family usually stops in, or I turn on some music. I enjoy listening to it while I cook."

"You're really a great chef, you know," I tell her genuinely.

"You've chosen to eat the same things for the past month, so I can't really trust your judgment."

I cock my head with amusement. "So you notice what I put on my plate every day, huh? *Interesting.*" I stroke my jawline, knowing I'm getting to her.

"No, and you're a lunatic. It's time to go now."

She's right. I've been here for over an hour and have a ton of shit to do, but I don't want to leave. "Okay, fine. Same time tomorrow?" I quirk a brow.

Maize huffs. "No! I already told you, I don't date men who work on the ranch, so you can stop doing"—she waves a frustrated hand in the air—"whatever it is you're doing."

"Only tryin' to be your friend." I cross my arms over my chest.

"I don't think that's a good idea."

"Why? You don't have any guy friends?"

"Not exactly," she breathes out. "And you're reminding me why I don't."

I slam a palm to my chest. "Ouch."

"Well, I warned you."

For a moment, I thought she would let her guard down, but she's smarter than that. As soon as she showed a sliver of her vulnerabilities, it's like she realized it and locked it away.

Maize Bishop isn't gonna make this easy, but I do love a challenge.

Once I'm back in the barn, Jackson strolls in with Knox and Kane behind him. They're laughing and smacking each other, but immediately stop when they see Kiera. I hold back laughter at how obnoxious they are, but even at twenty-one, they know to quit playing when their mother's around.

"What are you boys doin'?" she asks as Jackson kisses her.

"Making them clean stalls and organize the tack room. Then after that, they'll be washing all the work trucks and tractors."

Kiera's hands fly to her hips, and she scowls as if she knows this is a punishment. "What'd they do now?"

"Stole the Cotton's goats last night and hid them in our sheep barn," Jackson explains, shaking his head, but I can tell he's trying not to burst out laughing.

"Seriously?" she scolds, but then her expression softens. "That sounds like somethin' you'd do." Kiera teases Jackson. "Have them wax my car, too." She smirks before walking to the office.

"You're making this way too big of a deal, Dad," Knox complains. "The goats are back safe and sound. No one got hurt."

"Except when you pushed me and I tripped, nearly doing a face-plant in the gravel," Kane interrupts.

Although they're identical twins, they have different personalities. Knox reminds me a lot of myself, confident and ready to take on the world, whereas Kane is more reserved and loyal. Though I have a feeling he gets roped into doing crazy shit with his brother, then has to deal with the consequences later.

"Too bad Kaitlyn isn't here. I'd pay her to do my half." Knox barks out a laugh.

"Who's Kaitlyn again?" I ask.

"Our little sister. She left for college right before you arrived," Kane explains, but I remember Jackson telling me about her.

"How old is she?"

"Nineteen. Just started her second year of college," he answers.

"Don't get any ideas," Jackson snaps.

My eyes widen at his demanding tone. "No, sir. Absolutely not."

Aside from the fact that Jackson's my boss and I wouldn't want to lose his trust, nineteen is too young. Plus, the only woman on my mind right now is Maize Bishop. Her being twenty-five is pushing my minimum dating age limit, but she's mature, and our chemistry is undeniable. I find so many things about her sexy as hell. Though I've had flings with younger women, I'm done with all that foolishness. I want to put down some roots and start a family—sooner rather than later.

Perhaps Maize's not at that stage of her life yet, but she was the one who pointed out she was behind because she's not married with kids. She laughed as if it were impossible for her to find a partner in five years, yet here I am. I'd be willing to let her call the shots if she'd actually give me a damn chance to prove that what we had that night was real.

CHAPTER FIVE

Gavin

TWO MONTHS LATER

I've been working at the ranch for three months, and I thought Maize would've admitted she remembered us being together by now, but she hasn't budged. I've helped her in the kitchen a few times, but she went back to pretending I didn't exist afterward. Though I don't have time to play her childish games, I've come to accept Maize Bishop's stubborn as hell.

Way more stubborn than most of the wild horses I've trained.

I try not to let it bother me, but every time I see her, memories of her soft skin pressed against mine flash through my head. It's damn near impossible not to think about when she's around. I could understand if she was embarrassed or even regretted being with me, but why lie? I'm determined to find out, even if it takes me years.

Now it's the day before Thanksgiving, and all the Bishops are working double-time to finish their chores so they can eat and be with their families tomorrow. Luckily, I don't have as much to do—the stalls are shoveled, food and water stocked, and the tack rooms organized. Though I've been working with Cooper, he went to visit family in Alabama this week, so I just have to worry about the horses.

"Gavin! Wait up," Grayson shouts as I walk toward the B&B.

"What's up, man?" I'm already on the porch, reaching for the door.

"You got holiday plans?" he asks.

"Not really. I'll call my parents and work out after I feed the horses, but that's it. Why?"

"John and Mila invited me to eat at their house. You should come," he says as we walk inside.

"Not sure that's a good idea. Maize hates me enough as it is."

He shrugs. "So? Kenzie wants to murder me, and I've been invited for the past three years. We shoot daggers at each other, then eat pie."

I snort, heading toward the buffet. I'm starving, and the turkey potpie Maize made for lunch smells delicious.

"You don't think John and Mila would mind an extra person?"

"Nah, they told me to invite you too. Everyone eats with their families, then we show up here for dessert."

I like the idea of seeing Maize outside of the B&B, where she can't disappear or make excuses for why she can't stick around. She'll have to play nice in front of her parents.

"Alright, I'll go."

I load a plate, and Grayson fills his too. "Cool, I'll let Mila know to add a chair for ya. But get ready to nap for three hours after."

Chuckling, I find a table and take a seat. I look around, wondering where Maize is today because she's usually in the dining area during the rush.

"She's in the kitchen," Grayson tells me without asking. I blink and furrow my brows. "Maize. She's prepping all the desserts for tomorrow. Kenzie's helping with dishes while Sandra and Jane refill the buffet and prep for dinner."

I skipped breakfast and opted for a protein shake, so I didn't get to see her this morning. "So I assume you ran into Kenzie then?"

She's been away at college and came home a couple of days ago.

"Like an asteroid."

Laughing, I shake my head and dig into the best potpie I've ever had.

"So, tell me the truth about you and Maize. There's way too much…" He waves around his fork. "Sexual tension. Did you two meet before or something?"

I keep my head down and focus on my food.

"Dude, that's a yes." He points at me.

"That's a 'mind your own damn business.'"

He scoffs and acts offended. The kid is ten years younger than me, and I don't have the energy to gossip like a teenager.

"I knew it." He beams, and I roll my eyes.

"Kenzie's hated me since the first day we met, and I honestly have no idea what her problem is."

"You ever thought about askin' her?"

"I have a million times, but she's determined to bust my balls." He shakes his head, swallowing down his food. "She tells me to 'fuck off,' 'eat shit,' and—my personal favorite—'go to hell, jackass.' I'm convinced she's confused me with someone else because I didn't do a damn thing to her."

That seems suspicious, and I halfway wonder if they slept together, and *he* doesn't remember her. It's not out of the realm of possibilities, considering Maize claims she doesn't. Except I think Grayson's being genuine, which makes it worse.

So I ask him. "Any chance you two hooked up, but when you officially met at the ranch, you didn't recognize her?"

"Not possible. I'd remember Kenzie."

"You sure about that?" I challenge, finishing the last of my food.

Grayson wrinkles his face. "About eighty percent."

I chuckle. "Or maybe you did something else to her? Ran over her dog, called her fat, fucked her best friend?"

"Jesus," he mutters, laughing. "I mean, I don't think so. But I wish she'd tell me already."

"Well…" I stand, grabbing my empty plate. "Good luck with that."

"Ha, thanks." He follows as we put up our dirty dishes. "I'll see you tomorrow then. Lunch is at one."

"I'll be there."

We walk toward the front door and wave to a few guests on the way.

"Oh, and dress nice," he warns me. "Everyone's expected to be in their Sunday best."

"Seriously? Alright."

"Yep. Slacks, button-up, nice shoes."

"I'll see what I can do. See ya later, man," I say, then we go our separate ways.

After digging through my closet, I finally find something "nice" to wear. I can't remember the last time I dressed up, but I have a couple of pairs of black slacks and a few button-up shirts.

Once I've showered and dressed, I grab the flowers I bought from the grocery store yesterday and head to my truck. I arrive at John and Mila's at the same time as Grayson, and we walk to the front door together.

"Lookin' pretty sharp," he taunts as he knocks on the wood.

"I know how to clean up when I have to."

Grayson looks at the flowers. "Those for Maize?"

I grin. "Nope."

Mila answers with a smile and moves to the side to let us in. "Hey, boys. Glad y'all came."

"Thank you for the invite," I tell her, handing over the bouquet. "These are for you, Mrs. Bishop."

"Oh, Gavin. You didn't have to do that." She sniffs them and smiles wide. "They smell lovely, thank you."

"Of course."

Grayson and I follow her to the kitchen, and I immediately smirk when I see Maize's expression go from happy to annoyed. By her reaction, she didn't know I was coming.

"Maize, can you find me a vase, please? Gavin was so sweet to bring these for me," Mila asks, setting them down on the counter.

Maize studies me, and replies, "Sure, Mom."

"John's just finishing up some paperwork at the B&B and will be home any minute. Then we can dive right in," Mila explains.

"Where's Kenzie?" Grayson asks.

"Actively avoiding you." Maize snorts, carrying a crystal vase. "Wish I could say I was doing the same." She glares at me.

Grayson puts a hand on his chest over his heart. "You mean she hasn't missed me? I'm hurt."

I chuckle at his sarcastic tone, knowing damn well he wishes she *would* miss him. I'd almost feel bad for him if I wasn't dealing with my own Bishop woman issues.

John enters just as Kenzie comes down the stairs.

"Ugh, come on. I was hoping this would be the year I had something to be thankful for." Kenzie slams her shoulder against Grayson as she walks to the dining table.

"I'm here, so you do." He winks at her, but all she does is roll her eyes, then takes a seat.

"Where would you like me?" I ask, not sure if it's assigned seating or not.

"Preferably outside." I hear Maize mutter as she carries a hot dish.

"Across from you?" I ask loudly. "I'd love to."

She groans as she sets the food on the table.

"Mrs. Bishop, do you need some help?" I follow Maize into the kitchen.

"Take this," Maize says, handing me a scalding ass bowl without warning.

"Oh shit." I quickly set it down and grab a potholder off the counter.

"Warning, it's hot," she muses.

"Gee, thanks."

This girl really is trying to kill me. Though I don't know why, because she's the one who denies everything. If anything, I should be the one pissed at *her*, considering she bailed on me the morning after.

Once the food is on the table and we all sit, Mila says grace and thanks Grayson and me again for joining them.

"Dig in," she announces.

John passes the turkey, then we pile on corn bread stuffing and roasted veggies. Once I take a bite, it's confirmed it tastes as delicious as it smells.

"This is amazing," I say, smiling at Mila.

"Maize makes the best turkey," she confirms.

I look at her from across the table, then smile. "Should've known."

"Uh, *excuse me*. I helped," Kenzie blurts out, causing us all to laugh.

"Adding the marshmallows to the sweet potato casserole doesn't count…" Grayson teases. Kenzie gives him a death glare and looks like she's going to knock him out.

"You weren't even here, so zip it." Kenzie snarls, and I swear, the tension between them could be cut with a knife.

Everyone chats while we finish eating, then Mila offers seconds.

"I'm always ready for more turkey." Grayson pats his hard stomach.

"Don't forget about dessert later," Mila reminds him.

"No, ma'am. Maize's sweet pumpkin pie with homemade whipped cream is unforgettable."

Kenzie rolls her eyes and stands, then takes her empty plate to the kitchen.

"I made extra this year…" Maize says, pointing her fork at Grayson. "Just for you."

"You're my favorite Bishop, Maze. Don't tell the others…" he whispers, and she laughs. I hate that it makes me jealous, knowing she's sweet and kind to him but treats me like a walking STD.

I watch the way she lets her guard down, and as soon as her gaze meets mine, she looks away, but not before I see the faint blush on her cheeks.

When we're all stuffed to the max, I help clear the table. Kenzie and Maize rinse the dishes while Grayson helps Mila put the leftovers in containers. John and I break down the table to its normal size.

"Your house is beautiful, Mrs. Bishop. I love the modern décor. Much different than the B&B," I tell her once everything's clean.

"Thank you. We had fun decorating." She smiles at me. "You want a tour of the house?"

I glance around and notice Maize's reaction, and she tenses when Kenzie speaks up. "I'll give you one, Gavin! Let's start with my sister's room."

Maize elbows her in the ribs, and Kenzie dramatically coughs. "Shut up. I better do it, or you'll be telling him all kinds of embarrassing childhood stories about me."

With an unapologetic shrug, Kenzie smirks. "Well, duh." She looks at her incredulously, which makes me wonder what they're hiding.

With a sigh, Maize walks around me and tells me to follow her. I hear Kenzie chuckle, then she tells Grayson off, which makes me smile. These Bishop sisters don't make anything easy.

"You already saw the dining room and entryway…" She waves a hand to the left as we walk down the hallway. "The living room is here, though we don't get a lot of time to hang out or watch TV. Most of us are usually working or sleeping."

"Looks cozy, though," I say, shoving my hands in my front pockets so I don't do something stupid like reach out and touch her.

She takes me through the rest of the lower level, then we go upstairs, and she points out her parents' and Kenzie's room.

"Mine's at the end of the hallway."

I silently follow her, not taking a second alone with her for granted. This is the most she's talked to me since I moved to the ranch.

"It's very you," I admit after she opens her door and allows me to peek inside. Three walls are a neutral tan color, and one is a bright teal. Pictures of her and Kenzie on the ranch are framed and hung on the walls along with dreamcatchers. A white comforter is neatly spread across her bed, and fuzzy teal pillows are stacked high.

"You don't even know me," she states.

I study her. "I know enough."

She swallows hard with her eyes locked on mine, but too quickly, she lowers her gaze and breaks our contact.

"It's embarrassing to live with my parents at my age," she blurts out. "I just turned twenty-five and still sleep in my childhood bed." Maize groans, then shrugs. "But until they can marry me off, I'll stay here."

Bringing a hand to my chin, I scrub my fingers over my beard as I remember a similar conversation we had at the bar. "Marry you off, huh? To who? What happened to becoming a nun?"

Maize blinks hard, then shakes her head as if she has to remind herself not to react. "What? No, not like an arranged marriage or anything. But when you work on the ranch, it doesn't make sense to move away. Especially when I work as much as I do," she explains, leading me back toward the staircase. It's amusing she ignored the nun part and is still playing her little game.

"Doesn't hurt that it's cheap rent."

"That's definitely a perk," she says as we enter the kitchen, and when she checks the time on the wall, she adds, "Crap, I gotta go to the B&B and set up the desserts."

"Let me help. It'll go faster," I offer, not giving her room to argue.

She sighs. "Alright, fine."

After Maize announces we're leaving, they tell us they'll meet us there in twenty minutes. It will give me more alone time with her.

Since the B&B is only half a mile from her house, she leads me to a side by side, and we climb in. The silence slices through the air on the way over, and once we enter the kitchen, she gives me orders, and I quickly step into action.

"Pies over there, cakes and cookie bars on the other table, then fruit on the third one." She pulls items from the fridge, and my eyes widen at the assortment of desserts laid out.

"Shit. You feedin' an army?" I grab two pecan pies and inhale the sweet aroma.

"Just wait till you see *all* the Bishops together. There are a lot of us…" she says. "Then add in the ranch hands too."

As I help her move tables around the dining area, I wonder how everyone will fit in here, then remember the rocking chairs and tables on the back porch.

Once we've set the desserts out, Maize puts the serving utensils in each dish and directs me to find the dessert plates. Then I grab the whipped cream and start the coffee maker as ordered. Once I've done what she's asked, I head out of the kitchen and hear her talking to someone.

"Elle! It feels like it's been forever." Maize hugs her, and I immediately see the Bishop resemblance. Elle has long, dark hair and features similar to Maize.

"Came to see if you needed help, but I see now that I'm interrupting…" Elle looks me up and down, and Maize quickly turns around.

"No, no. Gavin's training horses with Jackson and Kiera. Mom invited him to dinner."

"Mm-hmm."

"Nice to meet you, Elle. I'm Gavin." I hold out my hand, and she quickly takes it.

"A pleasure. I'm Elizabeth, but only our grandmother calls me that." She smiles.

I chuckle. "Noted."

"Elle works with Dr. Wallen," Maize explains. "Which is why I hardly ever see her anymore."

"I met him shortly after I started here. Seems like a nice guy. I bet you're learning a lot from him," I say to Elle.

"Yeah, well..." She inhales sharply. "We don't call him Dr. Dickhead for nothing."

My eyebrows raise in curiosity.

"Speak for yourself," Maize chimes in. "The rest of us call him Dr. VetDreamy." Maize chuckles, giving Elle a hard time, but the thought of her thinking he's good-looking annoys the fuck outta me.

"Do *not* call him that," Elle warns. "Just because he's good-looking doesn't take away the fact that he makes my work life miserable."

"It can't be *that* bad." Maize waves her off.

"Not for you, maybe. You have a great view." Elle smirks at me, and Maize gives her a dirty look.

Deciding to play along, I step next to Elle and wrap my arm around her. "Glad to see someone appreciates me 'round here."

"Is Maize being rude to you?" she asks.

"If by that you mean she ignores and tells me off, or straight up groans any time I speak, then yeah, I guess so." I shrug, giving Elle my best puppy dog face.

"Maize Bishop!" Elle scolds, folding her arms over her chest. "I know your mama taught you better than that. Be nice to the new trainer. He seems sweet."

Maize perks a brow, and her nostrils flare with rage. "I'm *plenty* nice."

"That's you being nice?" My eyes widen with a grin. "Shit, I'd hate to get on your bad side then."

"Keep talkin', and you will be," she snaps.

"Okay, I'm sensing some kind of...tension here, so I'm gonna go find me some pie," Elle says, then quickly walks away.

"Unbelievable," Maize mutters before storming off.

I don't let her get too far before following her into the kitchen. "You ever gonna tell me what your problem with me is?" I ask as she grabs something from the fridge.

"My problem is you're always around. I'm not interested, and you aren't getting the memo." She slams the door and turns to face me.

"Whoa, whoa, whoa…" I hold up my palms to stop her before she runs off. "You're not interested? I didn't ask you out or anything." The last time I offered to take her on a date was a couple of months ago.

"I can read between the lines, and I'm good with body language."

"Is that so? Enlighten me then. What am I insinuating?"

She sets down the container and puts her hands on her hips. "You're intrigued by me and want to ask me out again even though I've given you a million signs I'd say no. Yet, here you are."

"The only thing that intrigues me is you refusing to admit we've met before. Why is that?" I cross my arms.

"Because we haven't." Her upper lip twitches, and it gives her away. It's obvious she's full of shit. It's only a matter of time before she confesses the truth. The sooner, the better.

"Okay, have it your way then." I shrug and walk away. Before going through the door, I look over my shoulder and smile. "I have a feelin' you'll be remembering very soon." Then I flash her a wink and leave.

The B&B fills up with Bishops, and for the next hour, I eat Maize's delicious desserts and chat with everyone. I hear her talking to someone behind me, but fight the urge to look since I can feel her eyes on me. She may not like that I called her out, but too damn bad.

"Gavin," Grandma Bishop sing-songs my name as she opens her arms and wraps me in a tight hug. Though she's not *my* grandma, it's what everyone calls her.

"Happy Thanksgiving," I say, squeezing her back.

"How was your dinner at John and Mila's?"

"Delicious. Maize didn't disappoint one bit," I emphasize her name, knowing she's listening close by. "Her desserts are even better."

"She's a precious gem, ain't she? We're lucky to have her." Grandma Bishop smiles proudly. After another minute, she excuses herself to make her rounds.

"You keep talkin' about me, then wonder why I think you're obsessed with me," Maize quietly says so no one can eavesdrop.

"Obsessed? You keep avoidin' me and say there's no reason for it," I retort. "Our night together is nothing to be embarrassed about, Maize."

"You're absolutely delusional."

I take my time and check out her body before meeting her intense gaze.

"Then why do you always have goose bumps when I'm around? Coincidence?" I pop a confident brow.

She narrows her eyes while simultaneously rubbing her bare arms. "Shut up. I don't."

I chuckle, bringing a hand to her shoulder and sliding it down to her wrist, feeling the bumps against the pads of my fingers. "Right. I believe you."

Maize groans, creating space.

"Stop denying it, sweetheart."

"You're so full of yourself. Even if we had met before, I doubt it would've been anything memorable. So perhaps my mind did me a favor and blocked it out." She flashes an *eat shit* grin, then stalks off.

Moments later, Grayson comes over and pats my shoulder. "Wanted to officially welcome you to the Bishop wrath."

CHAPTER SIX

Maize

FIVE WEEKS LATER

After an insane and busy Christmas, I'm excited I get to spend New Year's Eve with my cousins because I'm not working for once. I did an enormous dessert bar on Christmas Eve and then served a special brunch on Christmas Day. Since I gave my employees the holidays off, my mother and Kenzie helped. Having them around is always fun since we love baking cookies together, but it took four twelve-hour shifts to prepare everything.

Having Gavin at our house for Thanksgiving was awkward and tense. Thank God that pregnancy test Rowan made me take months ago came back negative, or shit would be hitting the fan right now. Giving him a tour and then him later confronting me was irritating as hell. I don't understand why he won't drop it and put the past behind us. It's been four months, and if I have to see him every day, I'd rather him not have the satisfaction of knowing I *do* remember.

How could I forget?

Still doesn't mean I want to admit it.

Denial, denial, denial.

That's my motto.

It wouldn't be that hard if he'd just stay out of my way, but he shows up at the B&B every damn day looking like a Southern temptation. If I don't push him away with my attitude, I'll end up right back in his bed.

And that *cannot* happen.

The last time I let a smooth-talking cowboy sweep me off my feet, I paid the price. Seeing him every day afterward was hell, and I won't allow it to happen again.

But tonight, I'm going to let loose and drink away my thoughts of Gavin Fox. It's no wonder they called him "The Fox" when he was bull riding. Not only was he talented, but he had the looks to back it up too.

The worst combination.

My phone dings with a text, and I see it's my sister.

> KENZIE
>
> You coming soon? It's starting to fill up!

Kenzie and Ethan are bartending tonight, so Elle and Rowan are supposed to meet me there to drink and hang out.

> MAIZE
>
> Be there in 30.

I finish getting ready, leaving my hair down in beachy waves, then put on some red lipstick. It's a contrast from my everyday look, which consists of a ponytail and mascara. It'll be nice to dress up and hang out with the gang.

Before I leave, I find my mom in the kitchen and wrap my arms around her. "Happy New Year, Ma."

She pats my hands before spinning around with a smile. "You headin' out?"

"Yep. Gonna keep Kenzie company."

She snickers. "I doubt she'll need it at the bar."

"True." I laugh. "Dad at the B&B?"

"He should be home at any moment. I told him the house would be empty tonight, so he better hurry. And hopefully, he'll bring wine."

I exaggerate a gag. "Gross, Mom."

"What? You think just because we're older, we don't need *alone* time?" She quirks a brow. "We had to get creative when you girls were younger."

"Aaaaaand that's my cue to leave." I kiss her cheek, then grab my bag and hop in my truck.

By the time I arrive at the bar, the parking lot is packed, and I have to park on the street. I enter and squeeze my way through a ton of people drinking and dancing.

"Finally!" Kenzie scolds when I manage to find a seat. "Thought you were gonna bail on me."

"Are Rowan and Elle here yet?"

"No, but they're on their way. Hopefully, this crowd weeds out soon, though."

Ethan comes up and hands me a coaster. "They will. Most of them stop in and have a few drinks before they go to house parties."

"Start me off with a Jack and Diet," I tell her.

Moments later, Elle walks in, and I hug her. "I'm so happy you could make it."

"Only because Dr. Dickhead gave me off tomorrow." She rolls her eyes like she's surprised.

"Which means you need to take full advantage and drink!"

She orders a cocktail, then turns to me to catch up. "So, you gonna tell me more about this Gavin?"

"There's nothing to tell."

Kenzie snorts, then strolls to the other side to help a customer. After Kenzie embarrassed me at Thanksgiving, I told her to butt the hell out. She's the only one who knows the whole story, and though Elle is aware of the one-night stand, I've kept the details to myself. I was with her and Rowan the morning after it happened. Elle begged us to help birth a calf, so I arrived hungover as hell and asked them if they knew anyone named Gavin. Since they didn't, I had hoped he was just passing through, and I'd never have to see him again.

My luck would have it otherwise.

"When we were officially introduced at the ranch, I acted like I didn't know him, and he's been torturing me ever since," I say quickly before sucking down half my drink.

"But you *do* know him."

"Yes, but I don't want him to know that! I want to pretend our night never happened, but he's hell-bent on not letting me."

Elle laughs, sipping her own drink. "Well, it sounds to me like Gavin wants round two."

I groan, shaking my head. "Not happening. I'm already embarrassed enough."

"Perhaps you're just so memorable, he can't get you out of his head." She shrugs with a cocky grin. "I mean, you are a total babe."

"Well, he can find another *babe* because it's not gonna be me," I say matter-of-factly.

Elle smiles and chews on her straw, looking behind me. "Speakin' of the devil."

I quickly glance over my shoulder and see Gavin with Grayson, Diesel, and Rowan behind him.

Fuck me.

Of course they'd invite him. Dammit.

"Hey!" Rowan rushes toward us and wraps her arms around us.

Kenzie squeals and takes their drink orders.

"Hey, Maize." Gavin's hoarse voice makes me shiver.

"I see you've turned your obsession into stalking."

"Is it really stalking if this is the only pub in town?"

I turn and see his flirty grin, which causes me to look away and motion for Kenzie to refill my glass.

"Let me buy you a drink," he says, taking the seat next to me.

"That's not necessary." I inch away from him.

"Maize, shut up and order the expensive shit." Kenzie waggles her brows.

"Round of shots?" Gavin asks, and I relax my shoulders. "For everyone," he confirms.

"Vodka," I say. Gonna need it if he's determined to bother me all night.

Kenzie pours the liquor, and soon we're three shots in. Diesel and Rowan are in their own little world as Grayson taunts Kenzie at the other end of the bar. Elle is playing pool with some guy, leaving me alone with Gavin.

"Looks like you're stuck with me."

"I've noticed." I groan, taking a sip of my drink. At this point, I can't taste the Jack or the Diet Coke.

"C'mon, I'm not that bad. You should give me a chance like you did four months ago."

I nearly choke and hope he doesn't notice, but by the sly grin on his face, I know he does.

"You're delusional."

"You keep sayin' that, but I'm not buying it, Maize Bishop."

I roll my eyes, not giving in to this little game. Maybe if I keep drinking, I'll be able to tune him out.

"Hey, we're all going to Wyatt's for the ball drop," Rowan tells me. "Wanna come?"

"Y'all leavin' now?"

"Yeah, we're gonna drink and eat snacks there," she confirms.

I look at Kenzie, then back at Rowan. "No, I'm gonna stay with my sister." Though she's a grown-ass woman and can take care of herself, I don't want to leave her here without company on New Year's Eve.

"Okay, babe. Text me if you change your mind." She kisses my cheek, and I watch as all the guys and my cousins walk out the door.

"You aren't going with your friends?" I ask Gavin, shocked he didn't even consider it.

"You're all the company I need." He smirks before taking a drink and looking at me over the neck of his beer. It shouldn't be sexy, but as I watch the way his throat tightens, I realize I must be drunker than I thought.

"I'm not here to entertain you, so go to the party." I wave my fingers toward the door. I can't be trusted alone with him.

"Who said I expected you to? You're quite presumptuous." He turns his body toward mine so our knees touch.

"I'm presumptuous?" I balk. "I beg to differ considering I keep telling you to go away and you never do."

"I'm just sittin' here," he says calmly, motioning for Kenzie with his empty beer bottle. "You're the one who keeps lookin' at me like I'm your next meal."

I shake my head. "You've lost your mind."

"That's not what you said the first night we met."

"Okay, now I *know* you've lost your damn mind."

"What can I get you lovebirds?" Kenzie asks casually, and if looks could kill, she'd be dead.

"Maize and I are gonna shoot some Fireball."

"No, we are not," I interject.

"It's no fun playing drinking games by myself," Gavin says, giving me a sly grin. I want to slap it off his sexy face. "You only have to drink if you lose anyway, so what do ya say?"

Kenzie waggles her brows when I glance at her. I sigh with a shrug, giving in. "Fine."

She lines up four glasses, then fills them full. "Have fun, you two." Flashing a wink, she moves to the other side to help more customers.

"Alright, Cowboy. What's this game?"

"Ever heard of two truths and a lie?" he asks.

"Unfortunately, yes. You really wanna play this game with me, though? I'm pretty good at reading people," I say matter-of-factly, but it's the booze talking.

"So you keep sayin'. And now I'm even more certain I do." He chuckles, scooting my shot closer. "If you don't guess the lie, you drink."

"And if I do, you drink."

"Let's play. Ladies first." He gestures toward me, and it takes me a minute to think.

"Okay. When I was six years old, I fell off a four-wheeler and sprained my ankle. I'm left-handed. And…" I tap my lips, thinking of the final one. "I've never had a one-night stand."

The corner of his lips tilts up, and I wonder if he's going to guess right or not.

"Jesus, you're playin' dirty. Alright, well, then I'd have to say your lie is the last one." The corner of his lip tilts up.

"Wrong. I was eight, and it was a horse." I glance down at his shot then back at him.

Gavin shakes his head "Oh, I see you're *really* doin' me dirty. Two can play that game, darlin'." Without arguing, he downs the shot.

The alcohol is definitely buzzing through my body because I can't take my eyes off him. His buff biceps, the way his veins pop in his arms, and how his eyes focus on me as if I'm the only one in the bar are hypnotizing.

"Your turn."

"Okay, get ready to lose." He flashes an arrogant smirk. "I rode my first bull when I was nine. I won my first championship when I was nineteen. I've never had a one-night stand, then left the morning after without as much as a goodbye."

I glare at him, knowing he purposely said that last one to see how I'd react. Well, too bad for him it won't work.

"Nine years old? Bullshit. More Fireball for you," I tell him confidently.

Gavin grins, placing it to his lips, but then sets it down in front of me. "Wrong, sweetheart."

"No way! Nine years old?"

"Yep. Believe it."

Groaning, I swallow down the shot. If I'm not careful, I'll drink too much and let my guard down, which cannot happen.

"Well, we're one and one. What's the tiebreaker?" I ask, noticing two shots left.

"How about I ask you a question, and if you tell me the truth, I take both of these."

"And if I lie?"

"You kiss me at midnight."

I sit up straighter, keeping my eyes focused on his. Is he for real?

"How will you know if I'm telling the truth?" I ask.

"Because I already know the answer."

"I might be drunk, but I'm not stupid," I tell him.

"Never said you were, but you wanted a tiebreaker, and I gave you one."

"How about we each take one and call it even?" I grab one of the glasses and hold it up.

"Why? Afraid you'll actually have to be honest for once?" he challenges, and I can hear the hurt in his tone.

Instead of answering, I down the whiskey, then slam the empty glass on the bar. "You don't know me, Gavin."

He leans in close, causing heat to ripple through me. Then his mouth lowers to my ear. "I know enough to know you like your ass slapped." Gavin licks his lips, then continues, "*Hard.*"

I squeeze my eyes shut, and flashes of our night resurface. Every time he's near, memories flicker through my mind, and as much as I've tried to ignore it, with him so close, it's impossible.

For a second, I want to give in to the desire and have a round two, but nothing good would come of it. He's older, more experienced, and more likely to break my heart. It won't end well.

"Excuse me," I say, pushing off my stool.

I rush to the bathroom and look at myself in the mirror. I'm completely red and flushed, and I'm pissed at how my body reacts to him. Our night together was the hottest sex I've ever had, but I'll be damned if I give in to his good looks again.

After I wash my hands and steady my breathing, I step into the hallway and gasp when I see Gavin leaning against the wall with his arms crossed.

"What are you doin'?" I stutter.

"Making sure you weren't running off on me again."

"Again?"

Gavin moves toward me, closing the gap between us. "Yes, *again*. The morning after we had sex, you bailed on me. No note, no explanation, just up and left. And I want to know why."

"I have no idea what you're talkin' about." I hold my ground, not giving in. "Perhaps you have me confused with another girl you slept with." I shrug, acting as if his accusations don't faze me.

"Trust me, I'd never forget you, Maize. We drank, I kicked your ass in a game of pool, and by the end of the night, I had you screaming my name in bed."

His words have a shiver running down my spine. Damn him.

"So you wanna tell me why you keep denyin' it?"

"Because it didn't happen." I snort.

"It's almost midnight."

I nearly get whiplash with his topic change. Kenzie shouts that there are thirty seconds left.

"Yeah?"

"Since you're so hell-bent on refusing we were together, then perhaps I should remind you what it was like." Gavin flattens his palm on the wall next to me, and when his mouth moves closer to mine, my breath hitches. "Let me kiss you," he whispers.

"That's not a good idea."

"Everyone should get kissed on New Year's Eve. Even a frustrating, gorgeous woman like you."

"Maybe I want someone else to kiss me." I shrug, mocking a smile. "You're not really my type. No offense."

"You sure about that? I was your type the first time."

"Again, that never happened."

People chant the countdown, and we're only seconds away.

"Ten, night, eight..." he says. "The opportunity might not come around again, Maize."

Five, four, three, two...

Without thinking, I fist my hands in his shirt and pull his face to mine. Our lips collide, and Gavin quickly catches on, reaching down and gripping my waist. As our bodies mold together, he slides his tongue inside my mouth. I taste cinnamon and inhale his musky scent as fireworks erupt between us. His hand cups my cheek, and he tilts my head back to deepen the kiss. Every nerve sparks with electricity as our mouths battle for more. We release moans as we devour one another, similar to the first time but more heated and desperate. Memories of how he touched me and satisfied my every need rush through me, and it's then I know I'm losing my resolve.

Slowly, I pull away and lick my lips. I blink, unable to look at him as we stand in the dimly lit hallway and try to catch our breaths.

"This doesn't mean anything's changed between us," I blurt out, finally glancing up at him.

He slides his tongue along his bottom lip. "I beg to differ."

"After a bad experience, I don't get involved with men who work on the ranch, so get whatever thought you have in that head of yours out because it's not happening," I say sternly, though by the smug look on his face, he's not buying it. "We had one night. Let's just end it at that."

"So that's why you've been lying?"

Inhaling a sharp breath, I finally nod. "Fine, yes. I froze the day you showed up at the bar and decided to bail instead. I never expected to see you again, especially not on my family's ranch."

"Just to confirm, you do remember?"

Nodding again, I admit it. "Yes, but like I said—"

He dips his head and brings our mouths together again. Softly, our tongues tangle, and then all too soon, he backs away.

"Nothing's happening," he finishes my sentence. "Got it." He flashes me a mischievous wink.

Hearing Gavin say those words is like a punch to the gut. Even though I'm the one who said them to *him*, knowing my secret is out in the open makes me feel more vulnerable than before.

"It's not you, Gavin. I mean, it is but not because I wasn't attracted to you. You're older than me, you work for my uncle, we both work long hours, and if shit hits the fan between us, we'd be stuck seeing each other all the time. Trust me when I say that isn't a good time."

"Maybe if you'd give me a chance, it won't end like your past relationship did."

"I can't risk that. I'm sorry." My heart couldn't take it again.

"Well, if you change your mind, you know where to find me." He bites his bottom lip. Damn those lips are gonna get me into trouble—*more* trouble. Considering we've already hooked up and now have kissed again, I'd say it's already messing me up.

"I'm sure you have no problem getting women. You had fun chasing me until I admitted I remembered you, but now that it's all out in the open, you can stop this little cat and mouse game and go back to hooking up with belt buckle bunnies."

Amusement is written all over his too-perfect face. "You're gonna be fun, aren't ya?"

"Excuse me?"

"You're more stubborn than the bulls that tried to buck me off. I've had dozens of injuries, been stomped on, and had one charge and flip me on my back. And still, I think you're gonna be the hardest to break in. But I like a good challenge." His smirk only fuels my annoyance even more.

"I'm not some animal you can train," I snap with a scowl.

"No, sweetheart, you aren't. You're going to be more work. But Imma prove that I'm worthy of a real chance. Don't worry, I'm up for it. But don't you dare think I'm going away anytime soon, sweetheart."

Gavin grabs my hand, presses a kiss to my knuckles, then winks before walking away.

I blink hard as I stare at his ass in jeans that fit him like a glove.

Wait, what in the hell just happened?

CHAPTER SEVEN

Maize

The last month and a half have been a mix of emotions, but mostly excitement and dread.

Lately, I've been trying to keep myself busy to ensure my mind focuses on anything other than Gavin and the way his lips felt against mine New Year's Eve. Trying to forget him is proving to be a lot harder than I ever imagined. Nine times out of ten, I want to punch him for being so handsome and smelling so damn good.

As I'm cleaning up after the lunch rush, the night crew comes in and begins prepping dinner. They're busy chopping onions and having a conversation about their teenage daughters, which has me snickering as I wash dishes. Over the past month, I've been doing a lot of soul-searching. I'm not getting any younger, and if I ever want to move out, I have to hustle harder. Though I've been dreaming about starting a catering business, I've done nothing to pursue it. I typically don't make resolutions, but I promised myself I'd make it happen this year. It's scary but exciting, and I'm not sure where to start, but I think I'm ready.

Once I finish cleaning, I tell everyone goodbye. Just as I'm heading through the dining room, Grandma Bishop enters as if an angel called her. "Hey, sweetie."

I tilt my head, wondering what she's doing here. Grandma's always up to something and is in the know with all the town gossip. "So, I've got some news. A little birdie shared something with me today."

My blood pressure rises, and I hope to all things holy she didn't catch wind of what happened between Gavin and me because I'd literally die. "Oh really?"

I try to play it cool, but I'm actually crumpling as my heart rate rushes.

"So, I was at my quilting club meeting and was chattin' with Rebecca Blanchard. She mentioned the rodeo was coming to town in a few months, which we all know is typically a big deal and brings lots of business to the B&B. But she *also* mentioned something else."

My palms are sweaty, and my mouth goes dry. Any time someone mentions the word rodeo around here, Gavin's name comes soon after. I nearly stop breathing as I wait, and the anticipation might kill me. Grandma eats it up as I wait. Sometimes she's so dramatic.

"Come on, just go ahead and spit it out," I finally say, the dramatic pause being too much.

"Maize Grace! Watch your manners. This is my story, and I tell it how I want." She gives me the evil eye, then goes back to being nice granny. "Anyway. Rebecca told me about the barbecue contest, and she mentioned you should enter your famous smoked brisket. The one you did for the food drive fundraiser last year. It was incredible, Maze, and we all took a vote and believe you could win first place." Grandma beams as if I already had the trophy.

"You really think I have a chance or are you just saying that?" I ask, nearly laughing that my food was the topic of their conversation at their meeting.

"I can admit I give a bunch of frivolous compliments, but honey, I'd never set you up to humiliate yourself. If your brisket wasn't worth a lick, I wouldn't mention it, because I can't have you embarrassing yourself or the

Bishop name," she confirms with a nod. "You went to that fancy culinary school for a reason. So, you need to enter and kick some ass."

I burst out laughing. "Grandma, you just said ass."

"I'm old enough to have earned that right."

"This is very true."

She grins at me and places her hand on my shoulder. "The last day to submit the application is Friday, then the judges choose who qualifies to compete. I think the grand prize is five grand, and I know you've been wanting to start that little catering business, which I fully support. So I think this could help with startup costs. Even though I've offered to fund it, I know how proud and independent you are, just like your dad."

My whole face lights up thinking about what that money could buy for my business. While Grandma has been super supportive, she's right. I want to do this on my own. It's the Bishop way.

"So whatcha think?" she asks, beaming.

"It would be an amazing opportunity. And if you think I have a chance, then heck yes, I'll do it," I say, and she wraps me in one of her infamous hugs.

When we break apart, she looks me in the eyes. "Honey, I think you're a shoo-in to win. Plus, once you start your business, there are tons of ladies at church who want to hire you. They've got daughters who are getting married, birthday parties, and holiday events that none of them wanna cook for. Don't blame 'em, though. It's easier to have someone else do it these days."

I snort. "You all deserve to be pampered."

"I'm no spring chicken anymore. It's why I love my grandbabies so much. Always willing to help." Grandma pulls a packet of papers from her giant purse and hands it to me. "Here's everything you need. Turn this into the Chamber before the deadline."

"Yes, ma'am," I say, flipping through the big packet. "I'll make sure I fill it out tonight."

Grandma waves goodbye, and when she's out of sight, I let out a loud squeal. I'm smiling so wide my face hurts.

Dad rushes into the dining room and looks spooked. "Are you okay? I heard screaming."

"Fine, just fine! Grandma thinks I should enter the rodeo's barbecue contest." I hand the packet to him, and he flips through it.

"So who's gonna be on your team?" he asks.

My eyes go wide. "Team?"

"Yeah, it says here you have to put a team together and list their names. It has a place for five to ten people." He gives the papers back to me, and I scan over them.

"Well damn," I mutter, and he doesn't correct me. "Um, you wanna help?"

He chuckles. "Of course, as a last resort, though. You should ask your sister, Rowan, Elle, Riley, Zoey, Knox, Kane, and force Diesel to help too. And if they say no—"

"Then I'll threaten them," I say.

"If you want, but I was going to say, I'll get your uncles involved. And either they'll cook because I'll tell Mama you need to put together a team, or they'll force their kids to help."

"Good idea! Guess I've got some work to do once I get home," I say, wondering if I should group text them or do it individually. I'm not in the mood for excuses, but I think they'll be on board to help without kicking their asses. One thing's for certain, us Bishop's usually stick together.

"Let me know if you're able to round them up or not." Dad grins, and I leave with a pep to my step.

It's been a few days since my cousins said they'd help me at the rodeo, and it only took a few friendly threats. Elle was even able to commit after she told her sexy as sin boss she needed off. I've got Riley, Elle, Kenzie, Kane, Knox, and even Diesel. Rowan's planning to close the bar during that week because it'll be really busy. I should find out any day now if I've been accepted, and if not, Grandma will have a few choice words with the Chamber of Commerce. No one crosses that woman when it comes to her grandkids, and I mean absolutely no one.

Today is Valentine's Day, and I'm already dreading it more than usual. I've decided not to go onto social media so I can avoid the ridiculous photos of couples so happily in love with candy and flowers. I'm already gagging thinking about it. Even though I'm a known love hater, as Rowan says, I still like making the day fun for the B&B guests.

The weather is brisk, and I crank the heat on full blast on the way to work. When I step out of my truck, frost crunches under my feet as I walk, and I honestly can't wait for the spring flowers. Once I'm inside, I immediately get started. After I mix the strawberry pancake batter, I pull out the giant heart molds and the smaller ones for the sausage patties. Each year, we get tons of compliments by keeping the theme.

My employees arrive, and it's a madhouse when breakfast starts, but then again, when is it not? We're running back and forth between the buffet and the kitchen, and I swear we make hundreds of heart-shaped pancakes. The next time I go into the dining area, I see Riley and Diesel ragging on each other as Knox and Kane instigate the situation.

"He totally called you a pussy," Kane taunts.

"I did not." Diesel shakes his head.

"Shhh," I say, rushing over to them and grabbing Kane by his ear like he's a kid. "We have guests in here, so you need to shut the fuck up," I whisper. "I will tell your mama in a heartbeat that you're using that language in the B&B."

He rolls his eyes but straightens up as soon as Dad comes into sight. "Y'all behaving?"

"Yes, sir," they all say in unison. I give them an evil look, then smile sweetly at my dad. He nods and walks away as I return to the kitchen.

Just after eight, my cell phone buzzes like crazy on the counter. It's from an unknown number, but I answer it anyway.

"Is this Ms. Maize Bishop?" a man asks.

"Yes, it is."

"Great, I just wanted to call and congratulate you on being accepted to compete in the barbecue contest at the rodeo. We would've gotten back to you sooner, but we had a ton of applications to sort through this year. You're still interested, correct?"

My heart flutters with happiness. "Oh my God, yes, absolutely!" I throw my hand up in the air, giving a fist pump as Jane and Sandra glance over at me.

"Fantastic. We'll have a pre-meeting in a few weeks that you'll need to attend. Please make sure you read over the rules for your team so you're not disqualified. We're happy to have you on board and can't wait to try your brisket."

"Thank you. Thank you so much."

The call ends, and I let out a hoot. I know I'm being loud as hell, but this is the best news I could've received today. I thought I wouldn't get picked for a few days because I hadn't received a call yet, but now that I have, that means I need to start preparing.

Knowing I have to tell Dad the good news, I go and search for him. He's in the dining area pouring coffee into a mug.

"What's going on?" He grins.

"They chose me for the contest!" I'm so excited my voice is an entire octave higher than usual.

He gives me a side hug. "See, told you! You're gonna win this, sweetie! I just know it!"

"That would be incredible," I admit, imagining it, then notice we need more bacon and biscuits. "Gotta get back to it."

I'm floating on cloud nine as I slap bacon strips on the griddle. Since Grandma mentioned it, I've been trying to perfect my honey barbecue sauce, but honestly, the meat is so juicy and tender that it's not even needed. When I deliver the food to the buffet, I see Gavin enter. His eyes meet mine as I carefully stack a pile of hot buttermilk biscuits under the lamps.

He winks at me, but I can't let his presence distract me, so I immediately turn around. I know what he's doing, so I'll keep avoiding and ignoring him the best that I can.

Twenty minutes pass, and Dad announces that we need more coffee. After I grind some beans and fill the giant container, I carry it out there, and that's when I overhear Gavin and Grayson's conversation.

"Yeah, I'll be at the rodeo for sure," Gavin says, then continues. "I'm still training Cooper. He's trying to qualify so he can compete at the next level."

"Oh yeah, hasn't he been riding for a while?" Grayson takes a huge bite of pancakes.

"He's determined and listens. He has what it takes," Gavin tells him.

"Well, he's got a world champion giving him instruction. I might come watch." Grayson smiles.

Gavin pauses for a second, and I don't even dare to look at him, though I don't mind eavesdropping. "Determination can be deadly, though. Most don't realize how dangerous it really is out there, and the moment you get sloppy, is when you could lose everything, including your life. Rodeo life, though, I really loved it."

I swallow, fill the sugar packets and stirrers, then go back to the kitchen, not wanting to hear any more. If he loved it so much, why would he want to stay on the ranch? Eldorado is small and simple. Moving from big town Houston to here is probably nothing more than a temporary getaway for him. I give him a year before he gets bored and finds some other place. I wasn't good enough for Timothy. Considering Gavin's history, I don't think I'm enough to make him stay. Or at least that's what I keep telling myself while keeping my distance. At this point in my life, I'm not looking for a fling.

The rest of the morning goes by in a blur. As I'm preparing for lunch, I call Grandma to tell her the good news, and she's ecstatic for me.

"If you ever need a taste tester, call me," she says with a laugh before we say our goodbyes.

Sandra washes the dishes, and considering how many people were in and out today for breakfast and lunch, I decide to do a deep clean. It's something I typically do once a week. Since Jane has already swept, I grab the mop and bucket and then drag it out to the main room.

I freeze in place when I see a dozen white roses in a vase on the buffet table. I look at them like they're a poisoned apple, then glance around, confused. Slowly, I walk up to them and notice a card is attached with my name written in chicken scratch. My eyes go wide, and I just hope Dad isn't around to witness this because it would cause too many questions.

I open the envelope.

Happy Valentine's Day, Maize. If you'd let me, I'd make it worth your while, since you no longer have amnesia.

I hurry and tuck it in my back pocket, and then grab the roses and take them into the kitchen.

"Whoa!" Sandra says with wide eyes.

"I know, I know." I set them down because while they're beautiful, they're also heavy. The sweet smell fills the kitchen, and I try to steady my breathing. My heart pounds hard because there's only one florist in town, which means Gavin *had* to speak to them about sending flowers. This is exactly how rumors start around here.

"Who are they from?" Donna questions, pulling me from my thoughts.

"Didn't say." I'm being truthful because his name wasn't actually written, just insinuated.

"Someone's got a secret admirer." Dad speaks up from behind me, and I nearly jump out of my shoes.

I roll my eyes, wishing I could disappear. "I guess."

"Hmmm." Dad rubs his chin. "I wonder who it could be."

"I dunno!" I look around, trying to find my escape. "I gotta get back to mopping."

I rush to the dining room and have never moved so fast in my life. I'm thankful I took the card because I know Dad would've peeked, and that's the last thing I need right now. After I'm done with my tasks, I grab the roses and tell everyone goodbye.

I'm tempted to text him on the way home and demand he stop, but I realize I don't have his number. Truthfully, it's probably a good thing because it means I can't drunk text him. Knowing we'll be at the rodeo together excites me but also makes me anxious. He's well-known in the area, and the last thing I want to witness is women flocking to him. Hopefully, I'll be too busy to even notice.

When I park, I look over at the roses. It was a sweet thought, and while I want to be angry, I'm not sure I can. If we were two different people, maybe we could work. Part of me wishes it was possible, but the other knows it's not.

CHAPTER EIGHT

Gavin

"He's bein' a bastard, ain't he?" Jackson asks, hanging on the railing.

"Oh yeah," I respond, nearly breathless.

A new colt was delivered last Monday, and he's my special project. They named him Demon for a fuckin' reason too 'cause he's a little shit and doesn't want to cooperate. If he keeps it up, we'll be doing laps around the corral for the next two weeks. One thing I've learned while training horses is to have patience and be gentle. These animals don't trust humans on instinct. It's something that's earned.

"Rodeo's next week, right?"

I glance at him over my shoulder. "Yes, sir."

"Good deal. I'm gonna try to watch your trainee ride. Hopefully, he places. Anyway, I'll let you get back to it."

"Alrighty, thanks," I say, then slowly walk up to Demon as he backs away. Eventually, his curiosity gets the best of him, and he takes a few steps forward. Holding out my hand, I let him sniff me and keep my movements slow. The last thing I want is to spook him.

I touch the softness of his nose, then create some space so he can get reacquainted with learning. Right now, he's ready to bolt, and if the gate was open, he would.

After a minute of staring each other down, I grab the rope and start lead practice. He trots around in circles, and I swing the extra ends of the rope in the other direction, and he turns around. We do this for thirty minutes, and then I give him a break. Demon eyes me.

I click my tongue, encouraging him to come toward me. I clip the rope to his halter and lead him around the pen, then we go back to our training.

As he makes his way around the pen, I notice Maize from my peripheral. She's watching me train, and a smile forms on my face. She's no different than the horses—resentful, hesitant, but also interested—and I'm determined to break her too. The chase keeps me going, but I also like the thought of being with her too. I may be a retired bull rider, but I'll always be a champ, and I'm ready to win her over.

When I turn my head, our eyes meet, and she freezes in place. She's carrying bags, and I'm sure she's bringing Kiera and Jackson breakfast. Sometimes she does that when they're not as busy at the B&B. Wiping the sweat off my brow, I keep my eyes on Demon. As he does laps, she moves closer and hangs on the gate.

"Hey," she coos, her voice soft and sweet.

"Hi." I don't stop my training session even though I want to do nothing but pay attention to her right now. Not sure what it is about Maize Bishop, but the chemistry we share and the way she makes me feel are different from all the other women I've ever been with. She's not the type you have a one-night stand with and forget, but rather the kind of lady you bring home to meet your mama.

"What're ya doin' for lunch?" she asks.

"No plans," I say with a half-grin.

"Why don't you come down to the B&B and eat? I know this sounds silly, but you lived rodeo life for a long while, and I'd like your opinion on something."

I lower my arms, and instantly, Demon stops trotting and stands twenty yards away and stares at me. Bringing my gaze to her, I walk closer. "About what?"

"I cooked the brisket I'm entering into the contest and want you to try it since you've been all over the state. Barbecue is a whole food group in Texas, and I know you've probably eaten truckloads of it." She hesitates. "I just don't want to go embarrassing myself. The only thing is, you'll have to promise to be truthful no matter what."

I study her lips, then meet her soft eyes. Something about Maize drives me absolutely fucking crazy, and right now, all I want to do is swipe my lips against hers until we're both breathless.

"So, what do you say?" she finally asks.

"Sure. I'll be there, but you owe me one," I tell her with a wink.

She chuckles, a sound I don't get to hear too often. "Add it to my tab. See you at eleven."

Once Maize is out of sight, I go back to Demon, and we try saddle training next. When I look down at my phone, I realize it's nearly time to meet Maize. Quickly, I finish up, then I pop my head into the office and let Jackson know I'm going to the B&B for lunch in case he comes lookin' for me.

On the way over, I can't stop smiling because this is a step in the right direction. Though Maize and I have played tug-of-war for months, her reaching out for my help feels like progress. She's smart to ask me because I *have* eaten a lot of barbecue over the years. It's a staple at every damn rodeo I've ever been to.

I pull up to the B&B and park. Though it's only the end of April, it's already hot as hell. Can't even imagine how summer's gonna be, but I'm not looking forward to it because I'll be working outside. When I enter, I immediately smell the smoky meat wafting through the whole place. My mouth begins to water, and my stomach growls.

As soon as I sit at a table in the corner, Maize steps into view and looks around the room. When she spots me, she smiles, then holds up her index finger and walks away. I get up and pour myself some sweet tea, and when I return to my seat, I notice she's carrying a tray full of food toward me.

"Whoa," I say with a grin when she sets it down.

The laughter that releases from her sounds so sweet. Maize hands me a set of silverware and sits in front of me. Before I take a bite, I notice she's fidgeting with the hem of her shirt. She's so nervous about me eating, not something I've witnessed since being here. I push the fork into the meat and watch the juices run from it. It's tender as can be as I eat it. The taste isn't like anything I've had before, and I swear it's the best damn barbecue I've ever had.

I grab the dinner roll and dip it in the barbecue sauce, take a few bites of smoked sausage, and finish off the brisket like I haven't eaten in a decade. Maize's cheeks turn pink as she bites her bottom lip. "Okay, so what do you think?"

With the rest of the bread, I wipe it across the plate until it's perfectly clean. "Do you have more?"

"You're just saying that," she chides, crossing her arms.

I place my hand over hers and lean forward, lowering my voice so no prying ears can hear. "You're gonna win this, sweetheart. It's the best I've ever had. Cross my heart."

Her smile grows wider. "Really?"

"I wouldn't lie. The texture. The flavor. It's not dry at all like some briskets are. And the sauce, holy shit, woman. I'm tempted to get down on one knee and ask you to marry me right here, right now."

She pulls her hand away, and I realize I crossed the line, but I don't care. It's the damn truth.

"So, about those seconds...?" I linger, not just referring to her food.

Standing and scooting in her chair, she grabs the tray, leaving my tea, then walks away. I almost thought she was pranking me until she returns with a heaping pile full of her soon-to-be award-winning barbecue. "I gotta go help my employees, so I'll be right back. Okay?"

I give her a nod and dig in. It's so delicious I eat every morsel, not wasting a crumb. About an hour passes before she comes back.

"There's no way you ate all that," she says, her eyes wide.

I lean back and suck in a deep breath. I might've gone overboard, but it was too good to pass up. "I did, and now I'm full as hell and have no idea how I'm going to work for the rest of the day. I can already feel the food coma coming. It was so good, and if I had any room, I'd eat more." I throw her a wink.

"You're not shitting me, right?" she asks again.

"Never. You'll win, hands down. I'd even bet on it." I hold out my hand, hoping she shakes, but she doesn't do anything but smile wide.

"Thank you," she whispers. "Means a lot to me. I'm just nervous about all this."

"Shouldn't be. You're a pro, Maze. That prize is yours," I stress, wishing she'd believe me. I look around and notice the B&B is empty. It's just her and me. The place is a mess, so I stand and help her pick up the remaining dishes left on the tables. We grab as much as we can so we don't have to make another trip, and I follow her to the kitchen area.

Maize sets the dishes in the sink and then steps slightly out of the way to give me more room to add what I'm carrying. Our arms touch, and electricity shoots through me. She must've felt it too because I notice goose bumps form on her arms. Though she denies anything between us, moments like this remind me there is something. Nothing she could say would make me think otherwise because her body gives her away every single time.

"Maze," I whisper, watching her breasts rise and fall. I place my palm on her warm cheek and brush my thumb against her skin. She swallows, and I'm tempted to kiss her, but I don't want to press my luck when I'm gaining ground.

My phone rings, and I glance down to see it's Jackson. I'm sure he's wondering where the hell I ran off to because I've been gone for a while. "I don't want to go, but I have to," I admit.

"I know," she whispers.

I look down and reject the call, not ready to go just yet, but knowing I have to.

"Do you want a hand?" I ask.

She tilts her head. "Not unless you want Uncle Jackson bursting through those doors and dragging your ass back to the training facility. You've helped me more than enough already."

Leaning over, I place a soft kiss on her head, then turn away just as her employees are walking through the door with baskets of veggies from the garden.

"See you later," I say, then leave. I sent her flowers on Valentine's Day, and the note I left wasn't a joke. I would make it worth her while if she'd let me.

When I get in the truck, I call and let Jackson know I'm on the way. Apparently, a mare's being delivered this afternoon. It slipped my mind that I needed to check her in, but I got to the barn in record time.

Jackson pulls hay down from the loft, and I grab a few bales and help distribute it to each stall. It's a revolving door with training now that three of us are doing it. Kiera and Jackson have been happy with how much we've grown the facility, and the word has traveled fast. We're booked nearly two years in advance, and the waitlist is a mile long too. Wouldn't be surprised if they hire a few more people to keep up with the demand.

Before long, a truck with a gooseneck horse trailer comes traveling down the rock drive. A man parks and pops out of the cab and walks over to me. "You Gavin?"

"Yes, sir," I tell him.

He nods. "I'm Billy Gibson. Own the ranch a ways down. Ready to unload her?"

"Sure am. And very nice to meet you."

Billy goes to the back and lifts the bar to the trailer gate. The mare instantly starts throwing her hoof out, ready to kick one of us. She's pissed.

"We call her Angel," he tells me with a thick Southern accent.

I chuckle. "Sarcasm, I assume?"

"Absolutely, son."

"Perfect, I've got one named Demon right now. They'll probably get along just fine."

Just as I'm assisting Billy, I see Grayson and Diesel pull up in the old beat-up Ford. They go inside the office, and I do a walk around of the horse. We like to make a note of any injuries before accepting them. I lift her hooves, and she's not having it, but thankfully, she's not too big or hard to handle yet.

"Whatever you do, don't walk behind her," he warns and pulls me back.

"Thanks," I tell him.

"She might've kicked your balls right off. It's one of her bad habits," he explains. "Her only goal is to take out anyone or anything that gets behind her flank. My dog learned his lesson real quick."

I nod and check the other side. "Noted. Well, she looks good."

"Y'all gonna earn your money with this one," he says, patting her.

It makes me chuckle. I've yet to meet a horse that was easy to break.

"You'll just need to sign some paperwork inside, and then you'll be all set," I explain and point toward the office. He gives me a head nod and goes that way.

As Angel is tied to a post, I take a step back, crossing my arms and looking at her. She's a beautiful gray leopard appaloosa with a black mane and white socks. Holding my hand out, I allow her to make the first move and sniff me. Once Angel seems calmer, I lead her to her stall. By the time she's settled in the barn, I walk to the front, and the owner is long gone.

Diesel and Grayson step out of the office, ragging on each other.

"If it weren't for me, you wouldn't even be at work this morning," he tells Diesel.

"And that's why you're my right-hand man," Diesel explains. "You keep me in check."

Grayson rolls his eyes and grins. "There's Casanova."

"What?" I chuckle.

"I heard Maize got roses on Valentine's, and I've been meaning to ask you if you sent them," Diesel says.

I tilt my head at them because there's no damn way either would know 'cause Maize's sealed like a vault. "I'm not the type of man who kisses and tells, boys. So, you need to go on with all that rumor mill shit."

"You're no fun," Diesel whines.

"I'm plenty of fun, or at least that's what the ladies say." I shrug and laugh.

"The rodeo's next week, right?" Grayson lifts his cowboy hat and smooths his sweat-covered hair down before setting it back on his head.

I nod, answering him with Maize on my mind. I wonder if we'll ever be anything more, and chasing women isn't in my forte. Feeling the constant hot and cold from her is a new experience for me, and I'm not sure I like it. Though I do enjoy the chase of it all.

"How's Cooper doing? Nervous yet?" Diesel asks.

"Actually, he's doing really well. Wouldn't be surprised if he placed. I know the competition won't be easy, though. As long as he stays on his A game and gets out of his damn head, he'll make it happen," I explain. "We're actually meeting tonight to continue our lessons. Most of it's mental, but a large portion is physical too. You ever thought about riding?"

Diesel's a big guy with lots of muscle, and with the right training, he could probably go far.

He snorts. "Hell no!"

"Big D here's too much of a pussy," Grayson snaps with a chuckle. "He nearly cried when he saw a spider in the truck last week."

I burst out laughing.

"I did not!" Diesel scowls and takes off running after Grayson, who's way too fast for him. I remember being pretty much the same at their age.

Diesel bends over and picks up a rock and throws it at Grayson. It nails him right in the back of his head. Wanting to retaliate, Grayson starts throwing them back.

"What in the fuck are you two doin'?" Jackson yells.

I cross my arms and watch them chase each other like kids.

"Nothing!" Diesel says, finally dropping his ammunition.

Jackson looks at me and shakes his head. In that split second, Grayson nails Diesel in the forehead.

"What the hell!" Diesel screams and starts the chase again.

Jackson claps his hands to get their attention, but they're lost. Seconds later, he puts two fingers in his mouth and lets out the loudest ear-piercing whistle I've ever heard. They both stop moving.

"Get your asses in the truck and get the hell outta here. Actin' like rowdy children," he demands, but he's smiling.

"Learned it from you!" Diesel pops off, and Jackson rears up like he's going to charge them.

It's enough to scare the shit out of them, and they climb into the truck without hesitation. When I see the look on their faces as they back out of the drive, I chuckle. They're giggling like schoolkids, and so is Jackson.

I shake my head, and Jackson pats me on the back. "Guess it's time to get back to work."

"Yes, sir," I confirm, then head to the barn. One thing about working on the Bishop ranch is that there's never, ever a dull day around here.

CHAPTER NINE

Maize

I can't believe today's the competition. I've been counting down to this ever since I got that phone call, and now it's finally here. My nerves have gotten the best of me all week, and I've been a wreck, trying not to overwhelm myself. I know what winning could do—give me the opportunity to jumpstart my business.

When I was in culinary school, it was very competitive. I received job offers from many of the chefs who taught me after I graduated. I could've gone anywhere—San Francisco, New York, Dallas, or Chicago—and worked for upscale restaurants and fine dining experiences only, but the stress would've been too intense for me to handle. Instead, I explained I'd be working for the family business. Though it wasn't what they wanted to hear, it was respectable, and I don't regret my decision. Being under pressure like that isn't for me, which is why I don't enter cooking competitions.

When we arrived with the pit early yesterday morning and saw the competition lined up, I was ready to drink tequila straight from the bottle. Diesel and Riley got the wood loaded and the pit to temperature as I prepared the meat. Some contestants have been smoking meat longer than I've been alive. They take it seriously and want to win just as much as I do. Learning there were close to thirty teams nearly gave me a heart attack.

Mom, Dad, Grandma, and I arrived before the sun rose this morning. After we parked, I added more hickory to the pit as my parents put up the canopy with chairs, so we didn't bake in the sun. I brought a checklist with timelines for my team, and as soon as Kenzie saw it, she rolled her eyes. My cousins have been the best support system and have helped me so much, but not without complaint.

Dad gets up and stretches as Knox and Kane check the temperature of the food. Kenzie micromanages them, using her soon-to-be teacher skills, and it makes me chuckle.

"You okay?" Dad asks as I unlock my phone and check the time. I swear only ten minutes have passed since I last looked.

I shrug. "Yeah. I guess. As good as I'm gonna be until this is all over."

"Honey, you're gonna do fine. And even if you don't win, I'm proud of you for trying. It's hard to put yourself out there and allow people to judge and be critical of something you're so passionate about," he says, patting me on the back. "It smells delicious."

"You wanna try the first cut when I pull it?" I lift my eyebrows, already knowing the answer to that question.

"Damn right," he tells me.

I look around him, and Kenzie gives me a thumbs-up. We're on track to having the juiciest brisket to date. If I don't win, I will swear until my dying day the judging was rigged.

Dad walks back to his seat, and Elle comes up to me. "Almost ready?" She checks the time on her smartwatch. "We have about two hours before we have to pull the meat and deliver the plates to the judge's area."

"I know. Actually, only one hour so it can rest beforehand." I bite my bottom lip, knowing that the juices will run out without adequate time to sit, making the meat dry. The last thing I want to do after smoking it for twenty-four hours is to ruin it at the end, and damn, it's so easy to do.

The twins are responsible for making sure it doesn't get dry and checking the internal temperatures. Right now, it's just a waiting game. I've done this process at least a hundred times since I knew I'd be competing, but it still makes me anxious. If something can go wrong for me, it usually does.

"Girl, you got this," Elle encourages, noticing my mood. Kenzie walks up and bumps her hips against mine.

"Can we eat yet?" she beams.

"Not yet. I made an extra brisket just for y'all, though," I tell her, knowing they'd want some after smelling it all day.

"Seriously, if I could cook like you, I'd probably already be married," Elle says with a smile.

Her joke makes me laugh, and it's exactly what I needed. "But then you wouldn't be available for that hot boss of yours."

She rolls her eyes. "Don't even. He's still being a total and utter dickhead. Because I took today off, I have to work the next three weekends. How in the fuck is that fair?" I can tell she's upset.

"Oh no. I'm sorry," I offer.

She shakes her head. "Not your fault. That's just how rude he is."

"Sometimes that attitude makes them even hotter," Kenzie quips, giving her a nudge. When I hear Uncle Jackson and Kiera, I turn around with wide eyes.

"Oh my gosh, what are y'all doin' here?" I ask.

"I had to come and see my honorary daughter kick some ass," Jackson howls. He sometimes calls me his honorary daughter because I couldn't tell Dad and Uncle Jackson apart when I was a baby. Honestly, though, some adults can't tell them apart now, especially when Uncle Jackson reels it in and tries to trick people.

"I might not win, though. I'm trying not to get my hopes up," I admit.

"You're doing the best you can, sweetie. That's enough," Kiera says and grins. As we chat about the weather, I overhear Riley and Diesel talking to Grandma. "So when you gonna give me more babies?" She glares at Riley.

Immediately, his face turns red, and Diesel nudges him. "Oh, come on. Don't pretend you're not banging every day."

Riley's eyes go wide. "My grandma is literally right there." He points at her, though she doesn't look offended. She raised Jackson, who was a total hellion, so she's pretty much immune to everything.

"And that's why I didn't say the f-word. I got respect for Grandma

Bishop." Diesel lifts his cowboy hat and gives her a curtsey. I snort and shake my head.

"Thank you, Adam. But we're not done with this conversation, Riley," Grandma continues.

Somehow, Riley finds his escape, and Diesel follows in his shadow. The two of them are hilarious together and will be best friends until they're old and wrinkly. Now that Diesel and Rowan are more serious, so much more has been added to their friend dynamic.

I let out a calm breath, double-checking my phone, the meat, and starting all over. It's the chef version of pacing. "Maize, why don't you go check out the rodeo and walk away for a little while?" Dad suggests, noticing my unease. "We've got this under control. The boys are doing what they're supposed to, and as long as Mama is over there watching them, they won't mess this up. She's literally your own Southern mob boss right now." He chuckles.

I look at him with big blue eyes. "Daddy, you sure?"

"You need a break before you drive yourself crazy."

Sucking in a deep breath, I nod. "You're probably right."

"Of course, I am, sweetheart. Fathers always know best."

"Okay, okay, don't go getting a big head or anything," I say, then take off my apron and hand it to him. "The brisket needs to be pulled soon. Elle knows when."

He salutes me, and I give a small wave, then walk past the rows of pits toward the main area. I make my way past horse trailers and temporary corrals.

In the arena, hooves pound against the ground, and when I'm closer, I see it's barrel racing. The young teens' age group is competing right now. It brings me back to riding when I was younger, and I realize how much I miss it. I can't remember the last time I saddled up and took one of the trails. In high school, it was my escape and gave me a chance to think. Now, I spend most of my time in the kitchen.

Leaning against the gate, I watch this girl, who's probably no older than twelve, race her horse. Her brows are furrowed, and she wears a serious expression as her ponytail sweeps in the breeze. When the young girl finishes, a small group of people stand and cheer, and that's when I see Sarah Cooke.

Groaning, I roll my eyes. Even though it's been years since I graduated high school, I will never forget how she treated me. Sarah was the real-life Regina George, all the way down to the blond hair and the clique of girls who followed her around.

I notice Gavin and Cooper sitting with them, and I shake my head. It slipped my mind that Cooper's family was friends with hers. Though I shouldn't be staring, I can't help but watch the way she flutters her long eyelashes at Gavin when he speaks. He has her full attention as he sits next to her. She says something, and he gives her a smirk, and it's more than obvious how intrigued she is by his presence.

My skin feels as though it's burning when I see Sarah flirting with Gavin. Not being able to handle it, I walk across the stadium and keep my eyes forward. Outside of the arena, a carnival has small rides for kids and a petting zoo with ponies, chickens, a kangaroo, llama, and ostrich. I watch a few toddlers with their parents inside the pen, and it's absolutely adorable. As I'm leaning against the cool metal, I feel someone stand close to me, way too damn close. I turn my head, ready to tell whoever it is to give me some space, when I see Gavin.

"Thought that was you," he says with the same smile he gave Sarah.

"I was about to tell you to back the fuck up," I say, putting my attention back on the kids. From my peripheral, I see Sarah and Cooper waiting for him. My jaw locks, but I'm not sure if he notices or not.

"How are things going so far?" He keeps his eyes on me. "Wait, aren't you supposed to be cooking right now?"

I laugh and meet his gaze. "The brisket is almost done, just waiting for Elle to pull it, then we'll plate it. My nerves were so bad that Dad forced me to take a break to get my mind right. Though I'm not so sure how much it really helped."

"Gavin," Cooper speaks up, then points toward the food area.

"Your friends are waiting," I mumble, glancing over at them. Sarah looks like she wants to claw my eyes out, and it makes me smile.

"We were going to get corn dogs and sweet tea. Have you eaten yet?" I shake my head.

"You should come with us," he offers. His arm brushes against mine, and I hurry and tuck my hands in my pockets, hoping he didn't notice the goose bumps.

"I don't want to interrupt anything."

A hearty laugh releases from him. "What're you talkin' about?" He turns and looks at an impatient Sarah and Cooper. While I don't want to be petty, I will never forget what she did to me. Sarah stole the only guy I liked in high school just to prove she could. Because of her, I was forced to go to the Jingle Bell Ball alone. *Bitch*.

"Nothing," I say, refusing to allow Sarah to get the best of me. He holds out his arm, and I hesitate but grab it.

"Ready?" he asks.

"Absolutely," Cooper tells him. "I'm starving."

Sarah's eyes burn into me, but she doesn't say anything. Gavin moves past them and leads us to the food truck area. Immediately, the sweet smells of homemade cotton candy and fried everything float through the air. We stop in front of one of the trucks that's well-known in town.

"What would you like?" he asks.

I shrug. "Whatever you're having."

Cooper follows him as he waits in line, but Sarah stays behind. Though I haven't spoken to her in over a decade, she moves closer to me.

"Hey, Maize. How've ya been?" she asks.

I don't even look at her. "Great."

She crosses her arms, and I notice she's staring at Gavin. "The things I'd do to that man." There's a slight pause. "I mean, unless you two are a thing."

"We're not official," I admit, just in case she asks him.

"So, are you two exclusive?"

This causes me to turn to her. "I'd rather not talk about this."

Thankfully, before she can respond, Gavin walks up with two giant corn dogs in one hand and two bottles of water in the other.

"I thought you wanted tea?" I say as he hands me my food and drink. "Thank you!"

"They were out, and it would take twenty minutes. Didn't want to wait." He gives a quick eye roll, then grins.

"That's a bummer."

Cooper hands Sarah an order of cheese fries. With his mouth full, Cooper chats about competing later tonight and how he's feeling nervous. I quickly check the time and realize I need to get back as soon as possible.

"I'm sure you're gonna place," Sarah says.

Cooper beams as he takes another big bite of a cheeseburger with a donut bun. My eyes go wide because I've never seen anything like that before.

"How's that taste?" I ask. I'd never thought about combining those two things, and instantly my mind reels with how to incorporate that for breakfast at the B&B.

"Delicious," he tells me with mayo in the corner of his mouth.

A breakfast sandwich served on a donut might be added to the menu next week.

Gavin chuckles and hands Cooper a napkin as he goes on about riding. Sarah glances at me, then she focuses on Gavin. She laughs in all the right places and looks up at him with her big brown eyes. It's pathetic. After we finish eating, I listen to Gavin talk about rodeo life and how he nearly broke his hip.

My phone buzzes, and I pull it from my pocket then answer.

"Where are you?" Kenzie asks. "Brisket has been resting for thirty minutes, and we're waiting for you to cut it open, or at least that's what Grandma says."

"I know, I know. I'm heading that way now," I say, grinning as a rush of excitement streams through me, but I stay calm.

"Okay, hurry your ass up. It's your time to shine, sis," she tells me before ending the call.

Gavin's eyes meet mine. "Everything okay?"

"Yeah, just fine. I need to get back," I admit.

"I'll walk with you." He turns to Cooper and Sarah. "I'll meet up with y'all at the arena in about thirty minutes." Without waiting for a reply, Gavin walks away with me.

"You were quiet back there." He glances at me.

I give him a smile, realizing we're alone. "I am now."

We're almost to the competitive cooking are, and I stop walking and turn to him.

"Thanks for lunch," I say before continuing.

"Anytime. Least I can do, considering you feed me nearly every day."

This makes me laugh because in a roundabout way, it's true. Time seems to sit still as the warm breeze brushes against my cheeks.

"What are you doing later? After you submit your entry?"

My heart races at the prospect of him wanting to hang out with me at his stomping grounds. "Cleaning up, then probably going home. Won't find out anything until tomorrow when they make the official announcement."

"After you're done, I'd love it if you came with me and watched the guys ride the bulls tonight. Starts at five."

I brush fallen strands of hair from my eyes and grin. "Yeah, I'd like that."

He seems pleased with my answer, considering I've been pushing him away for months. "Oh, I don't think I have your number."

My smile widens. "Of course, you don't."

With raised brows, he pulls his phone from his pocket, and I take it, plug in my number, then hand it back.

"Text me when you wanna meet up," I say, tucking my lips in my mouth, then turning away.

"You better believe it," he says, but I don't look back at him.

CHAPTER TEN

Gavin

As soon as Maize's out of sight, I send her a text.

> **GAVIN**
> This is my number. Lemme know when you're free.

I imagine the little smirk she likes to throw at me.

> **MAIZE**
> Will do.

> **GAVIN**
> Good luck! See you soon!

When she makes it back, I know it'll be hectic for her. Maize's a perfectionist when it comes to her cooking, so I can only imagine how anal she's being right now. I'm sure Riley and Diesel will tell me all about it, considering they were wrangled into helping.

I text Cooper and meet him at the barrel racing area where his cousin's competing. My mind wanders, and my body buzzes from being with Maize, but I try to push it away. When I come into sight, Sarah and Cooper wave, and I climb the stadium stairs two at a time and sit. For the next couple of hours, we watch the teens compete like fearless savages. They take corners so tightly that they look like they'll slide right out of the saddle.

Every so often, I pull my phone from my pocket to see if I've gotten a text from her yet. Tonight, she'll either be in a great mood or a shitty mood, depending on how things go. Either way, I'm determined to show her a good time.

When there's a break between age groups, Cooper stands and yawns. "I'm gonna go to the RV and take a nap." He rubs his eyes. "Need to reset my mindset before I ride."

"That's a good idea," I say. "Want me to come get you an hour before?"

"Yeah, that would be good." He gives me a nod, then leaves.

Sarah grins when Cooper walks away, leaving us alone.

She scoots closer, and I can feel the warmth from her body. "So."

I smile, and before I can say a word, my phone vibrates. Immediately, I pull it from my pocket and see a text from Maize.

> **MAIZE**
> Food is delivered, and we cleaned up. Judges are eating, and now I'm pacing. UGH.

> **GAVIN**
> Awesome! So, you're ready to hang out?

> **MAIZE**
> Yes! Please! I need to keep my mind busy.

A smile touches my lips, and I think of a few ways to do just that.

> **GAVIN**
> Wanna meet me at the mutton busting area?

Wanting to be alone with Maize, I stand and politely excuse myself. Sarah's face contorts, but she quickly smiles and tells me goodbye.

MAIZE

I'll be there in 10 minutes.

Once I'm out of the arena, I hear a crowd yell, followed by an eruption of applause. Parents and spectators are way more excited watching the toddlers ride sheep than the stadium is watching teenagers race barrels. It's adorable, and it's where I first realized I wanted to ride bulls when I was older.

I lean against the metal railing and see a sheep loaded in the shoot. A boy, barely five, sits on top of the fuzzy animal with a helmet and full gear. He holds on for dear life with his arms and legs. They open the gate, and the sheep zooms into a full sprint, trying to get the kid off his back. Five seconds later, the little boy is on the ground throwing a fit with elephant-sized tears. I chuckle, and so does everyone else.

As I turn, I see Maize walking toward me wearing a sexy smile.

"There's my champ," I say when she's closer and wrap my arm around her. For a second, I think she's going to pull away, but she doesn't. Instead, she leans in, giving me an awkward side hug, then creating space. Just like the curious horses.

"I haven't won *yet*," she reminds me, just as the next sheep bursts out with a little girl on its back. She holds on tight and ends up staying on until the announcer tells her to let go. There's a time limit to stay on just like in bull riding. She gracefully slides off, gets up, and dusts the dirt from her jeans, then gives a thumbs-up to the audience.

"Yes!" Maize hoots and hollers, then throws a fist pump in the air.

I chuckle.

"I love seeing girls break barriers like that."

"Around the states, mutton bustin' is gender-neutral. But she totally kicked ass."

When she walks past us, Maize claps loud and compliments her. I love her enthusiasm. A few more kids ride, and we decide to sit in the stands. We're so close the softness of her skin brushes against mine.

"If you're this excited about mutton bustin', you're gonna have a hell of a time in an hour."

She licks her lips. "I'm sure I will. Honestly, I've never watched the bull riders."

I tilt my head. "Why not?"

"Wasn't interested in the big egos." She shoots me a wink.

I clap my hands together and laugh. "Some of the assholes who ride love being in the spotlight, but most of the people who hung out with my circle kept to themselves. It was more about winning than being a celebrity. Super competitive."

She lightly elbows me. "I was just kidding. With my schedule, it just never interested me to take a day off and come out here. Plus, most of the girls my age flocked to the men who were in town just passing through. It's not my vibe, if you know what I mean."

I tuck hair that's blowing in her face behind her ear. "I understand."

"You were an exception," she says. "The *only* exception."

Placing my hand on my chest over my heart, I grin. "Means a lot. I'm honored. Shouldn't I get a trophy or something, though?"

She snorts. "Sometimes you're an ass."

"I'm not trying to be. Scout's honor."

My phone buzzes, and I realize it's the alarm I set to wake Cooper. He has an hour to get ready before he has to check in.

"Wanna walk with me to get Cooper?" I ask.

She nods, and we walk down the bleachers. I place my hand on the small of her back as we move through the crowd. There are more people here now than there were earlier, and that old excitement I'd feel before competing comes back. This time, it's a little different. While I'm not riding, I still have skin in the game because of Cooper. If he places, he'll get the qualification he needs to go to the regional championship, which is a big deal. Though it won't be easy, if he continues to rank, he could follow in my footsteps and make it to the world championship.

We walk past rows of trucks and horse trailers, and I can hear the generators buzzing from the campers. Most of them are luxury fifth wheels or buses, all bought by rodeo winnings and sponsors, I'm sure. These guys travel across the state to try to rank, and each time they win a title, they get paid too.

Maize looks at the different rigs, and she's amazed by how luxurious they are.

"Cooper is staying on-site even though he lives here?" Maize asks as we continue forward.

"Yeah. Considering you ride a few times during the rodeo, it's typically easier to be here than to commute."

When we make it to the giant fifth wheel, I get ready to knock.

Maize glances over at me. "Do you miss it?"

I look at her and contemplate my answer. "At times, but it's dangerous as fuck and a rough sport. It's well-known that each time you go out there, it's not a matter of if you'll get hurt, but when. After I went pro at eighteen, I pressed my luck a lot and knew I had to call it quits before I ultimately regretted it."

"Do you? Regret it, I mean?"

I don't have to think about it. "No. Retiring when I was at my prime was a good decision. I'll always be known as a two-time world champion who stopped riding after my final win. I still get calls for interviews and reunion rides, all which I've declined. I've broken too many ribs and tore too many muscles and ligaments over the years to have the desire to do it again. And concussions? I've lost count. Trust me when I say I don't regret stopping."

Maize's expression softens, and she shoos me forward. I tap on the door, and seconds later, Cooper opens it wearing just his jeans.

"Oh, sorry. I didn't realize a lady was present. I'll be right out." The door clicks shut.

I turn to Maize. "So, do you know the rules?"

"Of what?"

"Bull riding."

She shakes her head. "I know some, but you'll have to give me the CliffsNotes version, so I know what's going on."

A few moments later, Cooper comes out fully dressed in a nice button-down shirt and jeans. Of course, he has on his black Stetson and flashes his million-dollar smile.

"Ready?" he asks us.

I chuckle. "Ready as you are, cowboy."

Cooper leads the way, and we follow him.

"You gettin' nervous?" I ask Cooper, and he slows down his pace, stepping in line with us.

"Truthfully?"

I answer with a nod.

"I'm kinda losing my shit inside because what if I get hurt?"

I point at my temple. "You gotta get your mind right before you go out there. We talked about this before. Each time you get on a bull, it could be your last. It's why you have to respect the sport. When you're out there, what do you need to focus on?"

Cooper swallows hard. "Safety, my form, and the animal."

I pat him on the shoulder. "That's right because you already know the risk."

The lights from the arena splash across the ground, and I hear the noise of the crowd. Just seeing all the people causes a spike of adrenaline to rush through me. It's probably only a tenth of what Cooper is feeling. When Maize notices my shift, she grabs my hand and squeezes, but I stiffen.

"Great. Now I'm getting nervous," she tells me with a chuckle.

"We're gonna stay on the ground floor and watch. I'll be with Cooper when he climbs on the bull until they let him loose. Now, about those rules," I say, my voice dropping an octave.

I think I see her shiver. "I'm waitin'."

Cooper goes to check in, and Maize and I stand in the dirt by the bleachers. When I look down, I notice she's wearing cowboy boots, and it makes me smile.

"There's a rope around the bull's neck with a bell on it. The bell is supposed to help the rope drop when the cowboy falls off. We use this stuff called resin to make the rope stickier, so it's easier to grip."

"Learn something new every day." She gives me a genuine smile. "So why eight seconds? I always hear that being talked about."

I nod. "Ahh. Yes. Well, eight seconds is the amount of time it takes for a bull to wear out and for the adrenaline to decrease. So, it's a quick spurt of them being powerful motherfuckers, and then they kinda calm down after it. Trust me when I say seconds feel like minutes." Though I don't tell her that time seems to stand still in the same way when I'm with her.

Her mouth falls open slightly, and I can tell she's impressed. "That's insanity."

An announcer comes on the loudspeaker, and Cooper returns. "I'm rider number eight. I'm gonna go sit on the bench and meditate or some shit," he says with a grunt.

"You're gonna do just fine. We've practiced this over and over."

He gives me a nervous grin and leaves Maize and me to our conversation.

"So judging. The rider is judged up to twenty-five points, and so is the animal." I point over to where the judges are sitting. "Perfect score is a hundred, but it's as rare as getting struck by lightning or winning the lottery."

"Well shit," she mumbles.

Her response makes me laugh. "You know how you always see riders with their arms up in the air?" I lift my hand and show her.

She snorts and mocks me. "Mm-hmm, the typical cowboy riding a buckin' bronco pose."

"That's the one, and it's for a good reason. Once the gate opens, you can't touch yourself or the animal. You can only hold on with that one hand, and the other has to stay free, or you don't get scored."

"You get disqualified? That's messed up."

"Basically. Takes a lot of practice to keep that other hand away because you want to hold on with both because it's a long-ass fall to the ground."

Maize glances over at me. "I think I have a newfound respect for these cowboys. I had no idea it was so intense."

I take my hat off and tip it at her.

"Wait, how'd ya know what bull you're gonna get?"

"Ahh. Good one. You're matched up. At some competitions, you can choose, but usually, it's random."

"So it's not like Tinder where you can swipe right or left?" She snickers, and I join in on her sentiment.

Soon, the first rider is being loaded in the chute. Though the announcer says something, and the clock starts, I'm brought back to the last time I rode as soon as the gate opens. The bull was known for cycloning, which I fucking hated more than anything because I understood its dangers. When I fell off, he charged after me, and thankfully, one of the rodeo clowns deterred him. The moment I looked that big angry fucker in the face and stood on my feet, I decided right then it was my last ride regardless of how I placed. Little did I know, my score was ninety-seven, and I ended up winning the whole damn competition on one of the most notorious bulls at the championship.

The only thing that brings me back to reality is Maize's gasp. The guy falls and gets up and runs as fast as he can to the edge, where two people help him climb up. The clowns make a show out of getting the animal's attention, and the crowd goes wild. If it weren't so risky, I'd find it entertaining. Maybe one day, I will.

More men go, their scores not that high, and I know it's getting close for Cooper. I take Maize's hand and lead her to where the rest of the riders are impatiently waiting for their turn. Cooper comes and stands next to me, and I let go of her hand so I can give him a pep talk.

"The scores on the board right now, you can beat them. You've got the upper hand. Stay out of your head. Keep focused, and you can win this and qualify. Guaranteed. Don't be passive in that chute, Cooper. You gotta be aggressive and take control of that animal. If you need anything while you're in there, you tell those guys who are helping you load."

He nods and lets out a howl. "I think I'm ready."

The man before Cooper gets ready to go, and the chute boss lets him know he's next. Cooper waits to be situated on Troublemaker, a fire engine red bull who's already pissed as hell. I never understood why and how they got names like this. Doesn't make anyone feel good about getting on their backs.

Maize stands off to the side, and I shoot her a wink as I climb the metal railing and keep giving Cooper positive reinforcements. Safety is what I'm focused on right now because the last thing I want is for my rider to get hurt. We've practiced for months, and he's got it as long as he doesn't psych himself out when he climbs on.

"You've got this," I tell him one last time, then go stand next to Maize, watching his every move.

Cooper puts on his helmet and mouthpiece, then gets in the bucket shoot. The guy who's gonna be pulling on the rope to tighten it for him hands it over. He grabs the opposite side of the railing and puts his foot on the bulls back to let him know he's there and is about to get situated. After a few seconds, he sits, putting his feet forward so he doesn't break an ankle. Cooper starts loosening the rope and warms it up, then he asks for it to be tightened. The bull is already losing his mind, moving around and kicking the gate. A spotter holds on to Cooper, making sure he doesn't fall or break something before they let him go.

I've done this process a hundred times, but my nerves are fucking wrecked because it's all so unpredictable. Maize stands next to me, and I don't think she's taken a single breath.

He gets the rosin hot by roughly running his hand up and down it, and I can tell it's getting real sticky. After he taps his fists against the rope, the helper releases it, giving him enough slack to grab it when he's ready. The music is loud as hell, and the crowd is already excited. Funny how when you're in the pen, you can barely hear anything other than your heart and erratic breathing.

Once he's finished warming his rope, Cooper puts his palm in position and wraps it the way I taught him. At any second now, he'll give the nod, letting them know he's ready for the chute to be opened. Those ten seconds pass so slow, but when he does, it all goes by so fast.

His positioning is perfect with a straight back and his chin tucked. With his toes forward, Cooper rides with total control. I watch him and glance up at the clock. Five seconds. Six seconds. And right as it switches to eight, the buzzer goes off, and he purposely falls. He quickly bounces up with a big ass grin on his face and rushes out, waving to the crowd. I cup my hands around my mouth and yell his name. He sees me and points right in my direction, happy as can be.

Maize's beaming when I glance over at her. "He's going to win, isn't he?"

"Yeah! He just won this whole damn thing! There's no way the competitors can catch up to his score now."

She squeals and wraps her arms around me, and I love seeing her so excited about a sport I'm so passionate about.

Cooper eventually finds me, and he's on cloud nine. "I did it. I kept it simple just like you said. I felt like I was fucking flying!"

I pat him hard on his back. "Fuck yeah. You placed, man. That means if you keep it up, you could go pro, join PBR, and become a world champ."

Cooper gives me a tight hug. "Thanks, Gavin."

"You're welcome. Now get ready to go out there and smile real big for the cameras when you get your fuckin' buckle. Congrats. You made me proud."

Cooper's family meets him by the stands, and he goes over to them. They're head over heels excited for him, just as I am. I let out a deep breath as I lead Maize over to the stands. We finish watching the riders, and I can tell she's really into it. After it's over, Cooper's brought to the center of the arena where he's declared the Eldorado Rodeo winner. He does just as I said and shows all his teeth when he's handed his first buckle. I'm sure he'll win many more after riding like that. The crowd cheers for him, and he eats up the attention. Hell, when I was his age, I did too.

As the people disperse, Cooper finds me and lets me know he won't be staying on-site tonight, so I can have the camper if I want. I happily take the keys, glad not to be driving home after all the excitement. After Cooper's gone, I wrap my arm around Maize and pull her tight.

"So, whatcha think?"

She melts in my arms. "I'm impressed, like totally blown away by all of it. I'm just not sure how you did that for so long."

I grin. "Me neither."

We walk around the rodeo and grab some food because we're both hungry. When I look at the clock, I see it's just past nine.

"You nervous 'bout tomorrow?" I ask her just as we finish our blooming onion and fried shrimp.

"Yeah. But after seeing guys nearly get trampled by thousand-pound animals, I realize I don't have it so bad." She snickers. "And if I don't place, I'll just try harder next year."

"But if you do?" I ask.

"Then I might gloat a little," she admits.

"You should 'cause you deserve it. You work too hard not to be recognized on a high level like this."

A blush hits her cheek, and in the distance, I think I hear a band play. "You like to dance?"

She points at herself. "Who me?"

I laugh.

"Not getting amnesia again, are you?" I pop an eyebrow at her. She picks up a shrimp tail and throws it at me but misses.

"I've been known to two-step a few times," she admits.

After we clean our mess, I lead her over to where a cover band is playing. A temporary stage was erected, and some people have blankets on the ground watching while others dance in the grass.

I place my arms around her body as the group plays "Keeper of the Stars" by Tracy Byrd, a country classic. Her body fits with mine perfectly as we sway to the music. Maize looks up at the sky, and I follow her lead, humming the melody. The lyrics make way more sense with her in my arms like this. I silently thank the keeper of the stars for this moment.

"Oh look, you can see Regulus perfectly," she says, pointing up at the sky. I smile because all this time, I've been so amazed by her to notice the sky is full of stars. When another song begins, she looks up at me, and I place my hand under her chin and capture her lips in mine. Our tongues twist together, and that same fire I felt the first night we were together nearly burns me alive.

She becomes breathless, and I want to lose control with her again, but I refuse to be the one to pursue it.

"Gavin," she whispers when we finally pull apart.

"Hmm?" I say, leading her away so we can have more privacy.

"Take me home with you tonight," she tells me without hesitation.

"You're sure?" I ask, needing to know she wants me as much as I've always wanted her.

"Absolutely."

The confidence in her voice is all I need to hear. I thread our fingers together, and we rush back to the RV, barely able to keep our hands off one another. It seems as if the sexual tension between us has finally snapped, and I'm not complaining one bit.

CHAPTER ELEVEN

Maize

Right now, I need Gavin like I need air. He's the only reason I didn't completely lose my mind after delivering the food to the judges. Knowing I'd have the opportunity to spend time with Gavin tonight gave me something else to look forward to. As much as I've tried to turn off my attraction to him, I've found it impossible. My resolve has completely crumbled.

When he unlocks the RV, and I step inside, my eyes go wide. This is a huge change from the small campers we used to camp in as kids. It's like a damn mansion on wheels with a kitchen island, residential fridge, and recessed lighting. I rub my hand against the marble countertop, and my mouth falls open. "This is crazy."

"I know. They have way more options now than when I was traveling." He grins, the continues, "You thirsty?"

I pop a suspicious eyebrow and he chuckles, which is contagious.

Gavin removes the space between us and captures my mouth with his. Immediately, my heart races as his strong hands seem to memorize my body. A moan escapes me, and I want him to dominate me and make me his again. Carefully, he removes my hair from the ponytail I've been sporting all day, and it falls around my face.

"You're so goddamn beautiful," he says, studying me. "And you smell like barbecue."

A howl of a laugh escapes me. "Does this thing have a shower?" I ask, knowing it probably does.

Gavin takes my hand and leads me to the front. We climb a few stairs, and he opens the door to a full walk-in shower with glass doors and his and her sinks. There's even a real toilet. I turn and look at him with wide eyes because I'm actually shocked. "You're kidding me right now. This is nicer than my bathroom at home."

"I know, it's fancy. Shocks the shit out of me each time I walk into one of these things."

Slowly, he moves toward me and undresses me. His calloused fingers brush along my skin, and goose bumps form where he touches. I'm floating as he takes my chin and lifts my mouth to meet his again. I get lost as our tongues twist together, and I don't know how much longer I can wait to have him. I've been fantasizing about this as much as I've been trying to forget it.

Though we've had our ups and downs since he started working on the ranch, I've never stopped thinking about how he made me feel. Hell, I'd be willing to bet that's impossible. Now that he's standing before me, undressing me, I don't want to think about anything but his mouth and hands on me. I want to live in the moment with him.

After he unsnaps my bra and it falls to the floor, Gavin takes a step back and admires my body, lingering on my breasts.

"You're beautiful, Maze," he says, and it only builds my confidence.

"Thank you." I move forward and slip my fingers in the loops of his jeans and pull him to me before undoing his belt buckle and top button. I move the zipper down and forcefully push his jeans to his ankles, leaving him in only his boxer shorts.

Gavin bends over and takes off his boots and pants, then takes off his shirt. When I gaze down his body, I notice just how hard he is, and it makes me smirk. Gavin hooks his fingers in my panties and slides them down my body. It's the first time I've been naked with him in way too long.

His fingers thread through my hair, and I nearly melt into him as we greedily kiss. There's so much pent-up sexual tension between us that it nearly slices through the air as he leads me into the shower. The water is the perfect temperature as he washes my hair and body. One thing about the man is he pays attention to detail and doesn't miss an inch. When his fingers brush against my clit, I'm nearly putty in his hands. It doesn't go unnoticed as he palms my breast. After I'm washed, I return the favor.

It feels amazing to be able to touch him wherever and however I want. Considering it's been so long since we've been together, I drop to my knees and put the tip of his length in my mouth. Gavin places his palms on the wall to steady himself as I tease his cock with my tongue. His grunts only encourage me to devour as much of him as I can. Knowing how good I make him feel gives me all the confidence I need to continue.

His head rolls back on his shoulders, and his body tenses, but I don't let him come, not yet. When I stand, I brush my fingers over his thighs and up his stomach muscles, then give him a devilish grin. Gavin leans forward and plucks my bottom lip into his mouth.

"You wanna play dirty, sweetheart?" he asks.

With a popped eyebrow, I smile. "Maybe."

"Alright," he says, turning off the water and handing me a towel from the cabinet.

After we're dry, Gavin leads me to the bedroom. Seconds later, he removes my towel and moves me to the king-size bed. I sit and climb up, watching him intently. Swiftly, he grabs my ankles and slides me down to the edge. His warm mouth sucks on my clit until I'm squirming, then he flicks it with his tongue. Gavin goes painfully slow, allowing the orgasm to build to monumental levels before he slides a finger inside. Reaching up, he grabs one of my nipples and pinches. The sensation soars through me. My pants seem to please him, and before I come, he pulls away.

"Welp, that was fun."

I prop myself up on my elbows and look at him with wide eyes. "You wouldn't."

"You started it in the shower," he reminds me.

"Alright," I say, slowly moving my hand down my stomach and resting my fingers on my hard nub. "I'll finish myself. Trust me when I say I've had *lots* of practice."

Slowly, I massage my clit and close my eyes. Moans escape me as I love how good it feels even though I still wish it were his mouth.

"That's hot as fuck," he admits. Grabbing my wrists, he pulls them away. "But that's my job."

His tongue goes inside me, and he hums as he tastes me. "Delicious."

I don't know how much more I can take of him waging war on my pussy, but I try to hold the orgasm back as long as I can. Seems like an impossible feat and becomes one when my muscles tense and the build begins.

"Yes, baby, come for me," Gavin encourages. He finger fucks me as he flicks his tongue against me, picking up the pace. Seconds later, I'm crumpling beneath him, screaming his name. The orgasms nearly blind me, and I feel as if I'd been shot to the upper atmosphere. When I'm brought back to reality, all I can do is grin.

I move my head to the side and coax him toward me. He obliges and slides his tongue up my body until both of his arms are on either side of me as he hovers above.

"I've missed you so damn much, Maize," he admits.

I bite my bottom lip. "I'd be lying if I said I didn't feel the same."

"We're good together. You should just give up your game."

Before I respond, I wrap my arms around his neck and bring his mouth to mine, wanting to kiss him and taste myself on his tongue. The tip of his dick sits outside my entrance, and I want nothing more than to have him inside me.

"I should get a condom," he says before he continues.

"I'm on the pill," I admit. "I want to feel you. *All* of you."

"You're sure?" he asks, being the perfect gentleman.

I nod, begging him with my eyes. I've never wanted a man to take me as much as I want him to at this very moment. Slowly, he moves forward until we're one again. I gasp, forgetting just how big he is, and open my thighs wider to give more clearance.

"You okay?" he asks, making sure he's not hurting me, which I appreciate.

I nod. "Yes, feels amazing," I encourage, wanting him to lose control with me tonight.

Gavin takes it slow at first, his eyes meeting mine. Something boils between us, an energy I can't quite describe. It's magical and dangerous because I'm feeling things for him that I haven't experienced in a long ass time. I push the thoughts away, and my eyes flutter closed. Scratching my nails down his back, I hum his name.

"Fuck me, Gavin," I beg.

A second later, he's flipping me onto my stomach and moving me to the edge of the bed. I stick my ass into the air as he grabs my hips and slides inside. He slaps my ass with his hand, and the pain causes so much fucking pleasure.

"You like it when I do that?"

"Yes," I call out. "Slap my ass harder."

He does exactly what I say. The orgasm comes quick, without much of a warning, and I feel as if I internally combust. Sex this good should be illegal.

"You're so goddamn tight," he groans, moving in and out of me so quickly our skin smacks together. He grunts.

"Fuck, Maize," he moans, and then he loses it. Grabbing my hips, Gavin comes, and I feel his warmth inside me.

We stare at the ceiling, and my mind is mush. Gavin rolls over on his side and wraps his arm around my stomach, pulling me close to his body. I lay my head on his chest, listening to his heartbeat as he holds me. As his fingers brush against my arm, I close my eyes. Being with him was the perfect ending to my day, and somehow I instantly fall asleep.

The next morning, the sun blasts through the windows and wakes me. My eyes flutter open, and it takes me a minute to realize where the hell I am. When I look over, Gavin wakes up. He almost looks shocked and pulls me into his arms.

"Good morning," he says. "Glad to see you're still here."

I playfully smack him, and he laughs. "I guess I kinda deserve that. What time is it?" I ask, knowing my phone is probably still in my jeans on the bathroom floor.

"Almost eight."

My eyes go wide. "Eight? Shit."

"You gotta at least let me cook you breakfast. I kinda owe you for all the blueberry pancakes of yours I've eaten over the past few months," he says, and I laugh.

It's so tempting, but I know I have to go. "Can I take a rain check? Crap. I need to run home and grab a change of clothes so I don't get questioned by my entire family for wearing the same thing as yesterday."

Gavin sits up, giving me the perfect view of his bare chest and abs. My eyebrow raises, and right now, he's the only thing I want for breakfast.

"You like what you see?"

"Mm-hmm. I'm really enjoying the view right now."

He pulls me close and devours my lips. "So, if breakfast is out of the question, how about a quickie?"

I create some space so I can look at him, and I narrow my eyes. "Are you a mind reader or something?"

"No ma'am, it's your body that gives you away every time."

Seconds later, I'm crawling on to his lap, straddling him. He's already hard, and I want him so badly my entire body aches. We kiss as he slides inside, filling me full of his length and girth.

"Damn," I whisper as he digs his thumbs in my hips, steadying me as I greedily ride him. It feels so goddamn good being with him like this, taking full control as he gives me my body everything it needs and desires. The pace slows, and he thumbs my clit, and the build happens fast and quick.

"Maize, you feel so fucking good," he whispers as my mouth runs across his neck and up to his ear.

"I'm close," I breathlessly tell him, and then the orgasm rips through me. My head falls on his shoulder as he holds me tight, but I don't stop rocking my hips. Seconds later, he's riding out his release too, letting out a guttural moan.

After we clean up and I put on my clothes from yesterday that smell like brisket, I tell him goodbye. He kisses me so softly, and I just want to spend all day rolling in the sheets with him. No one has ever made me feel the way he does, and it's scary as hell.

"See you later?" he asks.

I nod and smirk. "I'd really like that. Want to meet me at the judging area at ten thirty-ish? They're supposed to announce who won then."

"I'll be there," he promises and pulls me in for one last kiss.

As I go to walk away, I look at him over my shoulder and smile.

"I already miss you," he admits, and I playfully roll my eyes at him as I go to the front door. He's everything I've ever wanted and needed, and I wonder what we'd be like if I actually gave him a chance. When I step outside, the sun is hot against my skin. I rush to my truck and try to think of what I'm going to tell my parents when I get home. It doesn't matter how old I am; they question me when I'm out all night.

I pull up to the house, and I'm relieved to see Kenzie's the only one home. Of course, she's still asleep, though. At least, I hope she is because she'll give me just as much shit about this.

I hurry and go to my room, grab a fresh set of clothes, and then jump in the shower. My only goal right now is to get back to the rodeo before my parents arrive. When I turn off the water and hear their voices, I realize that's not gonna happen today. I take my time fixing my hair and getting dressed. Then I grab my keys and try to sneak past my parents in the kitchen.

"Where've you been all night?" Dad asks, stopping me.

"John, leave her alone," Mom cuts in, thankfully.

He studies me. "You'll always be my baby no matter how old you are."

"And this is exactly why I want my own place," I say with a big grin. "Also, my business is only for me to know."

He sucks in a deep breath. "You are not moving out until you're forty-five."

I snort and pat him on the shoulder. "Nice try, Daddy."

Mom shakes her head and turns her attention to me. I'm scared she can see through me, or maybe she notices the glow I've been sporting all morning from having the best sex of my life. "Going back to the rodeo?"

"I am. Gonna check on everything, walk around a bit, then make my way to the judging area," I explain.

"We'll see you there," she tells me as she refills her cup of coffee.

"Okay, well, bye!" I sing-song and rush outside.

It's so quiet I can hear the birds chirping and the light breeze blowing through the trees. When I get in the truck, I become all sorts of nervous. Gavin was the perfect distraction to keep me out of my head about this competition, but now that I'm alone, it's all I can think about.

I drive to the rodeo as fast as I can. Once I'm parked, I text Gavin and let him know I'm back.

GAVIN

Good. I missed you. I'm still at the camper. Wanna meet me here?

MAIZE

I'll be right there.

A blush hits my cheek, and I realize I'm biting my lip. My heart flutters as I walk to the RV, and when I knock on the door, he comes out.

"Want to grab some coffee?" he asks, looking sexy as sin in tight jeans, boots, and a black button-up shirt.

"Thought you'd never ask."

We mosey to the food trucks, his fingers brushing against mine as we walk. I want him to grab my hand, but I also know we could get caught too. The smell of bacon and eggs makes my stomach growl, and Gavin offers to get us some breakfast burritos because I'm starving. As we sit at a picnic table and eat, I try to imagine what it would be like to be with him. How our life could be if we were together. Would my parents accept our relationship? Would I be enough to keep him here?

"Only one hour to go," he reminds me around a mouthful.

"I know. I'm getting super anxious."

He places his hand on my thigh, and that's when I realize my leg was bobbing up and down, and I stop moving.

"Sorry, bad habit," I admit with a smile.

He finishes his burritos and crumples up the foil wrappers. "Your breakfast has spoiled me. Nothing tastes good anymore unless it comes from the B&B."

"It's the secret sauce," I say, then nudge him.

"Do you bottle it up and sell it?" he jokes.

"Nah. The secret sauce is cooking for the love of cooking, not for the money," I explain.

He tilts his head at me and nods. "I understand and respect that so damn much."

After I finish, we make our way to the judging area. People are already in the seats they have set up at the pavilion, and I try to steady my breathing. The reality is I'm a nervous ass wreck. Time feels as if it's passing by so slow, and Gavin rubs my back to calm me down, but I tense. I quickly look to see if any of my family are around because if they saw this type of affection, the questions would come like crazy.

He moves his hand to his lap. I grab and squeeze it. "I just. I don't…"

"No, I get it. You don't have to explain, Maize. It's hard not to touch you after what we've shared. You know?" he whispers. "I'll be your best-kept secret. I have been for this long."

I smile, and my skin burns as I relive last night and this morning.

Soon, the family arrives and sits beside Gavin and me. The ceremony starts, and the judges go through each entry. As they talk about my brisket and the way it tasted, butterflies fill my stomach. After the judges have explained the rules, they announce the third prize winner. I'm relieved but also scared not to be called. Second place is next.

"And the first place winner is…" They hesitate. "Well folks, this was a hard one, very hard. There were so many incredible entries."

Uncle Jackson's sitting behind me and leans forward. Talking just loud enough for me to hear, he says, "Shut the fuck up and get on with it."

"Maize Bishop," the judge announces. Climbing to my feet, I look down the row at my mom and dad, who stand and wrap me in a hug. The crowd screams my name, and hoots and hollers fill my ears.

"Go, sweetie. Go get your prize," Dad tells me. I'm in complete shock and speechless, not able to comprehend what the judges are saying. Blood pumps through my body as I walk to the stage. They hand me an oversized check and a trophy, and I'm so overwhelmed with emotion, I instantly burst into tears. I never thought this would happen to me.

"Would you like to say anything?" the older man asks and hands me the microphone.

I take it and swallow. "I'm not good at public speeches so forgive me, but I'd like to thank my grandma for encouraging me to enter and my parents. Also thanks to all my cousins who helped out and made this possible. *And Diesel.*" I blow them all kisses. "And thanks to the cowboys who insisted I had a chance and believed in me." I look at Gavin, and our gazes meet.

Jackson lifts his hand to his mouth, and yells, "And what about your favorite uncle?"

Kiera elbows him hard in the ribs.

"And you too, Uncle Jackson," I say, handing back the microphone. As another judge speaks and entertains the audience, I'm brought to the back to sign some paperwork. They tell me a real check will be in the mail, and I guess I didn't realize the oversized one was just a novelty item. After I thank them nearly a million times, I return to my family, who are all waiting for me with smiles.

I'm surrounded by Bishops, and all I can do is cry because I'm so damn happy. A few older guys who have been competing in competitions like this all over the state come over and congratulate me.

After the onlookers disperse, I realize how much my cheeks hurt from smiling.

Gavin walks up and wraps his arms around me, nearly swallowing me whole. "Congrats. I knew you'd win."

"Thank you!" I exclaim as we linger for a few seconds, but he looks around and backs away, creating space between us.

"Congrats, baby," Grandma tells me, then looks back and forth between Gavin and me with a lifted brow but doesn't say a word. "Knew you had it in you."

After I've spoken to every single family member, we return to our cooking area and finish packing up the supplies. Once everything is loaded, Gavin walks me to my truck. Before I unlock the door, he looks around, then dips his head and gives me a soft kiss, and I get lost in it.

I pull away breathless, and I meet his eyes, mesmerized by him like he put a spell on me.

"Hopefully, we can do this again sometime," he suggests.

"Maybe," I say, liking I can keep him on his toes.

He chuckles and shakes his head. "It's all about the chase with you, woman."

"And it's a marathon, not a sprint." I climb inside the truck and give him a wave, which he returns. I back out and drive home, feeling the happiest I have in years. I think about the contest, my family, watching the bull riders, and being with Gavin. I've had a perfect weekend.

Right now, I don't know what we are or where this is going, but the chemistry we share is undeniable. The way he makes me feel is incredible. But is he in this for the long term?

Deep down, I want to give him a chance, but I also have to protect myself and my heart.

CHAPTER TWELVE

Maize

It's been a week since the rodeo, and I'm still riding the high of winning the barbecue contest and being with Gavin again. We haven't talked about it and have just shared side glances and texts with each other. He knows I'm wary, given my past, but I have a feeling I'm about to break my rules for him. If our feelings are mutual, then we need to decide where to go from here.

Our work schedules are hectic, and we haven't been alone since the rodeo. While I have some free time, I decide to drive to the training center, hoping to get a few minutes alone with him. This isn't a conversation to have over texts, and it'll be better to grasp his reaction if we're face-to-face.

I smile when I see him brushing one of the horses in the stables but quickly come to a halt when I notice Knox and Kane walking toward him. Those boys are the *last* people I want to run into here. They have loud mouths, and everyone would know I was visiting Gavin before dinner.

Instead of turning around like I should, I quietly hide behind a stack of hay. They can't see me, but I can hear them clearly.

"Hey, guys. How's it goin'?" Gavin asks as they lean against the gate.

"We heard a rumor," Knox says, crossing his arms.

Gavin chuckles. "Okay. And what's that?"

My heart hammers because I don't know who saw us together at the rodeo. If they speak my name, I'm going to have to make sure I keep my mouth shut. The dramatic pause makes me roll my eyes.

"Are you leavin' the ranch?" Kane finally blurts out.

I blink hard, inching closer to make sure I heard correctly.

"Yeah, Dad said you got another job offer," Knox adds.

What in the actual fuck?

Is it possible he's leaving the ranch for me? Or for good? I have so many questions right now.

"I did," Gavin confirms calmly.

"So you're takin' it?" Kane asks.

"Not sure." Gavin moves to the other side of the horse to finish brushing it. "Cooper wants me to train with him full-time year-round, which would mean traveling around to all the competitions and rodeos in Texas."

That news makes me sick to my stomach. He'd be gone most of the time, and a long-distance relationship would be complicated. Dating or even trying would be pointless.

"So you haven't decided yet?" Knox kicks his boots against the ground, clearly upset about this. I guess they've grown close with Gavin. We all have.

"Not yet, but I'm considering it because I love the lifestyle. It's been in my blood for years, but then again, I also love being on the ranch, so I haven't made up my mind yet. Right now, I'm juggling working here and training him, and it's hard to balance both. He wants me full-time, or he'll search for another coach."

"Tell him to find someone else then," Kane blurts out.

Gavin chuckles. "It's not that easy, but once I make a decision, I'll let y'all know."

Crossing the line with him was a mistake. I should've stood my ground, but the more I pushed him away, the more he pursued me.

Stupid, stupid, stupid.

I should've learned my lesson in getting tangled up with cowboys, but I obviously didn't. My heart can't take this.

Before any of the guys can catch me, I sneak out of the barn and go back to the B&B. Trying to keep busy, I decide to text my sister.

MAIZE

> We're drinking tonight.

KENZIE

Uh-oh. What happened?

She's the only one who knows Gavin and I hooked up after the rodeo and the only one I can talk to about him. Kenzie graduated from college a few days ago and is home now, thankfully. I missed having her around.

MAIZE

> Gavin. I'm an idiot for getting my hopes up.

KENZIE

Why?

MAIZE

> I just overheard him tell Knox and Kane that he got a job offer to work with Cooper full-time and travel with him. What was the point of chasing me if he planned on leaving? I'M SO STUPID!

KENZIE

No, you're not, so stop that right now. Did you ask him about it?

MAIZE

> No, I don't want him to know I was listening, and I especially don't want him to think he has to stay for me. If he wants to go, then he should. I refuse to hold him back. Plus, he should've told me himself.

KENZIE

Oh Maze. Tonight, I'm all yours. We'll talk and watch movies.

MAIZE

> I'll bring the booze.

I should've known better. Why would a retired bull rider be content in small-town Texas after years of traveling? Gavin craves excitement and probably enjoys the attention of multiple women too.

As I finish cleaning up while Donna and Becky prepare dinner, I get a group text.

RILEY

> Just a reminder, Zoey and I are throwing Zach a birthday party this weekend. You're all required, I mean expected to come. Yes, even you, Grayson.

I snort at Riley calling out Grayson. They already know I'll be there since I'm helping with the food. Gavin will hopefully be too busy with Cooper to stop by since he's having a hard time juggling it all.

As I'm cutting potatoes to roast, I dodge Gavin's calls and ignore his texts. I'm annoyed he hasn't told me this news and that my cousins heard it before I did. If he's leaving anyway, then I might as well cut things off between us before they have a chance to blossom.

Though my heart already feels like it's cracking, so it's probably too late for that.

At seven, I say goodbye to everyone and head to my truck. As soon as it comes into sight, I see Gavin leaning against it. He's waiting for me.

"Can I help you, sir?" I keep my tone flat. He's wearing dark jeans and a gray shirt. He looks good in anything, especially when it accentuates his muscles.

"As a matter of fact, you can, ma'am. I've been trying to get ahold of you all afternoon." His arms are crossed as if he's preparing to stay there until he gets an answer.

"I've been busy, ya know, working and all." I shrug, not giving him the attention. "I have plans tonight, so I need to get home."

"Why are you avoiding me again?" he blurts out, blocking me from my door.

"Look, Gavin," I say with a straight face. "Hooking up at the rodeo was a bad idea. A huge mistake. It shouldn't have happened, but it did, so let's allow the past to be in the past."

He squints, tilting his head as if he's waiting for the punch line. "Well, I can't say I'm surprised."

Now it's my turn to narrow my eyes at him. "What's that supposed to mean?"

"Running away is your MO, Maize. The second things get too real, you bail. You keep people at arm's length to avoid getting hurt again, and if you keep it up, you'll never find love."

I cross my arms over my chest, shaking my head in disagreement. "I'm not running or bailing. I just don't think you and I will work." I stand my ground, not willing to let him see this is breaking me.

He pushes off my truck and closes the gap between us, moving my chin up until I look at him. "I'm too old to play these games, Maize. You either grow up and take a real chance on us, or you don't. I won't chase you this time."

"Good," I blurt, my emotions boiling inside me. I'm seconds from telling him what I heard and have to stop myself from asking him not to go with Cooper. I won't be that type of woman who stops him from doing something that makes him happy. I saw how his eyes lit up at the rodeo, and I'll never take that away from him. "Being together meant nothing, Gavin. So let's pretend it didn't happen."

"That's what you really want?" His gaze burns into mine, and I swallow hard.

"Yes. Stop bothering me. It's time you moved on." I take a step back so I don't do something stupid, like kiss him.

Gavin retreats, brushing his hand over his scruffy jawline. "Alright, Maize Bishop. Have it your way." He sucks in a deep breath, then walks away.

I fight the urge to look at him over my shoulder and quickly slide behind the wheel, holding back tears. Even though this is what I told him I wanted, it nearly destroys me. But I have no right to be sad about it.

Once I get home, I take a long shower and let my thoughts wander. The only thing that'll numb the pain is alcohol, and I plan to imbibe once I'm dressed.

"Hey," I say, popping my head into Kenzie's room.

"I've got *The Longest Ride* on standby." She snickers, knowing damn well the premise revolves around a bull rider and a sappy love story.

"Hard pass." Walking in, I hold up the bottle of whiskey I found in Dad's liquor cabinet. "I've got the good stuff."

Kenzie pats the space next to her and gives me a sympathetic expression as I sit on her bed.

"Don't give me that look," I scold, opening the bottle. "And we're not watching anything from Nicholas Sparks."

She laughs and flips through Netflix before landing on *Scary Movie 4*. It's so ridiculous and stupid, and it's just what I need.

After twenty minutes of watching Anna Faris be a doofus while passing the whiskey back and forth, I finally speak. "Gavin was waiting for me by my truck after work."

"What'd he say?"

"He wanted to know why I was ignoring him. Instead, I told him what happened between us was a mistake and to move on."

"Maize!" she squeals. "What the hell is wrong with you?"

"I'm being smart, Kenzie!" I defend.

"No, you're pushing him away before he can do that to you."

"Duh." I take another long sip.

"But you're not even giving him a chance. He could stay. You don't even know what he's going to do yet."

"No, but he's considering it, which means it's only a matter of time before he does leave. And at that point, I could be stupidly in love with him or some shit, and it'd be a hundred times worse. It's better that I break it off now before anything more can happen," I tell her matter-of-factly. "I have to be the rational one. Though I don't want to hurt him, it's better than getting in too deep where the pain is unbearable."

"How'd he react to that?"

"I'd say less than pleasant."

She snorts, shaking her head as I tell her his exact words.

"You're too jaded and really will become a nun if you keep pushing guys away. Especially one who seems to like you and obviously wants to be with you."

"We're clearly at two different places in our lives, so it's for the best," I say with certainty.

"Or…" Kenzie grabs the bottle out of my hand. "You could just communicate, tell him you overheard his conversation, and ask if he plans to go or not. That way, you aren't making an irrational decision to end things and can choose together."

I flash her a glare, curling my lip. "Who the hell are you, and what have you done with my sister?"

She blows out a breath, then rolls her eyes. "I'm just being reasonable because someone has to."

Now that has me snorting. "Oh really? Do I need to bring up Grayson?"

Kenzie scowls, taking a gulp of the booze. "Shut the hell up."

Her sudden change of tone has me bursting into laughter. "That's what I thought."

"Guess we'll both become nuns," she confirms.

"Fine with me. I don't believe in love anymore anyway." I grab the bottle from her and take another drink.

"Yes, you do," she says, trying to reason with me. "You're just scared."

The whiskey goes to my head and makes me dizzy. Leaning against the headboard, I close my eyes. "Maybe you're right."

"Hope Mom and Dad didn't want grandchildren." Kenzie laughs as she rests her head on my shoulder.

"They know I'm working to get my catering business off the ground. What will your excuse be?" I tease.

"Focusing on my teaching career," she says with a giggle.

"You're already hired at Mom's school."

"Exactly, I need to let lesson plans and teaching on my own be the center of my attention. I don't want to disappoint her or the students."

I shrug. "Alright, that sounds like an excuse she'd buy."

We both laugh, are tipsy, and finish watching this ridiculous movie. It's just the kind of night I needed—to let loose, complain about my pathetic non-love life, and have my sister—my best friend—by my side.

CHAPTER THIRTEEN

Gavin

Three weeks ago, Maize was in my arms, and we had another amazing night together—a night I'll never forget.

Two weeks ago, she told me it was a mistake and to move on.

Now I'm left deciding if I'll take Cooper's offer or stay at the ranch. Though I'm tempted to live the rodeo life again, even if I'm not the one competing, I'm also not ready to give up on Maize Bishop. She's running because she's scared I'll hurt her, but that's the last thing I want to do. I've given her space as she requested, but when I catch her staring at me, I know something's still lingering between us.

In the next twenty minutes, the family vet is coming to check on a horse with an infection. Sugar and Georgia got into a little tiff, and now Sugar has a nasty bite on her back. I've separated them and won't allow them in the same pasture.

"Dr. Wallen, hey," I say, reaching out my hand, and he shakes it. "I'm

"Gavin, how's it goin'? I'm Connor."

"Nice to meet you. It's goin' alright. Just dealin' with these horses fightin' each other. Ya know the drill."

He chuckles, grabbing his bag and following me into the stables. "I sure do."

"Jackson tells me you've been working with the family for a while," I say as I lead him to the barn.

"Yeah, several years. Big family."

"I didn't realize that until Thanksgiving last year. It was a never-ending line of Bishops."

Connor grins as I take Sugar's lead rope and bring her out. He examines her, softly petting her to calm her as he inspects the area.

"So Elle works with you?" I say after he injects an antibiotic.

"Elizabeth? Yeah, she's been working with me for a couple of years now."

"I've only seen her a few times, but she seems nice. I hear she's brilliant, too."

"She is a very smart young lady."

His expression tightens as he talks about Elle, and I wonder if there's a reason for it. I've overheard Elle call him a dick, but Maize and Kenzie think he's a hot piece of ass.

If I had to guess, he's around my age, and since the majority of the friends I have here are much younger than me, I invite him to my party tonight. He seems friendly enough and as though he'd get along with everyone.

After he finishes with Sugar and packs his things, I put her back into the stall and turn toward Connor.

"So I'm having a little get-together tonight with a few of the Bishop guys. You should stop by for a beer if you can," I offer as we walk to his truck.

"Uh, sure. I should be able to swing it."

"I'm staying at one of the ranch hand cabins on the east side," I tell him.

"Yeah, I know where those are. I'll see you later."

I wave once he jumps in his truck and takes off. Next, I head to the shop where I know the guys sometimes hang out during their breaks. When I open the door, I immediately hear Diesel and Riley being rowdy and messing around, which causes me to laugh. Though they've been up since the ass crack of dawn, they're always having a good time.

"Hey, Gavin," they greet when they see me. "How'd it go with the vet?"

I shove my hands in my front pockets and nod. "Fine. He gave Sugar an antibiotic and said to inject her with it for five days. Hopefully, that does the trick."

"Since it's Friday, we're gonna hit up the pub tonight," Diesel says. "You should meet us there."

"Actually, I was gonna have a party at my place and invite all the workers."

"Party!" Riley shouts. "Hell yeah!"

"No, no..." I shake my head. "It's just a *small* gathering for my birthday, so if you'd rather drink at the bar—"

"Are you kiddin' me? We'll be there!" Diesel slaps my back.

"With a cake," Riley adds. "How old are you now, old man? Fifty?"

I snort at the way he gives me shit. "Thirty-six, asshole. I'll bring the beer since I'm not sure you're even legally allowed to buy it."

They laugh, and I tell them to come around nine. I plan to have finger foods and play some horseshoes. I'm happy to just hang out with the guys since we're always working and don't get to relax too much.

"Let Grayson, Ethan, and the others know. Cooper will be there, too."

"We're on it," Diesel confirms.

"But really, just a small gathering," I tell them. "We all gotta get up for work tomorrow."

Moments later, Alex comes in and scolds them for slacking off, so I head out and get back to work. I finish earlier than usual so I can get ready for tonight. When I picked up the alcohol and snacks, I grabbed extra just in case they came super hungry.

I throw on a button-up shirt and clean jeans with my boots. Tonight will be a nice distraction from thinking about Maize. Since no one knows about us, no one will bring her up.

At nine, Diesel and Riley come barreling in with a pan and whiskey.

"Hey! Birthday boy!" Diesel shouts, holding up the bottle.

"We made you a cake!" Riley adds, setting it on the counter.

"You *made* it?" I pop a brow, rounding the table to see this shit. "Is it edible?"

"Hell yeah, it is." Diesel removes the tin foil, and I nearly bust my gut as I laugh at their "cake."

"What the fuck is that?" I squint at the weird-shaped concoction.

"It's a dick and balls," Diesel tells me. "Well…kinda. It's a little slanted because dumbass over here"—he throws a thumb in Riley's direction—"messed it up."

"And I'm guessing these brown squiggles are pubes?" I point.

"You betcha." Riley grins. "It's Funfetti."

"Wow, I'm speechless." I cackle. "Thanks, guys."

I set the pan next to the sandwiches and chips. After I offer them each a beer, more people show up. Cooper comes, and I introduce him to the others. Ethan and Grayson arrive wearing grins, then soon we're all standing around with bottles and paper plates full of food.

Thirty minutes later, we go outside and play horseshoes in teams. Of course, I'm kicking all their asses, which isn't hard considering how much they suck.

When I purposely lose so others can play, I head into the house for more beer and to catch up with Grayson, who's standing in the kitchen.

"Hey, man," I say. "Need another?"

"Sure."

"How are things going? Anything new with Kenzie since she's been home?"

"Pfft." He grunts as I hand him a bottle. "She's a complicated egg I'll never crack. These damn Bishop women are confusing as hell. Maize and Elle are nice to me, but Kenzie? She'd murder me if given the option."

"Dude, you must've done somethin' to her." I lean against the counter and take a sip of my beer.

"Wish I knew. I'd apologize if she'd just tell me already, but instead, she insists on busting my balls every chance she gets." He groans.

"You like her," I say. "Or it wouldn't bother you so much."

Grayson shrugs casually. "I do. From the moment I met her, I thought she was beautiful and wanted to get to know her, but it's never been reciprocated. So instead of pursuing anything, I've just pushed her buttons since she won't tell me what the fuck her problem is."

I chuckle, having seen their back-and-forth banter firsthand. It's comical.

"What about Maize? Figure out why she hates your guts?" he asks.

"Which time?" I sigh, frustrated as hell. "Honestly, we do have a history."

He snaps his fingers and grins. "I fuckin' knew it!"

"We had a one-night stand a couple of weeks before I got hired, and on my first day of work, she acted like she didn't know me. She introduced herself like normal, and for months, she pretended she didn't remember me. Drove me crazy until she finally admitted it on New Year's Eve. But she doesn't date men who work on the ranch because she's been burned. Then at the rodeo, something happened, and we hooked up again."

Grayson's jaw nearly smacks the floor as his eyes bug out. "Dude. I should've known. I could always tell there was something between you two."

"I've been chasing her since the day I got here, and all she does is run." I sigh, chugging my beer. "I thought we'd gotten past all that at the rodeo, but then two weeks ago, she said it was a mistake and that I needed to get over it." Doesn't help my ego that I've never had to pursue a woman before, but Maize's different. The connection we share isn't like anything I've experienced before.

"Ouch." Grayson cringes. "That's not good."

"Especially since I still want her."

"These damn Bishop women are difficult, I'm tellin' ya. Just when you think you're making progress, they go and rip the rug out from under ya."

I laugh at the truth of his words. I haven't felt sparks with a woman in years, nothing like what I feel when I'm around Maize, and I hate that she won't give us a chance. Some people never find love once in their lifetime, and it's even more rare to find it twice. I'm not ready to walk away from someone who I'm falling so hard for—not after all this time. Especially not when I know how it feels to be inside her. I'll always remember the way she screams my name as she comes. She felt it too, and I'll do whatever I can to prove I'm worth the risk.

"Maize's a sweet girl, and from what I know about her, she's reserved and keeps to herself a lot. Don't give up on her yet," Grayson genuinely tells me.

"Trust me, I don't plan on it."

We leave the kitchen, and when I get to the door, I see a group of ladies walking across the yard toward Diesel and Riley.

"Ah shit." Grayson says what I'm thinking. "Looks like they told their women about the party."

Rowan, Kenzie, Elle, Maize, and Zoey come into view.

"Who are the guys with them?" I narrow my eyes at Kenzie and Maize as frustration and jealousy ripple through me.

"No idea, but I think they're townies. I've seen them at the pub before."

Just great.

We walk outside and say hello. Kenzie smiles at me but avoids Grayson, while Maize pretends I don't exist.

"Sorry, man." Diesel pats my shoulder. "Rowan overheard me and decided to invite the girls. Hope that's okay."

I nod. "Sure, no problem. Plenty of beer and food inside."

Looking around, I realize my *small* gathering is now at least thirty or more people.

"Get used to it because nothing on the Bishop ranch is a small affair. Ever." Grayson chuckles.

A few people walk inside and return with plates and drinks, but one guy has two bottles, then hands one to Maize. She smiles and squeezes his arm. What. The. Fuck.

Did she seriously bring a fucking date to my party?

After getting no closure and waiting six months for her to acknowledge we hooked up the first time, this is how dirty she wants to play?

I want to confront her, but that'd make a scene, and I don't want everyone seeing or hearing our conversation. I'm too old for these childish games, but dammit if it's not working.

For the next hour, I do my best to keep my eyes off Maize and her little boy toy, but it's nearly impossible when she purposely stands in my view. I've learned her friend's name is Leo, and if his arm wraps around her one more time, I might snap off his fingers.

"I'm gonna use the bathroom, be right back," I overhear her tell him. As she walks away, his gaze lingers on her ass, and my jaw nearly cracks in half.

A few moments later, I head inside, using the opportunity to be alone with her. The bathroom door is wide open, and when I walk down the hallway, I see Maize snooping in my bedroom.

"Can I help you?"

She jumps, quickly spinning around. "Jesus!" Her hand presses against her chest as she catches her breath. "You scared the shit outta me, Gavin."

"Well, imagine my surprise when I catch you *not* in the bathroom but in my bedroom. Lookin' for something?" I lean against the doorway with a smug grin on my face. She's not getting out of this easy or walking away this time.

"I got lost."

"Is that so?" I don't feed into her bullshit for a second as I push off the doorframe and step toward her. "You wanna tell me what you're doing here tonight?"

Maize crosses her arms, pursing her lips. "I was invited. That a problem?"

"Considering you've ignored me for two weeks and brought a date to my party, I'd say yes, it *is* a problem. You and I need to talk."

I nearly close the gap between us as her arms fall to her side, and the way her breath hitches doesn't go unnoticed. She licks her lips as her eyes flick up to mine.

"We have nothing to talk about, Gavin."

"Sure we do. For starters, why don't you tell me who your little friend is?"

"None of your damn business."

"You gonna sleep with him, then bail the next morning, too? Should..." I throw a thumb over my shoulder. "Should I warn him? Give him the Maize 101 on what to expect?" I lean down until my lips nearly brush her ear, then whisper, "Tell him you like it fast and deep and to slap your ass real hard. Save him the trouble of having to hear you talk."

"You asshole," she spews when I back away. "What's your problem? We hooked up, twice, and that's it. Move the fuck on!"

I smile in amusement because seeing Maize fired up is fucking hot as hell. She's trying to keep her walls up by being bold, but I see right through her façade. When I catch her staring at me when I'm eating at the B&B, it's with intent, not disgust. I see the way she bites on her lower lip, and how her chest rises and falls any time I'm near. She tries so damn hard not to be affected by me even when her body aches for my touch.

"You're adorable, Maize. A little spitfire even, but a *horrible* liar."

"What?" She gasps. "I'm not lying. I've already moved on, and you should too."

"You mean, that little Leo dude?" I bark out a laugh. "He couldn't find your clit even if you drew him a map with color keys."

She rolls her eyes, folding her arms.

"Alright then, go out there and kiss him. Stick your tongue down his throat and prove to me you're over us."

"You're ridiculous." She steps around me and moves toward the door.

I spin around, walking into the hallway to watch her ass. "But make sure you're not thinking about me the whole time when you do!"

"Fuck off, Gavin!" She flips me the bird over her shoulder, and I stifle a laugh.

Her mouth says one thing, but the way her body reacts is another—*the actual truth.* She doesn't want me to play this game and start dating for the hell of it. Or maybe she does?

Perhaps it's time to test that theory.

CHAPTER FOURTEEN

Gavin

I t's been two weeks since Maize pulled her little stunt and showed up at my birthday party with Leo in tow. I'm still annoyed as hell about it and determined to make her feel the fire that scorches me each time she's around. I'm not stupid and know she planned to make me jealous. Maize makes the rules to this game, and it's time for me to break them.

I've chased her enough, and if she really wants me to get over her, I've come up with a plan to see if she'll believe her own bullshit. When we were at the rodeo, I remember how she looked at Sarah Cooke like she may steal me away. Though I'm not the type of guy to lead a woman on, I asked Sarah if she'd like to join me at the big Fourth of July celebration at the Bishop ranch. Riley encouraged me to bring a date, and she was the only woman who I've really spoken to who wasn't a Bishop or married to one.

I drive over to pick up Sarah from her house, and she's dressed in a mini skirt, boots, and a strapless shirt showing off her summer tan. Though she's beautiful, I'm not really into blondes. When she climbs inside the truck, she immediately grins.

"Hey! How have things been going?" she asks. As soon as she buckles, we head toward the ranch.

"Good. I don't have any complaints." I smile at her as we continue to make small talk. We chat about the rodeo and Cooper placing and how he won first place again.

"I heard him tell my daddy he was planning to go pro and wanted you to travel with him full-time," she tells me when we park and get out of the truck.

"Yeah, that's all true." I leave the conversation there. I've lived in this town long enough to know that rumors travel like speed trains 'round here, so I'd rather not get into the specifics.

I grab a blanket from the back seat so we can sit on the grass comfortably. A tip Diesel offered when he told me he'd be proposing to Rowan today. As soon as we walk up to the crowd of people, I watch everyone's eyes zip to Sarah, but no one says a word. I've never brought a woman with me anywhere, so I'm sure it's a shock. Considering Maize is like a vault with her secrets, I doubt any of them would notice something's off except for her or Kenzie.

I spread the blanket and lay it flat, then we sit next to Rowan, Chelsea, and her boyfriend, Trace. I met her once before and say hello to the group. She recently moved back so Diesel could see his son more and she could see where things go with Trace. Sarah leans into me and laughs as Riley runs all over the place chasing after Zach. He's a cute kid, but I can already tell he's gonna be a handful when he's older.

John and Jackson are grilling burgers while a few of the others set up the fireworks. I watch as Alex takes Diesel and Riley off to the side. A moment later, "Life of the Party" by Shawn Mendes blasts through the speakers. Diesel walks across the pasture to Rowan and takes her hand. Dawson moves on to his mama's lap and twirls his fingers in her hair.

Watching Diesel and Rowan dance is mesmerizing. It's obvious how much they love each other. She smiles as Diesel dips and spins her around. Above, an airplane flies low, and everyone looks up to see the message drifting behind it.

It reads: Will You Marry Me, Rowan Bishop?

All eyes are on them as Diesel clumsily fidgets and tries to pull the ring from his pocket. As soon as he flips open the box, tears spill down Rowan's face. Diesel drops to one knee and tells her he knew she was his the first time they kissed. My eyes fall on Maize, who's standing with her hand on her chest over her heart, and she looks so goddamn beautiful with her hair pulled back. Even from a distance, I can see the softness of her neck and have the urge to run my mouth across her skin.

She may be anti-love, but I'm convinced it's all a ploy.

Rowan hesitates with her answer, and eventually, her grandma Bishop speaks up. "Rowan Bishop, you better give that man an answer and not keep him and the rest of us waitin'."

With a grandma like that, no wonder she's a spitfire.

"Yes, yes, yes! I will marry you," Rowan yells, loud enough I'm sure everyone in San Antonio could hear her answer. They have a little make-out session, then Diesel slips the ring on her finger. It's adorable, and I'm glad they're so happy and will officially start their life together.

After they walk away for some privacy, Jackson and John serve everyone what they've been grilling. I get up and grab food for Sarah and me, then deliver it back.

"I'm so happy for them," she says, taking a bite of her burger. "I love engagements and weddings. Mama says I'm a hopeless romantic, always have been, if I'm being honest," she admits.

"I can see that," I say. "It's not a bad thing to have a heart. Shows you're compassionate."

After we finish, the fireworks are nearly set up, and they'll start lighting them any minute now. I see Maize, who looks like she's ready to internally combust when Rowan walks up to her. It's obvious she's pissed. When Rowan pulls her away to talk to her, I nearly chuckle. While her anger shouldn't bring me joy, it does. It's proof she's jealous as hell. Once they head to the drink table, I turn to Sarah. "You thirsty?"

She nods, leaning back on the blanket.

"I'll be right back," I tell her and stand.

As soon as I'm close to Maize, I gently pull her away from Rowan so I can get a few words in.

"I've put the pieces together, Maize," I say in a lowered tone. She looks at me like she wants to throw daggers at my face.

"What are you talkin' about exactly?" she asks, playing dumb like usual.

I glare at her, allowing the silence to pass between us as she stares me down. Unfortunately for her, I'm immune to her act because, at this point, I could write a book on her reactions. The thought has me laughing, which only infuriates her more. "I've tamed wild horses, Maize Bishop, and I'll tame your attitude too. I like a good challenge."

She scoffs and rolls her eyes at me, but I can tell I've gotten under her skin. "Is that a threat or something?" she asks with shakiness in her voice.

"Not a threat, sweetheart. That's a damn promise," I confirm, meaning every word. I give her a smirk, then walk away. Before I make it back to Sarah, I grab two waters from an ice chest. I can only imagine how angry Maize is right now, and it fills me with joy knowing I can see through her.

I hand Sarah the water, and she thanks me. When I sit next to her, she scoots closer and leans her head on my shoulder. When I turn around, I catch a glimpse of Maize watching us and chuckle. I've got all the goddamn proof I need. She tells me to move on, then is ready to murder me when I invite another woman to join me. One thing is for certain—Maize needs to make up her mind because, at this point, I'm damned if I do and damned if I don't.

The firework show starts, and it's incredible. I've seen displays this big at rodeos, and I'm amazed they're able to pull it off so flawlessly. The booms from the mortar shells echo in the distance, and the colors are bright and spectacular. Some crackle and pop while others glitter and fade.

The summer breeze brushes against my skin, and I realize how much I love being on the ranch. It's been almost a year since I took the job, and I haven't once regretted it. I've found my second family, and I can't imagine how hard it's going to be to leave this behind.

When it's over, the big group of us burst out into applause while some hoot and holler. Considering nearly fifty people are here, it takes a while to tell everyone goodbye. I pick up the blanket, and we walk back to my truck so I can take Sarah home.

"Want to go to the bar and have a drink?" she asks when we climb in, and I start the engine.

"I'd love to, but I have to be up early. Should probably get some sleep."

She sticks out her bottom lip and pouts as I turn toward her house.

When I pull into the driveway, I park and smile at her. "Thanks again for joining me. That was a lot of fun."

"It was. Do you want to come in?" she whispers. She leans in and tries to kiss me, but I pull away before our lips can connect.

"Whoa, whoa," I calmly say. "Sarah. Because I'm a gentleman and I don't like to lead ladies on, I think I should set the record straight. While I think you're a very beautiful woman, we're just friends, and that's all we can be."

She rolls her eyes, obviously annoyed by the rejection. "Wow. Okay. Is it because of Maize?"

My heart rate quickens, and I meet her eyes. "All that matters right now is that you understand where you and I stand. I'm sorry if I gave you the wrong impression."

She sucks in a deep breath and lets it out. "It's fine. I feel really stupid now, but thanks for a good time."

"I'm sorry." I want her to know I genuinely mean it, but I don't think her embarrassment will allow it. She gets out of the truck, turns, and gives me a wave before going inside. On the way home, I feel like an utter asshole. If I were in my twenties, just passing through, I probably would've followed her inside. I'm a different man now, and my door no longer revolves. The only woman I want pushes me away continually, and it's frustrating as fuck.

By the time I walk into my house, I'm more than annoyed. I go to the fridge and pull out a beer, then sit on the couch. After I kick off my boots, my phone vibrates in my pocket, and I pull it out and see it's Cooper.

I open the message he sent.

COOPER

> Hey man. Just checking to see if you made up your mind about traveling the road with me and coaching me to pro level.

I read his text message a few times. I think about Maize and the way she looked at me with disdain today. Her words repeat in my mind, and how she's said several times she wants me to just go away. Regardless of what I think, Maize believes we were a mistake, and it only fuels the fire burning inside me. Closing my eyes, I set my phone down and lean my head back.

I weigh the good and the bad. I loved rodeo life, but I hated how dangerous it was, and I won't be risking myself. If Cooper wins, I get a percentage of his money. He's a good rider, and he has learned quickly, taking all my instruction to heart.

My mind is made, and I know what I have to do. After finding the right words, I send a text to Cooper, lock my phone, and then go to bed. I don't wait for his response because I already know what he's going to say. Tomorrow is a new day, a new beginning, and I know I made the right decision.

There's no going back now.

CHAPTER FIFTEEN

Maize

Rowan shows up carrying a bottle of tequila, and it makes me smile wide. She knows exactly what a girl with a broken heart needs, and it usually starts and ends with Patrón. In her other hand is a bag of limes, salt, and shot glasses.

"The traveling bartender. I love it!" I exclaim, helping her with the items. I move some things from the top of my dresser and set everything down. A minute later, Kenzie bursts through the door with cookies, popcorn, and a giant ass bowl of M&M's. Elle's trailing behind her, and she looks exhausted.

"This should do the trick," Kenzie tells me.

Elle nods. "Booze, snacks, and reality TV. You literally can't be upset after all that."

"I hope you're right," I say, sucking in a deep breath as Rowan pours the shots.

Elle kicks off her shoes and sits on the bed, and Kenzie follows her.

"So, catch me up." Elle waves her hand. "I need to know all the details of what happened, considering we're having a drinking party over a man."

I let out a huff and roll my head on my neck. I've been cautious to keep everything to myself—except for Kenzie, but she'd never spill my secrets. I'm grateful I had someone to talk to. Otherwise, I might've driven myself crazy over the past year while dealing with Gavin's shenanigans.

"You're stalling," Elle sing-songs and Rowan snickers, then turns around and hands us the tequila. She goes back to the makeshift bar as we shoot it down, then takes our glasses.

"Just needed a little liquid courage first," I admit, then start from the beginning. I tell them about the one-night stand and how it was the best sex of my life, how we kissed, the stolen glances, and unspoken words we've exchanged over the past few months. Then I go into detail about the rodeo and how elated I was to spend time with him.

"So what's the problem?" Rowan asks.

I suck in a deep breath. "I overheard the twins asking him about traveling with Cooper full-time, and he hadn't made up his mind at that point. So I pushed him away and stupidly brought a date to his birthday party. I honestly didn't know it was his birthday, though, so I wasn't trying to be a bitch. Anyway, he confronted me about it, and I told him I'd moved on, and he should too. So what did he do?"

I glance at them. "He brings Sarah motherfucking Cooke to the Fourth of July party. She was so hateful to me growing up and did some messed-up things just because she could."

Rowan shakes her head. "Maze. You told him to move on, and he did."

I throw my hands up in the air. "I know. I'm a damn idiot, and now I don't know what to do to fix this. I've messed up big time, and I've realized this entire time that he deserves better from me, but I'm scared."

"I was actually pissed when I saw Sarah there," Kenzie admits. "And she was being so flirty and touchy. I wonder if they had sex afterward."

Elle throws a pillow at Kenzie. "That is *not* helpful. Gavin is a gentleman, so I bet even if she begged him, he would've denied her. I'd bet money on it."

"Yeah, I don't think he did either," Rowan says, bringing us more shots, then continues. "Gavin's more mature than that. He didn't seem like he was *that* into her. After you two had your little confrontation, I watched him.

Each time she tried to make a move, he tensed. He was playing games with you, Maize. It was so obvious."

We gulp down the tequila, and I try to think back to Saturday. I was in a blind rage and didn't notice the way he reacted to her. I just saw the two of them together, and that was it. Shaking my head, I roll my eyes. "If he did that…"

"Wait, so is he going to travel with Cooper?" Elle asks. "Did you ask him?"

"I'm pretty sure he is because Uncle Jackson mentioned he was looking for another trainer. Why would they need someone else if Gavin wasn't planning to leave? I thought about it, and that's the only solution. It's not like I can just come out and ask him because we're not really on speaking terms at the moment," I explain.

"That does make sense, but it could be coincidental." Elle places a hand on mine. "I'm sorry. Men are dickheads."

"Speaking of dickheads, how's that boss of yours?" Kenzie asks.

"I am not talking about him tonight. This is about Maize, not me," she announces.

"He's just so hot. I literally thought about getting an assistant job just so I could stare at his tight ass in those jeans all day long." Kenzie grins, then shrugs. "It's not a lie."

I snort, and I'm so happy to have them as my support system. "Maybe you should apologize," Rowan suggests. "Tell him how you feel. You won't know what you're missing out on if you don't give him a chance. You have no idea if he's going to break your heart until he does. Sometimes, finding love is worth the risk. I know you're asking yourself, what if it doesn't work out? At least you would've had a good time. The flip side of that is, what if it does? What if he's your match, and you're so determined to push him away that you lose that opportunity?" Rowan stares at me, waiting for my answer.

I have nothing, though. She's right.

"When did you become so logical?" I ask.

She gives me a small smile, and I see her glance down at the gigantic diamond on her finger. "Love does that to a person, I guess. If I hadn't given Diesel a chance or allowed him to explain himself, I wouldn't be where I am right now. I was convinced marriage wasn't in my cards too, and the whole time the man of my dreams was right in front of me."

"I'm so damn happy for you," Elle exclaims, and Kenzie pipes in too.

"It was the sweetest proposal I've ever seen," Kenzie tells Rowan.

I look at her as she grabs our glasses and the tequila, and that's when I realize she hasn't drunk a sip. "Are you gonna have some Patrón, or are you trying to get us all drunk for a reason?"

The alcohol streams through my blood, and my face is starting to feel numb. "Well…" She hesitates.

My eyes go wide, and my mouth falls open. "Are you pregnant?"

A hint of pink meets her cheeks.

"You are!" Elle says, and Kenzie gasps.

Immediately, we stand and move to her, then exchange a group hug.

She places her finger over her lips. "Shhh…I don't want your parents finding out before mine do."

"You haven't told them yet?" Kenzie asks.

"No, and I was hoping I'd get you all trashed before you noticed I wasn't drinking."

"This is so amazing!" I admit, really meaning it. "More Bishop babies!"

She places her hand on her belly and laughs. "Told you they'd love you."

"Diesel knows?" Elle asks.

She nods. "After he proposed, I took him off to the side and told him. He's ecstatic to give Dawson a little brother or sister and so am I. Diesel's already an amazing dad, and I'm so happy he'll get to experience all the nuances of having a pregnant wife. He's already excited for the doctors appointments and making me tacos whenever I demand them." She laughs, and I notice how she's glowing. "You all better keep that secret because if Grandma finds out she didn't know before you three, she will kick my ass."

"You're right." Elle nods. "She'd lose her shit."

"But, back to you, Maize. Time to admit you were wrong and give the man a chance. Also, what did he say to you when he pulled you to the side?" Rowan asks.

I roll my eyes again. "He said he tames wild horses, and he'll tame my attitude too."

Kenzie slaps her hands together. "That's fucking hot. If you pass up the opportunity, I might let him tame me."

I playfully smack her. "You are too much sometimes."

"You need some grand gesture to show Gavin that you're sorry for being an asshole," Elle suggests as we move back to the bed. "You were literally being an asshole because of your insecurities, and that's not fair to him."

"If I've learned anything over the years, it's that communication is key. Apologize and put all your feelings on the table, then see what he says. You're gonna have to talk to him, and it won't be easy. Hell, it might even be a little humiliating, but you're gonna have to humble yourself a bit and do it anyway," Rowan says.

"Do you think it's too late?" I look at her.

She shrugs. "I dunno, but you don't want to look back five years from now with regret like that."

"You're right. It's just all so…"

"Awkward?" Elle says. "I understand that."

Kenzie looks at her. "Because of Mr. Hot Vet, huh."

"Shut it." Elle points her finger at her.

"I have a lot of thinking to do," I admit. "A lot."

Kenzie hands me the M&M's, and the four of us sit on my queen-size bed and get lost in trashy reality TV. Rowan gets up to go to the bathroom every so often, then comes back and makes us shots. I lean against the headboard, not paying attention to anything on the screen. All I can think about is Gavin and how I'll even begin that conversation. I feel lost and confused, and it's all my own doing.

After the girls leave, I lie down, unable to go to sleep. I toss and turn all night, thinking about Gavin and wishing I had the courage to text him, but I don't. The things I need to say should be said in person, but after the way I treated him, I wouldn't be surprised if he ignores me. At least that's what I deserve.

It's been almost a week since I hung out with the gang, and many of the things Rowan said have played on repeat in my mind. I know communication is key, but I'm also stubborn as hell. Half of me wonders what good it would do to talk to him about it, especially if he's planning to go on the road anyway. Then I remember how he said he doesn't regret retiring the night of the rodeo. My stomach is in knots thinking about it.

All week, I've looked for him at the B&B, but I haven't seen him once. I feel as if I ruined my chances by not giving him a fair one, and the thought crushes me.

"Did you hear me?" Dad asks from the doorway of the kitchen.

I was lost in my head again, something I've been doing a lot of this week. "No, sorry. What did you say?"

"We need more tea out here, please," he says with a smile.

I nod and suck in a deep breath. Instead of turning and walking away, Dad comes over to me. The lunch rush is nearly over, and I was prepping for dinner while my employees washed dishes.

Dad stands beside me as I grab the teabags. "What's going on with you this week?"

I shrug, not really wanting to talk about this with him, though he is a really good listener.

Dad grabs the sugar. "Is it about a guy or something?"

I could lie, but at this point, I don't even have the strength for it. "Yeah, actually it is."

"Not that I'm an expert or anything, because I'm not, but I can tell you that when I met your mom, I pushed her away as much as I could because I wasn't ready for a relationship. Sometimes though, you find the person you're supposed to be with when you least expect it. Your mom was only supposed to be here for a little while, and I didn't want to get involved with someone who didn't have roots here. My heart did what it wanted, and I fell so madly in love with her that I couldn't deny her anymore. The point is, you gotta be willing to give people a chance. I know Timothy broke your heart. I know it destroyed you, and I've also noticed how you've rejected every single man who's been interested since then. But honey, in the long run, you're only hurting yourself."

My eyes soften when I look at him, and I'm so emotional I almost burst into tears. He notices and opens his arms, and I fall into them. I'll never be too old for my daddy's hugs. "Thank you," I tell him.

"I love you so much, sweetie. And if your grandma doesn't get more

467

great-grandkids, she might freak the hell out. I'd like some grandkids of my own one day too. No pressure, though." He gives me a wink and presses start on the tea maker.

"I'll bring it out once it's done brewing," I say, feeling the weight sitting heavily on my heart.

Once Dad is out of sight, I know exactly what I have to do, so I text Gavin.

CHAPTER SIXTEEN

Gavin

I'm knee-deep in mud and frustrated as hell. Jackson and I struggle to capture one of the new wild horses in the pasture that's transformed into a playa lake. We've gotten a shit ton of rain lately, and it's caused a huge mess for us. Doesn't help this horse is an asshole and doesn't follow instructions. "C'mon, Lacey. Let's go," I beg softly, ready to go home and shower.

"I think her foot is stuck," Jackson says, sticking his arm down and reaching for her hoof. "Gimme just a second."

As I tightly hold her halter, Jackson tries to get her free.

"Ah, I think I got it."

As soon as his words come out, Lacey becomes more agitated. Quickly, I tighten my grip before she hurts one of us.

"Alright, girl. You're okay." I smooth my palm down her nose.

Jackson stands and shakes his and, whipping muddy slop all over me.

"Ugh, thanks." I wipe mud from the only clean part of my shirt. At this point, my clothes need to be thrown out.

"Sorry." He chuckles. "Hazards of the job."

"So I've learned."

Together, we pull Lacey out and take her to the barn. Like the other six we rescued this morning, she'll need to be bathed. According to Jackson, that'll be Knox and Kane's job, which means they probably got themselves into trouble again.

"I'm going to head home early," I tell Jackson. "I'm gonna have to shower three times to get this smell out of my hair." Taking off my hat, I brush my fingers through it.

"I hear girls like that." He smirks.

"Very doubtful." I snort. "See ya tomorrow."

I hop into my truck, and when I check my phone, I blink hard to make sure I'm not imagining a missed text from Maize. We haven't talked since the Fourth of July party two weeks ago. Though I've seen her plenty at the B&B, she's ignored me as though I don't exist. She was so pissed when I showed up with Sarah Cooke, but I'm not sorry about it. She shouldn't have brought a guy to my fucking birthday party. The moment she saw me with another woman, jealousy radiated off her.

Before I drive off, I unlock my phone and open her message.

MAIZE

> We need to talk in person. Can you meet me at the B&B tonight? Around 7:30?

What in the world would she want to talk about now, after weeks of this cat and mouse game she's played?

I'm too shocked to reply, so I decide to text Grayson since he's the only one who knows about Maize and me.

GAVIN

> Maize just texted me to meet up with her tonight. What do you think she wants?

GRAYSON

> *eggplant emoji*

470

GRAYSON

peach emoji

GRAYSON

tongue emoji

GAVIN

Wow, you're a lot of help. Thanks, asshole.

I shouldn't be surprised, considering Grayson's basically a country frat boy. Though it did make me laugh a little.

GRAYSON

My pleasure. Take condoms.

GAVIN

middle finger emoji

Deciding to just man up, I respond to her.

GAVIN

Do I need to bring groin protection, or are you not going to bust my balls for once?

MAIZE

Guess I deserved that. But no. I genuinely want to talk to you.

GAVIN

Alright, I'll be there.

Once I'm home, I take an extra-long, steaming hot shower. My mind races with the possibilities of what Maize wants to talk about. Considering her sudden change of tune, I'm half wondering if she needs me to donate a kidney or something.

I put on a black T-shirt and blue jeans with boots. Making sure I don't reek, I add cologne and put some gel in my hair. Once I'm finished, I grab a beer and eat something. With some time to spare, I decide to watch TV to keep my mind off her, but it's no use. My thoughts wander as the memories of us together play on repeat. Talking and laughing at the bar and rodeo, then falling into bed together. Waking up with her next to me was a nice contrast to the first time, and I wished it weren't so short-lived.

At twenty after seven, I jump in my truck and drive to the B&B. I'm nervous to hear what she has to say, but I don't let her know that. Once I park, I walk in with all the confidence I can muster and look around.

"Hey." Maize greets me in the dining room. I hold back a smile as I take in her beauty. She's in a sundress that makes her blue eyes pop, and I resist the urge to lean in and kiss her.

"Hello," I say, pushing my hands in my front pockets. "You look beautiful."

She brings her gaze to mine with a smile. "Thank you. So do you."

I furrow my brows because the sudden flip in her attitude is confusing. "So, wanna tell me why I'm here?"

"I want to talk about us but not in here. Outside." She glances over her shoulder to the back door that leads to the wraparound porch.

"Alright." I motion for her to lead the way.

The moment she opens the door, I spot a small round table filled with food.

"Take a seat."

I sit across from her and look down at the spread. "What's all this?"

She blushes nervously and shrugs. "Wanted to make you dinner."

"Okay, I'm gonna be honest with you. I feel like I'm in the twilight zone right now, Maize. After everything, I'm not sure what the hell is goin' on." I swallow hard. "One minute you're hot and the next you're cold. Your mood swings are givin' me whiplash."

She nods. "You're right. I have been, and it's what I want to talk about."

"Okay, well I'm all ears then," I tell her.

Maize grabs a roll and pulls it apart. "I'm sure you know by now that I'm not great in the sharing my feelings department or talking things out when my emotions get the best of me. While my past is no excuse for how I've treated you, it really messed me up. I had basically given up on dating, and the morning after our night together, I was embarrassed I jumped into bed with a man I had just met. We didn't know that much about each other, and I was judging the shit out of myself."

She stuffs her mouth with food, and I silently wait for her to continue. I can tell she's nervous, so I don't want to speak until she's done.

"It was really shitty of me to pretend I didn't know you. I should've owned up to it long before I did. You didn't deserve that kind of treatment, so for that, I'm truly sorry. Even though I'm in my mid-twenties, I'm not experienced with dating or having one-night stands. I get shy and anxious, so I resorted to playing dumb instead of acknowledging you. The fact that you even wanted to talk to me after that shows what kind of man you are. I should've realized you had good intentions."

She pauses to take a sip of her drink. I look down at my untouched plate and dig in while she continues.

"I'm far from perfect, and while you don't owe me a damn thing, I'd really like it if we could start over. I'd love for us to get a second—well, *third* —chance. No more ignoring or avoiding you, no more acting like a brat, and I'll definitely work on communicating better." She chuckles, and it makes me smile to hear that sound again.

"Well..." I swallow. "Honestly, I'm not sure if that's possible. You've been running this whole time, and I'm kinda tired of chasing you. I thought we started over at the rodeo, and then you blindsided me and pulled a one-eighty on me. So..." Shrugging, I hold back a smirk as I watch her squirm. As much as I want to give in and taste her lips, I won't make this easy for her.

"Okay, well first, Leo is just a friend, and I didn't know it was your birthday until after. Don't forget you brought Sarah Cooke to the family Fourth of July party!"

The anger firing through her voice causes me to chuckle. She really didn't like me bringing her.

"You told me to move on, so I was just following orders." I smirk, stabbing a piece of meat and taking a bite.

Maize groans with an eye roll, and it's adorable how worked up she's getting. "The only reason I said that was because I overheard a conversation and got spooked. I should've talked to you about it, but I didn't."

I tilt my head, curiously. "What are you talkin' about?"

"Knox and Kane asked about your job offer with Cooper, and you confirmed it. I knew if you took it, we'd be over, so I thought if I ended it before anything started, then maybe I'd save myself from heartbreak."

Fuck. If I had known that, things would be different between us right now.

"Wow. I'm glad I finally have an explanation at least."

"I'm sorry. I know I fucked up big time. My sister and cousins basically had to smack some common sense into me before I lost you for good. Or perhaps I already have...to Sarah."

The sad expression on her face is just too much, so I put her out of her misery. "Sarah and I are just friends. She understands I have no romantic feelings for her."

"Okay." She flashes a small, relieved smile. "We weren't friends in school, and she made my life hell. Seeing her with you made me hate her even more."

I frown. "I'm sorry to hear that." Had I known that, I would've never invited her. Now I'm twice as glad I turned her advances down.

She shrugs. "It is what it is."

"This is really delicious, by the way," I admit as I inhale another bite. "Beef tips are one of my favorites."

"That's a relief. I wasn't sure."

"I'm not picky, but you're an amazing cook, Maize. If I hadn't picked you up at the pub that night, I definitely would've tried after eating your pancakes."

Maize snorts and laughs again. This is the side of her that I adore. I'm just not sure if it's here to stay.

"You picked a great spot," I tell her, looking out at the sunset.

"I love it out here." She watches the clouds float across the sky. "Figured if you were gonna tell me to take a hike, at least I'd have a nice view to console me."

Smiling, I shake my head. "You knew feeding me would keep my ass here until my plate was at least cleared."

"Ha-ha." She playfully rolls her eyes.

Once we're both finished eating, I've made up my mind. Standing, I lean in and grab her hand, then place a soft kiss on her knuckles. "Thanks for dinner. It was delicious."

She looks up at me in confusion. "You're welcome. Thank you for coming."

Then I push in my chair.

"Are you leavin'?" she asks in a panic.

"Yep. I accept your apology, but I'm not sure where we stand right now."

She quickly rushes to her feet when I walk down the porch steps toward my truck.

"Wait, you're leaving before we finish our conversation?" The hurt and shock in her voice along with her scrambling to keep up with me has me holding back a smile. It's the first time she's chased *me*.

When I make it to my truck, I spin around to face her. "I've accepted your apology, but if you want to start over, then it's time for you to work for what you want."

Maize folds her arms over her chest and narrows her eyes. "Are you serious?"

Smirking, I open my door and hop in, then roll the window down. "Sure am, Maize Bishop. I've been chasing you for months. It's your turn."

"What?" She throws her arms to her sides.

"Gonna have to prove you're serious, sweetheart. You're a smart girl. You'll figure it out." I flash her a shit-eating grin and reverse out of the parking spot.

Her jaw drops, but before I drive off, I add, "Appreciate dinner. Already lookin' forward to breakfast." I throw her a wink, then speed off.

Watching her pout in my rearview mirror has me releasing a bellow of laughter. I can't imagine the thoughts running through her mind right now.

I've never stopped wanting her, but if she truly wants us to be together, she'll have to show me she's one-hundred-percent committed this time.

And I can't wait to watch her try.

CHAPTER SEVENTEEN

Maize

Dust flies in the air as my jaw drops in shock. I can't believe he fucking left!

Gavin drives off, and the anger pumping through my veins has me stomping my feet back to the table where I poured my heart out to him. If he forgave me, then why do I need to *prove* I want to be with him? Shouldn't my apology and spilling my truths be enough?

Ugh!

Did I need to spell it out for him? I thought I was clear when I said I wanted to start over. Didn't he realize that meant I wanted us to go out on a date or hang out and get to know each other again?

I basically pleaded for another chance, tried to work through my humiliation, and now he wants me to grovel. Gavin knows exactly what he's doing.

While I deserve it, I don't know how the hell I'm supposed to show him

After I clean up and put the dishes in the dishwasher, I call Rowan.

"Hey!" she greets eagerly as if she'd been waiting to hear from me. This was her idea after all.

"Listen to what this asshole did!" I blurt out, then tell her the whole story.

Once I finish, Rowan bursts out laughing.

"Are you seriously laughing?"

"I have to commend Gavin actually. He's a genius. You admitted you were wrong and apologized, but now he wants you to fight for him."

"That was me fighting for him," I deadpan. "What else am I supposed to do? Show up in lingerie and seduce him?"

"Girl, I'm not sure, but I'm living vicariously through you, so whatever you do, I wanna hear about it."

I groan, rolling my eyes. "Ugh. You're no help!"

"You fucked up, and now it's your turn to win his heart. You hurt him, and he needs to know you're serious about him now."

"But I am! I said I wanted us to have another chance and to start over. Should I have explained in detail what that meant?"

"You're gonna have to put some effort into it."

"Fine, fine. But hell if I know how or what to do…"

"Well, better get brainstorming." She chuckles.

Once we hang up, I head home and find Kenzie in her room. I explain what happened, and though part of this night was her idea, she says she's still "Team Gavin" and can't wait to see how I win him back. After getting zero advice from her, I lie in bed, thinking about everything. Before any ideas come to mind, I fall asleep.

The next day, I go through my early breakfast routine at the B&B and run into Gavin earlier than expected. He gives me a shit-eating grin, and I somehow restrain the urge to strangle him for leaving so abruptly last night.

"Howdy." He tips his hat after taking a seat.

"Howdy?" I arch a brow.

"That's what I said, ma'am. How're you on this beautiful day?"

Now I'm really confused. "Are you runnin' a fever or something?"

He chuckles, stuffing two pieces of bacon in his mouth.

"What? I'm always in a good mood when I see your gorgeous face in the mornin'."

Grayson barks out a laugh, and I finally realize he heard everything as he sits down across from Gavin. By the way he looks at us, I know he's aware of our situation.

"He knows, doesn't he?" I place a hand on my hip and scowl.

"You sayin' your cousins don't?" he counters.

I rock on my feet. "They might know a little." With a shrug, I continue, "But girls talk. Didn't know you and Grayson were that close."

"Hey," Grayson chimes in.

"He's the only guy around here who isn't consumed with a chick, so we have more time to talk and hang out. Plus, he's not related to you."

"Dude, thanks." Grayson grunts. "The girls around here are batshit crazy."

"Hey," I scold. "Maybe we're just not willing to put up with your antics. Ever think of that?"

"Antics? Y'all must be talkin' about Grayson." Kenzie comes to Maize's side, crossing her arms over her chest.

"And you've just made my point." Grayson flicks a piece of sausage in his mouth.

"So Gavin…" Kenzie directs her attention to him. "Heard Maize made you a nice dinner last night."

I groan with an eye roll.

"She sure did," he responds with a smug grin. "Best meal I've ever had."

"Well, I just want to say…" Kenzie looks over her shoulder at me with a mischievous smirk. "I'm rooting for you. But if she fails, I'm single. Just a heads-up…"

Oh my God. I'm gonna kill her.

"Is that so? Well, thank you. It's refreshing to have one Bishop girl on my side."

"Don't you have a job to get to?" I elbow her ribs and push her out of the way. "Mom won't like it if you're late."

"I'm not afraid of her," she taunts. Kenzie talks a big talk, but she'd never be late, considering she's teaching now.

"Ha, don't let her hear you say that."

Kenzie quickly looks around in a panic, and I laugh. Point made.

"Well, I have to get back to work. If you need someone on your side,

Grayson you have my number." I flash him a wink to get under Kenzie's skin, and luckily, it works.

"Why does he have your number?" she asks. At the same time, Gavin says, "He doesn't."

Chuckling, I head into the kitchen to clean. Lunch is baked chicken casserole and doesn't take long to prep, especially with Sandra and Jane bouncing around. Once it's baked and served, I meet Elle at the diner for a late lunch. My employees are more than capable of handling the kitchen while I'm gone. Right now, I need another woman to talk to about Gavin since my sister insists on antagonizing me about it.

"Hey!" She stands from the booth and immediately hugs me.

"I'm so excited you were able to come," I say, taking a seat.

"Me too. Honestly, it's been so hectic."

We grab our menus and flip through them even though we know what they offer.

"Yeah, same. Lunch rush is over, and my employees were fine." If I'm lucky, they'll start washing dishes too.

"Oh good, so we have time to chat." She smiles up at me.

"Yeah, I owe you an update on Gavin."

"Girl, yes. I wanna hear *all* about it."

I go through all the details– the nice dinner I made and our conversation that quickly shifted to him getting up and leaving. It takes me nearly twenty minutes to explain it all.

"Wow…Gavin's not messin' around this time." She snickers. "Sounds like he's trying to protect his heart just like you. What would you want a guy to do if the tables were turned?"

I hadn't thought about it that way. Shrugging, I draw a blank. "I don't know, I guess…a nice gesture of some sort. Something that shows he's thinking of me, but not just materialistic things. Something from the heart and thoughtful."

She waves out her hand. "There ya go."

"I don't even know where to start," I groan. "I tried to win him over with my cooking, and that didn't work, so I'm kinda screwed."

"What's he interested in? Obviously bull riding and horses since he trains them. But you gotta go deeper than that. What kind of music does he like? Or movies? Figure out some personal things, go out of your way to find out his favorites, then make it special."

"Hmm…that's not a horrible idea." I tap my bottom lip. "I have a lot to think about. But anyway, enough about me, what's going on with you? How's Dr. VetDreamy?"

"If it's possible, he's even moodier and more asshole-ish than before. He glared at me the whole time at Gavin's birthday party, then barely said a word to me the next day. It's like, no matter how well I do every task he gives me, it's not good enough or even acknowledged. I'm ready to open my own business, but even if I did, he has all the contacts. Everyone around here trusts him, and I'd go bankrupt within my first year."

"Have you ever just asked him? Like hey, you want to hate bang this out so we can work together or hey, need help gettin' that stick outta your ass so we can be civil?"

"When he was super edgy, I snapped at him a few times, but it barely fazed him. He'll hardly look at me when he gives instructions, then freaks out when I don't pay attention. Like talk about a double standard. I have to listen to his every word, but he pretends I don't even exist."

"My best guess is that he's actually attracted to you and is trying really fucking hard not to be. He's pulling a Maize."

She frowns. "A what?"

"A Maize. Me! He's pushing you away so you can't get close because he's scared he'll get hurt, or that he'll hurt you. Probably worried it'd ruin your professional relationship too. I mean, he's basically me in a man's body."

"I think you're reading into this *way* too much. He gets phone calls throughout the day, but one woman calls almost every hour, and he'll walk out of the room or distance himself to answer it. So I think he has a girlfriend, which makes your theory moot."

"You're sure it's a woman?" I ask.

"Yep, based on the few seconds of conversation I overheard."

"You don't know it's a girlfriend, though. For all we know, it's his drug dealer."

Elle snorts. "Yeah, that makes me feel better, thanks."

I shrug. "Gotta think of all options here."

The waitress comes over and takes our order. Surprisingly, I'm not super hungry, so I order a salad and a sweet tea.

"Maybe you should join a dating app," I suggest. "Then let it slip into your convo and watch his reaction."

"After your disasters, you want me to suffer through that?"

"Well, you don't really have to participate to see what he thinks about it. Maybe he'll try to find you and swipe right." I waggle my brows.

Elle rolls her eyes. "Very doubtful. Good looks aside, his personality is dull, humor is dry, and don't get me started on our one-sentence conversations."

"You need some kind of drastic change and see if he notices. Wear something different and tight, cut or dye your hair, put on a padded bra. If he looks even a tiny bit fazed, then that means he's looking."

"Okay, I can do the first two, but I'm not wearing a padded bra. Aside from being uncomfortable, I wear scrubs, and they're tight enough as it is."

"I would love to see you with bleach blond hair!" I exclaim. "It'd look hot with your tan, too. Get some layers or side bangs." I move my head from side to side as I imagine it in my mind. "Yep, it'd look sexy as hell."

"You know how long it'd take to get my dark hair to blond?"

"Well, good thing Zoey has all the mad skills!" I smirk. "I'm sure she'll help you out."

Elle groans but nods. "Alright, but I'm *not* doing this for him. I could use a change."

Smiling, I grab my phone to set a reminder to call Zoey after lunch. "Maybe I'll get some highlights myself. See Gavin resist my charm then."

She snorts as she takes a sip of her water. "Trust me, he's probably just as anxious to get you back in his bed. He just wants to play hard to get first."

"If Gavin grew up here, I could do recon and ask his best friend questions and get intimate details about him. Grayson would be my best bet, but I don't want to get him involved. Maybe Cooper would know? I don't have his number, though, and he might be traveling right now." The thought of Gavin leaving nearly suffocates me, but I push it away. I realize he never told me what decision he made. Regardless, I think I'd try long distance for him.

"Ooh, this is starting to sound like some kind of detective mission." Elle rubs her palms together. " I think Connor's been called out to their ranch before. I'll look in his files and see if I can find his number, or maybe you can just stop by randomly."

"Oh my God, that'd be amazing. You're a genius!"

Elle snorts. "I didn't go to vet school for nothing. But you probably know more than you think. You can't tell me in the past year you haven't eavesdropped on him while he was eating at the B&B."

She makes a valid point. I've heard a lot of his conversations. But I don't want to screw this chance up because it might be the last one he gives me.

Once our food is delivered, we take our time eating and chat.

After we finish, we pay, then stand. Neither of us wants to go back to work, but we know we have to. I miss hanging out with Elle and make her promise to do this again sometime soon.

"Well, good luck wrangling your cowboy." She pulls me in for a hug. "I'll text you if I find Cooper's number."

"Thank you."

We say our goodbyes, and before I drive back to the ranch, I text Gavin. Just in case she can't find Cooper's info, I need a plan B.

MAIZE

> I want to give us a real chance this time. Are my words not enough?

GAVIN

> You're adorable. Actions always speak louder than words, sweetheart.

I groan while simultaneously getting butterflies at the way he called me *sweetheart*. Damn him.

But if that's how he's going to be, then fine.

I just hope whatever I come up with is enough to win him back because right now, I'll do whatever it takes.

CHAPTER EIGHTEEN

Gavin

After two days of silence, I'm wondering if Maize's given up altogether. Though I've accepted her apology, and she's said she wants a real chance, I won't be falling back into bed with her that quickly. I've been burned too much by her already. She's spent the past year giving me whiplash with her mood swings, so she needs to prove she's serious.

I'd love nothing more than to hold Maize Bishop in my arms until the sun rises, but I'm patient.

It's Monday morning, and I'm heading to the B&B to meet up with the guys for breakfast. It'll be the first time I've been around Maize since Friday, and I'm anxious as hell to talk to her.

"Mornin'." John greets me when I enter. I tip my hat and flash him a small smile while scanning the room.

Grayson's already sitting at a table and looks up at me with a grin. "Hey,

I go to the coffee station, fill a mug, and add a little sugar. When I walk toward Grayson, I finally see her.

"Good mornin'," I drawl when she approaches. My eyes widen as I get a glimpse of her hair. It's pulled back as usual, but I notice blond strands. "You changed your hair."

"Morning. I did. I made you a special breakfast." She clamps her hands together.

I eye her suspiciously, pulling out a chair and sitting. "Is that code for poison or something?"

"Of course not." She flashes a wink, then leans down until her mouth brushes against the shell of my ear. "I promised to win you back, and since I know how much you love my food, I figured I'd better start there."

Shit, I'm impressed. There's no denying I'd eat anything she cooks. They say the way to a man's heart is through his stomach, so I guess she's testing that theory.

"What kind of favoritism shit is this?" Grayson complains the moment Maize returns carrying two plates.

"There might be enough for you too if you don't piss me off," she retorts, setting them in front of me.

My eyes widen in shock when I study the spread. I can hardly contain my excitement to try it all.

"Strawberry-stuffed French toast with maple syrup…" She points at the second plate. "Cheesy grits 'n sausage and blueberry streusel coffee cake."

"Maize, wow…" I look at the breakfast my grandmother used to make. Every Saturday morning, I'd go for a visit, and without fail, she'd cook this feast. Unfortunately, she passed away five years ago. I wished Mimi would've been able to meet Maize. She would've loved her.

Maize takes a step back, but I grab her hand and pull her close. "How? How'd you know?"

"I did my research." She smiles proudly. "Told you I was serious."

"Serious about what?" Grayson blurts out, trying to tear off a piece of my streusel.

I smack his hand away. "None of your damn business."

"Oh like I can't put two and two together." He scoffs.

Looking up at Maize, I smile wide. "Thank you. It smells amazing and really means a lot to me."

"You're welcome. I hope I did it justice."

Standing, I cup her face and press my lips to her. She melts into me, but I pull away all too quickly. Normally, she would've freaked out because she's at work, but she didn't this time. Though I'm sure her dad wouldn't appreciate the PDA.

"I'm sure you did. Thank you."

With flushed cheeks, Maize goes to the kitchen, and I sit.

"What the…?" Grayson's jaw hits the floor. "You wanna explain what is goin' on?"

"She's tryin' to win me back," I reply with a shrug. "I need to know she's not gonna run away from me again."

"You got a Bishop to admit she wants you, and you're not jumping at the opportunity to have her right now? You have some strong willpower." He chuckles.

"I've been chasing her for a year, and after being told it was a mistake, I'm a little hesitant."

"So you're playing hard to get?" He chuckles.

I nod. "Something like that."

The next day, she's bubbly and full of smiles, which makes me think she has something up her sleeve.

"Mornin', beautiful," I greet and quickly plant a kiss on her lips when no one's looking.

"Morning. You have plans after work?" she asks softly.

"Hmm…" I brush my fingers over the stubble on my jawline. "Stripper joint, beers, and hookers."

Maize groans, crossing her arms with an unamused expression. "That sounds like a productive Tuesday night."

"I mean, unless you have something else in mind? I'd cancel for you." I flash her a wink, and her cheeks tint red.

"Well, since you didn't call me last night to say you were taking me back,

I do. Way better than a guys' night out. And if you wanna join me, be ready by eight."

"I chuckle at her annoyance. "Alright. Where should I meet you?"

She licks her lips, then smirks. "I'll pick you up."

By the time the workday is over, I'm a giddy, anxious fool. I have no idea what Maize has planned, but I can't wait to find out.

I drive home and shower. Without knowing how I should dress, I play it safe by wearing jeans, boots, and a dress shirt. At eight, a knock sounds on the door, and when I open it, Maize nearly takes my breath away. Her hair is in two braids with loose strands around her face, showing off her new blond highlights. She's wearing cutoffs with a Texas tank top that leaves nothing to my imagination.

"I feel a bit overdressed," I tease, scanning down her body again. I'm not used to seeing her like this, but I'm not complaining.

"As long as you're comfortable, that's all that matters." She smiles in return. "I hope you're ready."

"I don't think I have a choice." I chuckle, closing the gap between us and kissing her cheek. "You're so pretty. I love your hair."

Maize flips one of her braids and blushes. "You do? Thank you. Elle and I got our hair done over the weekend."

I hold a piece between my fingers and imagine how it'd look spread across my bedsheets.

"You better take me somewhere quick before I come up with another idea."

She snorts, shaking her head. "Is this all it's gonna take for you to give me another chance?"

"I don't know. I guess we'll both see." I wink, then close and lock the door behind me.

Following Maize, I squint when I see a jacked-up truck. "What's this?"

"I'm borrowing it for the night."

"You know how to drive that thing?"

"Well, mostly." She laughs. "C'mon, Cowboy. Don't you trust me?"

I help her into the driver's side, and when I round the truck and hop into the other, she hands me a blindfold.

"Are you serious?"

"Yes!" She laughs. "It's a surprise, so put it on."

"Hmm…alright."

After a bumpy ten minutes and hearing her laugh at my uncertainty, she finally parks.

"We're here."

"Can I take this thing off now?"

"Yep."

I open my eyes and squint as I look around the partially wooded area. There's a large firepit surrounded by grass and hay bales.

"Where are we?"

"It's what I like to call the secret spot."

Scanning the area, I notice we're on a hill, and the ranch is in the far distance. "Okay, so what're we doing here?"

Maize opens the door and hops out. "Follow me and find out, Cowboy."

I do as she says, and when I turn around, I see a large white screen on a pole. Then she opens the tailgate and gestures for me to get in the back.

"Wow…" Blankets and pillows are spread out on the truck bed along with a cooler and picnic basket.

"I thought it'd be more fun to watch a movie under the stars."

I walk toward her, tilting up her chin. "No one's ever done anything like this for me before. I love it." I kiss the tip of her nose.

"Good. I even picked out a really awesome movie for us to watch."

"Is that so?" I climb into the back and help her up.

She messes with the projector while I grab some drinks and food.

We get comfortable on the blankets, and I pull Maize into my body during the previews.

"No way." I glance at her. "How'd you know?"

"Know what?" She plays innocent.

I smirk. "*No Country for Old Men* is my favorite movie. Now, how'd you know that?"

"I maybe did a little internet stalking."

"There's no way you found that online. Who'd you talk to?"

She sighs, realizing I'm not gonna drop it. "You're really gonna make me reveal my sources?"

"Yes, ma'am."

"It was Cooper. He gave me some great…intel about you."

I groan with a chuckle. "Shoulda known, that bastard."

"What's wrong with that?" she asks.

"He likes to joke around, so I'm wondering what else he said. I'm a little concerned, to be honest."

Maize laughs and snuggles closer. "Don't worry." She pats my chest and meets my eyes. "I already knew you secretly cried to *Big Daddy*."

I fucking hate Cooper.

We end the night wrapped up in each other, and I can't seem to take my hands or lips off her. I want to be as close to Maize as possible. While I want to lose myself with her, I keep control of the situation and only allow her to kiss me.

"Thanks for a nice evening," I tell her once she drives me back to my house. It's late, and we have to be up early, but that doesn't make it any easier to leave.

"You're welcome." She smiles in return. "I'll see you at breakfast."

By six, I'm dragging my ass outta bed and wishing I had an extra hour or three of sleep. Though I'll be paying for it today, last night was worth it. I'm enjoying Maize's effort and appreciate the lengths she's already gone to. When I look around the B&B, I don't immediately see her, so I load a plate with food. After chatting with Grayson, Riley, and Diesel, Maize appears wearing a wide, bright smile and greets everyone.

"Do I get a *special* breakfast this mornin'?" Grayson flashes a cocky smirk, and I kick him underneath the table. By the looks the other guys give him, Grayson spilled the news about Maize and me.

"You wish." She snorts.

"How about me? Your favorite cousin?" Riley muses.

"Or your favorite future cousin-in-law?" Diesel adds with a grin.

"You know…" Maize puts her hands on her hips. "It really surprises me you two managed to find women. Sorry, Grayson. Kenzie will get the stick outta her ass one day."

They laugh at the way Grayson glares at her. "Don't put that juju in the air."

Maize snorts, shaking her head. "Well, anyway. I do have a surprise for you." She licks her lips, bringing her gaze to mine. "Be right back."

"So you datin' my cousin, now?" Riley asks pointedly.

"Maybe."

"Shut the hell up," Grayson blurts out. "They've been screwin' for months."

I kick him harder this time. "Dude."

"For *months*?" Diesel asks, chuckling. "I think these Bishop women get their rocks off from sneakin' around. Don't get me wrong now, it's hot as fuck, but I'm bracing myself for the day Grayson and Kenzie come clean."

"Not happenin', bro." Grayson groans.

"We'll all find out when she's giving birth to his baby," I tease.

"You guys fuckin' suck. I hate you all." He grunts, then shoves food into his mouth.

Maize returns and sets a platter in front of me. It's a round cake covered in cream cheese frosting with purple writing on top.

Meet me where we first met. Tomorrow. 8pm.

The guys lean over to read it. "Where's that?" Diesel and Riley simultaneously ask.

Maize leans down and whispers in my ear, "I want to recreate that night. But this time, no cheating."

I smile wide as I think back to when we played pool together almost a year ago.

"What kind of cake is it, Maze?" Diesel dips his finger into the frosting, and Maize smacks his hand away.

"Carrot cake, Gavin's favorite."

My mouth waters, and I glance up at her with a grin.

Maize flashes me a little wink. "Told you I did my research."

Then she walks away.

It's Thursday, and I'm meeting Maize at the pub in an hour. Since she wants us to recreate the night we met, I wear the same shirt. The real test will be if she notices.

By the time I arrive, she's sitting at the bar talking to Kenzie and drinking. I walk up to her, and Kenzie's eyes light up when she sees me. Maize quickly turns and releases a gasp before I cup her cheeks, and our mouths collide.

Our tongues tangle together, and before we get lost in the moment, we break apart.

"What was that for?" she asks, doe-eyed.

"Just a thank you for the delicious cake." I smirk. "Grayson's all butt hurt I didn't share, but I refused. Best carrot cake I've ever had."

She blinks up at me with a shy smile.

"I don't recall that happening last time," Kenzie blurts out, watching us closely. "Am I getting the R-rated version?"

A blush hits Maize's cheeks, and I laugh at Kenzie's boldness.

"Might be X-rated. Not sure yet." I shrug, stepping closer and wrapping an arm around Maize. "One thing's for certain, I'm not wasting any time tonight. Plus, I'm like an elephant and remember every detail. The conversation about you becoming a nun, crooked dick pics, and—" I lean in so only Maize can hear me. "Spanking your ass."

She gulps and bites down on her lower lip.

"But right now, we have drinks to order and a game of pool to play."

"Dude." Grayson slams his palm on the table. "I can't believe you still haven't put her out of her damn misery. She's given you the first-class treatment all damn week, and you *still* haven't agreed to give her a second chance?" His eyes widen with disbelief.

I shrug, scanning the dining room for Maize and frown when I still haven't found her. We've been here for almost twenty minutes.

"Trust me, I appreciate her effort. I'm shocked, honestly. And I want to be with her. I'm just concerned she'll change her mind next week. But I'm enjoying every second."

"You better stop makin' her chase you before she gives up and the tables turn. This back-and-forth shit is giving me a headache. It could all backfire because Maize isn't that patient."

His words nearly gut me, and I realize he's right.

"Shit, I didn't think about it that way." I rub my sweaty palms down my jeans, looking around for her again but only see Jane.

"Hey," I say, grabbing her attention.

Jane walks over with a bright smile and rests her hand on my shoulder. "Hey, Gavin. How's your breakfast?"

"It's delicious, ma'am. Do you know where Maize is this mornin'? I haven't seen her yet."

She gives me a suspicious look. "She took a vacation day, so Sandra and I are handling everything today."

"Oh. Is she sick or somethin'?"

"Not that I know of." She shrugs.

After she walks away, Grayson points at me with his fork. "Told ya. You got greedy." He snorts.

I brush a hand through my hair before putting my hat on. Then I set my plate in the dirty dish bin and leave.

If Grayson's right, I'm gonna kick my own ass. Or better yet, let one of the horses do it.

CHAPTER NINETEEN

Maize

I'm standing in Gavin's cabin wearing red lingerie with black cowboy boots, and though I'm not snooping, I feel like I'm invading his privacy.

But maybe he should've thought about that when he started this whole *prove I'm ready to be with him* crap. For the past four days, I've gone out of my way to create some memorable moments.

Has he put me out of my damn misery and taken me to his bed? No.

Gavin kisses me like his life depends on it, then leaves me hot and bothered.

That ends *tonight*.

He'll give me a damn answer about us being together or I'm walking out of here.

I have candles lit, his favorite music playing softly, and my outfit doesn't leave anything to the imagination. Either I'll successfully seduce Gavin or he'll turn me down for good.

If the latter happens, I'm never going to be able to face him again.

When I hear the front door open, I lick my lips and wait for him to find me.

"Uhh, hello?" His voice echoes.

"In the kitchen," I respond sweetly as our dinner warms in the oven.

I even made dessert, assuming we'll have the energy for it later. I lean against the counter and hear his footsteps down the hallway.

"Holy fuck."

I blink at him with a small smile.

"Uh…" Gavin brushes his hand over his scruffy jaw, and I blush as his eyes study me. "H-how did you get inside?"

"My uncles have a master key for all the housing." I shrug. "I decided to borrow it."

He swallows hard and looks around. "You wanna explain what's goin' on here because I'm…"

I boldly step toward him. "I'll tell you exactly what's happening. I've been doing my best to show you just how ready I am to be with you and how I'm not gonna run, yet each night, I wait for your call and nothing. So I decided to try one more time—a less subtle approach," I say, placing a hand on my hip. "But it comes with an ultimatum."

Gavin crosses his arms, wearing an amused grin. "An ultimatum?"

I tilt my head. "You decide right now if you're giving me a second chance or I leave for good this time. I don't know how else to convince you. Hell, I've literally waxed my entire body and found a vinyl of Diamond Rio to play in your ancient record player—which was not easy to figure out, mind you."

"Of course you knew I was a fan."

"I overheard you talkin' about how you saw them in concert when you were a teen. Then something about how they were your grandpa's favorite and that was when you started listening to their music."

"Eavesdroppin'?"

"Please." I roll my eyes. "You and the guys are loud as hell. Everyone hears your conversations at the B&B. Including the ones about me."

The corner of his mouth twists up. "So tell me, Maize…" He sets his hat on the counter before threading his fingers through his messy hair. "You ready to be my girl?"

My heart races, and my breaths turn shallow as his husky voice sends shivers down my spine. He walks toward me, never breaking our eye contact.

"If you haven't gotten the hint by now…"

"Oh, I have." Plucking the strap of my dress, he leaves goose bumps as he brushes the pad of his finger down my arm. "I just wanna hear you say it."

Releasing a groan, I roll my eyes, then smile. "Fine, I'll stroke your ego this one *last* time, but then that's it."

"Mm-hmm." He smirks.

Instead of giving in to his cockiness, I inch closer and make demands of my own. "Make me yours, Gavin. I want you."

He cups the back of my head, pulling me toward him until our mouths collide. I gasp as he holds me into his body and captures my bottom lip between his teeth.

"*Mine*, Maize," he growls, sliding his hands down my back until his palms reach my ass. "Fuckin' mine. Got it?"

I nod and release a rush of air. "*Yes*. All yours."

Gavin lifts me, and I wrap my legs around his waist. His erection presses against his jeans, and I know he's as desperate and eager as I am.

Instead of taking me to his bedroom as I'd hoped, he sets me on top of the kitchen counter and stands between my legs.

"Waxed everywhere, huh?" He moves his mouth down my neck.

"Yes," I pant, tilting my head back.

Gavin slides his hand over my thigh and over the thin fabric. His fingers roam under my panties, and I release a moan of anticipation.

"Fuck," he groans in my ear. "So damn soft."

His thumb finds my clit, and soon, my breathing turns ragged and needy. He plunges two fingers inside me as he sucks on the softness of my neck.

"You're so tight and wet, baby. Shit, I wanna fuck you so hard."

"God, yes." My head rolls back.

He thrusts his fingers faster and harder until I can no longer take it and dig my nails into his biceps as I scream out my release.

Our mouths slam together, hot and greedy, as I claw at his clothes.

"Off…now," I order.

As he strips, I do the same, not wanting anything between us. He cups my face and crashes our lips together again. His tongue tangles with mine.

"Goddamn, baby."

"You've been teasing me all damn week," I tell him. "With your little kisses, then leaving me all hot and bothered. So *rude*."

He chuckles. "Imma make up for it, baby. Turn around and put your palms flat on the counter."

I do as he says, and anxious butterflies swarm low in my stomach as I look over at him studying every inch of my body.

"Now spread your legs and let me see your sweet pussy."

I obey, watching him stroke his hard cock.

Gavin closes the gap between us, brushing the tip of his erection along my slit. "Say it again, Maize. Say you're mine," he whispers in my ear.

Licking my lips, I look at him over my shoulder. "I'm yours. Have been since that first night a year ago."

"That's fuckin' right," he hisses, pushing in slowly. "'Bout time you realize it."

I smile at his possessiveness. "Now fuck me, Cowboy."

Gavin squeezes my hips as he thrusts deep inside, jolting me forward until I'm nearly flat on the counter. God, it feels so good.

"Shit," he whispers. "You're so tight."

Gavin pulls out slowly before ramming back in. Our bodies form a rhythm as we slam together over and over. Wrapping an arm around my waist, Gavin aggressively rubs my clit until I lose myself. My release is intense and harsh, and when I float back to earth, he squeezes my breast.

"Don't think I've forgotten about your ass…" He pulls back, then slaps a cheek, hard and sharp.

My body jerks, and I moan in response.

"We fit together perfectly," he says in my ear, his voice hoarse and raw. "We always have."

"Yes," I whisper-moan.

My back arches as the sensations build inside me, but then Gavin slides out and falls to his knees. Just as I'm about to ask what the hell he's doing, he grips my thighs and spreads my legs apart.

My stomach is flat on the counter as he slides his tongue up my center. He flicks and sucks, tasting every inch of me as I claw at the granite. I can barely fill my lungs with air as he draws out another orgasm, his mouth devouring my pussy like it's the last thing he'll ever taste.

When Gavin stands, he grabs my arm and spins me around until I'm facing him. Our lips fuse, and he lifts me.

"Oh my God," I squeal as he leads us out of the kitchen.

"Hang on." He grins.

When we enter his bedroom, we fall on top of the bed, and he quickly positions me to straddle him.

"Ride me."

I move until his cock presses against me, and I slowly slide down his hard length. He grips my hips, and we rock together, fast and hard.

Gavin massages my breasts, smacks my ass, and pulls my hair until I scream his name. I love how demanding and rough he is, but he's also sweet and soft. After my fourth orgasm, he flips me on my back and kisses me until he groans my name. He spills inside me, and slowly, we resurface to reality together.

"Wow…" I breathe out.

"Yeah, wow," he echoes, lying next to me.

Gavin brushes his knuckles over my cheek and gazes into my eyes. "I'm really fallin' for you, Maize Bishop. I hope you feel the same."

"As much as I didn't want to admit it, I do. No doubt about it," I confess with a smile.

"More stubborn than a mule, aren't ya?" He chuckles, pulling me into his arms.

"Well, I've learned what it takes to get your attention. Lingerie and an ultimatum."

His bright blue eyes light up. "Can ya blame a man? You're downright gorgeous with a smart mouth to boot. I was hard the second I saw you tonight."

"Romantic." I snicker.

Gavin tilts my chin and brushes his mouth softly over mine. "I really want this to work out, so no more games. I want to be together, and we can wait to tell people when you're ready."

His declaration has my heart beating wildly. It's been years since I've wanted a man as much as I've wanted him. Though it scares me, I want this to work.

"I agree," I tell him. "And we'll figure out the long-distance thing and take it one day at a time."

He quirks a brow, giving me a puzzled expression. "Long-distance?"

I suck in my lips, releasing a sigh. "When you start traveling with Cooper."

"Maize…"

"It's okay." I pull back slightly so I meet his eyes. "You have to follow your heart, and you love bull riding, so it only makes sense—"

"I turned it down," he blurts out. "A month ago."

My brows rise. "You did? But…when I brought it up at dinner last Friday, you acted like it was something you were pursuing."

"After you admitted to overhearing my conversation, I never said I was or wasn't, and you didn't ask."

I blow out a breath of annoyance. "And you couldn't put me out of my misery and just tell me you weren't leaving?" I scold.

Gavin laughs with a shrug. "It was nice to see you sweat for once."

"Soooo funny," I mock. "Why'd you say no?"

"Realized the ranch was my second home, and while I enjoyed being on the road, I want to settle down, and I want to do that here. With you. I love seeing you every morning, and it's something I looked forward to, even if you ignore me. Your family feels like my own. It just feels right to be here."

My heart swells as my eyes fill with tears. "I'm really happy you're staying."

He tips my chin. "Me too. Now I get to slap that fine ass anytime I want."

With a loud smack to my bare cheek, I yelp and laugh. "I kinda like sneaking around with you. Well, my cousins and Grayson know, but I want to wait until we get to know each other better to tell my parents. Are you okay with that?" After my last relationship backfired, I don't want to introduce my parents to any man until we've been dating a while.

"I'm good with waiting until you're ready." He flashes a wink. "Just promise me it won't be another year?"

I can't stop the ridiculous smile from forming as I look at him. "I can definitely promise that."

After we eat dinner and devour the dessert, Gavin cages me against the counter while I rinse the dishes. He feathers soft kisses on my neck. "I could get used to seeing you in my kitchen half-naked. It's giving me ideas."

"Yeah? What kind?" I muse.

"Really dirty ones. Bending you over the table for one, putting whipped cream on your delicious tits, then licking it off, you riding me. Those are just a few."

His hard cock presses against my back. "Mmm...I think that could be arranged."

He wraps his arms around my waist and pulls me close. Gavin's tall and big, which I love, and it makes me feel so small and cared for when he does that.

"Promise you'll always hold me like this?" I whisper, leaning my head against his chest.

"Always, Maize. I'm not going anywhere."

And when he presses his lips to my temple, I fall even deeper in love with him.

CHAPTER TWENTY

Gavin

Sneaking around with Maize for the past month has been incredible. I wish we wouldn't have wasted so much time chasing each other, but it's better late than never. While all her cousins know about us, and so do the guys, none of the Bishop adults do. And tonight is the big reveal to her parents.

While I'm nervous as hell, I'm also ready to yell from the mountaintops how much she means to me. We've spent all our free time together, but it never seems like enough. I genuinely want to know everything about Maize Bishop—her likes, dislikes, dreams, and aspirations.

Though it took a while, I think she finally understands I'm not some twentysomething looking for a one-night stand. I'm a man searching for my forever woman, and I've found that in her. I'm ready to settle down, and she is too. While she doesn't want to rush into things, I'd marry her tomorrow, but I keep it to myself. I selfishly want to wake up next to her every day and see her pretty smile before I leave for work.

After I get out of the shower, I put on my Sunday best, comb my hair, and rehearse articulating the way Maize makes me feel. While John and Mila are amazing, being introduced as her boyfriend could be a disaster. I'm not sure what their reaction will be, and that makes me nervous.

I'm falling hard and fast for Maize in ways I never imagined was possible. I've not loved anyone or anything as much as I loved bull riding and training, but I'd hang my saddle for her.

What we have is the real deal.

As I slip on my boots, there's a knock on my door. I open it and see Maize standing in a sundress with velvety red lips. A cute smirk forms as she looks me up and down.

"Damn," I say, pulling her into my arms and devouring her mouth. "Do I have lipstick on me?" I ask when we finally break apart.

"No, silly. It'll last fifteen hours." She steps inside.

"Really? I'd like to put that to the test then." I waggle my brows at her.

"I'd be up for the challenge," she admits. "Are you ready for this?"

I check the time and grow more anxious. I let out a cool breath, and Maize notices. Tilting her head, she moves closer and wraps her arms around my waist. "It's gonna be fine. I promise. My parents already love you."

I create just enough space so I can look into her baby blues. "They love me as an employee on the ranch, not as their twenty-five-year-old daughter's boyfriend. There's a big difference."

Her face softens. "I know that, but I also know how unconventional my dad's relationship was along with all my uncles. It's kinda a Bishop thing, if I'm being honest."

I grin. "How so?"

"Mila was my nanny before she was my mother." Maize shrugs. "So Dad has no room to talk."

"Wow." I remember Maize telling me about this before, but it slipped my mind.

"And Uncle Alex knocked up his now wife on vacation in Florida, then she showed up here, pregnant. Uncle Evan met his wife at a wedding, had a one-night stand, then found out she was the new doctor at the hospital."

My eyebrows go sky high. "What about Jackson?"

This question makes her laugh. "He's the only normal one. I know it's *very* hard to believe. He and Kiera were best friends growing up. There was drama, but it wasn't a random hookup. He chased after her for fifteen years." She chuckles.

"How do you know all this?"

"One time, Grandma Bishop was wine drunk after a quilt meeting and told me all their dirty secrets." Maize throws me a wink.

I grin at her. "Still doesn't mean your dad and uncles won't kick my ass or fire me."

She pulls me closer. "As long as you don't break my heart, I think you'll be safe."

"I'd *never* do anything to hurt you," I promise her and seal it with a kiss.

"I believe you," she whispers. "But we should really get going. Don't want to be late. It's one of Dad's major pet peeves."

I nod. "Okay, okay. I guess I am stalling."

She interlocks her hand with mine and leads us outside. I jump in the truck with her, and my mind spins on the drive over. Any other time, it would seem far away because the ranch is so large, but we arrive in a blink. We get out, and she stops and turns to me before we walk in.

"A kiss for good luck." She paints her mouth across mine, and her tongue darts inside. For a moment, I forget where I am, but when she pushes away, I remember.

"Let's do this," I say, finding my confidence as she grabs the knob, and we enter. Whatever her mother's cooking smells amazing, and I realize just how hungry I am. When her parents turn around and make eye contact with me, I immediately lose my appetite.

"Wait, Gavin's your boyfriend?" John asks, staring me down, and I'm not sure if it's with approval or rejection.

Maize nods with a smile. Then she takes my hand and leads me to the table, and we sit.

"Oh thank god," Mila says. "I was worried to death trying to guess who you were bringing tonight. Happy to see you again, Gavin."

It's a relief to know her mom is on board, but I still can't read John. He's typically quiet, especially compared to Jackson, but this seems more intense than usual.

"I made lasagna," Mila announces. "I hope you're both hungry."

"Sounds amazing," I say.

"Yeah, Mom. Can't wait. I'm starving." Maize looks around. "Did Kenzie already leave for work?"

"She did," John mumbles, not making eye contact with either of us.

A knot forms in my throat, and I can't seem to swallow it down. "What would you like to drink?" Mila asks.

"I got it." Maize gets up and pours us all glasses of iced sweet tea. I drink it down, wondering what John's really thinking. Maize helps set the table, then brings the salad, and eventually, the lasagna is set in the middle. John and Mila sit across from us as we pass serving spoons around and fill our plates family style.

"So, you're now dating my daughter?" John finally says once we all have our food.

"Yes, sir," I confirm.

"How long has this been going on?" he asks.

"Dad. That's really none of your business, is it?" Maize snaps. I can tell she's getting frustrated, and I try to put myself in his shoes. I understand his response.

Mila places her hand on John's lap. I'm sure to help calm his unease.

"You're much older, Gavin. Do you plan on stayin' in town?" John continues with questions.

"If we're counting, Gavin's about ten years older," Maize answers for me. "That's no secret. Older means more mature, and he's not a fuckboy like all the other men around here who only want me for one thing."

"Maize, language," Mila says.

"I've thought about my age more times than I can count. Maize's mature and thinks on a higher level. She knows what she wants in life, and I support that one hundred percent. And yes, I plan to stay here indefinitely. I love the ranch, and I love your family. I've already lived a full life and have traveled around the world and have no desire to go back to that. I'm ready to settle down, start a family, and do what I love, which is training."

Mila looks at me with adoration and smiles. "That's nice, Gavin. There's something magical about this place. It's one reason I moved here, well and because my grandmother lived here, but I fell in love with the ranch and John, and you too, Maize. It was home in my heart," Mila tells me. "Seems like it's yours too."

"Yes, ma'am. It is. Growing up in Houston has made me appreciate all this land, the quietness at night, and the stars. I've never seen so many. I know our relationship seems like it's coming from left field, but I can promise this has been brewing between us for a long time," I admit.

Maize snickers. "Over a year. And I'm happy, Daddy."

The room is silent for a minute before I speak up, but I know I can't leave without admitting my true feelings. I want her dad to know this isn't a fling, and I'm not sure how to convince him, so I let my heart speak for me instead. "I love Maize with everything that I am. I can't imagine my life without her." I smile and look over at Maize, who has tears forming in her eyes. It's not easy for me to be so vulnerable and honest, but it was the only way.

"I love you too," she tells me, then leans over and presses her lips right against mine. I kiss her back, but damn, the fire this woman has is blazing hot right now.

"I know you both have concerns about me breaking Maize's heart, but that's not going to happen. Finding love like this is rare, and I'm not going to let the opportunity pass me by," I profess, meaning it with all my being.

John's mouth tilts up into a smile, and he lets out a sigh. "Okay. Okay, you two. You don't have to prove anything to me. I just don't want you getting hurt, sweetie. And if you break her heart…" John glares at me and doesn't finish his threat.

I nod. "I'd kick my own ass if that happened," I admit. "But it won't, I can guarantee that. I'm a man of my word."

"I'm so happy for you two," Mila says in a high-pitched tone. "Now, let's eat before this masterpiece of a meal gets cold."

I grab Maize's hand as Mila chats about the school and how many kids they have enrolled this year. There are so many stolen glances and unspoken words that I can't wait to be alone with her.

"How's your planning going with the business?" Mila inquires.

John points his fork at me. "You support her starting this catering business?"

"Yes!" Maize raises her voice an octave with a laugh. "Gavin's been helping a lot. I ordered a ton of equipment, and he's kept me on schedule with my launch. Also, he's strong and has helped me lift all the heavy items that have already arrived. Free labor." Maize gives me a wink.

"I know you're gonna be successful," I say, beaming at her. I can't wait to see what she accomplishes. Grandma Bishop has already gotten her booked solid for months with ladies from church.

"And I'm about to be twenty-six, and even though I still live at home, I'm grown. I can do whatever I want, date whoever I want, and make whatever decisions I want."

John cracks a smile. "I wouldn't expect anything else from you, but I'll always be your father and will always have your best interest in mind." He pauses for a second, then looks at us. "I know the two of ya are waitin' for my blessing, so you have it. Once your grandma finds out, that's if she doesn't already know about this, she will be publicly asking for more great-grandbabies. Just please, wait until you're married."

"And don't wait until I'm old and gray to get married and have kids," Mila says. "I'd like to enjoy having grandkids."

Maize nearly chokes on her food and places her hand on her throat before chugging tea. "I've announced I have a boyfriend, and you're already planning a wedding and kids. You both need to chill out. We're taking it slow. There's no need to rush because I want this to last forever."

"It will," I say with a big grin.

Mila shrugs. "I was serious, though."

"Okay, so ring shopping next week?" I turn to Maize.

Her eyes are as wide as saucers, and her cheeks turn rosy pink. "Don't you even!"

I wrap my arm around her, and she leans in. "One day."

"Not right now," she says with a smile, but the look in her eyes gives her away. It's as if she's imagining a future with me, and it makes my heart swell with happiness. My face actually hurts from smiling.

After dinner, Mila makes coffee and pulls out a coconut cream pie.

"Just because Maize's a chef, doesn't mean I don't buy store made pies," she admits as she slides pieces onto plates and hands us forks. I take a bite and grin.

"It tastes great. I wouldn't have known the difference," I say.

"Maize still has a lot to teach you then," Mila says, grinning at her daughter.

Maize snorts. "I'm a little snobby when it comes to desserts that aren't made from scratch."

"A *little*?" John scoffs and holds his arms as wide as they'll go.

It makes me laugh. John watches the way Maize and I interact, and eventually, something snaps in him. It's almost as if he can see how much I love her. After we finish eating, I get up and help Maize with the dishes. Once the kitchen is clean, we go to the living room and tell her parents good night.

John stands up and gives me a firm handshake. "Take care of my daughter."

"Yes, sir. I won't let you down," I say, meeting his eyes, and we hold a silent conversation. I have his permission to date Maize, and it's enough.

"I'll be home later," Maize says, tugging at my shirt and pulling me away.

"Thanks for dinner. It was great," I say to Mila. "Good night, y'all."

"We'll do it again sometime soon," she tells me as Maize leads me to the door.

Once we're outside, I can breathe again. Maize leads me to the truck, and I pin her against the cool metal and kiss her. "So your dad didn't kill me."

"*Yet,*" she says with a snicker before returning her mouth to mine.

CHAPTER TWENTY-ONE

Maize

It's been two weeks since my parents learned that Gavin and I were officially dating. Dad took it as expected, but he quickly accepted it. When Gavin promised he wouldn't break my heart, I nearly melted on the floor like a popsicle in the middle of summer. Not having to hide my feelings has been such a relief. We've even gone on a few dates in town and hung out at the bar together. The two of us are inseparable.

News spread around town like wildfire, and I was actually happy about it. I want everyone to know he's *mine*.

Today, we're driving to Houston so I can meet his parents. It's a five-hour road trip, which gives me way too much time to think. I kinda understand why Gavin was so damn nervous to be introduced as my boyfriend to my folks, but at least he wasn't a stranger to them. This is on a different level. Gavin's promised he's said nothing but amazing things about me.

It's scary how fast I'm falling for him, and I don't ever want this to end.

Gavin's my past, present, and my future, and it's a big deal to meet his parents. He hasn't dated seriously in over a decade, so to say I'm feeling anxious is an understatement.

"What're you thinking about over there?" He grabs my hand and kisses my knuckles as he turns on the cruise control.

"What if your mom and dad don't like me? What if I'm nothing but a big disappointment or something?"

Gavin lets out a howl of a laugh. "Are you kidding me? They already love you and are ecstatic to meet you. My mom can't wait and even called me this morning to make sure we were still coming and I wasn't going to chicken out. They're down to earth and will be just as supportive as your parents are." He glances over at me. "Well, now that your dad is on board with the idea of us," he adds.

"That makes me feel a tad better. And hey, Dad just needed to warm up to the idea. He knows he can control me as much as he can control Kenzie," I tell him, and we both laugh, knowing Kenzie does whatever the hell she wants and doesn't care who knows.

"Okay, so I need to ask a million questions, and I have about four hours to do it," I say, wanting to ask everything I can before we arrive.

His smile is contagious. "Ask me anything you want."

I let out a breath. "Tell me about your parents' relationship."

"That's not a question," he says, chuckling. "But they were high school sweethearts. Mom barrel raced growing up, and Dad rode bulls too. He never went pro like I did because of an injury. They got married before they both turned twenty-one and had me soon after."

"Aw, that sounds sweet. Do you have any brothers and sisters?" Even though I know so much about him, I realize I still have a lot to learn.

He shakes his head. "Not that I know of. It's a good thing, though, because your family is so goddamn huge."

"This is very true," I admit. "There are *a lot* of Bishops."

Gavin grins. "And we're gonna add some more to that list."

I shake my head. "One day."

We blow through San Antonio without getting stuck in traffic, and the rest of the way to Houston goes by way too quickly. When we take the loop away from the city, I'm amazed at how quickly it transforms into open pastures. It's not Eldorado, but I see barns and horses and even some cows grazing in the distance.

Those five hours passed in a snap. Gavin makes another turn, and we drive down a long rock road until the two-story home with white shutters comes into view. We park, and I suck in air.

Gavin's palm rests on my thigh, and he squeezes. "They already love you. Trust me."

I smile. "Okay, let's do this then."

Gavin comes around and opens my door, and he holds out his arm for me to take. Having him this close is comforting in every sense, but as we climb the steps leading to the front door, I grow more nervous. He rings the bell, and his mama swings open the door. Before saying a word, she pulls me into a big hug and squeezes me. "It's so nice to meet you, Maize. Sorry, we're huggers 'round here. I'm Rose, but you can call me Mom."

I laugh and hold her for a second. "I'm a hugger too. Nice to meet you, finally."

"Come on in now. Y'all must be tired from that drive. Your daddy will be back any minute. He's out feedin' the horses," she explains, going to the stove and stirring something. Instantly, my mouth begins to water.

"Whatcha cookin'?" I ask, taking a few steps forward.

"Seafood gumbo," she tells me.

"Oh, I love shrimp!" I admit.

"Don't be shy. Come see. Gavin told me you were a highly regarded, award-winning chef," she adds.

This makes me laugh. "He's just being kind."

Gavin's mouth falls open. "No, I'm not. She won first place at the rodeo's barbecue contest."

His mom turns and looks at me. "Honey, that's not easy to do. Some people travel around the state and enter those competitions just for the prize money. Now, I want barbecue."

A blush hits my cheeks. "Thank you. I didn't think I'd win because of that, but the brisket spoke for itself. Gavin gave me the confidence I needed to continue because I was hesitant about entering."

With a quick turn of her head, she glances over at him leaning against the counter. "That's my boy. He's good at encouraging people to follow their dreams. Now, come and have a taste of this homemade roux."

Grabbing a spoon from the drawer, she dips it inside the giant stockpot and hands it over. I blow on it for a second, then sip it up. My mouth explodes with the different spices. With wide eyes, I can't seem to speak fast enough. "That's the best I've ever had."

"Really? It's a family recipe, top secret. Once you and Gavin get married, I'll have to share it with you."

Gavin moves forward. "Don't say the m-word, Mom. Kinda freaks her out."

"Hardy har har. It does not. Okay, well maybe a little," I admit. "But when you know you've found the one, why does it matter?"

"Is Maize Bishop turning a new leaf?" he asks, just as the back door opens and shuts.

Moments later, Gavin's dad waltzes in wearing a grin. Gavin's the spitting image of his father, and if he ages just as well, I'm in for a treat. He's tall and handsome with slivers of gray in his hair. "Oh, you must be Maize, the woman my son has fallen head over heels with," he announces, walking forward and hugging me.

"I already warned her about us being huggers," Rose tells him with a chuckle.

"I'm Wyatt. Welcome to the family," he says with a huge grin.

"Thank you!"

When his parents aren't looking, Gavin gives me a thumbs-up.

His dad grabs a cup of ice water and chugs it. "Horses are fed, and I'm starving. Smells so good." When it's empty, he refills it before sitting at the table.

Gavin pulls bowls from the cabinet and sets them next to the stove.

Feeling out of place, I turn and ask, "Is there something I can help with?"

He gives me a wink. "Nope. You're the guest of honor. Let someone else cook for you for once."

"Maize, do you want rice?" his mom asks.

"Sure. I'm not picky," I say.

"Only with your men," Gavin adds.

She carries two bowls, and Gavin grabs the others.

After his dad says grace, I gobble up the gumbo so fast it seems like I inhaled it.

"Help yourself! Have seconds and thirds. Don't be shy around here," Wyatt says.

"This is true," he tells me.

"So tell us a little about you, Maize. How'd you and Gavin meet?" his mom asks.

I swallow down the big bite I'd just taken, and thankfully, Gavin steps in. "We met before my interview at the ranch. Her family owns it."

"Oh, that's right. You know me, I forget so much these days," she admits.

"I work in the family bed and breakfast and plan all the meals each week. I'm responsible for making sure everyone is fed and full. Not any of that processed stuff either. We serve homemade everything and lots of comfort food. I have a few employees to help me because the workers will eat ya out of house and home."

"Bed and breakfast? Sounds like a place I'd like to visit." She grins.

"You should. Could get you the family discount." I laugh and give her a wink.

Rose claps her hands together. "Don't tempt me with a good time," she warns with a big smile. "You might spoil me so much I'll move in permanently."

"The more, the merrier," I offer, finishing my second bowl of gumbo. "I grew up on the ranch and am in love with the scenery and how peaceful it is. Small-town living is the best."

"It really is," Gavin agrees. "I don't think I ever want to leave."

"Well, if you won't move back home, then we might sell the house and come up there, especially if you have kids." She looks directly at Gavin, but I don't think she's joking.

My face heats. "My parents gave us the kids and marriage talk too," I explain. "It seems everyone's ready for that."

Gavin gives a chuckle and a head nod.

Once we're finished eating dinner, Gavin and I volunteer to clean up while his parents go to the living room to catch the evening news. We stand next to each other as he scrubs and I rinse the dishes.

"Told you they'd adore you." He softly bumps his hip against mine.

"Your parents are so nice. Seriously." I speak loud enough for only him to hear.

He bends down and kisses my forehead. "That makes me so happy. You have no idea."

After we finish, he takes me on a tour of the house. On the mantel sits framed pictures of him riding bucking broncos and bulls. When he shows me his childhood bedroom, I nearly gasp at all the trophies, medals, and winning belt buckles decorating the room.

"Welcome to my shrine," he says, holding out his hand.

I step inside. "Gavin. This is...*amazing*."

"I guess," he mumbles, entering behind me.

I feel like I'm walking into a time capsule full of his past memories. Moving around the room, I take it all in. "I didn't realize you won this much because you've acted like you weren't a big deal. Gavin, I'm so impressed." I wrap my arms around his waist and pull him close. "I didn't realize I was dating a cowboy celebrity of sorts."

He shakes his head. "I'm not."

"But you are. Look at this. Wow. No wonder people try to reach out to you all the time for training and stuff." I stand on my tiptoes and slide my mouth against his. We get lost in the kiss, in the moment, and the only thing that pulls us away is the sound of footsteps down the hallway. Not wanting to make it awkward, I create some space between us. A knock rings on the door, and it cracks open. She peeks her head inside.

"I made pudding parfaits if you'd like some dessert," she tells us.

"Thanks, Mom. We'll be right down," he says sweetly. She slowly closes the door, and after a second, Gavin pops a brow at me and brings me back to him.

"Right now, you're the only thing I want for dessert," he hums in my ear.

"If we weren't at your parents' house, I'd consider it," I admit. "But we better go downstairs before they get suspicious."

"This is true." He grabs my hand and leads me to the kitchen, where we fill ourselves full of pudding and cake. It's so good that I'm contemplating adding it to the B&B menu when I get home. Gavin and I watch TV with his parents until we nearly fall asleep. Both of us keep yawning, and eventually, we say good night, then he leads me upstairs. We fall asleep in his bedroom surrounded by all his accomplishments. To say I'm proud is an understatement.

The next morning, we wake up to a breakfast that's as big as the ones I serve at the B&B. We chat about the weather and Eldorado, and everything under the sun. When we're done eating, Gavin leads me outside to the barn.

"Want to go for a ride?" he asks.

A smile fills my face, and I nod. "Absolutely. I would love that."

"Then let's catch some horses." He grabs two lead ropes from the tack room, and I follow him out to the pasture where at least five quarter horses are grazing.

"Choose whichever one you want. They're all as tame as can be," he explains.

I walk with the rope behind my back and my hand out, the same way Kenzie and I did as kids with the trail riding horses. It works like a charm, and I snap the lead rope on the halter, then turn to Gavin.

"Meet you at the barn," I tell him with a hop to my step.

By the time he walks inside, I've already saddled up, adjusted my stirrups, and am waiting for him.

"Look at you! Hot as fuck!" he exclaims.

I chuckle. "I thought for a second I was gettin' rusty 'cause I haven't ridden in a while, but putting on a saddle is something you never forget. It's like riding a bike. By the way, this is a nice one."

"It was a prize saddle," he explains, then points at the branding and the date burned into it.

"You never seem to stop surprising me." I meet his eyes, wishing he could see what I see.

After Gavin's ready, he gets in position, and we head down a trail that looks well-traveled. As we ride into the path that goes through the forest, I can't help but grin the entire time. Beams of sunshine leak through the tree limbs as I follow him. Thankfully, a cold front came in over the weekend, so the weather is perfect. Eventually, we come to a clearing, and I see a giant pond with a canoe tied to a small floating dock. This is not what I expected.

We hop off our horses and tie them to a few posts. Gavin takes my hand, and we walk toward the water. He sits, takes off his boots, and rolls up his pants before sticking his toes in the water. I follow his lead and lean my head against his shoulder as we look out at the reflection of the tall pines on the water.

"Mom really loves you," he says, smiling. "And I do too. I love you so damn much, Maize."

"I love you too, Gavin. You're everything to me," I admit.

He turns and places his rough palm on my cheek, then dips down and memorizes my lips with his. Our tongues twist together, and by the time we pull apart, I'm nearly gasping for air.

"Thanks for joining me this weekend. I know it was a big step," he says, running his toes across the water.

"We should visit more often. I can tell how much your parents miss and love you." I steal another kiss.

"You mean it? You'll make the drive with me again?"

"Yeah, I'd love that. Your parents have already adopted me and made me a member of the family."

He kisses my forehead. "Thank you."

After twenty minutes of enjoying the view, we put our shoes and socks back on. He stands and offers his hand. I take it, and the moment I meet his eyes, there's not a doubt in my mind that he's the man I'm supposed to spend my forever with.

"One day, Maize, I'm gonna make you my wife."

I bite my bottom lip and smile. "That a promise, Cowboy?"

"You better believe it, baby. And I'll spend the rest of my life making you happy."

"Lookin' forward to it," I admit. He takes my hand, and we go back to the horses.

CHAPTER TWENTY-TWO

Gavin

It's been four months since Maize and I have been official. Today's Maize's birthday, and it's the first time I'll get to celebrate it with her, which means I'm going all out.

Though she told me not to make it a big deal since she's "only turning twenty-six," I absolutely am. There might be ten years between us, but age is only a number. Without a doubt, I know my future involves her, and tonight, she's going to know that.

I was able to get off work early so I can get everything ready at my place. She's always cooking for me and everyone else, so I'm returning the favor and plan to make her something amazing. While I'm no gourmet chef, I can follow a recipe.

Since she loves food so much and has a thousand favorite dishes, I had to get creative. Seafood isn't served regularly at the B&B, so I start there. She mentioned she loved shrimp when we visited my parents, so I found something I think she'll love. Knowing her love for spicy foods, I've decided to make Cajun seafood pasta with homemade garlic toast. It'll take me a good hour to cook the scallops and shrimp, so I hurry and take a shower, then get dressed beforehand. I want her to eat as soon as she gets here.

GAVIN

Dinner's almost ready! It smells so good...can't wait to see you.

Though she slept over last night, and I saw her this morning at breakfast, I always miss her and want to be with her all day. It's a sickness really—one I don't want a cure for. With our busy work schedules, there's never enough time.

MAIZE

On the way! Had to do laundry and pack a bag since you never let me sleep at home anymore ;)

I smile at her smart mouth, and hell, she's right. I'm downright addicted to her body being next to mine and getting to kiss her before we start our days.

GAVIN

See you soon, baby.

Ten minutes later, I hear the rumble of her truck and rush to the door. I open it and go down the steps to meet her before she gets out.

"Allow me," I say, opening her door.

She takes my hand. "Ooh, well thank you. What a gentleman."

"Only the best for my lady." I tilt my hat and press a kiss to her soft lips.

She giggles, then I grab her duffel. Taking her hand, I lead her into the house and set down her bag.

"Wow, you weren't wrong. It smells amazing in here." She lifts her nose and inhales. "Seafood for sure."

Reaching the oven, I take out the skillet, and her eyes widen.

"You made this?"

"Don't sound so surprised." I scoff. "I can cook. You just never let me." After setting the pasta on the stovetop, I remove the garlic bread.

"If it tastes as good as it smells, I'll gladly put you in charge of the kitchen from now on." She grins, eyeing everything.

"Not sure I'd go that far. This took a lot of planning. I honestly don't know how you make three meals a day for so many people."

"Lots of practice and prepping ahead of time," she responds effortlessly. "Also helps that I have help."

"Now, I didn't make dessert because I'm only so capable in the kitchen, but I did get Grandma Bishop to bake a cake for you."

"You didn't!" She gasps when I uncover it. "My favorite! German chocolate cake with chocolate mousse."

I chuckle at how adorably excited she is. "Of course."

She wraps her arms around my neck and pulls me down for a kiss. "That was really thoughtful. I haven't had that in years. Thank you."

"Anything for my love." Lowering my hands to her ass, I squeeze with a smirk. "You look beautiful, birthday girl. I love it when you wear easy-access dresses for me."

Maize snorts. "Let's see how good this meal is first before you get any ideas."

The table is set, and I pull out a chair for her to sit so I can serve her. Once our plates and wineglasses are full, we dive in, and I swear she's seconds away from an orgasm when she takes her first bite.

"Holy God, this is incredible," she moans around a forkful. Before she even swallows, she takes another bite, inhaling it. "I'm gonna need this recipe. My parents would lose their minds over this."

I don't admit that I've already spoken to her parents and told them what I was cooking. They're anxiously waiting to hear all about how tonight goes.

"Glad it turned out good," I agree. "Don't forget the garlic bread. I made that baby from scratch."

She grins, putting a piece in her mouth. "Mmm...so good."

"Did you have a good shift?" I ask when we're almost finished eating. Though we text nonstop, I always like hearing her talk about her day.

"Yeah, I did. My dad surprised me with flowers and balloons, as usual. My mom wrote me the sweetest card that made both of us cry. Kenzie bought me something that I'm currently wearing under this dress..." She waggles her brows. "And a few of the guests sang me 'Happy Birthday.'"

"Wow, sounds awesome."

"And now I'm ending it on a high note and get to be with the man I love." She gives me a sweet grin, and I can't stop the burst of happiness that radiates through me.

After we finish eating, I take the opportunity to do what I've been anxious about for the past month.

"What would you think about spending *every* birthday night with me?"

"What do you mean?" She tilts her head in confusion.

"And all *my* birthdays too," I add.

"Well, of course." She licks her lips.

"Forever?" I ask.

She furrows her brows in confusion. Deciding it's now or never, I stand and pull the velvet box from my pocket, then kneel in front of her.

"Wh-what are you doing?" She turns her body to face me.

"I have a special gift for you—well, two actually—but the most important one is this." I open the box so she can see the diamond I picked out for her.

"Oh my God…" she whispers barely over a breath as her eyes zero in on it.

"I'm not looking for a girlfriend, Maize. I don't need to date you any longer to know you're the one for me. I want to fall asleep with you every night and wake up to you every morning. I'm ready to settle down and start a life with the woman I'm madly in love with. I want forever with you, baby. Now the question is if you're ready for that too."

Maize licks her lips, her eyes catching mine for a split second before she looks back down at the ring.

"I love you so much, Maize. Will you marry me?"

Her hands fly to her mouth as tears spill from her eyes. She nods furiously. "Yes! Yes, I will marry you."

Her arms quickly swing around me, and she buries her face in my neck. I capture her to my chest and squeeze her tightly as my emotions start to boil over.

"I love you," she tells me, cupping my face, then kissing me. "I can't believe you just proposed!" She's half-laughing, half-crying, which causes me to chuckle.

"I have something else for you, sweetheart." I dig into my other pocket and pull it out. "This key is hypothetical since you already have a key to my place, but it's a promise."

She takes it from me and squints. "A promise for what?"

"A promise to build us a house with your dream kitchen so you have all the counter space and top-of-the-line appliances you want. But really, it's a token that I'll provide for you and our family, as well as support any goal you have in life. I know you want to stay close to your family and work, and your dad's already helped me scope the land for us to build on."

Tears fall down her cheeks as she looks at me with awe. "I honestly can't believe this is happening. It seems too good to be true."

I brush the pad of my thumb under her eye. "I know what I want, Maize. And that's you. Since the moment we met, you're all I've thought about. I've told myself that if I had the chance to be yours, I'd do anything in my power to make you happy."

"I love you with all my heart, Gavin. *You* make me happy." She leans into my palm, and I kiss her once more.

"Good." I grin. "Wanna put on the ring?"

Her eyes light up as if she forgot about it. "Yes! Oh my God, it's so beautiful."

I slide it onto her left ring finger, and our emotions get the best of us.

"I hate to ask, but…" She lingers on her words for a beat until our eyes connect. "You didn't happen to ask my father, did you? I know it's kinda lame in this age, but my family is—"

"Traditional, I know," I interject. "And yes, of course I did. I'm sure your mother's pacing the living room waiting for your call."

Maize bursts out laughing and grabs her phone. "You're probably right. Let's quickly FaceTime them so we can dive into that cake!"

Seeing Maize this happy is all I've ever wanted, and I'm not sure I could ever come down from this high. I knew it was risky to propose only months into us dating, but I've loved her much longer than that. I don't want to waste any more time. When I spoke with her parents, they were shockingly supportive. Mila cried and John gave me a bear hug, which was hilarious considering I tower over him. But I'm damn glad I'll be a part of the Bishop family now, even more so that Maize will be my wife.

"Alright, you crazy kids, you have a great rest of your night," Mila says with a knowing grin.

John takes the phone and looks directly at me. "Remember what we talked about, son?"

"Of course, sir."

He nods. "Good. Go have fun celebrating now. I have Sandra and Jane lined up in the kitchen tomorrow."

"Thank you. I love you guys," Maize tells them before hanging up. "Wow, we get to sleep in tomorrow? When's the last time that's ever happened?" she teases.

"Oh, don't be getting any ideas, future Mrs. Fox…" I pull her into my arms. "There'll be minimal sleeping happening tonight."

"Hmm…Mrs. Fox," she tries it out. "Or you could take my last name and be Gavin Bishop." She quirks a brow. "Or we could hyphenate?"

"Not to sound biblical, but my wife is taking my name. If you wanna hyphenate, that's fine, but Maize Fox sounds sexy." I squeeze her harder.

"Okay, Mr. Arrogant." She rolls her eyes but laughs. "Bishop-Fox would be a mouthful."

"It would. Plus…" I lower my lips to her ear. "I can think of other things to fill that mouth of yours."

As soon as the words leave my mouth, Maize's lips crash against mine. "Naked now, cake later."

"Fuck yes," I growl, scooping her into my arms and carrying her to my room.

"In my bed, tangled in my sheets, naked underneath me…" I whisper against her mouth.

"Forever," she says in return.

We rush to strip off our clothes and jump under the covers. My cock is so hard, but I need to taste her first. I slide between her thighs as they wrap around my shoulders, giving me full access to her sweet pussy. She fists her fingers in my hair, which I love, and I suck her throbbing clit between my lips.

"Yes, right there," she hums, tilting up her hips.

The best part about being in love with someone is how much better the sex is. When those feelings started to surface with Maize, I knew what we shared was special. I didn't want to acknowledge the void I felt before I retired, but it started to fill again when Maize entered my life. She's the woman I'm meant to be with.

I make love to my fiancée all night long. From the bed to the shower to the kitchen, and when we finally make it back to bed again, we pass out in each other's arms. Everything's perfect, and if someone had told me a year ago that I would be engaged to Maize, I wouldn't have believed it.

Goes to show what can happen when you don't give up and keep fighting for the one you love. It's even sweeter when the feelings are mutual, and her stubborn ass finally admits she wants to wrangle you in.

But I wouldn't have it any other way.

Gavin

ONE YEAR LATER

"Did you turn on the heat?" Maize calls from the kitchen as I take care of our laundry in the living room.

"No," I answer with a chuckle.

I'm folding clothes while watching the football game, but Maize's hot flashes have me cracking up, especially in the middle of November.

"God. Why's it so hot in here?" She comes into view, and I nearly burst out laughing when I see she's taken off her pants and shirt.

Meanwhile, I'm in joggers and a sweatshirt since she's turned on the air conditioner.

"I think it's you, sweetheart," I tease, standing to meet her. My palm automatically lands on her belly, and I'm overcome with pride. "You're not only eating for three, but your hormones are raging." I smile, thinking about the two babies inside he̶ ̶ ̶hat I can't wait to meet.

She pouts with a groan, and I pluck her bottom lip from between her teeth. "I'll turn down the thermostat, baby. Go sit, and I'll grab the fan, too."

"You're amazing." She sighs. "I feel like a freaking oven."

"It'll pass," I reassure her. It typically does anyway. "I'll grab you a sweet tea, too." Pressing my lips to her forehead, I grab the fan from our bedroom, then go to the kitchen for her drink. Lately, she's been getting hot flashes all the time and even in the middle of the night. To combat it, Maize has started sleeping with the fan blasted on her face, nearly naked, while I'm wrapped in a blanket.

Once I'm back in the living room, I make sure she's comfortable before I sit next to her. One hand rests on her bump as she sucks down her tea. Without even trying, Maize is the most stunning woman I've ever laid eyes on. Making her my wife was the best day of my life, tied with the day we found out she was pregnant with twins.

We hadn't expected it to happen so fast, but I was ready since I'm not getting any younger. Though if you ask Maize, she'd argue that her biological clock is ticking since she's closer to turning thirty. Undoubtedly, she was ready to get knocked up as soon as humanly possible. Apparently, the Bishop legacy of having multiples lives on.

My parents were undoubtedly thrilled when we told them the news. They visit at least once a month but I have a feeling they'll be coming a lot more or even moving here after the twins are born.

I go back to our clothes. We're finally having our housewarming party now that everything's unpacked. We moved in right before the wedding five months ago, but it wasn't completely finished. I helped the crew between shifts, and since I didn't want Maize to have to juggle unpacking and working, I took care of it all.

Once we learned we were having girls, we started decorating the nursery. Now that it's painted, it's time for all the furniture to be built and baby gear stored. I'd be lying if I said I wasn't nervous about taking care of two infants at once, but Mila's already offered to help as well as Grandma Bishop. They're over the moon excited, and her mom can't wait to be a grandma.

John keeps going back and forth about what he wants the girls to call him, and he's excited about our growing family. Kenzie was her typical overdramatic self and screamed with joy.

"You excited for this weekend, babe?" I ask, trying to match socks.

"Yes, I am," she says with a gleeful smile. "I can't wait to show off my hot house-building husband."

I scoff. "I *helped*, but I'm definitely not taking all the credit. The crew did the hard shit. I basically pointed and made sure nothing got messed up."

"That's pretty sexy in my book." She waggles her brows while lowering her eyes down my chest.

I chuckle, shaking my head. Another symptom of pregnancy is raging hormones that make her want sex all the time. Not that I'm complaining, but we have a party happening in three days. We've invited the whole damn town, it seems, but I don't mind. It's a potluck, so Maize isn't stuck preparing food for a crowd since her catering business is booming. Kenzie helps on the side, but Maize does all the cooking. Her doctor has warned her to take it easy with the stress of extra work since it's likely she'll go into preterm labor.

Moments later, my phone vibrates with a text, and I see it's Connor.

CONNOR

Would you mind if I brought someone with me to your party this weekend?

I read the message to Maize, and her smile drops. "He's bringing a *date*?"

I'm not sure what's happened between him and Elle, but their work relationship hasn't been the best as far as I've heard.

"I guess." I shrug.

GAVIN

No problem. The more, the merrier.

"I hope you told him absolutely not!" she pouts.

I snort. "Why not? Elle isn't dating him."

"Well, she could be if he wasn't such a jerk. And now she's gonna have to see him with another woman. It's a dick move."

I'm not sure how to reply and don't wish to get in the middle of whatever's going on, so I stay quiet.

"Whatever. I'm gonna tell her to bring someone then. Ha! See how Dr. Dickhead likes that."

I narrow my eyes in confusion. "Thought you called him VetDreamy?"

523

She scowls. "Not anymore."

That doesn't sound good, but I also don't ask. Connor and I see each other at least once a week at the ranch, and if there's drama, I stay out of it.

"There," she says as she sets down her phone. "Now it won't be awkward, and she won't be alone when he's hanging on some other woman."

After the clothes are done, I sit back and pull Maize into my chest. "Any kicks today?"

"I feel a little fluttering on my right side," she tells me, and I move my hand around.

"You're gonna be the hottest pregnant mama-to-be when you're ready to pop. I can't wait." I smirk.

"Ugh, shut up. I'm fat and only gonna get fatter."

"You're growing two babies," I remind her. "I can't wait for a houseful of girls." Smiling, I press a kiss to her cheek. Due to Maize being high-risk with twins, they took a bunch of bloodwork, and we found out the genders early on. "Which means we're gonna have to try for a boy next."

She relaxes against me and laughs. "I thought of what I want their names to be," she says, then looks up at me. "Madison Bailey and Mila Rose. Bailey after my biological mother. Mila after the woman who raised me."

"And Rose after my mother?" I ask, honored.

"Yes, and it's Grandma Bishop's first name too." She beams. "I thought it was a perfect tribute to the amazing women in our life."

My heart beats with pride and excitement. "I love them. It's a great idea, sweetheart. Mila's gonna love that you named one of the babies after her."

"I wanna surprise her, though. Announce it after the babies are born."

"She's gonna cry." I chuckle, and Maize does too.

"Oh, she definitely will."

Maize

I can't wait to see everyone today. Though I frequently see my family, I'm usually too busy working to visit for more than five minutes. Plus, I'll get to spend more time with my cousins and sister without being interrupted by guests. Not that I mind, but a break is definitely nice.

Now that I'm pregnant with twins, I need to slow down, which is hard when I'm trying to keep up with my catering business too. I book parties for up to fifty people a couple of times a month, and it's rewarding for me. I hope I can continue after the twins are born, but I'll hire someone if not.

One of the best things about growing up with a ton of cousins is that our kids will get to grow up together just like we did. My grandparents are in their late seventies and want to be more hands-off with the business side of things. They've already discussed passing the operations entirely over to my dad and uncles, which is a significant milestone. Bishops have run the ranch for generations, and the legacy will continue.

Although the idea of getting pregnant again after twins seems crazy, I do want to try for a boy. My nephew Zach is two, and he'll have a little brother soon since Riley and Zoey are expecting baby Zealand in just two months. There are Bishop boy cousins for him to grow up with, plus I know Gavin would love to teach our kids about bull riding and training horses. Mutton bustin' is already on the list for the girls when they're old enough. I'd be willing to give Gavin a houseful, but for now, I'm focusing on these two precious babies inside me and soaking up every minute I get to carry them.

"My girls," Gavin says, wrapping his big hands around my belly and grinning into my neck. "You're beautiful." He looks at my reflection in the mirror, and I smile in return.

"This bump is cute now, but in a couple of months, I'll be surprised if I can see my feet."

"You'll be waddling all over the B&B like a cute penguin," he mocks.

"Thanks," I deadpan, adjusting my dress so it covers my boobs that have doubled in size.

"Your mom's here. Kenzie too."

"Oh yay! Tell them I'll be right down." I turn around and kiss his lips. "Assuming it doesn't take me an hour to climb down the stairs."

"I could carry you. You're on your feet too much as it is, no wonder they're swelling."

"My feet are swelling?" I squeal in panic, then look down at them. "Do I have chubby ankles already?"

"Uh…" Gavin removes his hat and brushes a hand through his hair, a tell that he's about to bullshit his way outta this question. "I think I hear more people at the door. Meet ya down there, sweetheart." He quickly kisses my cheek before leaving.

He's lucky I love him too damn much to scold him. I didn't think it was possible to love him more than I did the day we got married, but when I found out we were pregnant, I fell for him even deeper.

By the time I enter the living room, it's filled with Bishops and friends of the family. I greet people and swipe Rory out of Rowan's arms. He's seven months now, and his little personality reminds me so much of Diesel.

"Hey buddy." I blow raspberries on his cheek, and he giggles. Rory is a perfect blend of his parents with adorable little dimples. Rowan and Diesel got married two months ago, and I hope they'll try for baby number two soon. Grandma Bishop hasn't stopped reminding them.

"Is Elle here?" Rowan asks.

I look around. "I don't see her yet, but…" My eyes widen when they land on Dr. Wallen, her boss. "Oh my God," I mutter quietly, and Rowan's gaze follows mine.

"I thought you said he was bringing a date?" Rowan whispers, taking Rory from my arms when he starts to fuss.

"I-I assumed he was…" I have to pick up my jaw from the floor at the little girl's hand he's holding. "He asked to bring someone."

"Elle's gonna be *so* mad at you." Rowan chuckles.

Kenzie comes over to us, and we fill her in. "Wow." She eyes Connor up and down. "He's somehow hotter now."

"Kenzie, ew. He's way too old for you anyway." I scoff.

"Really? You gonna talk to me about age?"

I roll my eyes. "Shut up. I better text Elle and warn her."

"Too late," Kenzie mutters, staring at the front door.

"Shit."

Elle walks in with a man I've never seen before, and he's dressed in black slacks and a sleek black button-up shirt. He's tall, with broad shoulders, and fit. He looks like a guy her mom would set her up with. Perhaps he's a doctor from the hospital Aunt Emily works at, but nevertheless, things are about to get awkward.

"Maize..." Gavin comes to my side and brushes my elbow.

"I saw," I say before he can speak. "Is that his...daughter?"

"Yeah, Olivia. She's six. He shares custody with his ex-wife," he informs me.

Well, *fuck.*

Elle spots us and walks over with a bright, friendly smile. "Hey, guys." We exchange a hug.

"Hey, who's your date?" I ask.

"This is Stephen. He's a doctor and works with my mom."

Nailed it.

"Hi, Stephen, nice to meet you." I shake his hand. "I'm Maize, Elle's cousin."

"A pleasure to meet y'all."

He shakes Kenzie's, then Rowan's, and Gavin's hand next.

"You have a lovely home. Elizabeth's informed me it was recently built."

Elizabeth? I nearly cringe at the way he uses her full name, considering none of us do.

"Yes, well, it's been a few months, but it took some time to finish. Plus, the Bishops love any reason for a party." I chuckle because it's true.

I turn to Elle, and my eyes widen. "Can I talk to you for a quick sec?"

"Uh—sure." Just as we're about to walk off, Connor comes over with a pointed glare as he holds his daughter's hand.

Elle's eyes bug out of her head as she stares at Dr. Wallen and the little girl next to him.

"Hey, Connor," I greet sweetly. "I heard you brought a little guest with you." Smiling, I lean down and take her hand. "I'm Maize. Thanks for coming to our party."

"Hello, ma'am. I'm Olivia."

"Oh my gosh, what a sweetheart," Rowan coos.

"How did no one know you had a child?" Kenzie blurts out.

"Well, you never asked." He shrugs. "Her mother lives in New Mexico, and we share custody. She visits over the summer and holidays. I picked her up early for our Thanksgiving celebration."

That explains why he asked at the last minute.

"She looks a lot like you," Elle says, breaking the awkward tension. "Hi, Olivia. I'm Elle. I work with your daddy."

Olivia shakes her hand with a cute smile. "Nice to meet you."

"Connor," Stephen says curtly.

Dr. Wallen stands up straighter with furrowed brows. "Dr. Burk."

"You two know each other?" I ask, waving a finger back and forth between them. I shouldn't be that surprised, considering we live in a small town, and everyone knows everyone.

"We were friends in high school," Stephen explains.

"Yeah, well…that was ages ago." Connor takes Olivia's hand. "Anyway, I'm gonna get a couple of snacks for her. It was nice seeing y'all."

Before anyone can say another word, Connor walks away and heads toward the kitchen.

Rowan, Kenzie, and I exchange a look. "I'm gonna go say hi to Grandma and make sure she gets something to eat."

An hour later, people are scattered throughout the house having a good time. Some are outside on the deck and admiring the views of the ranch.

"Hey," Gavin whispers in my ear behind me as I stare out at the orange and blue sky. "You wanna sneak into the guest room?"

Chuckling, I glance at him over my shoulder. "Are you crazy? We have a house full of guests."

"So? You used to like sneakin' around with me." He winks.

That causes me to laugh hard. "That's true."

I grab his arm and lead him down the hallway into the room. Once the door is locked, he latches his mouth to mine, and our tongues feverishly fight for control.

"Think you can stay quiet, baby?" he asks in a growl.

"If you cover my mouth." I grin.

Gavin lifts my dress and moves my panties to the side, then plunges a finger into my wet pussy. I'm already aching for him, desperately needing his cock to fill me.

He wraps his hand around my head and slides his tongue between my lips as he finger fucks me hard and fast, building the orgasm until I fall over the edge. I moan out his name, and he quickly covers my mouth with his.

Without wasting another second, he undoes his jeans and boxers, and when his cock comes into view, I immediately wrap my hand around him.

"Mmm…baby." His head falls back on his shoulders. "As much as I love that, we need to make this quick."

He lifts me until my legs wrap around his waist, and his cock presses between my thighs. The tip rubs against my clit before gliding down and entering me.

With a throaty groan, I take in all of him, and we rock together in rhythm.

"You make me so damn happy," he mutters in my ear. "Happier than I ever thought I deserved."

I'm on the verge of tears as he fucks me against the wall. "You make me happier than I ever thought was possible," I tell him.

"I'll spend the rest of my life making sure you and our girls are always happy. No matter what, sweetheart."

"I know you will."

I have no doubt Gavin will do anything to give us everything we could ever want and need.

He captures my lips once more, and soon, we're falling over the edge, moaning out our release as quietly as possible.

"Fuck, baby mama. That was hot." He smacks my ass after I adjust my dress.

I snort and shake my head.

"You think anyone noticed we were gone?" I ask, smoothing down my hair as he zips up his jeans.

"Nah. I think everyone's distracted as hell from seeing Connor with his daughter, Olivia. Especially Elle and Stephen."

I cringe, feeling awful that I'm the one who told Elle to bring someone. "Elle's gonna murder me. I still can't believe no one knew he had a kid."

"Connor's a private guy." Gavin shrugs, pulling me into his arms once he's dressed.

"As if things weren't tense enough between Elle and Connor, it's about to get a lot more awkward," I say.

"Considering that Stephen guy seems like the type Evan and Emily would approve of, I imagine he could be here to stay."

"You think so?"

"And if I'm being honest, Stephen seems more of her type than Connor."

"I wonder why he's always so short-tempered and rude to her. If he truly didn't care for her personality or the way she does things, why would he have hired her in the first place? Unless..."

"You think he likes her?" he asks.

"He could purposely be pushing her away like I did you when I didn't want to admit my feelings. I've had this theory before, but I think it's safe to say he just might be doing the same."

"Maybe." Gavin shrugs, pressing a sweet kiss to the tip of my nose. "We should go back out there."

I nod in agreement.

"Well, either way, when they go back to work on Monday, it's gonna be hella interesting." I cackle. "And I can't wait to hear all about it."

Continue reading for Grayson & Mackenzie's story in *Winning the Cowboy*

Winning the Cowboy
GRAYSON & MACKENZIE

Working on the ranch and settling down is all Grayson's ever wanted in life. When he meets the woman who could make that a reality, he learns she hates him with every fiber of her being.

He knows she's being unreasonable since their bickering is the hottest foreplay he's ever had.

Mackenzie Bishop's an elementary school teacher and can tolerate a lot, until it comes to Grayson. He may act like he doesn't remember what he did, but Kenzie will never forget. Not when the memory of that night still lingers in her mind years later.

She denies her attraction, but she can't hide it forever, especially when there's no escaping him.

Although she refuses to give him the time of day, they form a truce and everything changes—just not in the way he expected.

'Cause it's always one step forward and three steps back
I'm the love of your life until I make you mad
It's always one step forward and three steps back
Do you love me, want me, hate me?
Boy, I don't understand

"1 step forward, 3 steps back"
-Olivia Rodrigo

Grayson

"Grayson, I'm sorry. I really thought he was yours," Bella tells me, but there's zero remorse in her voice.

"Or you figured since Grant and I are brothers, he'd look like me no matter what," I retort. I've fed into her bullshit long enough to know when she's lying through her teeth. I've given her the benefit of the doubt for too long.

"No, I'm serious. I *want* him to be yours. And he will be. DNA shouldn't matter when we're in love." She steps closer and places her palm on my cheek. "I made a mistake. Don't let it affect our future."

For a split second, I'm pulled into her trance but somehow manage to blink it away. "No. *You* cheated on *me*. You made me believe that was *my* son." I point at her belly. She's seven months pregnant and convinced me that we were starting a family. After I caught her getting railed doggy style by my brother, I demanded a paternity test.

"We're engaged, Grayson. We can work through this."

I almost buy into her pleading voice, but I've lost the desire to be near her. If the baby was mine, I had considered giving her a second chance because I wanted to make it work for his sake, but that's not happening now. There's no doubt that she'll run right back to Grant. God only knows how long their affair has been going on. When I asked her, and she refused to give me a straightforward answer, it was all I needed to know.

When we fell in love during high school, it was effortless. The two of us were inseparable, and I knew she was the woman I'd marry someday. Finding out she was pregnant was one of the happiest days of my life. Even though we were young and clueless, I was ready to become a dad and husband. Each day had started and ended with Bella.

She took our future and ripped it apart.

I take two steps back, shaking my head. "No. The thought of touching you makes me sick."

"Grayson!" she snaps with a glare, crossing her arms. "I'm not giving you back the ring. You're breaking us up, not me. Right before Christmas, nonetheless."

I fight the urge to roll my eyes. On a good day, Bella's a manipulative bitch, so this comes as no surprise. She'll tell our family that I called off the wedding while conveniently leaving out her infidelity. Bella will say whatever it takes to paint me as the bad guy. But I'll know the truth—so will she and Grant—and as long as it means I get out of this nightmare, I don't give a fuck.

"Fine with me." I swipe my keys and wallet off the counter.

"Where are you goin'?" she demands, following me to the door.

"Don't worry about it. I'm none of your concern anymore, Bella. I expect Grant will move in shortly," I tell her with a forced grin, then grab the bag I packed earlier.

Before she tries to stop me, I go to my truck. Though my windows are up, I can hear her screaming at the top of her lungs. "You'll be back, Grayson! This isn't over!"

I don't know if I should be amused or upset by how narcissistic she is and how I always ignored it. My eyes have finally opened, and nothing she could say or do will convince me to stay with her.

After I check into my hotel—my new home until I can find another place to stay—I shower and order food. Then I turn off my phone and pass out to reruns of CSI.

The following morning, I'm flooded with voice messages from Bella, but I ignore each one. I send my mom a quick text so she knows I'm okay, but I don't tell her where I am. I wouldn't put it past Bella to get it out of her somehow.

Though I'm grateful I don't work this weekend, I could've used the distraction. Working in construction in the San Antonio heat isn't for the weak. It's miserable most days, but I love staying busy and working with my hands. At the end of each shift, I have a sense of pride knowing I'm making a good living for my family. Now I'm wondering why I even bothered.

One of the worst parts of this whole situation is that my brother hasn't apologized. If not for having an affair with my fiancée, then at least for hurting me and lying. Considering they're both self-absorbed, perhaps they're meant for each other then.

"Hey, man," my friend Jase says when I answer his call. "Let's go out tonight."

I groan. "Not sure that's a good idea."

"I know you're sulking, and that ain't good for ya. Let me buy you a few drinks and find you a good lay for the evening." He chuckles, though I don't find any humor in his words. I'm not a one-night stand kinda guy, never have been. I was always so devoted to Bella.

Stupid, stupid, stupid.

"Where?" I ask.

"Downtown...we'll barhop until we find the ladies."

Since I have nothing else to do and don't want to think about *her* anymore, I agree. We plan to meet in a couple of hours, so I take a shower and get ready for a possible disaster.

"Duuuuude. Ya came!" Jase wraps me in a bear hug against my will, and I try to relax.

"You coerced me with *free* liquor." I shrug.

"I gotchu. Four double shots of tequila."

My eyes widen, then blink a few times at the shot glasses lined up. "Jesus."

"Gotta find you a rebound. Can't let you do it sober." He hands me one, then clinks it with his. "Bottoms up, Harding!"

I'm usually a beer guy, but I shoot it down because why the hell not?

"By the end of the night, you'll be pushing the girls off ya," he reassures, handing me the second one. "You won't even remember their names in the mornin'."

"If we keep this up, I won't know *my* name."

Jase laughs, and we slam the tequila down. When I can't taste the liquor anymore, I switch to beer.

This goes on for hours.

Eventually, we make our way to the dance floor and find a group of ladies. My mind is clear for the first time in weeks, and I relish it. The more I drink, the happier I feel, and I don't give a shit that I'll pay for it tomorrow.

My head throbs when I open my eyes and find the bright sun beaming through the half-opened curtains. Fuck, I forgot to close those last night but am glad I made it back to my room at least. The night is one gigantic blur, and I'm pretty certain I was one drink away from alcohol poisoning.

Jase is a bad influence, and apparently, I can't say no.

He kept feeding me shots, then we met some girls. Between the loud music, barhopping, dancing, and alcohol—a hangover doesn't give justice to how shitty I feel right now.

When I throw off the covers, I realize I'm buck-ass naked and not alone. Then I vaguely remember one of the girls coming back to my room. Most of last night is fuzzy, but I know we had a ton of fun.

Deciding to get in the shower, I leave her in the bed and start the hot water. As I wash off the night, more details flood in.

Kissing her felt foreign because I haven't touched a woman besides Bella in years, but I actually felt something that could turn into more. Though I'm not sure I'm emotionally ready for a relationship, I won't allow what Bella did to hold me back either. I refuse to give her that sort of power over me.

My heart races as I wrap a towel around my waist and contemplate asking the woman sleeping in my bed out for lunch. I'd love to know more about her, and maybe she can recall the events of what happened when we came back last night. But unfortunately, that part of my memory is fuzzy too.

"You son of a bitch." Bella appears as soon as I open the bathroom door and throws a pillow at me. I catch it and toss it aside. "You just couldn't wait to get into bed with some slut, could you?"

"What the fuck are you doin' here?" I glance around the room, noticing the bed is now empty. "What'd you say to her?"

"Nothing that wasn't the truth," she states with venom in her tone. "So I guess we're even now, right? You got your revenge even though I *apologized*."

I'm disgusted that she thinks this has anything to do with her. When I walk over to my suitcase, I pull out some joggers and a T-shirt.

"I didn't do it to get back at you. Believe it or not, I don't sleep with people out of spite."

When I first caught her cheating, she tried to blame me for seeking affection somewhere else. Bella claimed I worked too much, and when I was home, I was too tired to give her attention. Hell, I worked twelve-hour days and got stuck in traffic for two. Then after I wouldn't give in to her reasoning for breaking my heart, she said she only did it to get me to notice her and not take her for granted.

More bullshit.

Nothing I did warranted her sleeping with my brother and getting pregnant with his baby—then lying about it being *mine*. I put her on a pedestal and treated her like a queen. Her *actions* showed me how much I meant to her.

"I need to get dressed. You know where the door is."

"We need to talk about this, Grayson. You went out and had your little fun, so now it's time for you to come home."

Instead of arguing, I grab my clothes and go back to the bathroom. I don't bother assuming she'll be gone after I'm dressed and avoid her stare when I come back out.

"Why the hell are you still here?"

"Grayson, *please*."

I gently grab her arm, and she thinks it's to bring her closer, but instead, I lead her across the room. "You need to go."

As I guide her into the hallway, I give her one more look. "We're over. Deal with it or don't, but you're not welcome in my life anymore. You've stolen enough from me already, Bella."

"We're family, Grayson!" she shouts after I close the door, then pounds her fist against it. "You can't avoid me forever! I'm your stepsister!"

I close my eyes because she's right, and I hate that she is. Broken up or not, we'll always be linked together because our parents got married, and the baby I thought was mine will now be my nephew.

Maybe it's time I get the fuck outta this town. Right now, all I want and *need* is a fresh start.

CHAPTER ONE

Grayson

SIX YEARS LATER

She's lying to me and everyone else, but especially to herself.

I can see right through it, but I can't figure out why.

This has been going on for over five years, and honestly, I'm tired of her games. The way she dismisses me, acts as if I don't exist anytime I'm around, and purposely taunts me with her delicious curves.

Mackenzie Bishop will be the death of me.

I started at the Circle B Ranch to help with the cattle operation while she was away at college. The manager, Diesel, introduced us, and Kenzie stood there, giving me the side-eye. When I finally reached out to shake her hand, her jaw dropped as if I'd offended her.

I just mentioned how nice it was to meet her. *Though I was thinking how gorgeous she was and wondered how her lips would taste.*

Since that day, she's hated me for no goddamn reason.

After years of taunting and bickering, I had hoped she'd finally tell me why she despises me so much. Or we'd fall into bed together and work out our frustrations the fun way.

No such luck.

"So, Kenzie, you gonna wear my favorite pink thong down the aisle this weekend?" I ask while her back is to me. I can only imagine the glare she's sporting right now.

"You're gonna let me borrow your underwear? How sweet." She looks over her shoulder and smirks.

Diesel, Riley, and Gavin—the other ranch hands—shake their heads at me.

"Why do you even try anymore?" Riley, Kenzie's cousin, asks. The four of us are sitting at a table at the Circle B Bed & Breakfast eating together, as per our daily tradition. The B&B sits on the Circle B Ranch and hosts hundreds of guests a year, including the workers, who eat between morning chores. It's owned by the Bishops, and most of the family's involved with the ranch in some way.

Kenzie's a schoolteacher in town, and her older sister, Maize, is the head chef at the B&B. Occasionally, Kenzie will stop by in the morning for coffee and bagels before work.

"One day, she'll snap," I declare. "One day. Then it'll be on."

Diesel snorts, shaking his head. "The day Kenzie brings a man home is one I don't wanna miss."

"Me neither. Watching Grayson fight some guy for a woman who hates him would be the ultimate entertainment," Gavin adds. Not only is he Maize's husband but he's also at least ten years older than me and twice my size, so it's not like I can even sucker punch him for that comment.

"Hey, assholes. Workin' here has gained me a six-pack and an extra thirty pounds of muscle. So eat shit," I say, then shove more food in my mouth. Maize's cooking is so damn good and irresistible, but the carbs are worth it. Especially when I catch Kenzie staring any time I have my shirt off.

"I still can't believe Ethan and Harper paired you up to walk down the aisle together in their wedding. That's a catastrophe waitin' to happen," Diesel says.

"I was just as surprised as you were," I admit. "But I'm takin' full advantage to find out why she pretends to hate me so much. When she's drunk too much at the reception, I'll be there to drive her home. She won't be able to resist my charm," I respond with a shit-eating grin.

"So confident for a guy who she's kicked in the balls and dumped buckets of water over your head," Riley taunts.

"That's called foreplay, my friends. All leading up to the moment we—"

My jaw snaps shut the moment I notice John Bishop—the manager of the B&B— standing at the end of the table with his arms crossed over his chest.

He's *also* Kenzie's father.

"I wouldn't finish that sentence if I were you." He looks like he's daring me to give him a reason to kick my ass out.

"No, sir," I say politely.

When John walks away, it's so quiet I could hear a pin drop.

"Good job there." Gavin chuckles as he takes a bite of his biscuits and gravy.

"Your father-in-law hates me," I say.

"He's just reserved." Gavin shrugs, then adds, "But yeah, you're definitely on his shit list now."

Once I've finished eating, Diesel and I go back to the cattle barn. Since Ethan and Harper's wedding rehearsal's tonight, my work day's cut in half. Once we're finished, I go home and change, then head to the church.

Ethan's one of Kenzie's cousins who runs the goat farm. I help him sometimes, and over the years, we've become friends. After they announced their engagement, I was kinda surprised when he asked me to be a groomsman. Even more so when I learned they coupled me with Kenzie, but I wasn't complaining.

"You look pretty," I whisper in Kenzie's ear the first chance I get. We're practicing walking down the aisle in order.

"Eat shit, Cowboy," she murmurs without looking at me as Harper's mom gives instructions.

I hold back my laughter as I stuff my hands in my pockets. "Pretty filthy mouth too."

She faces me wearing her signature glare. "Don't get any ideas. Just because I *have* to be paired with you doesn't mean I *want* to be."

"Why? You'd rather be sittin' on my face? Because if so, that can be arranged."

545

Without warning, she stomps her heel on my foot. "Fuck." I hiss, trying to keep it together so I don't cause a scene.

"Keep it up, dumbass, and you'll also be sportin' a black eye in the wedding photos," she warns with fake politeness in her tone.

Goddamn, why does her feistiness turn me on even more? It's a true sickness, something I can't explain. She's turned me down more times than I can count, yet I still can't control myself around her. Ignoring the impulse to get under her skin as much as she gets under mine is impossible. Kenzie's worked me up for so fucking long, I crave peeling back her layers and figuring out what her problem is with me.

"That wasn't very ladylike," I murmur when she's forced to weave her arm through mine.

While brushing strands of bleach-blond hair from her face, she ignores me.

As we make our way toward the front, I lean in and ask softly, "You gonna finally tell me why you despise me so much?"

"You're annoying."

"And you're a raging bitch most days, but that's not an acceptable reason to be a jerk to you."

She whips her head in my direction and scowls. Before she can retort, we're separating and moving to our respective places. While standing next to the other groomsman, I glance at her. I should apologize, but honestly, she's never given me the same courtesy for the harsh shit she says. However, I hadn't meant it. I only wanted to provoke a reaction from her, but instead, I feel guilty as hell.

She's gonna make me pay for that one. You'd think at twenty-seven years old, I would've learned how to keep my foot out of my mouth.

The following day, I'm up bright and early to get my chores done before I have to go to the church for the ceremony. I never spoke to Kenzie after the rehearsal because she avoided me at the dinner like usual.

"See ya guys there!" I wave to Diesel and Riley as I walk to my truck.

After a hot shower, I change into my suit and comb my hair before driving into town. When I arrive, Ethan's parents and sister are in the groomsmen's dressing room.

"Grayson, you clean up so nice," his mother, Emily, says.

"Yeah, man. Lookin' good." Ethan smirks, patting my back.

"You gettin' nervous yet?"

"Nah. Been ready to marry Harper since I was a teen." He beams, and I'm happy for him. Ethan and Harper were childhood friends until last year when Harper asked him to pretend to be her fiancé. One thing led to another, and a couple of months later, they were *actually* engaged. Now she's pregnant, and they're due in the fall.

"Hey, can you give this letter to Harper for me?" Ethan asks his sister, Elle. "I want her to read it right away."

"Sure thing, bro. I gotta wrangle the other bridesmaids anyway."

At that, I go search for Kenzie first. The church isn't that big, and since the bridal suite is at the opposite end of the hallway, it's not hard to find her. Fortunately, she's alone.

As soon as she sees me, she groans with an eye roll. "What do you want?"

I rake my gaze down her body, appreciating every inch of skin that's peeking out of her dress. Wavy blond hair flows down her back, and I want to reach out and tug it. "Relax. Do you always come armed?"

"Around you, I do."

"I was just comin' to tell you how beautiful you look. Peach suits you."

"It's coral," she corrects.

"Alright, well whatever color it is, it's pretty on you."

She stays silent, and I see her looking me over. After licking her lips, she swallows hard. Kenzie's terrible at hiding her attraction to me. If I honestly thought it was one-sided, I wouldn't push her so much. I won't stop until she admits it or tells me why she's hell-bent on pushing me away every chance she gets.

"The proper response would be *thank you*," I tease.

"I don't need your compliments, Grayson. Get the hint already." She stalks off, but I follow close behind.

"Fine," I mutter. "You look horrible. That color with your lipstick is all wrong."

She halts, and I nearly collide with her back. Kenzie turns with a scowl.

"Was that better for ya, princess?" Lowering my eyes down her chest, I notice her hard nipples poking through the thin fabric. I raise my brows and rub my fingers over my chin. "I'm guessing you liked it a lot."

"Seriously. You're the fucking worst. Stop following me like a lost puppy."

"You like being degraded in the bedroom, don't you? That's why you always fight me." I step closer, and when she backs up into the wall, I cage her in with my arms. "It's our version of foreplay, and I'm willing to bet if I felt between your thighs right now, you'd be soaking wet for me. Am I right?"

With a mischievous smirk, Kenzie arches her back, showing off her delicious cleavage. Then she slams her hands against my chest, and I stumble back. "Too bad you'll never find out."

Jesus fuck. She's clawing at my patience.

"Fine," I say as she walks past me. "You finally ready to tell me what your deal is then?" I follow her until she spins around.

"You are."

"And what is it that I did?"

"If you don't know, that's your problem," she snaps.

Frustration rolls through me. "Woman! I swear. Just tell me so I can like, I don't know, apologize?"

She snorts. "I don't want your apology."

"Then what do you want? What's it gonna take for you to stop acting like a snotty princess?" I ask desperately.

A corner of her lips tilts up as she crosses her arms. "I want *revenge*. And maybe then we'll be even." The amusement in her tone makes my heart pound. If I've learned anything about her over the years, it's that she doesn't make promises she can't keep.

"You're insane. I didn't even do anything." I shake my head, moving away from her.

I've had enough of this crazy train, and if I don't get off, I'm going to get further tangled into her web. I wish I could say I've had random hookups, but between work and the limited selection of single ladies in town, there haven't been many chances. Even if there was someone else, I know I'd be thinking of Kenzie the whole damn time.

Once the wedding ceremony begins, it's back-to-back action. We watch the newlyweds exchange their vows and first kiss, then we're thrown into wedding party photos. Kenzie ignores me as we stand close and smile for the camera. It's hard not to notice those luscious lips or feel the softness of her skin when she's next to me. Hell, I notice everything about her.

By the time the reception begins, the majority of the guests are halfway to tipsy town. Kenzie's been dancing with her cousins, and I've been watching her while I drink. She might be the only sober one here, which means my plan to offer to drive her home has gone to shit. So instead, I drink myself stupid and try to have a good time.

"You lookin' pretty messed up there, Cowboy."

My vision blurs as I blink at Kenzie. She tilts her head and assesses me. I shrug, walking away.

"Whoa, whoa, whoa. Where do you think you're going, Grayson Harding?"

The sound of her using my full name grabs my attention, even if her voice is different. Oh wait, she's not scolding or shouting at me for once.

"To find someone to keep warm tonight," I blurt out.

Kenzie barks out a laugh. "Unless you plan to snuggle with Payton or Luke, your options are limited. Everyone's married or over fifty 'round here."

It's funny because Payton and Luke are the ranch hands who help Ethan with the goats, and they also very much like women. She's right, though, because most of the ladies here are taken or too old for me. That fact doesn't explain why she came alone. However, she's made it very clear she doesn't date ranch hands.

"And what would you do if I found someone else?" I ask curiously as I struggle to get my keys out of my pocket. "I'm not waitin' forever, baby."

She groans. "You idiot. You can't drive."

"Why do you care? You'd probably like me ending up in a ditch." I'm rambling and blurting out shit, but I'm too drunk to care.

"I don't, but I worry about who you might hurt in the process. Let's go." She snatches my keys out of my hand and finds my truck in the parking lot.

I press my cheek against the window as Kenzie floors the gas pedal.

Though she claims to hate me, she cared enough to keep an eye on me. She denies it, but she notices me.

"Alright, can you get yourself up the stairs?" she asks once we arrive at my cabin. It's not much, but living quarters came with the ranch hand job. I've added personal touches, but it's a shack compared to the other houses on the ranch. Someday, when I have a wife and family of my own, I'll build.

"Totally," I stutter, reaching for the door handle and missing it. After my third attempt, Kenzie groans and marches over to the passenger side.

When she whips it open, I nearly fall out.

"Jesus, Grayson. What were you thinkin' getting so drunk?" She steps closer and pulls my arm around her shoulders to steady me.

"I was drinkin' away my sorrows."

She snort-laughs.

"Honestly, I was trying to gain the courage to ask you to dance." I stumble as I move against her toward my house. "But then I got too sloshed and decided to just keep chuggin'."

"You really are a fool, you know that?" She opens the front door and leads us in. "Your room?"

"Down the hall...but it's clothing optional." I flash a smirk.

"Really? I figured it'd be common sense that's optional considering the bimbos I've seen you talk to."

"You jealous?"

She sets me down on my bed and looks at me. "*Hardly.*"

I scoff because I've only hooked up with two women in the past six years, and neither was from around here. One was my ex-fiancée, and the other was a woman I slept with the night after I found out the love of my life had cheated.

"You gonna stay?" I ask, managing to kick off my shoes. "Or at least help me out of my tux."

"You can't be serious," she deadpans.

"It's a rental. Can't return it if it's all in shreds." I flash a devilish grin, hoping she takes the bait.

"Fine. But don't get any ideas, okay?"

"Oh, sweetheart. It's too late for that," I drawl as she slowly unbuttons my dress shirt. Her intense gaze is on my chest as she avoids my eyes. "One is where I tie you up in my bed and—"

"You have some rope?" She arches a brow as she removes my tie.

"As a matter of fact, I do…cuffs as well."

She gives me a mischievous look. "No, I really like the rope idea…"

"Oh shit, you're kinky *kinky*. Don't gotta tell me twice."

Once I'm down to my boxers, I grab some rope from the storage closet. When I return, Kenzie takes them from my hand. "Lie down in the middle."

I arch a brow, tempted to argue but don't. Once I'm settled, she straddles my hips and grinds against me. Blood rushes to my dick, and my heart races as her soft hands rub up my stomach.

"Kenzie…" I growl, cursing the last five drinks I had because my head is fuzzy as hell.

"Isn't this what you've always wanted?" she taunts in a sultry tone, bringing her mouth close to mine.

"You have no idea."

She brushes her mouth against mine but quickly backs away.

"Raise your arms," she says seductively, licking her bottom lip.

"Yes, ma'am." I do as she says and watch her tie my wrists to the bedposts.

"Perfect," she whispers in my ear.

"Now I can't remove your clothes," I pout, lowering my gaze down her curvy body.

"Guess I'll have to give you a private show." She stands and slowly unzips her dress.

"Fuck yes."

The gown falls to her feet, and my eyes widen in shock at her sexy undergarments. Lace bra and matching thong, tan and toned legs, creamy skin. I'm already rock hard just looking at her.

"Kenzie…I need to touch you."

"Hold your horses, Cowboy." She grabs the other rope, twirling it around in her fingers. "I'm not done with you."

Once she's at the end of the bed, Kenzie grabs my ankle.

"No…" I yank my leg out of her grip, but she pulls it back.

"You play by my rules, or I leave," she threatens, holding a serious stare.

Goddammit, she's testing me, but I don't want her to go. Not after finally reaching this point.

"You need to lose the boxers, though."

Swallowing hard, I lift my hips so she can pull them down my legs. My cock springs free, hard and ready to feel her warm pussy. She ties my ankles, leaving me completely at her mercy. Gliding a finger along my leg, she inches closer to my shaft.

"Imagining you riding me has me hard as fuck, Kenzie."

As she scans over my body, she bites her bottom lip. I notice the way her breathing hitches when she looks over my abs and erection.

"C'mon, baby girl. You're torturin' me now." I pull against the rope, desperate to touch her hard nipples.

"I'll be right back…" She moves toward the door, and I panic. "Just gonna freshen up in the bathroom."

"Hurry up." I grin.

She flashes a wink and backs out of my room. My body buzzes with anticipation.

After all these years, it's finally happening. Kenzie's going to be *mine*.

Twenty minutes pass, and I call out for her. No response. Then I shout louder. "Kenzie!"

I flail against my hold, the ropes not budging no matter how much I try. She fucking tied them tight as hell. After ten solid minutes of shouting her name, I come to the conclusion she's bailed.

More time passes, and I realize she's not coming back. The anger viciously floods through me as I recall her earlier words.

I want revenge. And maybe then we'll be even.

Revenge for what, though? I still have no clue what her issue with me is.

My phone's still in the pocket of my pants and out of reach. It's gotta be almost three in the morning, and if the guys haven't barged into my house by now, they're already passed out and won't be coming. Usually, one of the Bishops or other ranch hands hangs out here on the weekends but no such luck tonight.

I'm fuckin' screwed.

When I wake up some time later, arms are numb, and my thighs are burning.

"Alexa, what time is it?" I call out to the little black box on my nightstand.

"It's six ten a.m.," she responds.

Surely, someone has to be up by now to start morning chores. But who the hell can I call who won't humiliate me more than I already am?

"Alexa, call Diesel."

Though he'll laugh his head off at me, at least he'll keep his mouth shut.

However, it goes to voicemail. *Fuck.*

"Alexa, call Riley."

Voicemail again.

Son of a bitch.

Then I call Gavin and a few more of the ranch hands. No one answers.

The last person I want to bother is Ethan, but I have to try.

I breathe a sigh of relief when he picks up.

"Dude, I'm sorry to call so early, but it's an emergency," I plead so he doesn't hang up.

"It better be. It's my wedding night," he says roughly like he just woke up.

"Kenzie tied me to my bed with rope, then left. I'm stuck," I say embarrassingly. "I had Alexa call everyone, and you were my last resort."

"I'm sorry, whaddya just say?" he asks with a soft laugh. "She tied you up?"

"Yeah, man. I'm buck-ass naked too. Can you please help me? I wouldn't ask if it wasn't urgent. My limbs are going blue."

"Holy shit." He bursts out laughing. "How the hell did that happen?"

I explain the evening and how it went from amazing to bad in minutes.

"Alright. I'll be there as soon as I can."

"Thanks, I owe ya one."

He hangs up, and while I wait for him, I plot my own revenge against Mackenzie Bishop.

CHAPTER TWO

Mackenzie

Knowing that Grayson's tied to his bed, unable to move or reach his phone, gives me the biggest smile.

Sure, it was a bitch move. But trust me, it's well deserved.

We have a history, even if he pretends we don't, and this payback was years in the making.

I hadn't fully thought it through, especially not the part where I left without my bridesmaid dress. Driving home in my bra and panties was a nice surprise for me too. Since I stole Grayson's truck and didn't want anyone to see it, I parked behind one of the barns close to my house and ran inside undetected. I was scared as hell I'd run into my parents, but luckily, I didn't.

By nine in the morning, I'm wide-awake. My internal clock doesn't let me sleep in since I'm usually up at six thirty for work. The drive into town only takes fifteen minutes, but if I stop by the B&B for my daily coffee, I have to leave by seven forty-five to get to the school on time. I don't mind the early hours, though. I love my students and my job as a first-grade teacher at the private school my mom started before I was born. Over the years, she expanded and added a daycare center—where most of my nieces and nephews attend.

Since it's Sunday and I have off, I go to the B&B for Maize's sundae crepes and some hot coffee. Though I imagine some of the ranch hands are already working, I cross my fingers Grayson hasn't managed to get loose yet. There's a chance someone's already saved him, and he's there waiting to unleash on me.

"Hey y'all," I greet when I enter and see my parents in the common room with Maize and Gavin on one of the couches. Their twin girls, Mila Rose and Madison, are crawling over Dad's lap and giggling. They just turned two last month and are full of energy. "No love for your favorite auntie?" I kneel and open my arms.

Maddy immediately crashes into my chest, wrapping her little arms around me. "Aunt Kenzie!"

Mila Rose hugs me next. She's the shyer one.

"What are y'all doin' here so early?" I ask when they return to the couch.

"Daddy brought us to see Mommy and Papa," Mila Rose responds.

"And eat cakes and sausage!" Maddy adds.

"Love that idea," I say with a smile, then give my dad and mom a hug.

As I make my way into the dining room, I see a table full of ranch hands stuffing their faces.

"Y'all look like shit." I snicker at their hungover expressions. Riley, Diesel, Luke, and Payton look like they didn't sleep a wink after the big wedding last night.

Instead of someone spitting out a smart-ass comment, they whisper amongst themselves.

"What's goin' on?" my mom appears next to me and asks them. "Y'all are actin' suspicious."

I keep my lips tight. No doubt they know what happened to Grayson last night. Quickly, I glance around the room to see if he's around and breathe a sigh of relief that he's not.

Before someone can respond, my uncles come barreling in and being loud as usual.

"Is it true?" Uncle Jackson asks.

"Considering I don't see him here, I'd say so," Uncle Alex responds.

"What happened?" my mom asks.

Diesel smirks. "Grayson went home with a chick last night, and she left him naked and tied to his bed."

Riley laughs too, unable to contain himself. Meanwhile, my parents and uncles look shocked.

"Who was he with?" my mom asks.

Riley's and Diesel's eyes move to me. *Fuck.*

"Don't look at me," I say defensively, crossing my arms. "I wouldn't willingly go within six feet of Grayson, nevertheless naked."

My mom seems to buy it and shrugs before going back to the twins. My dad and uncles go to the breakfast buffet, leaving me to find Maize in the kitchen.

"What did you do?" she snaps as soon as we're alone. "Gavin told me this morning, and Grayson claims it was you." Not that I'm surprised it's already spreading around, but I'm curious who untied him.

"Payback's a bitch," I reply, grabbing a muffin from the tray. "He had it comin'."

"Mackenzie Rose!" she hisses. "Mama and Dad are gonna find out it was you, ya know? And when they do…"

"I'm twenty-seven," I cut her off. "They won't do anything."

Maize shakes her head in disapproval. "When you gonna tell me what he did to you? Then maybe I could take your side…" She glances at me as she stirs a pot of soup.

"Never."

Or anyone, for that matter.

It's too humiliating.

My stomach growls, and I excuse myself to the buffet for the reason I came—crepes and bacon. Just as everyone goes quiet, I feel someone behind me and stiffen.

"You may have wanted revenge, but you just started a war, sweetheart." Grayson's voice is so low, only I can hear him. His breath blows against my ear as he invades my personal space. "I'm gonna get you back for that little stunt."

I roll my eyes and spin around. "Grow up."

His eyes narrow into slits, but he keeps his mouth shut. I can practically see the steam billowing out of his ears.

"I had to call Ethan to come help me. Hope you're happy I had to bother the groom to cut me loose."

I smirk, then pat him on the chest. "Guess we're even now..."

Grayson grabs my wrist and squeezes. "Far from it, darlin'."

Glancing down, I see the rope burns on his wrists, and for a split second, I feel bad. Then I remember what started all this and swallow down that guilt.

"Whatever," I hiss, yanking my arm from his grip. "Good luck with that."

Taking my plate, I walk over to where my parents are sitting with Gavin and the twins.

"What was that about?" my dad asks.

"Nothing. Just Grayson gettin' on my nerves, per usual," I say casually, avoiding his gaze.

I take my empty plate to the dish tub, then play with the girls for a bit. Once they've gotten tired, I say my goodbyes and walk to my SUV.

"Kenzie," Grayson shouts, and I blow out a frustrated breath.

Ignoring him, I open my door, but before I can slide in, he's at my side, slamming it shut.

"That was almost my finger!" I scowl.

"I need my keys since you stole my goddamn truck." He holds out his hand with an intense glare.

Digging them out of my bag, I say, "*Steal* is a pretty strong word."

"You took it, so what would you call it?" he asks as I hand them over.

"Borrowed. Maybe that'll teach you not to get so drunk you can't drive your ass home," I reply smugly. "You should be thanking me, considering you could've killed yourself."

Instead of dismissing me as I expect, he closes the gap between us. I jump slightly at the unexpected closeness as my back presses against my SUV.

"Why don't we figure this out like adults and fuck out our frustrations? Or hell, just tell me what your goddamn problem is." His mouth is close to mine, and I curse my traitorous body for wanting him to move just half an inch closer and kiss me.

"You will *never* get me in your bed," I hiss with as much disdain as I can muster.

"Don't make promises you can't keep." He winks, then pushes off my car.

I fight the urge not to roll my eyes at his confidence. "I need my dress," I say, changing the subject.

He shrugs. "Come over and get it. You know where my bedroom is."

I don't trust him, and he knows it. "God, I hate you."

"I might've been drunk off my ass last night and have a hangover from hell today, but I noticed the way your nipples hardened while you were straddling my dick. I'd say that's the furthest thing from hate, sweetheart."

His arrogant attitude makes me want to chop off his balls.

"You know what? You're right..." I step toward him and press my chest to his, bracing my hands on his shoulders.

He arches a brow almost like he's shocked at my admission.

"In fact..." I arch my back so my breasts press against him, then jerk my knee hard between his legs.

"Jesus fuck!" He collapses to the ground, holding his groin and cursing my name.

I bend down so he can meet my eyes. "If you learned your damn lesson, you'd stop gettin' yourself into these type of situations." I give him a shit-eating grin, and he scowls.

Before I can leave, four ranch hands walk out of the B&B. Diesel and Riley laugh as they come closer.

"Dude..." Riley snaps his gaze to mine. "What'd he do now?"

"Just doesn't know how to keep his mouth shut," I respond casually.

"C'mon, man. Back to work." Diesel grabs Grayson's hand and helps him to his feet. "Stop harassing her, and maybe she'll stop tryin' to kill ya."

Grayson flashes me a murderous look. "You'll pay for that one, too."

Instead of heading home, I go to my cousin Rowan's house. She married Diesel two and a half years ago, but since I know he's working, we can talk without any eavesdropping. They have two kids together plus Diesel's seven-year-old son from a previous hookup. Though Rowan manages the Circle B Saloon in town, she does a lot of the bookkeeping and scheduling at home. It's nice for her since Rory turned three this month, and Ruthie is a year and a half. I like when she's working at the bar because it gives me an excuse to go there and hang out.

"Hey girl," she greets me at the door. "I was hoping to talk to you. C'mon in."

"Where's my favorite little cousin?" I tease Ruthie, who's glued to Rowan's hip.

She lets me take her and hugs me as we walk into the kitchen. "I was just about to make another pot of coffee. Want some?" Rowan asks, filling the pot with water.

"Yes! Hook me up, please. I forgot to grab some at the B&B," I tell her, setting Ruthie down when I sit at the breakfast bar.

"You forgot?" She arches a brow.

"More like…distracted," I correct.

"So the rumors are true then? I want *all* the details." She smirks.

Since I know she'll hear about it anyway, I start at finding Grayson drunk off his ass, to driving him home, then ending with tying him up and bailing.

"Holy sh-crap! Diesel said he was trapped for three hours before he got ahold of Ethan. Was he at the B&B this mornin'?"

"Yep…he declared war, then I kneed him in the junk. Once he fell to the ground, I walked away." I shrug. "He deserved it."

She eyes me, knowing I won't tell her why but I'm sure she'll ask anyway.

"Trust me, it was payback. Maybe he'll stop being a shithead and leave me alone now."

Rowan snorts. "Doubt it."

Rory goes to Rowan and repeats my bad language. "Shithead. Shit. Head. Shit*head*," he says.

My eyes widen, and I grimace. "Sorry…"

"We don't say that, okay, buddy? It's not a nice word," Rowan informs him, glaring at me in the process.

"But Kenzie said it. Does she get a time-out now?"

Rowan blows out a breath. "Yep. She has to sit in the naughty chair for twenty-seven minutes."

Rory's eyes widen. "That's a *long* time."

"That's how old she is," Rowan says. "Why don't you take Ruthie to get some PlayDoh from the playroom?"

"Okay!"

After he runs out of the kitchen, I apologize again. "My bad. I forget there are little ears around."

"It's fine. Diesel slips all the time and gets put in a time-out daily." She snickers.

Once the coffee is brewed, I add cream and sugar, and we catch up. Since I was doing wedding party things yesterday and she was busy wrangling two kids, we didn't get to see each other that much.

"So while I know what happened after the reception, how were things before that?" she asks.

"Good, I guess." Grayson clung to me like a piece of lint, but after we took photos, I avoided him. He's like a puppy...I turn around, and he's so close, I nearly trip over him.

Rowan pinches her lips together as if she's holding back laughter. "Have you considered giving him a real shot? Whatever your issue with him is, it has to have been a long time ago. Why're you holding a grudge?"

It's a reasonable question, but without explaining the whole story, it's hard to answer.

"Let's just say...Grayson isn't who everyone thinks he is."

She narrows her eyes. "Like he's living a double life or something? Wait, does he have a wife and five kids we don't know about?"

I chuckle. "Not exactly, but when I'm ready to tell you, I promise you'll never expect it."

CHAPTER THREE

Grayson

"Of course it's raining again," I grumble to Diesel, who's covered in mud. We look like we went swimming in the goddamn pond with our clothes on, and we smell like it too.

"And that's why we get paid more than minimum wage," he tells me while pulling the old broken barbed wire from the wooden post. I carefully take the new from the roll and string it the best I can. Using power tools isn't an option considering the weather, so we have to do it the old-fashioned way with pliers and wire cutters. It doesn't help that the fence line is close to a ditch, which is holding water.

Thunder rumbles in the distance, so we pick up our pace. Being a ranch hand is a rain or shine type of job. It could be twenty or a hundred degrees outside, but the tasks still have to be done. Today, it's fixing a broken fence in shitty weather. Tomorrow it'll probably be something else. Regardless, I'd rather be out here, covered in filth, than sitting at a desk being forced to

This right here is the life even though it doesn't feel like it at this moment.

"I swear, it better not start lightnin'," I mutter as the angry sky transforms from dark gray into black.

Diesel looks at the rolling clouds, then back at me. "So, heard you got tied up after the weddin' last week." He hadn't said much about it since it happened, but it doesn't surprise me he'd want more details. No telling what he's heard.

I groan, thinking about how dirty Kenzie did me. It's been a week, and I've only run into her once—when she kneed me in my balls. I've been avoiding her since. As soon as I figure out how the hell to get even with her, I will.

"She tricked me. Her acting skills are incredible."

"No, you just let your dick do the thinkin' instead."

"I blame it on the alcohol. I should've never put an inkling of trust into Kenzie Bishop. Swear she was comin' onto me, though. *She* offered to take me home. Probably had the whole thing planned now that I think about it."

Diesel laughs. "She either hates you for real or wants to bang your brains out. After how she humiliated you, might be a little bit of both."

"Did Rowan act like that?"

"Oh, we fought like cats and dogs, but I never gave up on her. Eventually, she came around and saw what was right in front of her." A smirk hits his lips.

As soon as I focus back on my task, a string of curse words leaves Diesel's mouth. I snicker when I realize his ass is on the wet ground.

"Don't you say a damn word," he warns, trying to scrape off the mud, but it's no use.

While I want to rag him about being a clumsy ass, I keep it to myself. Diesel's a jokester most of the time, but right now, with the clouds rolling in, his demeanor's nothing short of serious. We attach five strings of wire in an hour, and after our mess is clean, lightning strikes a tree close by.

"Let's get the fuck outta here. I ain't trying to die today," Diesel tells me with his arms full of extra supplies.

"Yeah, me either," I say, throwing all the shit in the back of the ranch hand truck. The bottom of the sky falls out, and because it's pouring so hard, we can't see the trail we took to get here.

"You smell like shit," Diesel mutters, turning down the radio. The windshield wipers are going full blast, but it does no good.

"And you're a dumbass because..." I point, trying to warn him as he slams into an old creek wash. The truck feels like it's sucked into the pits of hell as it hits rock bottom. Wheels spin, but we don't move, and that's when I realize we're stuck.

I turn to Diesel and shake my head with annoyance.

"Time to get out and push," he says with a chuckle.

"Hell no," I snap.

With a raised brow, he gives me a stern look. "Last time I checked, you reported to me."

I roll my eyes. "Sure thing, *Cow Boss*."

"Now that's the correct response. Too bad it's taken you a few years to catch on." He grins, then nearly shoves me out of the truck.

I slosh through the creek bed that seems like a roaring river and push the back bumper with all my strength. Diesel guns it, but the truck only rocks as the tires spit huge globs of mud on me. The hole we're in is growing deeper as the water rushes by.

I walk over to his window, and he barely cracks it. "Better call someone. We're stuck as fuck!"

"Think we should keep trying." He rolls up the window and points toward the back end. I begrudgingly do what he says, knowing it won't help shit.

After fifteen more minutes of getting nowhere, Riley shows up. He's got on his rain gear and looks at me like I'm a clown.

"Did you bring some rope or a chain?" I ask, hopeful.

"Nah." He walks closer and shouts at Diesel. "Put it in four-wheel drive, ya dumbass!"

Diesel laughs hard, revs the engine, and the truck easily climbs out.

With flared nostrils, I shake my head. "I'm going to beat his ass," I grit out.

"Considering the way you look right now, he'd deserve it. Also, you should probably ride in the bed. I know it's a ranch hand truck, but damn, you'll be detailing it tomorrow with how filthy you are."

Diesel rolls down the window. "Did you get a pic of him at least?"

"Shit, I forgot." Riley whips out his phone and snaps a picture of me, but right before he does, I give him double middle fingers.

"I'm walking back. Fuck both of y'all." I start my trek to the barn.

Diesel slowly drives beside me, coaxing me to get in. "Get in, man."

I give him a dirty ass look. "I'm not playin' these games."

"It's not a game anymore. I can't afford for one of my workers to get struck by lightnin'. Get your ass in the back so we can change clothes and finish our day," he demands.

"Fuck off," I say, just as the thunder rolls. "You're still an asshole." It was all the convincing I needed to hop in.

During the ride through the pastures, I'm miserable as hell. I stink like sweat and earth, and I'm covered in mud. If I didn't know better, I'd say Diesel's driving like a grandma on purpose because we're moving as slow as molasses.

It takes nearly twenty minutes for us to arrive at the barn, and I'm pissed by the time he puts it in park.

"Cheer up, buttercup. Take off early since you've had a rough day," he tells me as if that's supposed to make me feel better.

I narrow my eyes. "Is this another one of your jokes?"

"Nope. We can start over tomorrow when it's not raining like this."

I'm waiting for the punchline, but instead, he gives me a pointed look and crosses his arms. "Keep standin' around, and I'll change my mind because there's plenty of shit to do."

"Okay, ya don't have to tell me twice." I wave him off, then go to my truck. Instead of getting the inside dirty, I strip down to my boxers and hop in.

The rain slams harder against the windshield, and I have to slow down to stay on the gravel road, which has turned into a muddy slop. I slow down and make my way around the curb when a vehicle comes barreling toward me.

I'm convinced whoever's driving doesn't see me, so I start honking and flashing my lights. Before there's a head-on collision, I swerve out of the way and end up in the ditch. The SUV stops, reverses, and when I turn my head, I see Kenzie.

Furiously, I hop out of my truck. "What the hell is wrong with you!" Her eyes widen when she sees me, and that's when I remember I'm only in my boxers.

"Where're your clothes?" she blurts out as the rain eases. "You lost a bet?"

For a second, I thought maybe she'd apologize for driving like a maniac, but nope.

"None of your damn business. Watch where you're goin' next time," I snap before climbing back into my truck, not wanting to deal with her attitude too. I've had enough for today.

When I glance over at her, she makes a show out of flipping me off. I shake my head, put my truck in four-wheel drive, and gun it. As I back out, mud splatters on the side of her SUV, and she honks. Leaving ruts, I slam on the gas and leave.

Once I'm home, I immediately get in the shower. I wash off the dirt from the day, wishing the hot water would calm me. I'm annoyed, but I also can't get Kenzie off my mind. Too often, she fills my thoughts and completely consumes me.

I grab my cock and begin to stroke my shaft. I place my free hand on the wall as my head falls back. I'm hard as fuck, imagining her straddling me as I pick up the pace. It's almost too much to handle, but I don't stop. Thoughts of Kenzie's plump lips wrapped around me, then swallowing me down fill my mind. My balls tighten, and I groan out my release as the orgasm rips through me.

My heart rate is erratic as I stand under the water until my body relaxes.

"Fuck," I whisper-hiss, trying to gain my composure, knowing she's going to be the end of me. After I dry off, I head to my room to put on some fresh clothes.

Considering it's Sunday and Diesel let me leave early, there's not much to do. I sit on the couch and watch some TV for an hour, then I'm ready to do something else. I text Luke and Payton to see if they'd like to hang out, but both are busy. I even text Knox and Kane, but they're still finishing their daily tasks. Instead of messaging someone else, I grab my keys and drive to the Circle B Saloon in town.

The rain has finally stopped, and the late afternoon sun slightly peeks through the dark clouds. When I arrive, it's not busy. A few locals are sitting at the end of the bar, and to my surprise, Kenzie's here too.

A smirk touches my lips as I sit next to her. I can smell the floral scent of her shampoo and wish I could bottle it up.

She turns and looks at me. "You're literally like an annoying fly that won't go away."

"Nice to see you too," I deadpan, then order a beer.

Rowan comes around the corner carrying several binders. She sets them down next to Kenzie, then glances back and forth between the two of us with raised brows.

"Don't even ask," Kenzie mumbles, taking a sip of her drink. "He doesn't know how to take a hint. I don't know how I can be any clearer about how I feel."

"Seems like love to me," I taunt, and she groans.

"Keep tellin' yourself that, Cowboy," she snaps with an eye roll. "Delusional with a capital D."

"At this point, you should just appease me. You owe me."

Kenzie scoffs. "I don't owe you shit."

She's literally building an invisible wall between us, but I refuse to let her. Over the years, I've wondered why she hates me so much and haven't been able to figure it out. Now, after her trying to seek revenge, I'm even more determined to make her crack.

Rowan snickers, and I almost forgot she was here. "You must really like gettin' hog-tied because you don't give up."

"It actually kinda turned me on." I waggle my brows, and Kenzie pretends to throw up in her mouth, but I'm certain it's all an act.

Since the day we met, Kenzie Bishop has wedged her way under my skin, and I'd be lying if I said I didn't like it—I just wish she'd finally admit our connection isn't one-sided.

CHAPTER FOUR

Mackenzie

My alarm goes off, and I roll out of bed with a smile because it's Friday. Other than hanging out with one of my teacher friends tonight, I don't have any big plans. But it does mean that I'm much closer to the last day of school next Wednesday. Summer break can't come soon enough, especially after all the work I've put into lesson plans and grades this year while trying to make the last few weeks of class fun.

I love teaching and wouldn't trade it for the world.

After I finish getting dressed and grab my keys, I notice Mom's already left. I check the time, then go on my way. Apparently, my sister made bear claws, and I'm already foaming at the mouth for one. The weather couldn't be more perfect as I park in front of the B&B and walk inside.

"Mornin'," Maize says when I poke my head into the kitchen.

"Hey, sis!"

She's got flour on her apron, and her hair is twisted up into a high bun

"I just took these out of the oven, so they're still warm, just how you like 'em."

I hurry over and grab one, but it's so hot, I have to set it back down.

"If it wouldn't burn the fuck out of my mouth, I'd eat it whole right now." I laugh, pinching off some of the sweet bread and blowing on it. Once it's cooled a bit, I pop it in my mouth, then moan at how delicious it is.

"Jesus," Maize says with a snort. "You really need to get laid."

"Yeah, you're telling me. But you know how it is 'round here."

She nods, twisting more dough, then setting it on the parchment-paper-covered tray. "I do. Honestly, I'd hate to be searchin' for love right now, *especially* here."

"Not many options," we say at the same time, then laugh.

"I got lucky," she adds.

"I need to *get* lucky." I waggle my brows, then check the time as I finish my breakfast. I walk closer to her and give her a little squeeze. "Thanks for makin' my fave."

"Welcome. Grab another one before you go!"

I chuckle. "You're as bad as Mom. Between you two, I'm gonna gain fifty pounds on breakfast alone."

Maize shrugs, then shoos me away.

I walk into the main area and grab a to-go cup for my coffee. As I'm adding cream and sugar, I feel someone standing close. Glancing over my shoulder, I immediately see Grayson hovering.

"You're lookin' real lovely this mornin'," he says with a gruff tone.

I shake my head and put the lid on my cup. Then I turn and meet his chestnut brown eyes. Something swirls inside me, but I ignore it.

"Suck a dick." I take a sip of my coffee and walk past him.

"I'd prefer you suck mine," he throws back.

I turn to face him. "I doubt I'd be able to find it."

He lifts his brows, brings his hands to the top button of his jeans, and acts like he's gonna whip it out and show me.

I clear my throat. "Go ahead. Prove yourself."

Grayson chuckles. "Nah. Wouldn't be able to keep you off me if you got a good look at the family jewels."

"I've seen them, remember? Or have ya already forgotten how good I am at tying Palomar knots?" I blink a few times, waiting for his response.

Grayson quickly removes the space between us and leans in to whisper in my ear. "You may think this is over, but it's far from it. Whatever's going on between us has just started."

I take a few steps back and glare at him for getting into my personal space. "Fuck off."

Riley and Diesel walk in laughing about something, and I take the opportunity to make my escape. As my dad finishes up with one of the B&B guests, I go up to the counter. "Hey, Dad!"

"Hey honey, headin' to work?"

"Yep. Don't forget Lacey's coming over tonight."

"Oh yeah. Thanks for the reminder. Also, don't worry about us gettin' in y'all's way. I'm sure your mom and I will be in bed early. Didn't get much sleep last night." He waggles his brows.

"Eww, spare me please. Don't say things like that before I've had a full cup of coffee."

Dad laughs. "Anyway, have a good day!"

"You too," I tell him before leaving.

When I pass the dinner tables, Grayson lifts his head and looks at me. Our eyes meet, and I make sure to give him a dirty look. Being an asshole toward him in the mornings has easily become a part of my routine too.

I arrive at school just as a few of my students are being dropped off by their parents. I quickly chug the rest of my coffee, needing it to start working sooner rather than later.

"Miss Bishop!" Jackie says, wrapping her small arms around me the best she can.

"Hey, sweetie! Happy Friday!"

"Yes!" She fist pumps in the air, then skips away, yelling, "Summer break is coming!"

As I'm watching her, I hear my name being called. I turn and see my cousin Elle, then move toward her.

"Hey, Elle, how's everything goin'?"

Elle and her husband run the only veterinary clinic in a fifty-mile radius, so I don't see her as much since they both work a lot. "As good as it can, I guess. Stayin' busy between the kids and the clinic."

"Oh, where's Olivia?"

Olivia is Elle's stepdaughter and was my student last year.

"Just dropped her off. She's already inside."

"That little stinker! She didn't even say hi to me. Apparently, I'm chopped liver now that she's no longer in my class." I pretend to pout.

"You know she loves you, probably didn't even see you," she offers.

Cars are lined up in front of the parent drop-off area, and Elle looks in the rearview mirror. "I should probably get going before these crazy moms start honkin'."

"Probably right," I tell her, then we say our goodbyes.

Walking inside the school, I avoid the energetic bodies in the hallway on the way to my classroom. I open the door, knowing my students will rush in as soon as the bell rings. I'm just hoping most of them didn't eat sugar for breakfast, but I quickly realize I wasn't so lucky.

They're bouncing off the walls, chitchatting, but as soon as I turn on *Frozen 2*, it all stops. Well, until the songs begin, then it becomes a sing-along, which I don't mind. For the rest of the day, I keep them busy with coloring sheets, games, and movies. I love how much fun they're having. Seeing my kids smile and having a good time is everything to me. Considering there are only three more days left, it's useless trying to do anything else.

At lunchtime, Lacey and I sit at a table where we can watch our students but still have some privacy.

"Ready for tonight?" she asks with a big grin on her face. Lacey's a year younger than I am and lives in town. She's been a teacher at the school for two years and teaches second grade. As soon as she got hired, we became instant friends.

"Yes, ma'am. More than ready, but I'm already exhausted."

"Right? My kids have been terrors today."

"Olivia actin' up?"

"No, she's the only one who listens to directions. Honestly, though, I'm grateful I'm not teaching older ones. Dealing with their pre-teen hormones sounds dreadful," she admits.

"Girl, same. What time are you plannin' on comin' over?"

"Six good? Thought I'd grab a pizza and some liquor first."

"That's perfect. Hopefully, the last half of the day goes faster than the first."

She nods in agreement, and when the bell rings, we head back to our classrooms. The rest of the day flies by, and as I'm walking to my car, I run into my mom.

"Three more days!" she reminds me with a cheerful smile.

"Lord. I just hope I survive."

"You always do, sweetie. Lacey's still comin' to visit, right?"

I nod, then add, "Don't you dare say what Dad told me this mornin' about your night."

Mom giggles. "I don't wanna know."

"Good," I say, pretending to gag, but the reality is I adore how much my parents love each other. It's adorable, and I only hope one day I find the same type of lasting relationship. My dad's my hero who treats my mother like a queen, so my standards are high. Maybe too high for any man in Eldorado to meet.

"See you at home," she says, and we go our separate ways.

Now that my sister is married with kids, I'm the last child living in my parents' house. I have no reason to leave, though. I'm not dating anyone or plan to anytime soon. It's convenient, plus the rent is free, so it's allowed me to grow my savings.

Mom has already changed into her pajamas by the time I make my way through the front door.

"Your dad's bringin' some food from the B&B. Want him to grab you a plate?"

"Nah, Lacey's pickin' up a pizza."

"Perfect. Hope you girls have fun," she says as she pulls a few of her favorite wines from the cabinet and sets them on the counter.

My lips tilt up into a smile. "You've been holdin' out on me!"

"You deserve it. You've worked really hard this year, and I'm so proud of you."

"Thanks, Mom. Learned everything from you, the best of the best," I admit.

She grins wide and pulls me in for a hug.

I let out a yawn. "Welp. Guess I'm gonna jump in the shower, then change into something more comfy."

"Sounds good," she tells me just as my dad enters the kitchen. He sets down the to-go boxes and leans in to give Mom a kiss. After I give Dad a side hug, I make my way to the bathroom.

The warm shower soothes my muscles, and I'm perfectly relaxed when I get out. I slip on some yoga shorts and a tank top, then throw my wet hair up into a messy bun. By the time I go back into the kitchen, Mom and Dad are nowhere to be found. I'm sure they're lying in bed watching TV. Turning in before seven isn't out of the norm around here, especially because Dad gets up before the sun rises.

Lacey arrives with a large bag and unloads a frozen pizza, a bottle of tequila, some grenadine, and a jug of orange juice.

"I didn't realize gettin' sloppy drunk was on the agenda," I mock as I preheat the oven.

"Might as well. We don't have anything to do tomorrow."

I shrug with a grin. "You're right." I place the pizza in the oven and set a timer.

Lacey opens the cabinet and grabs a glass. She's hung out with me so much that she knows where everything is around here. Mom's told her a million times to make herself at home, and she does.

"You drinkin' the hard stuff or wine?" She pours the tequila and juice on ice.

"Guess I'll take a sunrise then," I tell her.

"You can have this one!" She slides the one she made my way.

My eyes go wide when I take a sip. "Jesus, Lace. Did you add any OJ at all?"

"After one, you won't be able to taste it anyway." She snorts, then makes hers the same way.

We sit at the table and wait for the pizza to finish, nearly chugging our drinks.

"I had an idea for next year that I wanted to run by you," I say nervously. "Yeah?"

"I noticed there aren't any after-school programs around here. So I was thinking about starting something for next fall."

She instantly grins, and I continue, "I think it would help the parents who work later. And we could do different things like sports or dance or maybe even art classes. I haven't fully decided yet."

"Yes. That's an amazing idea!"

I feel relieved she agrees.

"I danced all through high school and college. I would love to help. I mean, if you want me to," she adds.

"Oh my God, yes. I was gonna ask if you'd like to be a part of it. I think it's going to take some planning and time, but it'll be worth it. I haven't run it by my mom yet. I want to get the details together before pitching it to her, but now that you're on board, I think it will be a lot easier. Mom knows I can't dance. Or paint. And I suck at sports."

She chuckles. "I love the idea. I really think the kids will too. It'll keep them occupied and allow them to learn new things."

"Yes. Exactly. It will provide opportunities for those who don't get to typically do things like that too," I say, my thoughts lingering on the few foster kids we have. I want them to have a good experience, especially after everything they've been through at such a young age. While I can't imagine what that's like, I want to be a positive light in their lives.

Lacey's eyes soften as if she can read my mind, but before she can say anything, the oven beeps. I stand, feeling the tequila rush through my veins, and take it out. Sloppily, I cut it in half and put it on plates. We grab our food and drinks, then go to the living room.

"I might've made our beverages a little too strong, but I think it's time for round two," she says when I land on the Hallmark channel. Before I can reply, she's standing to do just that.

When she returns, she hands me a glass, and we dive into our food.

The heroine and the hero in the movie are as cheesy as our pizza. It's more than obvious the two have an underlying attraction, but they're too stubborn to admit it.

"Oh look, it's kinda like you and Grayson."

I whip my head toward her and hurry and chew the bite I just took. "Don't think so!"

She arches her brow. "Sure 'bout that?"

"Absolutely. He's annoying. Not my type. And an asshole. I'm happy with my nonexistent dating life at the moment, thank you very much."

"Mm-hmm," she responds.

"I am! I mean, I haven't seen anyone since college, and even then, it was casual dating and nothing serious. I have high standards. You've seen my parents," I remind her.

"This is true, but there's still hope for you. Aren't there two new ranch hands? Either one of them single?"

"Oh yeah, Luke and Payton. They're as single as a dollar bill, but even so, I'm not interested. Though, Luke has flirted with me. He's just not my type either."

"'Cause ranch hands aren't your type?"

"Exactly," I say with a sigh.

"If you change your mind, there's always Grayson," she taunts.

I groan. "I mean, full disclosure, I *am* attracted to him." I point a finger in her face. "Don't you dare tell anyone I said that, but I could never go there, not after what happened between us all those years ago."

Lacey gives me a sad expression. "I get it. But honestly, you should confront him about it. So then he at least knows *why* you hate him."

Meeting her eyes, I shake my head. "I can't. It'd be way too humiliating, and then the last thing I want is his pity or worst—excuses for why he did what he did. I'd rather just write him off and pretend he doesn't exist."

She lifts her drink and makes a toast. "For all the single ladies who are DTF but won't settle for just any dick."

I snort. "Now, that's something I'll drink to any day of the week."

CHAPTER FIVE

Mackenzie

I wake up in the morning feeling like complete crap. Lacey's snuggled up on the couch with a blanket, and all I can think about right now is coffee and food. Since she drank too much to drive home, she stayed over.

I plop down by her feet, and she stirs.

"Why did we drink tequila, out of all things?" she mutters with a groan. "I'm blaming you for this raging hangover I'm dealing with right now."

She lies back down and covers her face. "I'm blaming me too. It was such a bad idea."

"I think I need some breakfast. Want to go to the B&B with me?"

Lacey forces herself to sit up and smiles. "Yes. God yes."

On the way to the B&B, we're both silent. After drinking a half bottle of tequila, we're miserable. At some point, it tasted like water, so we kept going until midnight.

We mosey up the porch steps, and I can already smell the crispy bacon

"If food doesn't work, they say to just start drinking again," I tell her as she follows me.

"I may never have tequila again after last night," Lacey admits.

"Yeah right!" I say with a laugh. "I'm surprised neither of us got sick."

The sounds of clashing plates and chatter ring out in the dining room. As soon as we make our way to the buffet table, Maize comes from the kitchen carrying a pan of buttered biscuits. She gives me a second glance.

"You look like utter shit," she mutters as I smooth down my wild hair.

"Thanks," I murmur as she greets Lacey.

"Oh, so y'all had a party? Sad I couldn't have come. But then again, not worth feeling like the way you two look." Maize snickers.

"It was fun until it wasn't," I say, adding extra gravy to my biscuits and snagging a few sausage links.

"I'm gonna become a nun after that." Lacey lets out a groan. "They can't drink, right?"

"Sex," I point out. "They can't have sex."

"Well, either way…" Lacey shrugs.

"The nun's life was my backup plan. See how well that worked out." Maize chuckles, then makes her way back to the kitchen.

We sit down at the table across from Gavin, Riley, Diesel, Luke, and Payton. Of course as soon as they see us, they start talking amongst themselves.

"What the hell happened to you two?" Riley finally asks the burning question they all want the answer to.

"Look like they got ran over by a tractor," Diesel adds with amusement.

"Hey, hey. Y'all are talkin' way too loud." I hold up my hand. "At least let me get some coffee in me before you start actin' like rowdy assholes."

This only encourages them to keep going. The next thing I know, the group of them are pulling up chairs to our table and joining us.

"Ugh," I groan, and Lacey smiles when Luke sits next to her.

"Everyone, this is my friend Lacey. She's a teacher too," I say, and they all politely greet her.

"You like bein' a teacher?" Luke asks.

"Love it," she admits, and I think I might see a hint of a spark between them.

The chair next to me slides out, and Grayson sits down.

"Well, this day just keeps gettin' better, doesn't it?"

"Good mornin' to you too." He shoves a biscuit in his mouth, then continues, "Nice to see you're in your usual mood."

I ignore him, keeping my back to him.

"So you gonna tell us what happened and why you look like you were hit by a bus?" Payton asks.

"Tequila. *A lot of it*," Lacey responds.

"Ahh. Explains it." Luke gives Lacey a smirk, and she blushes.

"So what're your plans today?" Grayson asks me.

"Don't talk to me. We aren't friends, and I don't like you."

Diesel shakes his head. "Dude. It's clearly not the time."

"It's *never* the time." Riley chuckles. "Kenzie obviously hates you, man. Give it up."

I turn to him with a sarcastic smile. "Listen to your friends. They're apparently smarter than you, which isn't saying too much."

"Hey!" Riley screeches. "I was on your side for once."

"Yelling again." I use my well-practiced teacher's tone. "Use your inside voice."

"This *is* my inside voice," Riley retorts, talking at the same volume.

Gavin finishes eating and stands. "Time to go, boys. We gotta do a lotta shit today and don't have time to lollygag."

Riley and Diesel are done eating, so they stand and put up their plates. Soon Payton and Luke clear out too. The only people left are Lacey, Grayson, and me.

I turn my body away from him and give Lacey my attention.

"Did you say you were gonna organize your closet today?" I ask her.

She finishes eating and pushes her plate away. "There's no way in hell I can manage that. I'm going home, taking a bath, then climbing in bed. I'll try again tomorrow when my head doesn't hurt."

I laugh. "Next time, let's stick with wine."

Grayson clears his throat, and then I feel something cold snap around my left wrist. When I look down, I notice he's handcuffed me to himself. I gasp and narrow my eyes at him. What the fuck is he doing?

As hard as I can, I jerk my hand away. "Let me go."

"No can do, sweetheart. Lost the key." He shrugs.

"Are you a dumbass?" I squeal, my heart rate climbing.

He chuckles. "Guess you're spending the day with me then?"

"I swear, Grayson, if you don't uncuff me right now, you'll live to regret it."

Lacey snickers, and I narrow my eyes at her. "Well. I guess you two have your afternoon planned."

"Please don't leave me with him," I beg, but she winks, then stands to leave.

"You'll be okay. Just let me know how it goes." She pats my head before walking away.

"Grayson," I say between gritted teeth. "This isn't funny."

"It's not supposed to be. This is payback, baby."

When my dad walks up, I jerk my hand below the table. The last thing I need is him noticing we're cuffed together.

He looks curiously between Grayson and me. "What are you two up to?"

"Nothin'," I quickly say. "Was just telling Grayson he needs to fuck off."

"Mackenzie Bishop," Dad snaps. "*Language.* We have guests around, and the last thing I want is them hearing my teacher daughter speak that way."

My head pounds, and all I can do is nod. "You look like you're up to something."

"We're not," Grayson interjects. "Kenzie just agreed to act as my shadow for the day, so we're gonna get to work once I finish eating." He purposely uses his other hand to shove food in his mouth.

"You did?" He tilts his head at me, confused.

I shrug. Though I want to snitch on Grayson and sick my dad on him, I decide not to. If he wants to play this game, even though I feel sick as hell, then I'll make sure to get him back a hundredfold. *This is motherfucking war.*

Dad eventually walks away, and I slam our wrists back on top of the table. "I'm not in the mood for your shit today, so unlock them right now. I know you didn't lose the key."

He chuckles, which only infuriates me even more. "No can do, sweetheart."

Leaning in, he comes close to my ear and whispers, "I'll make a deal with you. Tell me why you hate me so damn much, and I'll remove them as quickly as I put them on."

"Go to hell," I whisper-hiss.

"Alright. Well, you made your choice." Grayson stands, yanking me up with him. He clears our plates before leading me outside to his truck.

"Get in," he tells me, opening the driver's side door.

"How?"

"You're smarter than me, remember? Figure it out."

"You're so fuckin' annoying." I hop in and scoot over to the passenger seat.

"I could say the same about you." He cranks the truck and takes off toward the barns.

I scoff. "No, I don't go out of my way to poke at you. I avoid you like an STD, but you get under my skin on purpose."

"Remember when you left me naked and tied up with no phone to call for help? This is your payback, Kenzie. You get to work with me all day long. Today, I volunteered to clean out the stalls. "

"Asshole," I mumble, staring out the window and wanting to throw up.

We pull up to a cattle barn, and when we walk in, I notice it's a damn disaster. There's shit everywhere. Grayson leads me to the supply room and grabs a shovel for himself, then hands me one.

"Oh hell no. I am not helping you do your job."

"Well then, I guess this is gonna take twice as long to finish. You must really want to hang out with me longer."

I rip the shovel from his grip. "You're an idiot. There's no way we're gonna be able to work at the same time. Use your brain."

He chuckles. "Sure we can. We just have to sync up our movements. You act like it's impossible or something."

Grayson takes a step toward me and tucks loose strands of hair behind my ear. Though I don't intend to, I meet his brown eyes. My heart pounds, and though I want to deny the electricity that flows between us, it's undeniable. "Sorry you feel like hell."

"*Then. Let. Me. Go.*"

"Tell me why you hate me, and I will."

I immediately close up and build a wall around myself that's so high, he couldn't scale it if he had a thirty-foot ladder. I'm not opening that vault right now. "It's because you don't stop antagonizing me and purposely piss me off."

"I don't believe you. There's gotta be more to it than that."

"That's my answer, take it or leave it," I tell him.

"Nope, not good enough," he declares.

I give up, not wanting to have this conversation. I want to get this torture over with, so I jerk away and lead us to the stalls.

Shoveling shit together is difficult at first, but then we somehow manage to do it. Honestly, I can't remember the last time I did demanding and physical chores like this, and if I weren't hungover, I wouldn't be having such a terrible time. Grayson even carried the wheelbarrow closer as I walked beside him. When it's full, he wheels it outside.

"You're pretty good at this," he offers with a smirk after we've cleaned half the barn.

"I grew up doing this, Grayson. Just because I don't work on the ranch now doesn't mean I don't know how to do shit."

"Pretty cocky for someone attached to me. Not gonna lie, I kinda like it, though." He shoots me a wink, and I respond with an eye roll.

As I continue shoveling, I realize I have to pee. Not wanting to complain to Grayson, I try to hold it in the best I can.

"Fuck," I mumble after we drop another load of manure in the back. Thirty minutes have passed, and I know I'm in a losing battle with my bladder.

Grayson turns to me. "What's up?"

"I have to use the bathroom and can't because..." I lift my wrist, and his hand comes with it.

For some unknown reason, he finds this to be the funniest thing in the world, almost to the point of choking.

"I have to pee!" I shout, so he stops laughing at me.

"Guess you're gonna pop a squat in a stall with one of the bucket potties. I'll be a gentleman and not watch. I'll even hold the toilet paper for you."

"You can't be serious." If looks could kill, he'd be six feet under.

"Does it look like I'm joking?" He moves his hand around his face, being overly dramatic.

I lock my jaw so tight it hurts, but my bladder can't hold it much longer. There's no way we'd make it to a bathroom. We're at least ten minutes away.

Heading back to the supply stall, I grab a bucket, and Grayson finds one of the extra toilet seats that fits on top. It's not an ideal situation, but it works when the ranch hands have to take a crap in the middle of their shift. A majority of the barns don't have plumbing, and desperate times call for desperate measures. I snatch a roll of toilet paper from one of the drawers and shove it toward Grayson's chest. He grins wide the entire time.

"I can't believe this," I say, setting up my portable bathroom. Once it's all in place, I suck in a deep breath.

"If you look, I'll make you wish you were dead," I threaten.

"Only if you tie me up first," he snaps.

I lower my jeans and panties, then sit on the bucket. As soon as I do, my need to go vanishes. At this point, I'm ready to cry. I have to go so badly, but I can't under the pressure. Now, I understand when my kids at school tell me they're pee-shy.

I close my eyes, trying to pretend I'm anywhere but here. I think about oceans, summer rain, and even a faucet running. Nothing fucking works.

"You waitin' on something?" Grayson finally asks with amusement.

"Shut up. It's in my bladder, but it won't come out because you're so close I can hear you breathing."

His entire body shakes with the laughter he's trying to hold back.

Minutes later, a drop comes out, then a small trickle, and pretty soon a heavy stream. I sigh in relief.

"Toilet paper," I say, waiting for him to hand it to me.

"Uh-oh," Grayson mumbles under his breath, and I grow more ragey.

"What does that mean?" I ask with an edge.

"I left it in the supply room," he tells me.

"You've got to be kidding me. You expect me to drip-dry after sweating my ass off doing half your job?" My voice goes up an entire octave, and I feel like I'm going to internally combust with anger.

"I'm just kiddin'. I *should* make you, but I'm not as cruel as you are to me," he taunts, handing me the roll.

After I've pulled up my panties and pants, I grab the bucket. Grayson walks me to the pile we created so I can dump it and rinse it out.

For the rest of the day, I give him the silent treatment. He's humiliated me enough, and though he thinks we're even, we aren't, not by a long shot.

After the barns are cleaned, Grayson takes me back to the B&B. He climbs out and leads me over to my SUV. We're standing close, too close, and right now, all I want to do is push him on his ass, but I know I'd go down with him since we're still attached.

"Welp, thanks for being my shadow today," he sing-songs.

I glare at him. "Uncuff me."

He pulls the key from his pocket, then throws it in the bushes with a laugh.

My eyes go wide, and I push against his hard chest. "What is wrong with you?"

He chuckles. "Whoops."

I move to the bushes and get on my hands and knees, forcing him with me. I search furiously and, by some miracle, find the tiny silver key. With all my strength, I bring my wrist to my body and unlock myself.

"You're so fucked," I warn him when I'm finally free. "Totally fucked."

"We're even now," he tells me sternly. "You left me for the wolves naked, and I made you work with me all day."

"Even?" I scoff as I walk away. "That's what you think."

CHAPTER SIX

Grayson

I can't believe this year is half over. It's already the middle of June, which means it's time for cow branding. We do this every summer for the new calves and cows the ranch has bought. Branding is important because if our cows wander off, the locals will know who they belong to.

Today will include a lot of horseback riding, and it's one of the times I feel like a real cowboy. Especially since it's done just like those on the great frontier.

I'm supposed to meet Diesel on the far side of the ranch at the corrals built for this very thing. I make a quick cup of coffee, then head out. When I take the steps off the porch, I notice something unusual in the bed of my truck— there's a high pile of rotting cow shit, and it stinks.

"What the hell?" I curse aloud, searching around and waiting for someone to jump out. But it's quiet, and the sun has barely risen over the horizon. Knowing I don't have time right now to drive to a barn and empty it, I decide I'll have to deal with it after work.

As I travel down the gravel road, I see some of it settling in the back as some fall out. I look in the rearview mirror and see fresh cow patties layered on top.

I grit my teeth, knowing there's only one person who's out to get me —*Kenzie*.

It's been a month since she's told me our little war wasn't over. After a few weeks had passed, I assumed she changed her mind or wasn't bothering with it. But doing this on a day like today is a low blow. Then again, publicly embarrassing me is her style—always has been.

I make my way to the area where all the ranch hands are meeting. As soon as I pull up, it's more than obvious I'm hauling crap around. I get out of my truck, and Diesel walks over.

"What are...?" He shakes his head. "Why are you carrying a load of shit in the back of your truck?"

I glare at him. "You tell me. I found it there this morning."

He smacks his hand on his leg. "The only thing I'm mad about is that I haven't thought of doing that to someone yet."

"Yeah well. By the time I'm done with branding today, it's gonna be absolutely rancid. I'm pissed."

Diesel nods. "Yeah, sittin' out in the sun like this. You're gonna have a full-blown mess on your hands."

"When I find out who did this..." I grind my teeth, already imagining my revenge.

With a lifted brow, Diesel puts a hand on my shoulder. "I think we all know who's responsible."

"Kenzie," I answer.

"Yep. She's the only person who's out to get you right now. Especially after you cuffed yourselves together. Rowan thought it was hilarious."

I grin wide. "I did too. But lord she was angry all day. And she had a helluva hangover." I keep the bucket incident to myself though I should tell everyone after this stunt.

"You're terrible, man. Wouldn't be surprised if the cow shit ain't the worst of it. You know she's a Bishop. They can be...*a lot*." He'd know, considering he's married to one of them.

We make our way over to the main area. "You gonna tie or ride today?" he asks.

"Oh, I have a choice?"

"Yeah, you've been doin' it for a few years. Thought I'd give you dibs."

"I wanna ride."

The horses are already saddled and tied to posts along the corral. A smile hits my lips, and I choose one of my favorite Palominos named Striker. I put my foot in the stirrup and grab the horn, then swing my other leg over. Once I'm settled, I enter the cow pen, where they're letting them out of the chute. Once I rope one, two ranch hands tie their feet, then a couple of others brand them. It's a quick process, but with so many animals, we'll be working until sunset for the next four to five days.

It's almost like a game, choosing a calf, roping it, then letting the guys handle the rest. We're zipping through the herd like it's nothing.

Six hours later, Diesel pulls me out for lunch and to give the horse a break.

As soon as my feet hit the ground, my legs feel like gelatin, and I make a mental note to start riding more. Our lunch is delivered to us where we're branding so we don't waste precious time. I scarf it down quickly, not realizing how hungry I was. However, skipping breakfast will do that.

Our break ends, and I get back to work. I'm in my element, and it reminds me of why I left San Antonio. I'm lucky as hell I found something I like doing because ranching was never on my list, but it's changed my life.

The rest of the day flies by, and when I head to my truck, I had nearly forgotten all about the mess until I smell it.

I'm exhausted from being in the sun and sore from riding, but I'm also starving. So instead of dealing with the shit—*literally*—I stop by the B&B for some chopped steak and potatoes. When I walk in, I can smell myself from sweating all day, but I don't care.

I walk straight to the buffet and pile some food on a plate, then cover it all with brown gravy. After grabbing a glass of sweet tea, I sit at an empty table in the corner and dig in. When I look up, I see Kenzie. Her eyes meet mine, and she gives me her signature sarcastic *go to hell* smirk.

When she sits at the table next to mine, I glare at her. "I know what you did."

She lifts her brows with an innocent look. "Don't know what you're talkin' about."

"Yeah right! You filled the back of my truck with shit while I was sleeping last night," I snap. "And you knew I had branding today and wouldn't be able to take care of it right away."

Her expression doesn't change. "How about you come with the receipts?" she challenges. "I'm waiting."

"I don't need proof to know it was you. I made you help me shovel shit. So this is the perfect revenge."

I notice a flicker in her eyes. "Grow up, Grayson."

"Just be aware, I'll get you back. And it's gonna be a thousand times worse than handcuffing you to me for a day," I tell her as she sips her tea. "Or driving around cow shit."

She slams the cup down. "Don't threaten me."

"Not a threat, sweetheart. A goddamn promise," I say, then finish eating without speaking another word. However, it doesn't stop her from stealing glances.

When I'm done, I go to the barn on the east side to drop off the manure. I pull up and see Kane's on stable duty today.

It's no surprise that the pile that was once there is gone.

Kane walks out with a shovel in his hand and laughs when he sees me. "Whose Cheerios did you piss in?"

I glare at him. "No one's. This is Kenzie's doin' because she hates me so much. And fuck it reeks."

Moving closer, he scrunches his nose. "You do too. What've you been doin' today?"

"Riding, and now I have to deal with this, which infuriates the fuck outta me."

He smirks as he hands me the shovel. "Have fun with that."

"Not even gonna lend me a hand?" I take off my hat and smooth down my sweaty hair. Damn, I can't wait to take a shower.

"Hell no. I didn't piss Kenzie off. You did. Kinda clever, though." He smirks.

Narrowing my eyes at him, I drop the tailgate down. The motion causes globes of crap to fall forward

"*Clever*?" I narrow my eyes as I study him. "You helped her do this, didn't you?"

He shrugs. "I'll do anything if the price is right."

"Why doesn't that surprise me one bit?"

"You wanna get her back? Just let me know." He does a little finger motion insinuating if I pay him, he's on board.

"I'm not that desperate. But I'll tell you this… When I get my revenge, she might need your help to clean it up."

He chuckles. "Perfect. I like extra cash."

I hop in the back and get started because the quicker I finish this, the faster I can go home. My body's already hurting. Sweat starts dripping from my brows again, and I curse her name as I haul it out. If she weren't so beautiful, and I wasn't so fucking attracted to her, this rivalry we have would be a lot easier. But as I mentioned earlier, this is far from over.

When I'm done an hour later, I grab the hose and spray down my truck.

The first thing I do when I get home is take a nice, long hot shower. Tomorrow, we'll be back at it early, and I'm ready to crash for the night.

As I pull a beer from the fridge, I get a call from my mom. At first, I contemplate sending it straight to voicemail, but then I answer just in case something's wrong at home.

"Hey, son. I'm shocked you picked up."

I feel bad because I don't purposely ignore her, but between my working on the ranch and needing to sleep, we don't get the chance to talk a lot. "Guess today's your lucky day. Everything goin' okay?"

"Yes, everything's fine. Thanks for asking. Just wanted to see if you got the invite to the family reunion in October."

I look at the pile of mail that's sitting on the kitchen counter. It's been there for about a week. "I'm sure I did, but I don't plan on goin', and I'm sure you can guess why."

There's a beat of awkward silence. "I know you don't wanna be around Bella, but she won't be there."

"That's a big reason, but not the only one."

My brother who still acts innocent in all of this.

"I understand, but I miss you and wanna see you. And so does your gram. She's not in the best health these days. Your aunts Debbie and Vicky are coming too, and they haven't seen you in years. I don't know what I gotta do to make you change your mind, but I hope you consider it…"

I contemplate it since Bella won't be there. There are too many bad memories between us, and I've refused to go home for the holidays because of her. It's why I usually spend it with the Bishops. The few times I've seen her after what happened, I feel a rush of anger mixed with bitterness and sadness, and I'd rather not be in that position. I want nothing to do with her, but considering she's family, she'll always be around. She made her choices, and I made mine to stay away as much as possible.

"You're positive she won't be there?" If I know one thing about her, she loves to make a scene even when I try to ignore her.

"She has a work event that weekend she can't miss."

I let out a long sigh. "Okay. I'll think about it."

"Thanks, I can't wait to see you," Mom says, and I can hear the cheerfulness in her tone.

"I didn't say yes, Mom. I said I'd think about it," I point out so she doesn't get her hopes up. I don't want to let her down, but the thought of going back makes me anxious.

"But you also didn't say no. So maybe I'll see my son soon."

"Well, anyway, I've had a long day and am really tired so I think I'm gonna call it a night."

"No problem. Sleep well. Let me know when you decide. Your aunts are staying with me, but I can keep the couch free if you do come."

"Nah, it's okay. I'd book a hotel room."

"Okay sounds good. I love you, Grayson."

"Love you too, Mom."

I don't have the best relationship with my stepdad either so this reunion comes with a host of dread and nerves. But I do miss *some* of my family members.

After I finish my beer, I rustle through the mail until I find the invite. I look at the date, then decide to go ahead and book a hotel room. If I change my mind at the last minute, I'll cancel it.

I'll ask Diesel for that weekend off, and it'll be up to him if I attend or not. I'm just crossing my fingers that going is the right decision.

CHAPTER SEVEN

Mackenzie

After working all summer, I finally finished planning the after-school program. Lacey has been a huge help, and once we realized we didn't have enough staff or volunteers to do all the activities I initially wanted, we decided to do a dance program. Hopefully, we can expand it to more in a couple of years; but we're focusing on this one for now.

Registration forms were sent home with the kids during open house, and they were required to send it back if they wanted to participate. Right now, fifty kids are signed up, and I know it'll grow over the years.

When I pitched the idea to my mom, she was excited about it. After Grandma learned about it, she was ready to invite the whole town to our first show, which will be in December before Christmas break.

Today's the first day of school, and I'm expecting it to be chaotic. The kids are usually little bursts of energy, and I wouldn't be surprised if I pass right out after dinner.

Teachers and students always have so much built-up excitement, and there's underlying energy flowing throughout the halls. It's a new school year, a fresh start, and though I'll have to learn all about my new students, I'm looking forward to getting to know their personalities.

After I've gotten dressed and ready, I stop by the B&B. A few of the older ranch hands are sitting at a table with Grayson. Immediately, I groan at my luck.

It's been six weeks since I had the twins help me fill Grayson's truck with cow shit, and I've been anxiously waiting for him to retaliate. But he hasn't. It usually takes us weeks to get back at each other, and time's been ticking. Based on his reaction last time, I know whatever he's up to will be next level, and I'm completely dreading it.

I grab a cup of coffee, snag a blueberry muffin, then find a place to sit.

"You look very pretty today," Grayson compliments with a grin as he moves to my table.

"Thanks," I mutter, not wanting to get worked up before school.

"You ready to admit you filled my truck with shit, or ya gonna keep denying it?"

I glare at him. "Please don't start with me today. I really—"

He holds up his hands. "Fine. Just know, I haven't forgotten, sweetheart."

Grayson stands and puts his plate away, then leaves.

If he only knew what *I* haven't forgotten.

I open my lesson plan on my phone and read over it real quick as well as look over the list of my student's names so I can start memorizing them. Then I look over the choreography Lacey and I created for the after-school dance program. I'm both excited and nervous. After ten minutes, I get on the road and head to the school.

This year, I have a little girl named Ashlin, who's in foster care and is such a sweetie. Tracie, her foster mom, explained what Ashlin had been through when I met her last week at our open house. The little girl's mother was an alcoholic, and her deadbeat dad left them before she was born. At five years old, she was basically taking care of herself. Child Protective Services found out Ashlin was living in filth and starving. She's been with Tracie for the past year and quickly attached to me when we first met.

This year, I decorated my classroom with a magical creature theme. There's a giant castle on one wall and a dragon on the other. I knew it'd be a big hit with the little ones, and I wasn't wrong. Apparently, my room was the talk of the school, and several colleagues came by and poked their heads in just to see.

Before the bell rings, I go to my door to greet my kids. It also helps me memorize their names. However, right now, they're wearing name tags, so it makes it easier.

"Good morning, class!" I say, bright and cheery as I give them high fives on their way in.

"Good morning, Miss Bishop!" Their small voices fill the space.

The first week of school is all about learning boundaries, going over the rules and expectations, and how to properly ask questions. Throughout the day, I show them where supplies go, how to use glue, replacing marker lids, and other instructions that will make my life easier for the rest of the year.

After the final bell rings, I'm tired as hell but also eager about teaching dance.

Ashlin stops me in the hall. "I don't know where to go."

"For the after-school program?"

She nods sweetly, and I can tell she's a little overwhelmed. "I'm going there now, so you can follow me if you'd like." I hold out my hand, and she immediately takes it.

"Thank you."

We walk to the gym, and I turn on the giant fans.

Lacey meets up with me. "There you are! How was your first day?"

"As expected! I'm so tired," I admit.

"Is that code for you want to eat pizza and drink tequila?" She waggles her brows.

I snort. "No way. I don't know if I'll *ever* be able to do that again."

She chuckles and looks around. "Sure ya will. Are you ready to do this?"

"Yes, ma'am." I grab the megaphone and clear my throat before queuing it up.

"Hey, y'all! So excited you're here. My name is Miss Bishop, and this is Miss Garcia. If you have any questions, you can ask us or any of the other teachers here." Then I introduce the teachers who have volunteered to help.

"If you're in kindergarten, go to Mrs. Hallows, who's holding the green sign!" I point at the far end of the gym, then go through the other grades and match them with their teachers. A month before school started, Lacey and I recorded the routine and sent it to the teachers. Now, they'll teach the choreography to the students, and we'll eventually put them all together. I cannot wait to see how the final production turns out.

Each group has fifteen to twenty kids, which is what I was hoping for. Lacey and I chose to work with the first- and second-grade students and assigned the others to the age groups they typically teach.

"Miss Bishop!" Ashlin looks up at me with her dark brown eyes. "I need to go to the bathroom."

Lacey continues her instructions, and I show Ashlin where it is.

"This is a lot of fun," she says, and it makes my heart swell.

"I'm so glad to hear that!" I tell her as she skips into the restroom. Hearing Ashlin say that has made all the prep work we did this summer worth it, and it's only the first day.

She comes out and walks right up to me. "Thank you."

"You're welcome," I offer, and we return to the group. Ashlin stands beside a little boy and picks right back up where we left off.

They're adorable and are learning quicker than I ever anticipated. My eyes scan over the room and land back on our group. They're having the time of their lives.

As I stand beside Lacey, my mind wanders. One day, I hope to adopt. Since meeting a handful of foster children last year, I've been researching the foster to adopt program as well. I've had an easy life on the ranch with a family who loves and supports me, but I know not everyone has that. Some kids desperately want and need parents, and I'd love to provide that.

While adopting isn't something I've voiced too much over the years, it's embedded deep in my heart. No one else in our family has gone that route, but I know they'd be thrilled about my decision, especially Grandma Bishop, who is dead set on expanding the family. Of course I'd love to get pregnant one day and have my own kids, but I'm not sure that's in the cards for me.

"Five, six, seven, eight...turn around and bow!" Lacey tells our group on beat with an energetic smile. She's in her element. When they finish the next eight counts, I clap. "Woo! That time was amazing. You're all doing so great."

Lacey grins. "Okay, let's do it again from the top!"

We continue running through the parts they learned until it's time to give them a little break.

After an hour, it's time to call it quits and get them ready for parent pickup. The day went just as planned, and I think we got a lot accomplished.

"The kids looked like they were having fun," my mom says once the room is clear.

"They did. I'm surprised by how fast they've caught on. Can't wait for our first show," I say excitedly.

She grins. "I can't either. It's gonna be adorable. Ya know your grandma has already told her quilt club about it. They each requested personal invitations."

I snort-laugh. "Of course."

Lacey comes over after the last student leaves. "Phew. I'm too young to be this tired."

Mom chuckles. "Just wait until you're my age. It gets worse."

Lacey places her hand on her forehead, being overly dramatic. "Say it ain't so, Mrs. Bishop." She gives me a wink. "Can't wait to do it all over again tomorrow."

"Agreed! Hopefully, we'll get through teaching them the middle part of the first song," I say.

"Oh, we will!" she encourages before telling us goodbye.

Mom and I grab our bags, lock up, then head to our vehicles.

"Guess we can say the first day of school was successful?"

She climbs inside her Suburban. "Absolutely, honey. I think it'll be a memorable year."

"Me too. But aren't they all?" I muse.

She gives me a nod and a wave. As she drives away, I turn and look at the sun lying lazily in the distance. A smile touches my lips. I may be single as hell and still live at home with my parents, but I have a lot to be grateful for—my job being one of them.

CHAPTER EIGHT

Grayson

Another lonely Friday night awaits me when I get off work. As I eat breakfast with the other ranch hands, Diesel and Riley mention meeting at the bar tonight since Rowan's covering for Kenzie.

"Wait, why?" I ask, knowing Kenzie only bartends when they're short-staffed. More people were hired once she and Ethan got busy building their careers. During their college breaks, they'd worked there to make extra cash. Since Rowan manages the bar, she only begs them to cover when it's an absolute emergency.

"Kenzie's sick," Riley answers. "She was picking up a shift for someone who has the flu but then got it too."

Though I'm supposed to be retaliating, I'm also thinking of using this opportunity to bring her soup. Underneath all the pranks and snarky comebacks, there's an underlying sexual tension between us that she can't deny.

"Uh, maybe. I'll let ya know later," I tell him.

I clear my plate, then go back to the barn so I can finish early. Diesel gives me the go-ahead once my afternoon duties are completed. I make my way to the B&B to grab some of Maize's chicken noodle soup to-go. It's so good, I grab an extra one for myself.

As soon as I'm in my truck, I drive to Kenzie's, anticipating she'll slam the door in my face or toss the hot food right at me. Even though she's ill, I wouldn't put either scenario past her.

I hold the bowl in one hand and knock with the other. When she answers, I take in her appearance and hate that she's not feeling well. She's wrapped in a blanket, her hair is in a messy bun, her cute nose is red, and her cheeks are pale. When I gaze down at her body, I smirk at her horse slippers.

"You come here to gawk at me looking miserable or what?"

Sick or not, Mackenzie Bishop will always have an attitude with me.

"Actually, I brought you soup." I hold it out, and she looks at it as if I'm trying to hand her a ball of fire. Though I owe her for the latest stunt she pulled, I'd never mess with her food.

"Why?"

"Because I heard you were sick."

"You poison it with laxatives or somethin'?"

"Jesus, I'm just tryin' to be nice. Cut me some slack for once."

She narrows her eyes, like she wants to say something, but doesn't.

"Oh, Grayson." Mrs. Bishop appears, and Kenzie's shoulders slump at her mother's kind voice. "How sweet of you to bring soup. Smells like Maize's." Mila grabs it and inhales with a smile.

"It is. Figured it'd make Kenzie feel better."

"Aren't you just the nicest?" She pats my cheek and smiles wide. "I'll put this in a bowl for you, honey," she tells Kenzie, then walks off.

I flash Kenzie a smug grin as she scowls. "Your mom *loves* me."

"That's because she doesn't know the real you," she grunts.

"The real me?" I nearly burst out laughing. "A Southern gentleman who works his ass off and is naturally charming?"

"The one who's a liar," she snaps.

"What're you talkin' about? When have I lied to you?" I cross my arms in frustration.

Her lips twitch as if she's holding back again. Though I'm not sure why. She always tells it like it is, especially when it comes to me.

"Thanks for the soup." She grips the door as if she's contemplating slamming it in my face.

I flash a small smile and take a step back. "You're welcome. Hope you feel better, Kenzie."

With the long Labor Day weekend over, the bachelor auction is all everyone's talking about. It's an annual fundraiser event Rose Bishop hosts. She suckers the single men in town to be bid on for dates. Though I try to get out of it each year, I never do.

"Grayson, sweetie," Grandma Bishop calls as I carry two large buckets of goat feed. Ethan needed an extra hand today, so after I did my regular morning duties with Diesel, I swung by the goat farm.

"Yes, ma'am?" I smile, tightening my grip around the handles. Thankfully, I'm wearing heavy-duty work gloves since they're so heavy, and the metal handle cuts into my hands.

"Would you be a peach and pick up my catering order at the grocery store?"

"They aren't delivering to the hall?" I ask, knowing all the food is for the auction tomorrow.

"Oh yes, they are. But I also got a separate order of sandwiches and snacks for Elisa's first birthday party this weekend. I'd cook it myself, but with everything going on, there's just no extra time." Before I can agree, she holds out an envelope of cash. Saying no to Rose isn't an option.

Setting down the buckets, I take it from her with a nod. "Sure. I'll swing by there shortly."

She smiles widely. "You're a gem. Thank you. Just take it to the B&B kitchen, and Maize will put it in one of the big fridges."

Rose walks away, and I stuff the envelope in my pocket before getting back to it.

"Alright, your dinner's here, calm down," I tell Cupcake, Cheesecake, and Cinnamon Roll as they scream at me. I'm surrounded by hungry goats, and soon, both buckets are emptied into the troughs.

Once I lock the gate, I walk back to the barn and find Ethan.

"Anything else, boss?" I stand in the entryway of his office where he's sitting behind his desk with Harper on his lap.

"No, man, thanks for your help this afternoon."

I tip my hat to him and smirk at Harper. "You gonna pop soon?"

"God, I wish." She groans, rubbing her hand over her big belly. "Damn Bishops and their stubborn ways."

I chuckle when Ethan scowls.

"Well good luck. I'm off to the store for Rose."

"Ahh, you got roped into helping since I'm finally off the hook." Ethan smirks, tightening his arm around Harper.

"Yeah, yeah. I'll be stuck doing that auction for the next twenty years."

"Not if you find yourself a wife," Harper muses. "Or Kenzie gets her head out of her ass."

My heart races at the mention of Kenzie. She never bids on me even though I see the way her nostrils flare every time there's a bidding war for me.

"Probably not in this lifetime." I groan, then wave before I leave.

I drive the fifteen-minute trip into town and park in front of the store. As soon as I walk in the doors, I set my eyes on the deli but am quickly interrupted.

"Grayson!" Sarah Cooke stands in front of me. "I haven't seen you in a while. How are ya?"

"Just fine, thanks. How 'bout you?" I ask to be nice. She went to school with Maize, and from what I've heard, she tried to steal Gavin from her. Though I doubt that's how it really happened, I do know most of the Bishop girls don't like her. Sarah can be persistent, but I've never had any issues with her.

"I'm great! Lookin' forward to the bachelor auction tomorrow. You'll be there, right?" she asks eagerly.

"Yep. Until I'm married, I suppose," I say.

"Perfect! I'll be bidding on ya so we can finally go on a date." She smiles wide, and my stomach flips. I'll never hear the end of it if I have to take

Sarah out, and I don't want her to get the wrong idea since she's already so flirty.

"Alright then, I guess I'll see you there." I grin, then politely walk away.

Fuck, what the hell am I gonna do? With most of the Bishop girls getting married, not many are left—Kenzie and Kaitlyn are the only ones available. Though Harper's friend Hadleigh is single and will be there, she'll most likely spend her money on the twins since she's best friends with them both.

My head spins with thoughts about what I'm gonna do. I pick up the catering order and drive back to the ranch, already dreading tomorrow. I could ask Kaitlyn to bid on me, but she's younger and we rarely see each other, so it'd be awkward. My only option is to beg Kenzie, but considering we're still at each other's throats, I doubt she'll help me.

Unless I make her an offer she can't refuse.

The moment I'd mention Sarah Cooke, she'll make sure I end up with her just to piss me off. But if I suggest something else, maybe we'll both get something out of it.

I park in front of the B&B and see her walking inside.

Perfect timing.

Grabbing the sandwich platters and veggie trays, I head inside and make my way to the kitchen. As soon as I push through the double doors, Maize and Kenzie stare at me.

"Hey, thanks for getting these," Maize says, opening the fridge for me.

"No worries. Your grandmother is a hard woman to deny."

"Trust me, I know." Maize chuckles, closing the door. She flicks her gaze between Kenzie and me.

"I better go check on the buffet table." She quickly hustles out, leaving us alone.

"I need a favor," I blurt out.

Kenzie looks around as if I'm talking to someone else. "You're seriously askin' me, Cowboy?"

"You owe me one," I grind out, crossing my arms.

"For bringing me soup last week?" she asks as if she's unimpressed.

"No. After that stunt you pulled with my truck, it's my turn to get you back, and trust me when I say I've been planning something big."

"You're bluffing." She mimics my stance, folding her arms over her chest. My eyes automatically drop to her chest, and I swallow hard at the low-cut top she's wearing.

"I'm not, but do you really wanna risk it?" I raise a brow. "I nearly killed my back shoveling all that shit, so trust me when I say you don't want what's coming to you."

Kenzie relaxes her arms. "Fine. What do you want?"

"Bid on me at the auction tomorrow," I say, taking a step toward her, "and win."

She scoffs. "You've lost your mind. I'm not spending my hard-earned money to go on a date with you."

"If you win, we'll call a truce. I won't go through with my evil plan." I raise a brow, challenging her to say no.

She furrows her brows as if she's trying to read my thoughts. "What's the catch?"

Holding back a laugh at her resistance, I answer, "You agree to go with me to my family's reunion in a few weeks. Then we'll call it even. No more pranks."

"Why the hell would you want me to go to a family event with you? We don't even get along." She leans a hip on the prep table as if she needs the support to keep from passing out.

I shrug, lowering my eyes and feeling vulnerable at the personal shit I'm about to confess. "Things in my family are...*complicated*. My mom is begging me to come, and I'd rather not go alone. I haven't been home in years, and let's just say...it'd make things easier if I had someone with me."

"Why not bring one of the guys?"

"Because I'm asking you."

The auction is tomorrow night, and if she doesn't agree to this arrangement, I'm doubly screwed—by Sarah Cooke *and* going to my family's reunion solo.

"So what do you say?" I ask as she thinks about it. "We continue this little game of getting back at each other, or we finally call it quits. Up to you."

"After the way you handcuffed us together, I should feed you to the wolves. Lord knows all the single women are gonna be fightin' over y'all." She snorts.

I shrug as if I'm not bothered, but I'm ready to get on my knees and beg.

"Alright, but don't say I didn't warn ya. I plan to get ya back ten times worse, so…"

"Grayson." She scowls, her lips in a firm line.

"Oh and trust me, it'd be warranted after the way you left me tied up naked. Handcuffs and cow shit will seem like child's play."

"God! Fine." Kenzie huffs, dropping her arms. "But if you play me and do something—"

"You have my word," I say sincerely.

She inhales sharply. "Not sure your word means anything."

"What? When have I ever lied to you?"

She shoots daggers at me. "Never mind," she finally says. "Alright, I'll do it, and then we're even. Forever."

I nod in agreement. "Scout's honor."

She snorts as if that amuses her and pisses her off at the same time. Lord, this woman is confusing as hell.

"That means this event is our 'date,' right? Because I'm not going on some romantic evening with you."

"Trust me, I don't have a death wish."

"What's that mean?"

"That means I know better. After getting kicked in the balls by you a handful of times, water dumped over my head in my Sunday clothes, and you telling me off every week, I'm not stupid enough to wine and dine you. I'd either end up in the hospital with a concussion or lose my memory permanently."

"Wow. You think so highly of me, makes me wonder why you'd even want to take me to your family's party."

"As I said, I don't wanna go alone, and since this is a truce, I know you won't attempt to slit my throat in my sleep."

Kenzie pushes off the table, sauntering toward me with a cocky smirk. "Don't be so confident, Cowboy."

CHAPTER NINE

Mackenzie

I'm not sure what the hell came over me or why I agreed to Grayson's ridiculous offer but knowing the pranks would stop was too good to pass up. Getting him back always takes tons of planning, and I've been anxious while I wait for him to retaliate. As long as he keeps his word, it's a good deal.

However, bidding on him will make everyone think I want to go on a date with him.

Spending the weekend with him at a family event will only add to the speculation.

But it's just once, and then I can put this all behind me. *Hopefully*.

Grandma's been in charge of the annual bachelor auction for decades, and I've been suckered into going and bidding on someone since I turned eighteen. I've *never* bid on Grayson, so it will seem odd. While I'd love nothing more than to tell him to eat shit and go to his family's event alone.

I'm a sucker for a challenge. And *not* pushing Grayson off a ledge after one of his smart-ass remarks *will* be one.

"You hear Harper's in labor?" Hadleigh comes up and asks. She rakes her fingers through her curly strawberry-blond hair, then pulls it up and out of her face.

"Really? Guess they won't be making it tonight. That's exciting. Another second cousin in the fam!" I smile wide as I walk closer to the stage that'll be filled soon.

"Yeah, they're so excited. I hope to go to the hospital as soon as the baby's here." Hadleigh follows and scans her eyes around the room. She's already told me she plans on bidding on the twins, and she's ready to throw elbows if another woman gets in her way. Though she swears they're just friends, we all suspect there's more to it than that, but I don't ask.

Ten minutes pass, and the place is packed with eager women ready to win themselves a bachelor or two. Feels like the whole town is standing in here waiting for it to start.

"Welcome to another bachelor auction. I hope y'all brought your wallets because every penny raised tonight is goin' to the local food pantry," Kiera finally says into the microphone, grabbing our attention. She's the emcee this year. "I've been to my fair share of these, and it's safe to say, the selection gets better and better." She winks at the audience, causing a roar of giggles.

"Excuse me, woman?" Jackson steps on stage. "Better than me?"

"Who gave you that?" Kiera looks at the mic in his hand.

Jackson smirks, walking closer until he's standing next to her. "I have my ways."

She shakes her head. "Well you're no spring chicken, my darlin'. But I would've spent all my money to win you."

Jackson wraps an arm around her, pulling her into his large chest. "You tryin' to sugar me up now?"

"Oh my God." I hear Kaitlyn groan next to us. "Is there anything more embarrassing than your parents nearly making out in front of everyone?"

Hadleigh and I chuckle as they continue bantering until Kiera finally shoves Jackson off stage and tells him to stop stealing her spotlight. Kaitlyn's face burns with humiliation.

"I think it's adorable," Hadleigh says. "We'd all be so lucky to have a long-lasting love like that."

"It's all fun and games until it's your folks." She groans.

"You gonna bid this year?" I ask her.

She shrugs. "Not much of a selection other than the few ranch hands I'm not related to."

I chuckle at her bored expression. Before I can respond, Kiera introduces the first bachelor.

"I may be biased as his mother, but this first guy is a looker. At six-foot-three, Knox Bishop is tan, muscular, and will keep you on your toes just like his daddy."

"Mom…" Knox scolds as he saunters down the runway in tight, dark-wash Wranglers and a black cowboy hat.

"But he'll also keep ya laughing for days." She winks at him. "Let's start the bid at fifty."

A dozen paddles fly up at once, including Hadleigh's. She looks around in horror.

"Do I hear seventy-five?" Kiera says as a few paddles drop. Hadleigh keeps hers flying high in the air.

"One hundred?" Kiera looks around. "Only one lucky lady can claim this cowboy. One fifty?"

"Dammit," Hadleigh hisses. "I should've brought more cash."

"Two hundred?" There are still four paddles waving, and Hadleigh's sweating as she stays persistent.

"Alright, two fifty?" Kiera asks in surprise.

Knox gloats with a shit-eating grin at the way he's being fought over. Typical Bishop boy behavior.

"Three hundred!" a woman shouts. Hadleigh and I jerk our heads and see Sarah Cooke.

"*That bitch!*" Hadleigh hisses under her breath.

No one likes Sarah and for good reason. She's constantly trying to steal people's men. Even if Knox's single, there's no way he'd really be interested in dating her.

"Do we have three fifty?" Kiera prompts, looking around as paddles lower, and it's just Hadleigh and Sarah.

"Goddammit," Hadleigh grinds between her teeth before she loudly repeats the offer.

"Three seventy-five?" Kiera asks.

Hadleigh flashes Sarah a glare, almost daring her to try her. Slowly, Sarah bows out, and when Hadleigh's the only one with her hand raised, it's known she's won. She grins wide.

"Alright, three fifty to Miss Hadleigh Callaway!"

"Whew." She sighs, then a flash of panic rises over her face. "Shit, I'm not gonna have much left for Kane."

"Ask Ma if you can get a two-for-one special," Kaitlyn suggests, laughing.

"This next bachelor is six feet of pure muscle with chocolate brown eyes you could get lost in. If your ovaries haven't exploded yet, prepare yourselves, ladies."

I hate that even before Kiera finished her introduction, I know she's talking about Grayson.

On cue, he walks along the stage and struts down the runway. The sleeves to his plaid shirt are rolled to his elbows. He has it completely unbuttoned, showing off his dark chest hair and all six of his abs.

Motherfucker.

His teasing is working too. The ladies are losing their goddamn minds.

Probably to make me pay even more for him.

Grayson stands on the edge of the stage, resting his hands around his belt buckle and flashing a perfectly white smile to the audience. The ladies are nearly tripping over themselves to get a closer look.

"Based on your responses, let's start at one hundred dollars. Any takers?" Kiera prompts, looking around at the handful of eager women.

Groaning, I hold up my paddle and find two pairs of shell-shocked eyes on me.

"Did you hit your head or somethin'?" Hadleigh chuckles.

"I wish," I murmur.

"Are you bidding on him to prank him later on your date?" Kaitlyn asks.

"Again, I wish."

They watch me with furrowed brows, and I know I'll have to eventually explain the situation. For now, I just need to focus on not losing.

"Two hundred?" Kiera asks.

I glance over and see Sarah Cooke eagerly waving her paddle. *Fucking great.*

"Two fifty?" Kiera makes a show of walking around Grayson and staring at his ass. "The view ain't so bad back here either, ladies. Do I hear three hundred?"

Now it's just Sarah and me. I glare at her, but she ignores it, probably determined not to lose a second time.

"Three fifty?"

Grayson's gaze finds me, and I clench my jaw at the amount of money he's making me spend. He flashes a devilish smirk, loving this way too much. Asshole.

"Sarah!" I shout, grabbing her attention. "If you don't put your paddle down, I'm gonna shove it down your throat."

An echo of gasps surface, but I don't care. I give her a hard stare, daring her to keep her arm up. I'm not spending another dime on him. When I hear a masculine chuckle, I look up and see it's Grayson.

The bastard is *laughing.*

Perhaps I should feed him to the wolves and let Sarah have him.

"Three fifty going once, twice..." Kiera's voice rings out, and as soon as I step closer to Sarah, she yanks her paddle down.

"Sold to Miss Kenzie Bishop. Good choice, honey." She flashes me a wink, and I fight the urge to vomit.

"What the hell was that about?" Hadleigh asks.

"I owed him," I say.

As soon as Grayson's off stage, Kane enters, and Hadleigh's eyes perk up again.

"I only have two hundred left," she mutters. "So prepare to scare some women away for me."

"I gotchu," I say with amusement.

"These boys are so good-lookin', I had to make two of 'em," Kiera gloats as Kane shows off his biceps in a tight T-shirt. "Let's start the bidding, ladies. Who's got one hundred?"

A minute later, the bid shoots up to three hundred, and Hadleigh gives up. "Fuck, he's gonna hate me."

"Nah, he'll get over it," Kaitlyn says though I'm not sure by the way Kane's staring at Hadleigh in disappointment.

"Five hundred!" Sarah Cooke shouts above the noise. She's hell-bent on winning someone, and unfortunately for Kane, her paddle's the last one in the air.

"Sold!" Kiera announces, and Hadleigh winces.

"Kenzie!" I hear my name being called and turn around to find Lacey.

"Hey, you made it!" I give her a hug as she squeezes next to me.

"Took me a while to find a parking spot. What'd I miss?"

"Knox, Grayson, and Kane."

"Hope I brought enough money," Lacey says, pulling out her wallet.

"Now that Sarah Cooke's cleaned out, you might have a chance." Kaitlyn laughs.

Next comes Luke, and Lacey's face lights up.

"Guess you really did make it just in time," I tease.

Lacey ends up winning Luke for one fifty. After another comedic break from Kiera and Jackson, Payton walks on stage, showing off his tattooed muscles and newly trimmed beard. At the two-hundred mark, Kaitlyn waves her paddle and manages to win.

"Ma'am...what's the story?" I ask with a hand on my hip.

Kaitlyn waves me off. "We're just friends. Don't get any ideas."

"Oh those ideas are already planted...in *his* head," I taunt.

Payton's from another part of Texas, and he's quickly fit right in with the family. Though he's usually quiet, he gives off a bad boy vibe with his tattooed chest and ripped body. I've seen him shirtless a few times since most guys work that way in the heat.

After the final bachelors are claimed, the event comes to an end. Grandma Bishop tallies up the amounts and thanks everyone for coming. Then she reminds us to eat and bid on the silent auction items before we leave. We applaud her for her efforts, and a line forms at the food table.

Knox and Kane find Hadleigh, and I might feel bad for her if two guys weren't literally fighting over her. Hadleigh apologizes profusely to Kane, but he shrugs it off as if someone didn't shatter his heart, but it's more than obvious.

He's devastated, and I'd even say a little jealous too.

"There's my woman," Grayson sing-songs, flinging his arm around my shoulders like he's lost his goddamn mind. I quickly shrug him off and put space between us because we aren't friends.

"You owe me three fifty," I say, crossing my arms.

He steps toward me, bringing his lips to my ear and sending a wave of unwanted shivers down my spine. "That wasn't part of our deal, sweetheart."

When he pulls back, he licks his lips and flashes me a wink.

I'm regretting this so damn much.

"Maybe I'll tell Sarah she can have you after all..." I scowl, turning to walk away, but he grabs my elbow and pulls me into his chest. My breath hitches as I look up at him.

"Nice try, darlin'. You're all *mine*."

"Could you two get a room?" Kane bites out, and it's what I needed to break the spell that Grayson's suddenly put me under. I push against him and take a few steps back.

"Don't be bitter. I'm sure you and Sarah will have plenty to talk about," Grayson tells them, though the sarcasm in his voice isn't missed.

"If she lets you get a word in..." Kaitlyn adds with a chuckle.

Kane rolls his eyes before walking away in frustration.

"Nice work..." I shake my head at Grayson.

"He'll be fine, trust me." He shrugs it off. As I grab a plate, Grayson's arm brushes mine as if he's never heard of personal space in his life. "So this finalizes our truce agreement, right?"

His voice is so low that only I can hear him.

"I guess," I mutter.

"You almost sound disappointed," he taunts, grabbing a large piece of pie.

"Only in myself that I agreed to this in the first place. And I'm out three hundred and fifty dollars," I deadpan.

Grayson's whole body shakes next to me as he chuckles. "I think you're finally warming up to me. Only took what? Almost six years?"

I stop and look at him, nudging him to pay attention. "This truce in no way means I like you, got it? As far as my hatred for you, it's still there. I just won't act on it for the sake of our agreement."

"Fuck, I love that fire behind your eyes. Just imagine how hot the sex is gonna be when you finally succumb to your desires."

"Christ, do you have wax in your ears or something?" I roll my eyes at his arrogance. "You've lost your mind."

His lips tilt up in a smug grin. "We'll see, baby."

I groan, grabbing a mini sub and cookie. "Do not call me that. Or any other term of endearment."

"Now I know that was definitely not a part of the deal, *sweetheart*."

"Consider it added, or I'm calling Sarah over here right now."

He chuckles. "You prefer to be humiliated and demeaned in the bedroom, right?" His chest presses to my back, and the hair on my neck stands up as his breath brushes against my ear. "You wanna be my dirty little slut? My filthy little whore who likes to be handcuffed and teased."

I jerk my arm back and elbow him in the ribs as hard as I can. He huffs, nearly choking on his tongue.

My cheeks heat as the anger flows through my blood. "Call me either of those words again, and you'll lose the appendage between your legs, got it?"

He sucks in a breath, slowly covering his junk with both hands.

"Good, glad we worked that out," I mock, patting his chest and walking away.

Hadleigh tries to hide her laughter but fails. She's probably wondering what the hell is happening between us, and honestly, so am I. This was supposed to be a simple arrangement, a truce to end this five-year war, but now I'm fighting another battle—the way my body reacts to his.

CHAPTER TEN

Grayson

It's been four days since the bachelor auction, and Kenzie's been mostly keeping her word. I'm convinced she enjoys getting a rise out of me, which is why she's constantly forcing herself under my skin. Though I usually don't mind since it gives me leverage to return the favor.

"Good mornin', darling." I let out a whistle as she climbs out of her SUV. "Lookin' sexy as hell."

She gives me a side-eye as she walks toward the B&B. "Keep your dick in your pants, Cowboy. Just because I'm tolerating you doesn't mean I want you near me."

"Ya know, for someone who claims to hate me so much, you sure talk a lot about my cock," I say.

"Only in the ways I plan to castrate you if you don't stay away from me," she retorts over her shoulder. It's not even eight in the morning, and she's already threatened my balls.

"Alright, wait—" I grab her elbow and pull her toward me. "We're supposed to be gettin' along. My family will never believe we're friends if we can't even be in the same room together. The fewer questions from them, the better." The fewer *anything* from them, the better. The last thing I need or want is their interrogations into my personal life.

She crosses her arms, the movement lifting her breasts higher. Since it's Wednesday, she's dressed in one of her hot teacher outfits, complete with black heels that bring her closer to my height. She's hot as fuck.

"Eyes up here." She playfully kicks my shin, making me blink back up at her. "So what do you suggest?"

"We need to practice gettin' along. That means no more name-calling, threatening my most prized possessions…" I lower my eyes to my groin, and she shakes her head in annoyance. "And at least being cordial."

She releases a deep groan, but I find it adorable. "I guess you're right. But it won't be easy, considering you've been the enemy all this time."

"Enemy?" I scoff. "I'm insulted since I've been nothing but a perfect gentleman toward you. I should be the one angry for the way you've treated me all these years."

She opens her mouth, then quickly closes it. I wish she'd just tell me what I did to piss her off for so long, but it's a losing battle. Whatever it is, I need to help her get over it so we can cross the boundaries she's been so hell-bent on creating.

"Okay, so we'll be pleasant to each other?" I confirm, waiting for her to agree.

She sucks in a breath, dropping her arms and momentarily closing her eyes. When she opens them, she nods. "Sure."

"Great, let's eat breakfast together then." I open the B&B door and motion for her to go inside.

When we walk into the dining room, almost all the ranch hands are already sitting and eating. I say hello to a few of the guys I work with, then move to the coffee bar where I pour a to-go cup, then add cream and sugar just how Kenzie likes it. After grabbing one for myself, I bring them back to the table and set both down. Kenzie gets a muffin, then takes a seat next to me. She's not a big breakfast eater, but since I've been up working for almost two hours, I'm starving. I stack pancakes, bacon, and sausage on my plate. When I return to the table, I take a sip of my coffee, then realize all eyes are on us, including Maize's.

"What?" I ask, cutting into my food and taking a huge bite.

"What's goin' on with you two?" Maize asks, waving a finger between us as she stands behind the guys.

"Yeah, y'all are bein' civil for once. What's up with that?" Diesel adds.

"You're even sittin' close." Riley furrows his brows. "One of you lose a bet?"

I chuckle, trying to ease the awkward tension and wrap an arm around Kenzie's shoulders. "We're friends now."

Maize snorts with her brows raised. "Come again?"

Kenzie finally speaks up. "Acquaintances," she states, pushing my arm off her. "We came to an agreement to stop fighting. That's *it*."

Everyone continues to silently stare.

"I don't think I've ever heard it so quiet over here." John walks up. "What's goin' on?" he asks Maize, crossing his arms as if he's ready to break up a fight.

"Kenzie and Grayson are sitting together and acting…friendly," she explains in shock.

"Oh my gosh, y'all are being so dramatic. We're scolded for arguing, and now y'all freaking out that we're not," Kenzie blurts out.

"Maybe give us a warning next time," Diesel muses.

"Ha-ha." Kenzie sips her coffee, then takes a bite of her muffin.

"Leave them alone," John says.

They listen and go back to eating and talking amongst themselves. I eat my bacon and watch as Kenzie chews her food.

"Why are you watching me like a creep?" She narrows her eyes.

"Not used to you being so close." I smirk, waggling my brows. "Just gettin' used to it."

"Well don't. It's only temporary," she says matter-of-factly.

I ignore that and keep talking. "Maybe we can make this a tradition, eating breakfast together, then eventually, move to dinner. Then *dessert*." I flash her a wink.

"Don't push your luck." She lowers her voice, emphasizing every word.

"Tsk tsk. Friendly, remember?"

Kenzie pinches her lips together and glares at me. She moves her hand below the table and rests it on my leg. My entire body heats at the simple gesture, but I pretend it doesn't. Instead, her gaze intently focuses on my mouth.

Just as I'm about to speak, she slides it up farther, causing me to jump. I quickly reach for her hand, but she digs her nails in harder.

"Friendly enough?" she mutters.

The corner of my lips tilts up as my cock jerks. "Any friendlier, and I'll be tempted to take you against the wall."

Her fingers brush along my erection. She twists away but not before I notice her flushed cheeks.

"Can I walk you out?" I ask before she gets up. "As a friend, of course."

Kenzie's body freezes before she slides out of her chair. "Sure. I need all the practice not killing you I can get."

Her unamused tone causes me to chuckle. She tries so hard to keep me at a distance, but I see the way her body reacts to mine—goose bumps along her skin, hardened nipples when I'm close, and hitched breathing. It's not unnoticed, even if she tries to act unfazed.

After I clear my plate, we walk out, and I try to think of something to say, but she beats me to it.

"I need a favor," she blurts when we make it to her SUV.

She faces me with tense features as if she hates asking for help.

"Sure. What's up?"

"I'm planning a harvest festival charity event at the school next month, and I could really use an extra hand. I'm gonna need some of the ranch hands' participation, and it'd be nice if I had help organizing some things," she explains.

"Alright, shouldn't be too hard to wrangle the guys. What do you need exactly?"

"Can you meet me at the school on Saturday at nine? I'll give you a tour and show you exactly what I'm thinking. It'll be easier than just telling you."

"Sure, that shouldn't be a problem. I'll be there."

Hopefully, Diesel will let me take a break for a bit, but it should be fine as long as I can make up my work. Even though getting up earlier or staying later sounds terrible, I can't deny that spending time with her would be one-hundred-percent worth it.

"Great, thanks," she says in a voice so genuine, I'm almost caught off guard.

I reach behind her and open the door. "Have a good day at work. I'll see you tomorrow morning for another *training session* of being friendly."

Kenzie climbs into her SUV. "And I'll practice biting my tongue. No promises, though."

Grinning, I say, "Wouldn't expect anything less from you, sweetheart."

After Kenzie leaves, I drive to the cattle barn, where my mind floods with thoughts of her. The more I think about her, the more inappropriate positions I dream about putting her in. I've always been attracted to Kenzie but knew I didn't have a chance in hell. Since our truce agreement, I think I might actually be getting through her hard exterior.

"So when is your bachelor date with Kenzie?" Diesel asks as we walk through the barn.

"Next weekend," I answer. "But we're hanging out this Saturday." Then I explain how she needs help and how I need a few hours off that morning.

"First y'all are eatin' together, and now you're planning events?" He cocks a brow. "Sounds a little sus."

"It's not. We're just...being friends." I purposely leave out the part about her going to my family reunion. As soon as I bring it up, there'll be questions I don't want to answer right now.

"Mm-hmm. I've heard *that* before." He eyes me cautiously. "What's really goin' on between you two?"

"As I said, we formed a truce. She won me at the auction, and I won't get her back for filling my truck with cow shit. What she had coming would've been ten times worse, which is why she agreed."

"And let me guess, now that she's not threatening to murder you in your sleep, you think you have a shot, right?" He chuckles at his own comment before I can respond. "I don't think I've ever seen Kenzie with a guy, not even when they hit on her relentlessly at the bar when she worked there. In fact, I figured men weren't her preference."

I burst out with amused laughter. "Maybe not her *only* preference, but when she was tying me up and straddling my hips, she was aroused as fuck. For whatever reason, she's holding back...and I'm determined to find out why."

Diesel shakes his head with a hesitant smirk. "After Rowan gave me the run around for years, I can confidently say it's in the Bishop's genes not to take shit from anyone. They don't need anyone to take care of them, but when they decide you're it for them? You feel like The Chosen One. So if you think Kenzie really does have feelings for you, don't let her slip away, man. She'll make you work for it, that's a given, but your persistence will pay off. If she didn't like you, she wouldn't even bother getting even or wasting her time on you."

I let his words sink in and wonder if it's true. Kenzie has always been the independent, take no shit with a no fucks given attitude, type of woman. It's why I've always been attracted to her. She can take it and give it just as good. A vast difference from my ex-fiancée, who only took advantage of every kind thing I did for her. It's partly why I haven't had a serious relationship since then—that, and because I've been infatuated with Kenzie since the day I met her.

After work, I go home and shower. I fist my cock as the water streams down my back and imagine how Kenzie would look on her knees between my legs. Her thick blond hair in a knot on top of her head, her bright blue eyes staring into mine, and her perky tits bouncing as she eagerly sucks me off. It'd take me only minutes to explode in her hot mouth, and then I'd bend her over and fuck her senseless.

At that image, my balls tighten, and my cock stiffens as I explode. I suck in a ragged breath as I whisper her name, picturing her licking every drop.

Hopefully one day, this won't just be in my imagination.

CHAPTER ELEVEN

Mackenzie

I feel like I'm living in the twilight zone. It's a weird reality where Grayson and I are somewhat getting along.

Honestly, I never thought I'd agree to anything he asked, but there's something in it for me too. Now, I don't have to look over my shoulder every second waiting for him to pay me back. After his family's reunion, we'll be even, for *good*.

Though he seems to have no idea why I've hated him. The anger of what he did will always be there. I've just agreed not to act on it any longer. Which has been easier said than done.

The first couple of days were weird, but after seeing everyone's reaction, it's become a game of who we can freak out the most by being nice to each other.

The sun beams through my blinds and that combined with my internal clock, means I'm up by six thirty on a Saturday. Feeling nervous about being alone with Grayson today didn't help me sleep in either.

When I'm not actively avoiding him and reminding myself when I loathe him so much, it's not hard to notice the way my body reacts when he's near. Which, of course, I *hate* admitting.

Thankfully, getting up early gives me time to put up my guard so I don't succumb to his natural charm. No doubt he'll put it on thick, per usual.

"Where are you off to already?" Mom asks when I walk into the kitchen.

"School," I reply, grabbing my tumbler to fill with coffee. "Gettin' a head start on planning the Halloween Harvest Festival."

"Oh, do you want some help today?"

"No, it's fine. I'm just writing out a detailed list of what I need and figuring out where it should all go. The hard part comes later." I grab my cup, then kiss her goodbye.

"See ya later."

"Bye, sweetheart. Stop by the B&B after."

"Will do." I smile, then head out the door.

I'm arriving earlier than Grayson, but it'll give me time to check my email and organize my desk. I have a journal filled with ideas and drawings for the festival as well as businesses and vendors to contact. We'll need several sponsors and volunteers to help make sure it runs smoothly

Once I walk into my classroom, I flip on the lights and go to my desk. It's not messy but needs some tidying. Fridays are always chaotic after school, and my mind's usually set on going home.

I chug my coffee, begging the caffeine to spark life into my blood when my phone goes off.

GRAYSON

Almost there! Wanted to shower after being in the pastures, so I ran home real quick.

KENZIE

No problem. I'm in my class, room 104.

Though I give him a lot of shit, I appreciate him cutting into his workday to help me. I'll need a lot from him, especially with getting the other ranch hands on board, but since we're doing this "friendship" thing, I figure this is a good start. The more time we spend together, the more comfortable I'll be with him next weekend.

"Hey."

My head pops up at Grayson's deep voice. He's wearing black jeans and a white T-shirt. So simple yet attractive as hell.

"Hey," I reply, swallowing my nerves. "You made it."

"Yeah, sorry I'm late."

"No worries. Just wrapped up in here anyway." I turn off my computer and stand behind my desk. "But since you're in here, might as well give you a mini tour."

"Your classroom is cute. Love the ABC wall," he says as I walk between the little tables and chairs.

I chuckle. "First grade is fun. The kids are hungry for knowledge and love learning their alphabet and numbers."

Next, I show him the small class library I have in the back corner. "This is where the kids pick their books for the week, but I also use it in the event a child needs some alone time."

"Ah, yes. First grade's stressful."

I give him a look. "Not just that, some get overstimulated and need a moment to themselves. It's how I am after dealing with you for five minutes."

He flashes me a look. "So I overstimulate you?"

I try to hide my smile but fail when I burst into laughter. "You wish."

"Every damn day, Kenzie Bishop. Just say the word." He beams.

I shake my head as I grab my notebook and pen from my desk. "Let's go. Lots to cover."

He follows me to the empty parking lot, which helps me get a visual. While it's not a huge space, it'll work for what we need it for.

"So the plan is to have fifteen to twenty booths for trick-or-treating. Businesses will pay a fee and can set it up however they want, as long as there's a theme. Costumes are required," I explain. "All the proceeds will go to a good cause. Each booth will be decorated and hand out candy."

"That sounds cool."

"I also want to do a silent auction and bake sale, so I need sign-ups for that as well. Maize is already on board, of course, but it's nice to involve as much of the community as possible. Then I'd like an apple cider and hot cocoa booth, apple bobbing, and face painting. There should also be games where the kids can win prizes," I say, reading off my list. "Oh and I saved the best activity for last...the hay maze. I'll need some of the guys to load up the trailer and bring out dozens of round bales, then set them upright so the kids can run through it. Maybe have some of them dress up and spook them too."

"I'll put Knox on that job," he says, laughing. "But it should be easy enough to get done. I can draw out a design for it too."

"That sounds great, but not *too* hard. This is for kids, remember."

"Oh come on…" He smirks. "What's the fun in that?"

"Grayson," I deadpan.

He holds up his hands in surrender. "Fine, fine. Have it your way."

"Good. Moving along."

I walk him around, showing him where everything should go, including the tables and tents. After the kids get candy at the booths, there'll be other fun activities as well. I want it to be a memorable event that they look forward to each year.

"So I think that about covers it." I glance over my list one last time as we make it to the front of the school.

"Sounds awesome. Everyone's gonna love it, *especially* the kids," he says genuinely, turning toward me. His eyes scan down my face and land on my mouth. Instinctively, I lick my lips as he studies them.

"Thanks, I hope so. And I hope it raises a lot for scholarships and extra school supplies. These kids deserve it all."

"They're very lucky to have you and everyone who's participating."

I nod with a smile. "The first thing I need to do is contact all these businesses."

"I can take half of them to make it go faster. Most won't be able to resist my good looks and natural charm."

"Just when I thought you were maturing." I make a list and hand it to him.

"I'm very mature. But remember, you're the one who paid the twins to dump shit in my truck. Talk about being *mature*."

I chuckle with a shrug. "I ran out of ideas."

"Thank God because I don't think I wanna know what you'd try next."

"Luckily, neither of us have to worry about that anymore."

"Speaking of which, ya ready for next weekend? I know it's a lot to ask you to be around my family. But if all goes as planned, we'll show up and chat for a few hours, then head back to the hotel before dark. We'll leave the next morning after breakfast."

"Yeah, I guess. Parents naturally love me, though," I sing-song.

He grins, brushing a hand through his hair. "I'm sure they do."

"Well, thanks again for coming and offering to help," I say, lingering as the tension between us grows awkward.

"I'm glad to do it, Kenzie." He steps forward, making my heart pound harder. "Seriously. I'm relieved you're finally not pushing me away and letting me help. You can't do everything yourself. You'll burn out. Plus, I'll always be here as your friend, if that's what you want."

Is that what I want? Hell, I don't even know anymore.

Grayson nearly erases the space between us as he moves closer. When I don't respond right away, he tips my chin up and forces me to look in his eyes.

As I contemplate my next move, I wonder if his lips taste the same after all these years. Before I can decide, my phone rings, and the sudden interruption makes us jump.

Stepping back, his hand falls from my face as I look at my phone.

"It's Maize."

"Go ahead, I gotta get back to the ranch anyway." He motions to his truck, and I nod.

"Okay, see ya later." I wave and watch as he walks away.

Quickly, I slide my finger across the screen before it goes to voicemail.

"Hey," I answer. "What's up?"

"Hey, so sorry to bother you. I know you're at the school right now, but I'm in a pickle."

"What's goin' on?" I ask eagerly as I go to lock up the school.

"I need a babysitter for just a few hours. Gavin had to go with Uncle Jackson to deliver a horse, and Mom's watching the kids right now. One of the B&B housekeepers called in sick, and Dad needs help cleaning the rooms before more guests check in this afternoon so he needs Mom's help. I can ask Grandma but—"

"No, no. I can do it. I'm leaving now anyway."

"Ah, thank you! I owe ya one."

"Yeah ya do."

After we say goodbye, I hop in my SUV and drive to Maize's.

"Hey, Mom. I'm here to take over."

"Thanks, sweetie. I would've been happy to stay, but your dad needs some help."

"It's fine. I don't mind hangin' out with these little rascals anyway."

I kneel and tickle Maddy as she tries to escape my hug. Mom kisses the girls goodbye, then it's just the three of us.

"Did y'all eat lunch yet?" I ask, realizing I'm ready to devour anything within arm's reach.

Mila Rose hands me her snack cup that's filled with crushed Goldfish.

"Oh, thank you for sharing." I mimic spoon-feeding myself. "Nom. Nom. Let's go see what's in the pantry. Auntie Kenzie's still hungry."

Maddy and Mila Rose follow me to the kitchen, telling me everything they want to eat. I find a box of *Frozen*-shaped mac 'n' cheese and can't wait to give Maize shit for having processed food in her house.

"Hot dogs!" Maddy says when I open the fridge.

"Ahh, good idea." I take them from the drawer.

"And juice," Mila Rose adds.

"Of course," I say, taking that out next. "Anything else? Maybe we should balance this with some fruits and veggies."

I grab some strawberries and a can of corn. "Good enough for me." I put the girls in their booster seats, then find their iPad to occupy them while I cook. "What do y'all wanna watch?"

"*Bo On the Go!*" they shout and point as I scroll through the options.

"Never heard of that one but okay…" I click it and feel instant regret when I hear the theme song. It's gonna be stuck in my head for days.

The girls sing along and dance in their chairs as I prepare our gourmet meal. Though they're two and a half now, I can't believe how big they are. It still feels like yesterday when Maize announced she was pregnant. Now I can't imagine life without them. Someday I hope I can have a table filled with kids too.

"Well, what's the verdict?" I ask after they take their first few bites.

"Yum!" they say, keeping their eyes glued to the screen. I'm pretty sure Maize would kill me if she knew I let them watch TV while eating.

"So you girls wanna know a secret?" I say, pulling them away from their show. "But you can't tell anyone."

I don't know why I feel like I have to get this off my chest, but if I can trust anyone not to tell, it's my two little nieces who won't even understand what I'm talking about.

"So there's a boy I think I might like," I say softly. "Except I don't want to like him. At least when we were bickering all the time, it was easier not to, but now that we're not..." I pause briefly as I come to terms with the reality of our situation. "It's harder to fight that attraction between us."

The girls look up at me with their big doe eyes, chewing on noodles and corn.

"So what should I do?" I ask them.

"More Frozen," Maddy says, holding up her plate.

"Me too." Mila Rose mimics her sister's actions.

I chuckle at how unfazed they are about my predicament. "What's the magic word?"

"Pleeeeeease."

"Alright, you won me over. More mac 'n' cheese comin' up."

I grab their plates and add a bit more. When I return with more food, I sit and think about why I've stayed away from Grayson. If we didn't have a past, I'd probably have already admitted my feelings to him. But we have a history, and I know his secret.

He just doesn't realize that I know it.

CHAPTER TWELVE

Grayson

The workday is relatively straightforward, and luckily, nothing insane has happened this past week.

"You almost done?" Diesel asks as I throw some alfalfa out for the cows.

"Yep." I remove my gloves and shove them in my back pocket. "Just finished."

"Awesome. Did ya pack yet?" He grabs the tools we were using to repair the roof on the barn and places them in the tack room.

"Hell no," I say, trying to stay focused as I climb down the ladder. Before we leave, I check the water troughs

"Why not?" he asks.

I laugh as we walk to the truck. "I procrastinated last night and thought I'd just throw a change of clothes in my bag beforehand. It's family. Nothing fancy."

He shakes his head. "Dude. You're finally goin' out with Kenzie, and you're not bringin' nice clothes? What's wrong with you?"

"It's not a date," I explain for the umpteenth time.

"It's called dressing to impress, but suit yourself." He shrugs as we drive to the other barn and finish distributing the hay.

"Before Rowan and I got together, I did whatever I could to get her attention," he admits.

"I remember, but that's not always a good thing," I counter. "Especially when it comes to Kenzie." She's made it clear she didn't like my attention, which led to our war in the first place.

He smirks. "It worked for me, though, didn't it?"

I shake my head and park. After a quick walk around, Diesel lets me leave early since I'm driving three hours to San Antonio tonight.

I love my job so much and don't take many vacations. When I ask for a few days off, I usually get them.

"Don't do anything I wouldn't do," he says as I pull my keys from my pocket.

"That's not saying much." I laugh, and he flips me off.

I go home and take a quick shower before Kenzie meets me at my place. She's been busy with the after-school program and has been getting home later than usual. I didn't want to interfere with that, so I told her we could leave when she was done.

After I'm dressed and shove a few pairs of jeans and shirts into a bag, Kenzie arrives with a giant suitcase.

I step outside and load our stuff into my truck.

"What's all this for?" I ask. "We'll only be gone a day and a half."

"I like to have a variety of outfits to choose from. You should be thanking me for not backing out because you know I thought about it at least ten times on the way over."

I shut the door and turn to her. "Thank you. I really do owe ya."

"Oh, you're gonna work for it during the Harvest Festival. Trust me." She chuckles.

"I have no doubt about that." I wink, opening the passenger side door for her. She climbs inside with a sweet smile, then I go around to the driver's seat.

On the way over, we don't talk much since Kenzie grades papers.

Eventually, we stop and eat dinner. Once we're closer to downtown, the traffic gets heavier, and it takes us longer than I anticipated to make it to the hotel. It's nearly nine when we arrive, and I'm exhausted. I grab our bags, and we walk to the front counter.

"Hello, how may I help you?"

"Hi. I have a reservation for Grayson Harding," I tell the woman.

She smiles and taps on the keyboard. "Oh yes, Mr. Harding. I have you down for a room with a king-sized bed."

Kenzie tenses beside me, and I feel like a total dumbass for not remembering to change the reservation. "Can we change it to a room with double beds?" I ask.

She clicks a few times before giving me an apologetic look. "Sorry, we don't. Right now, king-sized beds are the only option we have. I apologize, it's a busy weekend."

"Not your fault. Thanks for checking," I reply. After she hands us the key cards, I give one to Kenzie, then we silently walk to the elevator. I know she's not happy.

When we walk into the room, I notice we've got a good view of the city. The huge bed is piled with pillows with a flat-screen TV facing it.

"This is really nice," I say, trying to lighten the mood.

"Ya sure this wasn't all a part of your plan to get me into your bed?" She gives me her signature glare.

"I booked the room before I knew you were coming, and I forgot to change the reservation. My mind has been all over the place lately. I swear it wasn't on purpose. Cross my heart and hope to die, won't ever eat another piece of Maize's pie." I add the last part to make her laugh, but she doesn't take the bait.

"Mm-hmm," she groans, placing her suitcase on the wooden rack and unzipping it. "There's gonna be some *ground* rules, or that's exactly where you'll be sleeping. I never agreed to share a bed with you."

"I took a shower before we left, and I swear I don't toss and turn. I don't snore either." I smirk, but she's not impressed.

"You'll stay on your side of the bed no matter what."

I hold up my hands. "I will. Promise. I'll be a perfect gentleman," I tell her as she grabs some clothes, then goes to the bathroom.

When I hear the water running, I imagine her naked body under the stream. But then I hurry and push the thoughts away because the last thing I need is to be rock hard when she comes back.

I change into some joggers and a T-shirt, then text my mom to let her know I made it to town. She immediately responds, letting me know how happy she is that she'll see me tomorrow. The only reason I even considered coming to the reunion is because of her. There are too many bad memories here, which makes it stressful to be home after all this time.

When Kenzie walks back into the room, I can smell the floral scent of her shampoo and body soap.

She plops down on the bed, grabs one of the fluffy pillows, and wedges it in the middle underneath the comforter. "There. Just in case you get handsy in your sleep."

I want to laugh at how adorable she is but keep it inside. Kenzie grabs the remote and flips through until she lands on the Hallmark Mystery Channel. "Oh God no," I groan.

"What? I love this stuff. The whole whodunnit aspect keeps me interested. Don't knock it till you've watched it."

"It's like a toned-down mystery where the couple only kisses at the end, right?"

She shakes her head. "No. Well, kinda, but still. I like it, so shut up."

I snort, then get under the blankets. Kenzie grabs her laptop from her bag along with a stack of papers.

Instead of asking her to change the channel, I watch it. For fifteen minutes, I'm bored out of my mind, but she doesn't notice. After thirty minutes have passed, she closes her laptop and puts everything away.

When she climbs back in bed, Kenzie turns to me. "Tell me about your family. I wanna know who I'll be meeting tomorrow."

"You'll meet my mom who I love very much even though things have been complicated and I haven't been home in years."

"Complicated, how come?" Kenzie snuggles in and lays her head against her pillow, keeping her gaze on me.

"When she remarried about eight years ago, my stepdad moved in with us. Then a bit after, things were strained between my brother and me."

The room grows quiet. I haven't told anyone from Eldorado about my past because I moved there for a fresh start.

"What happened between you and your brother?"

I lie down and meet her big blue eyes. "What are a few reasons brothers would fight?"

"If I had to guess, I'd say probably because of a girl."

"Yep." The word lingers in the air as all memories come to the forefront. At times like this, I wish I could open up and tell her about my issues, but I keep it to myself. The last thing I want to do is burden Kenzie with my shit before she meets everyone.

Her face softens. "I'm sorry, Grayson. I can't imagine how hard it is for you not to have a close relationship. I'd be devastated if Maize wasn't in my life. She's my best friend."

I inhale in a deep breath. "We were close growing up, but some things happened, and it changed everything. Certain situations show a person's true colors, and you realize they don't care about you. All I know is when I have kids, I'm gonna teach them the importance of family. Being around the Bishops all these years has shown me that."

Kenzie props herself up on her elbow and gives me a small smile. "Sometimes family is chosen too, Grayson."

"I agree. It's not always the easiest to deal with, but I try. Moving away was one of the best decisions I made for myself because the ranch changed my life. I'll forever be grateful for the opportunity your uncle Alex gave me all those years ago."

As she studies me, that familiar stream of electricity returns. By the way Kenzie's chewing on her bottom lip, I think she feels it too. I wish I were kissing her and contemplate making a move. We're close, other than the pillow between us, and I swear I see her lean in. Her eyes flutter closed, and right before I can, my phone buzzes, successfully pulling me away.

I clear my throat and grab it. Why the hell do we always get interrupted when we're about to kiss?

> **MOM**
> Don't forget it starts at 10 at the park by the house. Love you.

> **GRAYSON**
> I remembered. Love you too.

After I set the alarm, I lock my phone and lie back down. The moment between Kenzie and I pass as quickly as it arrived. When she turns off the bedside lamp, I know it was another missed opportunity—one of a thousand I've encountered with her over the years. At least now we're kinda friends and not at each other's throats.

"Night," she says, rolling over and putting her back toward me.

"Good night," I respond and wonder what would've happened had my phone not interrupted us. She would've either let me kiss her or punched me in the face.

Perhaps it's best I didn't because the last thing I need is to show up tomorrow with a black eye.

CHAPTER THIRTEEN

Mackenzie

I've been a nervous wreck since my alarm went off this morning. The damn sex dream I had about Grayson doesn't help. Each time our eyes meet, it's all I can think about.

I bite the inside of my cheek as I push the images away.

"Almost ready?" Grayson asks with a smirk as he looks at me from head to toe.

I narrow my eyes at him, smacking my red lips. "Is there something wrong?"

"Nothing. Just seems like something you'd wear in a wet dream."

"What's that supposed to mean?" I counter, grabbing my crossbody and stuffing my phone inside. I'm wearing a cardigan with a white button-up shirt and black slacks. It's literally something I wear to school and *very* G-rated.

"If your hair was in a bun and you were wearing some black-rimmed

"Oh God. Not the naughty librarian fantasy," I groan as we take the elevator down.

"Why not?" He shrugs as we hop in his truck. "Something about makin' a good girl...*bad*." His words have my entire body on fire.

"Ahh, typical," I offer while I stare out the window and replay the dream I had.

Grayson's sexy as hell, and I've never thought otherwise, but due to our complicated past, I've tried to stay away. However, right at this moment, I feel more comfortable with him than I ever have. We can laugh and make jokes, and I honestly don't mind his company when he's not trying to drive me crazy. After years of riding each other's asses and pulling random pranks, it's a nice but foreign feeling.

"Did you hear me?"

"No, sorry." I look at him.

"What did you dream about last night?" He raises his brows.

"I said something, didn't I?" I'm absolutely mortified at the thought of him hearing me talk in a sex dream.

Grayson looks like he's about to burst out laughing. "Maybe."

"Tell me." I hide my face with embarrassment.

After he parks his truck across from the park, he turns toward me. His gaze pulls me in, and I find myself lost in his brown eyes.

"I have a video, actually." He flashes an evil grin, and I study his lips.

I'm reminded of last night when I was staring at his mouth and imagining what it'd be like if he kissed me. Then I think back on our conversation and realize I forgot to ask if his brother would be here today.

"Just kill me." I lean my head back against the seat as Grayson reaches for his phone.

He takes his sweet time scrolling. I check the time and realize he's stalling. In the distance, I see a large group of people under a covered pavilion. An older guy is putting food on a barbecue pit.

"Ahh, here it is," he says, showing me his pitch-black phone.

"Grayson..." I hear my voice moan in a strained tone.

I reach out to grab it, but he snatches it away, so I change my tactics and pretend I'm unbothered. "Guess you were on my mind because you were sleeping right next to me."

He arches a brow. "Or...you were dreamin' dirty things about me."

"And what if I was?" I taunt. "Or maybe I was pranking you to get your reaction?"

"Nah. You're not that clever."

"No?" I cross my arms with a grin, so he'll second-guess himself. "Whatever you say, Cowboy."

Laughter escapes him. "Well damn, now I don't know what to believe. But I kinda like sexy pranks."

I'm sweating bullets, hoping he buys it.

He glances out the windshield and releases a deep breath. "Guess we should get goin', huh."

I nod, knowing this is gonna be difficult for him. All teasing aside, I'm happy to be here with him.

As we walk across the plush grass, I lean in closer. "What's the real reason you asked me to come with you?"

"Well, the ranch has become my home. It's everything to me. And when I think about Circle B, you always come to mind. So, I thought bringin' ya with me would kinda be like having a little bit of home with me too. 'Cause when I'm there, I can do anything, and I'm not scared of shit. But this…" He looks forward as more people arrive.

My heart melts when he meets my eyes, and damn if the butterflies don't return.

"You can do this. It took courage to be here because you could've easily skipped." I give him a reassuring smile just as a woman walks up and greets us.

"Grayson, sweetie!"

Immediately, she pulls him into a hug and then does the same to me before he can introduce me. When she steps back, I notice their similarities. They have the same bright smile and kind eyes.

"Hey, Mom. This is Kenzie Bishop. Her family owns the ranch. Kenzie, this is my mom, Patsy."

"Hello, Patsy." I hold out my hand, and she covers it with both of hers.

"So nice to meet you, honey, but you can call me Mom. I didn't realize Grayson was bringing a girlfriend, but—"

"She's just a *friend*," he corrects.

"Oh." Patsy gives a nod, but I'm not quite sure she believes him.

"Apologies. I was just saying, I'm glad you're here. There are some cousins here I don't think you've met before, Grayson."

He grins, but I can tell it's forced. Leading us around to the picnic tables where people are eating, Patsy introduces me as Grayson's friend, but I hear the inflection in her tone. If Grayson knows them, he offers a handshake or a hug, but he mostly stands quietly to the side.

When his mom gets pulled away, Grayson leans in close. His warmth brushes against me. "Sorry 'bout that. She's almost as bad as Rose."

I snort. "Oh, Grandma would've already known your whole life story and asked when the weddin' was if I'd have brought you to an event like this. Trust me."

"Grayson, we've missed you so much. Wish you'd move back home so we could see you more," one of his aunts says, grabbing his attention. Though we'd just met, I already forgot her name.

"I know, but I love my life out in Eldorado too much to even consider it. Open land. No noise. Plus, the sunsets and stars. San Antonio ain't got nothin' like that."

She nods in understanding and doesn't push further. Fifteen minutes later, we're finally done parading around.

Patsy puts her hand on each of our shoulders. "Please, y'all eat. We've got plenty of links, hot dogs, burgers, and even some grilled corn," she tells us, then leads us there.

Grayson and I grab a plate, and that's when I notice him tense. I assume the man in charge of the food is his stepfather. He gives a friendly wave, but that's as far as it goes. We find an empty place to sit and eat.

"Nothin' like Maize's barbecue," he says, taking a bite of dry sausage.

I try not to make a face but can't help the snort that escapes me. The hamburgers are the same way. Grabbing the ketchup, I pour it all over and hope it makes it edible.

It doesn't. "Shoulda warned ya. He loves to cook but sucks at it." Grayson tries a bite of everything, then throws his plate away. I hand him mine too.

"Guess that means we're spoiled on Maize's cooking," I admit.

"You're right about that," he tells me, watching a few of his cousins throwing a Frisbee. "Wanna play?"

"I suck at it," I admit. "My college friends used to make fun of me for not being able to catch."

"You can't be *that* bad."

I grin at his confident tone. "To be honest, I probably drank too much and couldn't see straight. Probably why I liked to experiment so much in college, too."

"Ahh, used to party a lot?" Grayson leads me over to the group of kids. An extra neon orange disk lay on the ground, and he picks it up, then hands it to me.

"Kinda, I utilized my wild days, especially when my friends and I would go to concerts. And if they were outdoors, someone always had a Frisbee."

"Oh yeah, I remember those days. Lots of concerts and raves around here." At first, he smiles, but then it fades. I wonder if it brings back memories of his ex.

I throw the disk right to him, and he catches it.

"Go long!" he shouts. I back up a few steps, nearly tripping over my feet. His whole face lights up when he laughs, something I haven't seen since we arrived in town.

It goes over my head, then flips across the ground.

"You did that on purpose." I playfully shake my head, then overthrow it to him too. "First one who misses, loses," he says.

We go back and forth until we're in a rhythm, and I think it's the best I've ever played. I throw the disc with all my strength, and Grayson can't run fast enough to catch it.

"I win!" I squeal, somewhat shocked. Grayson gives me a high five, then puts his arm around my shoulder as we walk back to the crowd of people.

"I can't believe I won," I gloat. "Seriously. You didn't let me, did you?"

"And give you braggin' rights? No way," he tells me with a laugh, then a clearing of a throat interrupts us. As we turn around, I watch the color drain from Grayson's face.

My smile fades when I see *her*, and I feel sick to my stomach.

"What're you doin' here?" he asks the same question I'm wondering. I hear the roughness in his tone, or maybe it's pain?

I immediately recognize her blond hair. She's still beautiful with perfectly clear skin and a bright smile. If you told me she fell out of a magazine, I'd believe it. Her green eyes study him, and then a sly grin slides across her plump lips.

"We'll always be family, Grayson. My business meeting out of town was canceled at the last minute, so I thought we'd come and surprise everyone. Honestly, I was hoping to see you. I'm glad you decided to come." She runs her fingers through her hair, showing off a gigantic diamond that sits on her ring finger. The last time I saw her, she was pregnant.

"Why?" Grayson's jaw is clenched tight as he crosses his arms. Over her shoulder, I see a man chatting with a kid who looks around five or six. When the guy glances up, I know it's Grayson's brother. They look too similar.

"Because we haven't talked in ages." She puts a hand on her hip. "We have a lot to catch up on."

He doesn't even give it a beat before he responds. "There's nothing to talk about."

She finally glances at me and flashes a wide smug grin. "I'm Bella." She offers her hand, and I reluctantly take it.

"I'm Kenzie," I tell her, my heart pounding hard.

"Have we met before?" She narrows her eyes as if she's trying to place me, but I could never forget who she is.

"No," Grayson blurts out.

At the same time, I say, "Yeah, we have."

He looks back and forth between us as a large lump forms in my throat. Nothing about her gaze is venomous, but I don't particularly enjoy the attention being on me, especially since things are about to get awkward. I told myself I'd never remind Grayson of what happened that night, and now here I am, crashing right into it.

"How?" Grayson asks.

Neither of us answers him.

"I never forget a face, but I can't place where I know you from," Bella continues.

"It was once. Almost six years ago," I confirm. "You were pregnant."

Bella's eyes widen in recognition, and that's when she gives me an evil smirk. "Oh *right*. I do remember now."

She turns to Grayson. "I can't believe you're still with your one-night stand. I'm actually shocked."

Confusion spreads across his features. "What the hell are you talkin' about?"

"Oh, wait...she can't be a one-night stand if y'all are still together. Even if you and I were still dating at the time." Bella's words linger. She opens her mouth to continue, but I can't stand to hear another word about the night that changed everything for me.

"Sorry. Excuse me," I blurt out, then move across the grass toward the truck.

Moments later, Grayson's calling out my name. "Kenzie!" He rushes toward me, but I don't stop.

"Wait. What's goin' on?" he asks in a panic as he falls into step with me.

Hot tears threaten to surface, and I'm pissed I got myself into this situation. If I'd known she'd be here, I would've never agreed to come.

Grayson grabs my elbow and holds me in place in front of his truck. I hate that his hands on me feel so comforting. I stop and look at him.

"Please. You gotta catch me up with what's going on. None of this is makin' any sense at all." His pleading voice lets me know he's desperate for answers.

I suck in a deep breath and release it slowly. "That's your son, isn't it? The little boy who was behind her?"

Grayson swallows hard and squeezes his eyes before refocusing on me. "*No*. That's my nephew."

CHAPTER FOURTEEN

Grayson

I have no clue what the fuck is going on, and it's stressing me the hell out. The fact that Kenzie knows my ex-fiancée is absolutely frightening. At first, I thought Bella was just acting like a bitch, but when Kenzie mentioned Bella was pregnant when they first met, I knew my past and present had collided.

Though I'm confused as hell about when they could've met because the timeline doesn't match up with when I moved to Eldorado. The more I try to figure it out, the more baffled I am.

"Kenzie, please don't make me beg. I never told anyone at the ranch about her, so I need you to clue me in here. How do you know my ex-fiancée? How'd you know she was pregnant when we were engaged?"

"We met the morning after you and I slept together."

I stare at her. "What're you talkin' about? When was this?"

"About six years ago." She swallows hard. "You were in the shower, and I was getting dressed when she knocked on the door. I opened it and saw a pregnant woman with a large rock on her finger. She made an off-hand comment about me being there, and instead of waiting for you, I bailed. I figured you were engaged and had just cheated on your pregnant fiancée."

"Hold up, the girl from that night was *you*?"

Her cheeks redden as if she's embarrassed, but I'm the one who should be. "Yeah."

"Holy shit. Wow." I scratch my cheek, trying to think back on that night and how much of it is still a blur. "She was my *ex*-fiancée at that point, but holy shit...I can't believe this. I remember waking up in a hotel room next to a girl I'd met the night before, getting in the shower, and when I came out, you were gone, and Bella was waiting for me in the room."

"So, she's the woman who came between you and your brother then?" she asks. "That's why she's here. She's your sister-in-law, and the litle boy is your nephew."

Before I can explain, Bella walks over, holding her son's hand. She feeds off drama, and she'd probably shrivel up and die without it. Somehow, I keep my mouth shut and try not to tell her to go straight to hell with my brother. It's a perfect place for them since she's basically the devil in Gucci shoes.

I haven't seen Leo in years, but he's a really cute kid. However, it's hard for me to look at him because I'm reminded of the family I should've had. Our relationship was nothing more than manipulation and lies. I was just the stupid one who fell for it and believed her every word. Too bad it was all bullshit, especially the I love you's and can't wait to spend forever with you's.

As if he's bored, he skips away to chase a butterfly.

"I'm sorry if I caused any problems between you two," Bella says with fake sincerity. "I honestly thought it was water under the bridge since she's forgiven you for being engaged the night you two hooked up."

Kenzie stays quiet as Bella pins us with a smug look. Whatever her problem is, I don't want any part of it. "We were broken up," I remind her harshly. "And it's none of your damn business, is what it is," I tell her. Given the little details Kenzie just shared with me, it's safe to assume Bella thinks Kenzie and I started dating right after.

"Well, either way, I'm happy to see you with the same girl. I'm just shocked y'all aren't married by now, considering how long it's been." She makes a show of batting her long lashes

I stare at her, hoping she'll go the fuck away. Before I can respond, Kenzie speaks up. "We aren't together. It was just one night."

Hearing her talk about our one night together is driving me nuts because all I want to do is get Kenzie alone and talk this out.

Bella playfully laughs. *"Oh sure.* I see the way you two look at each other. It's adorable. You can't tell me you're *just friends."*

There's a hint of sarcasm in her voice, and maybe a dash of jealousy too. She's like a stingy kid with broken toys. Bella didn't want me back then, but she sure as hell didn't want anyone else to have me either. It reminds me of old times when I was a doormat, and she walked all over me.

"Don't worry about it," I snap, losing my temper at her bullshit. I want to call her out for being a manipulative psychopath, but I don't want to cause a scene and hurt my mother. It'll only give Bella satisfaction that she still gets under my skin.

"Leo, come say hello to your uncle Grayson," she shouts at him, though he's only twenty feet away. I'm sure the whole family heard her too. As if he's immune to her outbursts, he runs over with a smile. At least he's a happy kid. I just hope he has a good life.

"Hi," he says, and my heart hurts for him. I give him a genuine smile and a fist bump. "You're my uncle?"

"Yep," I tell him, trying to be as friendly as I can. "I'm your daddy's brother."

"Cool," he says, then runs away again.

Bella watches our interaction, and I hate the smirk on her lips. It's obvious she notices the pain etched on my face, especially when it comes to Leo.

I glare at her and hope she takes the hint to go away, but instead, my brother comes over and wraps his arm around Bella. Then he kisses her in front of me as if she's a trophy he won, and I didn't. I've only been around them a handful of times and realized I couldn't handle it, so I've avoided them at all costs.

"Hey, brother," he says as if he's temporarily pulled himself away from Bella's trance.

He glances over at Kenzie. "Oh hey, I'm Grant. Grayson's brother."

"Kenzie," she says, forcing a polite smile.

"Nice to meet you. Grayson's never brought a woman home before."

I grow more agitated at the two of them. They parade around like what they did behind my back was nothing. I've calloused myself over the years and am no longer the man with a broken heart, but it still doesn't mean I want to be around them.

As I look at them together, I'm happy and relieved I dodged the bullet, regardless of how much it hurt at the time. There's no doubt in my mind I would've been miserable had I stayed with Bella.

"Baby, your dad wanted me to get you," Grant tells her.

"Oh, he probably needs help with something," she says but doesn't look eager to leave no matter how much I wish she would.

Grant glances down at my keys that I'm holding tightly in my hand. "You leavin' already?"

"Yep," I reply coldly.

The awkward tension grows.

"Okay, well it was so nice meeting you, Kenzie." Grant shoots her a sly grin, and I want to punch in his face for even looking at her.

"Hope we can see you two again soon," Bella says, digging the knife in one last time. The two of them grab Leo and walk away. Kenzie glances at her phone, then walks past the truck.

"Kenzie!" I say, chasing after her again.

"I'm gonna take an Uber back to the hotel. I don't want you to leave because of me," she tells me, and I hear the trembling in her voice.

"No, please let me drive you."

She stops walking. "Stay with your family, Grayson. They've obviously missed you a lot, and I don't wanna be the reason you cut your time short with them. I also don't want it to be weird, so I'll just go."

I shake my head. "Absolutely not. If you're leaving, so am I. And trust me, it's gonna be weird no matter what now that Bella has shown her ugly face."

Her expression softens. "This is too awkward. I shouldn't have come."

"None of this is your fault," I confirm. "Let's get the fuck outta here, and we can talk because I have a shit ton of questions."

"You and me both," she mumbles, climbing into the truck when I unlock it.

For the next fifteen minutes, we ride in silence back to the hotel. I texted my mom to apologize for cutting out so abruptly, but I promised to make it up to her. She understood, considering Bella and Grant showed up unexpectedly.

When we finally arrive at the hotel, she gets out of the truck and walks inside without waiting for me. I catch up to her just as she steps on the elevator. "Where're ya goin' in such a hurry?"

She sighs. "I just wanna go home, Grayson. I'm gonna pack my bag and Uber back to Eldorado. You stay here. Meet up with your mom and spend time with her."

"Absolutely not. We need to talk about this, Kenzie. It's something we should've done a long-ass time ago, and the time is now."

CHAPTER FIFTEEN

Mackenzie

I glare at him, pinning him in place when all I want to do is run away from all of this.

Never did I imagine I'd see his ex-fiancée today or that she'd even recognize me after all these years. It brought up those memories I've been fighting to forget.

As soon as we're on our floor, I rush to our room and scan my key card.

"Kenzie," Grayson says as I start grabbing my shit and packing.

"You aren't leavin' without me."

I zip up my suitcase as he comes closer. I try to move past him to double-check the bathroom, but instead, he reaches out and gently grabs me. I try to wiggle free, but it's no use. His grip on me is too strong.

"Quit being a damn caveman and let me go," I demand just as I sit on the edge of the bed.

"Now talk," he orders, crossing his arms over his chest. "Start from the

Too bad for Grayson, I'm not intimidated by him. I defiantly shake my head, and he moves forward until my back rests against the soft mattress. My breath hitches as he hovers above me and the memories of our night together resurface. That's when I lift my knee, going straight for his junk, but he blocks me. Guess he's gotten so used to my antics, he can predict my moves.

"Nice try, sweetheart. I know your tricks," he muses with a cocked brow.

"Grayson!" I seethe. "You're really not going to let me go until we talk?"

"That's right. And I can happily stay just like this all night long. You owe me the truth of our past, Kenzie. Knowing the girl from that night was you is fucking with me, and I don't like that."

His warm breath brushes against my cheek, keeping me caged in his arms.

"Fine. You really wanna hear how after we slept together, I assumed you were a cheater who used me, and if that wasn't bad enough, when you showed up at the ranch four months later and acted like you didn't know me, I was angry and hurt? I liked you and thought that night we shared something special, but by the next morning, my heart was shattered."

The smug grin from his face fades as he stands and stares at me. I've never said those words out loud before and hadn't told anyone. All this time, I kept it buried deep inside—a dirty little secret that's haunted me for so long. I felt so ashamed and used every opportunity to make Grayson's life hell over it.

I sit up and smooth down my hair that's a wild mess as I wait for Grayson to say something, *anything*.

Grayson's mouth opens and closes a few times before he finally speaks. "Start from the beginning. Where did we meet?"

"At The High Five Bar in downtown San Antonio when I was still in college. We hit it off and drank for hours, laughing and messing around. After closing, we went back to your hotel room, and well, one thing led to another..."

He looks like he's trying to solve a calculus problem in his head. "I really don't know what to say except I'm sorry. I remember goin' out and meeting someone special. I do recall the way I felt about you, but at the same time, my heart was broken, and my emotions were all over the place. I felt like absolute shit the next day because I figured when you bailed, the feelings were one-sided. Bella mentioned a woman leaving, but I couldn't remember your name, which of course made me feel even worse. When we met at the ranch, I didn't recognize you because despite remembering what I felt, a lot of that night is a blur."

Though I'm sure that's supposed to make me feel better, it doesn't. "We both drank a lot, but when Bella showed up, I made my assumptions, then got the hell out of there. She made it abundantly clear that you were *her* man. When you showed up at the ranch, I figured that y'all had broken up because you cheated. I kept waiting for you to admit that you remembered me and hoped you'd eventually break each time I told you off, but you never did. I really didn't expect to ever see you again, so when I did, and you acted like we'd just met, it pissed me off even more. I felt used and poured that anger on you as much as I could. However, even after I believed you'd cheated, I was still attracted to you and hated that about myself. The only way to deal with what I was feeling was to keep you at a distance. But after years of going back and forth, you didn't allow it and always pushed my damn buttons."

"Bella cheated on *me* with Grant. That's why I broke up with her. I was so angry, I needed to just go out and drink away my sorrows. I'm so sorry for not recognizing you. Trust me, I'm kicking myself really fucking hard right now."

"If she's the one who cheated, why'd she show up and act like I was a dirty homewrecker?" I ask.

"Because she's manipulative as shit. How do ya think she got away with having an affair for so long? Anything that seemed fishy, she had a way to explain it, usually making me sound like I was the crazy one. I didn't realize how narcissistic she was until later."

"So she slept with Grant while you two were engaged?" I meet his sad eyes.

"Yep, then got pregnant and made me believe it was my baby for seven months."

Oh my God. That's why he looked like he was in pain when he saw Leo. "How'd they sneak around for so long?"

"Because we all lived together. They'd hook up when I was working or out with friends."

I give him a confused look because I hadn't seen that coming. "The three of you did?"

"Yeah, she and her dad moved in when we were seventeen." He must see my head spinning and continues. "She's my stepsister, Kenzie."

I blink a few times. "You were *engaged* to your stepsister?" If this wasn't such a serious moment, I'd give him so much hell for living the stepsister fantasy so many guys have.

"Technically, yes, but our parents didn't get together until after we were already dating. They met through us. After a while, they moved in, and that's when she started fucking us both."

"Wow...and yet she had the audacity to be mad that you broke things off?"

"Yep, now you see why I drank myself stupid that night. I'd just found out the paternity results, then completely lost it. Their affair already had me fuming, but when I realized she made sure I was attached to that baby while knowing damn well there was a chance it wasn't mine, I was a fuckin' mess. I was planning our future and thought we were starting a family. She ripped it all away with her betrayal."

I hate hearing the anger in his tone, knowing he's probably reliving it all.

"I want to still be mad at you for not recognizing me, but I can't after hearing the whole story. I understand now. It doesn't erase how I felt, but I can see why you wouldn't have been in a good headspace at that time."

"I would've told you sooner had you been up front with me all those times I asked you what your problem was," he counters with a smirk, and I know he's right.

"I couldn't. Not only was I humiliated about the whole thing but I also knew it would've been embarrassing to admit regardless of the response. I was either forgettable or a cheap lay or hell, both. The last thing I wanted was to hear your excuses. The only thing I could do was to retaliate and make your life miserable."

"Well, I moved to Eldorado for a fresh start and to forget about them. Let's just say, meeting you at the ranch definitely kept my mind off it." He smirks.

"How come you never mentioned to anyone you'd been engaged before? No one knew much about you before you moved there."

"Mostly because I wanted to forget. Talkin' about it woulda brought up questions I didn't wanna answer, and if I pretended it didn't affect me, then I could try to move on," he explains. "After she tracked me down, I realized I couldn't stay in San Antonio anymore. She'd never let me move on, and it'd always be in my face, considering she's family. So, I found a ranch hand job a few hours away and tried to start over."

"Well, you found a good place to do that. Long hours working in the heat and other ranch hands to keep ya busy," I say.

"Agreed. Circle B saved my life. Kept me out of a dark hole, that's for sure. Perhaps it was destiny to meet again?" He winks.

I release a small laugh. "Yeah, *maybe.*"

I hate knowing that most of this conversation could've been avoided had I been up front with him sooner, but there's no way I could've known. Had Bella not cheated, Grayson would've never been out that night, and we would've never met in the first place.

"You deserve better than her," I whisper.

He nods. "I know that now, but it took a helluva lot of work to get there. I never thought I'd meet someone like you the same night I was tryin' to erase Bella's existence from my memory. Maybe it was best I didn't recognize you because, at that time, I wouldn't have been able to give you what you deserved."

I pull in a deep breath, and we remain quiet as thoughts drift around.

Eventually, he speaks and disrupts the silence. "I hate how much I hurt you for forgetting. If I'd known you were *her*, I would've said something as soon as I saw you at the ranch. Kenzie, I'd be lyin' if I said I hadn't thought about being with you over the years. So to know we were already together but all the important details are missin' from my memory is fuckin' torture."

I hold back a smile as heat rushes through me. As much as I hate to admit it, being with him is a memory I've replayed in my head hundreds of times. "I didn't realize you were going through so much shit and honestly didn't even take that into account. I thought you were another asshole who was just lookin' for a piece of ass, and I was the dumbass who fell for your charm. Come to find out, I was the asshole all along."

"*No.* You have every right to be upset. I would be too if the roles were reversed and you didn't know who I was. Just wish you woulda said something sooner. I would've fully explained myself and apologized for hurting you. That was never my intention, and though I can't take it back, I hope you forgive me now that you know everything." The silence temporarily returns as his words sink in. "But I promise you this, I will never forget the day I met you at the ranch, ever. There was always somethin' about you I couldn't quite put my finger on. It all makes sense now, though."

I meet his kind eyes, and then I gaze down to his kissable lips. He swallows, and I think he might lean in and brush his mouth against mine. A part of me wishes he would. The other part of me knows how bad of an idea it is, considering how vulnerable we are right now.

All of this—the way I feel and what I've learned—is so overwhelming, and I know I need some alone time to process all of this. There's no way I'll be able to do that with Grayson sitting so close and smelling so good.

After an awkward few seconds pass, I clear my throat. "I really am sorry for not bringin' it up and just confronting you sooner. I let my pride get in the way and didn't know how to talk about something so conflicting, but I'm glad everything is aired out now."

"Me too," he says, nodding. "Feels good to finally have all the pieces. You don't know how much it drove me crazy not knowing why you hated me for so long. Honestly, I should've put it all together at some point. I knew you went to college in the same town I was from and that there was a chance we could've met, but I never assumed you were that girl. I always hated that I couldn't remember your name. Made me feel like a giant dick too."

I let out a deep breath and a slight chuckle. We both made mistakes that ultimately led us here, but there's really nothing more to say. The awkwardness streaming between us is ready to swallow me whole. "Can we pretty please just go back to the ranch? I kinda wanna be alone. It's nothing against you, I just…"

"Sure, if that's what you want. There's no reason to stay anyway. I'm not heading back to the reunion. Plus, it'll give me the chance to work tomorrow." He looks down at his phone and checks the time, then packs his small bag. It doesn't take him long to get his things. Within ten minutes, we're pulling out of the parking lot.

I have a million questions in my mind as we drive home.

Where do we go from here?

What does our future look like?

Now that it's all out in the open, I can already feel the dynamic of our relationship shifting. We're no longer "enemies," so are we friends? More than friends? I don't know.

After an hour of driving, Grayson turns down the radio. From the expression on his face, I'd say he's been going crazy with his thoughts too. "So, I have to ask. Given that you know all the details now, do you think we could get a second chance? Start over and see if that same spark still exists?"

I swallow hard, not wanting to make any rash decisions, though I'm relieved he mentioned it first. "I think I need some time before I can make that decision." My heart and head are still trying to catch up.

"Sure, that's fair." He flashes a genuine smile. "I'm still helping you with the Harvest Festival, though, right?"

This makes me laugh. "You're damn right."

He grins, and the thick air between us slightly dissipates. So many streaming emotions are playing in my head that I turn the radio back up to block them out. I don't know where we go from here, but I'll need to quickly figure that out.

CHAPTER SIXTEEN

Grayson

This past weekend didn't quite go as planned, though I'm not really sure what I expected.

Never in a million years did I anticipate Bella and Kenzie knowing each other. I could've gone the rest of my life never seeing Bella's face again, but considering she's family, there's always a chance I will. However, if anything good came out of this shit show, it was finally getting answers from Kenzie.

But now, I hope to win her back and get a second chance.

She asked for time to process everything, so I'll give her that. Even though seeing her at the B&B every morning will be torture, I'll give her space.

"You dumbass, what'd you do that for?"

"Me? You're the moron who forgot to turn the electric fence back on."

Jesus Christ. It's only eight on a Monday morning, and the twins are already arguing.

"You're just pissed Hadleigh wanted to hang out with me," Knox throws in his face, and I know it's only a matter of time before fists start swinging.

"Wanted to? More like *had* to. She won you at the auction and was just keepin' her end of the bargain." Kane shoves him as he passes.

I should break it up and tell them to knock it off, but it's good entertainment. So, I keep eavesdropping.

"Exactly, she won *me*. Not you. Get over it already," Knox retorts.

"There's nothing to get over except the fact that you'd never be good enough for her," Kane says as Knox trails him.

Everyone knows Kane's in love with Hadleigh, but who she has feelings for is still up in the air. One week, she's all about Knox, and the next, she's all over Kane. They should have a joust already, and the winner gets the lady.

"The hell does that mean?" Knox grabs the back of Kane's T-shirt and yanks him back.

Kane looks murderous as he shoves his brother away. "It means you'd just fuck her, then ghost her and leave her brokenhearted. Just like you do every chick you've hooked up with. You wouldn't know how to have a genuine relationship if it bit you in the ass. So yeah, my best friend deserves better than you."

Before they start fistfighting, I make my presence known and casually whistle as I walk toward them.

"Y'all okay over here?" I arch a brow, crossing my arms.

"Just fine," Knox grinds out between clenched teeth.

"That true?" I ask Kane.

"As long as he stays away from Hadleigh, it will be," he blurts, scrubbing a hand through his hair, then putting on his hat.

"Not that it's any of *my* business…" I begin, hoping neither of them decks me for intervening. "But Hadleigh's old enough to make her own decisions, even if you don't agree with them." I glance at Kane. "You can't control who she dates."

"Maybe not, but if he touches her, it'll change everything," Kane hisses, directing his attention to Knox.

Kane stalks off, leaving Knox and me alone.

"Is what he said true? You ghost women after sleepin' with them?"

Knox avoids my gaze for a few seconds before glancing at me. "You know how it is. Our lives are this ranch. There's no time to get serious."

"Plenty of ranch hands are married and have kids. There's time if you make time."

"He's just bent out of shape because she likes me. Meanwhile, he's too much of a pussy to tell her how he feels, so he directs his anger at me instead of manning up."

"You sure that's all?" I ask.

He shrugs. "Who knows. He's been pissy ever since she won me at the auction instead of him. Now he's acting like it's a competition when I didn't tell her to bid on me in the first place."

"Give him a break. He's in that weird friend-zone place where he's contemplating risking their friendship for more. If he confesses how he feels and she doesn't feel the same, it could ruin everything. Trust me, I saw Ethan go through the same damn thing."

"Yeah, but it was obvious to everyone that Harper liked him too. Hadleigh gives mixed signals." He says it like he knows from experience and has the same risks to overcome.

I scratch my cheek and nod. "Yeah, I know that feelin' too."

After a busy workday, I run home and shower. Though I know Kenzie's working the after-school program, I send a text anyway, so she'll see it when she's done.

GRAYSON

Wanna meet me at the pub tonight? My treat ;)

I'm certain she'll deny my invite, but I have to at least try. I can still give her the space she requested while hanging out as friends. I just want to see her.

MACKENZIE

Sorry, Cowboy. After being on my feet for ten hours, I'm taking a bath and going to bed early.

I read her reply after I get dressed. My smile turns into a frown, but I understand.

GRAYSON

Damn, you're gonna miss out on hearing the drama from earlier. But I get it. Can I bring you anything?

MACKENZIE

Don't try to seduce me with gossip!

GRAYSON

Well, if I tried using anything else, you'd call me bad names.

MACKENZIE

Ha! Probably true. But since you teased, spill it.

GRAYSON

Alright fine. FaceTime me later when you're soaking in the tub.

MACKENZIE

When I'm conveniently naked, huh?

GRAYSON

I'll be a complete gentleman. Pinky promise.

MACKENZIE

Yeah, I'm sure. But okay. You better be spilling some piping hot tea!

Though Kenzie's more modest than her grandma, she still loves knowing what's going on around here just as much.

While I wait for Kenzie, I decide to reach out to my mother. She's called four times and left urgent voicemails. We haven't spoken since Kenzie and I left the family reunion Saturday afternoon, and I'm sure she's dying to talk it out.

"Hey, Mom," I greet when she answers on the first ring.

"Grayson, honey. *Finally.* I was gettin' worried ya wouldn't call back." She sounds out of breath or perhaps relieved.

"Sorry, Ma. I was workin'. Just got home and about to find somethin' to eat."

"Honey, I'm so sorry about Bella," she blurts out. "She and Grant surprised all of us by showing up. I would've never pushed you to come had I known they'd be there."

"I know. I don't blame you at all," I reassure her.

"Your friend looked pretty upset about it. I assume she knows?"

"After the fact," I admit. "There was a huge miscommunication because it turns out Kenzie and Bella met before, which spiraled the whole thing."

"Oh, sweetie. I'm sorry to hear that. Is she alright now?"

"Once we got back to the hotel and talked, things made more sense. She's okay, though. We have a past and are only friends, but I asked her for a second chance to make it right. I've wanted her for a long time and didn't know why she wouldn't give me the time of day until this weekend."

"What'd she say?" my mom asks eagerly.

I explain how Kenzie wants some space to process it all. "I see her every morning, and we text, but I'm not pushing her to make a decision or anything. Not yet anyway."

"Don't let her get away, son. Even though we didn't get much time together, I could see the spark between y'all. In fact, I think it's why Bella made a show of going by you. She was jealous."

"Pfft. Of what? She made her decision six years ago."

"Though I don't agree with what they did to you, Grant's my son too, and I love him and Leo. I tolerate Bella, but she's a good wife and mother at least. However, women never forget their first love. Even if they're happy now, there's always a little bit of envy seeing the other person move on too."

I know how that feels, except mine was mixed with anger.

"Doesn't excuse how she blindsided me." Bella had to have known I wouldn't want to see or talk to her, but she made sure I did.

"I know, honey. You don't have to forget what they did, but I hope one day you can forgive them for your own sake. You'll feel lighter, and it'll help you in future relationships too."

I hate that my mother knows this from personal experience. My dad cheated with her childhood best friend. They had a four-year affair before she found out and filed for a divorce. The bastard was too chickenshit to admit what he'd done and fought her on everything—except Grant and me. He was more than willing to leave us behind to start a new family.

I haven't seen the asshole since I was ten years old.

We chat for another ten minutes before we say our goodbyes. I know she worries about me, and I hate that San Antonio holds too much pain. Hopefully I can plan to go back and visit her soon without the unnecessary drama.

When my phone rings an hour later, I smile wide when Kenzie's name flashes on the screen.

"Hello, gorgeous," I say when I see her bright blue eyes.

"Hey, yourself. What're ya up to?"

"Sitting here, thinking about you."

"I bet you are. Keep your hands where I can see them, Cowboy."

I chuckle. "Lower your phone for me."

"Nice try. The tub is full of bubbles anyway." She flips the camera, giving me a view of her toes peeking through the suds.

"Damn, such a tease."

"Hardly. So, what's this gossip? I have my glass of Merlot ready."

Kenzie flips the camera back to her stunning face. She's makeup free, and her blond hair is up in a messy bun, looking sexy as hell.

"I think Hadleigh's in some threesome drama with the twins."

Kenzie chokes on her wine, and I wait as she clears her throat. "Grayson! You nearly killed me."

"Not my fault you can't swallow."

She narrows her eyes at me. "I can swallow just fine when I'm not taken off guard."

"Not sure that helps your case."

"Shut up and elaborate please."

I repeat what the twins said while they were fighting and my conversation with Knox afterward. Though I shouldn't be spreading their business, it gives me a chance to talk to Kenzie about something unrelated to us.

"Wow, so you think she's playing them?"

"I don't think so. But honestly, who knows. I can tell they both want her or, at the very least, Kane doesn't want Knox to have her."

"They've fought for as long as I can remember, which is unfortunate because they're twins and should be really close."

"They're too different," I counter.

"My dad and Uncle Jackson are different, and they still have a strong brotherly relationship. Though according to my aunts, it wasn't always sunshine and roses either. Hmm…maybe they'll eventually grow out of it." She contemplates as she takes another swig of her drink.

"Maybe Hadleigh likes them both, and since she can't decide, she won't end up picking either of them," I suggest.

"Honestly, that's her best bet. Though they're my cousins so I don't see the appeal of either of them." She shrugs.

"If she doesn't figure out what she wants soon, I'm afraid next time fists will be swinging. They're both muscular as hell, so I wouldn't put it past them to do some real damage," I say, walking to the fridge for a beer.

"Maybe I can get some details out of Harper. She usually knows what's going on, but she's been busy with the new baby." Kenzie tucks her bottom lip between her teeth, and it has me fantasizing about all the places I'd love for her to bite me.

"So not to change the subject, but don't make plans this weekend," I say casually, hoping she doesn't call me out.

"And why not?"

"Just promise me you won't, okay?"

"Grayson."

"Mackenzie," I mimic her same tone.

Finally, she relaxes her shoulders and gives in with an unamused eye roll. "Fine, but I haven't given you my answer yet."

"Yes, I'm aware."

"It's driving you insane, isn't it?" she asks, trying to hold back a grin, but I see it behind her wineglass.

"Nope. Didn't cross my mind at all today."

"Good. I'd hate to know you were thinkin' of me."

"Oh, I never said I wasn't, darlin'," I retort.

She arches a brow.

"Had some *very* inappropriate thoughts, in fact. So filthy they can't be repeated."

Kenzie snort-laughs, and I love the sound she makes when she's trying to hold back. "Good night, Cowboy. I'll see you at breakfast."

"I'll be there...painful erection and all."

"Better get that looked at. Maybe a trip to the ER. I'm sure Uncle Evan works tomorrow."

"Hard pass." I shake my head. "Don't worry, I'll take care of it in the shower later."

I flash her a wink, then tell her good night.

After the call ends, I decide a second shower for the night wouldn't be such a bad idea after all.

CHAPTER SEVENTEEN

Mackenzie

After years of being angry with Grayson, it's foreign to suddenly not feel that toward him anymore. I redirected those feelings of hate toward the woman who cheated on *him*.

I only wish I knew the truth when I was face-to-face with her. Instead of quietly standing there, I would've given her a piece of my mind for being a shit human being. Sleeping around on your fiancé is bad enough, but to do it in the same house with his brother, then getting knocked up? All this time, she deserved the hell I'd given Grayson.

After sleeping on it a couple of nights and processing how I made assumptions and came to conclusions, I didn't want to dwell on it anymore. Grayson wants to move past it, so I need to as well, especially if we're really going to try for a second chance.

Every morning this week, I'd eat breakfast with Grayson at the B&B. It still freaks everyone out, which is hilarious. I already know they're placing bets behind our backs for when we'll finally hook up. A part of me wants to wait it out and make those assholes pay up, while the other part wants to show up at his house and jump his bones.

In the evenings after work, I'd come home and relax with a glass of wine and FaceTime Grayson for a bit. Every time we talk, those same butterflies from the night we first met surface. Though if I'm being honest, it's taken a few days to get used to this. We still tease and give each other shit, but it's not filled with hate and revenge. It's exactly how I imagined it'd be if our past was different.

When Grayson told me to keep the weekend open, I anticipated he'd ask me out. Considering it's now Saturday and he hasn't, I can't help but feel disappointed. The only person I've kept in the loop about this is Lacey, who's now seeing Luke. She's been telling me to *tie him down* for months. And hell, if he keeps me waiting for this "date," I just might have to get some rope.

"Mornin', Dad," I greet when I run into him at the B&B.

"Hey, sweetie. You're later than usual today." He checks his watch. It's nearly noon, but I shrug. I didn't have the motivation to get out of bed.

"Only coming for coffee and food," I mutter.

"Wouldn't expect anything less." He winks. "Maize made cinnamon rolls this mornin', and there might be some left in the kitchen."

"Ooh yum. Thanks for the tip." I smirk, passing a few guests as I make my way there.

"Hey, sis." I jump up on the counter and snag one.

"About time, I was about to send the National Guard."

I slouch and cross my legs, then shove half of the sweet bread in my mouth. "Felt like sleeping in."

"You look love-sick. What's goin' on?"

I try not to choke. "Nothin'. I need something to drink." I try to change the subject.

"Coffee?" Grayson's voice rings out. Maize and I snap our heads toward the doors, and my eyes widen in shock. "Two cream, two sugar."

"Aww..." Maize sing-songs. "I'm so goin' to win."

"Win what?" Grayson asks.

"Ignore her. She's just being dumb," I remark, taking the warm cup from his hand and watch Maize walk toward the door. She gives me a look that makes me roll my eyes, and I wonder if they really *are* placing bets on us. "Thank you. Impeccable timing," I tell him.

"I saw you when I was parking."

"Were you stalkin' me?" I pop a brow teasingly.

"Haven't you learned by now, Kenzie Bishop? My life consists of following you 'round like a lost puppy."

I nearly spit out my coffee at the same words I've said to Rowan about Grayson. "I'm gonna kill her."

He chuckles. "Don't worry. I didn't take offense."

"That was the anger talkin'. And probably pre-caffeine."

"I'm sure." He smirks, taking a few steps to close the gap between us. Grayson reaches up and grabs a loose strand of my hair. It's then I remember I look like I just rolled out of bed because I literally did.

"I'm a mess right now. Please don't judge me."

"You look adorable. And *hot*." He wraps the blond curl around his finger, then leans closer until his lips brush my ear. "I'm done waiting, sweetheart. Come over tonight. I'll be ready for your answer."

When he backs up, I can barely breathe. My stomach flips, and I fight the urge to kiss the smirk off his arrogant face.

Finally, I swallow and blink hard. "What time?"

"Six? I have plans for you."

All I can do is nod.

He grabs my hand, then kisses my knuckles. "See you tonight."

I watch as he walks toward the door, then gives me a mischievous wink over his shoulder before leaving.

Dammit, I'm so doomed.

I'm not sure how I'm supposed to hold back my feelings anymore.

I want Grayson Harding.

Badly.

As soon as I got home, I shaved, exfoliated every inch of my body, slathered lotion on all four limbs, and waxed my brows and lip.

Men have no clue about the insane process we go through just to be disappointed by them later in bed.

Though I don't have to worry about that with Grayson because he's already proven he knows what he's doing in the bedroom, even while drunk. If tonight goes as planned, he'll be reminding me all over again.

I put on my favorite black cutoffs, white crop top, and cowboy boots. Then I pull my hair into a high ponytail so the waves can flow down my back. My makeup is more natural than intense, but it's how I've always done it, so I know he'll like it. As I make my way to his house across the ranch, my nerves are all over the place. It's just a few minutes before six when I walk onto his porch and knock.

After a few more taps against the wood without him answering, I let myself in. Not surprisingly, it's unlocked. His house isn't small, but it's not huge either. A two-bedroom ranch style that could use some updating, but it's still cute.

"Grayson?" I call out, then hear water running in the bathroom. He must still be in the shower.

I tap my knuckles on the door and slowly open it. The room is filled with steam, but I see his naked silhouette under the hot water. Fuck, he's really tempting me, and it takes everything I have not to tear off my clothes and join him.

"Grayson," I repeat.

"Hey, sorry. Got home late, just gimme one second."

Instead of giving him privacy like I should, I stand and watch. His hard muscles flex as he rinses the soap off his sculpted body. I bite into my lower lip as I admire his perfect ass. When I hear the water turn off, I snap my attention toward his face.

Grayson grabs the towel as he steps out. Instead of covering himself, he uses it to dry off his face and shake out his hair. He gives me a direct view of his cock, and it's much bigger than I remember. When he catches me gawking, Grayson smirks and wraps the towel low around his waist.

"Gettin' a free show, are ya?" He threads his finger through his wet hair, causing water to drip down his chest.

"Pretty sure you gave me VIP access," I taunt.

He flashes his perfect white teeth as he comes to me. His closeness causes me to back up into the countertop.

"That depends. You have an answer for me?" His large arms come on either side of me, nearly caging me against the mirror.

Grayson's mouth is inches from mine, tempting me in all the right ways.

"You're not playin' fair." I can't concentrate with him so close, especially with his hot breath brushing against my skin.

The corner of his lips tilts up into a knowing smirk. "There are no rules when it comes to getting what I want. I play to win, sweetheart."

I stare at him, trying to form words as my heart races.

"Say the words, Kenzie. Are you giving us a second chance?"

His question is one I don't even need to think twice about. Not anymore.

"Yes, now kiss—"

Grayson cups my face, and our mouths crash together. I gasp at the immediate intrusion, then flatten my palms against his bare chest. As I part my lips, his tongue dives in, tangling with mine as I seek more.

"Grayson," I murmur.

"Damn, baby." He groans, lowering his hands down to my ass to pick me up.

As I sit on the edge of the sink, my thighs wrap around his waist, and I pull him closer.

"You're driving me insane," he whispers as he brushes his lips down my jawline. Tilting my head, I give him access to my neck. "You taste so goddamn good."

I feel his erection beneath the towel and know he wants this as much as I do. Lowering my hands, I grip the towel, but he quickly grabs it and stops me.

"Wait," he states as if he's in agony over his own words.

"What, why?" I blurt out a little too harshly. He's gonna give me lady blue balls.

"I want to properly take you out first."

Is he joking right now?

"Grayson. Don't you think we waited long enough already?" I pout like a child who's just been told they can't have ice cream for dinner.

"You have no fucking idea, but I promise…you'll like this surprise."

I push him back, causing him to stumble toward the wall. Jumping down, I remove the space between us, then wrap my palm around his dick, and he immediately groans.

"I truly believe you'll like my surprise too." I smirk, yanking the towel away. Before he has time to deny me, I kneel between his legs and stroke him.

"Jesus, Kenzie. You're a real-life fantasy come true." He wraps a hand behind my head.

I lick my lips, then pull him into my mouth. The way Grayson's head rolls back combined with the deep rumble of his moan has me more than eager to please him. His thick veins and velvety-soft shaft have my panties nearly melting.

"You feel so goddamn good, baby. Fuck, I bet you're wet right now, aren't you?" He gazes at me, and I happily nod as I play with his balls.

Hollowing my cheeks, I speed up my pace as I suck and stroke him. Grayson's hand tightens around my ponytail, and he grunts. His body tenses, and I know he's close. "You have a hot little mouth, sweetheart. Shit, I'm gonna—"

I nod, and he comes down my throat. Grayson's burst of curse words and groans make it even hotter. Releasing him, I lick my lips and swallow all of him down.

"Christ, woman." He lifts me to my feet, then spins me around before I realize what he's doing. "Bend over and plant your hands on the counter. We don't have much time if we want to get there before sunset."

I do as he says and yelp when he shoves my shorts and panties to my ankles.

"Spread those beautiful thighs, baby."

Grayson squeezes my ass cheeks apart as he dives in and sinks his tongue along my slit. The intrusion nearly has me blissfully flying to the ceiling.

"*Oh my God,*" I pant, arching my back.

Grayson smacks my ass as he flicks my clit, then sucks it hard between his lips.

"Don't stop," I beg.

Moments later, he shoves two fingers inside me and moves his mouth toward my tight hole. "So sweet and wet, just like I knew you'd be."

"Grayson, please."

"Not gonna lie, hearing you beg for me drives me so damn wild."

"I'm *so* close."

"Come on my tongue, baby." He removes his fingers, then sinks his tongue back inside me while pinching my clit.

I don't know if it's the years of buildup or if Grayson just knows how to please a woman, but I've never come so fast in my life. Tingles shoot up my spine as my muscles tense, and an orgasm erupts through me. I didn't just fall off the edge; he pushed me with so much intensity, I can't feel my limbs anymore.

"Holy..." I pant out, slumping against the countertop.

Grayson pulls my panties and shorts up, then spins me around and lets me taste myself on him. "Give me five minutes, and I'll be ready to go."

"I don't think I can walk," I mutter.

He chuckles, giving me one more kiss. "Don't worry, I'll carry you." Grayson winks before leaving me hot and aroused in the bathroom.

CHAPTER EIGHTEEN

Grayson

I guide Kenzie out to my truck with the taste of her still lingering on my lips.

Fuck, that was the hottest moment of my life, and I'll be riding that high till the day I die. As much as I wanted to bring her to my room and treat her right, I had to get us out of there before we missed everything I planned.

"You made us leave so we could come to the B&B?" She glances out the window, then flashes me a confused look. "Where my father works?" she adds, and I chuckle at her unamused expression.

"Gimme a little credit." I hop out of the truck and walk around to her side, opening the door. "Just *trust* me."

I extend my hand out, and Kenzie takes it. Then I lead her around the back of the B&B to the steps.

"Where are we going?" She furrows her brows as we climb up.

There's a third-floor balcony that can only be accessed from the two windows at the top.

"We're crawling through them?"

I chuckle, opening them wide. "It's just a couple of steps out. You'll be fine."

"If you seduced me up here just to push me off the roof, I'll come back and haunt your ass," she threatens.

"I wouldn't expect anything less from you, honestly."

Holding her hand, I help her step over the windowsill, where she sees her surprise.

"Grayson...you set all of this up?"

On the balcony, a picnic with her favorite foods and wine has been set up. And from this vantage point, we have a perfect view of the ranch and sunset. "Sure did. Thought we could use a quiet evening to talk." I stand next to her and gesture for her to sit.

"Wow, I haven't been up here since I was like thirteen. Knox and Kane convinced us all it was haunted, so none of us girls wanted to risk it. That was after Riley fired a water balloon at me when I was standing underneath."

I chuckle, uncorking the bottle of Cabernet. "Sounds like him."

"Oh, it wouldn't have been so bad if he hadn't filled it with green Jell-O. My hair smelled like limes for three days! Little shitheads."

"I bet y'all had a blast growing up here, though." I grab two wineglasses, fill them, and hand her one.

"Thanks. And it was. Truthfully, I can't imagine bein' raised in the city. Or living anywhere else, actually."

"It's a contrast from San Antonio. I couldn't get out of there fast enough, and once I landed here, I knew this was the place for me," I admit. "Though my mother wishes I'd move back, I can't imagine ever leaving."

"Your mom misses you, that much I could tell." She takes a sip of her drink and gives me a sad smile.

"I know, and I do plan on making more of an effort to see them. I'd love to show them around here too, so I might invite them out soon," I tell her. They'd immediately fall in love with the Bishops just like I did.

"You know my parents will set them up in the best room here, so just set the date." She grins, peeking in the basket. "What else do you have in here?"

"Shrimp po'boys in toasted Brioche rolls and fruit salad."

Her jaw drops as she eyes the container. "I love shrimp po'boys!"

"I know, you mentioned it a while ago, and I never forgot."

"Oh wow. You're spoiling me already?" She arches an amused brow as I hand her a plate full of food.

"Just showin' ya what you've been missing out on." I flash her a wink.

She groans, giving me an evil eye. "Don't gloat. I know I messed up making assumptions, but I wasn't gonna ask after you forgot our entire night together. So, it's only partially my fault."

I hold back laughter as she sulks. "Alright, I'll take half the blame. Deal?"

Kenzie snickers, then takes a big bite of her sandwich. "Mm…now that I've tasted this, I'd agree to almost anything," she states after she chews.

I arch a brow, stabbing a piece of fruit. "Anything, huh?"

"Yep." She moans loudly as she chews. "Please tell me you have like five more of these?"

"Maize made a whole bunch actually. I came up with the menu, and she agreed to cook."

"She never fails, I swear." Kenzie shakes her head.

We continue chatting as we devour the best shrimp po'boys I've ever had. Even the fruit salad is top-notch. By the time we finish eating, our glasses are empty, and I refill them.

"Watching the sunset out here never gets old," she says as the sun disappears behind the hills.

"I agree."

"It's one of the reasons I'm still living at my parents'. Though they love me being at home, I feel like I'm gettin' a little too old to still be there. I want my own space, but until I can afford to build, I'll be stuck."

"What about those prefab or modular homes? They have lots of options nowadays, and it's cheaper and faster," I suggest.

"Hmm…I never thought of that. But that'd probably be ideal, especially since I want to become a foster parent soon. I've already gone to the informational orientation, but it can take three to six months to be approved."

"Really? I had no clue you wanted to do that. I love that idea, though."

"Yeah, I really want to foster to adopt, but I'm not sure I'd be approved if

I live with my parents. They do home inspections, and the child would need their own room. Right now, my mom's using Maize's old room for the twin's playroom. And I don't want to make them rearrange their house for me, so it'd just be easier to move."

I think for a quick moment before blurting out my idea. "Use my address. It's a two-bedroom, and I was thinking about fixing it up soon anyway."

"Wait, *what*?" Her lips part as she looks at me unexpectedly.

"After some fresh paint and new carpet, it'd look pretty good. I was even gonna check out some new appliances. Once it's redone, it'd be perfect for you and a child to live in."

"Grayson, I can't just take your home." She shakes her head. "Where would you go?"

"Could probably crash with Luke or Payton. Well, maybe not Luke now that he's banging Lacey every damn night." We both laugh. "Payton wouldn't mind, I'm sure."

"I appreciate the offer, but I couldn't. If I can't afford to buy, I'll just wait to apply until I can."

I set down my glass and move closer, grabbing her hand. "Mackenzie." She looks in my eyes as I stare at her. "Let me do this for you. I feel like I owe you after all the pranks and everything."

"That went both ways," she retorts.

I shrug, not giving a shit about technicalities. "Please. I want to make a home for you."

"You'd do all that for me? Just so I can foster a child?"

"I'd do anything for you, Kenzie. I've had feelings for you for so long. I just want to see you happy, even if we only ever stayed friends. This gesture comes with zero expectations from you." I run my finger along her cheek and capture a piece of her hair before placing it behind her ear. "So, whaddya say?"

As she contemplates my offer, Kenzie bites her bottom lip. There's no pressure for us to become something. I'd do this for her either way.

"I'd say you're insane..." She chuckles. "But I can't deny that I love this idea. Being able to put on my application that I have a safe and quiet place for a kid and he or she would have their own space would be amazing. Even more so if there's an option to adopt."

"Consider it done then. I'll get started as soon as I can so it's ready for you."

"I don't know how to thank you for this."

Kenzie grasps my face and crashes her mouth to mine. Wrapping my hands around her waist, I gently pull her onto my lap. She straddles me as I devour her soft and eager lips. It's a fucking dream come true, one I wasn't sure would ever happen. This woman has consumed me for so long and to finally have her in my arms is heaven.

Her moans turn me the hell on. When she grinds harder against my erection, I nearly groan at how badly I wish we weren't on the roof of the B&B. I want to strip off all her clothes and kiss every inch of her.

"Goddamn, you're killin' me here," I breathe out, squeezing her breast through her shirt.

"Since you can't recall many details of that night, you want me to tell you the things I remember about our first time?" she teases, nibbling on my bottom lip.

"You still recall after all these years, huh?" I ask with amusement. "Must've been an unforgettable night for ya."

She pushes back and awards me with a playful eye roll. "Spare me your arrogant attitude for once."

I bark out a laugh, pulling her closer. "Tell me everything. I wanna know," I urge her as I feather kisses down her jaw and neck. "Remind me how good you felt wrapped around my cock."

"God," she hisses, rotating her hips and moving against me.

"As soon as we walked into your hotel room, you were tearing off my clothes. You couldn't keep your hands off me, and I couldn't wait to see you, so I frantically unbuttoned your jeans. In the midst of tryin' to get you naked and us being drunk, we tripped and stumbled to the floor."

I chuckle into her neck. "That sounds embarrassing. Maybe I hit my head and got temporary memory loss."

Kenzie threads her fingers through my hair and squeezes. "We laughed it off and continued undressing. Once I was down to my panties, you spread me on the bed and yanked them down with your teeth. In theory, it was hot, but in reality, you dragged your teeth against my leg and left marks."

"Jesus, maybe don't tell me."

She tilts her head back and laughs. "I told you to fuck me, and you quickly grabbed a condom before diving your mouth between my legs. I orgasmed so fast on your tongue, you thought I was faking it, so you demanded me to do it again. So, I wrapped my thighs around your head as you finger fucked and ate me out. Seriously, I've thought about that moment every time I've brought my vibrator out."

"I do still have a strong oral game," I taunt with a wink. "As you've already experienced tonight."

Kenzie shakes her head at me while raking her nails down my chest. "Then you bent me over."

I swallow hard as the image enters my mind. "Please don't tell me I came in two minutes."

"After the amount of alcohol you had, surprisingly no. You twisted your hand in my hair, spanked my ass, and drove inside me so deep, I came a third time. I swear we went for a solid hour. I woke up with your finger marks on my hips, bite marks on my legs, and a red ass."

"You're making my dick rock hard, Kenzie...fuck."

"Are you flushed, Cowboy?"

"Damn right I am. Jealous as hell of my past self too. And pissed I don't remember much." I bring our lips together and sweep my tongue inside. She shifts her head so I can slide in deeper and taste her sweetness.

"Take me back to your place so we can make new memories," she whispers.

"Kenzie. There's no expectation to jump right into sex. We're starting over, right? Giving this a second chance?"

"Or we could start right where we left off? We've known each other for almost six years."

I groan as she reaches between us and rubs her hand along my shaft. "But if you'd rather jerk off in the shower instead..." Her torturous teasing continues as her lips find my throat.

Hell no. Now that I have Kenzie in my arms, I don't ever want to let her go.

"Fuck it. You win." I grab the hem of her shirt and pull it off her.

Her eyes widen as she looks around.

"No one can see us up here, plus it's almost pitch-black. Just keep your moaning to a minimum." I smirk. "No screaming my name either. Unless you want us to get caught."

She waggles her brows. "Don't threaten me with a good time."

"Jesus Christ, woman," I growl, pulling down the cup of her bra, then squeezing her breast into my mouth. "Right now, I can't taste every inch of you like I want, but I promise to later."

"If you don't lower your jeans, I swear..." She moves against me, and I can tell she's already close to her release.

"Lean back a second..."

After she does, I manage to drag my pants and boxers down just enough to give her the access she needs. She quickly removes her shorts and panties. Before she climbs back on my lap, I sit against the balcony. As she lowers herself on my dick, I grab the back of her head and press our mouths together.

"Holy fuck, baby. You feel so good," I whisper against her lips as I thrust my hips upward. "You ridin' me is a wet fantasy come true."

"It's better than I remember," she admits, breathing hard as she sinks me deeper.

Kenzie leans her forehead against mine as we pant and moan together. I squeeze her hip with one hand and pinch her nipple with the other. Blond hair from her ponytail falls around her shoulders, and I take a chunk of it in my fingers, forcing her head back.

"Ah," she yelps, clinging to my shoulders.

As she sucks my neck, I lower a hand between us and find her clit.

"Yes, *yes*," she pants out.

"You're so wet, sweetheart. Come on my cock," I encourage. "I wanna feel you squeeze all around me."

"Keep rubbing me," she demands. "Almost there."

As our bodies mold together, I thumb her swollen bud and continue thrusting. Her breathing increases, and I can feel her pulse racing as she teeters on the edge.

"I can't wait to spread your thighs and eat your sweet pussy again. Slow and teasing until you beg me to let you come. Shit, I can taste you now," I say into her ear.

Kenzie's back stiffens as her pussy tightens around me. I continue circling her clit as she falls off the edge, but when she loudly groans out, I cover her mouth with my hand. I keep it there as she rocks her body and moans against my palm.

"Oh my God, that was so intense," she whispers.

"Hang on, baby. No screaming."

With my hands grasping her waist, I thrust up inside her, deep and fast, chasing my own release. She buries her face in my neck, trying to contain herself, but as soon as my balls tighten, I release inside her with an animalistic groan I can't restrain.

"Fuck," I say a little too loudly.

"You came inside me," she whispers, and for a moment, I freak out that she's going to be mad. "Guess that means you're mine now."

I take her face in my palms and place a relieved kiss on her lips. "I've been yours since the day we met."

And I'm not bullshitting her either. I couldn't even imagine being with another woman because all I've ever wanted was her.

"Take me home," she pleads. "I don't wanna have to be quiet next time."

CHAPTER NINETEEN

Mackenzie

The moment Grayson unlocks the door to his house, we're all over each other. Lips and hands fighting for skin as we tear off our clothes, tripping over random shit on the floor. I giggle when we nearly face-plant, but luckily, Grayson catches us before we do.

"You're gonna kill me...literally," he mocks, then picks me up like I weigh nothing. He throws me over his shoulder and walks us through the dark living room.

"You caveman!" I smack his ass. "Put me down."

"It's my turn to tie *you* up." His taunting voice gives me butterflies. Grayson sets me on his bed, then towers over me. "I still have the rope."

"Not sure I'd trust you." I narrow my eyes, then wrap my legs around his waist and pull him to my chest.

"Don't worry, it's not like I'd leave you naked and helpless..." He lifts my arms above my head, pinning me down, then brushing his lips against

"You wouldn't dare," I counter, then lift my hips and feel how hard he is. "You want me too much."

Grayson squeezes my wrists and brings his mouth to my ear. "Goddamn right, I do. I've dreamed about you being in my bed for so damn long, Kenzie." He sucks my neck, and I gasp when he bites down. "And let me be clear, now that you're in it, you're *mine*."

"Yes," I breathe out, widening my legs so he can press harder into me. The friction of his erection against my pussy is almost too much to handle.

"Say it," he demands, holding my arms with one hand as he lowers the other down my body. He grabs my bare breast, and it feels so good in his calloused palm.

"I'm yours, Grayson," I reassure him, breathing hard as his brown eyes focus on me.

The corner of his lips tilts up into a satisfied grin. "That's my good girl. Now let's remove these panties." He flashes a wink before grabbing the cotton and yanking them off.

I widen my thighs, and Grayson pulls them over his shoulders, then settles between them. Looking down, I hold my breath as he takes a long lick up my slit and immediately circles my clit with his tongue. I pinch my hard nipples and eagerly pant.

"Oh my God," I moan, my head falling against the pillow.

Grayson plays with my pussy, his tongue and fingers working me up so damn much, I can hardly control myself. I fist my hands in his hair, keeping his head right where I need him.

"Yes, right there."

Grayson's mouth moves in perfect rhythm, and soon, my body shudders as I ride my release. My back arches, and I scream out my orgasm, his name lingering on my lip.

"You comin' on my face is the hottest damn thing I've ever experienced," he tells me in a deep, gravelly voice.

My chest rises and falls as I watch him remove his boxers, and his hard dick springs out. Lying beside me, he grips the back of my head, and our mouths crash together. I love tasting myself on him and can't wait to return the gesture, but I need to feel him inside me right now.

"Fuck me, please." I nearly beg, clawing my nails down his chest.

"How do you want it, sweetheart?" He presses his lips against my neck.

I grab his cock and stroke him. Grayson groans in my ear, and it sends shivers down my body. God, hearing him pant from my touch will never get old.

"I wanna ride you again." I push him onto his back and straddle him. He immediately grips my hips, and his biceps flex as he tightens underneath me.

"Hell yes, baby." He lifts me so our bodies line up, then I slowly lower myself on him.

"Holy shit," I hiss as the tip of his cock hits me deep and hard. "That feels so good."

"So goddamn amazin'," he growls.

We form a rhythm, and he brings the pad of his thumb over my clit, rubbing torturous circles.

"So close, oh God." I squeeze my eyes shut as he adds more pressure. Once again, I'm falling apart.

"Your pussy's so tight, fuck." He groans like he's trying to control himself. Grayson fists a hand in my hair, then pulls me to his chest and captures my mouth with his.

As our tongues twist together, he brings a hand down and cracks it against my ass. I yelp out in surprise but love the way it burns. Picking up my pace, I ride him harder as he palms my breast.

"Your tits bouncing in my face is pure heaven." He smirks, squeezing them together as he kisses my chest.

Wrapping an arm around my waist, Grayson quickly flips us over. He towers over me, sliding between my legs and thrusting hard.

"Jesus," I moan out.

"Flip over," he demands, giving me room to roll onto my stomach. "God, this ass." He smacks it again. "On your knees, babe."

Grayson takes me from behind, hitting all the right spots. I arch my back and lift my ass as he speeds up. When his fingers dig into my skin, I know he's close and rock back into him.

"Shit," he hisses, pulling my head back by my hair.

I look over my shoulder, and our eyes meet. The feelings I have for this man are so complex, yet I'm not scared. Perhaps I should be since I've never had a real relationship, but he makes me feel safe and secure. I know he'd never purposely hurt me or cheat on me. We can give each other shit one minute, then we're sharing an intimate moment the next. That's exactly how it should be—someone who can make me laugh and orgasm in the same breath.

As his eyes bore into mine, an overwhelming burst of emotions hits me. When his muscles tighten, I realize I've been falling for this man for years. Though I didn't want to admit it, the lingering feelings were there all along.

"You're so beautiful, Kenzie," he says between heavy breaths. My pussy clenches as he slams harder, then he spills inside me.

After a moment, he releases me and realizes how hard he was hanging onto me.

"Damn, marked ya up real good. Sorry 'bout that." He brushes a finger over the impending bruise.

I lie next to him and rest my head on his chest. "Just wait till the guys see the hickey I left on your neck."

He immediately goes to touch it, and I chuckle at his horrified expression.

"Whoops. My bad," I say innocently with a smirk.

Grayson pushes me to my back, trapping my arms underneath his large body, and shoves his face into the softness of my neck. "Guess I better make us even then."

"Grayson, no!" I squeal. My students will notice it in a heartbeat. Not to mention, my parents and co-workers.

"Fair is fair," he taunts, sucking harder.

I wiggle beneath him, but it's no use. He's too strong.

After a moment, he pushes away and flashes a shit-eating grin. "There. Now everyone will know you're mine."

"You damn vampire." I glare. "I'll get you back for that."

He grins wide. "I'm sure ya will."

After an amazing night of being naked in Grayson's bed, we decide to finally get up and shower for the day. Of course, he joins me, and it takes us twice as long, but I didn't complain.

"Think we'll get to eat without being interrogated?" I ask as he drives us to the B&B.

He chuckles and kisses my knuckles. "Doubtful. They'll freak out, I'm sure."

When we arrive, we decide to walk inside hand in hand. It's past nine so most of the guests have already eaten and left for the morning. However, since it's Sunday, the ranch hands arrived later than usual and are all sitting at a table.

"Holy shit." Diesel's the first to blurt out.

They all turn and face us, including my father, who was chatting with them.

"Fuckin' finally," Ethan adds. "I've had to hear him talk about you for way too damn long."

My cheeks redden at the attention, and before I can talk to Dad, Maize bursts out of the kitchen. "Yes! Pay up, assholes! I finally won a bet." She high-fives Gavin, who's sitting at the end.

"You *seriously* had a bet going?" I ask, narrowing my eyes at my traitorous sister.

"Hey, you can't be mad at me. I made your favorite dish for your little date last night," she tells me matter-of-factly, crossing her arms.

"Alright, fair enough." I grin. "They were delicious by the way."

"What's goin' on?" Dad asks.

"By the massive hickeys, I'd say they're together," Riley mocks.

Dammit. Instinctively, I bring my hand up and cover my neck. "Shut up."

Grayson chuckles next to me. "Are y'all done now? Can we eat?"

"I could guess what he's been eatin'…" Diesel mutters with a chuckle as if we can't hear him.

"Dude." I give him a pointed look, then nod toward my father.

"Someone give me the PG version please." He lifts a brow.

"Grayson and I are together," I say simply. "And these goons are just freaking out about it for no reason." I wait while he processes what I said, then he finally flashes a smile.

"Wow. Can't say I'm that shocked, but if you fuck this up..." He directs his gaze toward Grayson. "I'll make sure there's more than cow shit in your truck."

"Yes, sir. No worries. I've waited years for this chance, so I'm not about to mess it up by bein' stupid." I look over at him, resisting the urge to climb him like a tree and kiss his perfect lips.

Dad gives us a nod and helps a guest as everyone else goes back to their conversations.

Shortly after we fill our plates and take a seat, Grandma Bishop rushes in and finds us. "Oh my goodness, I heard the news. I'm so excited. More grandbabies!"

My eyes widen as Grayson chokes on his food. "Lord. How'd you find out already?"

"Oh, honey. I hear everything. You can't keep secrets from me." She flashes a wink.

"Well before you get your hopes up, I'm not popping out any babies."

She waves me off as if I've lost my mind. "You'll change your mind."

Grayson leans over and whispers in my ear, "We can have fun practicing, though."

I fight back a smile.

"I heard that, Grayson Harding. You better plan to put a ring on her finger then."

"Oh my gosh, Grandma!" I panic. "That's like years away."

"Hmm...that's what they all say, then they make the engagement announcement at Christmas dinner." She winks, and I groan because it's only two months from now. The only thing I'll be announcing is if I get approved as a foster parent.

Just as Grayson and I finish eating, my mother walks in, no doubt summoned by my father. She gives me a joyful look and pulls me in for a hug.

"Only took five year's worth of Thanksgiving dinners, but y'all finally figured it out."

I chuckle in amusement. "Oh yeah, was your big plan to get us together? Make us eat turkey and stuffing next to each other?"

"Well, y'all are so stubborn, I had to try something."

Mom's invited Grayson over for Thanksgiving every year since he's

675

started, and I always dreaded it. We'd give each other shit, then I'd do my best to ignore him. Since he never went home during that time, Mom refused to let him spend it alone. Now I know why he always stayed here. This will be the first year we'll be going together, and the thought has me smiling wide.

"I'm just relieved I won't have to separate y'all from now on," she teases.

We finally escape the B&B without anyone else stopping us, and I breathe out in relief. I love my family, but they can be a bit much when they're excited about something.

"Any guesses how my mom's gonna react when we tell her?"

I grin at how suspicious she was of us. "She'll definitely call us out."

"Oh yeah, for sure." He takes my hand and leads me to the passenger door. "And I'll tell her she was right…my feelings for you were always more than just platonic. I just had to wait for ya to come around."

"And I'll tell her if her son hadn't forgotten our night together, this wouldn't have gone on so long," I counter as he cages me against the truck. That anger I felt when I thought he'd cheated would've dissipated as soon as he explained, and I probably would've forgiven him right away.

"Correction: I *didn't* forget that our night happened. I just didn't remember that the girl was you. There's a difference."

"Oh yeah, that's *so* much better." I snort, rolling my eyes.

Grayson cups my face and brings his lips to mine. "Just admit that you liked our little war and labeling me as your enemy. It made you burning hot. You're a little masochist."

"I am not!" I playfully smack his chest. "You just got on my damn nerves."

He chuckles, pressing a kiss to my forehead. "And I'm sure I still will."

We get in his truck, and I ask him to take me home so I can change clothes. My parents are still at the B&B so we'll have the house to ourselves.

"Wanna come to my room?" I taunt when we arrive, waggling my brows.

"Hell yes I do, but what if your folks come back and catch us?"

"Guess that's a risk you'll have to take…you in or not, Cowboy?" I walk toward the stairs, looking at him over my shoulder.

Even though we just spent the entire night together, I can't get enough of him. Now that I know what it's like to be with Grayson, I don't want to stop.

"Fuck it. You win again." He rushes toward me, and I scream as I run upstairs. "Better keep it down, baby." Grayson catches me in my room and kicks the door shut before pinning me against it. "Think you can do that?"

"No." I smirk. "But I'm willing to try."

CHAPTER TWENTY

Grayson

It's a perfect October day for a Harvest Festival. Kenzie was worried about the weather, but it's in the low sixties with a brisk breeze.

I've spent the past week helping her set things up at the school in the parking lot and playground. Since it's a huge charity event, the teachers and local businesses sponsor booths that they decorate in different themes. Some people get really into it and go all out and use Halloween movies as inspiration.

The community comes together to give the kids a safe space to trick-or-treat with a ton of activities for them to do. The best part is all the money that's raised will go toward scholarships and school supplies.

"Babe, you ready?" Kenzie asks from the other side of the stable. She's dressed like the sexiest Dorothy from *The Wizard of Oz* that I've ever seen. I'm tempted to peel that blue dress off her body, but I know we don't have

"Almost." I grin, then hang the lead rope in the tack room. I turn around to glance at my girl in pigtails.

"What?" Lifting a brow, she flashes a devilish smirk.

I remove the space between us, and she captures my lips. "You're hot as hell," I whisper, deepening the kiss.

It's easy to get lost with her like this, and as if she reads my mind, she pulls away. "We can't be late."

"I know, I know. I told Diesel I'd stop by and check on things before I left."

She smiles. "It's not a biggie, but we gotta go."

"Can you snap your heels together three times and make my dirtiest fantasies come true?" I tease, then stack a few buckets on top of each other. When I'm done, I open the gate and walk toward the front of the barn where we're parked. Kenzie grabs my hand, and I lift her knuckles to my lips.

"Maybe." She bites down on her bottom lip that I want between my lips.

"If only we had more time…" I wink.

"Trust me, Cowboy. I know," she tells me as I open the door to my truck. Kenzie jumps in the seat and turns to me. Wrapping my arms around her waist, I hold her as she wraps her legs around me.

"Don't be a tease," I say.

"I'd never." She slides her lips across mine, then puts her pointer finger in her mouth.

She's always loved teasing the hell outta me, and that hasn't changed. Running my hand up the inside of her thigh, I slip a finger inside her panties. She's soaked.

"Damn, baby." I groan, adjusting myself.

"Later," she teases, tracing the shell of my ear with her tongue.

"I might have to get you back for this…" I warn.

"I'd love it," she admits.

Creating space between us, I go to the driver's side.

"Did you remember your hat?" she asks with a sly grin.

Reaching into the back seat, I pick up the scarecrow hat and put it on. "Yep."

"Did you get Kane on board to be the lion, or was he still fighting you about it?" I ask as I turn on to the main road that leads to the school.

A chuckle escapes her. "I told Grandma on him."

"Oh, you played dirty."

She shrugs. "Don't I always?"

"Yes." I laugh. "Yes, you do."

"So is it a coincidence you made Kane the cowardly lion? Or did the costume fit too well?"

"You mean, Hadleigh and him admittin' his feelings to her, or rather not admitting them?" She chuckles. "It might've been a shot at him."

"He needs to get over himself and go for it. Better to just get it out there and know than sit back wondering," I say.

"Not sure he ever will." She shrugs.

"Guess we better start placin' bets, huh?"

"Oh my God, yes. Maybe I'll actually win some extra cash!"

I laugh as we pull into the parking lot across the street from the school.

Grabbing Kenzie's hand, I interlock my fingers with hers. "Did you get the yellow brick road figured out?" It was the last piece of the puzzle she needed to finish the design on her booth this year.

"I did! Elle helped me," she tells me as we make our way there. Kenzie wanted to do a *Wizard of Oz* theme and finally got enough adults together to play all the characters. Her sister is even dressed as Glinda the Good Witch.

"Ya nervous about today?"

"Nah. I know it's gonna go off without a hitch…" Her voice lowers. "Because of *you*."

"Me?" I lift a brow.

"Yeah. You took care of a lot of the stressful things, which made it easier on me. I'm grateful, babe, and I appreciate it so much. You have no idea."

I grin. "I can't take all the credit. You busted your ass to make this happen. But with that bein' said, I'd do anything for you, Kenzie."

"Anything?" She pops a brow and licks her lips. I'm tempted to pull her aside and kiss the fire outta her, but we're interrupted by one of her students.

"Miss Bishop," a little girl calls. "You look awesome!"

"Thank you, Ashlin." Kenzie bends down and gives her a hug. "You're the most gorgeous witch I've ever seen in my life."

The little girl blushes just as a woman walks up. "Miss Bishop, so happy to run into you. Thought you'd like to know the adoption was finally finalized yesterday."

Kenzie's eyes light up, and she exchanges a hug with her. "Congrats. I'm so happy for you all."

"Thank you," she says before they're called away by other parents.

"Ashlin was in foster care, and her foster mother submitted for adoption a while ago. Now it's official, so it's a big deal."

"Wow, that's incredible," I say, wrapping my arm around her.

"I hope that's us one day."

"It will be, sweetheart. Can't wait to have a home full of kids with you." I lean over and steal a kiss. "Maybe Grandma Bishop is on to something after all. The bigger the family, the more fun."

She grins wide. "Or drama, but yeah, having a house full would make me happy. I wish I could adopt all the kids who need parents. I'd do it in a heartbeat."

"That's because your heart is huge, Kenzie Bishop."

She sucks in a deep breath, and I can tell she's thinking about it.

"You know I'm gonna bust ass on gettin' the house perfect for you," I tell her.

"I know, Grayson. Don't know what I ever did to deserve you."

"I could say the same about you. It was meant to be."

After we pass at least twelve other booths, I finally see the yellow paper that's taped to the ground. Kenzie loops her arm with mine and we skip to her version of the Emerald City. Hadleigh and Kane are filling small bags full of candy for us to hand out just as Maize comes over with Mila Rose and Maddy. They're our little munchkins.

Elle walks up carrying Elisa, who's dressed like Toto, and I can't help but snort.

"Now that's adorable," Kenzie admits, stealing Elisa and placing kisses on her chubby cheeks.

"Where's Gavin?" Kane asks.

"The tin man should be here any minute. He was parking the truck," Maize explains.

"I'm ready!" Olivia raises her voice and spins around for us to see her lollipop guild costume. When Gavin arrives, I hold back laughter at how huge and perfect he looks for the part.

Once the festival begins, people of all ages arrive. Kenzie knows nearly every student's name that comes to our booth, and I love how attentive she is as she listens to them. They look at her like she's their hero, and I understand why because Kenzie's nothing short of amazing.

The trick-or-treating is supposed to last three hours, but it passes quicker than I thought it would. Most of the kids have made their way through several times, and when we run out of candy, we decide to clean our space. A handful of business owners volunteered to make sure the school grounds are cleaned after the event is over and everyone's gone. It makes my job a lot easier, honestly.

While we're packing up the tent, Rose Bishop walks over to us dressed like a queen with the crown and all. It makes me snort because she's basically Eldorado royalty.

"Y'all did so good. Did you see all the costumes that entered the contest? It just gets better every year, doesn't it?" She glances at all of us. "Goodness, I need to capture my grandbabies lookin' so cute. And you too, Grayson." She winks, then digs in her oversized purse and pulls out her iPhone.

She struggles with it for a few seconds until Kenzie goes to her. "I'll help ya, Grandma!"

After a few seconds, they've figured it out, and the pictures begin. Once she's gotten her fill of photos, she hugs and kisses each of us, then goes on her way.

"Just wanna tell y'all thank you," Kenzie says to everyone.

"You're welcome!" Hadleigh gives her a hug. "It was a lot of fun."

"Yeah, yeah," Kane grunts, but I see him flash a smile at Hadleigh.

We part ways with them, and for the first time since we arrived, Kenzie and I are alone. The sun's setting, so the temperature is dropping.

"Apple cider, oh my goodness," Kenzie shrieks when she sees the booth. We stop, and I get us each a cup. A slice of apple sits on the edge of the cup along with a huge dollop of homemade whipped cream covered in caramel sauce. She takes a sip, and when she pulls away, whipped cream sticks to her nose.

Leaning forward, I smirk before licking it off.

She pulls me toward her and captures my lips with an animalistic growl. We get lost in the moment and quickly realize we're making out in the walkway when someone clears their throat. Parting, we glance over and see Kenzie's mom.

"You two." She shakes her head. "Dorothy and the Scarecrow making out like they're on HBO."

"*Mom*." Kenzie interlocks her fingers with mine, tightly holding her drink with the other hand.

"Did you try the pumpkin pie?" she asks. "It's so good. I'm gonna go buy a whole one right now."

"Save some for us!" Kenzie tells her with a laugh before she walks away. When we're alone again, Kenzie turns to me.

"I've been waiting to kiss you all afternoon," she whispers.

"Well, just wait until we leave here," I say, waggling my brows. We find our way to the line for some pie. We're handed our slices, and it nearly melts in my mouth. Mrs. Bishop wasn't lying. It's the best damn pie I've had in a long time.

"I know why Mom got one to go now," Kenzie says around a mouthful, checking out the line that's even longer than the one we waited in. Playfully pouting, she shakes her head.

"I'm not *that* patient. I'd rather go home and eat something else..." Kenzie smirks. "But not until we've been through the hay maze. I gotta experience it firsthand."

"Deal," I say with a laugh. "You think ya can beat the fastest time?"

"You guys installed a freakin' clock?" she asks in shock.

"Of course we did. Then the ranch hands took turns racing. You're currently lookin' at the champ, baby."

"That's not fair because you knew the design."

I chuckle as we continue forward. "Doesn't make it any easier."

"We'll see 'bout that," she challenges as we buy a few tickets. After a few minutes, it's our turn to go inside.

"Do you wanna be chased?" one of the teenage volunteers asks us.

"Up to you," I tell Kenzie.

"Nah, I got a record to beat," she says with a cocky grin.

"I'm followin' you and won't get in the way. Good luck!" I offer with a snort.

Kenzie rushes through, thinking she made the right turn until she comes to a dead end. I take a few steps forward. "Givin' up already?"

"Not yet!" She rushes past me, giggling.

She takes another wrong turn, though she doesn't know it yet.

"We're getting close. I can just tell," she says matter-of-factly.

I chuckle, trying to keep it to myself. It's the worst move she could've made because it leads back to the start, and then you gotta backtrack without getting lost again.

Five minutes pass before she realizes she fucked up. The sound of children's laughter and voices float around as Kenzie throws a small fit.

"You're already three minutes behind my time," I mumble when she walks by.

Seconds later, Kenzie turns around and nearly mauls me with her mouth. She presses me against the giant hay bale, then slides her tongue against mine. As I groan, she wraps her arms around my neck and barely comes up for air.

"*Fuck*," I whisper when we finally break apart. "Keep this up, and we won't ever make it out of here."

She brushes her swollen lips against mine. "Sounds like a good time, Cowboy."

"Two people makin' out in the maze!" I hear Knox yell from up above the bales. He volunteered to help watch the participants in the maze because some kids get scared. "Wait. I think it's my cousin Kenzie and ranch hand Grayson Harding! Kenzie and Grayson standing in a maze, F-U—" he taunts.

"Shut up! I swear, you're like a mosquito!" Kenzie shouts. I take her hand and lead her to the exit, laughing.

When we're out in the open, she turns to me. "You were right. Knowing the design didn't help at all."

"Told ya, but I thought it was adorable you tryin' to figure it out."

We make a few more laps around the festival and pass the cakewalk and pumpkin carving booths. Once we've seen it all, Kenzie turns to me with a seductive smirk. "Let's get the hell outta here and go back to your place." She chews on her bottom lip. "I want you, no, *need* you, like right now."

"What's that saying again? Ahh yes, there's no place like home," I say as we head to the truck, not able to keep our mouths and hands off one another.

CHAPTER TWENTY-ONE

Mackenzie

"Mmm, baby. I know we're about to eat Maize's dessert buffet, but your tits are the best thing I'll taste today."

I snort, trying to keep my focus. "Please don't say my sister's name while you're inside me."

He chuckles in amusement as he circles my nipple with his tongue. It's been seven weeks since we've officially been together, and we still can't get enough of one another. My feelings for him get stronger every day, and having his support while I go through the process of becoming a foster parent makes me fall deeper and deeper.

"Speaking of which, we're gonna be late, and my parents will know exactly why." I tighten my arms around him as my thighs squeeze his waist.

Grayson got up early this morning so he'd be finished with his duties before my mom served lunch. I stayed in his bed and waited for him so we could show up together, but he basically jumped me in the shower as soon as he came home. Now he's pinned me against the wall as the hot water turns cold.

"I can't help myself, baby. I crave you all the goddamn time," he murmurs in my ear as he wraps a hand around my throat and playfully squeezes. "I'm so in love with you."

My eyes snap open, and my body tenses at those six words. He notices and looks at me.

"Shit, I'm sorry. Too soon?"

My mouth goes dry as I open my mouth to speak, but he beats me to it.

"Ya know what? I'm not sorry. I love you, and I won't apologize for that."

My heart flutters, and I can't help the stupid grin that covers my face. "If you'd let me talk, I would've said, no, it's not too soon because I'm so in love with you too."

I've never said those words to someone I was dating before, and though it feels foreign, it feels so damn right when it comes to Grayson. In less than two months of being with him, we're already planning our future. I have no doubt he's the one for me. I thought about telling him those words weeks ago, but I chickened out.

"Oh, thank God." His mouth crashes to mine as he continues thrusting and holding me to the wall. "Shouldn't be surprised. I've been obsessed with you for quite some time."

"Really? I hadn't noticed," I deadpan.

"Don't sass me." He nips my neck, then sets me on my feet. "Alright, baby. Bend over. I'll make sweet love to you later, but right now, we're runnin' outta time."

I giggle as I steady myself, then moments later, we moan out our releases. Grayson kisses me so passionately, I almost lose my footing.

By the time we get dressed, we're already late. I quickly blow-dry my hair and put on some makeup before we rush out.

"Well, well, well..." Maize chastises me as soon as we walk in. "The lovebirds are finally here."

"Relax. We're eight minutes late." I swoop Maddy up in my arms as soon as she comes for me. Mila Rose skips over next, begging Grayson to pick her up.

"Auntie Kenzie! Mommy has a baby in her tummy!" Maddy pats her own belly, and I laugh.

"No, she doesn't." I tickle under her arm, then glance at Maize, who's giving eyes to Maddy. "Wait. Are you pregnant?"

Maize nods with a big smile. "Yeah, we found out a few weeks ago."

"Oh my gosh!" I wrap my free arm around her and squeeze. "Congrats, that's so exciting!"

"Yeah, thanks. We're terrified of being outnumbered, though," she explains. "But excited."

"Well, this'll keep Grandma off my back for a few months at least."

Maize glares at me. "Yeah, that's exactly why we did it."

Gavin comes over, and Grayson pats him on the shoulder. "Congrats, man. Heard you'll be chasing three little ones around."

"I guess so." He crosses his arms with a grin, then shrugs. "Just couldn't get the wifey off me."

"Gavin, oh my word. Shush. If I recall, I told you to let me sleep," Maize throws back, and we laugh.

"What if you have twins again?" I muse.

"Don't you dare send out that energy." She points a finger at me. "After this, he's gettin' snipped."

"I beg to differ," Gavin retorts.

Maize leans in close. "If you ever wanna have sex again, you'll do it, especially after I pop out three humans. *Got it?*"

Gavin holds back a smile as he nods in agreement.

Moments later, Mom calls us into the kitchen, and we help bring the food to the table. I've been staying with Grayson almost every night, so I don't see my parents as much.

"Kenzie, how are things goin' with the foster program?" my mom asks after we take our seats and dig in.

"Really good. I'm going through some of the classes now, then they'll do a house inspection. After the training, they'll review my application and determine if I've been approved or not." I told them about my plans to do a foster to adopt program a few months ago but haven't updated them.

"Oh, they'll come to the house?" Dad asks.

"Yeah, they need to make sure it's safe and meets all their requirements but actually…" I hesitate and inhale a deep breath. "Grayson and I are fixing up his place, and then I'll be moving in."

After we became official, Grayson told me he wanted to be involved with fostering too, so we've been doing a lot of planning together. We agreed that updating the second bedroom was first on our list. Though I was ready to do this alone, I was so damn happy when he suggested we apply as a couple.

"As if you aren't already living there?" Maize chuckles.

"That's really great, sweetie. I'm excited for you guys," Mom says. "Just make sure you come visit often."

Dad nods in agreement.

"Of course. I'll still see you at school and Dad at the B&B. You couldn't get rid of me if y'all tried." I smile and am relieved to have their support. It's a big change but one I'm definitely ready for.

"Do you get to pick what age or gender?" Dad asks.

"You can specify those things, but I didn't. I'll be happy to help any child who needs it," I reply. Some kids are only short-term, meaning they could be there for one night or a few months, whereas some end up staying for years. I just hope to match with one I can eventually adopt.

"That's pretty neat," he responds. "You're doin' an amazing thing, kiddo."

"You really are," Mom adds.

"Well, I was inspired by you and always admired y'all's story." I grin.

"Wait, I don't think I know this one?" Grayson chimes in. "Do I?"

"Mom was Maize's nanny before she and Dad got together, and then she raised Maize like she was her own."

Maize looks at Mom and starts to tear up. "Ugh, damn hormones." She wipes her eyes, and we chuckle.

After lunch, Maize escapes to the B&B to set up for our traditional dessert buffet. The entire family shows up, and we feast on pies, cakes, cookies, and bars. Though I'm as stuffed as a turkey, I can't wait to have one of everything. Grayson and I help clean the kitchen while Gavin chases the twins around.

"Y'all are goin' to San Antonio tomorrow, right?" Mom asks as I wipe the countertop.

"Yep, we gotta be on the road early to make it there by noon," I say.

Grayson has made good on his promise to his mother that he'd make an effort to visit, especially during the holidays. Though everything's out in the open with his brother and stepsister, they haven't completely made amends. I'm not sure they ever will, and I wouldn't blame him for not wanting to. However, for his mom's sake, he decided we'd go and keep the past in the past. I know it's not easy for him to be around the people who betrayed him, but it's a step in the right direction, and I'm proud of him. Maybe it'll be water under the bridge this time next year, and they'll have a relationship again.

"I hope to meet your family someday, Grayson," she tells him. "You should invite them out for Christmas."

His eyes widen as he searches for the right words. "Maybe."

"Whatever you're comfortable with, no pressure."

"Thanks, Mrs. Bishop." Grayson smiles, giving her a side hug.

Once the kitchen is cleaned and the leftovers are put away, Grayson and I go to the B&B early to help Maize. We walk in, and I realize I wasn't the only cousin who thought to show up before the rush. Ethan and Harper are already here with baby Hayden and Grandpa Scott.

"Hey, Gramps. Happy Thanksgiving." I wrap my arms around him for a tight squeeze.

"Hey, kiddos. Don't tell your grandma I'm here sneakin' extra pie." He puts a finger over his mouth.

"Your secret's safe with me." I flash him a wink.

Harper comes over, and I steal Hayden from her. He's only a few months old and still so little. "How's the nighttime routine goin'? Getting any sleep yet?"

"What's sleep?" Ethan groans.

I chuckle at his exhausted expression, then hand the baby back so I can help Maize. She's wearing her favorite apron and blasting Justin Bieber.

"Thought you grew out of your Biebs phase," I tease.

"Dude, his new song is a whole ass vibe, though. Can't help it." She dances around, and it causes me to giggle.

Within thirty minutes, the dining room's packed with sweets and family. I notice Kane and Knox are in the living room having a heated argument. Though it's nothing new for them to be fighting about something, this seems more serious than usual.

"What are the twins bickering about?" I ask Harper as she rocks Hayden.

"Same thing they've been for the past few months...*Hadleigh*," she confirms.

"Uh-oh. What happened now?" I move closer to her on the couch as I soak up the gossip. Harper knows all the gossip between Hadleigh and the twins.

"She and Knox hung out alone last weekend when Kane was away. He flipped his shit when he heard Knox didn't come home till the morning after."

"Oh damn. So, he thinks they slept together?"

"Yep. Kane got so jealous, he marched to Hadleigh's and told her Knox isn't good enough for her, then confessed how he felt."

"Shut. Up! Oh my God. What'd she say?"

"She said she needed time and space to think about what she wanted. I know she doesn't want to hurt either of them, especially Kane because he's her best friend. Now she's torn between what to do, and it doesn't help that the twins are hardly speaking. Well, unless you count their arguing."

At this point, the only thing I'm missing is a bucket of popcorn and some spy gear so I can hear what they're saying.

"Jesus. Who knew the tea was gonna be so hot today. Is Hadleigh coming?" I ask since she usually does.

"No, she picked up an extra shift at the hospital 'cause she knew being here would be awkward."

"Dang. I would've paid for the premium package." I chuckle. "Guess that makes things a bit tense, especially with them working together."

"Oh yeah...they've been at each other's throats a lot more than usual. Ivy's been helping me at work, and we've already placed bets on who she'll pick."

Ivy is Hadleigh's little sister who works for Harper and her soap business. She's been helping more often since Hayden was born.

"I want in on this bet, considering there was one going for Grayson and me."

"Yeah, I lost that, by the way. Thanks."

I snort. "Serves y'all right."

Kane shoves Knox, then walks away before Knox can retaliate. By the look on Kane's face, he's devastated.

"Okay, now I kinda feel bad. But still, my money's on Knox," I say.

"I told her to choose both," Harper says, giggling. "Hot twin brothers who both want her…sounds like the ultimate fantasy."

"I might agree if I wasn't related to them." I gag. "Honestly, though, the only way this isn't gonna blow up in their faces is if she picks neither of them. She'd be better off dating someone else anyway. Or she should do what I did in college—date a few girls and really learn what an orgasm is before you settle for a man."

Harper looks at me as if I've grown a second head. "Wow, learned something new about you."

I shrug with amusement. "Had some making up to do. Growing up in bumfuck nowhere didn't give me many chances to release my wild side."

Harper glances around before lowering her voice. "When I'm allowed to drink again, we're goin' out, and you're sharing some of those stories with me."

"Deal." I flash her a wink.

"What was that all about?" Grayson walks over and asks, nodding toward Knox.

"I'll tell ya later," I say, glancing at Harper. "Right now, you need to roll me out of here because I ate way too much."

"Prepare to feel the same way tomorrow. Mom booked a caterer for the big event of me coming home." He sighs.

"Aww, how sweet. She wants it to be perfect for ya." I grab his hand and squeeze it. "We should probably go home, though, because I'm exhausted, and neither of us has been sleeping much."

Harper looks at me with a knowing smirk. "You two have fun."

Grayson pulls me off the couch, and I grin. "Oh we will."

CHAPTER TWENTY-TWO

Mackenzie

SIX MONTHS LATER

I cannot believe another school year is ending. When I first started teaching, Mom would always tell me how the years pass by so fast. Now, I understand. Some of the kids I taught years ago are going into junior high. They were sweet little babies, and now they're hormonal teenagers.

The spring program will start in thirty minutes, and I have pre-show jitters since most of the town will be attending. I know the students will do amazing because they've spent countless hours rehearsing.

"Did you find Silvia's yellow shirt?" Lacey asks a few teachers who are standing on the side of the bleachers.

"I did and already gave it to her," I tell her.

Lacey blows out a breath. "Thank God. She was having a complete meltdown just a while ago, so I went searching high and low for it."

"She left it in her classroom," I explain.

"Awesome. I think we're ready then. I'm gonna go make sure," Lacey says.

The kids are currently waiting under the covered walkway outside with another group of adults and will enter when the program starts. Their shirts are color coordinated by grade, and they'll each do their own dance number, then finish with a combined grand finale.

"That's a good idea. I'll be out in about ten minutes," I explain, looking for Grayson.

Before I meet the kids outside, he finds me.

"Break a leg, baby," Grayson says, painting his lips across mine. "Isn't that what they say?"

"I guess, I was never into theater. But I think that's the right sayin'." I lean forward to steal another kiss.

"Kissin' you here feels scandalous," he whispers in my ear.

I hold back laughter and shake my head. Sometimes, I think about all that wasted time we could've been together, but regardless, I'm grateful we eventually found our way to each other. And maybe Grayson was right. Us being together could've been destiny. Sure as hell seems like it after everything we've been through.

"I'm so happy you're here."

He tucks loose strands of hair behind my ear. "Of course. I wouldn't miss it for the world."

"Gah, it's gonna start soon." I brush my lips against his, and he pulls away with a smirk.

"Time's a tickin', sweetheart. Better get out there. Y'all are gonna do great! It'll be one to remember, I promise," he encourages, then gives me one last kiss before walking away.

As I look out in the gym, it's crammed full, and some people are standing. Granted, it's not a huge space to begin with, but I think this is the most we've ever had since we started. It makes sense, though, because we have nearly fifty percent of the student body participating now. The program grew faster than I ever imagined it would.

As some of the teachers round up the kids, I take one last look at the crowd. I grab my megaphone and gain their attention. Once I key it up, all their eyes are on me.

"Are y'all ready and excited?" I ask and look across their smiling faces as they nod.

"Alright, well, it's time we get started." I clap my hands encouragingly, then lead them inside the school. They'll wait in the hallway until it's each grade's turn to go out.

As soon as the music starts inside the gym, the kindergarteners rush in. The room fills with cheers as soon as The Jackson 5's "ABC" comes on. I sit in the front, nodding and smiling along as they perform. It's absolutely adorable.

Each grade's performances pass by in a blink, then it's time for the group dance.

As the song for the finale starts, I'm overwhelmed with pride and begin to tear up. The kids are so well practiced that they don't miss a single beat. When the song finishes, the room erupts into applause.

My mother walks up as the kids take their bows, then rush off.

Just when I think she's about to thank everyone for coming, another song starts. I'm confused and think there's a mistake, then look at Mrs. Lattice, who's controlling the music. She smiles and waves, so I know she's up to something.

After a moment, I realize the song is "Marry Me" by Jason Derulo.

The kindergartners come out holding signs, smiling and moving to the music. I rush to read them.

This is our love story. One that we've written.

I look around, and everyone looks just as confused as I am. The chorus starts, and the first and second graders walk out with more signs.

You're the only one for me.
I thank God for our second chance.

After they leave, the third graders come out.

I know we're meant to be.
I can't imagine life without you.

Last but not least come the fourth and fifth graders.

Will you marry me, Kenzie Bishop?
Be my wife and spend forever with me?

As soon as I read my name, my mouth falls open, and I cover it with my hands. Grayson walks into the center of the gym as all the kids stand to the side, and that's when I realize they have signs that read, "Say yes!"

"Go on," Mom beams, placing her hand on the small of my back and pushing me toward him.

Tears spill over as I go to him. He leans forward and kisses me, wiping the pad of his thumbs over my cheeks. "Don't cry, baby." He flashes me a wink, then drops to one knee and opens a velvet box. As everyone cheers, I'm completely speechless.

CHAPTER TWENTY-THREE

Grayson

K enzie's face is priceless. She's completely stunned, and I'm so glad I was able to surprise her with this moment.

"Will you marry me?" I ask, just loud enough for her to hear as the entire audience watches.

"Oh my God, yes," she squeals, and I immediately slip the ring on her finger. As I stand, she wraps her arms around me, and we kiss like we're the only two people on earth. I slide my tongue between her lips, unable to hold back. Happiness soars through me, knowing I'll get to spend the rest of my life with the woman of my dreams.

The kids give some awws and ewws, and we eventually pull away when we hear Knox yell, "Get a room!" Then I see Hadleigh smacking his chest and shushing him, which causes me to laugh.

Soon we're being bombarded by Kenzie's family and students. They congratulate us and praise Kenzie for an amazing show.

"I'm so happy for you!" Maize squeals, pulling Kenzie into a huge hug.

"And amazing job, Grayson. It went off perfectly. Kenzie's face, the shock —pure gold," Maize says, turning her phone around and replaying the video.

"Y'all knew?" Kenzie blurts out. "I seriously had no idea!"

"Good, that means the people in this town *can* keep a secret," I taunt.

After the gym clears out and Kenzie says goodbye to her students, she interlocks her hand with mine. "How the hell were you able to pull this off without me knowing?"

I laugh, leading her to the parking lot. "I had some help from Lacey and your mom."

"Wow, I can't believe you pulled it off. But I'm really glad you did. That was the sweetest proposal."

I lean over and steal another kiss when we get to her SUV. "I'm so damn glad you said yes."

"You really thought I wouldn't?" she teases.

"You never know. I tend to have the worst luck, and if you'd said no, I would've been so embarrassed and moved outta town."

She gives me one of her signature looks and tilts her head. "And give all these single women permission to snag you? I don't think so. You're mine." She wraps her arms around my neck and pulls me closer. "I love you," she whispers against my mouth. "I can't wait to spend forever with you and tell our children all about the pranks we pulled on one another."

"I love you too, Kenzie. So damn much." I take a step forward, pressing her back against the door. She grinds into me, rubbing against my erection. I've finally got everything I've ever wanted and needed and am looking forward to marrying the woman of my dreams.

"Let's go home, Cowboy," she suggests. "Meet you at your house."

"Sounds like a plan," I say.

Kenzie and I pull into my driveway in record time. I don't even think the sheriff would've been able to stop us.

As soon as she gets out of her car, my mouth is on hers. We're desperate for one another. At this rate, we won't be able to make it inside. Eventually, we pull apart, completely breathless, and I pick her up and carry her to my bed.

When I set Kenzie down, she smirks. "I can't believe you're my fiancé."

"Soon to be your husband," I remind, leaning over and capturing her lips. We rip off each other's clothes as we kiss, lick, and moan in pleasure. It's not long before we're making love.

I take my time tasting, pleasing, and making her scream my name as my tongue flicks against her clit. Kenzie fists the sheets as her back arches. "Yes, yes, yes..."

"Tell me what you want, baby," I whisper, pulling away, teasing her as she teeters on edge.

"You," she groans. "Please."

I move back to her clit as I shove two fingers inside her tight pussy. She writhes under my touch, and soon, she's screaming out her release. As she catches her breath, I trail kisses up her stomach until I meet her mouth.

"Fuck me," she demands, tugging on my bottom lip with her teeth.

"I love seein' you like this," I tell her, slamming my cock into her over and over. I'm overwhelmed with emotions and feel myself quickly crumpling and don't know how much longer I'll be able to last.

Kenzie digs her heels into my ass, forcing me deeper as I'm about to unravel. "I'm so close..." I groan out as she sucks my neck.

With a few more thrusts, I'm a goner. My body convulses as the orgasm rips through me. She scratches her nails down my back and lets out a satisfied hum.

"Thank you for loving me," she whispers.

"Thank you for *finally* letting me," I tell her, and she giggles.

I place a kiss on her forehead and let out a content sigh as I hold her naked body. It took a while to get here, but I wouldn't change our path. It's made me appreciate how amazing she is.

"God, I love you," I say.

"I love you more."

EPILOGUE

Mackenzie

ONE YEAR LATER

"You're gonna wake her up," I whisper-hiss as my eyelids fight to stay open.

"Then you better stay quiet, Mrs. Harding," Grayson kisses his way up between my thighs. "Don't scream."

"Easy for you to say," I groan as he swipes his tongue over my clit.

Though I really could've used another thirty minutes of sleep, waking up to my husband between my legs is worth it. However, ever since we got Amora, I'm more cautious of how loud we are. The little girl has been through enough during her life, and the last thing I want is for her to hear her foster parents having sex.

Grayson thrusts two fingers inside me as he licks my pussy, bringing me closer to the edge. I reach for a pillow and place it over my head as I moan.

"Come on my tongue, baby. I need to taste you before I go to work."

My back arches as he finger-fucks me deeper and sucks harder. It only takes minutes to set me off before I'm screaming.

"That's my girl. Fuckin' perfect." Grayson crawls up my body, removes the pillow, and grins at me. "Nothin' like starting my day with you on my lips."

"Keep that up, Cowboy, and you're gonna be late for work."

He shrugs, then leans in to kiss me. "After the number of times I've covered for Diesel not showing up on time, I'm not too worried."

Before I can respond, a small knock echoes. "Oh my God." I panic and throw Grayson off me. He's caught off guard and can't stop himself before he plummets to the floor. "Shit, sorry," I whisper, then dig for my shorts that he tossed aside.

"Coming sweetie, just a minute," I call out, rushing to my feet to get dressed.

I open the door with a smile and see Amora standing with her blanket and stuffed bear in her arms.

"Mornin', sweetheart." I kneel and give her a hug. "You sleep okay?"

"Mm-hmm." She smiles. "I'm hungry."

"Me too." I playfully boop her nose. "Let me take a shower and get dressed, then we can go to the B&B. That sounds good?"

She nods.

Amora is a six-year-old black girl who moved in with us eight months ago. After we got married, our application was approved. We got the call about her a week later, and she's been with us ever since. Her father died soon after she was born and her mother passed away two years ago. Since she had no other family, Amora immediately went into foster care. We've adjusted better than expected, and I fell in love with her as soon as we met. There was no doubt in our minds that she was meant to be with us. I can't imagine my days without seeing her bright smile and hearing her laughter.

Since it's Saturday, we don't have to rush to school and can hang out until Grayson's off work. We're busy during the week since she participates in the after-school program. By the time we get home and eat dinner, she's nearly falling asleep on the couch.

"Where's Daddy?" She loves seeing him in the mornings before he leaves.

Amora surprised us about a month ago when she started calling us mom and dad. We told her she could call us whatever she was comfortable with. After we discussed adoption and asked if she'd like to live with us forever, she confirmed she did, so we're now in the process of making that happen. She seemed relieved to have a place she could finally call home. Of course, I wept like a baby, but I was too happy to keep my emotions in.

Grayson pops his head up and holds back a groan. "Right here. I'll be out in a minute, honey."

"Did you sleep on the floor?" she asks, furrowing her dark eyebrows.

"Yeah, sore back," he responds, and I turn to glare at him.

"Why don't you find something to wear, and when I'm out of the shower, I'll do your hair," I suggest, and her whole face lights up.

After she goes to her room, I get cleaned up.

"Pretty sure I'm gonna have a bruised tailbone because of you," Grayson taunts when I'm out of the shower.

"You'll be just fine," I muse, patting his ass. "Tell the guys it's a sex injury."

"Don't worry, I will." He winks.

Amora's outfit choice makes me smile. She loves unicorns and anything rainbow-colored, so I'm not surprised by her pink tutu, purple tights, and unicorn shirt. She's even paired it all with her favorite pink cowboy boots. When she first arrived, she only had one suitcase of clothes, but Olivia was sweet enough to pass some items down that no longer fit her. Shortly after, we took Amora shopping and let her pick out whatever she wanted. Now one of her favorite things to do is shop in San Angelo, not that I can blame her.

"What do ya think?" she asks, spinning around.

"It's perfect!" I squeal. "How do you want your hair?"

"In piggy braids!"

I lead her to the bathroom, and she steps up on her little stool in front of the mirror. I get to work, doing it exactly how she likes.

"Alright, sweetie. What do you think? Look okay?" I ask, holding up a handheld mirror so she can see the back.

"It's the best, Mom!" She smiles wide, and it fills me with so much pride. "Can we go eat some of Maize's pancakes now?"

"You bet!"

We say goodbye to Grayson, then hop in the SUV and drive over. A couple of days after Amora came, we introduced her to the entire family. At first, she was a bit overwhelmed, but she's high-spirited and has had no problem adjusting to having so many people around. Grandma Bishop absolutely adores her and so does my mom, who loves taking her out for lunch on Sundays after church.

"There's my girl," my dad says as soon as we enter. She wraps her arms around him and squeezes as hard as she can.

"We came for coffee and pancakes," she tells him.

"Um..." I clear my throat. "Coffee's for *me*, pancakes for *her*," I clarify.

Amora giggles, then skips toward the dining room. A handful of ranch hands are eating, and she goes to each one and gives them high fives.

After I help add butter, syrup, fruit, and whipped cream to her pancakes, I place her plate next to Gavin and the kids. The twins turned three a couple of months ago, and their baby boy, Maverick John, will be one soon, so it's safe to say their hands are full.

Right before Amora came into our lives, Elle and Harper both announced they were expecting, and a month ago, they gave birth within days of each other. Connor and Elle welcomed another baby girl named Evelyn Grace, who we call Evie for short. Ethan and Harper also had a girl who they named Hailey-Mae Rose. You'd think with all the new babies on the ranch, Grandma wouldn't be asking me when I'm getting pregnant, but she hounds me at least once a month. Of course, Amora then confirms she wants to be a big sister, and well, I'd do almost anything to make her happy.

"Mornin', Mom," I greet when she comes over.

"Hello, my sweet babies." She gives kisses to Amora and Maize's three kids.

"Am I chopped liver?" I scoff.

Maize walks over with her apron covered in flour. "We are now that she has grandchildren."

"Not true..." Mom squeezes Maize's cheek.

"I beg to differ," I blurt out. "I called to talk to you last night, and you spent thirty minutes chatting with Amora first."

Maize chuckles. Mom shrugs.

Though I give her a hard time about it, I love how much Amora is already a big part of the family. She's the same age as Riley and Zoey's son,

Zach, and they play a lot, along with Dawson and Olivia, who are a bit older. There's almost always a birthday party, pregnancy announcement, engagement, or wedding around here, but honestly, I wouldn't change it for the world.

Grayson

I've been looking forward to today for months. Pulling this off without Kenzie knowing hasn't been easy, but luckily, Amora and the after-school program have kept her busy. However, since the school year ended a few weeks ago, I'd been worried she'd come across her surprise before it was ready.

"She's gonna freak." Maize beams.

"She's gonna love it." Gavin stands next to me as we stare at the prefab house I bought for us.

We've talked about getting a larger place, and though we could build, I know she wanted something sooner rather than later. So after I had the land developed, I started planning. Giving Amora a larger bedroom was my top priority, as well as adding another bedroom in the event we had more kids. I also know she wanted a deep jet tub, and since I knew every detail of what she wanted, I made sure to get her dream home. I can't wait to see her face and give her the full tour.

"I hope so," I say, brushing a hand through my hair. "Or she'll be pissed I didn't tell her so she could micromanage every aspect." I bark out a laugh because it could go either way with her.

"Trust me, she's gonna be so happy," Mila confirms.

I brought out the entire family to witness the big reveal and make sure everything was in place. Though it's been ready for a few weeks, I wanted it landscaped first. Then her sister and mom helped with some decorating while a few ranch hands put together furniture and installed the appliances. The property Grandpa Bishop gave us is on a side of the ranch Kenzie hardly visits, which is how I've kept it a secret.

"Alright, well…I'm gonna go pick them up. Don't go anywhere," I tell them.

My nerves are on high alert as I prepare for my speech. I'm as anxious as I was the day I proposed.

"Kenzie?" I call out when I walk in the door. Amora greets me in the living room, and I pick her up for a hug. "Hey, sweetie. Where's Mommy?"

"She was gettin' dressed."

I kiss her cheek, then set her down. I can't wait for Amora to see her new room. "Can you get your boots on? We gotta leave soon."

"Okay, Daddy!" She scurries to her room.

"Sweetheart, you in here?" I open our bedroom door and find her sitting on the edge of the bed, hunched over and crying. "Baby, what's wrong?" I rush over and kneel in front of her.

She finally looks up and wipes her cheeks. With a grin, she hands me a pregnancy test that says PREGNANT.

"*Oh my God.*" I blink at the stick, my heart pounding. "We're having a baby?"

I wrap my arms around her and pull her to my chest.

"Yeah, I guess we are." She chuckles, tightening her hold on me. "I'm in shock because we just started trying."

A month ago, Kenzie stopped taking her birth control, and we decided to go with the "if it happens, it happens" motto, but neither of us expected she'd get pregnant so soon. However, I'm not disappointed.

"I'm so excited, babe. Amora is gonna be the best big sister," I say.

"She really is. I can't wait to tell her."

"Well before we do, I actually have a surprise for the both of you." I stand and grab her hand. "But we gotta go right now."

"Now? My face is all red and splotchy."

I take her cheeks in my hands and press a kiss to her lips. "You're beautiful."

On the way there, I make the girls wear blindfolds.

My heart is still racing, especially after finding out we're expecting, and now I know this couldn't have been better timing. I park the truck, then help them out of their seats.

"Where are we?" Amora asks, wiggling in my arms as I hold her.

"Smells like the ranch so I don't think we're far from home." Kenzie chuckles. "Oh great, now my senses are gonna be heightened. Hope it doesn't make me sick."

Two loud gasps echo, and I glare at Mila and Maize for making a noise. Shit, they overheard that and are gonna know *exactly* what Kenzie means.

"What was that?" she asks.

Purposely dodging her question, I tell them to remove their blindfolds. Kenzie blinks a few times, notices her family, then looks at me. "What's this?"

"Is that our new house?" Amora squeals.

Kenzie's eyes widen as I smile and nod. "It sure is, sweetie. All ours."

I set Amora down so she can run to Mila.

"What do you mean? *How...*" Kenzie stares at everything in disbelief. "How are you always pulling off these surprises?"

I grin at how stunned she is. "Do you like it? I picked an exterior design I thought you'd love the most, and it has an open floor plan that you said you wanted. And it's a three-bedroom."

"Grayson, I can't believe you did this..."

Maize and Gavin walk up with their kids. "C'mon, I've been dying to give you the tour," Maize says. "And show you the pictures we hung."

"I think I'm in shock." She pretends to pinch herself.

I give her a sly grin. "Did my best to keep you busy and away from this part of the ranch."

"Busy baby-makin'." Maize snorts.

"Y'all heard that, huh?" Kenzie grins, unable to contain her excitement. "We just found out before we came here."

Mila wraps Kenzie in a tight hug. "Congrats, honey."

"I hope it's triplets," Maize taunts, and my eyes go wide at the thought.

"Don't you dare curse me." Kenzie glares at her.

"What does baby-makin' mean?" Amora asks, interrupting them.

Kenzie gives Maize a pointed look, and she shrugs. "Guess that's payback for telling the twins that spiders crawl in their mouths while they sleep."

"That was an accident!" Kenzie counters. "They weren't supposed to be listening."

"They slept with tape on their faces for a week!" Maize grinds out, and I bite back laughter.

I kneel in front of Amora and hold her hand. "It means Mommy has a baby in her tummy. You're gonna be a big sister."

She releases a loud gasp and squeals, "I *am?*"

Kenzie joins me and smiles wide. "Yep. Are you excited?"

Amora wraps her arms around our shoulders and nods. "I can't wait!"

After all the excitement, they're given a tour of the house. Grandma Bishop and the rest of the family were impatiently waiting inside, along with my mom and stepdad, who were excited to be a part of Kenzie's surprise. Instead of keeping the pregnancy a secret, Kenzie and I share the news since they'd find out soon anyway. Of course, Rose said she knew it all along.

"I still can't believe you did this, and I had no idea," Kenzie admits as we lie in bed that night. We'll start packing and officially move in next weekend.

"Good. That was my plan." I lean up on my elbow and rest my palm on her stomach. "I can't wait to hold our baby."

"Me too. Is it weird that I kinda hope it's twins? One of each…"

I arch a brow, waiting for her to tell me she's joking. Except she's not.

"Amora says she wants a sister and a brother." Kenzie grins. "I told her we wouldn't know the gender for a while but that we'd love the baby no matter what."

"Well…I guess that means we'll just have to keep goin' until we give her one of each." I flash her a wink.

"I'd love nothing more than a houseful of kids with you, Cowboy. You make me so happy."

I bring our mouths together. "And I'll spend the rest of my life making sure it always stays that way."

Amora

NINE MONTHS LATER

February is my favorite month of the year.

It's the month my adoption was finalized and when I became a big sister.

I watched Mommy's belly grow and even felt little kicks. She let me help decorate the nursery, which was so much fun. Daddy and I bought lots of toys, and at the baby shower, I got to open presents.

Though they told me we couldn't pick what the baby was, I prayed hard every night for one of each. The day of the ultrasound, I got to go and crossed my fingers and toes on the whole way to the hospital.

That was the day we found out there were *two* babies in Mommy's tummy. They decided not to find out their genders beforehand. It was a surprise to all of us when they were born—a boy and a girl.

I was so excited and told them I prayed for it, but they just smiled at me

However, I knew better. God always answers children's prayers. It's how I found my new family. I asked for parents who'd love me, and shortly after, I was sent to them.

My mom before Kenzie loved me a lot too, and she promised to always look over me. She got sick with some kind of cancer, and sometimes I feel her presence though I'm not sure how. When I asked if I could name my sister after her, they immediately said yes. Then told me I could name my brother too.

Since I'm seven now and *very* responsible, Mom and Dad let me hold them for as long as I want. Or until they cry. When I talk to them, Matilda makes the silliest noises, which usually wakes up Micah, and then he squirms. We call them Tillie and Mikey.

"What're you doin' up, sweetie? You should be in bed," Mom says when she catches me peeking into the nursery. Though they normally sleep in my parents' room, Mom comes in here when Dad's sleeping.

"I heard the babies crying and wanted to help."

"Oh, you precious angel. Micah doesn't like his diaper changed is all." She grins. "You wanna rock Tillie while I feed him?"

I nod frantically, then jump into one of the rocking chairs. Mom wraps her up in a blanket burrito before setting her in my arms. After adjusting the pillow underneath, she presses a kiss to my forehead. Mom takes Mikey and sits in the other rocker while he eats.

"So what do you think about having two newborns in the house? Pretty big change, huh?" she asks softly.

I smile and nod. "I love it! Can we have two more?"

Mom makes a funny choking sound, then laughs. "Oh, sweetheart. I think we're gonna have our hands full with them for a while but tell your aunt Maize it's her turn since Maverick turns two soon."

I giggle, then Mom does too. Soon, Daddy walks in and asks what's going on.

"I got Tillie to sleep," I whisper proudly.

"You sure did, honey." He picks her up and lets me know he's going to put her back in the bassinet. When he returns, he lifts me and says I need to go back to bed too.

"But I'm not tired," I tell him.

"Your body needs sleep. It's how you grow to be big and strong. Just like me," he teases, tickling my belly.

I squirm until he stops and tucks me back into my big girl bed. I love my new room; it's big and decorated with unicorns. "Can you tell me another bedtime story?"

"Sure, kiddo. How about I tell you the one where I finally won over your mama." He laughs, handing me my teddy bear.

"You mean when *I* won you?" Mom interrupts from the doorway. "That auction started it all."

"Is that true?" I ask him.

Dad winks at Mom, and it gives me a warm fuzzy feeling. "Nah. She had won me over long before that."

Continue reading for Knox & Hadleigh's story in *Claiming the Cowboy* or read *Jackson & Kiera*, Bishop Family Origin, #4

About the Author

Brooke Cumberland and Lyra Parish are a duo of romance authors under the *USA Today* pseudonym, Kennedy Fox. Their characters will make you blush and your heart melt. Cowboys in tight jeans are their kryptonite. They always guarantee a happily ever after!

Connect with Us

Find us on our website:

kennedyfoxbooks.com

Subscribe to our newsletter:

kennedyfoxbooks.com / newsletter

facebook.com / kennedyfoxbooks

twitter.com / kennedyfoxbooks

instagram.com / kennedyfoxduo

amazon.com / author / kennedyfoxbooks

goodreads.com / kennedyfox

bookbub.com / authors / kennedy-fox

Books by Kennedy Fox

CONNECTED DUET SERIES

CHECKMATE DUET SERIES

ROOMMATE DUET SERIES

LAWTON RIDGE DUET SERIES

INTERCONNECTED STAND-ALONES

BISHOP BROTHERS SERIES

CIRCLE B RANCH SERIES

BISHOP FAMILY ORIGIN

LOVE IN ISOLATION SERIES

ONLY ONE SERIES

MAKE ME SERIES

Find the entire Kennedy Fox reading order at
Kennedyfoxbooks.com / reading-order

Find all of our current freebies at
Kennedyfoxbooks.com / freeromance